David Br. ._ ,

THE SAGA OF BARAK

Re-Published by
HawkMedia

IMPORTANT FOR 2017

Updated in the last moments of publication

New Game available soon on mobile devices from late 2017.

Please check out our website for the latest details

At http://sagaofbarak.com/

ISBN-13:978-1545416136

ISBN-10:1545416133

Re-Published (2017) by HawkMedia

53 Stucley Road

Bideford

Devon

Ex393eq

http://www.hawkmedia.co.uk

About The Author

I was 23 when I started writing. No one inspired me to write, I just had a need to. Now I have a young daughter who has given me an urgency to get on with it.

A man in my middle years, I've had a varied working life, from starting life as an apprentice in Newcastle Upon Tyne to working on the railways for some years. I then travelled through Europe working in forests and on building sites in both East and West Germany as well as all over Eastern Europe. Here I worked with many interesting people, many of them perhaps should not have been there for various reasons. Eventually on returning to England after some seven years give or take I did some forestry work in Northern England. (This involved cutting down the trees and hauling them out by horse.) Horses have always been a part of my life and are now a part of my daughter's.

After this I moved south to Devon and worked in the building trade but when the recession hit I became a taxi driver.

I have throughout my life written poems and fiction but never taken it seriously until now. I have a seven year old daughter who has been a steadying and inspiring influence in my life and so now I am taking my writing seriously. I am in the middle of writing a trilogy of an historical fantasy novel.

The first I have completed entitled 'The Saga of Barak', the second I am in the middle of entitled 'Land of the Picts'. My writing is now a big part of my life. It is easy for me to find time to write but I don't have a specific place. If something comes to mind I just jot it down no matter where I am. Sitting in the taxi waiting for fares gives me lots of time to think.

I don't come from an articulate background and so my writing may not be precise or from a writer's view, 'well written', but it is a story the way I would say it.

Although I have enjoyed most of the various jobs I have done, nothing gives me more passionate feelings than when I am writing. I cannot express how I feel to see my work published and, God willing, a best seller.

Dedication

I would like to dedicate this book to all who believed in me, all my family, extended family and especially my daughter Ellie-May who gave me the incentive to go on.

Acknowledgments

I would like to say thank you to all the people who have helped me to get this book published. Firstly without my daughter's inspiration would never have got to the end of this first book let alone be almost finished the second and putting together the ground work for book three.

To my very good friends Lorna and Bill who were there for me when I needed a computer to write the book down and all of the hours that they spent translating my longhand and who have pushed me every step of the way and still do.

Also a mention for Jim Burns and Triden Elite who have been working so hard to get a game of the book ready for launch in June 2017. To HawkMedia who have republished this edition of the book.

Finally to you for buying my book.

I hope you enjoy it and look forward to the second book in the trilogy and if you enjoy a challenge look out for the game based on the trilogy which is due to be released in June 2017.

Details can be found on the website http://sagaofbarak.com

Thankyou..

David Brierly.

Contents

Introduction
Part One
The Saga Of Barak

Barak is at once the ultimate hero, or perhaps anti-hero; he is a giant of a man who stands nearer seven feet than six feet tall.

The Ogre has of course immense strength and awesome physical power, and is an expert in all forms and manner of weaponry.

For over three decades now Barak has stood out supreme over his contemporaries and the great slayer has seen most of them come and go, off to meet with their various very hard of hearing gods.

The giant is a ferocious looking man, a man who is completely tattooed from the top of his big shaven head right down his huge body all the way to his great booted feet.

The great slayers well-kept teeth are filed sharp and dagger-like into little more than wolf-like fangs. This somewhat painful operation the ogre had undergone some years earlier to join a tribe he once lived with in the darkest and most dangerous part of the African jungle. However, the end in this particular case, well, it more than justified the giant's means.

Still though, it must also be said Barak's eating habits were at best described as most dubious, and perhaps even a little more than sinister.

But then again as the old saying goes, 'to each his own.'

And now at fifty years of age Barak's vast physical and mental powers had neither wavered nor in any way had they waned. And as well as this, besides preserving all of that awesome natural power, the giant was still just as stubborn and uncompromising as he always and ever had been.

Now after commanding a campaign for the eagles of Rome the ogre had at last finally returned with his mission, as always and ever, accomplished; returned back to his adopted home.

For the giant Barak, home now lay nestled under the southern side of the great wall of the long dead Emperor Hadrian.

From both of these cold grey shores, from the westerly and turbulent Irish Sea to the cold great grey North sea on the eastern side of the island. This, impressive towering wall stretched out, winding its way in a snake-like fashion across the bleak rugged landscape of cold wild northern Britain. Hadrian's great

7

wall, just as planned when constructed years ago to separate the more civilized Romanized Britain from Pictdom. Gratefully the wall kept apart the savage ruthless barbarism that lay in the dense forests and the ever snow-capped mountains beyond from its most northerly province.

This mighty construction with its many turreted garrisons and its ever growing settlements was commonly known as the 'Wall in the Sky.' And as said it was also the Emperors farthest flung and bleakest northern outpost in Rome's still vast but dwindling Empire.

But bleak and far flung or not, it was here in this place upon this small green island the giant had planned upon spending the rest of his remaining days.

Aye it was here the ogre would bide in a bliss, full retirement hunting down the swift deer and the lurking wolf in the dark woods. It was here he would course the fleet hare in the lush meadow, and it was here the great slayer would fish for trout in the great Salmon River. This was a river that started its life off springing up as no more than a trickle in the land of the Picts. But then after flowing for many a winding mile, the now mighty river ended its fresh water days surging boldly into the cold grey North Sea.

Here with the great wall on one side of his home and the river on the other, here was where Barak would bide.

Well anyway, this was at least the giant's well thought out plan for his retirement and his future. But then again, plans of course as everyone knows did not, nor indeed still do not always work out as they are quite intended.

Chapter One

It was late summer moving into early autumn, but even now the leaves upon the trees of the forest were changing colour from a deep lush green to a rich golden brown. Aye, and it was also the first mild frost since the ending of the last Spring; this early chill giving the promise of a long and hard cold winter ahead.

Smoke dwindled slowly skyward on that windless morning from a cluster of turf-roofed hovels in the early morning half-light at the start of a crisp day. Mangy half-starved cur dogs yapped and cringed at the approach of a stranger meandering slowly down through the early morning mists.

This lone rider had emerged unheralded and unannounced from a dense forest of ancient oak, ash, birch and chestnut trees. It was a forest that flanked the southern side of a great wall, and this was a wall that was both high and broad. So broad was it, why two chariots that were even hard driven could pass by each other with plenty of room still to spare. Aye, indeed, this stout lofty wall, was considered by most to be quite a marvel of its time. And this high broad wall, well it was also a long and lengthy thing. Indeed here was a high, mighty construction that stretched from coast to coast across the island's wolf infested wilderness. Here the Romans last northern fortification ran all the way from the western shore by the Irish Sea, across the cold rugged land to the bustling and prosperous harbours of the east coast. This great wall spanned the most northerly and perhaps also the most inhospitable part of Britain.

Beyond the great border wall there was nothing, well nothing anyway but Pictdom and savage primitive barbarism. Not only was the now deceased Emperor Hadrian's great wall the most northern part of Britain it was also, as already said, the most northerly outpost in the whole of the still vast but now dwindling Roman Empire.

The 'Wall in the Sky' the men of the legions called it. While there were others in the ranks who would unflatteringly say it was simply the end of the world, well at least the end of the civilised world. Some of them, well these men just called this place the end of the very road itself. No, no, oh no, the great wall was perhaps not in the least way a favourite and sought after posting for those who hailed from the warmer climes.

But still and no matter, the lone rider wound his way slowly on down past the peasant hovels of the peat diggers and the pig keepers. This grim faced, somewhat unforgiving looking man sat astride a huge mountain of a horse.

And this beast was a huge Gaelic war horse. A great hairy legged powerful looking thing with a long flowing flaxen mane and a silken tail that trailed all the way down to the very ground. This creature was at least, so it seemed by its striking appearance, a most well cared for animal. It was both a well groomed and a well fed thing with bold dapples upon its broad backside that testified to its good condition. Also as well as all of this, the great hairy legged thing was fresh shod all around with the very thickest of iron shoes. And this same big chestnut gelding with the long flaxen mane and the equally long tail carried upon its big broad back, sitting there most casually and regally, a very giant of a man. In a most relaxed fashion this huge man was sat perched upon the big chestnut horse. It must be said that both horse and rider looked most impressive. And the warrior, for warrior the big man obviously was, sat enclosed in a very expensive high-backed high- fronted Arab saddle. And here was a comfortable saddle that supported the warrior's huge frame most snugly. Obviously this intricate expensive piece of wonderfully handcrafted leatherwork had been designed to fit both horse and rider.

Two tall grey long eared mules, gaunt but strong animals, followed on behind the horse and rider, submissively in tow. These were both weary-worn looking creatures, and also heavily laden. One of the mules carried the big man's weapons of war, his well-worn chain link armour and a small round spiked metal shield. Also there was a long lance and perhaps some half dozen throwing spears. This honest uncomplaining beast also carried an impressive looking longbow made of black wood inset with fine ivory writing of some sort. All of these weapons the docile creature carried as well as a Turkish crossbow. Oh, and some other items of the big man's other personal affects. Meanwhile the other mule was laden down with cooking implements such as large cast iron potbellied stoves, as well as an array of copper pots and pans. Strange items these seemed indeed for such a mighty man of war. Also as well as cooking pots and pans, there were sacks of seeds and plants, none that hailed from this cold green island. Aye, there was all of this, as well as strange exotic fruits and vegetables. Oh, and these edibles also hailed from warm distant places that lay far far away to the east of this island. Slowly and wearily the tired animals laboured on down then upward along a well-worn path to an impressive looking castle. And know you this, it was a stone castle mind you, not one of those hastily thrown together timber and mud affairs. Nor was this castle topped off with either turf or straw thatched roofs to keep out the sting of driving northern rain and the cold winter snow. Oh no this tall mighty castle made of stone, had sitting upon its shoulders a blue slate roof which was obviously cut, then fitted by the very best of craftsman. This place where the stout castle stood was called Coriosopium. Here, was both a settlement as well as a small garrison; this place was one of many of such situated in measured distances along the great northern wall.

Now the big chestnut gelding was reined up close alongside the thick solid oak gates of the castle. Meanwhile the big man sitting upon the big horse knocked upon the stout door with the great boars head iron ring inset there. The stern faced man waited only for but a moment before banging once again, this time though the warrior knocked a little louder and a little harder.

'Will you open up these gates now for me you foolish rustics?' the large warrior demanded gruffly. 'Or must I tear the very things down myself to gain entry here?' The rider roared this out somewhat impatiently. 'For I must say to you all now, I do have upon me the most ravenous of hungers. Aye, and also an even more powerful throat-burning thirst. Oh yes, and also fools, as well as these immediate needs. Well, I would most urgently bathe myself in the very hottest of soapy sudsy scented waters. Not though that I would expect many, if any, of you earth worshiping ditch dogs to understand that pressing need of course.' The huge man rumbled these words out with just the slightest hint of a sarcastic chuckle. From behind the great gates the big man's keen ears could hear movement and men talking nervously in hushed whispered voices. And the large warrior by the by, was now becoming more than a little irritable.

Of a sudden an armed guard shouted down a little timidly an order from the battlement above to the guarded gateway below. And then, almost at once the thick heavy oak doors began to creak themselves slowly open.

Rumbling and grumbling the big man spat, then the warrior growled and grunted with discontent. Aye and all of this while he cursed out loudly at being kept waiting for so long a period of time. A moment later when once this complaining was done the warrior urged his big mount on with a nudge to its ribs and it trotted forward into the castles stone cobbled forecourt. As ever the big grey mules followed on behind the large mounted warrior, obediently in tow. Once inside the stout gates the big man yawned as he looked all about him. Seemingly the warrior was taking in all and everything at a single glance of his dark eyes. When this observation was done with the huge man looked down from his saddle a little reproachfully at those who stood there before him. Now this huge horseman looked down at the five castle guardsmen standing there a little uneasy and more than a little cowed before him. The very big horseman atop the big chestnut gelding knew only one man of their number. And that man was Hubert. Hubert was a long time soldier and servant of the castle, and was the eldest of the small group of most dejected looking men. Hubert, well it must be said this particular castle guardian indeed looked a most sorry forlorn and downcast figure. Aye indeed, he appeared to be a worn out weary looking shell of a man, a man who was perhaps starved of many a good night's sleep. As well as the weary looking Hubert there were also two young Britons with a most vacant expression about them. It was an expression these young men wore whilst they were stood standing there quaking in their worn out boots. These badly bred looking things, well the pair of them were little more than spotty gangly nervous fidgety looking youths. Youths, who, by their stale and earthy stench were also infrequent bathers, and strangers to soapy water. Meanwhile the other two brave and noble guardians of the castle gates, who were a little older than the rank smelling Britons, these were doubtless of German origin. Barak was the name of the huge rider, and he reasoned this quite rightly judging by their fish scale armour and their general dress. Oh, and also of course by their bulging goatskin drinking gourds that hung heavily at their ample waist. And also this unwashed duo from the Rhineland, well they were both quite unsteady upon their booted feet. This while their stale breath, smelling strongly of beer would have got a nun drunk.

And the Germans, well here was a breed of men who seldom wandered or went very far without a strong drink of some sort strapped at their side. That whether it was in peace time, or even in a time of full blown bloody warfare. However, though, this was a habit that in the big man's opinion was not to be considered in any manner a failing on their behalf. Oh no far from it, this, the large warrior thought was a most wily and astute practice that lay to the Germanic tribesman's undying credit. After all if you are indeed marked for a slow lingering death in battle, or even while ploughing a field for that matter, well then, why on top of all that misfortune, as well as everything else should you also die a thirsty man?

Once again the large rider looked about him as he observed all and everything. A worthless, skinny, half-starved collie dog cur yapped then scratched at its sad flea ridden body. Also a trio of large white geese gaggled and hissed out loudly as a drunken soldier who had stayed out far too long stumbled across their path. No doubt, this the fool did while trying to find his way back to his home. Of a sudden the big man's dark, almost almond eyes settled once again upon the man Hubert affixing him with a steady most stony stare.

'All is not well here in this place my old friend,' the warrior said evenly. 'I sense it, I smell it, aye and above all else I do know it.' In a solemn tone the horseman said this while easing himself down from his mount onto the stone cobbled courtyard. These five fidgety onlookers noticed the huge warrior did this somewhat a little stiffly from his high backed expensive Arabian saddle.

At the first sight of the very big man sitting atop his very big horse it must be said the other four guardians of the gate, who were unfamiliar with the warrior, had been taken very much aback. In fact the four of them were in all truth shocked, aye, and perhaps even afraid in a strange way by the giant's fearsome appearance. Aye, and all of this even though the warrior had come to them as a friend, not as a foe.

'Speak up man,' the giant demanded of the downcast Hubert. 'For have we not many years ago hunted down the savage Picts together over the great wall of Hadrian? Why, we have drank and diced and we have slept in the snow together, aye all of this we have done with our blue stained itchy enemies not a sling shot away from where we lay. So with this in mind tell me my friend, why am I now to be treated as no more than a stranger here in this solemn place? Aye, and a stranger who must guess and be left to ponder, as to what dark misfortune is obviously afoot here? '

Hubert's hairy weather-beaten face wrinkled as he fought back tears. The troubled man bowed his head as he fumbled nervously with his ample ever greying beard.

'Barak my Lord, you are indeed as ever and always correct in all things,' he mumbled in a most distressed fashion. 'Aye and all is not well here at the great castle; no, no, it is not well at all my Lord.'

Hubert spoke these sad solemn words in an almost hushed and mumbled whisper as he stood there with his bearded raggy head bowed.

Now the huge man in reply to these words grunted and scowled as he gave off a most disconcerting growl. And this as the warrior prepared himself for the bad tidings that he already guessed was obviously sure to come. While silently contemplating this disaster, next the overly large warrior swayed his bucket sized head that had atop of it a well-worn chain link helmet. A much repaired chain link helmet at that, draped down to Barak's broad shoulders. The huge warrior swayed his head gently at first from side to side this way and that, and then he gave it a sudden violent jerk. His great heavily muscled neck creaked then clicked itself with a loud crack into place. With this done the giant, for giant the man truly was gave out a low lion-like growl of both relief and pleasure. And this he did before once again continuing to speak out in a low rumble.

'Please believe me, that much I had already surmised friend Hubert,' the man called Barak said frankly and evenly. As said previously it was in a somewhat stiff and painful manner by the looks of things that the giant had dismounted from the big gelding after his long ride. Now after clicking his thick neck back into place the ogre stretched his huge arms skyward. With this done the huge warrior began stamping some life back into his big booted feet, and indeed so hard that the ground it fair shook.

Standing there now towering high above the castle guards Barak was indeed a true giant of a man. Aye indeed Barak was a colossus of a man. And a man who in appearance was every bit as awesome and as fearsome as he had been described and depicted to these four new sentinels in the past weeks and months they had eagerly awaited his return. Indeed it would be true to say Barak was without any doubt the most frightening looking warrior in the very extreme. Now this ogre stood standing there, well he was indeed nearer seven foot than six foot tall. From the top of his huge shaven head, aye and also over almost every part of his massive body the famed slayer was adorned with the most elaborate of tattoos. Vivid colourful images of scaly dragons and giant jungle serpents intertwined in their bloody heroic death battles covering almost every inch of this huge being. Etched all about the giant's massive frame were the likenesses of strange animals none there in that company had ever before set their eyes upon, or for that matter ever would. So tattooed was the giant that only through small

13

spaces between these life-like dragons and serpents could you glimpse his tanned weather-beaten skin. And thus make out big Barak was a European not an Asian or a Moor of some sort.

When this painted giant spoke his teeth flashed white and these were most pointed things; in appearance the teeth were just like the fangs of the forest wolf. Long ago these teeth had been filed and sharpened for the most dubious of reasons. Obviously this little piece of dentistry of course only added to the warrior's already fearsome and most frightening appearance. Also this man of war's huge body was like that of a man some twenty years younger than his approaching fifty years of age. Aye, Barak was trim at the waist while being massive at the chest and shoulders, and his arms, well these hung by his side like huge ham shanks. Obviously the giant was immensely strong, and his vast body, well this it did fair ripple with an awesome power and a raw savage vitality. Long years of bloody carnage and warfare as well as the years he had spent hunting down his food; this coupled with his harsh vigorous outdoor lifestyle had given his flesh no time to decay or to soften. Nor had the ogre's great body become wasted or jaded in any way, or his great strength, as his great muscles were forever in constant use. For if indeed the huge warrior had succumbed at all to the ravages of the years and the constant non-stop violence and warfare, well then he would of course been a long dead thing by now. Aye for it was only the strongest, the most cunning and the most ruthless of men that survived in his blood spattered trade. But in the here and now, well then here was a true man of war, here was a killer, here was a slayer of both man and beast. Barak lived it, indeed he even breathed it. Alas the ogre, well for his many unaccountable sins, had in the not so far distant past supposed he once even loved it. For warfare and the slaying of his foemen and his enemies had been all he had ever really known since being little more than an ungainly very lanky boy.

Still though besides all of that, nothing the spotty local youths or the half drunken Germans had ever even heard or ever imagined about Barak and his frightening appearance; nothing, no nothing any of them even wildly expected had quite prepared them for this most frightening formidable slayer.

Now then, here standing before them in huge booted feet was a man you could follow into war, any war. Barak was a giant of a man, a man who could lead you and your friends and brothers in arms headlong into any battle; this no matter how savage or bloody the fray may be. Oh yes under his great vast mighty shadow a lesser man could feel safe, aye very safe, why he could feel confident, protected even.

While Barak talked with Hubert the Germans drank from their gourds as they spoke to each other in their own native tongue. And this the pair did somewhat excitedly about the arrival of the much famed notorious giant Barak. The slayer listened intently as he grinned wolf-like on hearing their words. For it just so happened, the German tongue was one of the many languages Barak spoke with ease. In fact the Germanic tongue, as well as Norse and of course the language of the Britons was perhaps his most favourite language of all. Still the giant listened to them chattering away for but a moment or two longer then he spoke up answering the question the Germans had so carelessly put to one another. And the giant when he spoke back to them both easily and fluently, well this gave the men of the Rhineland somewhat of a shock. As this of course, after all was something neither of the men were quite expecting. Barak, when he spoke, the ogre even mimicked and mastered their Thuringen dialect off to perfection. Now the warriors from the Rhineland, both of them at once glanced at each other most sheepishly. At once the Germans instantly both bowed, apologising for their unwise and perhaps ill-chosen comments.

However, the giant merely grinned as he had taken no offence on hearing their words. In fact Barak was quite used to such slightings and offhand derogatory comments. After all is said and done the ogre had a lifetime to get used to them. Strange though it is how sometimes even the slightest of slurs can be taken as more as an offhand compliment than an insult.

Barak handed the reins of his big horse as well as the mules lead ropes to the humbled looking Germans. This done the giant most politely bade them to care for and feed and water his honest and weary animals. All three beasts, Barak instructed, were to have double corn as well as the very best of hay. And this as it so happened was a task the German guards were both most keen upon undertaking. After all it is not every day you get to assist such a slayer as Barak, this even if the task is a little bit on the menial side. Now the giant in the meanwhile, he walked casually off with the still very downcast sullen Hubert across the newly cobbled stone courtyard toward the inn of the Seven Stars.

'What did you say to them my Lord Barak?' Hubert asked while looking back over his shoulder toward the Germans. Who, by the by were already drinking their own brew of frothy beer from their gourds as they made their way to the stables. 'For I do think my Lord, whatever it was you said caused them to take a fright. ' Hubert said this with just the slightest trace of a smile crossing his craggy bushy face.

The old guardsman liked the Germans well enough as they were good company on the gate and even more so in the tavern. Sometimes though the men of the Rhineland did just have that little bit too much to say for themselves, but this was more so in drink. Barak gave a thin smile then he answered his old friend.

'The Germans spoke to each other saying I was some sort of a cannibal, Hubert. Apparently the Rhiners had heard that I was an eater of men's flesh, can you believe that my old friend?' Barak said this with a most sinister and dangerous grin about him. 'Oh I don't know Hubert, you see some people just don't realize how sensitive a man I truly am,' the giant added with a weary sigh. Barak then yawned, this followed by a cough as he next spat onto the cobbles. Then, the ogre cleared his throat before once again continuing to speak to Hubert.

'So anyway my friend, I merely told them, our beer drinking sausage eating cousins, I only eat men when there is nothing to catch. Nothing else about if you know what I mean Hubert, because after all men are not near as fleet as the stag nor are they as big and ferocious as the bear are they? Aye and I do suppose all in all, and taken on one at a time I must admit I do find them, men I mean very poor sport. Why I do suppose they are not much more exciting in the hunt or the kill than catching and killing a rabbit,' the giant went on in all earnest.

Even under these present somewhat sad bleak difficult circumstances Hubert could not help but sneak out another slight smile. Barak, as always and as ever had a grim and a sharp ready sense of humour about him. This was a common trait so it was said amongst the men who spent their lives under the constant shadow of death. In fact it was well reported and rumoured the gladiators of Rome's arena mocked at their peril-fraught unlucky lot most of their waking hours; well at least that was the rumour. Because after all said and done, bitter tears coupled with complaints as well as screaming and cursing at the distant moon and the stars above well this would not change a single thing in their violent, bloody and mostly short lived lives would it?

'Oh by the by, anyway Hubert while we are talking of meat,' Barak continued. 'Know you this with the right sauces, with some good spices and a few fresh herbs thrown into the pot. Well, I do swear you can just about make anyone taste like a nice roast chicken, or even a rabbit come to that. Oh, oh I am so sorry Hubert, I mean of course you can make anything taste like chicken or rabbit.' Barak added this very quickly thus hopefully correcting his somewhat careless slip of the tongue.

Hubert, well the old guardsman in a very diplomatic fashion simply made out he had never quite heard Barak's verbal blunder. After all too much information can at times often spoil a perfectly good friendship.

The two men next walked slowly over to a heavy much used oak bench. It was an oak bench that of course was sat outside of the small sturdy stone built inn. This was the only inn within the castle walls as it so happened. Aye and truth said it was quite a prosperous little place at that was the inn of the Seven Stars. And there above the doorway to the place hung a black wooden board carved in the shape of a star, this with seven gold painted stars emblazoned neatly upon it. Barak, once there outside the premises, banged loudly upon the tavern's door with a great fist, the ogre demanding loudly and urgently drink and food be brought for both himself and the downcast Hubert. After but a short while in waiting had passed them by it was a bleary, bloodshot eyed innkeeper that opened a small window above the tavern door. It must be said the landlord was perhaps not at all best pleased at being so rudely awoken so early on that chill morning. But before complaining and once seeing who the huge caller was at this early hour the innkeeper very wisely saved his insults for another less large and less dangerous customer. Hastily the landlord at once dressed himself, this done he next hurried himself downstairs to attend to the giant's urgent needs. So with some ale inside them, both Barak and Hubert sat there outside by the bench while they talked together at some length. The early morning drinkers were brought yet another jug of cool ale from the deep, well stocked cellar of the Seven Stars. And this one was to follow the other three which had already been hastily consumed. Also, as well as the cool frothy drink there was a large platter of goat's cheese, this with slices of thick cold meat the fat red faced landlord kindly provided, aye and all of this was free of charge.

Hubert was a tired tearful man now with a few drinks inside of him, oh aye the old guardian of the gate was full of sorrow worry and woe. Barak scowled, grimaced then lit up his long clay pipe with the expertise of a man who was well used to striking flints. Barak sat puffing away on his strong black mountain weed; he said nothing for now, no the ogre said not a single word. As now the giant chose instead to let the distraught Hubert pull himself together. And this Barak did instead of pressing him and badgering for any immediate forced information as to the cause of his obvious distress.

This castle, this impressive stone castle had been built quite recently by the Romans themselves, it had been a present, a gift no less, as a token of thanks to King Aulric. It had been Aulric who had helped the northern legions of Rome in the long years past with border wars, aye Aulric had assisted them wage war against the savage Pictish raiders. King Aulric, who years ago when he Barak and Hubert had been much younger men, had tamed and fought nonstop against the savage warlike Picts who dwelled north of the great wall. Then, as well as defeating the savage but primitive Picts, Aulric with big Barak as his warlord had also united the scattered feuding northern clans together. Even the warring unruly tribes and the outlaw bands had all sworn an allegiance to both Aulric and the old hated enemy that was Rome itself. Aulric was just a young chieftain then, tall strong and proud he had always been and still was a highly principled most moral man. But back then in those far off days Aulric was both a brave and fearless warrior, as well of course as also a good leader of men. Times though they are ever changing, it had now been many years since Aulric had been forced to take up his sword. Well, this other than to knock apples down from a tree for the children of the village.

But that though was perhaps another story.

Anyway at long last after several jugs of the landlord's good if not very strong beer Hubert had at last spilled out his tale of woe to the patient pipe smoking giant. Aye and when he finally did so, well what a sorry tale it did indeed turn out to be once delivered. Barak sat there both silently and patiently while puffing away upon his long clay pipe, the slayer was still at this time not saying a single word. No, the ogre instead listened most intently as Hubert told him of these recent sad, very strange very sinister events.

Apparently Aulric had hidden himself away these past days hiding inside his great hall; the king was now both a weeping and broken man. Aye Aulric sat even now in an empty hall. And it was a hall that had been in only the recent past, a site of great banquets and lavish festivities. It was this hall, or well it least had been, a place of great merriment, a place of high fellowship that was open to all rich or poor alike. But oh how things had changed though, aye and they had all changed in less than just a week. Now the kindly king's beloved son, the good and noble Prince Kye lay a broken dead thing, all struck down with assassin's arrows. And then on top of this dark sinister tragedy, there was yet another liberty, this just as foul and just as cowardly. Aulric's daughter, the Prince Kye's much loved popular younger sister Ellena had simply vanished without a trace. This double disaster had all happened when brother and sister had been riding out together in the dark woods south of the castle. Perhaps sadly she too had been slain, and mayhap her body for now was merely concealed. Aye, hidden in a woodland thicket, or maybe and at very best she had been kidnapped. Perhaps she had been abducted and kidnapped for a ransom yet to be demanded. But if so, then by whom and for why was the wonderment of it all? As of yet no one knew the answer to these most perplexing of riddles, all were left to ponder. So far there had been no contact from the killers of the Prince or from the abductors of the Princess, who were of course obviously the same cruel callous people. And as well as all of this, these cruel perpetrators had no apparent reason for this heartbreaking outrage. Well at least none other than perhaps greedy bounty. But then, with this being so why then had there been no ransom as yet been demanded?

Barak after some while sitting deliberating upon the bench seat arose to his big booted feet somewhat stiffly. Next the ogre yawned as he stretched his huge arms out with the weariness of his long travels. Once again the slayer moved his great neck from side to side, and this he did, until once again, just as it did earlier, creak then click itself into place. With a grunt of both pleasure and relief Barak next bent over to speak to his long time friend. Now the slayer shook Hubert's hand, this while thanking him kindly for the information the guard had at long length managed to convey over the past hour or more.

'You say our good friend Aulric is right now in the great hall of the castle Hubert?' Barak asked this question with yet another long stretch and another mouth gaping yawn.

Hubert took a drink of his ale then nodded his head.

'Aye Barak, but he will see no one my high Lord, the King is fuelled with too much drink and fuelled with even more black sorrow. Sadly I must say this, our friend the king is not at all the same man he was when you left to retrieve the lost Roman Standard. '

Barak grumbled something in a strange tongue as he smiled thinly and peered down at the bearded much troubled Hubert.

'Well my old friend, king or no king, believe this, he will most certainly see me', the ogre said this with some element of conviction. 'Oh yes please believe me my old brother in arms, we will talk Aulric and I. Furthermore we will waste no time, we will talk now without any further fuss or delay' Barak rumbled out. 'Know you this Hubert, I was there on the day of the birth of both those children—aye also I was charged with guarding them, to look out for their safekeeping and protection. But now alas for my wanderings and my other many sins I have failed them both.' Barak sighed a little sadly as he next spat then cursed once again in that same foreign tongue, this whilst he stared up for a moment towards the angry grey skies above him. The weather in the north of Britain was ever fickle, it being bright and sunny one minute, then dark and stormy the next. Aye the weather in this part of the turbulent ever changing world, well it was more than just a little like the moods of the giant in many ways.

'However my troubled friend, as I say things are not always as dark as they might at first seem to be Hubert.' Barak said this after several moments of grim silent contemplation. 'Anyway Hubert, I must at once send off now, this very moment in time, an important message. Aye and then with this message once dispatched I will go to speak with the much distressed Aulric. Only after we have this conversation, will I decide what must be done to make all right once again. Oh aye, also of course, in what manner we must do it.' Hubert stared ever upward at the giant slayer with tear-filled eyes from where he still sat upon the wooden bench. Both men had long been and were still close to the King and also to both of his children. Hubert in fact had known Aulric all of his life, indeed they were brought up as boys together in the harsh northland. Together as children they had hunted played and fished, aye together the lads had also plagued the very life out of the Roman soldiers. All of this when they were no more than but snotty ragged children dressed in itchy woollen rags. Barak after but another moment or two of deep thought changed the subject.

'By the way Hubert, this innkeeper who has tended us is not Tom. Oh no, no it is not Tom with the purple nose and the few uneven teeth in his head. Where is he Hubert? Tell me whereabouts is the Tom fellow?' The giant asked this whilst sucking upon a painful rotten tooth at the back of his mouth. And here was a tooth that by the by had of late forever been troubling him. 'He is a good man to drink with, the Tom fellow,' Barak stated in a matter of fact fashion. 'And this despite the fact he does not put his hand into his pocket as often as he might for a wealthy man. Aye and believe me on this Hubert, Tom upon this early hour would have charged us for the food and drink we have breakfeasted upon. Oh yes, and also this service would have been costly too more the likes. And this just for rousing him from his blissful drunken slumbers.' Hubert gave only the hint of a smile in reply, and a nod of total agreement at these words followed by just a slight chuckle. Next though and only a moment later the old sentry smiled as he scratched at his ample bushy beard before speaking.

'You know the big fat merchant Edward, the one with the dyed black hair and a gap in his top teeth?' For just a moment the giant was thoughtful then grunted as he gave a slow but positive nod. After all what was big Edward to Hubert, well he was only little Edward to Barak.

'Aye, aye I think I know the fellow well enough. If I remember rightly the man is a fool, he is a fool with far too much mouth, also with far too much money is he not? ' the giant asked.

'Yes, yes that is the same man, and indeed he is the same fool', Hubert at once agreed before continuing with what he had to say. 'Well anyway Tom he sold this Edward a horse, a black horse, a mare called Kate.' The giant at once smiled then next scratched at the snow white well groomed goatee beard that adorned his huge square jaw.

'Kicking Kate?' the giant next enquired knowingly.

Hubert at once nodded, 'Aye my Lord Barak that is the very same beast.' Once again the giant smiled, most wryly this time, and then he spoke.

'Say on Hubert, for that mare I think was perhaps just far too much animal with far too much fire in its heart for fat Edward to handle.' Hubert, well he was now thankfully perhaps not quite as forlorn as he might have been just a short while ago. In fact the castle guardsman now in these last moments even seemed to be enjoying himself just a little in the giants company.

'Well that black Kate she struck Edward so hard with one of her back hooves one morning, I was there Barak, I saw it, funniest thing I ever did see,' Hubert chuckled. 'It was a bright sunny most busy morning this summer gone, aye in this very square too. Edward being Edward, well the fool sought as ever to impress the market day crowds with the black mare's turn of speed, so he gave her the whip over her backside. Bad idea Barak, and all this in his best chariot too, a chariot that very quickly ended up as kindling wood. Well, as you know Edward was a most foolish man before that morning, but now, well now he is even more of a total idiot Barak. ' Hubert once again chuckled to himself as he took a drink of ale before once again continuing with his tale. 'Why, poor Edward, since that kick cannot now even string two words together without stammering and stuttering. Aye and all of this while spitting and slavering all over his fruit and vegetables. Know you this also my Lord Barak, by the time the man eventually manages to shout out the word "carrot", or "turnip". Why by then the rest of the stallholders have sold up, packed up and gone home, money in their purses with their day's trade done and dusted. The giant first chuckled at these words, but then he leant back with hands upon his hips as he laughed out long and loudly as he imagined in his big bucket sized head the comical scene.

'And so, so tell me, where is Tom now Hubert?' Barak asked at length when his laughter ceased. 'Tell me, for I will find him and drink with him on my return from this venture I must very soon undertake. But only to drink with him mind you, I have no intentions of buying a horse from that rogue..' Hubert chuckled as he wiped beer froth from his beard before answering the giant's question.

'Tom, once away from here bought the Greyhound Inn, which lies in the village of Condercum. And this inn, well, it sits nestled by the great wall. From this place the Greyhound is only a day's ride to the east from here on a good horse, or two days ride on a bad one.' Barak on hearing this grunted then the ogre gave a nod of approval at Tom's choice of a new inn.

'Good tavern, I know it well. Aye and Condercum, it is also a small but growing garrison with many thirsty soldiers, very astute of Tom,' the giant muttered to himself. 'But anyway besides all of that, drinking with Tom for now it must wait..' Barak of a sudden affixed Hubert with a friendly look. 'Now you hear this, and hear this now what I say to you, but most of all believe it Hubert..' Suddenly the giant's face now changed and this in but an instant, and now it contorted into an angry grimace. And this just as suddenly as it had earlier broken into a broad smile which had then cracked into laughter. 'Upon my good dragon-sword, I do swear here and now I will hunt these dogs down. Also, I do swear these fools will all die screaming for their mothers or whatever other sickly thing it was bore them into this savage world. ' Barak promised this in all earnest as he next put a huge reassuring hand upon Hubert's drooped shoulder.

All of a sudden a cold shiver ran up the Briton's stooped broad back. Hubert had never for one moment thought he would or could have possibly felt any pity for these men Barak would hunt down. But somehow now he did, for they were all in his considered opinion no more than walking dead men. They each and every single one of them were all men who were merely living on borrowed time. And this was time these brigands had before meeting with what would doubtless be a very violent, very sudden demise. Because simply for this very reason, not even the wildest stormiest of seas, or a desert, however vast and barren. Nor a mountain range, however high and snow-capped or the darkest deepest of forests. All of these natural elements would neither slow nor deter Barak upon his blood hunt. Nor for that matter even any dark demon or imagined demi-god could stand against the wrath and power of the great war Lord. Oh no, oh no, these foolish callous men who had brought so much sorrow and woe to the castle, whoever they were, these men would all die screaming. And of that simple brutal fact Hubert, well the guardian of the gate was in no doubt whatsoever. As sure as night is dark and day is light and the old world turns each day as it does, these fools would all meet their well deserved end by Barak's massive broken hand.

Barak after a little while longer bade a much happier Hubert a good morning then the slayer strode off purposely towards the King's Hall making just a slight detour on his way. There was so much to discuss so early in the morning and Barak despite being a little travel weary was keen to be getting on with it.

Chapter Two

Barak's great big hide boots fair echoed loudly down the long stone slabbed corridor toward the King's Hall as he moved there with great and purposeful giant strides. The standing guardsmen stood there at ease, well that is if ease is the suitable word. And this stance the men took as they first heard the heavy unmistakable footfalls then saw Barak as he fast approached them. Now the guards very wisely at once lowered both their gaze as well as their weapons. For to try and stand in Barak's path, even while by being so ordered for Aulric to have privacy for his grieving, well, this of course would have been no more than sheer suicide. The last two remaining castle guards drew open the doors to the Great Hall, Barak gave to each a polite nod then at once strode forward and entered the dimly lit room.

Aulric's chamber as it happened was a great long most impressive Hall, also of course it was a place the ogre had drank and feasted in many, many times before. And here was as has already been said, a place of good friendship and high fellowship, and above all a place of good warm honest cheer. Aye up till almost this very moment in time it had always been a happy gracious proud place to meet up with friends and comrades, but not now, no not now on this sad gloomy day.

Barak looked about him as he always and ever had a habit of doing, taking in all and everything around him in what seemed at just a moment's glance. Aulric was sat there at the far end of the room in his high backed throne, his body leant forward slumped across the table. At this particular time the good king was snoring loudly, indeed he was fast asleep and dead to the world. Now, the giant at this point sniffed the air as he gave off a low growl followed by that most disconcerting grunt of his. To Barak's disgust this place was not tidy, it was not in good order, not neat. In fact the great hall, well it was not a clean place at all. After his brief observations the great ogre then sniffed in once again the stale rank air about him. Grumbling and rumbling curses, the giant spat in disgust upon the stone slabbed floor then he ground in the spittle with a huge booted foot. Sadly this noble place, this great once proud hall, why it stank to high heaven. With huge measured strides the giant next moved to the tall windows. Once there he tore aside the heavy closed red velvet curtains to let in the early morning light through the crisscross leaded glass windows. Even now there was still at this early hour something of a bitter chill in the gloomy hitherto sun starved room. Barak who was a man who was ever tidy in all things at once stoked up the four fires one at each wall of the long hall. With this done the ogre next threw what available logs he could find into the dying embers.

'Ah good, that's much better,' the giant muttered to himself as the long dried out logs took alight instantly. After this task the ogre next moved with some haste along the long banquet table helping himself to such food that was neither stale nor sour. Cheese, bread, boarsmeat and chicken, the great slayer eagerly devoured. Next after consuming this fare the ogre washed it down with a big goblet of good strong mead. Barak being a huge man also had a huge appetite so despite just dining at the Seven Stars the ogre could always find room for a little more food in his ever hungry belly.

Some half dozen of Aulric's best and most favourite hunting dogs lounged ever sleepy about the great hall. These noble beasts were tall, rangy lean broken coated animals of mixed collie and greyhound blood; hardy animals that could run down a stag or a hare when required. Alas though these were lazy docile beasts at rest, it would be fair to say these fleet running dogs only came to life upon the day of a hunt. At all other times these long lanky dogs were more than content just to lounge around for days on end scrounging food, then sleeping on again before the hearth of the blazing fire. And please believe this, the dogs had indeed lounged, lounged then slept and once awake the dogs had also fed well from the long table. However, sadly the beasts were unable to take themselves out of the great hall for these past days; this through no fault of their own. Well the big running dogs had, because of their confinement, made quite a considerable mess of things. Barak after but a moment gruffly summoned a most nervous guardsman. The slayer bade him send servants at once to clean up the dogs stink then wash and scrub the floor down. Also, after this most urgent task was completed, the kitchen staff were to be roused from their beds and bring with them fresh meat to the hall. Oh, oh aye and of course, more much needed drink. Once this was done the guardsmen were next ordered to walk the dogs out into the woods for a run, oh and of course to do what they must. As ever and always with the giant Barak organization was the key to all and everything. Aye, without any sort of organization then of course all and everything was lost and in utter hopeless confusion.

After all, well these Britons were a simple folk, aye here were folk that needed much guidance Barak had long thought. Oh yes, these rustics were not quick thinking things at all. Honest enough that was all very true, their cooking and brewing skills were not of a high standard. Aye these Britons were not anywhere near as adept as the Germans when it came to making beer or sausages. So for that reason it was mead the giant demanded to be brought for him to help his thirst, not the wishy washy ale the locals drank. For that indeed was a sad pathetic brew that in the ogre's expert opinion could not even get a decent dog drunk. Now though, the monks from the small island of Lindisfarne to the north east of the wall, well, these saintly scholars knew only too well how to make a good full bodied drink. Aye, big Barak could well stomach that holy lovingly brewed refreshment. Mead and strong cider, yes that at least had some sort of bite to it. Aye, and this even more so when mixed together in the same drinking pot, this with whisky from the North West added to the brew. True, this was still nowhere near as good as the powerful clear steppes vodka the giant favoured above all and everything else. But still after all and everything, this mead was easily better than anything else about the ogre supposed to himself. Barak drank down greedily another goblet of the freshly brought mead, then the ogre licked his lips with an element of satisfaction. Next the slayer gnawed most readily upon a whole leg of lamb, ripping the flesh away easily with his sharp filed down teeth. Now the giant after devouring this tasty piece of flesh poured for himself another drink. After a loud burp of satisfaction the ogre lit up his long clay pipe concealed under his thick leather hide waistcoat. With this done, then in blissful satisfaction the ogre let out a long weary sigh as he blew near perfect smoke hoops into the still chill morning air.

Oh, through all of this whilst the giant drank and smoked, he watched Aulric as the king slept and snored loudly. Doubtless though, this was a troubled drunken sleep, a sleep that was filled with nightmares and demons as well as all manner of other horrors. Barak watched Aulric all this time as he sat upon a shaky three legged stool. Barak was warming his outstretched legs in front of the blazing fire as he sat only a yard away from the King. The giant muttering away to himself, next kicked off his big thick hide boots and extended his large thick woollen stockinged feet toward the fire. Barak had already decided he would finish off his pot of strong relaxing black weed before waking his troubled slumbering friend.

Now the great slayer ran his dark, almost black eyes over his old friend Aulric. Indeed he looked a very aged most worn out thing, aye the good king appeared jaded and tired out in the very extreme. Hubert, well at least the loyal trusty guardsman was sadly most correct in his description of the heartbroken king. Aulric was not at all like the strong able man the giant had left behind some months ago at the very start of the summer.

Barak had been off abroad of late these past months, far away across the sea fighting for the glory and the pride of the Legions of Rome. And the mission, well it was what he himself had called no more than a fool's errand, this was an undertaking to retrieve a lost Roman standard. Aye a worthless Roman standard that had been taken forcefully by the savage barbarian horsemen far to the east of Rome's now much troubled borders. To be perfectly honest the whole sorry venture had turned out to be a lot of trouble and a lot of blood loss for what was no more than a wooden stick with a painted eagle sat atop of it.

However, this sad fact aside the giant had nevertheless retrieved Rome's glorious unyielding emblem of power. This though had proved to be both a tricky and dangerous task eventually achieved after more than some element of difficulty. Anyway the ogre, who by the by never failed in anything violent, had brought this gold painted stick back to Britain. And this along with the Standard of the Legion he had taken with him to retrieve the first lost Eagle. The first standard was lost by some idiot high bred nobleman who was in charge of damned good men. Oh and of course, these were men he had no right to command anyway. And the fool and the coward that he was, fled the field, his post as well as his undeserved command. Aye the coward deserted his soon to be slaughtered infantrymen and simply rode off upon his fast pricey Spanish horse away from danger. By all accounts the fool was now in exile somewhere, hiding both his shame and his cowardice from his disgraced family as well as his disgusted peers. Rightfully so, after all he had brought black shame to both his kin and his very expensive military academy. Bravery is something you are born with, not something a man is born to, had long been Barak's view of things. In the past the giant had witnessed unarmed peasants fighting to their very last gasp and their last drop of blood to protect what little it was they owned. And all of this while the so called high-born had scurried away on their fine horses in a panic at the first sign of any danger to themselves. Still, those Roman standards though, well they were all the giant had brought back with him however, as over a thousand good Roman cavalry soldiers, then another five hundred hired German mercenaries had perished in the final three days of hand-to-hand fighting. This battle was the conclusion of months upon months of sneak skirmishes with the savage plainsmen. Only Barak had as ever and always survived, only the slayer prevailed, only he alone had survived the last savage fray on the cold windswept rainy plains. Then, when all of his men were lost and slain and piled high all around and about him, the giant was the last man standing before his victorious enemy. But big Barak, who was as ever and as always a quick thinking man was undaunted by the stark face of almost certain death. And so now, the smiling mocking ogre, knowing full well mens' failings, at once insulted, spat upon, then challenged the barbarian chieftain who had led the savage horde of horsemen. Aye the great ogre had most cleverly challenged the clan leader to a duel of honour. Of course this would be a straightforward death fight, man to man and back into the very earth where they had once come from. Thankfully, aye perhaps very luckily, for big Barak the barbarian chieftain, while being high in courage but low in brain power, had foolishly and willingly accepted this offer of combat. So with offer accepted the fight was on. They had fought warrior against warrior in a glorious blood duel; this of course as always in such matters was to the very death. And also of course this great exhibition of bravery and showmanship was all done for the very glory of it all. But in all truth, this fray was in Barak's opinion nothing more than a formality, no more than entertainment. However, glory entertainment or not, this duel had been a very brief, bloody and a most one sided affair. And there was of course only ever going to be one winner in this glorious mismatched duel. Big Barak, well to be honest the wily ogre had known this simple fact all too well before the onset of the fray. However, though the other hapless warrior, who was by the by, a tall lanky one- eyed man with long greasy ginger hair and a big red unkempt beard, while being a brave soul was perhaps not privy to this stark simple fact. Aye sadly for him this unpleasant looking itchy fool with a row of broken teeth, he was a man apparently less educated than the fearsome ogre Barak. Anyway bad wagers put aside, the victor of this fight was to place the loser's head high upon a pole in the middle of their last battlefield. This gruesome trophy was to be placed there for all to see, well, all but the multitude of dead men strewn about here there and everywhere all about. However this grizzly macabre act was not a gesture of insult in any way. No, oh no far from it, no it was more of a promise, a pledge each warrior had made to one another before the fight had even ensued. Both Barak and the savage one eyed high smelling chieftain had sworn whoever the victor was he would then simply lop off the loser's head. Barak had perhaps pledged this with a sigh a yawn and a handshake. While knowing full well whose greasy ginger skull would be the closer to the heavens on that cold starry night. Anyway with this deed once done the head would be placed upon the high pole to stare down upon the vast crowd with unseeing eyes, well one unseeing blue eye. The fierce code of the so called barbarian tribes in many ways carried a lot more honour to it than that of the back-stabbing Roman high born nobility. Because at day's end after all said and done, the giant's hairy unwashed, very itchy enemies, which of course were still many in number, could have stood well back from the fearsome giant and shot Barak there and then full of arrows. And this until the ogre dropped down onto his knees and simply bled to death. For it must be said there were still many thousands of the savage horde about that stood silently watching their former leader meet his swift but noble end upon his final day on earth. Perhaps there were still over ten thousand hairy itchy men or even more wild looking open mouthed things who witnessed the brief but savage duel between Barak and their ferocious but mismatched one eyed clan chieftain. However, for their own reasons the horsemen did not do this. No their arrows stopped in their quivers and the warriors to their credit upheld their savage code of conduct. Thankfully for Barak the savage unwashed horsemen kept to their word, to a man they bowed to the giant's power and his skill with a sword and of course to his courage. Later after the fight, after the blood and dust was finally settled, these now leaderless horsemen simply let the slayer ride off with both of the Roman Standards.

And so it was a victorious Barak who rode away from the battlefield. However though, this was not until the following morning. Because as ever with the giant, and having manners about him, Barak had thought it would not be polite to leave without having at least one night in toasting the savage chieftain who he had so quickly and recently slain.

So there under the tall pole that carried the one eyed chieftain's hairy grinning head, aye under the cold starry steppes sky, Barak had sat his broad back against that pole whilst he drank much vodka and feasted upon thick steaks of horse flesh. Oh and all of this with the unwashed itchy horde for company and until sunrise of the next day. And what a drink that was by the by, the giant had found the barbarian chieftain was also quite good company, well, good company for a dead man that is. As for Barak, well he being ever polite the giant had toasted the chieftain most sincerely, the ogre did this many times before the coming of that following cold red skied dawn. And then when the giant finally arose upon

26

to his great booted feet on that dawn. Well he had quite simply bade his former foemen a farewell, well those who weren't speechless with drink that was. The great smiling ogre had bade them as brothers of the sword and lance all a fond farewell. Barak had wished them all good fortune in their future battles, oh and also better luck in their choice of a new leader. Perhaps one with both eyes and more intellect might be of some help the giant had joked quite uncaringly. Finally once his words were spoken and all was done and dusted. And when big Barak thought he had received sufficient adoration and homage from the newly won over horde of savage horsemen. Well, the giant had then quite simply ridden off, and the slayer did this on the best horse available. Oh and this horse as it so happened was the former mount of the now deceased and headless chieftain. But still after all said and done that brave fool had no further need of it. And also as an added bonus as well as a certain amount of good luck, the horse to its former owner's credit, was a fast spirited beast. Aye the tall grey horse crossed many cold rivers with Barak astride its back. And the gelding proved that it was a damned good swimmer as well as a good galloper. To the savage bloodthirsty horde that watched the great ogre ride away, singing an out of tune ballad as he did so. Barak, well, he was no different a man to what they were, in fact, these unwashed warriors supposed he was one and the same. Aye this great tattooed slayer to them was neither a god nor a king or even an ogre, nor was he indeed a Roman commander. No, the great slayer was only a barbarian, though except Barak was of course quite the biggest barbarian any man there had ever seen before, or for that matter ever would.

Barak had smiled and whistled, why the slayer even sang a little while he had mounted the dead chief's horse. Once mounted and with his mission accomplished, the ogre had smiled again broadly to himself as he rode away from the killing fields of the cold eastern plains. Above him now as the ogre rode off in a westerly direction the skies were already darkening with the gathering of huge black vultures. These creatures were always and ever hungry for human as well as animal flesh. And aye these, screeching feathered carrion were most greedy things, and also things keen to be getting on about their gory breakfeast. Barak the meanwhile had at this time both standards heads pushed upside down very disrespectfully inside one of his bags of weapons. Concealment in the giant's opinion of such trinkets was always and ever the wisest move. To some misguided fools these pieces of wood with gold painted eagles atop of them were held as great prizes. For gone now were the days when the standards were made of pure gold with ornate silver trappings about them. Rome quite simply at this moment in time was in decline, aye and a rapid decline at that. Now the Empire, well it just could not afford such lavish expense. Still though, out of sight out of mind was always the safer more sensible option Barak had always thought. Anyway besides all of that, tomorrow or perhaps even the day after Barak mused to himself as he sucked upon both his bad tooth and his long pipe. Then, aye then he would ride off to Vindolanda to drop off the standards, oh and also to meet with the Prefect who had sent him on this pricey ill-fated mission. Oh and what a foolish mission this had been, and a mission that had cost the lives of so many good soldiers and brave men.

Barak was still musing over what might be the Prefect's reaction as to the cost of this most recent foolish campaign when Aulric began to stir himself into some sort of sense. Barak upon seeing this first sign of life at once pulled upon his great hide boots. For some reason not quite known even to him-self, the ogre always liked to be well shod whenever in company.

'Fools, I ordered this Hall to be kept empty, who is it who dares break my ruling and my order, who dares to trespass here in my great hall?' Drunkenly the King shouted this while he dribbled and slurred out his words in a sad most pathetic fashion. Aulric was not at this time even looking up at the intruder who drank his drink and ate his meat. Aye and Aulric however, well the king never quite finished whatever it was he was about to say next.

'I do dare Aulric, for it is I your friend Barak.' The giant he almost bellowed these words out. 'I am returned here to this place of yours, I am returned from my foolhardy quest for the Eagles of Rome.' In the meanwhile as the giant spoke between gulping down his drink Aulric merely sat there in his carved ornate oaken chair in a most pathetic state. Alas the sad king did this while he snotted like some sort of lost child, and all of this while he wept into his baggy shirt sleeve. Now the king after sobbing sadly next made an uncaring dismissive gesture with his right hand.

Barak rumbled out a curse then sucked upon his sore tooth before spitting bile and blood into the fire. Once with this cleansing of his mouth done the giant said on.

'You are unwashed my old friend.' Barak grumbled this out more than a little taken aback by his friend's dishevelled appearance. 'Indeed, I must say in all honesty that you are a most unkingly and also a very sad sight to behold,' the giant further added with a low rumbling voice. 'Aye, in all fact I must also add this to my observations, you do also stink to high heaven Aulric my friend.' Barak said these profound but honest words as he reached out then next poured a nearby jug of water over Aulric's throbbing head. Angrily the King cursed while he banged upon the long oak table with his fists as the cold water ran over his face then coursed down the back of his neck. Barak once again sucked upon his painful bad back tooth then spat a little more blood and bile into the raging fire before speaking up.

'Aulric you must trust me, for I do say this speaking as a long-time friend. But I do hope you understand just what it is I say to you Aulric? ' Barak had said these cruel but honest words with just the slightest hint of sympathy to his sad heartbroken friend. But sympathy, however, with Barak was not and never had been a long running thing. And, so the ogre quite simply next got on with the business in hand. 'Now then good Aulric, now you must stir yourself, and now you must shake your fuzzed up head and come alive. Oh, aye, now my old friend you must pull yourself together as best you can. '

Aulric spluttered and cursed himself into some sort of life as next the King reached out for his sword hilt, this out of the sheer sadness and madness at his most troubling situation. Sadly this however was to no avail, as in a most pathetic manner the king fell back against his great carved oak throne in a most untidy heap. Indeed, it was then the king would have tipped himself up and fallen into the fire had not Barak with rapid reflexes caught him and held him firm by his skinny wrists.

Barak scowled then growled as the ogre sighed deeply to himself in concern for his long-time friend's sadness. Now Aulric close up, well he indeed looked an even more beaten, broken down thing the nearer Barak was to him. As already said the heartbroken king looked a most worn out tired creature who appeared to look much older even than his years. Aulric was a man who was a little younger than the giant but despite this he had always looked far older than his overly large friend. It was obvious to Barak that Aulric was by his shabby appearance alone a most broken and beaten man. On top of all of that the fallen king stank strongly of ale vomit aye and even other nasty more odious things.

Of a sudden the good King suddenly drooled as he frothed at the mouth, just like some sort of demented madman from out of the back streets.

'Barak, Barak, is it truly you who stands there before me my good and most faithful of all friends? Is it indeed you Barak? Or perhaps I have indeed gone totally and hopelessly mad? ' the king stammered out at length. 'I had thought in my dark madness you had forsaken me, deserted me and never again would you return to this place. Yes, yes in all truth I did think this in my mind's troubled darkness big Barak. ' The good king sobbed this out while hanging onto the giant like a frightened babe to its mother as he did so.

As for Barak, the giant warrior, well, even the slayer was moved in the very extreme to see his friend in such a sad pathetic distress. But still and despite all of this, Barak remained just as stalwart and just as stern as ever he always had been. So with this being the case, for now at least the giant in front of his weeping friend showed little or no emotion.

'You have cried and you have sobbed here in this great Hall of yours these last days for long enough now' the ogre declared almost with a fatherly voice. 'Now Aulric, now you must please believe me in what I say, weeping, well it achieves nothing. Oh no my friend this achieves nothing at all.' Barak with these words said then swallowed down another mouthful of mead and then once again he spoke. 'So my man, now of course you must pull yourself together, you must talk to me now.' Barak said this a little sternly while the king turned away from the slayer and cradled his throbbing troubled head in his boney hands as Barak said on. 'My friend you must talk to me' Barak insisted. 'Aye and talk to me right now this very minute, this so that I might find a cure. Talk to me Aulric so

I might find some sort of a remedy, a cure for this sinister unspeakable tragedy, this evil wrong doing that has befell you and your family. '

Barak after saying this gently sat Aulric back down upon his carved wooden throne from where he had risen.

'There will be no more drink for you my friend, well at least not yet anyway,' the giant said firmly as he placed a huge hand upon Aulric's quivering shoulder. 'You must first sober yourself up, and then next when your head clears a little tell me all and everything. Please believe me Aulric I would know every single little detail of this tragedy, aye all and everything mind you. You must take good care Aulric that nothing you tell me is left out; do you understand me my friend?' Barak had now discarded his shaky stool and he pulled himself up a good heavy chair. With this done the ogre next sat himself down facing the broken forlorn king. Aye and now the giant the meanwhile held Aulric's gaze firmly with those black eyes of his. Barak after another swig of mead next bade the king recount the events of these last few sad grim days. For this outrage, well, it was altogether a most strange sinister affair, aye and that was to say the least. Strange because the King of the northern Britons he had no known enemies, why the King was strongly allied to Rome itself. Aye and also as well as all of this, Aulric had the respect as well as the friendship of every tribe from one end of the great wall to the other.

From the Irish Sea to the west of the island and the cold North sea to the east Aulric was most well thought of by both the rich and the poor alike.

And as for the foolish childlike blue dyed warring Picts, well, those fools could be easily dismissed for any involvement in this black crime as their days of savagery and fear spreading was over long ago, well at least for now it was anyway. Barak, well perhaps he more than anyone else had most brutally crushed these unholy savages into a cringing submission. So for now at least these blue dyed fools were happy and contented enough to fight steal and butcher among themselves far north of the great wall of Hadrian. Aye these savage simple but brutal souls thrived in the cold far off snow-capped mountains feasting upon giant deer and the abundance of salmon that swam the northern rivers. As for Aulric, well the kindly King had wanted and hoped to end his days peacefully with his children all about him, aye and in good time perhaps even their children also. His wife alas was no more as she sadly had died giving birth to his young daughter a dozen years earlier. So now in his most unexpected grief the good king was all alone, the rest of his family all dead or gone on to who knows where or what? Aulric suddenly shook his head as he stirred himself into some sort life. Then while still in a drunken daze the King looked up blearily eyed and he addressed the giant. His words though were however not overly kind, no they were harsh and not quite complimentary at all.

'Had you been here with me in this place Barak, here instead of being off warring for the foolish arrogant pride of the Legions of Rome, my children might yet still be safe.' And this the Briton blurted out both sadly aye and also more than a little bitterly. 'Damn Rome, damn Rome with its pompous arrogance to hell and back,' the heart-broken king cursed out loudly. Aulric had meant no offence toward his friend Barak but nevertheless these words cut most deeply into the giant's very large heart, even more into his very soul itself if the truth was to be known.

Aye, what made matters worse as it so happened, as has already been said, this disastrous quest, well it was no more than a foolhardy disastrous folly. A lot of good men had died on those cold windy plains to retrieve what was after all only a symbol of dying Roman power. But still despite all and everything even in the face of Aulric's harsh bitter but honest words Barak still showed no outward sign of either remorse guilt or even anger. Perhaps because after all was said and done, and for better or worse, what had happened had happened. Aye what was done was done. And therefore, well it could of course not be undone. But then again though, on the other hand however, well this could and it would always be avenged. So now with this black retribution firmly in Barak's mind, now it was a time to listen. Yes it was a time to listen now, time to learn of these past goings on. And then, and only then, and when he had gathered enough valid information would the ogre act. Barak of course being Barak, well then no doubt he would of course act quickly, aye also very possibly and more than likely the ogre would act most violently.

After some little time in passing whilst listening very carefully to Aulrics every word the great tattooed giant relit his long much loved weed filled pipe. Now the ogre appeared to be more relaxed, in fact the slayer appeared quite at ease with himself. Barak listened most intently most carefully to every single word Aulric said to him, the ogre as always and ever overlooked nothing. Often the slayer would ask the king to repeat himself over and over again. This way the giant was making quite sure Aulric was accurate in his every single detail of this recent tragedy. But in the meanwhile the heat from the blazing fire warmed Barak's huge body, while the monks' mead from the flagon warmed his belly and the black mountain weed from his long pipe warmed his very being. For well over an hour Aulric went over and over again repeating in parrot fashion the grim events which had brought a once proud king to become a sad shambling mess of a man.

Aulric ran a rough scarred gnarled hand through his long greying somewhat unkempt lank and greasy hair.

'Seven arrows, seven arrows that were black shafted and with black flight feathers you say?' Barak asked a little whimsically.

'Aye', Aulric replied simply in answer to Barak's question, a question the giant had asked him several times before already. 'How many more ways can I answer you the same question Barak?' Aulric asked this a little sharply. Barak sucked upon his pipe with some gusto as the slayer simply ignored Aulric's irritable anger completely.

'Where is the young Prince Kye now Aulric? Tell me my friend where does the boy lie? For I would like to see him, I would like to look upon the prince once more.' Barak said this while rising a little stiffly to his huge booted feet and then warming his backside by the blazing fire. The long night's ride, this and also the lack of a decent night's sleep was making his huge tired body feel a little chill. Now the king sighed sadly and most wearily at Barak's request. Aulric in his own way was perhaps even fearful to look upon his son's lifeless corpse whilst in the company of Barak, this less he once again unman himself and weep. In truth the king seemed just for now lost in his much troubled thoughts for a moment or two. But then after but a second or two in thought the sad king shook his weary head as he rubbed his pounding skull. Next, and with what seemed was a great effort Aulric began to stir himself as he rose somewhat unsteadily to his feet.

With this task done Aulric next pointed towards a heavy red crimson velvet curtain that hung just to the left of the fireplace from where the two men had been seated. Barak who had already been up on his big booted feet moved instantly to the side of his friend to offer assistance if needed. After all the slayer did not want to see the shaky Aulric fall headlong onto the stone floor and hurt himself. However the king though as it happened managed with great resolve to steady himself and he waved Barak away.

'Draw back that curtain Barak, a concealed chamber lies there behind it.' Aulric indicated with his bony forefinger toward a heavy red velvet curtain. This curtain hung under the tapestry of an elaborate boar hunt hanging from the stone wall just left of the fireplace. Barak with but a few huge strides stood by the curtain, once there the ogre drew back the drape. Just as Aulric had said a solid studded oak door lay hidden behind the heavy velvet curtain. Barak at once turned the key already in the lock and followed by Aulric who had pulled himself together a little entered into the room. As ever the king seemed to draw strength from Barak's very presence. Although still obviously shaken and grief stricken Aulric appeared now at least to be in some sort of control over his troubled emotions.

This room was like no other room in the castle, aye it was a cold place, a place just like a Roman death chamber of rest. As the floor, the walls and even the ceiling, these were cut from the finest quality of Roman pastel coloured marble. And this was also by the look of it carved out by the very best of Roman craftsman. Barak at once glanced all about him, as ever and always taking in all and everything. Now there before him upon a large marble table lay the lifeless body of the young Prince. The long limbed youth was naked save for a leather loin cloth. Also the young prince had been washed cleansed then scented with the crushed pollen of wild forest flowers. Prince Kyes arms were placed across his breast as was the custom for the dead and also an ornate golden band had been placed upon his black haired head.

Now it was the king's resolve seemed to break for but a second as he gazed with tear filled eyes upon his one and only son. But still despite this emotional attack, to his credit Aulric held himself strong in front of his grim giant retainer. Aulric slowly and shakily lowered himself down as he knelt by the side of his son. And the king somewhat grimly took the boy's hand in his as he interlocked fingers. Once again to his eternal credit the king did not weep nor did he buckle. As in all truth Barak had expected him too, perhaps though this was alas merely because there were no more tears left to be shed.

Aye indeed perhaps now the good and kindly king had ran himself quite dry.

Barak noticed that in the corner of the room there lay a thick wolf skin cloak a leather tunic and also a pair of thick hide boots. Doubtless these items of clothing were how the young Prince was dressed at the time of the cowardly attack. Aye and also as well as the Princes' personal affects seven long black shafted arrows also lay there. Most of these offending missiles were now broken, this by Aulric in his disgust his anger and his very hatred of the things. It was Aulric alone who had washed and tended his one and only son, allowing no one else to touch the lifeless body. Even his physicians the king had dismissed as he cursed them in his anger and his sorrow. For after all, it was they who had pronounced his beloved son to be now a dead and lifeless thing.

Barak after a brief moment observing the youth next moved over to the corner of the room as he carefully examined the black arrows very closely. And then of a sudden the giant gave out a savage grunt as he cursed in a language that Aulric was not totally familiar with.

Over the many years he had spent with Barak the good king had heard the slayer speak in this strange unknown guttural tongue before. But this was mostly when the ogre was either roaring drunk or was talking to his big red bloodthirsty dogs his many horses or his great black very unfriendly eagle.

'When exactly did all of this occur Aulric, tell me when did it all happen? And you must think most carefully now and you must make no mistakes in your accounting of things. For believe me my friend this is a most important question that requires a most important answer..' Barak said this as he ran a finger over the arrowhead of the black shafted arrow. The kindly King sniffed, coughed, then he paused for just a moment, this as he struggled to gather his wits and his ravaged senses together. Aulric was thoughtful for but a moment then he at last spoke up to give his reply to the ever calculating ogre.

'It was on the night of the last full moon, so I suppose Barak it must have been two or three days ago,' Aulric answered after some long and careful deliberation. 'Aye, aye I do remember because I looked into the heavens on that sad starry night and swore I wanted to die before I ever saw another full moon.

Know you this now, without my children I am nothing, nothing my friend Barak. No I am nothing at all, I am not a king, I am not a man and I am not even a father. Though father I would choose any day over being a king or anything else for that matter' said the heartbroken Aulric. For a moment the king paused as he gathered his composure then spoke once again. 'But know you this Barak, I will build for my only son Kye a great funeral pyre. A pyre higher than even the great wall of Hadrian itself to send his ashes off to the gods of my fathers' Aulric said this while placing a hand gently upon his son's forehead. 'But as for my beloved daughter, well who knows where my child Ellena is, or what has become of her? Is she alive do you think big Barak? Indeed does she still live and breathe the cold crisp air? Do you think my child, she still walks the earth? Aye and anyway my old friend, why oh why did this accursed outrage happen to me and my children in the first place? Can you tell me that Barak? If not I am lost, as no man I know has ventured further or knows more about the way of things than you do, so tell me then, why has this foul crime transpired?.' Aulric asked this question with his voice shaking with emotion. 'I am at war with no one Barak. I have no enemies left to fight with, remember, you killed them all for me. Well for me and also for the glory of Imperial Rome of course - do you remember my friend?' the King asked solemnly before continuing. 'This thing, it is an outrage I tell you,' Aulric declared his rising anger now taking over from his grief.

Barak sighed most deeply then the ogre grunted and growled a low rumbling growl, it was a growl like that of a wounded bear, then the ogre spoke. 'No more of an outrage than it would be to suffer the good noble and handsome Prince to the flames Aulric' Barak said this in a slow matter of fact fashion. Aulric stared up at his towering friend in both horror and sheer disbelief at these unbelievable words. As slowly there across the giants scarred tattooed face there next crept just the very faintest hint of a crooked smile.

Now the king felt, well rather he fumbled for his sword for the second time since Barak's return. Aulrics brain at this time was still addled with both drink and grief but the King neither understood nor liked what Barak had just said to him.

Was he being mocked now the king thought dimly to himself? Aye and was he being mocked by the very man he trusted more than any in the whole cruel world. As ever the ogre well he apparently could read Aulrics very thoughts.

'Be still, be calm with yourself my old friend, and leave your blunt sword where it rests. And then listen well to me, listen carefully to what I say to you Aulric.' Barak demanded this as the ogre once again repeated that which he had just said to the dumfounded king.

'Your boy is not a dead thing, oh no, oh no he still lives Aulric.' Barak went on with his voice sounding firm and also most convincing. 'The good prince like I have said is not dead at all, do you understand me Aulric? Your boy, well he for now merely sleeps the very deepest of slumbers.'

For just a brief moment in time Aulric wondered to himself if it was not he but Barak who had finally gone stone mad. Had the giant at last gone insane? Aye perhaps it was the great slayer who had finally taken leave of his senses? True it was he himself had almost drowned himself in drink with his grief and his sorrow over these last few days. Aye, but surely though to this bitter indulgence he was most entitled given the present grim circumstances. But still for what he had drank in his Great Hall was out of his sadness and madness, this as well as his sheer heartbreak. Why these few goblets of ale he had drank down these past days would scarce cause the giant to be even unsteady upon his great flat booted feet. Barak, why the great slayer drank that and perhaps even three times that amount just as an everyday social event, aye this just to quench his great never ending thirst. Oh and this not to mention all of the strong brain destroying black weed the slayer puffed relentlessly upon almost every single moment of every day. No, no surely it was Barak who had finally gone totally insane, aye Barak it was who had gone stone mad. After a moment or two of slow pondering and careful deliberation Aulric at length spoke up even if it was a little shakily.

'But my own physicians have examined my son Kye, saying he was no more alive than the table he lies upon,' Aulric explained somewhat gloomily. 'So please believe me my big friend the young prince is now nothing more than but a dead thing lying there before you. Aye, alas he is now nothing but a corpse Barak, no more than that.' Aulric said these words very sadly. 'Please believe me big Barak my friend I would only wish it was otherwise,' Aulric protested sadly.

But big Barak, well he would have none of it. Instead the ogre shook his big bucket sized head in a most dismissive fashion.

'No,' the giant then answered both simply and bluntly. 'No, no you are wrong, Kye is not a dead thing Aulric, nor will he die, well at least not for another fifty years or so. Well that is of course providing the boy does not fall off his horse and he leaves the heavy drink and the black weed alone.' Barak said this with a sort of lop sided smile, then once again the ogre went on to explain things as they were to his very baffled friend. 'Now hear me out, and you must listen to every word I have to say to you without any sort of interruption, do you understand me? Aulric gave a slight nod, the king at this particular time had not the strength or the will to argue with Barak. 'It has been four full days now since the full moon Aulric, not two or three as you had thought it to be. Aulric feeling somewhat dizzy and groggy of course let the giant say on without any sort of argument. 'So, tell me my friend, and answer me this, why then has the young Prince not the death stiffness about him?' Barak asked bluntly.

Aulric was much taken aback by the giants well put question, also on top of that Barak was of course most correct in what he had just asked. As the young prince by now, well, he should be laying there upon the marble slab just as stiff as a broad sword. Yet, here the lad was now laid before them still soft to the touch, why the Prince was even a little warm.

'Look you here at these arrows Aulric, the tips are not finished with off steel heads, no these are blunt and wooden things. Then look you at the wounds inflicted upon the boy's body, the legs the arms aye and even one in the backside. So, this attack, however foul and cowardly, however pre-planned and wrongful was not done with any murderous intentions. Aye and of that Aulric I am most sure and certain,' Barak added positively. Aulric was at once struck numb and dumb with both shock and sheer disbelief. All of this information was just far too much for him to take in at once. Perhaps because of this reason, quite simply the information Barak had gave him, well it was yet again both correct and accurate. Aye on reflection all and everything big Barak had just said to him made total sense.

At length after some while deliberating this new situation the much confused king spoke up.

'But my own physicians, they said the young prince my son was dead Barak, aye they to a man looked to him and all and every single one of them had him slain. '

Barak grumbled away to himself angrily at these words, the ogre as it so happened was a man who had long been most unimpressed by Aulrics so called healers.

'Umph, your physicians Aulric, why, those imposters are not fit to doctor a worthless hill sheep,' the giant declared angrily. 'Truth said these fools of yours are little more than witchdoctor's who cast the bones of chickens and scream at the stars in childish and vacant wonderment. Aye indeed your so called doctors are no more than uneducated morons each, all and every single one of them.' Barak said this with some conviction, and with a certain degree of rising anger. After all had he not returned earlier than planned the young prince would of been placed upon a high pyre and then burnt to ash, aye and all of this while he was still alive. However, Barak had the feeling Aulric perhaps needed a little more solid proof that his son lived. Being so, then proof the king would have.

'Now look you here Aulric..' Barak next produced from one of the front pockets of his thick knee breeches a small burnished copper mirror. Next this mirror the ogre held close over the lips of the young Prince. Aulric stood back a pace or two as the king was in all truth not quite sure what he was even looking for, or even looking at for that matter.

'Here, look you my friend, do you see it?' the giant pressed offering the copper disc to Aulric. 'That my friend is the boy's life's breath, indeed, it is his very being, look Aulric do you see it now? ' the ogre asked urgently. 'The young prince still breathes, the boy he lives, can you see it now Aulric?' Barak repeated this question a little urgently as he held out the polished copper disc toward Aulric. Now the king with his bloodshot eyes popping from his throbbing troubled head at once clasped the mirror in gleeful disbelief. For a moment or two Aulric stood silently examining the misty covering from his son's slight but still steady breathing.

'But how is this at all possible - how and most of all why?' the king exclaimed in a dreamlike shock when the gift of speech eventually returned to him. 'I swear upon my blunt sword, I do not understand it, no I do not understand any of this at all Barak.' Aulric said this as his head was still spinning with the very confusion of these strange recent sad events.

Barak gave out a grunt and a low growl as he sighed deeply then next the ogre shrugged his massive shoulders. Cursing under his breath Barak looked to his long time friend who was alas still broken and much confused as to the way of things. After but a moment in passing the giant glanced down at the young Prince laid upon the cold marble slab. Oh yes, this indeed was a most messy affair; it was also an affair that would take some time in explaining, aye also even more time in its solving.

'Come Aulric my old friend, for I do think it is time now that you will need a drink.' Barak said this while affording Aulric a somewhat dubious smile. 'But you hear this aye and you hear this now Aulric,' Barak said in a most serious tone of voice. 'Your young prince, he must lie here in this place; Kye must lie upon that very slab until my return here from my quest. Oh aye, and of course also my bloody vengeance,' the giant rumbled out in a most menacing fashion. 'Here is the best and the safest place for him, it is cool here, free from decay as well as dirt,' the ogre further explained. 'Also the coming winter chill will not harm the lad as he feels nothing, the prince must stay as he lays, now do you understand me? '

Barak asked this question while putting a huge hand upon his friend's trembling shoulder, Aulric made no reply at this time as quite simply he could not find his tongue to speak. With this being so then of course the great ogre said on. 'Yes Aulric, here in this cold chamber is good for your boy, do you truly understand me?' Barak asked this question most firmly. Aulric only nodded in agreement to this, even though the king did not really know in all truth what he was agreeing to. Or for that matter did the much baffled king even know to where and to what and to why Barak was apparently going to be venturing off. After some time passed the two men did leave the young handsome Prince lying there upon the cold marble slab. And this task the men managed even though Aulric was most reluctant to do so. Once out of that cold but clean room Aulric locked the stout door behind them. Next the befuddled king tested it with a push then once satisfied all was secure the men reseated themselves by the hearth in front of the blazing fire. Aulric shakily took a goblet of drink in both hands offered to him by Barak and took a big swallow. Then with this done the king waited patiently for his friend to continue with his explanation of these recent sinister events. First though before all of this Barak had decided he would take another long drink of the monks' mead, this, and also refill his pipe with yet more strong weed.

Chapter Three

'You say to me that these men were assassins Barak? But then if so, well how is it with seven arrows these so called killers missed the heart and the throat of my young son?'

Barak gave a long deep and a most weary sigh on hearing these words. Now the giant could see this explanation of things was going to be something of hard work.

'Aulric was a good brave sincere man, a man of high morals. However, at times the king was perhaps not the brightest of men Barak had ever met. Still though despite all of this he was of course entitled to an honest explanation, this being so then the king would have it. 'As I have already said to you Aulric, this was not in any way a murder mission. And know you this my friend it is harder not to kill a man using seven arrows that have all struck the body than kill him. No, these men without any doubt were good bowmen please believe me on that score. If these men had wanted your son the Prince Kye a dead thing, then one sharp arrow would have been enough to seal his fate and so send him off to the ever after.' Barak explained all of this after a long leisurely puff upon his pipe before once again continuing with Aulric's education.

'Aye, now look you here, see for yourself,' the giant went on as he handed one of the offending arrows to Aulric. Next the giant pointed out the hollows in the arrowheads which were wooden and not steel tipped as was the norm. Here it was in these wooden shafts the sleeping potion was contained. Aye here within the thin carved out grooves held firm with pressed bee wax the potion rested. Later this wax would dissolve once inside the warm body of the victim. And it was then the potion would go to work and bring about the sleep of death. 'Look you Aulric the arrowheads are short blunted things, this so they would not deeply penetrate the flesh, can you see that? ' the giant asked hoping his friend was grasping the situation. Aulric though was still much confused but nevertheless despite everything the much muddled king seemed to understand what the giant was saying to him.

'Yes, yes I must admit that I can see that now, now you do mention it Barak..' Aulric exclaimed this as he pulled at his hair in the sheer anger and the very frustration of it all. 'But why Barak, Tell me why is my only son in a death sleep and as for my little girl; what of my beloved daughter Ellena? Is she then a dead thing now? Tell me my friend is she discarded and abandoned in some thicket or ditch or other? Or mayhap she is a slave, aye a slave for sale in some dark dingy rat-infested dungeon far to the east of here?' Aulric said this as his body trembled with emotion and his pale eyes welled up with tears before he once again said on. 'Or perhaps, just perhaps something even more evil and sinister has befallen her, if that is at all possible? '

Barak at once cursed as he growled away to himself at seeing his friend so broken and forlorn. So once again feeling the need of a little comfort the ogre took a big swallow of mead. Of course this was followed by another long puff upon his long clay pipe before answering his friends well put question.

'No, no Aulric please believe me, she, the princess Ellena is none of these things.' Barak put in quickly before his friend upset himself becoming saddened and perhaps even more tearful than he was before.

Now the good and kindly King Aulric affixed Barak his long-time friend with a sad worried questioning stare. Barak had over the years travelled both far and wide and spoke in many foreign tongues. Yes the great slayer of both man and beast knew many, oh so many things, far more than did he. Aulric was a man who had never even left his own little island or in all truth had he even ventured very far at all. Why Aulric himself supposed he had never even lost sight of the great wall, aye and this since being a small boy. Barak, however, on the other hand, well, he was a most learned man. The great slayer could read and write in the Latin, Persian and Greek, aye these as well as many other languages besides. Aulric, well he in all truth had never held any man higher in esteem than Barak, this in either courage, integrity or intellect.

Barak knew he had much to explain to Aulric and the ogre sighed heavily at the very thought of it. Nevertheless the ogre very casually blew a perfect smoke hoop into the still air despite all of these imminent problems. Barak then spoke some comforting reassuring words to his forlorn friend.

'Ellena, she is safe my friend, please believe me she will be kept so until the time I go and fetch her, aye and believe me, fetch her I will..' Barak said this in between his drinking his smoking and also a little bit of unhealthy coughing whilst spitting into the glowing fire. 'Fetch her and bring her back to you - aye and fetch her like I say I will, you have my word upon it,' the giant said most sincerely.

Barak spoke now with such a matter of fact certainty that Aulric with some effort drew himself up from his carved oak throne. For the first time on that chill but sunny morning Aulric looked a little more like the man he had been before Barak had left in search of the Roman standard.

'I will come with you Barak upon this dangerous vengeful venture my friend, aye together we will slay these bringers of sorrow in a good and honest fashion will we not?.' Aulric said this as he drew his blunted rusty sword and hunched up his shoulders, this whilst puffing out his somewhat feeble chest.

However this was a plan of action which did not at all appeal in any way to the great uncompromising slayer.

'No, oh no.' Barak replied straightaway and very bluntly. As the giant knew only too well this request, which he had by the by expected, was also a request he must in all honesty refuse. 'No you must bide here in your stone castle Aulric, you must care for the boy. No one else can be trusted with his safe keeping, deceivers and knaves could still abound; do you understand this Aulric?' However, in simple truth Barak did not want Aulric along with him on this long and dangerous venture. As ever there was to be only Barak and Barak alone in charge on this perilous mission. And just as ever and always the giant would brook no interference of any sort from anyone on this long hazardous quest that lay ahead of him. With the good hearted but fumbling Aulric along Barak had surmised the whole affair would be no more than a total disaster.

Barak spoke softly but firmly and king or no king Aulric made no offer of any argument whatsoever. But he never did with Barak, then again no one ever did with the towering glowering ogre. Whatever the giant said and whoever he said it to, well this was the norm, taken to be the last absolute word on all and anything. Aye, and that be whether these souls were kings, pharaohs or emperors. Wherever or whatever task it was Barak undertook, the giant was always in charge, he was always the commander, always the leader of the men.

'I will take with me a dozen of your best warriors, men who know the princess well, men she will feel safe with and be at ease with on her homeward passage. These rogues who have your daughter do have a start on us that is true, but that is of no matter. I will overhaul these fools, catch them, then of course I will slay them all. Once this simple little task is done I will have the princess returned back to your side in all haste.'

Barak spoke with such confidence the slayer made the whole affair sound like little more than some sort of a rabbit hunt rather than a dangerous rescue mission.

'I though must travel on as she sails homeward to you Aulric. I must travel on to obtain the antidote that will awaken the young prince from his deep slumbers. Alas this journey will take me some time, some months in the doing of it. But still, never the less you must care for the boy in my absence. Do this Aulric and believe me all yet will be well.' Barak's confidence reassured Aulric, the king smiled, he even chanced a moment's nervous laughter. Now Aulric spoke up as he wanted yet more information. However, though now it was Barak's turn to look somewhat glum, Barak's turn to look somewhat downcast.

'Barak my large friend you must tell me how you know so much about these men, these men who come to my land to cause such sorrow and upset. For I would know the whys as well as the wherefores of this cruel most uncalled for of all outrages.' Aulric said these words calmly, now he was sounding like a man who at last was regaining both his composure and also his confidence.

Barak gave a slight nod, then the ogre spat out a wad of black phlegm into the blazing fire. He was, the giant thought to himself, both smoking and drinking far too much than was mayhap at all good for him. Perhaps with this in mind he would cut down just a little on his unhealthy habits after this next venture, aye but then again perhaps not.

'First though Aulric, before we do go into the whys and the wherefores of things you must answer me this question. '

'Aulric, tell me since I left this cold place to do the foolish bidding of Rome, have any strangers arrived here - by here I mean in this place or around about if you know what I mean?' Barak asked this question while swallowing down another mouthful of the monks' strong sweet mead. 'Traders, gypsies, new men to the garrison even, anyone strange or unknown to you at all. And think now most carefully Aulric for this is indeed very important. ' Aulric pondered while he deliberated for some time; the king, as Barak advised, was indeed most thoughtful. In fact he was very thoughtful, as the king knew well this question was somehow crucial to all and everything. At long length after what seemed like an age in passing Aulric smiled then he spoke up. Aye and when he did it was also the answer Barak had fully expected, the answer the ogre wanted to hear.

'Prospero the Magistrate at Vindolanda, he has a new secretary, they tell me he is a foreigner by all accounts. I have seen him several times on my visits to speak with the Prefect about this and that. ' On hearing this, the ogre gave a wry grin as he motioned for Aulric to say on. 'Aye Barak this man if I remember rightly he began his work in the magistrate's office the very same week you left this place.' Barak smiled once again and the ogre urged with a nod of his great link clad head for Aulric to say on further, which of course the king did. 'This fellow is a tall thing, aye he is a lean cagey sort of man. And also the fellow has a most shifty sly untrustworthy look about him. Well, that is when you can catch a glimpse of his ferret like face.' Aulric said this only after he had given the matter some considerable thought and further long deliberation. 'He is always and forever a lofty hooded figure dressed in a long red robe that reaches down to the very ground. Oh aye, and this hooded robe he wears even when at his writing and his reading. Indeed Barak, I must say he looks to me more like some sort of a sinister holy man than any sort of a book keeper, if you know what I mean?.'

Barak gave out a very satisfied grunt, then the ogre took yet another deep swig of the sweet heady mead.

'Can you tell me this then, how does the man sound to you Aulric? When he speaks I mean, how does this tall hooded stranger's voice sound to you?' Barak paused as he watched Aulric with his hands shaking unsteadily pour himself a drink of mead. 'Tell me my friend,' Barak pressed, 'is this man's dialect or his accent familiar to you in any way at all? Once again I ask you to think now, aye and to think upon this question most carefully, for this is most important. ' Aulric paused at this point as he scratched at his greasy hair then at his unkempt beard. All the while the king fidgeted nervously then suddenly he smiled before speaking up once again. Somehow the king had the feeling this sad strange affair was about to piece itself together just a little bit more.

'Like you Barak, aye now that you do mention it, when the tall hooded book-keeper talks, well I do suppose he sounds a lot like you. '

Big Barak grinned in a most dangerous wolf like fashion, the smiling ogre refilled up his empty goblet with yet more monks' mead before speaking.

'You know Aulric my friend, I thought somehow he just might,' the giant said after a huge swallow of drink and yet another long puff upon his pipe.

Aulric was now a much happier, much more confident man, Barak was after all behind him in this sad sinister mess. And also the giant had sworn upon his famed dragon sword to put all right that which was wrong. Why, that pledge alone made by the fearsome unstoppable ogre in itself was more than enough for Aulric.

'Now then my large friend, you must tell me about these assassins. Oh and aye, you must tell me how it is you know so much of their dark cunning and their evil ways Barak?' Aulric pressed this question as he leant forward in his throne. 'And tell me this also, why did you ask if a stranger had arrived here in this place? Here in these far flung northern parts my most trusted learned friend?' Aulric asked eagerly.

Barak stalled for but a moment or two, and in all truth the slayer did not straightaway answer Aulric's most direct and honest question. Indeed the giant was most ponderous and he was very thoughtful before making any sort of answer.

'Well Aulric, let us hope that we can always remain so, as friends I mean. ' This was the giant's final reply after some sombre deep and very thoughtful deliberation. Barak next gave a weary sigh with just a slight shiver, this due more to tiredness than anything else. 'You had I suppose better make yourself comfortable Aulric.' Barak said this while topping up his friend's goblet whilst once again refilling his own. 'For this tale I am now about to tell you, though I do say so myself might take some time in the telling of it. '

Oh aye and just as Barak had said, well the tale indeed did take some time in the telling. Later when the story was at last told and Barak had finished with his explanation of these sad recent events, well it must be said, poor Aulric once again had the look of a man who was totally utterly lost to all and everything. It was only after some passing of time as the ogre silently puffed away upon his pipe Aulric at length found his voice.

'So you mean to tell me Barak that you are a king, aye and you are a king by birthright at that?' Aulric asked this question in utter amazement at his very large friend's strange new revelation. Aulric, well he might have carried the title of a king but in all truth he was in reality no more than a clan chieftain, a chieftain who had with the help of the Romans been promoted somewhat slightly in rank.

'Aye, aye Aulric I am, I am a king, though not by choice I must say to you. Anyway, tell me why is this, a fact that you find so hard to believe Aulric?' Barak asked this question somewhat indignantly.

Aulric gave a thin smile, the bemused Briton coughed a little before draining his goblet down in a single swallow. It was not yet noon and so far this day he had been told his dead son now lived, and also his most trusted friend and long time retainer was a king. Aye and Barak, well he was a real king at that. Barak was apparently the ruler of some far flung kingdom; the slayer was not some made up king as he was but a man of royal blood. Apparently the giant was lord and monarch of some vast powerful hidden kingdom that lay far away to the east. Barak, by his own honest account of things had left his homeland many years ago as no more than a boy. Not wishing to be entrapped by protocol royal goings on and the mundane life in the palace. The young prince, as he was, then had simply saddled his horse and rode off into the wild.

Apparently his father, the great and powerful king Bartok had alas died in a fall from his horse. Being so then literally overnight the young prince had become the new king of a vast far reaching empire. However, this was an illustrious title and a position the young Barak did not crave or want. No this was not at all for him, the constant deceit coupled with the trappings of protocol and the non-stop treachery of everyday court life, Barak, even as a youth had despised.

Instead the lanky young Barak with his heart broken by his father's sudden demise had opted instead for a wanderer's life. Then much later on, after a certain amount of even more tragedy and heartbreak in his young life the youth had out of pure hatred chosen another path. Barak had turned to live the life of a bounty hunter, later after this he had next become a mercenary, a very highly paid mercenary at that. Finally after much gore and blood letting Barak had become perhaps the most famous commander and warrior in the known world. For even as a gangly spotty youth Barak had always figured it was better to die by the sword in the heart from an enemy who had at least the courage to meet him head on. Aye at day's end this violent but honest demise was far better a fate than that of a dagger in the dark. Well this or perhaps that other cowardly method of killing a man without actually facing him, which was of course the poison in the cup from a so called friend or palace aid. Still though, despite all and everything, as the eldest son the kingship and the throne had went to him. This was regardless of whether he wanted the title or not, or also indeed even whether Barak was there or not. And so now as the great slayer had so far not abdicated, been slain or died of the drink, the weed or some other natural ailment. Well this being so, despite all and everything he was still the rightful King of the empire of Krozakistan. But now though as the giant approached his fiftieth year there was a time of great change, even more great protocol. Barak, well now the long absent slayer was stuck with little choice as to what to do next. By the laws of his kingdom he must either abdicate the throne then hand it down to the next in line. This or else Barak must argue the point and fight for the right to keep the kingship.

As said it was the law of the land and they demanded Barak return to his kingdom so he might give up his throne publicly or defend his crown. By 'they', well that meant the nobles, the magistrates and the high ranking governing bodies. These as well as all of the other pocket lining lying privileged scum. Or if you like it better put, then the so called elite of the land, the wealthy and the powerful. The men in waiting, those who like so many jackals lay in ever eager readiness to seize yet even more power for themselves. As ever this breed of selfish carrion, these unworthy fools cared not at all for the common people. People who in all truth it was their responsibility to look too, no such men as these cared only for their own comfort and greed.

Barak had a brother but this sibling was no more than a babe when he had rode off from Krozak the capital of Krozakistan a long, long time ago. Over the many years while Barak had been away from his homeland the great slayer had learned from here and there his brother was a weak man. Apparently for most of the time his younger sibling was mostly a sickly unwell thing, a man who was rarely ever seen. Aye and also he was, well as so word had it, an ill advised man who had become no more than a puppet for those who would take power and rule in his stead.

Barak had been brought up by his father who himself was a warrior king, a man born of the most fierce of the warrior elite. Just like his son Barak, the King had been a huge looming giant of a man, a man who lived by the sword, oh and of course his sacred word. Barak being brought up by his father, well he of course knew only too well of honour and honesty. His younger brother however, well alas he had no such guidance, no strength of honour instilled into his very being as he grew up into manhood. Many times over these past years Barak had felt a great guilt. Guilt and even a kind of cowardice for even leaving his brother alone in that gilded but corrupt cage. Many times in the past, even more so of late, this guilt had ruined his sleep, tormenting his dreams, turning them into no more than recurring nightmares.

Their mother she had died at the birth of Barak's younger brother Zark. Perhaps deep down Barak had resented his brother, blaming him in some way for her early untimely demise. But either way besides all of that, this was all a very long time ago, such maybes were all lost in the misty past of time. Now though there were other matters, aye urgent matters that must be dealt with in the here and now. Aye the ghosts of the long past, well these would not have to wait much longer to be settled with once and for all.

Barak with his dark musings over decided he would next further educate Aulric.

'This tall red robed stranger you speak of, this hooded scribe for the Prefect and the Magistrate's office. Well no doubt it was this fellow who was an agent, or at least in league with the Black Guards, these men were responsible for this terrible outage..' Barak stated this fact to Aulric at long length, and the ogre did so more than just a little solemnly.

Aulric leant back in his throne, the king of the northern Britons looked just momentarily more relaxed now than he was before.

'These Black Guards Barak, who are they? Who are these bringers of sorrow and chaos to my land?' Aulric asked. The intrigue of the whole affair had his fuzzed up head suddenly once more in a spinning dizzy turmoil. Much more of this strange intrigue and the king thought he might end the day lying beside his son joining his forefathers in the hereafter. Oh aye, and this without any sort of antidote to assist his recovery. Barak merely grunted as he downed yet another mouthful of mead to fortify his resolve. And then once again the ogre continued to explain the sinister plot to a very much baffled and overawed Aulric.

'As I have already said to you my friend these men are assassins, well at least when required they are. The Black Guard can be a deadly legion. In some ways these men are a secret force made up of a mish mash of lunatics who will do the bidding of whoever rules Krozakistan. When I say a secret force, well by that I mean this legion do most of the dirty work for the royal house. But besides that with the darker part of the legions purpose aside, well these soldiers are still a public legion. Yes this is very true, and fine soldiers the Black Guard are at that. But many in these Black Guard ranks are quite fanatical, some of them are a little unhinged shall we say,' Barak added with a slight smirk. 'Most of them come from well born military families with a long history in soldiering and warfare. These men are trained almost from birth in horsemanship, in the mastering of the sword the lance and the bow. '

Barak after this long explanation of things paused as he next sucked upon his painful back tooth. A tooth which he had quite forgotten about on that particular morning, then clearing his throat after a spit on the ground the ogre spoke up once again.

'And so my friend, by sticking young Kye with these black shafted arrows, well the men of the Black Guard have left a most clear message - aye a message that only I myself could read.' Barak said this with a grunt followed by a most resolute sigh. 'Do you understand me, do you understand what I am saying to you Aulric?' Barak asked with a sense of urgency in his voice. 'These sad and bad most treasonous fools, well I do suppose they want me to follow them. For of course they know full well I must go back to Krozakistan to obtain the antidote of the black lily sometimes known as the black lotus needed to save the boy. This plant is found growing only in the volcanic foot hills about the capital itself.''

Barak paused for a moment just to make sure that a bewildered looking Aulric understood just what it was he was saying to him. Then once satisfied the ogre slowly yet again continued with his explanation of things as best he could. 'When crushed then left for a week or so to settle this becomes the antidote. And this, well this is the potion I must retrieve to save and awaken the young prince. Once again Aulric took on the expression of a man who was lost in total bewilderment, despite this obvious bafflement the giant continued to speak and say on. 'Trust me Aulric, this potion will restore your son to you just as he was before this terrible outrage.' Barak paused for a moment while Aulric took all of this information into his dizzy spinning head. After this moment the giant once again continued with his explanation of things as they stood. 'It is a far journey I must travel to make all that is wrong right, but still nevertheless this trek I can and I will undertake Aulric. As I have already said, I will pledge my word upon my good dragon sword on this. Indeed I will give my very life itself if needs be to make right this terrible wrong that has befallen your family. ' The giant said this with honest conviction

Aulric upon hearing these words arose from his throne, now the good king was perhaps not quite as unsteady on his feet as he had been. The Briton paced to and fro anxiously as he took another swift drink of mead before addressing Barak.

'Well let us hope it does not come to that my large friend' Aulric said his voice full of concern. 'But tell me this, why was my daughter Ellena taken along with these Black Guards then Barak? Had these accursed Black Guards already not caused me enough grief and sorrow without abducting her as well?' The giant all of a sudden growled and snarled in a most unsettling manner, next the slayer shrugged then scowled as he took for himself a deep draw upon his relit pipe.

'Because Aulric, quite simply she was there for the taking, aye also perhaps just as a little extra bait to lure me back to my homeland.' It was most reluctantly the giant had said all of this. Barak after all was more than a little ashamed and perturbed as to what upset his countrymen had done here in his adopted home. 'But fear not Aulric my friend for she is safe, aye you can believe me when I tell you she will be kept that way,' Barak said in all confidence. These men who came here from my land for whatever bad misguided reasons, well these fools will guard her with their very lives. Aye and this no matter what' the ogre growled out. 'It is truly a sad shameful thing that has been done here.' Barak next sucked long and heavily upon his beloved pipe. This was a long draw that brought a strange eerie sort of smile across his tattooed face. Barak next took another mouthful of drink before speaking up once again. 'Ellena she is but a child, you can believe me she will be kept from any harm, aye she will be kept well away from the others.'

Aulric, well the King paled and almost dropped his goblet from his hands upon hearing these words.

'The others, the others, what others?' Aulric put in sharply almost choking upon his own drink as he did so. 'Tell me what others Barak? Do you then mean to say there are more devils to deal with than these accursed Black Guards of yours?' the king blurted out. Big Barak cursed his own tactless clumsiness, perhaps the situation could have been explained a little better. So after yet another deep drink, another long draw upon his pipe to ease his stress Barak gave a slow but most positive nod in reply to the king's question.

'Know you this Aulric, my people are from the vast deserts, the rolling steppes and the snow capped mountains. So alas my friend, mariners we are not,' the giant next explained simply. Aulric scratched at his itchy head then at his unkempt bearded chin in frantic agitation at these honest words. This whole sinister plot once again as ever, well it was becoming the harder to follow, not the easier in its tracking. Why it had more twists and turns to it than one of his fast dogs coursing a good hare in the big buttercup meadow. After a brief pause so he might choose his words perhaps a little more carefully Barak once again continued to speak, explaining the way of things with a little more tact.

'They, these men of the Black Guard have crossed the seas with rogues and reavers, aye it is pirates they have with them for company, there is no doubt in my mind of that', Barak further explained. 'And as for this company of brigands, I would say these are without any doubt north men who hail from the northern fjiords.' Barak said this quite profoundly as he rose up from his chair that creaked and groaned under his great weight. Once the giant was upon his great booted feet he paced up and down a little uneasily in front of the fireplace sucking rapidly upon his pipe as he did so. The king of the northern Britons sighed heavily then reseated himself, slumping back into his throne at these words before speaking again.

'Tell me, why must those in league with the Black Guard be north men Barak?' Aulric next enquired. 'For please believe me my large friend there are pirates a plenty out there in the open seas and the oceans, why these rogues are everywhere all about us,' Aulric declared. 'These thieving ruffians are a scourge, aye they are a plague with their plundering, looting and general mischief. You must please believe me these rogues will do on both land as well as sea.' Barak grunted and growled but he made no argument, in fact the ogre was in total agreement with his friend on that score. The giant paused for a moment to briefly puff upon his pipe before answering Aulric's well put question.

'Because my friend the men of the north have sturdy shallow broad beamed boats. Good strong vessels that can sail directly up the Salmon River, then later on these same vessels can put out to the open sea. Riding upon fast horses from here you can be at the old hunch backs port on the river in but a matter of a few short hours the giant next explained. Barak's sensible practical assessment of the current grim situation as ever and as always made a lot of sense. The huge ungainly, hard to sail galleons of the southern races would have to stop anchored where the Salmon River met with the cold North Sea. Aye and that busy bustling harbour, well it was many days away across rough ground and through thick dense woodland. With this being so, well of course the passing of such a band of foreigners, it would not go at all unnoticed, nor would it go unchallenged. No, not even the boldest of assassins and kidnappers would dare such a desperate mission. Of a sudden the giant gave out a broad grin then the slayer afforded himself a most fearful growl that even startled Aulric.

Barak's keen brain coupled with his animal instincts was working ever quickly now as the sinister plot unfolded itself inside of his big bucket sized head.

Luckily the ogre had returned home to the castle of Aulric much quicker than had been expected of him, about some seven to ten days quicker as it so happened.

Barak, well he had planned on biding in Gaul a good while longer, this even though the ogre did not like the Gauls one little bit. In his last communication to the Prefect, this sent by carrier pigeon. Well the giant had indicated it might yet be some time before his eventual return to the land of the Britons. Barak as chance would have it had a certain fondness for an overly large farmer's daughter. She was a big hairy armed thing who helped out in the evenings in one of the taverns Barak frequented. Well at least she would be an overly large thing for anyone else that is, but Barak however had found her a quite perfect creature. Things though do happen however, aye and not always for the best, unfortunately Barak was sadly forced to end his courting days a little bit early and leave Gaul rather rapidly. Barak's countryman, the one who had afforded the information to the masters of the Black Guards, well he would not have known this however. No, the spy would not have known at all that Barak would be more or less passing the Black Guards so close, so close but only in the opposite direction. It was obvious when Barak had set out many months ago to retrieve the foolishly lost Roman standard. Well now it seemed doubtless even then the Black Guards had also left on route to cause their mayhem and misery.

As it has been already said, it was very true the somewhat beguiled giant had planned to bide in Gaul a while longer. This was of course with the view to treat himself to one or two more romantic weeks with the large hairy armed lady. But alas things did not work out for the lustful Barak after a bit of a fall out over the newly purchased chestnut gelding Barak had rode back to Aulric's castle upon. Barak after a dispute had killed the horse's former owner. Apparently there had been an argument over the price of the noble beast some days after the purchase of the animal. Then with the owner already dead and headless, Barak just for good measure had also dispatched two of the luckless horse dealer's friends. Drink fuelled men who had been foolish enough and unlucky enough to draw their blunt rusty weapons against the ogre. Fools after all are ever fools, they always have been and always will be. With this being so, these men died as such twitching away their last moments on the tavern's floor. Of course the ogre was unconcerned at the death of the Gauls, after all it was they who drew their steel first. As for Barak, well the ogre in his opinion had bought the big handsome horse fair and square. Aye it was true to say the ogre had paid the price agreed for the huge beast on the very night of the deal, cash on the table and sealed with a handshake. Mind you it was also very true to say that Barak had managed to get the man in such a state of complete utter drunkenness the fool could barely speak let alone haggle over the big horse. But in all fairness, well that after all was not the giant's problem. Still nevertheless the giant had somewhat reluctantly left this place of blooming romance and the large hairy armed tearful farmer's daughter. This of course as well as three dead men and a magistrate's summons for his immediate arrest. Feeling no longer welcome the ogre had with some haste made off to a nearby harbour to begin his journey homeward. Of course this was to be better if not good news for Aulric and bad news for their new found enemies. Enemies who were expecting a much better head start towards their final far off destination, either way this slim start was well to the giant's advantage.

'In two or perhaps three days hence from now I will leave this castle Aulric' Barak next explained. 'Then I will set sail from the Salmon River to start my manhunt, believe me my friend I will overhaul these foolish, soon to die ditch dogs. Aye I will have the princess back with you before the next full moon, before this moon even wanes, believe me my friend you have my life upon it. ' Barak's matter of fact profound statement was declared both bravely and confidently.

As for Aulric, well the gloomy king felt quite elated all of a sudden, indeed these past hours his emotions had been up and down at an alarming rate. Barak was of course innocent to these past events he could not, nor would not be held accountable in any way for the crimes of others. Still though this promise of having the Princess returned to his side so soon, well this did seem a little bit too ambitious even for the ever confident sometimes over flamboyant Barak.

'Sail you say, aye and sail in two or three days hence Barak,' Aulric exclaimed. 'No, oh no surely not, this is of course quite impossible,' Aulric further added with just a trace of doubt in his voice. 'There is after all still so much to do my friend. Why Barak we have as yet not even a ship with which to pursue these dogs,' Aulric said this with a weary sigh followed by a shrug. 'So tell me, how is this possible Barak?' Aulric asked this question sounding once again a little disheartened and perhaps a little daunted at the thought of the formidable task that lay ahead. Barak though was more cheery. The ogre had by now refilled his pipe's bowl once again with yet more strong black weed. Barak had a wolfish grin about him as he puffed away quite contently.

'Oh, but we do have a ship my friend and I must say this to you, that we have a damned good one at that.' Barak boomed this out proudly after another long suck upon his long clay pipe. 'Aye Aulric we have our good Norse friend Ragnor's dragon boat, we have the stout speedy Falcon to assist us on our quest for justice and of course bloody revenge. Why, this very morning before I even came here to the great hall to speak with you I sent off a good hawk. It was one of my own birds of course, not one of your slow useless pigeons, on a flight to the seadog. The big red bearded Viking, he will I think not fail us, well at least the big fool never has done in the past,' said Barak with a wry smile. 'Doubtless the rogue will be here in two or three mornings hence, this with his sea going killers to assist me on this trek. Well that is of course if he is not by now a dead thing or lying rotting in heavy link chains somewhere in a damp dark place. Or perhaps the big hairy Viking has been lucky, maybe the drink and the high living he so loves has taken him off to hell or Valhalla. Who knows Aulric my friend, as such good luck it often happens' Barak chuckled to himself. 'Though for now

I must say this would be most badly timed if Ragnor was with hairy pot bellied gods..'

Barak had said this with a slight smile, the giant was, he supposed, quite pleased with his forward planning of things. Aulric shook his greasy fuzzed up head in disbelief at Barak's quick thinking.

'How did you know you would have need of a ship Barak? You had this morning not even talked with me before you sent off your bird. And also you had not even seen my son, or knew of the grim tale I had to tell to you. ' The giant Barak laughed warmly, he placed a huge gnarled right hand (it was a hand which had been broken several times in the past) upon his friend's shoulder.

'Because my little brother, no one here on this sad backward little island of yours is either stupid enough or brave enough to shoot your fine son full of arrows. Then after this black cowardly liberty make off with your much beloved daughter. Did you really think these dogs would still be hiding somewhere in Britain? No, oh no my friend I think not,' the giant said with a slow shake of his mail link clad head. Aulric had to pass a grim smile at his large friend's cunning and reasoning, as always and ever Barak was as astute and as wily as he was fearsome.

After a moment or so of thoughtful pondering over what Barak had said Aulric then spoke up.

'You know I had at first thought the Druids, those fools from the western mountains far to the south west of here had some sort of a hand in this dark deed. Aye I did truly think this. I had thought these men of Cymru might have had some part in this foul cowardly crime upon my family, Barak,' Aulric looked about him strangely. The troubled King had said this to Barak almost in a whisper, as if the very walls had ears.

'Why so? Tell me Aulric why did you think this of the foolish childish Druids my friend?' Barak asked this question quickly and simply. Aulrics answer came back almost as quickly as the question was put to him.

'Because Barak, the Druids who hold sway there in their wilderness have long hated Rome, aye also the fools hate any allies of Rome,' Aulric further explained. 'In fact I think sometimes to myself perhaps these fools are not much wiser than the cursed Picts. Damned Druids they hate all and anything or anyone without a great white beard sticking out a full foot from their weak pointy chins.'

Barak on hearing this smiled then he chuckled away to himself. Aulric must have come to these semi-sensible conclusions long before the drink and the sorrow had made him useless for all and anything.

'You know Barak, high in the snow capped mountains and in the deepest forests that are their domain it is strongly rumoured these druids still give human sacrifice to their pagan gods..' Barak gave a positive nod on hearing this then a grunt of disgust in silent reply as the slayer had also heard such tales of human

50

sacrifice on his extensive travels. Barak took a swig of mead then puffed once again upon his long pipe as Aulric continued with his unflattering remarks concerning the social habits of the druids.

'Aye believe me my large friend a tribe that offers up their virgins to their earth god, well these are in my opinion not folk to be trusted. Damned druids spend far too much time with their ragged flea bitten hill sheep if you ask me,' Aulric hissed scornfully. 'Must be something not quite right there don't you think Barak?'

The giant gave another positive nod, the ogre agreed with Aulric's point as he himself was a man who had no love of priests of any kind. Aye also the astute slayer had noted that these so called holy men themselves were never too keen to give up their own lives in loyal faithful homage to their various unseen deities. Whilst the giant was still thinking about this detail Aulric continued with his condemnation of the Druid brotherhood.

'Aye Barak know you this also, it is also rumoured these long bearded tattooed savages have cannibalistic leanings,' the king further pressed before thinking about his words. 'Oh, oh I am so sorry my friend, believe me I meant you no offence.' Aulric added sheepishly after realising what he had just said to his large tattooed flesh eating friend.

'None taken' Barak replied with a crooked cynical smile. The giant, well he did indeed find it so amusing that so many folk, these even including his closest friends all took such an interest in his supposed dubious eating habits. After a drink and a brief pause Aulric spoke on once again.

'Aye also my friend, I have heard the dwarfs live in the mountains and the caves of the snow capped mountains far to the north of here. You know the high mountains that lay even beyond Pictdom. Well, it is said these dwarfs grow ever stronger and ever more cunning in their ways. Aye and what these strange tunnel dwelling folk lack in height they more than make up for in strength and courage. After all Barak these creatures are only stunted giants. Barak puffed away upon his pipe. The ogre had met with only a few dwarfs in his time and he had found them much as Aulric had said. True it was they might be short of leg but otherwise the dwarfs were strong sturdy men with much courage and much fire about them. These short legged mostly bad tempered folk were in fact in many ways just like miniature Vikings. Aye the dwarfs were as it so happened as short in temper as they were in leg. As the long bearded long haired dwarfs were never found wanting when it came to a fight.

'You know Barak one of them, a dwarf I mean came here when you were away warring for Rome.'

'Oh aye, say on then,' Barak said while raising his dark eyebrows in surprise at this revelation.

'Aye, Drox he was called, the long haired big bearded stunted ogre got himself so drunk one night that he wrecked the Seven Stars. Tables, chairs, stools, benches, windows and everything else he also smashed to bits, this just for the very hell of it. Why the dwarf even jumped up atop a stool then knocked out Cedric with one blow to the chin when the captain had went to arrest him and put him in the cells. Though that is a sore subject which is even now never mentioned, if you know what I mean? Cedric after all is a very proud man and when he at length came around from the blow, well he was not a happy man..' Barak on hearing this amusing piece of news smiled to himself as he imagined the scene of utter carnage in the seven stars.

'What happened to this Drox fellow then Aulric, did the dwarf eventually spend a night in the cells?'

'No, oh no'' Aulric said with a shake of his still weary head. 'The dwarf after wrecking all and everything and causing much mayhem leapt aboard stuttery Edward's big white billy goat. Drox then rode off into the night laughing like some sort of a maniac as he did so. Edward, well as ever, was foolish enough to stand in the way and was at once flattened by the dwarf's heavy oak cudgel..' Both Aulric and Barak had a chuckle at the unfortunate Edward's expense, so far it appeared poor Edward had not had a good year at all. Aulric then suddenly ceased his laughter, he both frowned and scowled as suddenly a thought crossed his much troubled mind.

'Barak my friend, tell me, do they mean to kill you then, these sinister Black Guards with their brood of moonlight conspirators? Or do they perhaps merely wish you to return to your far off kingdom for a judgement of some sorts? And then once they have you there perhaps these men only want for you to give up your throne and to stand down publicly?' Barak gave off a grunt followed by an uncaring grin. Next the ogre gave a carefree shrug of total indifference to Aulric's well put question. Now the giant toyed with his thick gold hoop ear ring that dangled from his left ear. This as the ogre picked a small piece of meat out of that annoying broken tooth at the back of his mouth. By every passing day that sore tooth was becoming ever more troublesome and ever more painful. Still though this aside, the great ogre now had more pressing things to contend with that much outweighed a rotten tooth.

'Who knows?' the ogre answered in a most 'could not care less' sort of fashion to Aulric's question. 'But know you this my friend, either way I will no doubt disappoint them in their plotting and their scheming, and this no matter whatever their treasonous plans are. Well at least friend Aulric, that is my most avid and hoped for intention. ' Barak said this with a most crooked wolf-like sort of smile.

With this said and not another word spoken the giant was at once up off and gone from the hall. Barak had spun about upon his big booted feet, gathered up his wolf skin cloak which he had earlier discarded and was away striding down the corridor in most rapid fashion. After all the giant had so much to do over these next few days and also he had so little time to do it in.

Chapter Four

First things were always first with the very organized Barak, this being so the giant on leaving the great hall went at once to the stable to check over his war horse and the pack mules. The big gelding as expected was unsaddled, unbridled and stood inside a roomy straw filled stall. Also the great beast had been watered, groomed and cared for, now the gelding was chewing lazily and happily upon good freshly ground oats. Likewise the tall grey mules had been attended to, the animals were tethered up to the stable wall looking most content. Barak's mules had also been brushed down, watered and fed till they could eat no more. Lazily the noble yet humble creatures rested now contented with their bellies well and truly full. It must be said the mules were looking very sleepy animals as cleverly the beasts of burden leant against the wall. The heavy packs these beasts had carried for so far without any complaint lay by a small doorway that led out into a large garden at the rear of the stables. This was Barak's garden. It was a place the giant loved to spend many a happy hour digging away while planting and tending his varied crops of strange exotic fruits and vegetables. In this place the giant exchanged his beloved dragon sword and his chain link armour for a spade and a hoe. Here the slayer would and he could sit for hours on end just relaxing unwinding while forgetting all about warfare battles and other people's feuds and problems.

Barak scooped up one of the heavy hessian sacks then bending over almost double he made his way through the doorway out into his garden. Oh and what a garden, here was a garden like no other garden in all of the land, yes it was truly a splendid magical place. Most pleasantly the scent of fading but potent jasmine came instantly and most pleasingly to Barak's keen senses. After a short while of taking in the scents and sights of the garden the giant smiled broadly as a small, dark skinned curly haired boy of no more than ten years of age bounded forward to greet him. This small child shouted out loud the slayer's name as he ran towards him just as fast as his small sandaled feet could carry him. The child's arms were outstretched, his face was beaming with joy as he ran full tilt toward the towering ogre. Barak too with no one about to witness his humanity smiled broadly in a most kindly fashion as the boy leapt into his huge arms.

'Hassan, Hassan,' Barak said softly as the ogre held the boy high above him with his arms at full stretch. 'Our garden looks good my boy, you have done well, aye you have done very well..' Barak said this while giving the child first a hug then a playful shake.

'Everything has grown tall Barak. I watered the plants just as you instructed me to do. I also dug in the dirt and straw from the stables as you told me to,' the small boy said proudly. 'And over there by the wall there is a pile of dead things I have gathered to rot, birds, foxes, badgers and other things from the forest. And also as well as this, there is a big pile of seaweed from the coast the fat man with the donkey brought for us,' Hassan said on excitedly. Barak very gently put the child down and was next led by hand by the small black haired dark skinned boy. Then together man and boy walked around the vast garden that blossomed and flourished with all manner of plants blooms and fruits from all around the known world. Bananas, dates grapes, water melons, oranges even coconuts grew and flourished under sheets of glass cunningly strapped and held together to form small growing houses.

Barak, well he was after all well educated, the ogre could make glass. This was not some sort of magic. No it was just a clever skill that he had learned as a boy from the master craftsmen in the palace of Krozakistan. And as for his garden, well that acre paid well enough for itself, not that money was any sort of issue anyway. Most of the vegetables were sold to the people of the castle and the nearby villages at a very cheap rate on market day. Of course this benevolent transaction would doubtless have caused the stuttering Edward some loss of both sleep and revenue but that was a minor detail that did not bother anyone too much, least of all Barak. Also at the end of the day poor Edward was now apparently no more than a jibbering idiot anyway.

As a rule the exotic fruits were mostly purchased by the Roman nobles and the so called hierarchy of the Roman Legions. And of course Aulric being Aulric the kindly king would always buy whatever exotic fruits which were surplus just to give to the poor and the needy. For if nothing else the good king loved his people, aye he was ever a benevolent man; no one starved here in his domain, no one ever went without a meal.

Barak sat himself down on a wooden bench against a wall facing southward after a lengthy walk about his garden. Playfully the giant slayer ruffled the small boy's mass of black curly hair.

'Look you Hassan, I have brought for you the seeds and roots of plants from lands and islands from far away, far, far away.' Barak said this while tipping out the contents of the big hessian sack. 'Hassan, these seeds must be kept warm and kept dry in a dark place at all times,' the ogre next explained. 'Then in the coming of the spring, when the earth warms up a little you can plant them into the earth and make them grow.' Hassan grinned broadly as the boy gave a cheerful nod on hearing this.

'In the spring,' the young lad repeated excitedly.

'Yes, yes in the spring, boy, though there are some roots and bulbs that we can plant now if you would like, but only if they are dug in deep enough into the earth.' Barak said this seeing the young boy wanted to busy himself.

Hassan beamed with delight, the child loved to tend the huge garden, it had become his life, his passion even. Dimly the child could remember a time of fear, a time of stress, strife and hardship. That though was a dark time, a time before Barak had come into his life. Hassan alas was born into slavery and misery and the child could not remember his parents or did he know of any living kin. Barak was his family now, he was his friend, his mentor, his protector, the giant was all things and everything in the world to him. Barak gave him food clothing and a warm place to sleep at night. The ogre gave him security and even a fatherly love. Hassan was also very close to Aulric, the good king knew only too well of Barak's fondness for the boy, Hassan; he was like a son to the fearsome giant. Aulric, to his credit, cared and looked to young Hassan whenever Barak was away warring in far flung places for whoever it was paid him the most at that particular time. But this campaign, this last foolish one to retrieve the lost standard of a careless cowardly officer and a luckless Legion. Well this, so Barak had always said was going to be the end of it all, after this mission there would be no more warring. No more for him the clamour and the roar of blood-red battle. No more for him the cries of dying men and the pitiful bewildered screams of horses all stuck down with steel and arrowshafts. After all these long years the giant supposed he had done his share of killing, no, no he had done much more than his share. So once he had retired from battle and warfare Barak had planned to cultivate his garden even more, aye to make this his garden a veritable paradise. Also, as well as this garden in the castle's grounds, deep in the forest the giant had built for himself a lodge. It was a huge affair with out buildings, roomy stables and kennels to house a score of dogs. From here, from his very own home the great ogre could hunt and trade, aye from here he could barter and haggle. From here the slayer could buy and sell both good horses as well as fast dogs. Most importantly from here the giant could just get on with the rest of his life. Of course as an added bonus the great ogre could spend the remainder of his days with the young Hassan.

For over thirty years now the giant killer had fought and he had slain all that stood in his path. Barak had roamed the earth under his big booted feet and went just wherever he would have a mind to go. The ogre supposed he had enjoyed most of it, regretted some of it, but been ashamed of none of it. Still though despite this even Barak knew in himself his time living by the sword had gone on far too long. Even with his luck and good fortune, if not his strength and his speed with the blade must be now running low, if not running out altogether. Behind the great front and the huge bravado Barak was after all still only human, he was still only a mortal man. Why he ached more now than ever before. When the cold winter weather came his old wounds came back to plague him with a vengeance. In all truth these old wounds seemed to trouble him more now than on the day when first inflicted. Wounds Barak had long forgotten about in warm climes returned to remind him of their presence with the frost, the ice, the rain and the snow. Oh aye and of course mayhap most of all that fierce biting north easterly wind. Perhaps Barak thought to himself he was just an old fraud after all, he was not some sort of super human being as most believed him to be. Still if nothing else his trade in cold steel, warfare, blood and pain had paid him well, aye it had paid him very well. Barak would never have to starve, nor would he be lost for the price of a roof over his big bucket head for the night through poverty. At the end of the day Barak's many bulging chests of gold, silver coins and other riches that lay secure in Aulric's strong room, any one of those chests could buy him a kingdom. Not that the ogre wanted one of course, no far from it, after all the one that he had abandoned all those years ago was still causing him grief, aye and that even now.

The remainder of that day Barak spent in a most pleasant fashion with the young Hassan. Barak seeing the boy was unsettled and missing Aulric's daughter promised Hassan all would be well. Ellena, young Hassan's friend, would soon be returned to the castle and also the prince would be restored to life. Happily the young Hassan seemed more than pleased with Barak's simple explanation of the situation. So with this put to one side the great ogre and Hassan sat in the autumn sun to laugh and talk. Hassan as ever was most eager to hear all about Barak's latest adventure for the emperor of Rome. Together man and boy laughed and joked, then before it became too dark Barak took the boy for a ride upon his huge chestnut war horse. Only then after all his tasks were completed and Hassan was tucked up in bed for an hour or two of well deserved sleep. Barak with a little time on his hands went off for his long awaited much looked forward to hot bath. Aye and what a bath it was; indeed it was a most soapy sudsy regal affair. Barak after all was a man who was used to the extremes of both the freezing cold and the intolerable heat. So the giant now soaped himself as he lounged in near boiling aromatic water. Water that was awash with foamy scented bubbles. Here Barak soaked his huge body in a most contented fashion, here the great ogre warmed his aching bones. This the slayer managed all the while as he puffed in a most happy contented fashion upon his long clay pipe enjoying his strong weed. Barak had after all waited a long time for this hot watery heaven, yes he had waited a very long time for this pleasure.

With this being so the giant was in no hurry at all to leave the comfort of the small Roman designed spa. True by Roman standards this was a quite small pool. The bath itself, well it could only hold a dozen bathers at one time while the Roman baths on the other hand were huge affairs. Bathing to the Romans, well, it was more of a social occasion than any act of cleanliness. But still that was matterless, this bath was a lavish well put together pool that had been built into Aulric's private quarters. Sadly it must be said this was a very seldom used luxury in the giant's long absences. Other than being used by the princess or on occasion by the prince the marble bath, well it would remain a mostly dry place. Aulric, good man though he was had or at least seemed to have a dread of soap and hot sudsy water.

Anyway, after contemplating Aulrics lack of general hygiene for a while at long length Barak arose and somewhat reluctantly vacated his hot soapy sanctuary. Quickly the giant dried dressed then examined himself in a mirror that stretched from floor to ceiling. All though was apparently not well with the well groomed somewhat vain ogre.

'Oh no, oh no that will not do, that will not do at all,' the ogre grumbled as he spied a grey hair or two appearing upon his right eyebrow. The snow white chin beard that Barak carefully pruned and nurtured every day was one thing, as that of course was a thing of beauty. His jet black eyebrows though, well these must always one way or other remain black. Barak licked the forefinger of his right hand then dipped it into the bowl of his pipe. Next the ogre groomed the offending eyebrow darkening it with the black ash from his long clay pipe. Barak after doing this and once satisfied with the outcome smiled as he turned this way and that toward the mirror admiring his handy work.

'Good, yes that is very good, now I am repaired' the ogre muttered away happily to himself. Then with a grin childlike chuckle the giant twirled about on his great hide boots and he was briskly off about his most urgent business. Much refreshed the now radiant, washed, shaven giant next went and roused his sleeping ward Hassan. On that evening the giant and the boy dined in the small but busy tavern of the Seven Stars within the castle walls. Hassan as ever hung upon every word his giant protector said to him as they feasted on the very best food the inn keeper served up before them. Huge tasty game pies, pies that were filled with a mixture of rabbit' hare and squirrel meat. Also as well as all of this there were fat pork sausages steeped in rich onion and cider gravy all topped off with a nice thick pastry lid atop it. After that ample course was finished off there came an apple and blackberry pie covered with a generous portion of thick cream. Both man and boy devoured this pudding with eager relish then both lay back in their chairs bloated content and full.

'I thought you did not like the cooking of the Britons very much Barak?' Hassan asked this question while wiping cream from his dimpled chin. Barak grunted as he gave a nod of agreement at Hassan's comment.

'True as a rule I do not, but in all truth boy it was me who taught this woman how to make such pies when she worked for Tom. Aye and to her credit Hassan, I must say she makes them very well, aye very well indeed,' the giant chuckled. 'Who knows my boy, perhaps there is yet some hope yet for this primitive backward little island.' Both the big man and the small boy laughed together, the night went well but it was over all too soon all too quickly. At long length after that cheery evenings end Barak carried the happy weary Hassan off to his soft bed to sleep and to dream his dreams. But still nevertheless early on that next morning while everyone but the castle guards slept and slumbered on, the giant with the child, man and boy were up out and set off into the forest towards Barak's lodge. Hassan held on tightly to Barak's thick leather tan coloured tunic as the great war horse thundered on along through the woods at quite a pace for its great size. The beast was guided on by the ogre through the narrow forest pathways that Barak knew only too well.

First though before they would arrive at Barak's sturdy well built lodge there was a man Barak would meet and speak with. This man was a good man and a man Barak had long known well and also trusted most dearly. Barak had left his big red dogs with this fellow who was a hard working woodsman. Aye the giant had left his hounds there at the end of last spring while he was away on his last venture for Rome. And also at this place there was a present to pick up for Hassan, aye it was a gift the boy would love. In fact it was a gift that any little boy would love, love and cherish.

'Puppies!' Hassan shrieked with joy as he was lowered from the back of the big horse to the ground by Barak. In but an instant four fat red coated pups straightway were upon the boy. At once the child rolled about the ground in fits of laughter while being tugged this way and that by the boisterous pups.

This woodsman who had cared for the dogs in Barak's absence was a man of medium height and build, the forester had about him a weather beaten craggy face that made him hard to age. But anyway this man smiled warmly and had a kindly expression about him. Typically the woodsman was dressed in dark green woollen garments with a thick leather tunic atop that came down to his knees. Also this man wore a floppy sort of hat of green velvet, Barak had never seen him without this floppy cap, this whether the woodsman was asleep or awake. Barak nodded most cordially, then the giant dismounted a little stiffly from his big gelding. It seemed Barak's fast ride through the forest had sadly apparently taken more out of him than it had the big horse. Anyway the woodsman clenched hands in friendship with the slayer. Both smiled warmly while watching the boy playing with the four boisterous red coloured very fat pups. These pups were a couple of months old now and were big robust very well grown things. Boarhound pups, these pups in time would grow to be massive beasts capable of hunting large game and also well able to pull down an armed man of war. Barak looked eagerly about him for the proud parents of the litter. Suddenly his dark eyes found them. Yonder there, in the glade, just beyond the woodsman's lodge a pair of tall powerfully built dogs, red coloured like their offspring now bounded silently toward the giant. Moments later with a resounding crash Barak was deposited most rudely into a thicket of woodland heather. These huge dogs had bowled the ogre over with both their combined size and their quite surprising speed. With this done next the beasts fawned all over their laughing master as he lay amongst the forests undergrowth. Meanwhile the huge dogs wagged their long thick powerful tails in excitement at the giant's return.

It had been months now since their master had left them there in the dark forest, also it had been many years since Barak had been knocked so rudely to the ground. While the woodsman had cared for these great beasts as well as he could the hounds had only one loyalty and one loyalty alone. And of course that fierce undying loyalty it was to Barak and only to Barak. Hassan standing by the woodsman's side laughed loudly as Barak again and again was knocked off his huge feet by the great Boarhounds. Barak's dogs were so big that standing upon their hind legs the beasts could even lick the giant's fierce tattooed face. After some length of time the hounds at last calmed and settled themselves allowing their master to rise to his big booted feet. With this done, once upright after a few kind words from Barak the big dogs padded obediently behind their master towards the woodsman's lodge.

Erik the woodsman was a solitary man, in all truth he cared very little for the company of other men as a rule. Erik found that most men were quite boring and bland things and mostly they had nothing or little of any importance to say. Barak though, well he was a different kettle of fish, here was a man he both liked and respected, also big Barak could tell a good tale when in the right company. In fact with a few drinks down him and a few pipe fulls of that strong black weed he constantly smoked Barak was at times damn good entertainment. Later as the men settled themselves down before the fire in the long roomy very tidy woodcutter's lodge to drink cider.' cider by the way Erik had made himself, there came the sound of hoofbeats, a horseman fast approached. This horseman rode into the clearing at some speed as it happened then abruptly the rider reined his horse in sharply outside of the lodge.

Erik and Barak both glanced at each other a little bewildered, after all Erik was not a man who had many visitors.

'Is it your brother perhaps?' Barak suggested.

Erik shook his head.

'No, no my brother would fall off a donkey if it went any faster than a good healthy trot. No that's a good horseman who sits atop a good horse Barak, please believe me because of that fact you can be most sure.'

Barak grunted in agreement as he rose and moved to the open doorway. This so he could see for himself this good horse with its capable rider atop it. Now on seeing the rider Barak smiled broadly to himself as he recognized the rider of the sweating mount. It was Cedric, a man he had campaigned with in the past, a good man, a good soldier and a high ranking captain in Aulric's own personal guard. Barak gave a nod of welcome as he stepped forward a pace or two from Erik's porch. With another nod of greeting Barak next placed his hand upon the sweating mount's shoulder.

'Are there problems Cedric?' the giant suggested fearing as always the worst. This hard blowing horse belonged to Aulric and Barak himself had bought the mare for him as a birthday present with money earned from one of his campaigns. As it so happened he had bought the mare from Tom in the tavern of the Seven Stars, aye more than likely she was the only decent horse the innkeeper cum horse dealer had ever sold. Anyway Cedric shook his head in reply to the giant's question.

'Nay my Lord Barak', he said sliding down from the well put together bay mare. 'Well, at least I think not.' This man who was in his early thirties said as he removed his domed bronze helmet. Cedric next ran a hand through his short cropped dark hair as he wiped his perspiring brow free of sweat before entering into the lodge. Cedric was of course at once made both comfortable and welcome by the woodsman who had in the past met Cedric on several occasions on his visit to the castle. So now thus relaxed the soldier drank down more than a little strong cider. Cedric talked casually, the soldier was pleased to see Barak, these bad times he felt would now be somehow brutally corrected. After a short while Aulric's favourite captain next conveyed his important message to the giant, this done Cedric tarried there for a little while longer waiting until his horse had cooled down and rested itself. As it so happened the news Cedric had rode so hard to deliver had quite pleased Barak.

Cedric with eleven other of Aulric's men would accompany Barak to rescue the princess. Every one of these men would be selected by Cedric himself, the soldiers would be the cream of Aulric's warriors. This of course was information that was very much to Barak's liking. Also, as an extra bonus the well travelled Cedric was almost as good a mariner as he was a horseman. It was also revealed Ragnor could not get to the Salmon River for another three days, this as his vessel the Falcon was holed. So of course the Dragon boat much beloved by the large hairy berserker had of course to be repaired.

That little hiccup gave Barak a little more time to put some affairs in order, a little more time with Hassan. Oh and of course a little more time for a social drink as well as with some catching up on current affairs. After all said and done his life could end at any moment so now it was best to make the most of his time over these next few days. Well, at least this was the way the giant chose to look at it. Oh of course there were also the Roman standards to return to the magistrate's office. After this menial task was accomplished there was the hooded scribe to briefly interview, then once that interview was over the meddling fool would doubtless be executed. So all in all these next couple of days should be at least quite busy and sometimes even pleasurable. However that business, well it could all wait for now as for tonight he would relax and bide with Erik. As for Hassan, well the boy could play with the pups and pick one of them as a gift for himself. A young growing boy in these wild parts should after all always have the company and protection of his own dog, aye and the bigger the better.

Cedric after some time talking and drinking bade his farewells then climbed a little unsteadily upon the bay mare. After all by now the soldier had drunk down several big jugs of Erik's rough but very potent cider. So at a rather more sedate and somewhat unsteady pace the officer made off back in the direction he had so recently come from. Erik who was a man well used to solitude was however greatly enjoying the company of the giant and the boy. Sometime earlier the woodsman had killed a piglet in readiness for a feast. Less than an hour later this piglet was cleaned gutted and roasting upon a spit in the fireplace of his lodge. Now the remainder of that whole day and well into the evening would go perfect for all. There was after all good cheery company, this as well as good food washed down by good drink too. Later at nights end there was a good trouble free sleep at the end of it all, aye and this all in comfortable beds. On the next morning at first light as the old one eyed black cockerel crowed Barak awoke just as fresh as the day, the slayer did this atop of a comfortable straw filled mattress too. It was a mattress that Erik had cleverly extended to accommodate the giant's great length. Erik the meanwhile on that morning had cooked over the fire some goose eggs, this as well as mushrooms with thick ham all fried up in rich goat's butter. Hassan by now was already up and the boy was outside playing with the pups under the protective watchful eyes of both the huge dogs. Bears wolves and black boars as well as stealthy seldom seen mountain cats still abounded here in this dense northern mountain forest. Why here was not at all a safe place for a grown man never mind a small boy. Erik for a moment stopped his dining and turned toward Barak with a somewhat sad look about his weatherbeaten face.

'One pup died at birth, Barak, it was a small bitch pup with a black mask. She was a pretty little thing, and for the loss of her short life I am most sorry..' Erik said this honestly and earnestly as he drank some fresh foaming milk from a wooden cup. Barak sat upon the side of his berth. The slayer cursed under his breath then shrugged his huge shoulders, next the ogre sighed, then spoke.

'Sadly these things do happen, Erik, but whenever they do, well I am always deeply saddened. Everything, every man and beast I think should at least see both the moon and the sun at least once before they are gone off to wherever they might go. Aye, I do believe that all of the beasts of the earth, no matter how useless and lowly these creatures might be, are all at least entitled to this one pleasure. '

Barak went very solemn of a sudden, the giant did this at times, with strangers or with those folk who did not know the slayer this was something that could be a bit of a worry, aye a bit disconcerting. But Erik, however, he was a man who knew big Barak, aye the woodsman knew him very well.

'My brother, well as you know he has your great black bird, tell me when do you want it back Barak?' Erik asked and straightway, just as expected, this question snapped the giant from his obvious gloomy thoughts. The slayer stretched out his huge arms then he rose stamping his booted feet before turning about to face the woodsman. Now the relaxed looking giant looked the woodsman full in the face then he spoke up in answer.

'At the Salmon River, aye at the Salmon River, three days from now, I would meet with your brother there, can you reach him to say this? ' At once Erik without any hesitation whatsoever gave a positive nod then he spoke.

'Yes of course Barak, by a pigeon of mine I will send it off at once, well after breakfeast is finished. Trust me my friend, my unwashed brother will be there on time, you have my word upon it.' Erik said all of this before swallowing down his last big fat sausage. 'For somehow my friend Barak, well I do feel you will have need of that big black bird of yours. Well, she as well as the big dogs also on this venture you must undertake for the good King Aulric. This is of course if I am not most sadly and wrongly mistaken in my assumption. '

Barak said nothing, however the ogre gave a nod followed by a grim sort of smile. Next the giant refilled the bowl of his pipe with strong weed as it was time now for his first smoke of the day. Erik as it so happened was not far off at all in his assessment of the forthcoming situation.

'No, no you are not wrong,' the giant muttered in reply after exhaling a cloud of smoke. Erik gave a sigh, the woodsman was he supposed quite worried about the giant.

'She has killed many wolves that big black bird of yours Barak, my brother I think has used her well,' the woodsman said changing the subject. 'My brother, well he might as I have already said, not be a good horseman, but with dogs and big birds he is I think a lot better. ' Barak nodded and smiled then the giant asked a question.

'And your brother, has he kept for himself a good pup, Erik? ' With a smile the woodsman nodded as he passed a wooden plate of fried goose eggs, pork sausages, mushrooms and thick cured ham to the ever hungry giant. This was Barak's second breakfeast of the day, no matter, after one more long puff upon his pipe the ogre would dine once more. Barak as usual wasted no time in devouring his breakfeast. This was followed by a big jug of frothy goat's milk the ogre swallowed down to clear his throat. In the meanwhile the woodsmen said on.

'Aye they were all good pups Barak, perhaps the bitch pup that died was rolled upon by its mother who knows? For it was not born a sickly thing, no, no it was just unlucky in the way of things I do suppose,' the woodsman said sadly. 'But aye in answer to your question my brother has a good pup, he took the runt though, but then again he always does. I think this is because he is so small in stature himself,' Erik said with a grin. 'For under all the wolf skins he hides beneath my brother is only a thing of skin, bone, gristle and sinew. Why my brother, why I don't suppose he would even make a decent bowl of weak broth if he was put in a pot and boiled up.'

Barak smiled at Erik's words, as this description of his own quite unsociable brother was very accurate. Indeed Barak could not have described him any better, this even though he had met with him only the once.

'You're a good man Erik, you have looked to the dogs and the pups, the animals are strong and they are well.' This, the giant said when he finished with his grinning.

'Will you take the dogs with you also on your quest Barak? For if not then you know they can bide here with me in the forest if you so like? ' Erik offered most sincerely. 'For I do declare Barak, these hounds of yours are both good company, aye and both good guard dogs too. Indeed a man can sleep safely even in this forest with those two about. Barak shook his head as he swallowed down more, frothy goat's milk.

'My most earnest and sincere thanks to you my friend, but I must say no to that. For as you have so rightly already said Erik, I do think I will have much need of the hounds. Oh Aye, aye, just as I will also have much need of that big black bird. Please believe me Erik there is alas a lot more dangers to face on this mission for your king than the threat of mere mortal men. '

Erik looked a little worried on hearing these words, after all he was not a warrior, nor was he a man of war. However, he was a man of the woods; he was a man of the dark and dangerous forest. With this being so, well then Erik knew only too well about the animals that abounded in the wild, also he of course knew all about life and death. Erik knew well of the bear, the boars the wolves and the great deer of these woods. All of these creatures were all powerful fast and strong beasts, but even they could not go on forever, this being so neither of course could Barak. After all the giant was still only flesh and blood, aye Barak, he was only muscle bone and blood. Perhaps this ogre who hailed from a land far away was the most fearless and fearsome of all living men. But still nevertheless after taking all and everything of that into consideration, he was still a mortal being. Barak after all said and done was still only a very big middle aged man. Aye and in all truth looking at the great man now, well, the ogre did have that certain look of humanity and vulnerability about him Erik thought to himself.

Now at this moment in time, the giant appeared to be not only the hunter, he was also in many respects also the hunted. But then again perhaps this was just because the giant was sad and downcast he must once more leave the boy behind. However, whatever dangers the future held for him Barak still enjoyed a most wholesome and hearty breakfeast. In fact the slayer not only managed to consume two large breakfeasts he also finished off a large ham shank just for good measure. Next this done with the eating finished and his pipe relit Barak decided he would take with him not one pup but two. As a gift for tending his dogs whilst he was off warring for Rome the other two pups were to be gifts for Erik. Of course these pups would grow to be huge things that would make fine hunters and also good fearsome guards against both man or forest beast. On top of this the pups would keep the woodsman company in his self inflicted solitude deep in the dark forest.

Erik not wishing to be undone by Barak, well he had already planned a gift of his own for the young Hassan, oh and what a wonderful gift it was to turn out to be.

Erik told Barak as the boy slept he had a present; this was to be a surprise for Hassan on that following morning. However, the wily woodsman though would not even hint or say as to what this present was. Aye and try as he might Barak with all his guile and persuasive powers had still gone to sleep none the wiser as to what this gift might to be.

On that morning just as Barak and Hassan were about to head off back to the castle. This, after a brief stop off at his own lodge just to look the place over, the pair were led by Erik to a small corral behind a well stocked wood shed. There in the confines of this rounded roomy corral, whinnying and prancing about in a most proud regal fashion was a small clean legged pony enjoying the early morning autumn sun. Most merrily the pony bucked and reared as it stomped and rolled in a most carefree fashion. This, while the pony shook its ample double sided mane while the creature stared most curiously at these new strangers.

'Like her?' Erik asked the small boy, while already knowing the answer to his question. Hassan beamed at once while he clapped his small hands together gleefully. For that second the small child was speechless as he watched the young prancing pony enjoying the dawn of a new day. This pony which was completely spotted all over its body came boldly over to Hassan then she nuzzled the boy softly.

'You are far too big for her to carry Erik,' Hassan said with a broad mischievous smile as he regained his power of speech.

'You are much too heavy,' the boy added with a giggle. Erik merely shrugged then he smiled warmly before nodding in total agreement with the young lad.

'True, true this is all very true,' the woodsman answered without any argument whatsoever.

'As well as this she is far too pretty to carry you anyway,' Hassan went on jokingly.

'Aye that is also very true lad, but you are not too heavy, nor are you too ugly for the pony to carry. And that my boy, well that is why the pony is your pony, and she is not mine..' Erik said this with yet another warm smile as he ruffled Hassan's black curly hair. At once the young boy grinned broadly then Hassan laughed out aloud before doing a somersault of joy into the air. These past two days for Hassan had been a truly wonderful time, indeed perhaps some of the best times in his short life.

'Good enough Erik,' Barak said this as he reached for a purse of coins inside his leather tunic. 'This, my friend is a very fine present for young Hassan, indeed it is Erik,' the giant added with a cheery smile as he produced his heavy purse of roman coin. On seeing Barak's intentions the woodsman recoiled.

'Aye this is all very true, so tell me, since when was a present, which is a gift, to be paid for, Barak?' Erik asked this in a most matter of fact fashion. 'Stay your hand big Barak, as you have already said I am a woodsman not a horse trader, this pony is not for sale it is my gift to the boy. '

Barak said nothing in reply, but instead the slayer gave Erik a simple nod of his big bucket head in gratitude.

And as for young Hassan, well he could of course not have been a happier little man. Now the boy had two fat noisy pups to play with in the garden -(which he knew of course still had to be kept clean and tidy). Now the child had his own fat pup. He also had another one he was to look after for Barak. Then to top it all the boy now had his very own pony, oh aye and what a pony that was. Why, this could have been a painted thing such was the pony's well balanced markings. No other boy in the village or in the land for that matter had a pony quite like it or pups that would be as big or as strong and as bold as his. Hassan felt both very lucky and very proud. Indeed the child was very happy and elated with the gifts he had received, aye and these all within a day of each other. After all Hassan's once cruel troubled life was now at last carefree. Now Hassan had a warm berth above the stable and a snug room in the castle if and when he wanted it. Oh aye and also he had the great garden to work and play about in. Also while on the way to Erik's lodge Barak had even talked of making a small fish pond inside the large garden. Though Hassan, even as young as he was, knew only too well Barak never owned or neither did he do anything which was at all in anyway whatsoever small.

'This pony Erik, she is young and she is a spirited proud prancing thing. Tell me is she broke to the saddle, friend Erik?' Barak asked this question not wishing Hassan to hurt himself on an easily spooked pony.

'Aye, aye this is true, she is young and has much spirit Barak, but yes, she is well broke.' Erik said this with great confidence. 'Trust me I would not risk any harm to the young boy..' Barak gave a satisfied grunt as he next cursed and sucked upon his painful broken back tooth.

'I know this; you're a good man Erik, you are a man I know I can trust. The filly's markings though, they are most uncommon. I have seen these ponies before but not on this island. If I am not much mistaken she is from Jutland, I think she is a most valuable and expensive animal. ' Erik on hearing this gave a wry smile, as the woodsman knew just exactly what Barak was hedging at with his probing words. Of course the value of the pony was far more than any mere woodsman could ever afford, this just to stand about in a coral as some sort of an ornament. Oh and then if by chance Erik could afford such a beast, well it would be pure folly just to give the creature away on some sort of a whim. So either way, to come across, then buy such a rare pony, well this was a most strange occurrence the giant thought. Erik smiled to himself, Barak obviously wanted to know more about the small spotted pony but perhaps he felt it rude to ask too much. Still though Erik decided he would tell the slayer anyway just how it was that he came upon it, also how he came to own it. Oh and by the by, know you this, Barak was not the only one who could tell a good tale.

'Shortly after you departed and set out upon your last venture, when you left the dogs here with me, there came after a little while a band of wild looking gypsies. Aye these travellers were passing this way on the road westward, Barak. I met them in the forest by pure chance; later these gypsies stayed there over yonder in the clearing for a while. Some dozen or so rogues made up of a hodgepodge of red-haired men and women with another dozen red haired freckled faced children who scratched at their scalps a lot.' Barak gave a slight smile and next raised his dark eyebrows knowingly.

'Irish! ' Barak stated more than enquired. Erik at once nodded in agreement.

'Oh aye, mad, bad the wild quite insane unruly Irish,' the woodcutter answered with a shake of his velvet capped head.

'I bought from these rogues a big bay gelding for the hauling of the trees True the beast is a little clumsy but he is a good and honest worker, aye he is game enough and up for the task. Though I must say this Barak he is not anywhere near as big as that huge beast of yours, he is something completely different.' Erik after saying this hesitated for just a moment then he spoke. 'By the way my big friend would you do me a horse trade, if I perhaps sweetened the pot just a little?'

Almost at once the giant very quickly shook his mail clad head.

'No, oh no,' Barak said instantly with another most positive shake of his big head. 'I do like that big chestnut gelding, the big beast suits me well - anyway like you say you're not a horse trader, are you?' Erik smiled at the giant's clever reply so he merely shrugged his shoulders then carried on with what he had to say.

'As you say Barak, I am not a horse trader.' Erik, with this said went on once again with his tale. 'Anyway, I bought the bay gelding from these travellers at what I must say was at a very fair price, as I have said they camped yonder in the glade.' Erik nodded toward a small clearing he had cut away in the dense forest some time earlier. 'This band of gypsies, well they drank down my cider in great quantities. Also their clan ate my cheese as well as my bread and my meat with equal gusto. Ah but of course I charged them for it Barak, believe me I am not a greedy man, however, I still know how much these gypsies can both eat as well as drink. And also Barak I have noticed that folks, well they do tend to drink and eat even more so if the fare is free. Aye and you know yourself only too well big Barak, even good hospitality can go on for only so long. However and anyway, at about this same time, the bitch, your bitch was most heavy in pup

66

and lying inside my lodge. I had built inside for her a cosy den, this I filled with straw and made for her a most comfortable warm place. As I knew well from the dates you gave me it was soon to be her time to pup..' Barak smiled as he also knew well Erik was the best man to leave his big dogs with. As also was Erik's brother the best man to trust with the care of his great black and none too friendly eagle. 'Of course all of this was weeks and months ago, aye when it was high summer,' Erik said as he continued with his tale. 'Barak, those nights back then were light and warm, I must say they were the most pleasant of summer evenings that I can quite remember. However though, on one of those long pleasant evenings as I walked over to my beehives to draw out some honey to spread upon my toast. ' Erik then suddenly paused for just a second, he did this as if he were deep in thought. 'Yes, yes I do remember now, it was to be the eve of the horse traders leaving my forest before heading off west to the coast. '

Erik once again paused, this time he gave an involuntary shudder before continuing with his tale. 'Well all of a sudden Barak I was beset. Aye beset by two huge black dogs, big half bred mastiff things. And Barak I must say that these creatures, well they were all things at once. Aye these brutes were fighting dogs, gypsy dogs, camp dogs and all in all they were very nasty fearsome beasts at that. The Irish traders must have had them chained and hidden away up until that time. As I had never before seen them, or had I even heard them on my frequent visits to their encampment.

I at once felt for my hunting knife, I was in total fear you must understand Barak and the knife it was alas my only weapon..' Erik seemed to pale at the very thought of that summer evening. 'In an instant I was cornered, with my back against a stack of my own logs that were drying out for winter firewood. Erik wiped sweat from his furrowed brow at the very thinking of it before once again continuing. 'I had nowhere to go, nowhere to run nowhere to hide. I must say I thought my life was to be over there and then Barak, aye that I was to die in a most gruesome fashion.' Erik paused again for just a moment before continuing with his dramatic and honest tale. 'Barak I must say that things at this point did not look good for me, no, oh no they did not look good at all. As I have already said I thought my life was over and done with, that I would end my days as no more than dog food. For armed with only a knife I had of course no chance at all against such huge slobbering bloodthirsty beasts.'

Erik paused once again making quite sure Barak truly realized what exactly it was he was saying to him. Aye and of course that Barak was taking in the full seriousness of the grim life threatening situation he had been involved. Then when thus satisfied after some moments of thoughtful deliberation the woodsman once again continued with his exciting tale. 'My mouth it was dry with fear Barak, why I could not even call out for help.' Big Barak said nothing instead the ogre stood there silently listening on intently to the woodsman's story.

'But then it was that Tim came bounding forward, aye he came bounding most bravely in rapid fashion to my aid and to my rescue.' Barak looked a little baffled at these words, the giant knew most men in the forest but he had never heard of this Tim fellow before.

'Tim, Tim?' Barak asked with raised eyebrows. 'Who is this Tim that you speak of Erik - do I know of him at all? Is he a woodsman that is new to this place or is he a forest hunter perhaps?' Barak enquired at a little bit of a loss as to who this Tim fellow was.

'No, oh no, nothing at all like that Barak, I called your big dog Tim. You I know don't give your pets and animals names for your own unknown reasons. But me, well I call your big red dog Tim,' Erik explained. 'Tim it is a good name I think, anyway it is an honest name. Indeed it was the name of my father you know?' Erik had said this almost defensively. Barak, well the ogre merely smiled then nodded his bucket sized head in salute and respect to the memory of Erik's father who no doubt by now was a long dead thing.

'Please, please go on Erik', Barak said with a wave of his hand. 'I would like to hear more of this "Tim" dog', said a smiling Barak. Erik with this encouragement once again began to continue with his tale.

'Well Barak, these gypsy dogs were not only fighting dogs, they were also dogs of war too.' True these brutes were perhaps not as big as Tim, but never-the-less they were not small creatures either. No far from it, great slobbering unyielding fearsome monsters they were. Their great black hides carried many aged scars from steel weapons as well as the fangs of the beasts of the woods. I do honestly believe these hounds would have eaten me alive there and then on the very spot. Aye, well at least I think that was the intentions of these two black devil dogs. Oh aye Barak this I am sure would have been my fate had not Tim set about them both in good and heroic fashion. '

Barak struck his flints together and lit up his long clay pipe, the ogre was in truth quite enjoying this well told story.

'Anyway, the dogs fought and they fought and they fought on some more Barak, oh what a fight it was. What chaos, mayhem and raw savage courage did I witness here in these dark woods of my birth. I must say this to you in all honesty now, I thought I had seen all and everything in this my forest. You know I have seen great cave bears fighting with packs of savage forest wolves, black boars fighting with the lynx and proud red stags locking antlers while fighting to the very death of it. Surely these great beasts in my own minds eye could not be surpassed for their savage bravery.

'But how very wrong I was to have thought this, oh how very wrong I was to think that I had seen all and everything. Nothing I have ever witnessed or am likely to ever witness, was as savage or as noble as this blood duel. ' Erik paused for a brief reflection of that shocking incident then continued once again with his exciting story. 'Nothing, nothing I tell you could be its equal for sheer savagery or ferocity. ' Barak imagined in his big bucket head the ferocious duel, oh how he wished he too could have been there to witness the glory and the very sheer savagery of it all. 'This fight could not be stopped, you must understand that Barak. No not in any way, not even by you or by me or even the forest gods themselves, not in any way at all I tell you. I tell you this Barak the big dogs moved far too fast, they could not be leashed or called off. All three of these huge savage animals had the very lust of blood about them, it was total mayhem. Oh yes it indeed was a fight to the death, aye just as simple and as plain as that,' Erik went on.

Barak smiled proudly, his big red dog was here before him, he was alive and he was well. So obviously the giant of course already knew the outcome of the fight long before Erik could tell him the rest of the tale. But still though, the giant had the feeling this was going to be a very interesting story. Hassan by now as this tale was being told was away from the men, the boy had the pups playing at his feet while he continued petting his spotted pony in the corral.

Erik in the meanwhile went on with his story.

'The head man of the Irish clan was a one eyed man with a wild evil most wanton look about him. Aye he had a savage look, even with his one remaining eye he still looked a most dangerous fellow. But as it so happened however, his evil unkempt appearance belied the man's true worth. Anyway the disturbance of the dogs fighting and crashing about in the woods had roused the Irish from their drinking and their dicing. Alerted they had at once come a running and cursing through the brash and the thicket to see what was amiss. Once, and when I had at last scrambled myself up to a safe place high upon my woodpile. When I felt secure and had full control of my tongue and my brain, then it was we gambled on the outcome of the fight myself and the red haired itchy Irish.

Barak puffed contentedly upon his pipe as Erik paused for a moment before continuing.

'I have a fine legged grey mare of Arab blood, she is yonder in another clearing that I have cut and fenced off. Barak on hearing this looked quite impressed, apparently this woodcutter Erik had more horseflesh than he had ever expected. 'I bought the mare cheaply off a stuttery drunken fellow called Edward who was selling vegetables on market day..' Erik explained this almost as if he were able to read Barak's mind. 'I think the fool was afflicted in the head in some way. Still when dealing and making a trade this affliction of his, well this was of course not my problem was it? At once the giant smiled then he chuckled at the mention of the vegetable seller's name. 'You must understand this Barak, she though being a thing of beauty and grace is not my sort of horse. No, oh no far from it, the beast is far too fast for the likes of me, also she is far too small for the likes of you..' Now the giant of course fought back a peel of laughter, the ogre knew only too well who Erik had bought the horse off. Aye and Barak also knew only too well why the fool stammered as he did. 'Anyway besides all of that, we, the Irish and myself, well, we gambled horse for horse on the result of dog fight. Aye, we wagered me and the gypsy clan chief, my fine legged horse for the spotted pony. Erik then smiled proudly as he remembered the dog's victory, and also of course his own good fortune, the woodsman continued with the conclusion of his tale.

'Well Tim after some time crashing about amongst the brash and the thicket the great hound won the savage fight, in so doing I won the pony by his victory. ' Erik next smiled proudly as if he was the owner of the dog he had named Tim before next speaking. 'And that my friend, well that is quite simply why the pony is yours Barak and she is not mine,' Erik said on in all honesty. The giant was taken much aback as he had never realized just what a good teller of a tale Erik was. Why, the woodcutter was nearly as good as he was himself at story telling, well nearly.

'So tell me this Erik, what then of the itchy Irish gypsies, were they at ease and forthcoming with their bad wager? Or did you have to persuade them perhaps in some way to part with the spotted pony? ' Barak asked this question knowing full well all men were not always good and valiant losers when it came to parting with money. Oh aye and this, well this even more so, when their coinage was lost in the middle of some vast forest, and when also these losers had no witnesses to testify against their bad judgment.

Erik first shook his head in reply then he spoke up.

'No, no far from it Barak, the big one eyed man Boru, why he slew his own brother. This killing he did when the younger sibling suggested they neither keep their bargain then do even worse against my person. Aye the younger brother had moved they should slit my throat then steal your dogs and take my horses after this dark deed was done.' Barak spat venomously then he gave a grunt of disgust at such unsporting treacherous talk.

'Did these men know they were my dogs to begin with Erik? Did these red haired itchy Irish gypsies know to whom the dogs belonged?' Erik at once gave a quick positive nod in reply.

'Aye, aye they did that, for I told them as much when the clan first arrived here, I thought it wise to speak up, make them a little wary if you know what I mean? ' Barak gave a slow nod and a grim crooked sort of smile.

'Good enough.' Barak said spitting into the ground, this after sucking once again upon his annoying bad tooth. 'For a man he should always hold true to his word, true also to his fighting dogs and his fast horses, or else Erik he has nothing.' The woodsman gave a grunt followed by a nod of agreement, now Erik knew another reason why he liked Barak. 'And now my friend tell me, what of them Erik, what became of the black fighting dogs of the gypsy? '

Erik replied straightway with a wry smile across his creased weather beaten face.

'One of them, the bigger one of the two it was killed there and then in the fight with its neck broken, crushed between Tim's sharp teeth. The other one was badly hurt and it ran off yelping and howling into the woods. Well, it ran off as best the thing could Barak. For it was a blood covered creature, a front leg was badly mangled and its right shoulder was ripped clean to the very bone.' Erik, well he said this with a trace of pity in his voice. This even though the creature would have doubtless dined upon his flesh and then crunched his bones into little more than pulp. Barak, smiled grimly at these words, for he, despite what most believed was also not a man totally without compassion. However though, well this was something that for most times the giant kept very well hidden. 'This big black dog must have died of its many wounds Barak as some days later I stumbled across its corpse in the forest, it was indeed a most broken creature. ' Both men next shared a moments silence for the fate of the would be man eaters, then, the giant spoke.

'And the Tim dog?' Barak asked with a wry smile. 'Tell me was the big red beast of mine, was he hurt at all much in this epic heroic battle in your forest? '

Erik shook his head then blew through his thin lips.

'No, no not at all, the big dog was not at all hurt Barak. True it was that the big Tim dog bled a little from an ear wound, he was perhaps a little stiff and sore for a day or two. But then three days later the dog killed a big red stag as I worked away in the forest cutting trees. He is I think a great dog, he is a dog to be indeed very proud of Barak, Tim has I think no hound his equal.'

Barak puffed leisurely upon his pipe then the giant smiled casually at the thought of his big dog saving the woodsman's life.

'Yes, yes I know this only too well Erik of the dog's bravery. For indeed he has proved himself many times in the past against both man and beast,' Barak said proudly. 'But tell me what of the one-eyed man; what of Boru' I think you called him. He, this man Boru with his red haired itchy clan, what ever became of them? ' Erik gave a shrug and a sigh.

'The gypsies moved on the very next day toward the western shore, this as they and their kind so often do Barak. You know yourself, it is their way, and it always has been. Perhaps once there they intended on boarding a ship back to their homeland. But either way the one eyed gypsy said they will come back and return here next year. Aye the clan said they will return at the same time and in the very same month. Oh and also Boru further said he and his clan will bring with them both heavy horses and fast dogs, all of this, as well as perhaps some fighting birds to trade with. Also the clan leader Boru, the one eyed man was most hopeful you would be here yourself, and maybe have pups for him to deal for. I had already told him that none of these pups were for sale or trade.' Erik then paused trying to read the expression on the giant's tattooed face. Barak thoughts though were when he wanted them to be as unreadable as a hardened tavern gambler. 'Anyway and wisely I think now, the big gypsy offered no threat or even argument over either the pony or the pups,' the woodcutter said. This of course was both astute and very prudent of the gypsy, for to harm Barak's friends or his pets was a crime and an insult the ogre would not tolerate nor would he ever forgive. Suddenly the giant smiled away happily to himself as he blew smoke hoops into the air, aye this Boru had been both a wise and an honest man. It was his wisdom and his honesty that had not only saved his own life it had also saved the life of his itchy freckly red haired clan.

Barak puffed away upon his pipe as he sighed in a most relaxed contented fashion while lounging over the corral fence.

'Good, then I will be here to meet with them, Erik, next year. I must tell you now Erik I do look forward to the trade and the barter greatly. After all that is what retirement is all about is it not? Oh aye Erik, then we can drink, feast buy and sell, all will be good, please believe me all will be well. '

Erik looked up at the towering giant. The woodsman he had long known Barak. True of course they were perhaps very different men, but yet again they were the same in so many ways. Erik was not a man of war and blood and slaughter as was Barak, no he was only a simple man of the woods, a man of the wild. But so then was Barak, perhaps in some ways even more so than he was. Erik was from this place in the dark northern forest, here he was bred, here he was born, aye and here he would no doubt, when the time comes, die. All that Erik had ever known was this great green forest and this wild northern wilderness, but Barak, well the ogre knew many such wild places. The slayer could survive anywhere in the world, he was not just a warrior, he was more, much more. Barak, well he was a great hunter of beasts as well as a hunter of men. Aye quite easily the giant could live of the land, any land, whether it be desert, forest or even an icy waste in the middle of a frozen sea. Erik knew all of this and the woodsman admired and respected the giant because of it. Erik while looking forward to the giant's company in the early summer of next year still doubted though it would ever happen.

'How can you say you will be here, here in this place when bad Boru with his red haired itchy freckly clan return Barak?' Erik asked plainly. 'Why my friend you could be almost anywhere, anywhere upon this troubled earth, aye you could be anywhere at all.'

Barak was steeped in thought while still peering over at Hassan as he frolicked about happily with the young pony and the pups. After a stretch a yawn and a long puff upon his pipe the giant spoke.

'Trust me Erik, I will be here, I swear this is my last quest. After all this is done, when it is over, then, I want to go hunting in the forest and fishing in the great Salmon River. Aye I will be buying and selling horses while spending my time just as I want to. For I have I think at long last, finally had enough of warring and bloodshed and the killing of men. Men I mostly did meet with for only the last few seconds of their life, this, before I took it from them.

Aye, I have had enough of the non-stop killing, the sorting out of other people's problems and their trifling affairs. There are after all other things, more important things I must concern myself with.' Barak said this whilst sounding like a man who meant every word of what he said. Erik though was still not totally convinced.

'Yes, yes, you say this now but after a while you will return to the sword, it is alas your calling Barak.' However the giant disagreed, the slayer shook his big bucket head slowly, but he shook it in a most positive manner.

'No, as I have already said Erik there are other things that I want to do, more important things. '

The woodsman smiled yet again, Erik felt that he knew Barak now better than ever he had done before.

'Good, that is good, for he is a fine boy Barak,' Erik said nodding toward Hassan.

'Aye, he is that,' the giant agreed. 'But still my friend, it is now time we left you Erik,' the giant said with a sigh and a final puff upon his pipe. 'But know this Erik the next time we visit you, I promise we will bide here a while longer. And then you in turn, well you must visit me at my lodge, there I will cook for us a banquet. ' With this said and agreed upon, the two men shook hands warmly then Erik went off into the stable. The woodsman had no saddle for the pony but there was a well made pleated bridle that had come with the filly. Next the pony was bridled up then a very proud Hassan who was a good rider of a horse saddled or bareback, was put atop it. After another warm shake of hands and some sincere words of good luck both man and boy were once again on their way.

Hassan waved back to Erik until he could see him no more as they rode off into the dense forest. Once out of sight of the woodsman the riders trotted on along winding ways towards Barak's lodge. Hassan's spotted pony was only a tiny little thing compared to the huge chestnut gelding. In fact the pony was barely taller than the giant boarhounds that padded silently and steadily along behind it. Meanwhile the two fat well fed pups were dozing most contently in a hessian sack draped across the front of the high backed Arab saddle.

It was shortly after midday when Barak and Hassan reined in their mounts outside Barak's big roomy lodge. The pups had by now woken, at once they were set free to roam and play. Released, the yapping pups ran about wildly exploring the out buildings before finding the nearby pond.

Barak unlocked the stout oak door to his lodge with a key that was concealed under a big plant pot. This was a huge plant pot filled with earth, oh and of course an array of herbs. Barak had this plant pot constructed and designed this way so no normal man could possibly move it. Even Barak had to strain a little to get the base clear of his wooden porch. Now the slayer entered his spacious abode, here was a doorway which was one of the few the giant could enter without stooping. Of course this was because the ogre had engineered and built his home entirely by himself. Thankfully the lodge was just as he had left it all those long months ago, this of course was much to his relief. Once a winter or two back the giant had returned from a campaign to find that a large black bear had moved in for the winter.

The beast was of course most indignant when awakened from its winter slumbers, then even more insulted when it was quickly and rudely evicted out into the wild. On another occasion Barak returned to his lodge to find it in a total mess and disarray. Everywhere there were broken goblets and plates, also there was stale food lying about all over the place. Aye all of this, as well as broken furniture and also his well stacked log pile Barak had found much depleted. Now this outrage of his home being treated by some low life disrespectful riff raff as a doss house, this had infuriated him no end. True it was that the bear had torn down the back door to gain entry. However though, other than that, well the great black beast had merely slept and done no other damage. And to be truthful, well the creature had been a damn sight cleaner and a more considerate guest than the uninvited human visitors.

Barak's attention suddenly turned from the inside of his large tidy lodge to the outside of the building. Hassan meanwhile cried out most excitedly, the lad jumped up and down with glee as the pond it fair teemed with fish. Barak had stocked it up well with brown and rainbow trout the year before. The carp were long time residents and were already plentiful in the teeming pond, but it was the trout that were by far the tastiest eating. Both man and boy stood there for a short while staring intently into the ponds clear depths.

'Well my boy, we will have to be up early in the morning mind you Hassan. And then once dressed after a quick breakfeast we must be on our way at the hurry up.' Barak said this seemingly reading the boy's mind.

Hassan at once smiled, he clapped his hands with joy. Next the boy ran off laughing as he did so towards a lean-to at the side of the well built very tidy lodge. Barak in the meanwhile sat himself down under the shade of a well grown willow tree. This large pond was like some strange sort of oasis in the midst of the vast green forest. As for Barak, well the slayer always felt contented safe and above all most relaxed here. This place in the forest and of course his garden, well they both made him feel almost like a different man, a normal man even.

A stone's throw away among the many tall bull rushes something stirred under the surface. Next of a sudden there was a splash followed by a quick violent flurry in the clear water. Only a heartbeat later a rainbow trout leapt from the water and another fish followed in hot pursuit, this was a much bigger fish.

'What was that?' Hassan asked as he rejoined Barak with two long fishing poles.

'It was another hunter besides ourselves my boy, Barak replied watching the clear waters keenly.

'Aye, I do think that we have some competition my lad, look you there by the tall reeds yonder. '

The boy followed the line of Barak's finger as the giant pointed into the clear unspoilt water.

'Pike!' Hassan suggested excitedly. 'Is it a pike Barak?'

'Aye it is a pike and it is a big one by the looks of it my boy. Still live and let live, he is no enemy of ours. He must eat as well as we do young Hassan. Besides that of course a pike on the end of a pole is a good fight. Aye and if you are good enough and lucky enough to land it, well then it is also a good meal at the end of that fight. '

That afternoon was a most pleasant one, as well as catching half a dozen fat trout, but no pike. Both Barak and Hassan enjoyed watching the pups play and frolic until they were both completely exhausted. In the meanwhile both the big red dog along with the big red bitch dozed lazily side by side upon the porch of Barak's sturdy lodge. As the sunny afternoon turned into a wonderful red skied dusk both the huge tattooed man accompanied by the small boy ambled slowly and contentedly towards the lodge.

Once there Barak lit a fire inside his large tidy abode, inside the lodge there was as would be expected, a very large stone fireplace. Of course this was a good place for cooking meals as well as for keeping the lodge warm, this in even the coldest of northern winters. Apart from enjoying his garden Barak was also very fond of cooking and of dabbling about in a kitchen. Well in truth the killer even enjoyed cooking over a camp fire or brazier for that matter. Oh aye in all truth the ogre had, he supposed, quite a passion for preparing and cooking meals for his friends.

Erik had given the giant two gourds of cider before he had left and also some cheese, a large loaf of fresh baked bread and a skin of frothy goat's milk for Hassan. So it was most contentedly that man and boy sat down to a banquet on that pleasant autumn evening. Indeed it was a veritable feast, a feast of grilled trout with goat's cheese as well as wild forest mushrooms with fresh baked bread.

Barak sat back after his meal smoking his pipe while drinking his cider, the slayer sat upon a large but simply made chair that rocked upon curved runners in front of a raging fire. Relaxed and contented now the giant stared almost searchingly into the dancing flames, the slayer at this particular time looked like a most satisfied man. Hassan the meanwhile played outside with the pups laughing and chuckling with delight under the starry sky. Here now was a far cry from the little boy Barak had rescued some years earlier. With a yawn the giant puffed upon his pipe while he ran a finger over his somewhat arched and crooked nose. But then next suddenly the slayer cursed and he ground his teeth together as that broken cracked tooth at the back of his mouth began to bother him once again.

Both of the boarhounds had both been well fed at Erik's lodge upon pheasant carcasses and mashed goose eggs. Now the dogs had finished off a rough but wholesome gruel made for them from boiled up fish heads and innards. Barak was a man who after all and everything at all times despised any sort of waste.

Barak snuffed out his pipe but then after just a short while the ogre once again relit it once again, this just to ease his thoughts. He must, he supposed to himself, cut down with the weed smoking and the heavy drinking. But not now however, no, now was not a good time at all the ogre thought to himself. No Barak had already decided to cut down on both of these unhealthy and also quite expensive habits after this very tricky mission was over, well perhaps he would! A big male red stag called from deep within the forest, its bold challenge was answered only moments later by another rutting stag with similar interests. Then next and not long after, a pair of wolves howled from far off in the distance. Aye and this as an eagle owl hooted from high above in a tree just behind the lodge. Forest noises; the dark woods came alive at night this was the time in the day Barak had always loved the most.

The huge tattooed giant sat there with his thick very long legs outstretched toward the blazing fire, why so relaxed was he that the ogre had even taken his big boots off. Barak had sat there in a most content fashion with his cider, his weed and his many thoughts for the future. For the giant could do this in the here and now, aye he could think and he could plan for what lay ahead without any effort at all. Silently without any interruption the great ogre could sit and listen to the sounds of the wild woods all about him. Once in the not so long distant past Barak had actually thought to himself he was totally invincible, perhaps in truth he had merely brainwashed himself into thinking this. Or maybe then again the slayer had simply that insane self confidence instilled into him by lesser men. Lesser men who were constantly all around and about him, lesser men who were for ever wanting to be in his company. These were men the ogre had known from all over Europe, Asia and everywhere else upon the Earth where he had trod with his great booted feet. Men, who had held him in total awe, well this as also mayhap, as in some sort of dreadful fear. Perhaps this adulation at the time had made him feel god like and immortal. Barak chuckled to himself, he must have been a total fool to have even entertained such ridiculous thoughts. Now though sadly for Barak most of his old friends had dwindled and gone on, friends that had simply fell all about and all around him. These friends had mostly of course been slain in battle or had merely succumbed to the rigors of time and the very harsh years. In some cases these friends of his had for their many sins simply drank themselves or smoked themselves to an early death.

Understand this, a man who has trained for war and adventure all of his life then for whatever reason cannot take up his calling, well he never lasted long as a rule. For these men of war normally made very bad husbands, oh and also they made even worse farmers or labourers. Fish out of water that's what they were, lost souls with no direction or adventure left in their lives. Most of them had never even planned for old age thinking they would have died by the sword when their time came. Or perhaps these adventurers would simply meet their untimely demise in a tavern brawl in some nameless far off place. Aye but all of this was still adventure, much better than farming. So with a pocket full of gold on them for some sort of comfort as they lay bleeding their last moments away these men cared not at all where they died. Still though, however grim a future this might seem to the normal run of the mill type of fellow, well this was a fate that held no fear for men such as these. For the pirates, the rogues and the reavers were men who took what they could when they could take it. And as for reaching ripe old age, well that was something that seemed so very far away to these rough rugged men. Also of course this was an impossible goal most of them would doubtless never achieve anyway. But still to their undying credit, the pirates, mercenaries along with other foolhardy chancers, well all each and every one of them knew this stark fact only all too well. Barak though however, well the ogre was much more fortunate than his followers as he had many huge chests full of gold silver and other precious gems. These chests the slayer had amassed by plunder, it was a bonus so to speak. Also of course there were the many huge payments given him by Rome for his risky business. Indeed the great ogre had enough gold to buy any of the northern kingdoms, aye this he could do ten times over. But still riches aside, besides all of this up till now the giant had fought on quite simply because thus far he merely enjoyed his work. Barak had welcomed the wars the battles and the thrill of it all, in a way he supposed it was a distraction of sorts. Aye the ogre honestly supposed to himself he had enjoyed everything about his life as a cold blooded killer, perhaps though for the wrong reasons. Still, there was the travel, the adventure the glory, aye even the gore filled battlefields. Why the very conflict itself the great ogre had embraced whole heartedly. But now though, while sitting here in his warm cosy lodge reflecting on his blood soaked past, with the boy and the pups playing outside. Well, the giant now supposed he really did not at all relish the next long very perilous task that lay ahead of him.

As this mission was for him too close to home, aye in fact it was too close to both homes. The one he had long ago deserted, and the other one he had some time ago adopted. Still though despite all of this it was nevertheless a task he must not only undertake but it was also a task that must be completed. First the princess, she must of course be rescued quickly then returned safely as soon as possible. As for the young Prince Kye, well he of course must have his antidote to restore him back to his former health. Oh and then of course there was the little but most important matter of sweet revenge. After all someone had to pay in blood and pain for the plotting and the villainous scheming of this most devious crime. It was after all an uncalled for action, it was an action which had caused so much grief and upset to not only his close friends but also Barak himself.

However though, for now at least that time of black bloody reckoning would have to wait just a little while longer.

Barak of a sudden gave his huge head a shake free from his dark broodings then both he along with Hassan enjoyed the rest of that blissful evening. Much later on as that carefree night passed on into a new day together in the misty morning light of daybreak man and boy were saddled and off towards Aulric's stone castle. Aye and it was a most enjoyable ride too, this even though the spotted pony had to near gallop to keep up with the fast trotting, long striding gelding. Once again it was around noon when the riders arrived back in the castles courtyard, also it was a busy courtyard that fair teemed and bustled with activity.

Cedric had called in his chosen men in readiness for the off, Aulric's sensible captain had selected each and every one of these men himself. Just as Barak had advised him the officer had selected soldiers who had spent most of their time in the castle. These were men who were not just outriders, not just men that patrolled the dense forests and the misty fens. After all Ellena she would have much need of friendly familiar faces about her on her release. And most certainly, well she would according to Barak be very soon rescued, yes she would be rescued unharmed at that, of that the giant was quite sure.

Once Ellenna was safe and secure the giant wanted her ordeal to be finished, he wanted that part of the quest over and done with. Barak wanted for her a safe passage back home to her doting father with men she was both familiar and comfortable with. As this of course would quite rightly help the child recover from her harrowing unplanned ordeal all the quicker.

Chapter Five

Cedric had organized the horses to take his men off to the Salmon River, the animals were even now in the stables saddled and waiting for the off. On top of this Cedric had also organized food and drinks for their journey and had even secured money from the treasury for travel expenses.

Cedric greeted Barak in a most eager fashion as the giant dismounted from the big gelding.

'All is in readiness my Lord Barak,' Cedric said, quite pleased with himself on his planning of things so far. 'I have archers, spearmen, also a few good swordsmen here at your command. ' At once the giant gave an immediate grunt of satisfaction it was quite nice to have about him someone who could actually think for themselves.

'Good, aye that is very good Cedric, aye you have done well,, Barak rumbled with an approving nod of his big head. 'But tell me this, do any of these men know their way about a ship, Cedric?.' Aulric's most trusted officer at once smiled.

'Aye my Lord Barak, I have also picked three men who have sailed these north seas in traders and fishing vessels.' Cedric answered It was obvious by his broad smile he was once again quite pleased with his selection of men. Barak once again was quite impressed, the giant at once grinned as he congratulated Cedric on how efficient the officer had been in his arrangement of both men and horses. 'Barak you seem to have some idea in your head that we will soon have the princess rescued, have her back safely with us. Can I ask you why you might think this is so my Lord? ' Cedric asked plainly of the giant.

Hassan the meanwhile proudly led away both his own spotted pony as well as Barak's big horse. At this time the boy was followed by the fat bouncy yappy pups into the stables, aye and all of this whilst the children of the castle and the surrounding villages looked on in envy. All the time wondering to themselves how lucky it was for Hassan to have such a father figure and provider as Barak. Now the giant leaned back over, with his huge hands pushing hard upon his hips until his massive back gave out a creak. It was a loud creak, a creak that sounded all the world just like that of a giant pine tree blowing in the wind.

'You know my man if it's not my neck then it's my back, if it's not my back then it is my legs Cedric,' Barak complained out aloud. 'This I suppose my friend is from too many old forgotten wounds, as well as far too many cold nights out in the freezing windswept fields and the soaking fells. Aye who knows Cedric?

Perhaps just mayhap, also just too many hard years living the life I have lived since I was little more than a boy..'

Cedric was taken more than somewhat aback by Barak's very frank truthful and most honest statement. Here the living legend Barak, well, he sounded strangely just like any other man who was perhaps passed his best, past his fastest days. How though then could that possibly be? He was after all Barak.

'In answer to your question Cedric, well my good friend the Norseman Ragnor brings us his vessel the Falcon for this pursuit. Know you this, the Falcon, believe you me is by far the fastest boat you are ever likely to voyage upon. Ragnor is also a master mariner and a navigator without compare, true he does not perhaps bathe a lot though,' the giant sniggered. 'Then again this detail should be expected as he is after all a Viking. Still though besides that little set back you can take it from me whatever it is that we chase, and wherever it is bound for, well it is already caught. ' Barak stated all of this with such a degree of confidence the slayer instantly reassured the ever over cautious but very sensible Cedric.

Next Barak continued to further enlighten Cedric with his well worked out thoughts on this most recent of dilemmas.

'My guess is these raiders are without any doubt Norsemen of some sort, they are renegades, pirates, foolhardy chancers that is for certain. Or else these desperate fools would not dare risk such an outrage against such a popular well loved king. After all is said and done, my friend Aulric does have the blessing of the Emperor of Rome himself. Aye Cedric, a broad flat bottomed boat could sail up the Salmon River and dock at the very point where we ourselves rendezvous with Ragnor. South sea traders, the Greeks or the Persians in their huge galleons could not do this. As after all these vessels are but huge clumsy floating castles no more no less, well this at least is what Ragnor the red says anyway,' Barak explained with a wry smile. 'Aye, floating abominations such as these would have to harbour miles away down by the salt sea. That as you know my friend is many days hard ride from here, also the travel is over rough terrain..' Cedric listened on intently the officer was most impressed at Barak's cold logic and reasoning of this tricky situation, Barak said on. 'Therefore these desperate rogues would of course on such a trek run the risk of the princess being recognized,' Barak paused for a moment. 'I have already said this to Aulric, much as I have told it to you Cedric.' Once again the great slayer paused as he took a light for his pipe from another passing smoker. 'No Cedric, I think you will find that we hunt a flat bottomed dragon ship manned by cut throats murderers and the most commonest cowardly of all knaves.'

Cedric stood speechless he was a man who was ever impressed by the ogre's quick thinking and his reasoning of even the trickiest of matters. But still even though he had known the giant for some years the officer was at a loss as to Barak's quick practical simple explanation of all and everything. Matters that appeared otherwise hereto most complicated to all and everyone else seemed easily explained away by the giant. Barak now ordered Cedric's men be stood down for that day, the soldiers were to relax and take in refreshment at the Seven Stars tavern. On the morrow at sunrise, it was then the men could make their way unhurriedly to the port and of course the tavern that stood on the banks of the Salmon River. For no doubt it would be the following day after that, when Barak's avengers would sail off on the start of their adventure. Ragnor, if Barak was not mistaken would either be moored there this very evening, or he would perhaps come in with the morning tide. But either way, one way or the other, the giant had every faith the big noisy Viking would not let him, or Aulric down.

This being so doubtless tomorrow night would be a night spent reliving many old campaigns while pointing out both old and new battle scars. Of course there would be time somewhere between fast flowing drinks for analyzing and planning their present mission. Either way tomorrow would nevertheless be most boisterous as well as a most raucous night, of that both Barak and Cedric were in no doubt at all. There was of course on these occasions and gatherings always the big bravado, the ever egotistical bragging. Most of this was perhaps just a touch of nerves, or maybe just a mish mash of total nonsense altogether spoken by half drunken men. Still, in a way it was a kind of bonding, while many past adventures and exploits might be slightly exaggerated in the revelry. Nevertheless most of the brutal heroic tales were as true as the stars, as these were all hard fierce fighting men who Barak had called upon for the mission ahead. Viking warriors as a rule drank as they toasted each other's courage, pledging to watch one another's backs in the bloody fray that was sure to come. For whatever it was that lay ahead of them, Cedric as well as Barak both knew the only certain fact about this whole hastily put together mission was quite simply this, not all of these bold men who sailed down the great Salmon River would be sailing back up it ever again. Either way with that minor detail aside Barak put that sunny afternoon in pleasantly enough. And after a few relaxing drinks in the tavern with Cedric and his chosen men the ogre excused himself and then he made off to collect Hassan. The rest of the time on that afternoon was spent with the boy tilling the rich fertilized soil. Happily through Hassan's efforts in the past the earth was suitably prepared, so next a variety of strange fruits and vegetables from the far side of the world were dug into the fertile bedding place.

Barak went deep with his digging this so the coming frost would prove harmless to his newly acquired exotic plants. Barak had also discovered a new method of keeping his glass houses warm throughout the cold northern winter months ahead. Before leaving for his last quest the slayer had the very capable armourer make him several iron tubes, these tubes were at least six foot long and over a foot in diameter. These tubes Barak lay down under the ground then he had covered them with earth. Hassan had been instructed as to their purpose, the lad had been shown how Barak wanted fires lit before the boy retired to his bed. When the fires at length died out the embers and hot ash were to be shovelled carefully into these tubes. This in turn would heat up the metal which would then heat up the earth warming the roots of the plants. Of course the boy beamed with both excitement and pride at being entrusted with such an important task. However there was still much to do, so next after some while spent in the garden both man and boy begun to prepare the many supplies for the following day.

Fresh fruit, melons, dates oranges, bananas, even coconuts, all grown from his own garden, the giant loaded into hessian sacks. These important supplies of food would lie in the stable overnight in readiness for his pack mules early on the following morning. Metal armour the giant had already decided he would take little of, as this merely slowed and encumbered him. Also more importantly in the cold winter months that lay ahead armour would only chill his ageing bones. As after all cold steel offered little heat in what eventually would of course become freezing conditions. So instead the giant packed for himself thick hide and fleece garments, this as well as skins of the cave bear and the forest wolf for the long cold nights that lay ahead. Most of his many weapons the slayer would leave at the castle, a good dagger, a skinning knife, a couple of throwing spears, his favourite and famous dragon sword were all that he needed. Oh, but of course the somewhat vain giant must not forget his scissors for trimming his snow white goatee beard or his shaving knife. Nor, must be left behind the Persian sword given to him as a present when he was but a boy by his father. Anything else that was required the giant could and would rob off the dead, after all and at day's end, these dead would be many in number. Oh and also, well these unfortunates, well, they after all would not be in need of anything. Of course as ever the giant would take with him his own much used cooking implements on this quest. These were such items as copper pots and pans even a couple of small iron cauldrons for stews and broths and other gut warming wholesome meals to keep the snap of winter at bay. All of this ironmongery the ogre would take on his long journey, indeed his pots and pans far outweighed his weapons of war. Also as well as his cooking vessels packed ready to go were his many herbs and spices. Here were spices that came from Barak's own garden, flavoursome plants that would help with the flavouring of his cooking. Also there were needles and thread for the repairing and stitching of clothes and saddles, as well as injured flesh, back together. Any open wounds that required doctoring or stitching up was a task as a rule left to Barak. Oh yes, the giant was indeed a man of many parts. As well as all of this the giant had already loaded his big sacks with an array of other things. Aye and these were items that quite normal people would not even think to pack. Barak however was in no way normal, no far from it, he was you must understand a well travelled man. Barak by his own admission was a man with many a fault, forgetfulness though was not one of them, no, the ogre never forgot nor overlooked anything. Horse shoes for one thing, the slayer also carried these most necessary items. Aye the well prepared ogre had many sets forged and founded by the local blacksmith. Barak being a man of many parts was more than able to heat then modify with a good hammer these shoes to fit the particular animal when needed.

On that night after much last minute running about, Barak dined in the king's hall. He was accompanied by Cedric and the eleven chosen men selected to accompany them on their forthcoming mission. This supper though, well it was a most civilized toned down affair, aye in fact it was quite boring by big Barak's standards. Why no one there got drunk or were in any way even noisy or for that matter even cheery. But then again, perhaps such behaviour would after all have been most inappropriate under the present circumstances. Still though the mission was nevertheless discussed and planned out as well as it possibly could, well, until they would be at least under way and under sail. Cedric would be charged as already arranged with the safekeeping and the hasty return of the princess back to her father's side. If need be, perhaps because some of his men were lost in the taking of the child Ragnor would assign some of his rogues to sail back with Cedric. Either way, which ever ship the princess eventually sailed homeward in it would be a most well manned vessel, nothing at all would be left to chance.

Barak after dining, drinking and talking over the morrow's venue rose from his chair at length and bade everyone a cordial goodnight. With this done, the Slayer was up, off and away, now he was heading away toward his bed. Barak wanted to rise early, for a man of his habits he had drank very little mead over these last few hours. Aulric excused himself from the table and hurried after his friend who was making his way to the room above the stables where Hassan was sleeping.

'Barak,' Aulric called out, 'hold a moment I have this.' From inside his robe of heavy black velvet Aulric produced three equally weighted heavy leather purses. The king who was trembling slightly pushed them towards Barak. 'Here, take these with you for your journey my friend..' The good king said this while his voice as well as his body was quaking with nerves. 'They are yours Barak, coinage for you on your long journey.'

Barak recoiled and stood back a pace, the ogre shook his big head.

'No, no I need no payment for this task Aulric. I am not a mercenary, well, at least not all of the time you know?' the giant protested with just the slightest of smiles. 'As you so rightly said before Aulric, if I had not been on that fool's quest for Rome perhaps none of this would ever have taken place.' Aulric looked hurt and most apologetic for these words he had earlier spoken. Oh aye the king felt guilty now for saying what he had said in his anger and his bitterness, this in the great hall that first day of the giant's return. Still though, the king went on and pressed his case. 'Let's just say this coin is for unseen expenses Barak and let us leave it at that. Yes my friend, we can call it expenses, after all you will be away for many months so take it and welcome. Please, if it is only to buy the drinks and food or for buying the information that you need then take it. Take it Barak,' Aulric insisted. 'You know yourself a few well placed coins can often loosen the tongues of the unworthy. Also, unless that great rogue Ragnor has changed a great deal, well I don't suppose he will be opening his purse very much, if you know I mean?' Aulric said with a slight smile. 'I for my turn will look to the boy Hassan as I always have done in your absence, as for you well you must just do what you do best, kill people.' Aulric said this with a nervous chuckle. 'I know that you will not fail me, nor will you fail my children. Aulric's whole body of a sudden shuddered and he was quite overcome with emotion. But the king nevertheless steeled himself then he spoke on. 'And you, you yourself must also come back home, home here to my island safe and sound to us Barak. Aye, aye you must do this for the sake of young Hassan if nothing else. '

Barak said nothing for a moment, there was a short period of silence before the giant spoke again in a rumbling voice.

'I ride to the Garrison of Vindolanda to return the Roman standards in the morning's first light, this I will do before we set sail.' The giant said this as he somewhat reluctantly took the purses from Aulric. With a nod of thanks the ogre then placed the purses in the deep inside pockets of his leather waistcoat.

'Tell me Aulric do you know of anyone who is good with foreign languages? As well as this they also must have about them a good knowledge of the writing skills?'

Aulric was thoughtful for but a moment, then the king shook his head.

'Well, apart from yourself and the young Hassan no, no I don't. But tell me Barak why do you ask me such a question?' Aulric enquired a little bemused. Barak gave the most wolfish of grins in fact it was almost a snarl.

'Because my friend the noble Magistrate, well that misguided fool will have need of a new scribe before tomorrow morning is over.' Barak said this as he once again turned upon his heel and bade his friend a final goodnight.

Aulric watched in grim silence as Barak growled away to himself like some sort of a vengeful lion as he strode away down the corridor in a most purposeful speedy manner.

Now, the king scratched at his beard, which he had by the way trimmed and cleaned up a little since the giant's return. Aulric, well the man had his problems, aye that was very true, all so very true. Barak, though, here was a man who also had his issues, and also his own dark dilemmas. The great slayer was without doubt a troubled man, aye he obviously was not himself, no, the ogre certainly was not himself at all. Barak could and he would if possible sort out Aulric's troubles, aye even this hellish nightmare with a little time and a little butchery could be resolved. But who then could help Barak? Who was it who could solve his problems of both mind and spirit? For the giant after all was an island to himself, this because the big man quite simply was the best of the best. Being so there was no one who the ogre could really turn to in time of need. For at days end if the giant himself failed to win the day, then who might he call upon who could?

Chapter Six

At the cock's first crow Barak was already dressed, saddled up and before it was even full light he was off and away. Aye the ogre was off, and he was off at a headlong gallop toward the garrison of Vindollanda. The sleepy guards at the gate of Aulric's castle gave a shudder as the stern faced ogre disappeared into the misty gloom of that early autumn morning. Rumours were already circulating about the castle that someone was going to have their last breakfeast on this fresh chill morning. Fresh and chill it was, but nevertheless this was still, the giant thought to himself, a good morning for a gallop. That day was going to be cool and clear once the forest mists and the darkness of night gave way to the bright autumn sun. Both of Barak's great dogs followed on close behind the powerful gelding. Also the huge beast as it happened by the way was not a slow or clumsy thing either. And now, well the big dogs were running open mouthed after but a short time with the effort of keeping up with the big long striding chestnut. It had been a good long while now since either of the huge hounds had undertaken such a prolonged chase. Aye the big gelding for being such a huge beast and carrying such a giant of a man upon its broad back could certainly step along at quite a pace.

Barak smiled to himself as he patted the gelding's broad neck and spoke to the creature soft words of encouragement. Aye, if nothing else Barak was still a damned good judge of horse flesh.

A little later as Barak drew into the outskirts of the garrison of Vindolanda, a handful of soldiers marked well the ogre's rapid approach aboard his huge war horse. Aye a handful of rugged soldiers and each and every one of them hailed from a different place in Europe. These men cursed as they muttered their prayers of deliverance to their various gods hard of hearing. And this they did as the men now turned away completely ignoring the giant's arrival, instead the soldiers chose to resume their game of dice. As after all it would be far better to lose their pay, which by the by was a month late anyway rather than lose their heads. For this by the looks of things, well it was obviously not an early morning social call that the big killer Barak was making.

Barak as usual was clad in a leather waistcoat hide knee breeches and his thick stout boots - upon his big head as ever the ogre wore his chain link helmet. A long black wolfskin cloak streamed out from behind him as the slayer galloped past the crouching guardsman who chose to keep their heads down low as they watched the tumbling dice. On this bright morning the giant was armed only with a curved dagger and of course his favourite much famed ivory handled dragon sword. No shield or armour did the ogre carry about him, nor did he need. Other than this Barak was armed only with an intense hatred for the man who had obviously brought about this whole sad messy affair.

With a tug of the reins the big sweating horse was pulled abruptly to a dead halt in the centre of the garrison's square, the beast was blowing hard from its exertions and moved not an inch as its master dismounted. Barak dropped the reins over the saddle then he strode purposefully towards the magistrate's office. At this time the giant was followed closely behind by the big hard blowing gelding and his equally out of breath dogs. Barak paused for only a brief moment and stopped his long striding. Now the ogre stared across the town square to where the stone masons made ready for their day's work.

There were two very large completed statues already standing, these carved from local stone. One of them was of the now dead once very industrious Emperor Hadrian, the other one was dedicated to Trajan. Also there were two other builds in progress, one the giant knew was to the present Emperor Septimius Severus but who was the other one going to be dedicated to the giant wondered. Barak grunted as he ran a thick forefinger over his arched crooked nose. However the giant wondered this to himself only briefly as there was still of course an account here to be settled.

The big Barak carried with him a hessian sack that he had untied from the back of his high backed saddle. Within it were the two Roman Standard Heads, the symbols of Rome's power and its fast fading glory. By now both of the panting dogs had laid themselves down at a command from the giant as he entered the magistrate's office, the dogs guarded the doorway. Out of breath the animals rested themselves, but nevertheless were still wary and watchful as they lay at the doorway, nothing now could go in or out.

'Who or rather what on earth is that? ' This question was asked by a young centurion who was just starting his day's turn of duty. The centurion was a tall handsome young man who was fresh from the most expensive military college in all of Rome.

'Well, that there before you is death my young and noble friend. In any tongue and in any place on this wicked unfair earth of ours, that is certain walking death that you look upon. ' Now this question was answered in such a profound manner by an older centurion. He was also a centurion that by the by the young man was all in due time to replace.

Cassius Antonius was a long served soldier of Rome, aye and he was a damned good soldier as well as this. Truth said the man could have aspired much higher in the ranks had it not been for his wild ways and his unruly drinking habits. Cassius Antonius's replacement though was young and keen, also the young man had with him all the arrogance of an aristocrat. Oh and also the young man was fast promoted because of his family's wealth and its influence in the senate. After a few years in the legions with some quick promotion he would go into the world of politics then he himself would enter the Senate. Once there he would doubtless make long winded speeches and be taught to lie a lot while looking the good people of Rome straight in the eye. Oh yes, the young man's whole life had been planned out for him from the very day of his birth. Four experienced time served legionnaires stood close to both the older centurion and his young replacement. All of these men it must be said looked on most nervously at the events taking place before them, indeed the men were fearful even.

'I do sense the big man's intentions here are not at all friendly Cassius, this is not good, no it is not good at all. ' The young centurion said this as he drew his brand new shining short sword then advanced briskly and foolishly towards the office of the Prefect and the Magistrate.

Cassius shook his head in bewilderment at the young fool, he spat scowled then cursed in that order. Now the older centurion held one of the braver, nay one of the more foolish soldiers back by his thick red tunic as he made off to follow the headstrong young centurion.

'I would say this to you my young nobleman,' Cassius spat once again and shouted toward his replacement's back. 'I would say to you this, what you have just said is a most massive and gross understatement.' Cassius said this while raising both his gruff voice and his bushy greying eyebrows at the same time.

'Nevertheless Cassius, if the big man is indeed intent on law breaking, we, as soldiers of Rome must be equally intent on law enforcement. ' The young man argued as he suddenly halted and turned about to look back at the more experienced centurion. A centurion who by now stood several yards to his rear. 'Come with me men,' the young officer said trying to sound like a man who was in some way in command of the situation. 'We must of course do our duty, we must do it for the power and the glory of our Emperor Septimius Severus. Oh and also of course for Imperial Rome,' the young centurion was quick to add. 'But above all men, we must all stand together now, we must uphold the law. After all, it is both our duty and our calling. Apparently the young centurion seemed to like the sound of his own voice, so he said on. 'Come men of Rome, for even though this be the most far flung primitive of the Northern provinces. Its earth, its very soil by conquest is then that of Rome itself.' It was very obvious to Cassius that this young true blue blooded Roman was perhaps not the most attentive of persons. For if he had of been then the young pompous fool might have noticed that two of the soldiers were Germans and the other two were from Gaul. Indeed it was only Cassius and he himself who were of Roman origin. And to be honest the older centurion had been in Briton for so long now that he neither cared who the emperor was back in his homeland, nor either did he care who it was that might one day assassinate him.

Still, besides assassinated Emperors there were some immediate problems that needed very careful handling. Cassius the older centurion called out to his young over-keen replacement. He, who had by now begun to advance towards the Magistrate's office at a rather brisk pace.

'Sheath your sword, sheath your sword or I swear that you will die here and you will die now you young fool. ' The older man shouted out with an element of panic in his gruff voice.

'We are soldiers of Rome,' the young officer shouted back without even looking over his shoulder. 'And you must surely know by your long experience Cassius that by the very manner in which the big man rode in here then paced across this courtyard that he means violence against the noble Magistrate?'

Even as the young man spoke there was a scream from the magistrate's office, it was a scream of terror, after this there was a sudden deathly silence. It was the magistrate who had let out the shrill terrible cry of horror. Barak on entering the room had thrown the Standards of Rome across the room into the corner beside a doorway that lead off to an ante-chamber. Also the ogre had done this with some element of both anger and disgust before getting on with his more serious business at hand. Barak next after a very brief and very unfriendly word with his countryman next very promptly removed his head from his neck. Being polite Barak to his credit with this mission accomplished then explained the situation and the reason as to the scribe's sudden violent demise, albeit very briefly to the shivering law official. The quaking magistrate as it so happened, well he of course agreed with every single word of the explanation Barak had given him. Also the spineless magistrate then thanked the giant many times over for the return of the Legions Standards. Oh and also for ridding him of this foreign trouble maker who was apparently the bringer of much distress to this area of Rome's far flung province. For at the end of the day, no matter who, be they the Tribunes, Prefects, or for that matter the highest ranking ambassadors from the senate itself. Each of these all to a man knew they were all utterly powerless against this huge bloodthirsty and apparently uncaring ogre. Barak for one thing was not only totally physically unstoppable, the huge killer also had great influence in Rome itself. Why he was the Emperor's favourite commander and his most talked about warrior, Barak after all was his most trusted right hand. This was a well known fact, also it was a well known fact the other pure bred Roman officers hated Barak with a black passion. Their feeble efforts were swept to one side while Barak's victories and achievements were the talk of the Empire, rightly so the rank and file agreed. Not a soldier in the ranks, foreign or Roman, would choose another to lead them into battle other than Barak. By all the Gods at once there was once even talk of a statue being built in Rome itself in honour of the huge bloodletting murderer. In fact and come to think of it perhaps the new statue in the square could even be dedicated to the ogre.

Now the ashen faced magistrate bowed several times as he stammered out his admiration for the towering fiend standing there in front of him. Then in sheer panic the jibbering fool even offered the ogre some wine, this followed by a breakfeast of eggs, ham and mushrooms if he so desired. Thankfully though Barak, well he did most very politely decline the invitation to drink and dine.

Apparently the ogre had some urgent business elsewhere thanks be to all the stars and gods at once the magistrate had muttered to himself as he quaked with fear.

Anyway Barak very politely bade the distraught magistrate a very good day while sending his compliments to the absent Prefect who was apparently away on some urgent business or other. So without any further ado Barak most roughly scooped up the shaven head of the Scribe by a large bat like ear. Next the ogre turned about and before leaving the office he gave a slight bow as he apologized for not having time to clear up the rest of the gory mess. Of course the magistrate who was by now looking very frail, very pale, also a most sickly creature accepted Barak's apology most eagerly. Barak, the magistrate did understand, was of course a very busy man. So of course it was best he be on his way and about his business, aye and this all just as quickly as possible.

Once again the giant gave a thin smile then after another polite nod of his great big head emerged back out into the square in front of the magistrate's office. Once there with some disgust the ogre threw the scribe's head onto the cobbled courtyard. It landed there with a dull thud then bounced and rolled about for several yards before coming to a final halt. Now the dark eyes of the deceased were bulging from the bald head, as for the tongue, well that was sticking out in quite a comical fashion. By now some fifty or more soldiers, tradesman, market traders and other general busybodies had gathered to see what all the early morning uproar was about. Barak, who was an ever vigilant always observant man focused straightway upon the straight backed chest out young centurion. The slayer had never seen this man before on his many frequent visits to the garrison. Barak was under the impression that the young centurion had something to say, the ogre was as ever quite correct in this assumption.

Taking a pace forward the young centurion somewhat sheepishly addressed the huge slayer.

'Today you have killed a man here, so now you are under arrest and you must come with me to the cells, it is the law.' The young centurion said this while trying to sound brave and assertive. He then very quickly looked about him for at least some sort of moral support.

But there was of course none to be had however, and the centurion was, so it seemed, quite alone. Barak smiled most broadly as he too glanced about him into the mixed crowd.

'I am?' the giant asked; he was at this time still smiling.

'You are,' the young centurion replied after a thoughtful pause and a little shakily. 'Will you come along with me quietly to the cells?' The young centurion asked this question while trying to look stern and perhaps in some way in charge of this very tricky situation. Of course the centurion was not to be kept long in waiting for the answer to his somewhat foolish question.

'No boy,' Barak answered with a slow shake of his big chain link clad head. 'I will not come along with you quietly. In fact, I don't think that I will be coming along with you at all. '

On hearing this, the young centurion sighed heavily then cursed his parents under his breath for having him sent here to this far flung cold damp province. Wisely, the young man decided he must now choose his next few words very carefully, this lest they be his last.

'But you must understand you have committed a cold blooded murder, this man here he is dead.' This the young centurion said as he pointed a shaking finger towards the severed head. Barak gave the centurion, a couldn't care less, sort of shrug, then the killer picked at that back tooth which had been bothering him for some time.

'Well my boy, without a head most people are dead things I do suppose. Did you not know that was a harsh but very simple fact of life? ' At once these words brought a chuckle from the mixed crowd of observers. However they were words though that in turn brought a red flush to the young man's smooth whiskerless cheeks. 'Do they teach you nothing at all at your expensive military school back in Rome, boy?' Barak asked this question with a cold cynical grin.

Even in these brief moments that the giant had spoken to the young man Barak knew exactly what the young fool was all about. Oh aye the ogre knew only too well of his true blue blood pedigree, and also of his proud arrogant upbringing. Here was a young man who had never in his life been without, nor had the fool ever wanted for anything since the time of his birth.

At this point in the conversation Cassius Antonius had by now seen more than enough, and he had already turned his broad back on this very dangerous, tricky situation. Mumbling curses the older centurion was now heading off at a brisk pace towards his brother-in-law's drinking house, the well used Bacchus. If this stubborn young fool wanted to get himself killed so early in the day then so be it. But as for himself well he not only wanted a drink, now he most desperately needed one.

Cassius was due his retirement and his pension very soon, so the older centurion had no intention of getting himself killed here and now. At day's end this sad uncalled for tragedy would alas all have been caused merely by his young foolish replacement's stubborn folly. True it was that his brother in law would be getting knocked out of bed early this morning to open up his doors. But there was one thing most certainly sure, that was the penny pinching in-law was also going to make a lot of money on this day.

Of course the crowd the meanwhile all found Barak's wry humour most amusing, even though this humour was at the expense of the young and clearly very embarrassed very proud centurion. Oh and by the by also the panic struck magistrate was not long in following Cassius to the comparative safety of the

90

Bacchus. Now he hurried past the crowd with his head down not giving the young centurion or the giant a second glance. Later that day the magistrate had already decided that he would write his resignation out. Aye after all enough was enough of this cold hostile little island. But, this resignation would be scribbled out only when the drink gave him more courage to do so.

'This dead man here, well this bald bat eared head anyway. This it is not the head of any Roman or is it that of a Briton,' Barak explained calmly. 'No my boy, sadly to my shame the deceased thing is one of my own people. With this being so would anyone here amongst you die for this traitor? Die for a man who was treasonous to his own kind?' Barak asked this question as he strode toward the young centurion. As he did so the crowd parted fearfully and fell back leaving the young centurion standing quite alone. Now the centurion, well alas for him he was the only soldier left for the giant to talk to. The rest of them, well quite wisely they had ran away to join Cassius and the magistrate in the now very full Bacchus Tavern.

'For I tell you now, I, Barak would not throw my life away on such as that,' the giant said firmly as he nodded toward the scribe's head.

On shaky legs the young centurion Marcus, only now as he stood alone realized the size and power of the man called Barak. He looked skyward up and up at the giant, then he looked around about him for some sort of assistance, but alas there was none to be had, he was all alone.

Marcus was a high born aristocrat who was starting his army career as a centurion, a young man with a hundred men to command. A hundred men! what a joke that was, he looked about him, and yet again he could count not even one man of that hundred. The young noble had not yet been in the Northern legions a month yet here and now he was staring at a certain and doubtless death straight in the painted face.

On the other hand Cassius Antonius was a man with over twenty five years service in the legions. Cassius was a man who had started out his career as a water boy tending stock and making sure marching men had refreshment at day's end. While Marcus Agrippa Caesar in total contrast to the humble Cassius was a high born noble bred from the very highest nobility in all of Rome. Still though, the brash young man reasoned to himself as he was stood there alone before the giant. High born or not, perhaps it would be more prudent, if not valiant to simply walk away and join his fellows in the Bacchus. Even with all the confidence of youth, the military training, the brainwashing as to Roman invincibility and superiority. Of course the young man knew only too well he had not a chance in a million against the fearsome fiendish looking Barak. For only now did the centurion truly realise who and what it was that stood directly towering there before him.

This ogre was a real thing after all, he had always been just a little unsure of Barak's very existence. As a small child he would be frightened off at night time to his bed by his doting mother, saying to him as she did. That tonight the giant barbarian Barak walked the streets of Rome in his big booted feet. He walked the streets at the dead of night and that the giant slayer ate and gobbled up little children for his supper, this she would say to him. Oh and of course the tattooed ogre, well he was in particular very partial to feasting upon small Roman boys.

Barak gave a thin knowing smile as ever the ogre seemed capable of reading a man's mind, now the giant could smell the young man's fear, he could almost taste his sweat. While the giant smiled he stood now only an arm's length away from the Centurion. Then it was that the young roman noticed the wolf like teeth, he felt very sickly and very faint all of a sudden. If rumour was true and it often was, how many men had the giant chewed upon over the years with those fangs? Next the young centurion glanced at Barak's sword which had been cleaned of blood before being replaced back into its ornate leather scabbard. It was the ivory handled dragon headed sword, the giant's death dealer, a sword he had been told about since being just a small boy.

While the young centurion had heard much of the great slayer from his earliest childhood days to being a more confident youth, Marcus was in all truth never quite sure if Barak truly existed. Well at least existed and perhaps was at once the fierce demonic figure that had been portrayed to him from being a small boy. For it was later on in time as the boy grew into youth, then manhood that the giant's greatness was beginning to be played down little by little by his doting parents. After all Barak, well he was not of Roman blood so perhaps it was time now that his legend was pushed to one side. No, it was now Barak was depicted merely as no more than an unthinking ogre, a puppet and a slave of Rome. Barak was no more than a huge savage brutal mercenary, he was not of course from the family of Caesar as was his noble bloodline. Still though, the young Roman thought to himself as he quaked and sweated in his armour and winter clothing, Barak was without any shadow of doubt a living marvel to behold. And that sword he carried at his hip was, so they say, forged from star metal by some ferocious war-like yellow skinned race from afar. These were a race of ferocious warriors that were as yet not even totally known to Rome at this time. It was also said that the deadly weapon had taken a full year in its making, this with a dozen master craftsmen working at it day and night. All of this perhaps was merely hearsay, in all truth it sounded very unlikely the blade was made from a metal that fell from the sky. But then again the blade, well it was there before him and his eyes they at least did not lie.

From behind the young centurion there came a sudden loud shout that stirred the young man from his bleary somewhat gloomy musings. It was a familiar friendly voice, then there was another voice and yet another. Now the men of the northern legion they beckoned him, the rank and file called to the young centurion, beckoning him to the safety of the Bacchus.

Both Cassius Antonius and the Magistrate stood at the doorway to the tavern; both men hailed Marcus over to join with them. After all it would be indeed a shame for the young handsome man's career and his life to end here, so abruptly so far away from his large expensive home.

Barak would to his credit now show just a little bit of his much hidden compassion.

'Go, go now, go and drink your fill of your wishy washy Roman women's wine" Barak said with a slight smirk. 'Aye lad, you must enjoy this fine sunny morning my boy. For if I am not much wrong, then you will live long and you will prosper well young Roman, so go now and be gone" Barak firmly advised. 'Many years from now boy, when I am a long dead thing you can tell this story to your children, perhaps even their children..' This the giant added with a slightly whimsical tone. Barak had said this as he took his gelding by the reins and with a great leap swung himself up onto its broad back. Of course this athletic act giving the height of the horse must have looked most impressive to the growing number of onlookers. Why in all truth there was not many agile youths that could have made that lofty jump. Still though, vanity, well it always has its price. Aye and this being so, well once within the comforting confines of the high backed saddle the giant thought to himself it might have been far wiser just to use the stirrups to mount the great gelding.

'Live you long young Roman.' Barak said this with a polite parting nod of his big bucket sized head, 'and farewell to you. Oh and another thing boy, you must heed that fat fraud Cassius. He is a good man, even though some might say he drinks too much..' When the giant said this his voice was perhaps in just a slightly higher pitch than it was before he leapt with a youth like fashion aboard the tall gelding. Still, nobody there in the crowd seemed to notice the giant's somewhat squeaky voice, and if they did well they never said as much.

As one the people of the garrison sighed with relief as the giant spun about on his big horse then thundered away out of the market square with his great red dogs bounding close behind him. As for the young centurion, well, he might live long and indeed he might also prosper well. More than likely he would give his family's proud name coupled with their wealthy status. But besides all of that the young centurion certainly did have a story to tell, and as it so happened the young man was not going to be long in the telling of it. So as he watched Barak leave the garrison, Marcus on rubbery legs and with his heart beating like a madman's drum went without his normal swagger to join Cassius Antonius and the magistrate in the now bustling Bacchus tavern.

Oh and of course the young man was well welcomed.

'Congratulations to you young Marcus.' the older centurion said clapping him firmly on his back with one hand whilst passing him a cup of red wine with the other.

Marcus took the wine in a most thankful but very shaky fashion, and he at once swallowed it down with some panic and urgency in a single gulp. Clumsily the young centurion in all truth spilled some of it, if not most of the wine upon his new shining breastplate and his red tunic.

When the young man could at length catch his breath he then spoke up and to his credit the young fool spoke up honestly.

'If I were thrown into the arena with the man-eating lions of Rome, I swear I would not have felt such fear as I have felt this sunny morning,' he stammered out after a another cup of hastily drank wine. With a fatherly smile the older centurion gave out a grunt of satisfaction on hearing these honest words the young man had spoken.

'Your first lesson went well my boy, I am so proud of you.' Cassius boomed this out as he shouted out for yet more refreshment.

'Proud, proud, why do you say that you are proud of me Cassius? the young man asked with a very baffled expression about his ashen face. 'As I after all made no arrest of the giant law breaker, aye and remember this a man was most savagely killed here on this bright morning. Why, his head I believe it still lies in the town square even now staring with sightless eyes up at the chill blue sky,' the young centurion said shakily. 'No, oh no Cassius I have failed in my sworn duty to uphold the laws of my homeland and Imperial Rome. Thus I am unworthy of my office and my family name. Truly I am most ashamed of myself and alas I can say no other,' the young man went on whilst looking most downcast. Cassius raised his bushy eyebrows then gave a very dismissive grunt before replying to his future replacement's somewhat imagined self critical shortcomings.

'Listen, the man quite simply was already dead Marcus, so you could not have saved him, in fact no one could have saved him. Aye and anyway, from what big Barak said the fool was not worth the saving in the first place. Oh and by the by my boy, the Lord Barak is I admit a cold blooded killer, but he is not a liar when it comes to matters such as this,' the older centurion replied evenly.

'Oh, oh well how very refreshing that is to hear, then the great ogre he is a pinnacle of integrity,' the young man mumbled between sips upon his wine. 'Still though despite all of that I did not do my duty, did I Cassius? So I have failed in my appointed task here,' the young man answered a little sadly and ashamedly. With a frown the older centurion gave a grunt a growl and a could not care sort of shrug then he spoke.

'Yes, yes boy perhaps all of that is true, but nevertheless you have survived boy, you still live. ' Cassius Antonius said this almost in a whisper, Cassius was, he supposed, at last warming to the young, full of himself nobleman.

His arrogance, his self-centred pompous pride was gone now, the young man of a sudden struggled to fight back tears of sheer relief. As he realized only now that he lived and breathed when he could so easily have died in the square on that bright morning, aye and he would have died for what? Now it was the young man gave his troubled head a shake then he took another deep drink of wine, this done the young centurion spoke again.

'But Cassius, the soldiers the people of the town, what will they think of me now?' Most dismally the young man asked this question with his voice full of concern for his standing in the community. 'After this black most shameful day am I then no more to be looked upon than a coward? And am I to be no more than some sort of a laughing stock here in this cold hostile place that abounds with ogres, huge dogs and horses the size of elephants? What would my family back in Rome make of it all I ask myself?' After asking this the young noble was almost beside himself with shame and self-doubt. After all his privileged upbringing had not prepared him for anything quite like this morning's strange and bloody event.

Cassius was grizzled and experienced the old soldier comforted the young man, a young man who on first meeting he had little or no time for at all.

'No boy you did no wrong,' Cassius said a degree of sympathy in his gruff voice. 'Watch now and I will prove it to you, aye I will prove it to you in the here and now. Three cheers for Marcus Agrippa Caesar!' the older centurion shouted out. Instantly a roar of genuine support went up for the young man, then there was another and another. Aye and the last cheer it was the loudest and perhaps it was the longest of them all. Now at least it so appeared the proud young nobleman was at that very moment accepted by the men of the northern legion. These were the rank and file; these were straight honest and hardened men, each and every one of them veterans of the wall. Why these tough solid soldiers from here there and everywhere, these men were the backbone of Rome itself. Of a sudden the young man smiled nervously then he saluted his companions in a gesture of thanks. True it was that many there among them were not even Roman - they were Spaniards, Germans and Gauls, a mish mash of soldiers. But nevertheless these tough men made up the numbers now in this cold bleak Northern Province of Rome. These men took Roman pay when at long length it came to them, and these men did the empire's bidding without question or without complaint. Aye it was these rough rugged men that held the wall secure, the wall in the sky, the long dead Emperor Hadrian's wall.

For the second time in one day the young man felt suddenly very humble. But now although the centurion was humble, he was humble yet proud. Aye and he supposed he most certainly was more at ease with himself than he had perhaps ever been before in his short spoilt pampered life.

Here he was in the tough Northern legions now and there was no doubt about that. Now this was his new family, these men from all across Europe and even Asia were his new friends and his new comrades in arms. That be it all for the better or for the worse of it was to be his new life for the foreseeable future.

Cassius nudged the young man stirring him from his gloomy musings.

'Mind you boy, you still faired a lot better than the noble magistrate over there.' The older centurion laughed out loudly as he said this. 'Those aren't all just wine stains covering his expensive toga if you know what I mean?'

Prospero the Magistrate overheard those somewhat unkind words but in all truth and at this particular time he cared little. So the hitherto somewhat haughty official simply raised his grey eyebrows and merely shrugged, he then with a raise of his glass laughed off Cassius Antonius' somewhat crude and mocking remarks. After a morning like this one, well, who cared if his bladder had failed him, for he too at least lived when he so easily could have died? Aye at least his balding head after all the morning's horrors was still sitting on top of his scrawny wrinkly neck.

Now the shrewd innkeeper gave a rather cheeky salute to the bloodthirsty ogre Barak and then yet another loud cheer went up. After all the dead man had obviously done something seriously wrong to offend and upset the giant. Also besides all of that no locals had been hurt or even threatened by Barak. And in all truth the people and the soldiers of the garrison never had in the past felt under any threat by the giant's hand. Also in all honesty the smiling innkeeper could not remember the last time that he had taken so much money in so short a time, this so early in the morning at that. So really with all things considered it had ended up not being such a bad morning after all. Well that was providing of course you were not the magistrate's now headless secretary. As for big Barak, well the giant was now a contented if not a happy man. Now the treachery and the shame that his countryman had brought upon him was at least put to rights. True it was the trouble and treason the fool had caused could not be undone but at least it was still avenged.

Chapter Seven

Barak was at least in appearance a more settled and a calmer man when he later trotted back into the courtyard of the castle. Cedric was gone now, he had already left for the port an hour or so earlier. Slowly and somewhat unhurriedly the officer with his eleven men now wound their way down through the forests winding pathways towards the port on the great Salmon River.

Barak had some last minute arrangements to make and as always some running about to do before leaving on this his last venture. His mules had already left with Cedric so this meant Barak could at least travel fast and light to catch up with them at the river port. One thing was for certain the big horse could at least gallop when need be and it had been an age since Barak had enjoyed such an early morning ride.

After a quick search of the castle and its grounds the giant found Aulric sitting in the garden, the king at this time was watching Hassan playing with the fat very noisy puppies. Barak at once went and joined the king but neither men spoke a word about the task in hand - no not a word.

Everything had been said that could be said and Aulric knew everything would be done that could be done.

'When you return here to this place and I know well that you will, make sure that you bring that old sea dog Ragnor with you Barak..' Aulric said these words with some sense of emotion as the men rose then at last walked slowly together towards the stable. 'Then we will drink, we will feast and we will rejoice like we never have before. And I know only too well that the Prince Kye will be rejoicing along with us and he will give you praise for his life when we do so.' Aulric said these words while trying to sound both positive and confident. Any dark misgivings or doubts of any sorts the king did have he had simply pushed to one side, well at least for now.

Hassan ran to Barak's side before the giant could once again reassure Aulric that the quest would be completed, thus it was that Barak had said nothing more. Instead the giant ruffled the boy's black curly hair then he playfully hoisted him high into the air.

'The boy he will want for nothing not now not ever Barak, I will swear with my life upon that, Aulric said sincerely. 'If anything should happen to you on this quest, which as I have already said I do greatly doubt, then I want you to know that at least Barak. I would treat young Hassan as if he was my very own. True the child he is not of your blood nor is he of mine but believe me Hassan would be welcome in my house for as long as he would stay. ' Aulric paused for a moment his emotions getting the better of him, after a while though he regained his composure and said on. 'And now my large friend I feel that I can say no more.'

Barak removed his link helmet then bowed his big shaven head in thanks.

'I will not fail, I never fail, who knows perhaps that is my curse. You already know that to be fact only too well Aulric,' the giant said with a slight smirk. It was the king's turn now to bow his head to the stern faced giant. As always since their first meeting the King of the northern tribes was of course both grateful and proud to have such a friend, perhaps never more so than at this particular moment in time. 'Aulric when I do return and return I will to this island of yours, it is finally over for me, enough is enough.

'Over, Barak?' Aulric queried. 'Then you are in all truth serious, you do mean to settle down at long last and put away that much used sword of yours? Remember, you have said this to me many times before Barak. Aye you have often spoke of retirement, this more than often after a bad campaign, a bad wound or even on a more bad and bloody day than usual.' Aulric then paused while he looked up into the dark almost black almond eyes of the towering giant. Barak replaced his tattered chain link helmet upon his head and affixed Aulric with a solid stare. 'Barak, this time somehow I think you actually might mean it, do you?' Aulric pressed this question with his voice full of sincere concern for his long time friend. In all truth the king of the northern tribes after this recent heartbreaking event supposed he would also welcome the permanent protection as well as the company of the giant.

Barak fixed Aulric with his black eyes then spoke in a low rumbling voice.

'Please believe me Aulric; my days of warfare are done with on my return.' Barak replied this evenly without any hesitation whatsoever, 'It is all over for me at the end of this quest.' Aulric on hearing this, felt quite choked at the giant's words this was the end of an era after all.

'Will you then bide here with me my friend? Will you share your time between my mighty stone castle and your big lodge in the dark forest? Will you Barak? Aye and indeed can you Barak, after a lifetime of butchery and wholesale slaughter, can you lay down your well used dragon sword? You must forgive my doubting for you are my friend and I mean no offence to you. But I ask again, can you in all truth retire from the battlefield and your past love of warfare?' Aulric pressed this with still a trace of doubt in his mind.

'Aye,' Barak answered back once again simply and without any hesitation. 'And yes I will bide here in this cold forsaken island of yours, I will leave no more for war. We will hunt, we will fish, we will ride through the forest, the boy and me. Well, that is if this is to your liking young Hassan?' Barak asked this question of the small curly haired dark skinned boy who had returned to his side after running off with the pups again. Hassan hugged one of Barak's great huge long legs then, perhaps for the first time Aulric now saw the giant waver, to weaken and soften a little. He actually showed another emotion apart from outbursts of raging anger and of course his cold hearted steely determination. But then again perhaps Aulric was not quite as surprised as he might once have been. In fact, come to think of it he was not surprised at all. How on earth could he be after the strange revelations and all that had happened over these past few days, anything was possible, aye anything at all?

Of a sudden, thoughts both nightmarish and dreamlike coursed through Aulrics tormented mind yet again. How was it that his dead son now lived? And how was it that his best friend, a man he known for years was now the king in a far flung land? Once again the northern king looked most troubled and perplexed. Perhaps these dark mind-bending thoughts would never leave him, aye perhaps these thoughts would haunt and torment him till the very day he died.

Barak as always and ever noticed everything.

'Shake yourself from your dark musings Aulric. Put your trust in me just this one last time.' Barak said this as if he could read Aulric's very troubled mind.

'I do, I do trust you.' Aulric said taking Barak's advice and giving his head a vigorous violent shake. 'Please believe me my large friend, I do trust you above all others.'

Barak on hearing this gave out a satisfied grunt then he turned his attention once again to the small boy at his side.

'When I do return to this place Hassan we will have all of our time to spend together, this is my promise. But in the meanwhile look you to the garden, care for the pups and the spotted pony. As this will keep you busy and your mind active the time will fly by quickly. Believe me boy I will be back here in this place with you before you even know it. But in the meantime you are in charge of the garden and all that is mine, well ours. Oh, and Hassan, when I am not here then you are me, do you understand what I say to you lad - you are me? You speak as I would speak and act as I would act, do you understand me?' On hearing this, the small boy gave a very proud and a most positive nod of his black curly head.

'Yes Barak I do understand, I am you, but only I am a lot smaller, also I have lots of hair and of course proper teeth..' Happily the small boy said this with a bright smile that revealed his own most perfect white shining teeth.

Barak hoisted the boy high aloft once again as if he was no more than a toy as he spoke gently to him in the language of the Krozak people. This was a tongue which Hassan both understood and was now familiar with. Next the giant placed the small child back upon the ground with the playful yapping pups.

'And you, you take care also Aulric, don't take too much of that monks' mead or their cider. Take my advice and you stick to that weak women's beer you locals brew and are so fond of. You Briton's could never handle a good drink anyway,' Barak said with a wolfish grin. 'Look to my boy Hassan, when I come back we will feast and drink and I will tell great tales of this my last heroic quest..' With this said and without another word spoken Barak was atop his rested war horse. However, now though, the giant quite sensibly used the stirrups to mount the lofty steed. Then finally with a nod to both his friend and the boy the ogre was off out of the courtyard at the gallop, his great dogs lolling behind him.

'Father, be careful, come back safe to me,' the young Hassan called out imploringly as the giant clattered across the cobbles upon his huge war horse. Barak winced but nevertheless despite this he did not falter this even though the boy had never called him by that name before. Now the great giant kicked the gelding on and the slayer kept on riding without a backward glance.

Either it be by the brisk rising wind or the cold late afternoon air. Or indeed it was perhaps due to the very speed of the great horse itself as it passed him by. Whatever it might be, but as the giant waved Hubert a goodbye on his departure the weary and forlorn old guardsman standing at the gate could have sworn there was a tear in the eye of the black hearted slayer. Of course this though was something that would stay forever a secret with Hubert aye and it would stay with Hubert alone until his very death.

It was not quite dusk when Barak approached the tavern that stood on the last port of the great Salmon River. It was the furthest point that even a shallow bellied boat could manage to sail. For just a bowshot away, higher upstream towards the land of the Picts there was a high foaming wear. Barak had once again greatly enjoyed the ride upon his big warhorse towards the small port. This as the big gelding had galloped well on the few small stretches of open road. Also, and as a bonus Barak had a well grown roe stag the dogs had brought down tied at the back of his high backed saddle. Ahead of him now as dusk fell and the ogre neared the river, a small ragged primitive looking hill pony bravely blocked the giant's path. Atop it there was an equally small ragged primitive looking man sat upon a makeshift saddle made of wood, hide, oh and of course wolf skin.

Barak pulled the huge gelding alongside the unwashed man who was also dressed entirely from head to foot in wolf skin hides. At once the gelding snorted loudly as the big beast stamped its huge iron hooves. What was this strange combination of things that stood before them the great beast must have thought to itself?

Erik's brother, for of course it could be no other, was most definitely a man of the earth, the woods and the wild. In fact it would be true to say that he was more akin to the animals he hunted than anything that was at all human. Still besides this the men greeted each other cordially enough did the huge warrior and the small hunter. But then again they had good reason too, for both men were hunters and were, despite appearances, much the same in many ways. The giant himself had tracked, hunted and slain almost everything that ran over plains or

100

deserts or forests. Also he had hunted the fish that swam the rivers and the oceans, even the birds that flew in the skies the slayer had hunted with his crossbow and feasted upon their flesh. Yes the giant and this strange looking little man had much in common. But even so, Barak's over keen sensitive nostrils did still wince just a little at the wolf hunter's strong lupine scent.

'Be still.' Barak commanded of his massive dogs which were also not quite sure what it was that sat atop the hill pony, the huge hounds regarded its rider with some suspicion.

'They think that perhaps I am a wolf my Lord Barak'' the little man said quite proudly; apparently the hunter was pleased at the dogs' unsure reactions toward him. Next the wolf hunter smiled to himself and he revealed a mouthful of sharp, broken but perfectly white teeth. These teeth however, were the only thing about this strange little person that was in any way at all clean. Indeed it was little wonder that Erik did not invite his brother to bide long with him on his rare visits to trade or swap news of the happenings in the dark forest.

Barak did not even know the brother's name, he was simply known as Wolf to all and everyone who he had any sort of contact with, not that they were many in number. Still though and besides this, it was a title that the hunter seemed to like. Well leastways the wolf hunter apparently drew no offence from it.

'Your pup is it well?' Barak asked of the wolf hunter.

The small man atop the small pony gave a strange sort of smile come wolf like leer.

'Aye Barak.' the hunter replied with a nod of his wolf-capped head. 'It sleeps in my dugout with my other dogs, it will make a fine hunter of the wolf I do think. For it does have about it, both great spirit and the most powerful strength for a young pup. It is bred to hunt, it is bred to kill, my thanks to you Lord Barak'' the dirty little man said with a slight bow of gratitude. Well at least the strange little unwashed high smelling man has manners Barak thought to himself.

'Bred for the task, indeed that is very true what you say Wolf,' Barak declared proudly. 'And what of my big black eagle I do not see her, tell me friend why is that?' Barak asked this question leaning forward in his high backed saddle and fearing some accident might have befallen his beloved eagle. Now the little wolf hunter grinned, then he gestured sky ward with his dark shiny rat like eyes.

'Aye perhaps this is so great slayer, but she nevertheless sees you, after all you are not hard to find,' the wolf hunter added with a slight chuckle.

High in a pine tree directly above him Barak made out the great black silhouette of a huge bird sitting silently watching all that went on about it. At once the giant smiled; even in the gathering darkness she looked fat and well fed. Barak put two fingers to his lips, he next gave a shrill whistle, then, on silent wings the great bird floated silently downward to land on Barak's outstretched left arm. It was an arm which had been heavily strapped with a thick hide covering; this in turn was lined with sheepskin. From elbow to wrist this padded gauntlet ran to protect his flesh from the bird's wicked curved talons.

This great yellow eyed eagle was as black as a raven. It was birds such as these the Black Guards made their flight feathers from. These black eagles were sacred birds, aye they were the very Emblem and the standard of the Krozaky people. Only the King or his family could own or fly one of these airborne killers. This was an ancient law that had gone on for as long as the royal house of the Kings of Krozak had been established all those long distant years ago. Within the palace and the great halls and libraries of the city these magnificent birds flew free and unhindered. Every one of the eagles had full rite of passage in the palace and anywhere in the capital, indeed the whole vast kingdom was their sanctuary. All of these birds were well fed and well cared for, their valuable fallen feathers were gathered up and collected as they fell. Other feathers were either scavenged from vacated nests or taken from the carcasses of old fallen birds out in the wild. Aye, and the penalty for killing the black eagle was most severe, it was death by fire. Of course this was no doubt a harsh and a cruel law, but nevertheless it was the law of the land and a law that had stood for over a thousand years.

'She has taken for me many wolves Barak; even the golden eagle in the mountains of the land of the Picts has neither her great strength nor her courage. Even in full flight the eagles of the highlands are nowhere near to being her equal.' The little man said this full of praise and admiration for the big black wolf killing bird. 'Aye the best golden eagle I ever saw was one of my own, and while from a high swoop she could pin a wolf down, she could not kill it,' the hunter said honestly. 'But that huge bird of yours though, she can pick the biggest wolf up with ease then fly off with it to drop the unfortunate creature against a tree or a rock. Why Barak, I have even seen her crush a big she wolf's head till its eyes popped out of its very head. '

Barak noticed the wolf hunter's dark eyes danced with glee as he talked about the she eagle's unmatched prowess at wolf killing.

'No golden eagle could do that,' the wolf hunter added. Barak said nothing, he merely nodded in agreement in reply to Wolf's honest and accurate statement. As it happened the giant had always thought little of the eagles that hailed from the land of the Picts. In all truth Barak had long thought them lacking in both size and raw power. Not to mention flying ability and sheer courage.

Still though as he did not want to insult or offend Wolf by decrying his native eagle the giant very politely kept silent. Barak then whispered most softly as he stroked the bird's head gently while its yellow eyes blinked in the fast fading light. If only the wolf hunter knew how truly privileged he had been to fly the great black bird. After all is said and done the wolf hunter could not be further removed from imperial royalty. Still, royalty or not Barak had reasoned it was better the bird stay with a man who knew how to fly and use such an eagle. As this of course was far preferable, rather than have her chained up to a perch in the castle's hall.

Barak was for a moment most thoughtful then he spoke almost in a whisper to the hunter.

'Tell me, did she come to you at the call, Wolf?' Barak asked eagerly. 'Could you fly her from your arm? Tell me could you do this?' the giant pressed almost urgently. At this question the little man smiled wryly before he shook his wolf capped head most knowingly.

'No, no never my Lord Barak, she was ever faithful to you, she slept above my dugout in a great gnarled oak tree that was ancient long before the Romans ever came here as invaders to our island. ' Wolf said this honestly but with a hint of disappointment in his voice. In truth the hunter had set himself a challenge he had hoped to win the eagle over, but alas to his bitter disappointment he had not. 'Besides,' the little wolf hunter went on, 'I doubt very much that my feeble arm could bear her weight, she is so big and strong. She took meat from me on the wing though, from my outstretched hand or even from a lure. But no Barak, the she eagle never trusted me enough to sit upon my arm. Nor did she even sit upon a perch of my making within my den. ' Once again the little wolf hunter sounded a little put out and disappointed that he had not gained the great birds full trust.

Barak smiled both proudly and broadly as he spoke soft words once again in his native tongue to the bird.

'I raised her from a fledgling, for ten years I have had her or she has had me, in truth, I do not know if I am her master or she is my mistress in this partnership. Women, they may be unfaithful in their men's absence when they are at war or even at work in the fields or forests, Wolf,' Barak stated profoundly. 'But not loyal and noble creatures such as these, no these creatures cannot be bribed, bought, cajoled or conned.'

Wolf nodded his head in total agreement. The small hunter, as it so happened, was of exactly the same opinion as the giant.

'That's why I never wanted to take a wife Barak,' the little wolf hunter grinned. 'Doubtless though there are none out there who would want me either,' he then added with a smile and a shrug of total honest indifference. 'Anyway big Barak, well I must say that is something which suits me just fine,' the wolf hunter chuckled. With that profound statement the hunter next turned his small raggy hill pony about and began to trot rather unsteadily off into the gathering gloom. 'Fare well to you slayer, and good luck big Barak on your manhunt, kill them all,' the little wolf hunter said with another chuckle.

'Hold on there, I have a purse of silver for you Wolf, here take it,' the giant offered producing the leather purse from within his waistcoat.

103

'Keep it Barak, keep it for your strong drink and your weed, the black eagle has paid her way in pelts and bounty, aye and also I truly enjoyed her company. This, even though she might not have enjoyed mine. Live you long great ogre, slay you many, before you yourself are laid low,' the strange little man shouted back over his scrawny shoulder.

Big Barak gave a disconcerting grunt as he very gently stroked the underside of the great eagle's throat.

'Drink! Weed! Do you think that strange little unwashed thing was trying to say something to me my lovely?' Barak asked softly of the big black eagle.

With these last words said the little man atop his little pony faded off into the darkness of the woods like the mist of the forest. As he trotted steadily off the hunter took along with him as he went his own earthy scent as well as that of the wolves and the very forest itself. One day Barak thought to himself he would like to spend some time with both Erik and his brother together. As no doubt that event, should it ever happen, would be both very interesting as well as very entertaining.

Aye and if by some slim chance Wolf could be tricked into having a bath of some sort before this meeting, well that would of course be all the better. Perhaps though, well perhaps this little miracle was far too much to hope for.

Chapter Eight

By the time Barak had unsaddled and cared for his big warhorse in the spacious barn which lay just a stone's throw from the riverside tavern it was fully dark. Two of Cedric's men dozed lazily and casually there within the barn's ample confines. Cedric's soldiers had attended to Barak's gaunt grey big eared but kindly mules and also to all the other mounts as well. These two men with their chores done, reclined now most contentedly upon their sleeping blankets. Casually the soldiers were eating cheese and bread from their saddlebags while drinking the weak, wishy washy local ale Barak so despised.

Barak stayed there with the men for some time while the ogre talked about this and that, but nothing really in particular. Earlier these men had been in the tavern but they had found it far too noisy and way too packed out for their liking. Apparently the big Viking Ragnor had been there in the tavern since before mid-day. In the soldiers' own words the big Viking and his hairy itchy, very noisy men were in the very highest of spirits. That information to the Briton's credit, well it was a most polite and diplomatic way of saying that the Norsemen were all roaring drunk. This revelation however was no more than Barak had expected from a boatload of noisy northern pirates. Indeed if the savage seagoing rogues had all been sitting about calmly talking in a sensible fashion about this that and the other he would of been worried in the extreme as to their well being.

Barak tended his big gelding, which by the by the slayer was liking more by the day. Perhaps, the giant thought to himself this big horse was not quite right in the head in some ways. For it at times certainly did not behave like a gelding, no far from it. Indeed the creature's behaviour was more like that of a stallion, or even a rig. But then again every single animal in league with the giant was perhaps not quite totally normal one way or the other. Anyway besides this, the giant after a little while bade the soldiers a very goodnight. However the ogre did this only after he had commended them on their good sense to take themselves away from the ongoing revelry inside the tavern. For as it transpired neither of these men had ever even sailed the Salmon River before let alone the great salt sea. So obviously gorging upon food and drink all night before they set off on their perilous venture would be most unwise. Oh aye this indeed would doubtless make their voyage the following day a very long one, also a very unpleasant one.

The Norse on the other hand, well these were men who were of course all used to high living. Why these sea going rogues would often sail out from their berths three parts drunk whilst relying upon the sea air and the sharp wind to sober them up and bring them eventually around. Indeed, it was a harsh simple fact that any man who was in any way the least bit tender or delicate after a long heavy night of feasting and drinking. Well he or they would become the target for mockery and cruel ridicule, aye and this till someone else made a fool of themselves in their stead.

Aulric's soldiers, the two men Barak had earlier spoken to in the barn had said the locals who normally frequented the Salmon tavern were nowhere to be found. All of the farmers, peat diggers, woodsman and fisherman now concealed themselves deep in the forest. There was of course the possibility this long dragon headed ship could perhaps be a friendly one. But on the other hand the last long boat to sail up the Salmon River had brought nothing but heartbreak mischief and sorrow. So now under these present circumstances concealment seemed perhaps the most prudent and sensible option.

Barak entered the Salmon tavern having to crouch down to gain entry without knocking his great head upon the solid oak door frame. Of course the drinking establishment was smoke filled and was heady from the seaweed or whatever else the savage Vikings stuffed down their pipes for a smoke. Indeed when the giant finally drew a deep breath he certainly took their smoking material to be something coastal. Well it was either that or it was something even more horrible by the stench of it. Then again that would come as no surprise as the Norsemen were ever and always a most uncouth unkempt bunch of rogues. But that though was perhaps the very reason why big Barak liked their company so much. Barak looked about him whilst he smiled broadly; proper men at last the ogre thought happily to himself. These Vikings' well they were by nature and design all huge, fearsome and uncouth hairy looking men. All about the hairy headed, hairy faced reavers arm wrestled and played dice. This whilst singing their out of tune sea shanties.' There was as ever nowhere upon any of the tables a chess board in sight. No, oh no for that was a game of strategy which required an element of patience, aye and also a brain. True these men were tough and fierce, the Norse were without doubt bold and brave warriors. However though, it must be said that intellectuals, well alas they were not. Barak stood inside of the noisy tavern seeing all before him, the roe deer stag at this time was draped over the giant's right shoulder. Lying as it was over Barak's huge body with his great size and power the creature looked like little more than some sort of a fur wrap.

The uneven aged stone slab floor of the tavern was awash with spilt beer as well as discarded and spilt broth, aye and it was, it must be said, quite treacherous underfoot.

Looking about him the giant recognized many of Ragnor's big burly men he had fought alongside with many times before in the past. Sadly though there were also many old trusted faces that were missing from the noisy pack of sea wolves. It had been five long violent bloodsoaked years since the big Viking chieftain and Barak had last campaigned together and met man to man. And in five long warring years living as these men had chosen to live out their lives, well, there would doubtless always be a lot of casualties.

Of a sudden there was a roar of clamorous recognition as at last the giant's presence was noticed. At this the eagle hopped from its master's arm and up aloft onto one of the oak structural beams of the rickety old tavern. Barak had left his big dogs behind in the barn sleeping most soundly after their exhausting day. After all, the hounds had covered many miles at a good pace behind the big gelding that day. Aye, this as well as the running down of the roe stag which had to be said lead them a merry dance. Roe stags might not be as big or as awkward a beast to bring down as the larger red deer but they were certainly a lot faster and more agile through the woods.

Of a sudden a big red bearded man with ice blue eyes pushed his fellows rudely aside as he clasped Barak's massive shoulders with both of his hands.

'You've not changed Barak, why, you've not changed one bit,' the big Viking declared. 'I do swear that you are exactly now as I last remember you when we parted company in the tavern. I remember it well, why it was a tavern not unlike this one, all those years ago.' The big chieftain said this standing back a yard or so silently admiring his friend's fearsome appearance and awesome power.

Barak shrugged then he smiled before offering an explanation for his apparent good health.

'Clean living coupled with a clear conscience Ragnor, I do swear I have not had a drop of drink since that very day. Oh aye my raggy red bearded friend, I am now a reformed man. ' The giant said this without a trace or hint of a smile as he stared down at the big Viking. Aye and Ragnor was a very big man, a man that very few were ever lofty enough to look down upon him. Ragnor stood back another pace in both horror and sheer disbelief at the giant's words.

'No, no you do lie to me big Barak,' the Viking declared loudly and with a shake of his hairy head. 'Though I do love you most amongst all men, I do say to you now that you are a liar, you have not forsaken the drink..' With his blue eyes popping out of his head the big burly Viking bellowed these words out, his bull-like roar growing ever louder.

Barak's fearsome face suddenly cracked open as the ogre gave off a great grin that revealed each and all of his fang like teeth.

'Of course I lie, do you think I would ever give up the comfort of drink you great Viking fool?' On hearing this, the place at once became an uproar of rude coarse warriors banging upon tables with metal flagons. The Vikings liked this rough humour and the Norsemen all loved Barak. Well they loved him to a man save for one of their number. Aye, the shaven headed ever glowering Bull Neck, he was a man who had no love at all for the giant, no, Bull Neck harboured no friendship at all for Barak.

'What have you here then Barak lying over your shoulder? Is it mayhap a dead or dying pet? ' Ragnor asked nodding toward the Roe deer as he boomed out into full blown laughter.

'No. It is your supper you great fool,' Barak answered with a cheeky smirk. 'I will tonight, as I have always done in the past feed you fish-eaters with proper meat, red meat, man's meat.' It was now Barak's turn to burst into genuine mirthful laughter. Now the giant was amongst his sort of men, raw harsh brutal men.

True it was these Vikings were crude and they were rude and not, it must be said, to everyone's liking. But these men were big and were brave, and also they were the boldest of all warriors as well as the gamest of adventurers. All of these men lived for the day and whatever fortune it might or might not bring to them. Aye, yes indeed these wild rogues would do very nicely for Barak upon this very high risk, most dangerous of adventures.

Ragnor had one of his men take the roe stag away into the tavern's roomy kitchen for butchering. Once there it was handed over to the several hard pressed cooks who already busied themselves making broth, baking bread and preparing other culinary delights for their big hungry noisy guests. It was still only early in the evening but in two or three hours from now the venison would be well cooked and ready to feast upon. Well that as well as a few dozen rabbits, a couple of hares and half of a tough old ram that was already being prepared by the over worked kitchen staff.

Barak would of course much preferred to have prepared, then cooked the meat himself - nice and slowly, lovingly even. Slowly the venison he would have cooked of course with a plentiful dose of carrots onions and turnips, as well as plenty of herbs and spices to add to the flavour. But now and under these present circumstances this of course would have doubtless appeared a little rude and ignorant to lock himself away in a kitchen.

Together the two huge men Barak and Ragnor moved off to the end of a long rectangular oak table. There they sat themselves down relaxing and resting their bodies in front of a raging fire. Both the Vikings and Cedric's Britons banged their metal goblets on the oak tables in a noisy salute as Barak and Ragnor clasped their hands once again in genuine friendship and brotherhood.

All there in that hall knew only too well that this adventure was going to be a bloodthirsty affair - that of course went without saying. But still and even now the Viking chieftain had acquired some information that was very much to his liking. It also had to be said this recently obtained information would also bring much cheer to big Barak.

'You mean to tell me that you actually know this dog?' Barak asked of Ragnor in sheer disbelief at what he was hearing. The giant had barely finished his first goblet of mead when Ragnor gave him details of a black sailed dragon ship. It was a ship which had sailed from this very port only four days before the Norsemen themselves had pulled in to the dock.

'Aye, oh aye I know him well, the fool's name is Wraif,' Ragnor answered both bitterly and hatefully.

'He is then a Norseman, Ragnor, this fool of yours is he not?' Barak put in sharply leaning across the table towards his big red bearded friend.

Ragnor growled like a bear and spat bitterly into the fire then the Norseman sneered out his answer to the giant's question.

'Perhaps along the line the dog has some sort of bad Norse blood in him somewhere Barak. But know you this, Wraif is a hated man and he is despised among my people, I swear upon my father's sword I will have his head in my hands within the week,' Ragnor promised earnestly.

Barak smiled broadly and lit up his long pipe but only after stuffing the smoke bowl full of the strongest of black weed. Oh yes, this news was very much to his liking, yes indeed it was.

Apparently while the ogre had made his way along forest paths from the coast to Aulric's castle, well these fools were sailing past him down the Salmon River to the sea, aye and this with the young princess aboard their Dragon boat. Well these kidnappers certainly could not have cut it much finer than that the ogre thought silently to himself.

'Tell me all what you have heard, Ragnor? Inform me about this walking dead man who is very soon to feel your anger and the blade of your broad sword. '

Once again the men touched goblets, drained the contents then refilled them again hastily before exchanging more of their information. After all they had much to tell one another. When at last it was all told both men were quite taken aback and much impressed by what news they had learned from each other.

'So you are then a king, big Barak?' the Viking chieftain war lord and sea master asked somewhat incredulously. 'After all these years as friends and comrades I never knew that I had been mixing with royalty..' Thus joked the much bemused Viking, while at the same time he gave a slight bow of his hairy red head. Still broadly smiling Ragnor wiped beer froth from his big red beard before next pushing back his long tan hair and tying it with a leather thong behind his thick powerful neck. 'So tell me, how do I address you now Barak?' he then smiled. 'Tell me how do I call you Barak? Is it as Your Highness? Your Eminence? Your Grace or . . . ?'

Barak gave a grunt as he blew smoke hoops into the air.

'Just call me Barak you great oaf, after all my name has sufficed both of us for all these years so why change things now?' the giant answered with a smile and a shrug. 'Anyway Ragnor forget about all that nonsense, you must tell me more about your friend Wraif. '

Ragnor smiled wryly then he went on to tell Barak of what he had learned about the much hated and the much despised Wraif.

'Wraif's Dragon ship had been guarded by three black clad men, these men were ever vigilant, ever sober. Why the innkeeper says the black clad men touched not one drop of drink. Four other men also dressed in black had remained in the barn; they too had remained sober and ever watchful. These men within the barn guarded something, perhaps it was a prisoner. For four days and nights the sea raiders had drunk in the tavern, such a fool is Wraif.' Ragnor paused, took himself a long drink then continued with his tale, but he did this only after a long and loud belch. 'It was only when one of the black clad warriors had eventually grown angry and impatient did these rogues put to sail. Aye one of these sinister warriors had put a knife to Wraif's throat demanding they be gone from here. Wraif by all accounts and not surprisingly took a fright so did they sail away from this place. ' Ragnor went on with what he had learnt from the innkeeper as he continued to relay much valuable information to the attentive giant.

'According to the innkeeper who had overheard this and that from these over noisy and over confident rogues, they felt no need to hurry on their way to wherever it was they were bound for. No, that fool Wraif seemed to think he had all the time in the world to wile away. Either way there was apparently no love lost between the aloof and sinister looking black clad men and the pirates..' Ragnor further explained to Barak that his name had been mentioned and at this the pirate captain Wraif had merely laughed. Apparently the fool had said to any other fool that would listen to him it would be weeks before the giant would arrive on this sad little island, let alone be able to prepare a pursuit ship.

Barak drummed upon the table with his huge sausage thick fingers all the while his ever quick brain in his huge bucket sized head was working overtime.

'And you say we can catch and overhaul these fools within the week, Ragnor?' Barak enquired, a little taken aback by the suddenness of it all.

'Easily,' the big Viking replied straightway. 'We will sail on through the first night, then on the following evening we will moor up into one of the first main ports on our route. Once there we will no doubt find out even more information about Wraif and these black clad kidnappers. Who knows Barak, we might even be lucky enough to find these cocky fools all sitting around a table congratulating each other on their dubious deed..' True it was the Viking said this somewhat hopefully. 'Wraif is nothing but a coward, he is also a boaster and a braggart, and on top of that he is a damned liar. Aye and those my friend Barak, well those are some of his better qualities,' Ragnor said with a hateful sneer.

Barak had to smile slightly to himself his old friend Ragnor certainly had no love for this man Wraif, no none at all.

'The ditch dog will doubtless want to stop off at every harbour or small port on route he even remotely passes along the Germanic and Baltic coastline. Believe me the fool will do this just to brag and bluster to any who will listen..' Ragnor suddenly calmed himself, his agitation was making his hate filled heart pound all the faster. Aye and the last thing the big Viking wanted now, was to have a seizure of some sort. 'Anyway,' the Viking at length continued to talk after draining his goblet dry. 'This is the line the fool must take to sail to your distant homeland. I have had heard of your kingdom Barak, though I never thought I would have reason to be sailing towards it. I most certainly never ever thought I would be sailing there with its King,' he chuckled. 'I can take us as near as possible by boat, but you know as well as I do the rest of our journey will be both hard and arduous across rough and dangerous country. '

Barak was deep in thought now, though in all truth, he never missed a single word Ragnor had said to him.

'Before the week is out Wraif will trouble my shores and my settlements no more. Nor my dreams for that matter, aye no more will he raid plunder, burn and rape. ' Ragnor said spitting into the fire with a sneer of hate and contempt.

At long length and after much discussion between the two men the venison was cooked, prepared then brought before the noisy drunken Norsemen. Quickly the meat was then carved into slices by Ragnor and laid out upon wooden platters. As ever, the flesh was of course at once eagerly and quickly devoured. Perhaps it was a little dry and a little overdone but still the flesh was still tasty enough and was well appreciated by the ever hungry Vikings.

Barak watched silently as both the Norsemen and the Britons greedily devoured the meat. Now the giant had become suddenly silent as he smoked his weed and drank his drink. Barak the slayer was now deep in thought about the forthcoming mission. By the midnight hour it was all over, both the Britons and Norsemen alike had retired to their berths. Some had gone to the big barn to lay down their drink filled weary and throbbing heads. While some had returned to the dragon ship, the others just remained where they lay either on the tavern floor or across the long wide oak tables. Vikings it must be said lacked much in manners and social graces, aye here were men who cared little much where they slept. But best of all though, well these rough tough men to their undying credit also cared little where they died.

While all slept Barak alone was still awake. Now he with his dogs, which he had brought from the barn and of course the great black eagle together now feasted upon the very bones of the stag. Nothing was left, no nothing was wasted. The liver, heart and kidneys all provided the giant and his lethal pets with a tasty decent supper. Silently Barak looked about him at the sleeping Vikings who remained lying here and there all about the place. Big bearded men garbed in bits and pieces of link armour atop wolf and bearskin coverings. Their leggings were of thick wool and their boots stout and strong, no doubt filled with forest moss for warmth, as were Barak's. Also , each and every one of them were armed to the teeth with two axes apiece, great round spiked shields and hefty broadswords strapped either to their sides or across their broad backs. The Britons also were good men, and they also were garbed and armed well but in all truth there dress was more in line with the Roman militia than barbarian attire. Either way, both the Britons and Vikings were all well liked by Barak, well with the odd exception. And these men would as has been said already do very nicely for the giant on this most perilous venture.

Chapter Nine

At first light a Viking horn sounded out its awakening call and the Norsemen rose to their big booted feet like so many huge hairy automatons. The more disciplined Britons by now were already up and about their tasks quickly loading their horses aboard the big broad bellied Dragon boat.

'Ragnor says we can overhaul these pirates within the week.' Barak said to Cedric as he was leading his big gelding and his grey mules aboard the impressive Viking vessel.

Cedric raised his eyebrows in surprise.

'So quickly, surely not, is this at all possible Barak? He exclaimed. 'Or is this perhaps my Lord Barak, merely no more than drunken and boastful talk?' Barak gave an immediate shake of his head.

'No, no it is not boastful talk and aye it is indeed possible Cedric. It is possible simply because Ragnor says that it is so,' Barak answered with confidence. 'And know you this it is a dragon ship that we pursue just as I thought it would be.' Barak said this and he was obviously by his grin quite pleased at his educated guesswork. 'So Cedric, now knowing what sort of craft you will soon captain, can you, do you think sail this vessel safely back here to this place once it is taken?' Barak asked this question while hoping and knowing that he would get an honest truthful answer.

Cedric at once smiled then he gave a most positive and enthusiastic nod of confidence. As it happened the Briton was truthfully quite looking forward to being the captain of a Norse long boat, even if it was to be only quite briefly.

'Yes, yes I should be able to sail it Barak, depending of course how big it is. Although, I might need half a dozen of Ragnor's men if it is an overly big vessel,' Cedric answered honestly.

'You must understand my Lord Barak, I would wish no harm to befall my Princess. And this merely caused by my misplaced pride and my over confidence as a sea captain. '

A half dozen good men, these swords would be sore missed Barak mused to himself, but then again what must be must be.

'Spoken well,' Barak said with a smile and just a slight nod of his head in gratitude at Cedric's honesty. 'I have already spoken with Ragnor at some length about this particular matter. '

Barak as ever was always one step ahead of all and everyone else about him. 'Your men will become part of his crew over these next few days afloat. It will I think help them understand the handling of the ship, thus stand you all in good stead for your homeward voyage,' the giant went on. 'And by the by, the vessel you are soon to acquire is not as big as the Falcon.' Cedric glanced Barak a puzzled look and the giant explained more. 'The innkeeper, he was quite helpful quite talkative and he gave us good news. We will soon have Ellena back safe and sound,' the giant said confidently. Cedric smiled broadly upon hearing this information, the captain had known the young princess for some time now, he looked forward to seeing her safe and well again. Oh of course he also looked forward to bringing a smile back to his King's face when she was returned safely home to him. Also having to command a smaller vessel than the frightening formidable looking Viking ship of Ragnor, well that in itself was also good news.

A Viking horn sounded out once again long and loud as the last of the men brought aboard the dragon headed boat the supplies of food and drink for both man and beast. Now it was that the first part of the adventure had started. This being so the sleek well made craft was pushed off from the small port with long stout oars The voyage was begun. Within the hour the big red sails of Ragnor's dragon ship filled with breeze and the Falcon was heading swiftly off down river toward the great grey cold salt sea. Thankfully there was a good wind to assist them and the big red sail with a black falcon emblazoned upon it billowed outward growing taut with rushing air. The horses had been hobbled and tied securely and despite some small struggle on their part they could go nowhere.

After a few days of sailing no doubt the beasts would soon find their sea legs. In the meanwhile Barak's great black eagle soared high above them till at length it disappeared into the clouds completely from sight. A little while later by early afternoon the Falcon had passed the stone harbour of Arbeia; this was a busy place, a busy port that stood on the headland where the Salmon River joined the cold grey North Sea. Now the big red sails were wind filled and fit to bursting as the Falcon rode the foaming waves and headed out toward the open sea. Aye indeed the trim Viking vessel was now moving as fast as a galloping horse as it cut easily through the surf.

'Ah, the freedom of the sea Barak, don't you just love it Barak?' the big Viking roared out with his strong arms outstretched. 'Tell me my friend what delight will you cook for us tonight Barak?' Ragnor asked with a cheeky and sarcastic smile. Barak's interest in affairs of cooking and the kitchen had long been a subject that always amused the big uncouth Norseman no end.

Barak of course knew this only too well.

'You think cooking is only woman's work don't you Ragnor?' the giant asked a little accusingly.

Ragnor merely gave back a grin which was then followed by a carefree shrug of his broad shoulders.

'Perhaps I do, but then again perhaps I don't,' the Viking answered with a thin smile. 'But I do know this Barak, I know you do cook up better food than anyone I have ever met before. Better food than I have ever tasted, that be whether it was cooked by a man or by a woman toiling over the stove. I see also you have even brought your own pots and pans, aye and even your many spices and herbs along with you on our adventure. ' Ragnor added this with just a slight chuckle.

Barak looked down upon the big Viking giving him a fake stare of annoyance.

'Oaf,' the giant muttered under his breath before announcing the menu. 'Salmon, we will have salmon for our supper this first night. Fresh red salmon, that I myself caught on a gaff only hours ago in the River while you all slept and noisily snored your drink off. I Barak, I myself waded out into the ice cold becks in freezing water to secure your meal. Though I must admit, I did invest in some large fresh fish from the innkeeper early this morning. This I did when I settled up last night's, oh and of course, all of yesterday's bill. You know Ragnor, the tavern's bill for all the food and the drink that you and your men had consumed. I must say, though I am not of course complaining, this even though it was a considerable penny. The big Viking scowled then twisted his hairy face whilst he spat over the side of the ship upon hearing this apparent complaint.

'Bah, so you would begrudge paying for a few ales and a bite to eat for these brave rogues of mine? Ragnor asked jokingly but noisily. Barak smiled, the ogre turned his back upon the wind and the few drops of rain that were blowing side wards into his scarred tattooed face. Next after some mutterings in his own language the giant lit up his long clay pipe with a brand from a glowing brazier. This was a big three legged iron brazier that sat upon the flattened hammered out bronze shield of a fallen crewman, well pirate. Thus with the shield so preserved the memory of the long lost hero would never be forgotten, indeed he would sail on with the Falcon forever. But perhaps what was even more important the shield would also prevent embers from the fire setting the dragon ship ablaze.

'So Barak, on top of that hurtful slur your complaining of buying us, that is we your friends and comrades a few drinks. Now you say you want us all to sit down tonight to feast upon boiled fish at a cold day's end? Ragnor's voice was rising a little now but not in anger, no he spoke more in the line of entertainment. His rough rogues always liked to listen to any verbal duel that went on with their popular leader and the quick witted giant. 'I must say Barak, that you do disappoint me, I had thought far better fare was due these bold heroes. Yes I must say that you do disappoint me more than just a little Barak.' Ragnor said this enjoying his goading of his gigantic friend.

'Why some of these younger men here that you have never met came along, risking their very lives mind you, just to get a taste of your cooking. Cooking that I myself Red Ragnor have spoken so much about. Why, even the never smiling Bull Neck there whose jaw you broke five years ago over some stupid dispute. Aye even he loves your cooking that is true, though the somewhat unhappy soul might not admit to that openly. ' Ragnor was grinning like a fool now and in all truth he was quite enjoying his own wit. The rough Viking rogues also found this light hearted banter very amusing, as of course did the giant who sucked upon his pipe, for now he said nothing. Only Bull Neck as ever was a glowering gloomy figure. Aye the ill-humoured fellow was not amused, nor was he impressed that Ragnor should have mentioned his name in any sort of praise for Barak, this even in jest.

Barak exhaled his smoke then he pointed the mouth piece end of his pipe at Ragnor in mock anger.

'Know this you foolish man, the fish will be very slowly grilled, it will not be boiled. The fish will then be stuffed with fresh goat cheese. This done, next the fish will be dressed with herbs and spices from my very own garden. After this I will wrap the fish tightly in the best of cured bacon. This done I will replace the salmon, which by the by is the prince of all fish, once again back upon the brazier to finish off the cooking.' Barak, this said took another deep draw upon his pipe before speaking again. 'Aye, I tell you this now, Ragnor the fish will taste wonderful. Certainly much better than those leather like smoked cod you sea going fools are used to feasting upon on your long voyages away from your homes. Aye smoked cod that make your breathe smell so bad doubtless your wives or goats or whatever else you sleep with can smell your coming before they even see you.' Barak laughed a low rumbling laugh at his own humour. However, the big Vikings were less discreet bursting into a loud rough laughter.

'Anyway,' Barak then declared confidently, 'is that feast good enough? Is it good enough for you and your unwashed scurvy sea dogs?' Barak was now smiling smugly to himself, more so as he noticed that many amongst the listening Vikings were already licking their hairy lips in eager anticipation of their much deserved supper. As already said Ragnor the Red was a man who loved his food almost as much as he did his gallons of drink.

'Anyway Ragnor' Barak then continued after an unhealthy cough and a spit over the side of the speeding Falcon. 'As far as your big oaf of a pet Bull Neck over there is concerned. Well, the fool called me a liar. Should there ever be a next time,' the giant paused for another cough. 'I swear that I will break his back and not just his jaw.' Now though the great giant was not a smiling thing, no he was not smiling at all. At once the big Viking chieftain sensed that sudden anger in Barak's words, he responded in a most diplomatic fashion, well diplomatic for a barbarian that is.

'There will be no next time Barak.' Ragnor promised most sincere like as he took a pace forward toward the black eyed giant. 'If there is, why then I swear by Odin's beard that I will kill him myself. Though, I must confess he will be hard to replace, Bull Neck is a good boatsman, aye he is also a good and fearless fighter,' the Viking added just for good measure. All of this had been said to the giant in almost a whisper. Ragnor was still the leader of his men, their long time

115

captain and he was not a fool in any way. What he had said to the giant was sincere and Ragnor meant every word of it. Still though, he very sensibly wanted to keep harmony amongst his rogues, picking obvious sides so early on a dangerous venture as this was would doubtless prove foolhardy.

Barak meanwhile made no reply whatsoever as to the better qualities of Bull Neck; the giant merely sucked silently upon his long clay pipe.

Aye then he sucked painfully upon his painful back tooth.

Meanwhile the dragon ship sailed on and on, it sailed on into the eventual cold darkness of the starry northern night. Three big iron braziers glowed brightly, one at the stern, one at the bow and one mid ship by the towering mast. All three of these braziers rested upon the flattened shields of dead men. These blazing braziers though offered all the still living men aboard the Falcon some light and some much welcome heat on that chill night. But above all and everything else here was a place for Barak to do his cooking. All the while the stout dragon boat sailed further out into the open sea skirting the rugged coastlines at a safe distance. This way the experienced sea goers would keep themselves safe from the rocks and the hidden sand banks that, though concealed, were many. True it was they had some time to make up on the pirates' head start. Nevertheless big Barak had every faith in Ragnor's seamanship as well as the good ship Falcon's speed. Ragnor likewise, well the big Viking he had every faith in the giant's cooking skills. And although the giant Barak did seem an unlikely chef he as ever turned out a supper that night which delighted all aboard, even Bull Neck.

The following dawn found the Norsemen well on their way, aye in fact their progress was even better than Ragnor had anticipated it would be.

'We could sail on another night Barak if you so wished it?' Ragnor asked on the late afternoon of their second day out at sea.

Barak scratched at his trim snow white goat beard while he scraped the rest of his face clean of whiskers with a small but very sharp curved knife. The giant was ever well groomed, after all he was man who was most particular about his fierce appearance. Every day the ogre, no matter where he was, would set about his big head and his tattooed face with his needle sharp curved Persian shaving knife. Aye the ogre would be washed, soaped and shaved, his white beard and his black eyebrows trimmed with his scissors no matter what.

'No Ragnor, we need land I do think,' Barak answered firmly. 'As these horses are as yet unused to the sway of the boat, aye, they will need walking and fresh grass to feed upon. This lest they grow uneasy Ragnor, believe me I do not want them to become sickly things.' After admiring himself in his shaving mirror and some thoughtful deliberation the giant asked a question of his friend. 'Is there perhaps a place that you know of where we can dock the Falcon for tonight Ragnor, you know, so we can of course refresh ourselves?'

Without any hesitation what so ever the Viking gave a most positive nod.

'Aye, aye Barak we can pull in on the first port on the Germanic coastline. In truth it is not much in size, but it has two good inns and is a friendly enough and a welcoming place as a rule. '

Barak at once gave a nod of agreement.

'Friendly or otherwise my hairy friend, I do think that we should dock there for tonight Ragnor. ' Barak said rinsing his face and head once again free of any suds with fresh water.

Ragnor offered Barak a towel to dry himself off with then he spoke and said on.

'Wraif doubtless would have pulled in at this place Barak, we could I think gain some news here of his whereabouts. Who knows? Mayhap the fool might even still be there drinking and bragging as he is prone to,' Ragnor said once again speaking ever hopeful. 'You pray to your gods Barak and I will then pray to mine. Once again, who knows my friend perhaps together these gods might make it just so for us.'

Barak at once then gave his long time friend a slightly cold somewhat dismissive stare.

'I have no gods to pray to Ragnor, you of all people should know that to be fact.' Barak said this with a trace of both anger and bitterness in his voice. 'I have alas now faith only in my strength of arm and of course my good dragon sword. Thus far in my blood soaked life these have always been enough to see me through the times of darkness,.' After saying this the giant then went silent and sullen for a moment or two, Ragnor knowing Barak's strange moods said not a word. Then though of a sudden the ogre turned and glanced down at his most trusted friend. 'But of course my good faithful barbarian brother, now I do in all honesty need your sword and your strength also,' the giant added with a great degree of diplomacy.

Still when the giant's darker musings were put to one side those black eyes of his did light up a little merrily. Aye that was just with the thinking that Wraif might be docked up where they were about to pull the Falcon in. Oh if only he could end this chase to recover the Princess that very starry night. What good luck that would be if the hunters might find those which they stalked in their first port of call. Barak after thinking for a moment or two turned once again to face the Viking.

'Well, you're the captain Ragnor, so you have the final word. What do you say, do we dock or what? '

Barak was now being most diplomatic in the extreme. In matters of the sea and of the sailing of the Falcon the giant both wanted and he much preferred Ragnor to decide the final course of action to be taken.

'While I am the mere captain here on board this longboat, you my friend are the King.' This, the Viking said as he smiled crookedly back at his large friend, at the same time Ragnor gave a slight bow and a snigger as he did so.

Barak sucked upon his bad tooth then spat the slime over the side of the boat. Next the ogre gave a grunt of grudging satisfaction.

'Pull in then Ragnor for there are things that I must tell you, things that I have so far left out about this long perilous quest. '

At once the big Viking gave off a wolf-like grin and a carefree shrug.

'Then tell me now Barak why do you hesitate, why do you put it off? After all we are the greatest of friends, are we not? Barak was thoughtful for but a heartbeat before speaking.

'Aye, aye this is all very true, we are that Ragnor,' Barak said also in a most care free manner. 'But nevertheless friends or not, you yourself must know some things are best spoken about over a few drinks in a quiet friendly little tavern. Agreed?' Barak said placing a hand upon his friend's shoulder.

Ragnor gave a knowing grin. The Norseman then scratched at his rough huge ragged red beard.

'Something tells me Barak this new information of yours concerning this quest could perhaps be very painful to the ears,' the big Norseman suggested.

Barak paused for but a moment, he lit up his long clay pipe from a brazier then he puffed away quite frantically till the weed took hold.

'Aye Ragnor, perhaps it will be a little painful at that,' the ogre said after exhaling a mouthful of smoke. 'But still with a good quantity of German beer inside you, well it might not hurt nearly so much,' Barak added with a sly smile. Anyway for now the men said no more about the matter as the Falcon sailed on into the dimness and the gloom of the approaching night.

As the light of day eventually faded the Falcon with its red sails lowered drifted silently, aye even ghost like into the small harbour. Indeed just as Ragnor had said it was a most cosy little place, a friendly and sleepy little hamlet. With the Falcon secured to the harbour wall the horses were at once unhobbled and unloaded. Then with this done the beasts were led from the Dragon boat to graze contentedly inside a long fenced off field. This was a field that belonged to a very fat, very red faced and very happy innkeeper. Indeed the innkeeper appeared to be the type of a man who, if you told him you were about to rob him, drink all of his beer and eat all his food he would still be a smiling thing.

Just as expected the innkeeper was a most worthy host Fat pork sausages, thick well cured ham, goose eggs and smoked fish with fresh brown wheat bread were all served up in healthy quantities on the long pine tables of the warm cosy inn. These tables were laid out in four neat rows before raging well stacked fires. At once frothy tan coloured beer was hastily brought by a big fat woman who was very nimble on her feet considering her bulk. By the looks of her she was possibly just as strong as Barak judging by the size of her shoulders and her arms. She was as it happened the inn keeper's none too pretty wife, nevertheless a pleasant thing.

All the men of the Falcon sat there in the tavern in good spirits, aye the rogues sat and drank while they ate and they talked both of the past and of the future soon to come to them.

'How many men are we Ragnor?' Barak asked the Viking captain after returning from a conversation with the fat red faced innkeeper.

'I have thirty-eight fighting men under my command, also myself, and my two deck boys, these are my nephews Sven and Stefan. They are young but nevertheless can handle a broadsword and a longbow as good as anyone. I should know as I taught them both myself,' Ragnor added proudly.

'Forty-one men in total for you then Ragnor, you included, plus my twelve Britons and myself, that makes fifty-four souls in all.'

Ragnor stretched out his long legs with their thick woollen leggings towards a blazing fire. Now the Viking yawned and shrugged not really seeing the significance of Barak's questioning.

'Wraif's ship is smaller than yours, his crew also is smaller, it consists of thirty or so pirates but no more than that. Also of course he has the seven Black Guards along with him. That makes thirty-eight or thirty-nine men to handle, give or take.'

Barak paused a moment then said on.

'Then again we can always add another two or three of these scum as guarding their longboat and their cargo; men the innkeeper never noticed.'

Ragnor grunted then he pulled at his long beard which he had just plaited that night as they had sat there eating, drinking, plotting and talking.

'How do you know all of this Barak? Tell me how did you come by this sudden and most welcome information? ' Barak leant across the pine table while filling the bowl of his long pipe with weed.

'My new friend over there,' Barak said as he nodded toward the back of the tavern bar's counter 'The fat and smiling red faced innkeeper, Horst, the man is called. '

Ragnor had been drinking quickly to keep up with Barak, however, this was not always a wise practice.

'Horst! So you know the tavern keeper then?' Ragnor asked a little unthinkingly as he waved a thick very tasty pork sausage in Barak's face.

'Well I do now. Also my podgy friend tells me that Wraif and his scoundrels were here only two days ago. Two days ago, my wayward red haired reiver.'

Ragnor upon hearing this good news almost choked on the fat pork sausage he was so much enjoying.

'So we are upon them, just as I said to you earlier Barak, we have gained two days,' Ragnor boomed out gleefully. 'Soon then, soon these fools are to be ours,' the big Viking said leaning across the table toward the giant.

Ragnor had a mane of tawny hair that seemed to change in colour from red to blonde then back to red again with each and every days passing. The Norseman had just unplaited his great red beard but now because of his joyous agitation the big Viking was yet again replaiting it. This was something that Barak had always found a bit of an annoying habit. So fuzzed up was the big beard now that it stuck out a full foot from the Vikings square jawed face, now Ragnor both looked and roared like a lion.

'Wraif is mine to kill mind you Barak.' Ragnor said this while banging his great fists upon the stout pine table so loud that the rest of his men went silent and stared in wonderment at their leader. The big Viking had thick heavy gold rings upon each and every one of his big sausage sized fingers. Doubtless it was, these gaudy items of jewellery had all been taken from dead men. Well, dead men who were all quite alive and healthy until the moment they had encountered Ragnor that was.

'I ask nothing out of this venture Barak, only that I have Wraif to butcher for my own pleasure and vengeful satisfaction. Remember this Barak, I came along with you because you asked me,' the big Viking went on. 'You are my friend, as is the kindly Aulric a friend to us both. Though perhaps he is a friend in a different way as to what you are to me,' Ragnor said as he swallowed down the last of his sausages then washed it down with more good German beer. 'Because after all Barak we of course at day's end are both killers, that quite simply for the better or for worse is our calling.'

Barak was somewhat taken aback by this very stark but very truthful statement. So now with the giant, seeking comfort from this cold hard fact of life, at once puffed upon his pipe with gusto. Then, after he was immersed in heady smoke from his long pipe the ogre then swallowed down yet more drink. Ragnor coughed and spluttered as he accidentally inhaled some of the giant's strong weed. But after a little while in recovering the big Viking spoke up once again.

'And I know well Barak if I ever needed you or Aulric I would only have to do the asking the once. No gold, not Roman coins or any other treasure do I want or do I crave from this task, I want only Wraif. Do you understand me Barak? Ragnor went on. 'That dog Wraif made Stefan and Sven orphans. Also the coward killed and raped their mother who was my sister, this after he butchered and

120

murdered their father,' Ragnor said bitterly. 'You do understand my need for this bloodletting don't you Barak? At once the giant gave a grim and solemn nod of his big head, no wonder Ragnor hated Wraif as he did. Still though, big Barak said nothing in reply as Ragnor went on with himself. 'You can do what you want to with the rest of his crew and your black garbed assassins Barak as their fate does not concern me. But know you this my friend, the fool Wraif he is mine, aye he is mine alone to butcher.'

Barak leaned back casually in his chair, the ogre smiled as he sucked more leisurely upon his long clay pipe enjoying the strong weed. Then at long last, the ogre well relaxed now because of his vigorous smoking, spoke.

'Yes my friend, this is of course agreed Ragnor. For you as with me, this venture is about blood and revenge not glory or even riches. Any money or treasure that might be taken is for our men to divide between them, your men and my men.' Ragnor gave a nod of agreement then both men shook hands firmly while the eavesdropping Vikings banged loudly upon the pine tables. Apparently they all seemed pleased at their forthcoming wealth. Both men, Barak and also Ragnor were now happy and in good cheer.

'Two days, two days, three at the very most and I will have you Aulric's daughter back,' Ragnor promised. 'And I, well I will have that ditch dog Wraif to slaughter,' Ragnor said passionately.

'Good I do believe you Ragnor,' Barak said with a grin. 'Now my friend, shout us all one more round of drinks in for everyone, which as usual I of course will pay for,' the giant chuckled. 'Then we can have an early night, for there is much sailing ahead of us, also there is much killing to be done,' Barak said this with a happy contented sort of smile.

'Good idea Barak, but you have I do believe something to tell me, remember?' Ragnor pressed after he had shouted loudly out for more drinks to be brought to the noisy tables.

'Yes, yes, but it will keep for now, first things must always be first,' Barak replied somewhat evasively.

That night was the soberest night Barak and Ragnor had ever put in together inside a tavern that was full of good food and drink. But still once the Princess was taken from her captors, when she was safe and secure then there would be plenty of time for late night drinking and celebrations.

On that following morning, just before dawn the Falcon was loosed from its moorings and slipped silently out of the small German port out into the cold grey mist shrouded sea. One day, perhaps on their return sail homeward, if he was of course not killed in the meanwhile, Barak decided he would pull in back there to have a proper drink in that inn he noticed on leaving which was called the Dogfish. Aye he would do this, he would also have a lazy wander around the small but interesting port in the hope of finding other welcoming havens.

The wind that chilly morning was once again sharp and brisk, but it was in their favour and the wind quickly blew the morning mists away. Ragnor the meanwhile, well the wily Viking knew only too well Wraif would still be sleeping off his last night's drink wherever it was the fool had spent the night. Alone the Viking stood at the bow of the long boat and smiled a cold hateful smile to himself, they were still making good ground upon the soon to die Wraif; this fact made Ragnor a happy man.

Ragnor spat downwind as the Viking muttered away to himself while he urged the Falcon on as it cut its way over the cold grey sea. Now the speedy Falcon was closing fast on its prey and the big Viking knew this only too well. But nevertheless Ragnor was impatient and he was hate filled. The big Viking wanted both revenge and blood and he wanted this the sooner the better. But still though Ragnor thought to himself as he stared ahead out across the foaming waves, Wraif had best make the most of what living the fool had left to live. For the man only had three more nights left to do his lying and his bragging and that was at the most, the very most. The Norseman put in another night on the dragon boat, making the best of a light sky and an ever growing moon. It was turning much colder now, the sky was light and starry, doubtless there would be a slight frost before the morning. Ragnor stood warming himself by a glowing brazier, it was after midnight by now and most of the men were fast asleep. This or they were at least trying to get some sleep as they huddled for warmth under their winter wolf pelts and heavy bearskins.

Bull Neck was sat at the stern of the Falcon at the rudder, the fellow was mumbling out curses and oaths as was the norm for him. Bull Neck was a large unpleasant man, a man of bad disposition and a man who liked very few people. Aye and as well as this also the big oaf had inside him that overwhelming and acute hatred of Barak. Over the past few years they had known each other he and Barak had two or three fallings out, not with blades however. No, not even Bull Neck was so stupid, even that fool knew well of Barak's prowess with a sword or a knife or anything else sharp for that matter. Why even a soup spoon was deadly in Barak's big broken hand. And besides that the clumsy lumbering Bull Neck lacked any sort of finesse with a blade. The oaf's chosen weapon was a huge carved oak cudgel he had bought from a drunken Irishman some years earlier while they were trading in Jutland. Anyway in their last fall out Barak had broken the Bull's jaw with a punch that had lifted the heavy burly Viking clear off his feet and sent him flying over Aulric's banquet table. There he had landed upon the stone slab floor a twitching gibbering wreck of a man. Bull Neck had of course never forgotten that night, nor had he forgiven Barak for that painful humiliation. That particular evening as it so happened was also the last time Barak, Aulric and Ragnor had all been drunk together under the same roof. On another time, a time before that incident, Barak had slung Bull Neck headlong into the chill harbour waters at the Roman port of Arbeia. This was a very busy prosperous port which stood where the Salmon River joined the North Sea. And

122

this was for no other reason than the giant was caught in a bad mood, oh and of course because the giant quite simply just did not like the man one little bit, nor ever would he.

Bull Neck was as his name suggested a man of immense raw power with huge arms and broad shoulders. The Bull was perhaps a little over six feet tall, his huge neck was so big that it appeared wider than his dome shaped shaven head. His nose was a big fat bulbous thing that gave him a most piggy sort of look also it was a nose that had been broken more than once over the violent years. As well as this Bull Neck's small and also piggy squinty eyes were of a different colour to each other. One of them the right one was of a deep green the other one was a very light brown. As well as these afflictions, when the brutish fool spoke which was very little, well he spoke with a most comical sort of lisp like stammer. Not that many people ever mentioned this in jest though to the great oaf, if they did so then doubtless they lost teeth. This affliction of Bull Neck's was more obvious whenever he was in the presence of Barak. Still though despite all this the man was no coward, aye he was in all truth a good fighting man to have at your back. And if nothing else he would, Barak supposed to himself, come in handy over the next few hard months to come. Bull Neck by the way was also a man who was fiercely loyal to Ragnor. Truth said the oaf now only spent so little time with his captain these last few days because of the constant presence of the giant in Ragnor's company.

But still no matter while Bull Neck brooded at the rudder of the Falcon Barak stirred himself from under his great bearskins from where he had been up till then sleeping soundly. Barak had awakened for no other reason than bad dreams, nightmares of his violent passed, these often troubled him. As usual the Arab saddle had been his pillow that night and the giant had slept flanked either side by his great dogs who both warmed and guarded their master at all times. Also the big black eagle she sat nearby atop a makeshift perch, ever watchful ever alert to any form of danger. It was now somewhere between midnight and the breaking of dawn.

'We are close to him now, I sense it I know it.' Ragnor said this as Barak rose and moved over to his side where Ragnor stood by the seated Bull Neck. The giant first grunted then he spat over the stern into the blackness. Once this was done the ogre next lit up his long pipe from one of the braziers. Bull Neck cared little for the giant's intrusion but he wisely said nothing and moved away from his captain who in turn now took the rudder. Knowing the dislike Barak and Bull Neck harboured each other Ragnor instructed Bull Neck to get some sleep. With a simple grunt Bull Neck made off and lay himself down after covering himself in thick furs.

'How close, Ragnor?' asked Barak with a contented sigh as he inhaled his strong weed in deeply.

'Tonight, this dragon boat of mine has cut the waves like a hot knife through butter, it has flown, flown like the Falcon it is named after. Tonight when we dock, I will have him and you Barak, well, you will have your Princess.'

Barak gave out a satisfied grunt as he yawned stretched then ground his teeth together hoping in vain to dislodge that ever painful back molar.

'Good, very good, I said that I would have Aulric's daughter back with him by the full moon. So it can still be done, you think we will find him tonight Ragnor?' Barak asked almost gleefully. Ragnor gave a positive nod,

'Aye' the big Viking said simply in reply. The giant was most impressed, he had of course calculated it would be another two days till they eventually caught up with the pirate.

'Tonight, are you sure of that Ragnor?' the giant repeated, this news seeming too good to be true.

Without any hesitation the big Viking gave yet another most positive nod.

'Aye, I do that Barak, I swear this ship of mine has never cut through water like it does now. The gods are with us, tonight we will have him aye and we will have him in the best harbour on the whole of the German coast. We will have him in the harbour town of the Hundsruck. And know you this Barak my friend, this place has the most taverns the most trade stalls and the best market square along the whole of the coast. It also has comely women a plenty, it is full of buyers and sellers of everything that you could possibly want. Why there in the Hundsruck you can buy black skinned slaves from afar, these as well as fast horses, cattle, sheep and goats. This as well as fast dogs for hunting the stag and hare, also good fighting dogs to gamble on. All this as well as the best of fighting birds that come here from Asia and the far off Orient. Why there are even hawks and falcons brought from Arabia and beyond. Aye indeed my friend, there is all and everything in the Hundsruck that you might have a craving for.

Barak clicked his huge neck into place then the ogre stretched and yawned once again, next he gave out a grunt of satisfaction. 'Sounds like a good place to me Ragnor that I must admit my friend,' Barak said with a broad smile. The giant was a man who liked nothing more than a good market town to do a bit of trading and bartering. However, the slave market, there was a place that he would not be visiting. Barak, well the ogre had an intense dislike and hatred of slavers. In fact it was such a deep rooted hatred Barak would not even trust himself to pass close by to the cowardly greedy flesh peddlers, this lest he loose his black temper and slay them.

'Wraif will have stopped here, or he will be stopping here and that is for sure, aye and also for sure here is where he will surely die,' Ragnor said cheerily. 'We have made good time Barak and somewhere not too far ahead of us we will find him.' On hearing these words of glee and confidence Barak smiled then put a hand upon his friend's broad shoulder.

124

'That is a very curious name, for a place my friend, the Hundsruck I mean,' Barak said blowing out a mouthful of strong smelling smoke from his fired up pipe.

'Why so? What does it mean Barak? ' Ragnor asked.

'It means the back of a dog, or the dogs back if you like the sound of that better. Like I say it is a strange name, but then again I suppose that Germans are a bit odd to say the least. Still though, they do I suppose make good beer, well at least it is a lot better than that childish brew the Britons come up with anyway,' Barak said as he ground his teeth together.

'I like their sausages, you know the black ones that are made from pig's blood.' Ragnor put in with a lick of his hairy lips. 'In fact Barak, if I was not a Viking then I do suppose I would wish to be a German', he said in a low matter of fact mutter.

Barak merely smiled at these words, in a way that was more or less like saying if I were not a mule, I would choose to be an ass. This as Barak had always thought there was little difference between the Germanic tribes or the Norse. Next the giant chuckled to himself, he dallied there a while with Ragnor until he finished off his pipe full of weed. Then with this done he once again went back to his rest intending to catch a little more sleep before daybreak. Ragnor however he stayed by his rudder his brazier and his post. As now the big burly captain of the Falcon was far too full of hate and blood lust to find any sleep on that dark chill night.

It was late that same afternoon, just as the first hint of darkness began to fall when a sail was sighted far ahead upon the distant horizon - it was a black sail. Aye and of course it was a black sail the dog Wraif sailed under, a black sail set upon a sleek black dragon ship.

Barak moved to one of his hessian sacks, then returned moments later with an object Ragnor had not before seen.

'Here, take this,' Barak said passing Ragnor the long and quite elegant looking tubular item that was made of copper, leather and glass.

Ragnor took the object and examined it most carefully.

'Very nice my large friend, but what is it Barak?' Ragnor asked this question with a most puzzled look about his hairy unkempt face.

'It is Persian,' Barak replied simply and not going into great detail.

Ragnor still looking very puzzled held the object in his big rough hands, in all honesty he neither knew if it were some sort of weapon or one of Barak's cooking utensils.

So Barak, well, the giant noticing with some amusement Ragnor's obvious bewilderment then enlightened him.

'Bah, look you here Ragnor, I do forget that you are a most simple and uneducated man,' Barak said mockingly.

Next the giant held what was of course a spyglass to Ragnor's eye as he focused on the far off horizon the Viking instantly recoiled with the viewing of it. This the Norseman did in both shock and sheer amazement at what he had just witnessed.

'Wraif,' he exclaimed out loudly. 'Why, I can see that scurvy no good ditch dog as plain as day. I swear it is he, aye, it is that devil of a man, it is Wraif himself,.' Almost out of control the big brash Viking roared this out both loudly and gleefully as he replaced the spyglass for another look.

'Good,' Barak said, clapping Ragnor on his broad shoulder in congratulation. 'That is good, yes that is very good, then we do indeed have him..' For a long moment Ragnor seemed totally dumbstruck, then after but a little while he spoke up.

'What magic is this? For he appears to be no more than a stone's throw away from us Barak.' Ragnor said this as he next examined both ends of the leather bound spyglass.

'No magic Ragnor,' the giant rumbled. 'Well, at least it is not bad magic anyway. '

Ragnor muttered words out that Barak did not quite catch, still though the Viking seemed happy enough with Barak's brief explanation as to the qualities of the spyglass. Almost instantly the Viking's mind turned to more immediate things.

'Lower the sail,' Ragnor commanded. 'The fool Wraif must not see us, well not until tonight anyway,' Ragnor hissed, his cold ice blue eyes narrowing with hatred. 'We will drift for a while and let him get further ahead of us Barak. After all we know where the rogue is bound for and we are not far from the Hundsruck now my friend. But we must let him dock, we must let him and his scurvy crew be off and away from his ship before we slip into port,.' Ragnor said this somewhat thoughtfully as he brooded on dark revenge. 'Aye big Barak we will let him, and his band of fools, dock for just one last time.'

The giant said nothing in reply he merely gave a simple nod of honest agreement as to Ragnor's planning of things.

Barak then left Ragnor to his dark vengeful musings and he went off to speak with the good captain's nephews Stefan and Sven. These lads were twins and were perhaps of some sixteen or seventeen years of age. Also the youths were both tall handsome and well grown boys, true Norse breed. Their heads were topped with a mop of hair that was as white as snow and both boys had the brightest of blue eyes. Very similar to their uncle's when they weren't blood shot with the drink. Since Barak's arrival the boys had been inseparable from the huge dogs, the dogs as it so happened seemed to like all the attention and the non-stop affection bestowed upon them. Barak, well the great slayer had a task for the lads to perform, aye and it was an important task at that. First Barak would talk with the young brothers about this mission to make sure they were both keen to undertake it. Then this once done he would next talk to their uncle Ragnor for permission for them to do so. For this task the ogre had planned for them it must of course be carried out carefully and according to plan.

Chapter Ten

As darkness fell under a clear sky and a bright three quarter moon Ragnor's dragon ship slipped slowly and silently into a packed bustling harbour. The Falcon was then steered expertly out of sight and hidden in between two huge Roman slave galleys. These vessels were floating giants of things in truth they appeared to be more like castles than ships, in Ragnor's opinion such vessel were good only to hide the Viking longboat. Ragnor had always hated these cumbersome vessels with a passion, a waste of good trees he would often say with a grumble. Why the timber used in the building of one of these useless slow cumbersome floating fortresses could have been better used to make ten good fast dragon ships.

As the Falcon had silently slid into the harbour the Norsemen had noticed the black painted and it must be said, the very useful looking longboat of the pirate Wraif. This vessel was moored some six ships down from where the Falcon had berthed between the two large Roman galleys. Two or three of Wraif s pirates were singing loudly about their recent exploits as they sat drunkenly by one of the three blazing braziers on board the tidy ship. These braziers were placed in similar fashion to those upon the Falcon.

At each end of the dragon ship, by a brazier at the stern and the bow stood a black clad warrior warming themselves from the night's chill. Both of these men neither drank or sang or seemed to want to associate with the pirates in any way whatsoever. Also these hook nosed hawk eyed men had marked the Falcon slipping into the port, silently. However, the warriors had thought nothing of it as according to their information the ogre Barak would still yet be in the land of the Gauls somewhere. No doubt wherever he was the ogre would be drinking and smoking his black weed to excess. And so again according to the information given them by the now deceased scribe Barak well he would be there for some time yet to come.

With the Falcon made secure Ragnor was keen to be about his business The Norseman wanted Wraif dead and he wanted that long waited for deed done now. Barak though as always and ever was more cautious in this next episode of blood letting.

'It is still early yet Ragnor, best let Wraif and his foolish rogues drink themselves into more of a stupor, believe me it will make the killing of them all the easier. ' The ever practical Barak said this as he donned a black hooded wolf skin cloak that reached all the way down to the top of his knee high stout boots.

Ragnor grunted then growled and fidgeted with the hilt of his boar's head hilted sword a little impatiently.

'We have come this far and waited this long, so best I think that we do the job properly,' Barak advised.

In truth the impatient Norseman looked a little put out at these words as he once again fidgeted with the hilt of his boars head broad sword. Still though impatient or not Ragnor was no fool and he saw that Barak's words made much sense.

'Aye, aye I suppose this is true enough Barak,' Ragnor at length somewhat grudgingly agreed. 'But still, I would have liked to have this fool Wraif know exactly what I am doing to him while I am doing it, if you know what I mean Barak,' Ragnor protested.

The giant grinned and put a consoling hand upon his friend's broad shoulder, then he gave a shake of his head.

'My brother Ragnor, dead is always dead, so why then make an easy job a harder one?'

Still though, the Norseman seemed unsettled and agitated as he scratched at his big red beard then he gave a sigh before spitting overboard.

'So Ragnor my friend we do it my way, do you agree?' Barak pressed, confident of the reply. Ragnor was thoughtful for just one moment longer then he nodded in agreement.

'Aye' was his simple and only word on the matter. Through long experience the big Viking knew only too well that what Barak had said as always and as ever made good common sense. With this agreed and without another word spoken Barak pulled the wolf skin hood over his head then he shook Ragnor's hand. With this done and a parting nod, next the giant whistled his eagle down from the mast and silently the slayer drifted off into the shadows of the night.

Barak on that evening had left behind him his huge dogs, they were the meanwhile being petted and pampered by the young brothers.

'Where is the Lord Barak off to then?' asked a huge misshapen hunchback with a head of deep red hair that was braided and reached beyond his waist belt.

Ragnor merely shook his head and shrugged before answering.

'Who knows, death dealing no doubt, he wants us to wait here aboard the till he returns.'

Bull Neck who stood by the huge hunchback looked unimpressed on hearing Ragnor's explanation.

'I thought you w-were the m-m-master of this vessel and not that great lumbering oaf.' This Bull Neck stammered out grudgingly as pushed past the huge hunchback who towered above him.

Ragnor sighed heavily he was beginning to weary now of Bull Neck who was in truth his second-in-command. And also Ragnor was becoming ever more irritated with Bull Neck's constant belly aching as regarding his friend Barak, this quite rightly so. With this in mind it was now time the Viking chieftain had decided to himself just to put Bull Neck exactly in his place.

'Bull Neck, you are a good fighting man and your loyalty to me I know is unwavering, for that believe me I am grateful and I thank you. But know you this and know it now, one day you will say one word too many against Barak, then he will quite simply kill you..' Ragnor said this as he had turned about to face Bull Neck. The Viking chieftain then affixed him with a cold but honest stare. 'And this, this, your death, I must confess would sadden me greatly.

'So it is best I think that you let bygones be bygones Bull Neck. For Barak, well the ogre has killed more men than the plague, and in truth I know of no man who could stand any sort of chance against him. Aye and that be it either on the field of battle, inside of a tavern, or even on a cobbled street. I myself am a proud and an unbeaten warrior who has slain many good men in honest and bloody warfare,' Ragnor said proudly. 'But know this, the very idea of ever crossing swords or making an enemy of Barak makes my blood run just as cold as ice. For quite simply my friend the ogre has no equal in a fight, do you understand that Bull Neck? Do you truly understand that what I have just said to you?'

But big Bull Neck merely scowled and he made no reply as to Ragnor's honest and sensible advice, but inside of him his dark jealousy and hatred of Barak was ever growing the stronger.

'Now in answer to your question Bull Neck, yes I am the master of this ship when we are at sea. But we are harboured in the here and now and we are on the very verge of a glorious and long awaited bloodletting. So, in these affairs of cold blooded butchery I do admit that I bow to Barak. For the ogre is after all a master of both cunning and strategy, not to mention mayhem and even bloody chaos itself. And that Bull Neck is why the ogre simply still lives, aye lives and thrives after all these years in a violent gore- filled life. After all is said and done slaughter, well, it is his stock-in-trade. And I must say this to you now, I know of no better man at it than he, do you?' Ragnor asked plainly.

Bull Neck once again made no reply though as he felt bitter and greatly belittled by Ragnor's stark words. For all his faults he was a proud man and a brave formidable fighter himself, he too had fought and killed many good well respected fighting men over his years with Ragnor. Yet in the here and now, Ragnor had dismissed his chances in a straight fight against Barak as totally futile, non-existent even. Though he had of course not meant it Ragnor had just made the jealous Bull Neck hate Barak even more.

Bull Neck muttered oaths and curses under his stale breath then he stormed off angrily, brooding away to himself as he so often did.

'And you, you big Loki, you who are perhaps the closest if not Bull Neck's only friend, perhaps you also have some sort of a grievance against Barak?' Ragnor asked this of the big very large looming and most unpleasant looking hunchback. 'If you do for some reason have any grievance against him Loki, then you may as well say it to me now rather than later. '

The big hunchback Loki shook his huge slightly lopsided head then he paused just briefly before speaking making sure that Bull Neck was out of ear shot. However this caution was not out of fear of the brutish oaf, oh no, it was merely prudence.

'None,' the big man answered plainly and honestly. 'Despite my appearance that some might find offensive and my many other failings the Lord Barak has always spoken to me in a most kindly fashion. Not one word of abuse or ridicule has he ever said to me in all the years that I have known him,' Loki replied honestly. 'Bull Neck I consider to be my friend, I trust him with all confidence by my side in a tavern brawl or in full on warfare. But alas, in heavy drink he insults me and mocks me much as he does with most men who sit in his company. He is I suppose Ragnor not in any way a cheery drunkard. But I am myself no coward, Odin knows I have little enough to lose. I suppose my miserable worthless life counts as nothing, this being so I have no fear at all of Bull Neck. So far he has not laid hands upon me as he has done with other men he has drunk with. ' Loki paused at this point to wipe spittle from his thick red, almost dark crimson beard. 'For that is a liberty that I would not permit, then I would fight him, I would fight with him till my death or his, Ragnor.' When Loki said this Ragnor knew this man was stating an honest fact, the big hunchback was neither bragging nor was he boasting. 'Yes please believe me Ragnor if a blow was ever struck by him on my person then he would have to kill me, or I in turn would surely kill him,' Loki said passively.

Ragnor for the first time perhaps realized just how good honest and brave a man the big forthright hunchback truly was. Big Loki despite his appearance was not in any way a stupid man nor was he a man to be under estimated in any way. Aye come to think of it Ragnor had never seen Loki bested in a fight. Aye and also in all truth over these past violent years the chieftain had seen him in many.

'I also fear the same as you do Ragnor,' Loki went on after another little dribble from his somewhat lop sided mouth. 'It is not our enemies out there the brash oversure Bull Neck should fear, but the Lord Barak's black temper. Barak although he is a man I both like and respect he is nonetheless just as you say still a pure killer. Oh aye he is a man I much prefer to have as a friend rather than a foe'

131

Ragnor gave a grunt then a nod of agreement on hearing this. Loki might have indeed been a big misshapen thing and not a creature that at all endeared, but never the less he most certainly was not a fool.

Ragnor gave a nod of his head then clasped the hunchbacks hand warmly perhaps he had in the past overlooked this huge warrior because of his appearance. Now the clan leader felt suddenly very guilty, and he would not make that same mistake again.

'Go, go now and drink with your friends Loki, but not too much mind you,' Ragnor said with a wry but friendly grin as he stared up at the none to pretty Loki. 'I will call you when it is time for the killing. Oh and tonight Loki I would like you to stand with me, I would like for you to fight at my side.'

Loki on hearing this nodded his agreement then gave a sort of lopsided smile that caused him to dribble a little bit more than usual. The big hunchback at once wiped his mouth with his sleeve then he lurched off to join Bull Neck who sat with some other half dozen of the Viking crew around a brazier.

Meanwhile Barak by now was standing concealed in a narrow alleyway that stood directly opposite Wraif s ship. Patiently and silently the giant watched as his countrymen stood statue-like by their posts. This, the men of the Black Guard did while Wraif's foolish oafs the meanwhile drowned themselves with yet more drink, aye and weed by the smell of things, black weed at that. Careless reckless fools, little did they know it but this was to be the very last drink they would ever have, well at least in this life anyway.

Barak noticed that this harbour was indeed a busy bustling little place even as it was now a late hour in the evening. Aye it also had more than its fair share of shambling drunks roaming the narrow cobbled streets. Most of these were searching for their hovels or their ships after a long day on the drink. Suddenly from up above him there came a loud screech and then another. Barak watched with an element of interest as two huge gulls tried to hunt down in vain a small but overly quick bat against the bright moonlight.

And then distracting the giant from the Arial hunt there came of a sudden yet another stumbling fool passing by Barak's hiding place. This unsteady drunkard was by now one of many, although this one was different as he carried a torch in one hand and a bottle of drink in the other. Also this passer by, well he was a fat noisy one legged man with a wooden peg where his right leg should have been. Barak stared with some interest at the staggering unsteady man as he sang his soul out in the tongue of Germania. Quite comically this loud out of tune fool was dressed in bits and pieces of out of date Roman uniform and armour. Also, he was the giant thought to himself more than just a little familiar.

As the drunkard came hobbling unsteadily along, the man with a great deal of difficulty lit up the irregular placed street lights with his oil soaked torch. But never this must be said at his first attempt. It was also true that he was a few hours late at his mundane and menial nightly task, but then again wasn't he always. Aye and that was if he ever turned up for work at all.

Barak shook his head in disbelief then he smiled to himself and chuckled, indeed the ogre recognized this unwashed and most unsteady man.

'Horst, Horst is that you, you drunken unwashed fool?' Barak hissed out in a low hushed voice from the safety of the darkness of the alleyway.

At once the one legged lantern man dropped his torch in fright as the giant momentarily stepped forward and showed himself. This the ogre did only briefly before he once again stepped back again into the shadows of the narrow alley.

'Barak?' the drunken man declared in shock after a moment or two of bewildered hesitation. 'It is true then, it is true that you still live, you still breathe and walk the very earth with your great booted feet? I had thought by now that you, for your many past sins, would surely be a dead thing, well, this giving the life you choose to live' Now the drunken man paused for a moment to cough burp and fart. 'Well anyway that was what I had thought until only two days ago.' The fat man took a swig from his bottle. 'Then my largest and most colourful of friends, there came a whispered rumour that you approached this place of many taverns, approached with a band of killers.' Horst said this with a drunken slur as he bent over to pick up his torch. Barak at these words merely shook his big bucket head and the ogre chuckled again to himself before replying.

'No, as you can see I am not a dead thing Horst, true it is though that many wish I were. But sadly for some, well yes I, alas sadly for them, do still live and breathe. Barak had said these words with a grin of satisfaction before continuing his conversation with the unsteady German. 'But by my good dragon sword Horst, why you're an even fatter rounder little man now than what I last remember you to be.' Barak said this with a most mirthful chuckle. Horst staggered back a step or two then he peered ever upward at the towering giant. 'Aye and so tell me this, my little fat friend. How is it that every German I have ever met with who has the name of Horst is fat red faced and for the most of it are always in a drunken state?' Barak asked this question still with a broad grin about him.

Horst laughed as he gave back a drunken lop sided smile before managing to speak. 'I think my Lord Barak that all of we Horsts, well we are all just very lucky.' The German said this after first breaking wind then next belching out another loud burp.

Barak chuckled at this reply, Horst was a man who had always a ready wit about him, aye he was a man who could always manage to make the ogre laugh. Funny or not though, big Barak was after all on serious business this night. 'Keep that torch down Horst you fool, for I have an urgent task to complete here on this cold night. '

Horst blew through his thick rubbery lips and swallowed down a mouthful of strong vodka.

'Oh, who is to die this night my Lord Barak? Tell me my Lord, what poor misbegotten soul are you sending to hell or heaven tonight?' Horst asked this question while offering his vodka to Barak.

'Ah vodka, good Horst at last I have a real drink.' Barak said this most gleefully before wiping the top of the bottle clean. Horst was a good man and he was damn good company and that either in a tavern or around a camp fire for that matter. Oh and also and as well as this the ever drunken German was an amiable enough fellow in every possible way. But sadly the heavy drinking German was alas perhaps not the most hygienic of men.

In truth his teeth were very few and mostly black, oh and also his stale breath would kill a fox.

'It has been some years since I last saw you Barak. I had about me two legs then, well at least I think I did. ' Horst said this most light heartedly.

Barak gave a smile followed by a nod of agreement.

'Aye, that you had my brother, a matching pair so to speak. So tell me my friend, what then happened to your other leg, Horst?' Was it perhaps the gout, too much fine living, too much drink?' Barak suggested after downing another mouthful of vodka.

'No, oh no great ogre it was nothing like that, it was a fast chariot and alas on my part slow reflexes, my Lord Barak.' The German answered with a heavy sigh and a shrug before continuing with his tale. 'Sadly for me, well I must confess that I fell right in front of it, the chariot that is.' Horst said this without even the slightest hint of self pity or even a hint of bitterness at his misfortune.

'Well then I salute you my old friend,' Barak said as he took another big drink of Horst's vodka. 'As I am in no doubt, no doubt at all you were in a state of total and absolute uncaring drunkenness at the time of this impact? '

Once again the short fat German smiled as he gave a simple nod in reply to both of Barak's questions; also his correctly presumed answer.

'Of course I was my Lord, but luckily for me it was a Roman chariot driven by a young Roman nobleman that laid me low. And also I had many good Roman witnesses as well as a score of German observers to testify to the incident. This being so, the magistrate of this place' Horst then paused to burp and spit onto the cobbles. 'Well, he most very kindly gave me a wooden leg to replace the gout ridden, rather septic other one that I lost. Oh and then with even further generosity, they, the Roman powers that be gave me the job of the street lantern lighter..' This the drunken German added seemingly quite pleased with the way things had turned out.

'Oh well that's all very good Horst, things I see are looking up for you then?' Barak said smiling sarcastically.

Horst took no offence at all at the giant's quick wit so the short fat German merely gave a bow then chuckled away to himself. 'My Lord, a man, well he does what he must do to survive oh great one, you know that to be a fact perhaps more than anyone,' Horst slurred. 'But anyway tell me this, my Lord, when did you come here to this place Barak, aye and for why?' Horst next enquired.

'We came here but an hour ago,' Barak replied. 'And as for the why of it, well I will start with the killing of those five men aboard that long ship yonder. ' The giant said this blankly and in a most matter of fact fashion as he indicated with a nod toward his intended victims. Coughing and spluttering the drunken German turned unsteadily about and glanced over at the doomed guardians of the longboat.

'Horst, give me your spear I have a good use for it,' Barak then demanded.

Horst turned about again as he peered with blinking bloodshot eyes ever upward toward the towering giant

'Oh, Oh that is a very big bird that you have there with you on your arm my Lord Barak. But to be honest most sailors have with them parrots not big black vultures, did you not know that Lord?' It was a smiling Horst that said this as he passed Barak his Roman throwing spear.

'This is an eagle, it is an imperial eagle at that and not a vulture you drunken fool,' Barak smiled as he said this. 'I know that I have told you this many times before Horst, but you are quite a funny man, leastways for a German,.' Barak said this as he glanced down at Horst and as he felt and balanced the throwing spear in his right hand. 'Well my Lord Barak I do try to bring a smile and a little happiness to the savage faces around about me. ' Horst said this whilst giving a slight bow and almost falling over with the effort of it. Horst was one of those men who whatever the situation and no matter how drunk the fellow become he somehow was never lost for words. 'Why will you kill these unfortunates my Lord Barak?' Horst slurred out. 'Well that is of course if you don't mind me asking. Is it perhaps for no more reason than just too simply put the time of day in before your supper? Or is it merely no more than a little target practice for you perhaps?' he asked uncaringly between hiccups.

Barak gave out a grunt followed by a low growl then he clicked his massive neck into place with a sudden jerk of his powerful muscles.

'No, no, I do not mind you asking me this question Horst..' Barak rumbled this out as he took yet another swallow of vodka. 'It is an honest question and also a one that deserves an honest answer,' the giant continued. 'Those men aboard that boat have taken a young girl captive, she is the daughter of my good friend Aulric. Aye and these fools have also, as well as this outrage, stuck his fine young son full of long shafted arrows. And so my little fat friend for these liberties, those aboard as well as the fellows they sailed here with, well of course then these men all must die.' Barak he had said this in a most matter of fact fashion, Horst being sensible even when drunk, well he was not going to argue the point.

'Of course they must die my noble Lord.' Horst said in total indifference raising his grey bushy eyebrows as he did so. 'I agree with you, as of course I always do' the German slurred. 'So this being the case my Lord Barak, can I perhaps help you in any other way, apart from the loan of my spear I mean?'

Barak was not lost for words, nor was he long in replying to the humorous Germans kind offer of help.

'Yes Horst as it so happens you can help me, aye you can help by letting me drain the last dregs of your vodka before I send every man aboard that boat to hell. To hell mind you and not to any imagined heavenly place where the dead have blonde hair and white wings attached to their backs.

Horst chuckled then he smiled an almost toothless smile.

'Take it, take it, it is yours my Lord,' he slurred. 'I anyway have another flask hidden under my red Roman cloak.' This said the drunken German produced yet another bottle of vodka and of course he at once uncorked it. 'Forgive me my Lord Barak, but you will never make that throw from here. No, oh no my noble Lord, no not even you could do that throw from where you now stand.' Horst said this profound statement as he took his first drink from his fresh bottle. 'Why it would take a good bowman to make that kill from here, and you must remember my Lord you are not as young as you used to be. '

Barak grumbled angrily under his breath. As it so happened the ogre was quite happy and comfortable with his age. This even though everyone else about him seemed to think that he was either a dead thing or close to getting there.

'Mind you my lord Barak I do not know, for I do swear you look even bigger and stronger now than when I last remember you, well if that is at all possible. But then again perhaps that is merely because I have been spending far too much time with these short stocky garlic breathed Romans.'

Barak made no reply instead the ogre gave the German a look of total disdain regarding his age and his throwing ability. Then after but a moment passed the giant hoisted the great bird aloft with one hand as he threw the Roman spear at his chosen target with the other. All of this happened at the very same moment, this, well this it was to be double death.

Of course Horst's apparent lack of faith in the slayer was to be proven totally unfounded.

And this as the spear tip entered the throat of one of his unfortunate countryman who stood at the bow of the boat, then the great eagle struck the Black Guard at the stern of the vessel at the very same instant. Its talons dug deep into the skull of its victim tearing through the black turban and leather skull helmet underneath into his very brain. Luckily for him the Black Guard warrior knew nothing at all, and he was a dead thing in but an instant.

Barak by now was already off and away, the ogre was running up the gangplank of the dragon boat with long giant strides, indeed he moved with the speed of a youth. Wraif's three drunken fools had just time enough to see their huge painted slayer before they too were dead in the blink of an eye. Moments later these fools were, after being relieved of their gold and coinage and their black weed, floating face down in the cold dark still harbour waters.

Now the giant would free the princess, she doubtless was imprisoned in the small holding cabin that lay under the mast pole.

'Ellena, Ellena.' The ogre called out in a hushed but somewhat urgent tone from outside the stout little door.

Instantly the girl answered, calling out his name in an excited reply. Now it was a smiling Barak who at once turned the key to the door then threw back the bolt, beckoning her to him.

'Barak,' the girl sobbed wildly as she came out of the small cabin in a rush into the giant's arms. 'I thought I was lost, I thought that I was gone forever and I would never see you or my father again,' she said still sobbing wildly.

Now the giant scooped her up as though she was nothing more than a plaything and he held her high above him so he might look at her by the light of the three quarter moon.

'Are you hurt at all my child, tell me did these ditch dogs harm you in any way at all? For if they have Ellena, then, I will make their dying all the slower and all the more painful for it,' Barak promised her with an angry growl.

'No, no, I have not been harmed Barak,' she sobbed out tearfully. 'But my poor brother, they have killed him Barak, these men have killed the Prince Kye.'

Barak next set the young maid down gently as he took her by the tiny hand.

'No Ellena, your brother, he lives.' The ogre then explained all to the bewildered princess. 'Trust me and all will be well, but come my child we must go now quickly and quietly as we have no more time to dally or delay. '

On hearing this, the pretty, young dark haired girl smiled broadly at Barak's strange but most welcome and pleasing news. Her many questions though, well these would at least for now have to wait. Wait until they both had vacated the ship which had been her prison, and a prison for what seemed like an age.

Once back aboard the safety of the Falcon Barak straightway explained all and everything to the confused but attentive Ellena. She would sail home to her father in the morning with Cedric and his men in the black dragon ship, the ship on which she had once been a prisoner would now be her deliverer.

Wraif her kidnapper, well that pirate would have no need of the trim well put together vessel, that was one thing for sure. Barak had at once recruited Horst then sent him off into the Half Moon Inn to do a spot of spying. For that apparently was where Wraif and his pirates had all ended up after a drunken tour of the many other taverns about the busy harbour. According to Horst these rogues were all well and truly drunk by now, bragging and boasting while more or less pushing the locals out of the taverns with their wild aggressive behaviour.

The black clad Krozak warriors however, were sat at the far end of the long well lit tavern with only themselves for company. These dark eyed scowling men unfortunately were apparently both watchful and sober so obviously this of course was not going to be an advantage at all for the giant. Barak, well for his part, the ogre would have to get to these men first and deal with them before any of the other killing started. On their feet, armed in full flow, their years of training and their skill with the sword could cause some problems, this could and would cost the lives of some men. Horst had also further said that as well as being sober, these black clad milk drinking warriors were all armed to the teeth.

However, that though was already a stark fact and something Barak had more than expected.

Apparently there were nigh on some forty or so pirates in all inside the tavern. These rogues could all be easily recognized by their bright crimson satin sashes they each wore about their waist.

Apparently this seemingly was a symbol of their sea-going clan and their bloody brotherhood. However this gaudy decoration was a good thing as at least it would make identifying the doomed brigands from other revellers a lot easier.

After all it would be most unprofessional to chop up any of the locals Barak supposed.

'You know what you must do my boys?' Ragnor asked of his nephews. 'Aye uncle, we must slip the dogs on any fleeing pirates wearing the red sash,' Sven answered as he held the big male dog by its heavy studded collar. Stefan the meanwhile likewise held the snarling bitch in readiness. So as a smiling Ragnor left them, the boys with their orders understood concealed themselves behind the striped canvas of a closed up market stall.

Meanwhile the big black eagle had settled itself on top of the tavern roof pruning its black feathers as she waited patiently for her next victim of the night.

The big burly Norsemen had concealed their broadswords and double headed axes as well as they could under their bearskin cloaks. Their big rounded spiked shields had been left aboard the dragon boat, as this bit of extra armoury would make them stand out. Anyway against such drunken fools as were their targets the shields would not be needed. Slowly in twos and threes the Britons and the Norsemen drifted into the tavern mingling in with the bustling throng of drunken revellers. Each of them picking out and marking a target for the coming fray as they did so.

Barak was followed closely into the tavern by Ragnor, the big hunchback Loki and the ever brooding but nevertheless useful Bull Neck.

A black wolf skin hood covered Barak's chain mail clad head while a black satin face veil hid all but his dark almond eyes. Barak dragged his right leg and he stooped over to conceal his great height. Luckily the ogre was moving amongst big men, a fact that also helped in his disguise. There was the tall burly Ragnor and big Bull Neck while the hunchback Loki was well over six foot tall, in fact he was the loftiest of all the big Vikings. Perhaps, if it was possible that he could have been straightened out on a rack of some sort then Loki would be near as tall as Barak.

Ragnor halted not far away from where Wraif stood bragging and boasting telling all and everyone who would listen just how clever and cunning a fellow he truly was. Now the Viking chieftain could have reached out and touched him, aye he could have dropped him there and then on the very spot. For now though, with great fortitude the Viking resisted the temptation. Ragnor at this time was flanked on either side by Bull Neck on the left of him with the hunchback Loki to his right. These fellows despite their obvious faults were both more than capable men for the bloody job that was now only a few moments away. Meanwhile Barak had left this little group, the ogre stooped over limped on ahead, the slayer was alone now as he neared the five Black Guard warriors.

As just said the pirate captain Wraif was as ever for bragging and boasting to everyone and anyone who would listen to him. Still though despite his bragging it had to be noted that each and every one of the pirate crew were all well adorned with gold, all well put on with gold rings and gold chains about their grubby weather beaten necks. Whatever their short comings were these men had in the past obviously been at least a most prosperous band of brigands.

True it was that Ragnor had entered this hunt for revenge and not gain. Still never the less that heavy gold chain about his intended victim's neck would make a nice keepsake, a nice memento. As Barak approached the table where the five Krozak slayers sat he sensed that one of the facing men was suspicious by the arrival of a lot of new faces in the bustling tavern.

Three of the Black Guards sat with their backs toward Barak while two men faced him as he edged slowly ever nearer and nearer towards the group of his intended victims. Another step then another, only a heartbeat now then he would be right amongst them dealing out death with his dragon sword. One of these men in black however must be kept alive for questioning, but how much alive was another thing entirely.

Of a sudden one of the facing warriors cursed as he arose and reached for his sword as Barak's face veil fell away. The tattooed face, the size and the very power of the man standing before him, there was no doubt about it, none at all, it was the devil himself. This was Barak aye and it was doubtful that the ogre had just arrived in the tavern looking only for his supper. At once the black garbed warrior along with the man next to him leapt to their black booted feet calling out in alarm to their comrades. However, their cry was brief, very brief as just seconds later their turbaned heads rolled about on the sawdust covered floor staining it bright red.

Of course this was now the signal that Ragnor had waited for, at once all hell broke loose aye and it did so with such a savage vengeance.

Barak brought the ivory hilt of his Samurai sword down hard on the warrior's head who sat with his back towards him in the middle of his two companions. And at once the Black Guard fell back over to the floor without so much as a twitch, knocked clean out. This warrior was the lucky one, though he might not think that if and whenever the guard ever came around. The other two men of the Black Guard the giant skewered without even raising so much as a sweat. Apparently it seemed they just did not make assassins like they used to Barak thought grimly to himself, his task once completed. Both of these men had dropped to the floor as dead things still twitching away quite comically. Now the giant almost at once wiped his beloved sword clean on one of the deceased men's black cloaks.

Barak with the killing and cleaning of his sword once done then looked down around about him at the ensuing carnage in the tavern. Now so it seemed the slaughter that ensued and was going on all about him was at its very peak. But sadly from a sporting point of view, well it had to be said in all honesty this fray was looking a very loaded and a most one sided affair. Oh aye, indeed this evening's reckoning it was just all far too easy.

Wraif meanwhile, well that pathetic fool was already a dying man. The pirate was standing there, bleeding heavily from a chest wound, upon his high booted feet. Ragnor held him now firmly by his butter coloured forked beard. As might be expected the big Viking had a most crazed look about him as he rattled off some insults, spat in the pirate's face and then cut his throat. With this long awaited task done the Viking then threw the worthless pirate captain to the floor while he kicked the lifeless body in sheer disgust.

Bull Neck meanwhile had brained several pirates with his heavy club and now he was quickly going through their belongings, this while they still moaned out in their final death throes.

The unpleasant looking Loki also appeared to be enjoying himself and without any effort hurled another luckless pirate through the already broken tavern window snapping his neck as the luckless fool struck the cobbles outside in the street.

So all in all the fray it was no more than a complete and utter rout, in fact it would be fair to say that it was no sport at all. With the big brutish Norsemen and Cedric's more disciplined soldiers making short work of the drunken feeble opposition, in just a matter of but a few minutes it was all over. The pirates were outnumbered, out matched and incapable of defending themselves against this sudden most vicious mass attack by savage vengeful superior warriors.

Barak by now had moved over to the long bar counter of the tavern of the Half Moon. Here the two owners of the Half Moon themselves stood there horrified open mouthed and dumbstruck by the sudden outburst of merciless butchery. No one from Wraif's ship save the single Black Guard was left alive. All of them had suffered the sword, the axe, the cudgel, or of course been put through the windows.

This was a busy seaport tavern so obviously at times it was a dangerous violent place. Here in the Hundsruck the locals were used to brawls, even the odd stabbing. However this massacre though, well this was something totally different this had been no more than a one-sided blood bath, a slaughter no less.

Horst had been more or less accurate with his mathematics for a drunkard and forty three bodies in total were accounted for; thirty eight pirates plus the four Black Guards that had perished inside the tavern. Five more of Wraif's men had made it out into the cobbled streets of the harbour front only to be brought down by the dogs or the eagle. Horst the innkeeper from their first port of call had apparently been out a little with his head counting of the pirates but that had proved matter less anyway.

Both of the boys Stefan and Sven were overjoyed, they were proud at their part in avenging the deaths of their family as well as the people of their villages and the settlements. Wraif's reign of terror was now at long last at an end, the hitherto elusive pirate was no more.

Barak now pulled back his hood and completely stripped away his face veil altogether.

'Tell me innkeeper, have you vodka in this fine place of yours my friend?' Barak asked as he leaned across the bar counter. 'For I am most weary of ale and cider; even mead has lost its appeal,' the giant said casually. 'German beer is very good mind you,' the ogre added not wishing to offend, 'but tonight I do celebrate.' Barak said this as he dropped a bag of silver coins onto the solid bar counter. 'For you,' he rumbled with a care free gesture of his hands. 'Let us, let us just call this payment for any damages done to your fine establishment, eh? '

Both of the landlords of the Half Moon inn could only gape at each other in both horror and wonderment. Words as yet just would not come to them, then after some length of time one of them finally found his tongue.

'We have vodka, good vodka that comes from the steppes my Lord,' the fatter, bolder one of the two men said. After some deliberating and a little nervously the fatter one then pushed the bag of coins back toward Barak. Next the innkeeper took a mouthful of beer as he looked around his tavern at the carnage done to it. There were not only pools of blood held captive in the sawdust about the floor but blood was splattered all over the walls and even the ceiling. Stools, tables and chairs were broken into pieces. As for the windows, the two either side of the door were completely broken. All of this murder and mayhem had happened and not a night patrol of the harbour guard had yet appeared, nor would they if they had any sense. Handling a handful of the local drunks was one thing - handling killers such as these, well that of course was something else.

Already the victors were stripping the dead of anything of value, gold, silver rings and chains, these as well as leather boots, even crimson sashes as keepsakes and trophies were taken from the dead.

'Keep you money, Barak.' The bigger fatter man said trying to regain some sort of composure. 'But please my Lord, please kill no one else as I think there has been enough bloodshed for one night, even for you,' the fat innkeeper added bravely.

Barak smiled a warm cheery smile, not the smile of a man who just moments ago had slain four of his countrymen then put another one in a coma.

'To kill no one now, well, that will be an easy task my friend,' the giant laughed. 'For look about you my chubby host, there alas is no one else to kill,' the ogre added with a good humoured smile. 'They, our enemies that is, well these fellows are all now dead things, so you have nothing more to fear,.' The ogre said this with a shrug and a sigh then he most politely offered the innkeepers an explanation for the bloodshed. 'But know you this, innkeeper, these unwashed ditch dogs were all killed for a good reason,' Barak said cheerily. 'Oh aye these were all bad men, brigands and kidnappers, do you understand?'

'Oh off course they were my Lord Barak, we believe you totally,' the pair of fat innkeepers said almost as one. It was obvious the two fat red faced porky innkeepers were still visibly in a state of shock, but nevertheless to their credit they after a little while managed to calm themselves. Moments later after a few beers to fortify them, the innkeepers, with the aid of Ragnor's men organized a hasty clean up of their blood soaked establishment.

There still at this hour was no sign of those from the Roman militia who normally policed this establishment, nor of course would there be.

'Like it Barak?' Ragnor asked showing off Wraif's heavy gold link chain that now hung about his own broad neck.

Barak smiled then the ogre gave a positive nod of admiration.

'Aye it suits you Ragnor, I suppose it goes with your hair,' the giant chuckled. 'Well let us say the chain suits you more than it did the fool Wraif anyway. ' Now the two men laughed heartily as a big four wheeled flat cart was drawn up outside the tavern door. Without delay the dead were at once loaded upon it, then very quickly removed. Quickly, if not quietly the cadavers were most unceremoniously carted off toward the dense forest on the outskirts of the harbour town.

Winter draws in fast and cold in Germania, wolves as well as bears abound and as the freezing winter bites these fearsome beasts become ever the bolder, ever the hungrier. At such times the beasts of the forest move in from their dark woodland abode looking for domestic stock. Sheep, goats as well as cattle and pigs these are all easy prey to these creatures of the night. Why even the cur dogs and the drunks from off the narrow winding cobbled streets were not safe once the snows of winter came. Being so these dead bodies would at least not be wasted. Oh, no, far from it these corpses would keep the beasts of the woods well fed and satisfied for at least some time to come. Wraif and his band of fools, strange as it was, these men were to become more use to the community in death than ever they were in their living years.

At length the innkeepers Lothar and Sthal settled themselves down as their tavern was at last emptied of bodies. Three cartloads of cadavers had gone off into the woods and the place had been made once more clean and tidy. More tables and chairs had been brought from the taverns out buildings to furnish the place. Why looking about now, no one would ever have even known there had even been a disagreement in the popular ale house.

After some time the innkeepers were at length persuaded to take the purse of money for the substantial damage done. Then after this the podgy pair were given yet another even fatter one; this purse was to pay for the food and drink for the rest of that night's ongoing celebrations.

Not one man of Ragnor's crew had been lost in the brief one sided onslaught True a few of them bore scars and wounds but none of these fatal. Also the Britons had come through the brief but bloody fray unscathed without a man lost to the pirates.

Barak as ever had planned the attack to perfection. Why even the ever moody and broody jealous Bull Neck had to reluctantly acknowledge that simple fact to his fellows as they sat about celebrating the slaughter.

Cedric with his men drank their drink and ate their supper in a more sedate fashion than the noisy boisterous Norsemen. Once fed and with enough ale in them for a good night's sleep, Cedric bade his goodnight and along with his soldiers wisely made an early night of it. Only the three Norsemen who were slightly wounded in the fray would be lucky enough, or unlucky enough depending on view to be sailing off with Cedric back to Britain. Giving the smaller size of Wraif's ship Cedric was confident with the training his men had received from Ragnor all would be well. Aye that number of men would do well enough to man the pirate vessel and get them home safely.

Wraif s ship on close examination was a good vessel, in fact it was a very good vessel. Naturally the boat was long lean and light, also it was well put together, indeed as a bonus this ship was a very good prize. Since the thing was neither gold or gems or something that could be put in a pocket Ragnor had secretly decided that this ship would more than likely be better off with him. But this was a little detail however that would have to wait till their eventual return from this venture. Well that of course was if they ever did return safe and sound to the Salmon River. Ragnor was no fool, the Norseman knew only too well this was to be a most dangerous trek that lay ahead of them. Still that aside, either way the slender craft would be easy to handle, and this even for a Briton. Aye, so before the full moon had come and gone the Princess would be once again home safe with her much relieved doting father. So Barak, a man to whom his word was sacred, had upheld the first part of his sworn pledge. Aye the Princess just as he had promised, she would be back with her father before the full moon had come and gone.

Now though this aside, what lay ahead of them, well of course this was to be the hardest part of their venture. In all truth the giant, he supposed, had not been totally honest with Ragnor as to the full dangers the warriors must face on the remainder of this long and most perilous quest. True it was Barak had intended on telling him two or three times over these past days. Oh yes it was also very true the ogre had put off the Viking's enlightenment on a few other little matters. Still, after giving this matter some careful consideration and some long deliberation Barak had decided this information would keep for another day, or perhaps even two. In the meanwhile for now the men would drink, feast, and celebrate their easy if not quite glorious and heroic victory. For in truth it was a victory won over fewer and much inferior men, still though it was a victory nonetheless. In all honesty the giant supposed only his own black garbed countrymen were worthy of the killing.

Leaving Ragnor and moving toward the blazing tavern fire, standing there silently, alone, the giant first silently then mentally saluted them. But then, in almost the same instant the ogre cursed them for their actions, actions which had caused him to take their lives. If Barak did believe in a god perhaps he would have prayed for their souls, but the ogre did not. Barak, well he believed only in Barak.

'Tell me Lothar would you sell me this place of yours?' A loud and drunken Ragnor asked this as the fat innkeeper brought more drink and meat to the table where earlier the Krozaky warriors had sat by the fireside. This table was, as it so happened, one of the only tables which had went undamaged in the brief affray.

Lothar glanced over at Barak with a puzzled look about him, as now the innkeeper was looking to find some sort of explanation for Ragnor's most curious and unexpected question.

Barak merely shrugged swallowing down more vodka before speaking.

'He is drunk my friend, I have never met a Norseman yet who could handle a man's drink, a proper drink. Aye they might think they can drink, these hairy itchy Vikings, but alas my friend they cannot..' Now the giant laughed shaking himself from his dark gloomy thoughts. 'Well leastways the Norse cannot drink vodka, mostly they dribble it all over their long red beards. Beards that are already filled with bits and pieces of stale food, this and other things, moving things,' Barak smirked.

Since the slaughter Barak had already consumed several bottles of the most potent steppes vodka, but still he looked like a man who was just coming out for the start of the night.

Ragnor who had foolishly tried to drink vodka with his large friend fared less well, in fact he was totally wrecked as he sat there in his chair in a complete shambles.

'Well would you? ' Ragnor pressed sitting most unsteadily and slurring his words out. 'Would you sell me this place of yours? I like it here so I will buy it off you for a fair, no a good price. The big drunken Viking said while banging his great fist on the table so hard the plates and goblets bounced about as if doing an Irish jig.

'Perhaps, yes perhaps I might for the right price just sell up, yes I do believe that I would cash in the Half Moon. ' Lothar who was ever the bolder of the two landlords answered a little shakily. 'But I would of course have to talk with Sthal first over any sale. We are after all business partners and the inn is half his,' the innkeeper went on as he piled up goblets, plates and other items to be taken off to his kitchen.

'Good, then go and talk with him,' Ragnor said a foolish drunken smile across his face. 'When our quest is finished, when we Vikings have killed all and everyone, I can see myself wearing one of those leather aprons, Ragnor slurred. 'You must be making good money here, why, you must be making money hand over fist in this place.' Ragnor pressed while wiping beer froth from his bushy beard.

Quite sensibly the Viking had now by the looks of things forsaken the strong vodka as it apparently did not agree with him.

Lothar was a businessman, a shrewd one at that, and he always became cagey and nervous whenever money was mentioned. Quickly the innkeeper hastily excused himself from Ragnor's interrogation then he made off towards the kitchen with the goblets and plates. It was well after midnight now and Lothar as well as Sthal wondered with some trepidation what the rest of the morning was going to bring. Also they wondered about the lack of the Roman guards on night patrol, why had the guards not turned up for their nightly free drink and a bite of supper? Mind you, this was more than likely a blessing than a curse. As doubtless such an appearance would have just been more mess for them to clean up, more cartloads of dead off into the forest. Perhaps they were after all both just getting a little too old for this trade now. Being an innkeeper was after all a very demanding way of making a living. It was also tiring as they were both constantly on their feet from getting out of the bed until climbing back into it at day's end. Indeed both of the overweight innkeepers often wondered why and how they were just so fat.

No, a good offer from the Viking and for his part Lothar would let the inn go. Indeed Ragnor or whoever else for that matter that came along with enough money could have it as far as he was concerned. Aye he would sell up then move inland into the country. With the money from the inn he would buy some nice land and breed pigs, Lothar liked pigs. Oh aye there was plenty of money in pigs, also they tasted very nice and everyone ate them; well everyone in Germania did. What was also most important you were less likely to get killed in the business of breeding pigs than selling beer to murderers, pirates and hired killers.

Barak puffed upon his long clay pipe while he chuckled to himself at the very idea of Ragnor doing an honest day's work.

'You would never make an innkeeper Ragnor, well at least not a good one. After all the sea is in your blood, aye it is what you are and what you do You're a northern raider not a respectable innkeeper,' Barak said in a dismissive fashion. 'So why don't you do yourself a favour my friend, forget all about inns and innkeeping. No, inn keeping would never work out for you; besides Ragnor you have a family. Aye you have a wife, a son and a daughter, all of who must be well grown by now' Barak further added. 'Would they like life in the tavern? No I doubt it, with you drunk and doubtless gambling away your money all the time, I think not. '

Ragnor scowled at these harsh but somewhat sensible words then he spat venomously into the fire. Years ago the big Viking's wife was once a flaxen beauty, however, she had now somehow transformed herself into a fat ever complaining scold. And as for his daughter well she had married a ne'er do well, the village waster if not the village idiot as it so happened. Aye here was a man who could neither sail nor hunt, farm or even do a day's honest work for pay. So now Ragnor, as well as providing for his own lodge and keeping his family in food and drink, now also had to maintain his daughter's home and keep her worthless man into the bargain. And as for his son, his only son whose name now he never even mentioned. Well that huge bitter disappointment of a man was never happier when putting his time in with a needle and thread instead of a sword and shield. So all in all Ragnor's life at home was not one he had greatly loved or even relished. No, the big Viking had decided he could and he would buy himself a tavern with the spoils he had saved over the years of high adventure. Aye he could do this, then perhaps with a little time and a lot of drink he would forget about all else. Oh yes those problems which had troubled his recent years would be tucked away and forgotten about, of that fact the big Viking was quite sure and quite positive.

Who knows perhaps with a little bit of luck the Viking mused to himself, he could find a good fat bar wench to help him out with this that and the other.

Just as with Barak, Ragnor also wanted this to be his last adventure. Hopefully, and with a bit of the ever needed luck thrown in, he would live long enough to see the venture through till its conclusion. Anyway plotting and scheming for now put to one side, there was drink to be supped and meat to be ate. So now as was the norm the warriors drank and feasted on for a while longer, each man in the tavern with their own thoughts their own plans for the uncertain future.

As for Barak, well he suddenly became uneasy and unsettled with himself for no apparent reason. The moody giant without a word gathered up his wolfskin cloak and left the others drinking in the tavern while he walked the cobbled streets of the harbour and its outskirts. Barak did this with his great dogs following on behind him and with the great black eagle sat upon his arm.

As for the unconscious Krozaky warrior, well he earlier had been carried off to lie aboard the Falcon. Once there the warrior had been placed in a small holding cabin quite similar to the one the Princess had been held when aboard Wraif s ship. Outside the door of this cabin it was guarded by two Britons who no doubt would snooze there till they sailed off homeward. Now though the Princess meanwhile slept comfortably and well guarded by two more of Cedric's men in a warm room above the Half Moon. Ellena would rest there warm and safe dreaming her dreams until she was ready to sail off to meet her loving father in the morning. Of course since her release she had been well cared for the child had bathed in hot sudsy water, then after this she was fed on pork chops and goose eggs. Also the princess had been brought fresh clothes for her journey home, these the forward planning Cedric had brought along with him. When at long length the Norsemen left the tavern that morning at whatever unknown time they did leave, the streets were not at all deserted.

A large company of Roman harbour guards were standing in wait observing the goings on, these men were subdued and were cautious. However, these guards said nothing though; no these men merely watched with interest as the Norsemen retired to their berths aboard the Falcon.

Well harbour guards might not be a totally accurate account and description of the armed men standing there in the shadows fingering nervously their sword hilts.

Horst had earlier told Barak the prefect of the harbour town, a man called Milo, had been told to expect his coming, so of course also expect trouble along with it. Furthermore the prefect had also been told to give Barak the freedom of the port. He was not in any way to interfere with the slayers business here, these were orders direct from Rome itself. Apparently the Emperor Septimius felt in the near future he would be once more in need of both Barak's strength and cunning yet again. Whoever or whatever it was Barak hunted down, and no matter what he did in Hundsruck that broke the law it was quite simply to be ignored.

Obviously this of course was a communication which had not pleased the pompous Prefect Milo one little bit. For in his jumped up opinion it was he who was the lord and master here in the Hundsruck. So the very idea that one of Rome's foreign henchmen doing just as he pleased in his holdings impressed him not at all.

Also this was even more so of an affront as Milo was not a man who in any way whatsoever was in favour of the current Emperor.

Chapter Eleven

Recently there had arrived at the harbour town of the Hundsruck a new man, a new protector - he was a hero apparently. By all accounts he was a great and an unbeaten gladiator of Rome, a man who hailed from the very coliseum itself. With this being so, then he was of course a champion swordsman and duellist of some esteem. And also this fellow was some twenty years younger than Barak. Furthermore apparently this fellow had the support of the town's magistrates and all of the resident Roman nobles. Oh yes to these overstuffed pompous fools the one time gladiator had become both a favourite, a bodyguard and even something of a celebrity.

Milo, the prefect of the harbour town, was a man who also very much favoured this gladiator of the coliseum. So all in all, this paragon of Roman bravery was popular with the ruling hierarchy and the powers that be. As well as all this, he had become something of a hero among the legions of men that were stationed permanently at the Hundsruck.

But only the Roman blooded ones mind you. The foreign conscripts, the auxiliaries made up of Thraciens' Huns, Spaniards, and of course the Germans, these still adored and worshipped Barak with undying passion.

Anyway this esteemed gladiator's freedom had been bought by the wealthy family of some high ranking prefect, senator or some other sort of con man from the Emperor himself. Of late this Roman hero had apparently participated recently in several wagered duels while in the surrounding area.

Several duels followed by several easy victories, it appeared his admiring flock of Roman followers grew steadily in number. Talk had it this fellow was apparently an ambitious and a deadly warrior by any standards. Well anyway this at least was the rumour. But either way this gladiator would have everyone in the Hundsruck believe he was a most dangerous man to go against. A dangerous man who was to be both feared and respected; well at least the fool most certainly had a dangerous mouth. More than once in the recent past he had after drinking too much wine vowed to his doting followers he would in the future cross swords with Barak. And then after another glass or two, even worse, well the reckless fool had also bragged as to the outcome of such a meeting.

Horst who had known Barak for years, well he had carelessly spoken with Bull Neck about this ambitious and flamboyant swordsman. At the time of the conversation Horst was of course ignorant as to Bull Neck's hatred and jealousy of the giant. It was a conversation Horst would later regret this, if only briefly.

Still, indeed it would have been far better to have said nothing at all to the wayward stammering foolish Bull Neck.

Barak could have sailed off being none the wiser of the empty words of a young and foolish braggart. But of course Bull Neck being Bull Neck, well the wayward fool had in turn spoken to Barak. All be it in a stuttery and spluttery sort of fashion. Bull Neck had informed the ogre he might be in some danger from this new and apparently very confident slayer, a slayer who intended to lay him low. Bull Neck after saying this had also pointed out to Barak he was not getting any younger. And of course with this being so perhaps it would be wiser just to ignore the rantings and ravings of some ambitious swordsman who obviously thought he was the better man.

Bull Neck was of course a man who never spoke to Barak, well at least not without being pushed into it. Barak though was not a fool, no the ogre knew full well Bull Neck would like nothing more than to see him slain by a better sword, or at least by a younger one. So despite his better judgment Barak now stalked the streets followed only by his dogs with his big eagle upon his arm. If it was a duel this nameless fool wanted then it was a duel he would have. However, Barak's prowling was of course a fruitless foolish search. For no matter who Barak approached seeking information about this swordsman, they all at sight of the giant merely ran off into the darkness, afraid of the huge looming figure.

So with this being the way of things the giant headed off somewhat a little gloomily toward the Viking longboat. Just as Barak returned to where the Falcon was moored his gaze and his attention was drawn to some half dozen Roman legionnaires who stood talking loudly by the Roman galleon that lay next to Ragnor's longboat. Most of their fellows had retired to their beds earlier when Ragnor and his men had boarded the Falcon. But these noisy few lingered on for some reason or other that was unclear. All of these loud mouthed fools had about them all the confidence of both youth and far too much drink, a deadly cocktail. Nevertheless, that foolish and false bravery was soon to evaporate very quickly into the chill air.

Barak paused as he was about to step aboard the Falcon's gang plank. Of a sudden there was a name mentioned, it was a Roman name, and also it was the name the slayer was looking for. Now the giant stalled for but a moment then he turned about to view these fools. Slowly then did the giant approach the young soldiers till he stood but a spear's stretch away from their company.

At once the young men became very hushed of a sudden, now they no longer laughed and joked or voiced off their hero's name as of course this huge fearful looking man standing towering before them was doubtless the giant slayer Barak. It was obvious to even these foolish drunks this monster could be none other but he. One of their numbers dropped a clay jug half full of red wine onto the cobbled harbour floor in fright. It broke instantly, the wine trickled through the crevices in the cobbles; it lay there looking very much like pools of blood. Barak grinned wolfishly, the ogre well knew fear when he saw it, or indeed smelled it.

'You then know this fellow Maximus? Oh forgive me but I forget the rest of his long winded but insignificant name.' Barak said this with a vicious snarl as the ogre at this particular time was itching for a fight.

Meanwhile both of Barak's huge dogs circled and moved behind the Romans watching their every move, just as would a sheep dog do with its flock. One of the young Romans was so overtook with fear he at once vomited then staggered away into the darkness never to return. Barak of course was greatly amused by this and the slayer chuckled as he scratched at his neatly trimmed snow white chin beard.

'Tiberius, he is called Marcus Maximus Tiberius, my Lord Barak. One of the young terrified soldiers said in a hushed voice after some moments of long suffering deliberation.

Barak shrugged then growled out a word of thanks to the informant as he looked down at the small congregation from under the cover of his hooded cloak.

Now, it had begun to rain a lot heavier, as indeed it had done on and off these past hours. Also, the cold north easterly wind, this too was now rising with a chilly bite just a little. Luckily though, this wind was blowing in the right direction for the princess on her voyage home.

The giant took another pace forward; at this advancement those before him grew nervous and fearful. Foolishly and nervously these fools fumbled at their sword hilts out of sheer terror. Barak of course paid them no heed, why he could kill all of these fools together armed with only a chicken leg.

'I believe I knew this Maximus's mother,' Barak sneered mockingly as he pulled back his hood. 'She was a whore in one of those cheap run down pleasure houses on the outskirts of Rome. ' All there upon that harbour standing in the rain and the gathering biting wind suddenly sobered up, this on witnessing the black eyes, the fanged teeth and the elaborate tattoos of the ogre.

Indeed if these young men were afeard before Barak pulled back his hood, well now they were doubly so.

'Tell him that, tell him just that from me will you?' Barak paused for a moment as he ran his dark eyes over each and every one of the young Roman soldiers. This done then once again the ogre continued to speak. 'Tell this fool of yours, you tell him the very words I have just spoken. Who knows, he might even be lucky enough to be one of my many offspring. I did, you know, put much time in such places when I was a younger man. Tell him this also, tell him that I would meet with him, aye meet with him this very day before we set sail. ' Barak then paused for a second time as he looked down at the fearful cowed young men standing before him. These men the giant noted, were neither proud nor were they noisy now. 'Anyway you collection of fools, I must go now to my bed, tell this champion of yours I will be in the tavern of the Half Moon at noon today. In my eagerness to meet this soon to die fool I will put off sailing for one more day if I have to. Oh aye, please believe me, this I would do just to hunt him down should he not appear. For you must understand this, I have the patience of old age about me you see, aye the patience of an oyster? ' the giant said with a calculated snigger.

Barak, once these words were spoken, glared at each and every soldier in turn, straight in their brown watery eyes he looked at them. Now they each to a man at once bowed their heads fearful to return the giants icy stare. Barak growled then he spat with obvious contempt, the ogre next said something very insulting. With this insult delivered the slayer then turned to walk away, however he stopped suddenly and looked back over his shoulder. As ever on such occasions the ogre had that grim cold unforgiving smile across his scarred tattooed face.

'You tell him this; tell him, this champion of yours, if this fool does perchance come to the tavern at noon to meet with me, the fool need not worry himself what to choose for his evening meal. '

With these last words delivered Barak pulled up his hood and wrapped his black wolf skin cloak about him as next the slayer disappeared without another word back aboard the Falcon.

Much deflated the legionnaires were left alone now standing there in that cold biting wind and the driving rain. It must be said these men were a lot less proud and a lot more humble than they were before speaking to the slayer. Still such has ever been the folly of over confident youth when in the company of too much drink and also too much bravado.

Not long after Barak had laid down his big head the giant was roused from his slumbers. As now the Princess Ellena awaited him, she wished to say her goodbyes and give her thanks to him. Quickly Barak arose from under his bearskins and then he was down the gangplank and stood beside the princess on the harbour front. Now, at this time, it was just breaking daylight and luckily the wind was still in the right direction to carry the child swiftly home. On this somewhat breezy drizzly morning the princess was well put on with a thick woollen hooded cloak and stout boots fleece lined for warmth.

'Oh I wish you were taking me home Uncle Barak,' she said as the ogre scooped her up with one huge arm. 'We could ride and gallop through the dark woods together then out over the meadows. I have seen that great beast you have bought, he is a big thing but surely cannot be very fast of foot though,' she jibed. 'No, he is just far too big, far too clumsy to move at speed,' she giggled. 'I suppose in a way he is a bit like you, big feet and a big head,' she said still giggling happily and childishly.

It greatly pleased Barak to see her so happy, the giant smiled warmly as he placed the child back onto the cobbles.

'Well he is still faster I think for me, than a smaller, quicker one would be with me sitting perched upon its back.' Barak joked and laughed as he walked the princess to the deceased Wraif's black dragon boat.

Earlier, while the giant had slept, chests of gold and plunder had been emptied and then shared out fairly among all the men. So both those who were leaving for Britain and those who were going onward into the abyss were all at least happy souls. All were wealthy men now but true it was perhaps all would not live to spend their fortune, but that was another story.

'Take good care of her Cedric, the innkeeper at the Salmon River port will have horses waiting for you, I have already arranged this with him before I left.'

As ever and as always Barak had planned all and everything down to the very last detail.

Everyone aboard the black dragon ship was in high spirits now as they made ready and were about to sail off. For after all these men had come through their part of the adventure with only scratches, their bounty was secure and also they had their princess.

Perhaps the only gloomy souls aboard Wraif's vessel were the three slightly injured Norsemen. True it was these berserkers had much gold, but still gold was not everything. After all fame and legendary was far better, and all three of these big brave souls would have dearly loved to have sailed onward to complete the adventure, aye or die in the trying.

But no matter as at least they lived to tell of Wraif's slaughter, Barak waved off the princess till she at last disappeared off into the morning mists. With this done the ogre then went back to his bed to catch up on some much needed sleep. Aye, he wanted a little rest before his supposed meeting in the Half Moon tavern at noon. Barak a few hours later arose, this after a short while of contented slumbering. At once the ogre washed then as ever scraped his head and face with his shaving knife. Next with this done the slayer chewed upon the bark of some unnamed tree, this to clean his wolf sharp teeth.

All of a sudden Ragnor loudly hailed Barak, now there was a lone legionnaire standing by the bow of the Falcon; he would speak with the Lord Barak.

Barak at once on hearing this threw his heavy black wolf skin cloak about him and made off down the gangplank with huge strides towards the young Roman. The young man, who was well dressed in a brand new uniform of the Northern legions politely bowed and gave his name simply as Antonius.

'My Lord Barak, Marcus Maximus Tiberius awaits you now in the inn of the Half Moon,' the young man declared as he gave Barak another polite bow.

'He is? Is it that time already?, I thought I had said noon?' Barak muttered to himself a little disgruntled. For a moment the young legionnaire was hesitant in his answering, then he spoke. But mind you it took him all of his courage to do so.

'My Lord Barak, you see Maximus, well he had already arranged to be somewhere else at noon,' the young Roman explained sheepishly.

Barak yawned then raised his dark eyebrows awaiting the young man to enlighten him further as to the busy schedule of this fool Maximus.

'You see he has a prior rendezvous, this with an Arab trader, and this is to buy a fast horse my Lord Barak,' the young Roman went on to explain after yet another polite bow.

'Oh, oh I see, well I suppose that is two people that I must disappoint so early on this breezy day. ' Barak said this as he lit up his long clay pipe with a brand from a harbour brazier.

The messenger was silent for a moment or two upon hearing these words, but then in a state of slight confusion he spoke up.

'My Lord?' the Roman said a little hesitantly not quite knowing what Barak meant by his somewhat vague reply.

Baraks' eyes narrowed with pleasure as he took in a deep breath from his long clay pipe, the ogre then glowered down at the young legionnaire.

'Well, I firstly must disappoint the seller of said fast beast, for alas this Arab trader will not be selling anything fast, slow, or otherwise, well at least not to your soon to die friend anyway. Next, I will further disappoint the late to be Maximus, oh and whatever the rest of his name is. Believe me my boy this fool of yours will not be riding anything on this day. Well, apart from the slow boat across the river Styx that is,' the ogre chuckled. 'Where is the fool anyway?' Barak demanded. 'Ah yes I remember now he is in the tavern of the Half Moon.

Well boy, that is as good a place to die as any I suppose,' the giant muttered this in between puffing vigorously upon his pipe. '

Barak next stepped forward pushing aside the Roman messenger, then though not forgetting his manners the ogre turned and apologised for this rudeness, after all the young man was only a lackey. With this done the ogre was off striding purposely toward the tavern puffing away furiously upon his pipe as he did so. Of course the giant as ever was most eager to be about his business, Barak was keen for blood.

'What was said there Horst, did you hear anything at all?' Ragnor shouted this question down as he leant over the side of the Falcon. The one legged German at this time was sitting most unsteadily atop a harbour mooring peg eating a huge smoked eel and drinking from a jug of red wine. It was a jug of wine which had been discarded by the small congregation of Romans, those who had occupied this place several hours earlier. Thankfully for Horst the fools before leaving had the good sense to cork the jug before shambling off in fright into the gloom. Wine at best had little bite to it, so with rain water added then sadly of course it would have none at all.

Horst grunted, then and with a degree of difficulty the German with red wine running down his beard struggled to his feet, well rather his foot.

'A duel Ragnor, the great ogre he has a duel, a duel with some fellow called Maximus,' Horst replied.

Ragnor had a look of great surprise across his hairy face, after all who on earth was foolish enough to duel with Barak?

'No, no this is not possible' Ragnor declared in shock. 'If so, who is he Horst? Do you know anything of him, this soon to be deceased?' Ragnor asked as he combed some of Wraif s dried blood from his beard.

A mouthful of smoked eel prevented the German from giving an instant reply to the excited Viking's question.

First Horst coughed belched then broke wind, next he spat into the murky grey waters of the harbour.

'Aye the fool is a local hero among the Romans here in the Hundsruck. He is, so they say supposed to be good, very good, apparently he used to be a gladiator of Rome, once again, or so they say. ' Horst said this with a sneer of contempt as the German had no love at all for Romans.

Aye and also he had no love at all for so called roman charioteers.

'Oh that's good, very good news Horst. Then we might if we are lucky even find some fool stupid enough to bet on the Roman,' Ragnor said this quite gleefully as he began to descend the Falcon's gangplank.

Horst however shook his hairy itchy head in dismay.

'I very much doubt it,' he said in between bites of his smoked eel.

'Why so then?' Ragnor pressed, standing now before the ever drunken German.

'Because my big Viking friend, these Romans are proud and they are arrogant things, but alas they are not stupid, Ragnor. I mean after all the Romans do still rule most of the world you know? ' The short fat man from the Rhineland said this with a chuckle and a hint of sarcasm.

This wit though, well it was wasted on Ragnor as his head still pounded from last night's drinking. Now though the big Viking sighed heavily and a little grudgingly as he supposed Horst was correct in his assessment of the wagering situation. Still though, if he gave good enough odds then he might just be able to trick some fool into having a gamble.

'Come on Horst, there is no time to waste, as this fight could be, and very likely will be over very quickly. Well that is unless of course I am very much mistaken. ' Ragnor said no more as he was off at the run leaving the stumbling hobbling half drunken Horst in his wake.

Several others, those within earshot, Bull Neck included, at once downed their mundane chores, joined Ragnor and were off rapidly in the same direction.

Meanwhile the gladiator Maximus stood inside the tavern of the Half Moon one foot casually set upon a three-legged stool. Apparently the blowhard was already toasting his monumental yet premature victory with a cup of red wine. Also this fool had also very kindly filled the drinks in for his twenty or so noisy confident supporters. Some of these were high ranking Roman soldiers from the Northern legion. However, most were no more than well bred fops with nothing better to do with their time than to make a hero of a loud mouthed fool.

'Let us see what this man, this painted warrior, is like fighting a real swordsman and not some back woodsman with a wooden staff.' Loudly the former champion of the Roman arena roared this out with his cup of wine held high aloft above him. 'Who knows, if his pelt is as colourful as they say it is then I might well skin him and put him upon my wall,' the fool confidently joked.

At this the followers of Maximus were just about ready to clap, to cheer and applaud their bold champion's wit, aye until they heard the doors of the tavern being slammed open. So hard did the stout doors hit the walls of the entrance the tavern fair shook to its very foundations. Of a sudden there was a deathly silence, and it was a silence that seemed to last forever.

As in the past on so many occasions no description of the slayer Barak, of his height, his power and his overall appearance could or would ever match up to the larger than life man when he at last appeared in the flesh.

Lothar the innkeeper was a man who for whatever reason had no liking whatsoever for Romans. Now after putting up with the noisy arrogant Marcus for most of that morning the fat innkeeper smiled broadly. Why, he smiled almost as if Barak were an old friend and protector of his.

'Romans and gladiators of the arena,' the innkeeper said with a smile and a sneer as he raised his own frothy drink skyward. 'I give to you all here in my humble tavern of the Half Moon Inn, a toast to my good friend, aye my good friend the Lord Barak.

'Oh and by the by my noble lords, I will both take and also cover all bets in my tavern against Barak.' Lothar put this in very quickly thinking that he could perhaps win a little money toward his own retirement fund. 'You Cassius, I do believe just a moment ago you wanted to bet that rather heavy purse of yours that is hanging at your hip? ' Lothar said this with a greedy calculating smile.

Cassius was a young noble man recently arrived to the Hundsruck for no other reason than to drink and gamble with friends he knew here in the prosperous harbour. Cassius while being young and wealthy was not a fool however, and now the Roman aristocrat glanced briefly at the giant then at the gladiator Maximus. After this quick observation all of a sudden the young man felt more in the mood for drinking than he did for gambling.

'I will give you two to one Cassius, will you take these odds or have you perhaps lost faith in your so far undefeated champion?' Lothar pressed somewhat mockingly.

'I should gut you now you fat sausage eating German pig.' A very offended and most hostile looking Maximus said his big fist clenched towards the German's fat red face. 'You would dare insult me by giving odds and odds on an even fight? ' the gladiator declared angrily.

Barak sucked on his bad tooth and spat bad blood from it onto the floor before speaking.

'I do dare, I do dare at odds of ten to one, not some foolish and childish two to one. I will give you ten to one Maximus, or ten to one for any of your fools here who would bet against me. So will you choose him or me.' Barak said this while indicating toward the gladiator. Now in the meanwhile the giant was striding in a most purposeful fashion across the tavern's freshly cleaned floor.

Barak quickly discarded his cloak and threw it over the back of a chair which was still stained with last night's dried blood. With a savage growl the giant slayer next flexed himself as he creaked his great neck to and fro until it clicked itself into place.

There was a hushed gasp amongst the Roman camp as they were in truth not expecting to meet a man who was either quite as huge or quite as ferocious in appearance as this fellow.

Barak had already noted none of the Romans he had spoken too earlier that rainy windy morning were here to witness the outcome of the duel. These men had apparently already come to their own conclusions as to which way the fight would be ending. Aye, it was only a note one of their number delivered to one of the gladiator's night servants at his villa earlier that morning. And this apparently was just a simple scribbled roughly written note explaining the time and the place of the rendezvous for the duel.

'Well, well are then any takers here?' Barak demanded loudly as he threw two heavy leather pouches of gold onto the bar counter. 'Who here among you posturing fools has money to throw away this morning on him?'

There was a hushed silence among the friends of the hitherto confident Roman champion, but there were alas no takers as to Barak's generous ten to one wager.

'And you there Maximus whoever and champion of whatever have you then nothing to say for your sad sorry self. Tell me fool where is your gold? Where is your gambling money?' Barak demanded. 'And by the by, just who is it that you think you have slain of any note? Who is it that you have defeated that would make you contemplate you are even worthy to share the same tavern as me, let alone any sort of arena? '

Maximus glared up and up at the giant both fearfully and hatefully. He was now being belittled and bullied and most rudely ridiculed here in front of his very subdued so called friends. And all of this bullying, all of these insults were coming from a man who was old enough to be his father.

Barak was in the mood for slaughter today, perhaps he suddenly thought to himself he always would be. Perhaps he could not or would not ever change into the peaceful tranquil man of the woods he had long dreamt of becoming. Perhaps he just could not ever break the dark mould into which he was cast long ago. And also, perhaps after all the remainder of his life was to be lived on the battle field, and not in the meadow field.

'You would skin me would you? And you would put me upon your wall, you little Roman rabbit? Come then fool and try it.' Barak said these words with a fierce snarl across his face, now the ogre was looking to incite and provoke some sort of a challenge. However the result though, well it was perhaps not what he had expected and hoped for.

Maximus made no reply, as indeed the gladiator seemed totally overawed by the whole affair and this very dangerous situation. This even though, here was a situation that he found himself in through his own fault.. Barak was always and ever had been a most shadowy sinister figure. At times the giant seemed to be conceived as being more a myth than an actual flesh and blood man. It was even rumoured about the still vast but shrinking Roman Empire that Barak had died years ago, or that he simply did not exist and never had. It was also said he was merely now some fabricated ogre who was meant by use of his most fearsome reputation to keep law and order along the many Roman frontiers. For while in the past many people had met and clapped eyes upon the giant there were still also many people who had not. There were also many in the younger generation who had thought Barak was no more real than the Minotaur or the centaur. Still though despite these doubters the ogre did exist, he was here and he was here now. Whatever it took, the giant had decided he would stir this posturing fool before him into some sort of action before much longer. So with no more ado, and of course with little exciting happening around about him. Barak, well he next promptly slapped the gladiator violently across the face with the back of his hand. This blow was only a slap of contempt, but still the ogre slapped the Roman with enough force to send a front tooth flying out of this gladiator's mouth.

'Rabbit,' Barak sneered out spitefully. 'You are just as I had at first thought you would be You are just another little Roman rabbit.'

Ragnor had just made the door in time to see Barak seize this would be duellist by both of his ears. Next the ogre raised his would be foeman up effortlessly from the tavern floor till he dangled there like some sort of spoiled child. After a curse or two and a few insults Barak then head butted Marcus Maximus Tiberius full in the face with his big bucket sized head. At once there was a loud terrible sickening crunch and the handsome Roman's nose was at once smashed and most badly broken. With a heavy thud the gladiator dropped to the tavern floor as Barak released his grip upon him.

Now the face of the proud, loud mouthed Maximus was bloodied, it was also bruised and it was broken. On top of all this, the gladiator felt both sick and dizzy, indeed Maximus was at a total loss at what to do next. As after all this most certainly was something he had not at all expected.

'A duel, a duel do not make me laugh you posturing fool,' Barak said with an evil smirk. 'I advise that you go, aye and go now while you still have your legs to walk with,' Barak commanded pointing toward the tavern doorway. 'You disappoint me, as I most foolishly thought today I was to face a worthy opponent,' the giant sneered a little spitefully. 'Someone who was worthy of the killing, but all I find is some fop scented poser who moves among even lesser men than himself, this just to make him feel a great and glorious man. '

All of these friends of Maximus now felt both very foolish as well as belittled, oh and of course it must be said they were also very afraid. So now these much less confident men drank down their wine silently nervously and very hurriedly. Now each and every one of them thought, as a collection of barbarians entered the tavern, now would be a good time to leave.

Next, suddenly, with a growl of frustration and hate, this assisted by sheer fear as well as embarrassment. Maximus launched himself upward from where he had been so rudely deposited. Desperately the bloodied gladiator struck outward and upward, this with his short sword in his hand; after all, he was a gladiator of Rome. Well this at least Maximus thought somewhat dimly to himself as he made his futile attack. At day's end he was after all a champion swordsman, not some sort of common bar room brawler to be slung about and insulted. Oh and by the by, the man Maximus was in no way a little rabbit, he was a man well over six feet tall and of a powerful athletic build.

Anywhere else and in any other place than this, well the Roman would have looked an impressive foeman indeed, but not here, not now, not in this situation. Why, here in the Half Moon tavern standing against the size and power of Barak this so called gladiator just looked like a half grown boy.

Barak next drew his death dealer, his ivory handled samurai dragon sword. Without effort the ogre blocked the short sword with ease; there were sparks as the blades clashed together.

Maximus in an instant felt the awesome power of Barak as sword on sword he was forced seemingly without any effort backwards towards the bar counter. In a dreamlike panic the Roman instinctively spun about then he struck down low at Barak's lower leg seeking to cripple him, or at least slow him down some.

Ragnor, Horst together with the innkeeper Lothar, were all offering huge odds on a wager with the Romans as to the outcome of this sword fight. Of course it was an offer however that found no opposition, there were alas no takers at all.

Stall, Lothar's less robust partner, well he had vanished at some speed that morning at the very mention of the coming duel. After all, the fellow had seen quite enough blood and gore over these past few hours alone. So he was it must be said in no rush whatsoever to see even more of it.

Aye, perhaps now would be as good a time as ever to sell up and move on to pastures new. After all, the old Half Moon Inn had certainly served both of them very well over these past years. But still besides that, things certainly weren't getting any easier with the passing of time. Why there were more rogues, pirates and cut throats now than ever filling their popular drinking establishment. Aye and all in all selling drink was becoming an ever increasingly dangerous occupation.

Barak first sneered then smiled with contempt as he parried another sword swipe aside with an easy flick of his own keen blade. One of the gladiator's braver friends threw Maximus his small spiked fighting shield. It was plainly obvious that Maximus would need all the help he could get here against this man. Maximus gave a thin smile as he clasped the shield in his left hand, this smile for whose benefit no one was quite sure of. Still, nevertheless once again the gladiator either foolishly or bravely pressed forward with his futile attack. The Romans sword thrusts were both high and low, head, belly and legs, of course these moves were typical standard Gladiator training.

Barak of course knew and expected every move the Roman would make in his sad futile effort for a victory. After all, the ogre had fought in many arenas, not as a slave or a captive though but as a challenger to all comers. The giant had fought for a good purse and it was a purse the slayer had of course always walked away with. Barak had in the past taken on many a so called champion, most of them were a lot better than this one standing before him now. Still, you can at the end of the day only fight and kill what is in front of you Barak thought to himself a little wearily.

'Have we any money on this farce Ragnor?' Barak asked casually as he parried another badly timed sword swipe.

'No, no Barak there are no takers,' Ragnor said with a disappointed shrug. 'Why there is not a gambler or a sportsman in the place,' the Norseman said sullenly.

160

'No wonder,' Barak replied with a little chuckle as his sword slashed through the tough leather and metal spiked shield just missing the Roman's hand.

'Looks like a perfect half moon,' Lothar muttered to himself. 'I must keep that as a sign for above the doorway. ' On hearing the words of his countryman the fat German drunk had a better idea of decoration.

'Why not just put the Roman's head there?' Horst said as the fat innkeeper kindly poured him a drink of frothy beer.

Maximus snarled, he threw down his worthless shield then once more pressed home his fruitless desperate attack with his short sword.

Well, if nothing else at least he was a brave fool thought Barak to himself as he easily diverted two neck strikes with his own sword.

For five minutes the men fought, or in the case of Barak, well the ogre merely sparred with his inadequate foeman. For this little affair in all truth after all was little more than a little light exercise for the ogre. Still though Maximus did try, inadequate or not he was relentless if nothing else with his futile attack. Barak suddenly smiled, it was that cold thin most murderous of smiles. It was a smile the giant reserved for those who knew they were beaten and had no chance of victory. These men, even when as foolish as this one knew they were about to die on the end of his famed and greatly feared dragon sword.

Maximus was sweating, not with effort though for he was fit enough, no doubt of that, he was just not good enough. It was cold fear now that made the hitherto unbeaten gladiator sweat and shake. Now right here in front of him was something completely different to anyone he had ever fought before. Here before him now stood an excellent swordsman. Here was a man not only with great power, but a man with balance, speed and skill, here was an ultimate warrior, here was an ultimate killer.

Now the gladiator stood back a spear length from his adversary taking in for the first time the full size and appearance of the giant. What foolishness, what madness, what arrogance had overtaken him to make him even think that he could ever cross swords with this painted devil?

Maximus spat upon the sawdust covered floor and he took a deep breath as he muttered a prayer to his gods, gods who it so seemed had obviously forsaken him. Somewhat sadly, next the foolish gladiator turned to look upon his friends and his followers. And oh of course, this for what he thought would be the last time. After all, he knew only too well now he could not beat this giant of a man, this painted fanged demon. Now Maximus knew how all the men he himself had sent to heaven or hell had ever felt in their last moments upon this earth. Now the gladiator prayed to himself once again, this time he prayed he die both well and quick. As obviously he of course had no wish to be left to lie on this tavern floor twitching in agony under the gaze of his disappointed friends. Aye and then perhaps to die much later while laid upon a grubby mattress somewhere with his entrails hanging out. Still though Maximus thought grimly to himself what must be must be, and so he supposed he had just best get it all over with. Maximus Tiberius, gladiator of Rome, next cursed then screamed as he charged forward. He was hoping by now for no more than a quick clean death, this for himself of course.

In the very instant Maximus made his attack, for what he thought in all honesty would be the last time. Barak however then did the most curious of all things. In but an instant the giant moved with the speed of a cat quickly to his right side. And there and then the ogre lay down his much loved, much cherished ivory handled sword atop one of the long tavern tables.

Ragnor gasped in horror as did everyone else in the tavern, who, was not for the Roman gladiator. Well apart from Bull Neck that is. Bull Neck a deceiver who was at the point of rejoicing. Barak had left himself totally unarmed now as he stood statue like and motionless facing his younger armed opponent.

Maximus though, well he halted dead in his tracks and the Roman never followed through with what he had expected was to be his last thrust. A last thrust for what he knew was going to be an impossible victory against the far superior giant.

Barak stared down impassively at the bloodied somewhat bemused gladiator. At that moment the giant's appearance was that of a man who was totally uncaring as to what happened next.

Now the two young brothers who had been sleeping late had just arrived and burst through the tavern's doors. Sven seeing Barak unarmed reached for his own sword but Ragnor stayed his nephew's blade, this after all for better or worse was Barak's affair.

With a bemused look about him the Roman halted in his tracks, this with his short sword held above him ready to make his strike.

'Death wish, I have seen it before, this is sheer madness.' Ragnor hissed through clenched teeth, 'Sheer madness.'

A very confused Bull Neck looked on for a moment or two in silence before finding his black tongue.

'Ssstrike, why does he not ssstrike?' Bull Neck stuttered a little put out that the Roman did not press home his one and only advantage.

Horst alone had overheard these treasonous words and he was it must be said less than impressed.

'Perhaps you did not know this fathead, or Bull Neck or whatever else you might be called. But the Lord Barak, well he is on our side.' Horst said this with a scowl and a sneer of utter contempt. The German had no love for Bull Neck even though they had only just met a day earlier. Aye and also Horst knew him well now for what he truly was. Horst had always found it to his advantage to play the drunken fool. However, while he was often if not always drunk he was never a fool. No, and indeed he was far from being one. Horst also knew only too well now that Bull Neck was the mother and the cause of all of this nonsense.

'Strike why don't you Maximus?' Barak asked in a most calm and carefree fashion. 'I am standing before you, and also I am now unarmed, bereft of my dragon sword. '

Maximus gave a nod of agreement as to the giant's statement then the gladiator spat out blood and another tooth onto the freshly cleaned floor.

'Yes, yes you are indeed an unarmed man my Lord Barak, that is most true.' The Roman had said this with a bow of his head. 'But it was not I who disarmed you, nor ever could I if truth is told,' he said honestly. Next the Roman lowered his sword then threw it onto the table next to Barak's blade. 'I would sooner be a dead man than be called a coward, Lord Barak. Far better it is for me to die here and die now, a fool who was beaten by a better blade than strike an unarmed man. ' Maximus said this with a certain amount of both passion and pride, and also in a somewhat shaky voice.

Barak scratched at his well groomed white chin beard then he shook his head, the ogre chuckled in a most light hearted fashion to himself. Barak now removed his link helmet then scratched at his big shaven head before once again replacing the tattered headgear back where it belonged.

'Perhaps, perhaps I was wrong about you after all Maximus,' the giant conceded. 'You are a gladiator, aye and what is more, now you are now the most famous of all gladiators,' Barak said with a thin smile. 'That quite simply Maximus is because of this reason,' Barak said, clearing his throat before continuing. Maximus, the meanwhile stood there silent and cowed. Now the Roman was expecting to be ridiculed and belittled by this unbeatable ogre. Silently to himself, Maximus, well he supposed that he would deserve at least such a final insult for his foolish bragging and boasting. Barak though, well the ogre decided he would spare the gladiator at least that parting shame.

'Famous you are Maximus,' Barak continued, a smile across his face as he said it. 'Famous for this reason, as you, you Marcus Maximus Tiberius are the only man who has ever drawn swords and duelled with me, then lived to tell of it.'

Maximus stared up at the towering giant. The Roman was still bemused and bewildered by the ogre's strange dangerous actions. After a short while the Roman found his tongue and was able to speak.

'How did you know that I would not make the strike my Lord Barak?' he asked sounding both very humble, childlike even.

Barak then gave another thin smile followed by an indifferent shrug.

163

'I did not,' the giant replied evenly. 'You might well have chosen to carry on with your attack. But you chose not to, so young man that is good enough, agreed?' Maximus shook his head in sheer disbelief at the slayers strange words, then his legs of a sudden went to jelly. Without another word spoken and after a polite bow toward the giant the much humbled gladiator made his way a little unsteadily out to the back of the tavern, vomiting as he did so.

However Ragnor was not in the least impressed with that morning's entertainment, and this was more than obvious.

'Can we be off now? Can we sail Barak? Or do you perhaps wish to dither and dally and impress even more of these village idiots?' Ragnor asked this question with a little bit of anger in his voice at his friend's dangerous stupidity. 'We still have the tide with us if we hurry, that is of course if we waste no more time.' The big Viking was not well pleased, as well as not landing a wager, his long time friend's actions were of course most foolhardy.

'Aye,' the giant answered with a deep somewhat weary sigh. 'I suppose our business here in this place is for now finished Ragnor, so we must away.' Barak said this with a slight smile as he realised only too well that Ragnor was put out because he did not manage to secure a winning wager or up till now invest in the tavern.

'Well at least you lot of Roman inbreds are not quite as stupid as you look. ' Horst mockingly said this addressing the very subdued friends of the now missing Maximus. With this said the German then swallowed down a goblet of their red wine while he put his own coins brought out for a wager back into his purse.

These coins as well as the three gold rings he now wore upon his fingers were given him by Barak. Loot taken from those aboard the Falcon, those Barak had seen off the night before.

'Enough of the insults you drunken German ditch dog, come Horst you one legged fool we must away with the tide, the entertainment is now over. ' Barak said this with a broad carefree smile as he next picked up his dragon sword and made off hastily toward the tavern door. Now after this foolish time wasting escapade there was a prisoner that the ogre wanted to question.

'Lothar I will see you on our way back from this quest, well if we are not all killed that is,' Ragnor shouted back over his shoulder. 'About the selling of the Half Moon tavern I mean. Aye I will speak with you, well you and Sthal, as you will, I hope, think about my offer?

Fat Lothar gave a nod of his perspiring head then he gave a wave of his hand in farewell to the backs of his new found friends. After this when the small party of killers had left his premises the fat innkeeper straightaway discarded his frothy beer and reached for the vodka, for now he most urgently needed something stronger.

As they had left the Half Moon tavern Ragnor put a question to Barak, the giant had as he did so often become all of a sudden most sullen and very quiet.

'Why did you put up your sword my friend? Are you perhaps tired of living Barak? After all that man in there might not have been the greatest foeman you have ever fought, but still, he had at least a fool's chance.

'What you did was pure folly of the worst kind, Barak, you must remember your promise to Aulric. Suddenly the big Viking halted in his stride for a moment as did the giant; they were out of earshot of everyone else now. Ragnor felt he needed to know more, what exactly was going through Barak's big head. 'Once again my friend I must ask you, why did you put up your dragon sword?'

Barak paused for a moment the slayer had about him a far off distant look about his scarred tattooed face. Next he struck up his flints, lit up his pipe and blew out a cloud of smoke, it was then Barak spoke.

'Oh just to see if I had to kill, just to see if I had to kill the man to win the fight Ragnor. Just to see if I could content myself with merely proving a point without taking a life. Aye and as you saw for yourself, well I passed the test. I allowed the fool to live Ragnor. In all truth I do suppose that deep down I wanted to kill him, aye this is very true,' the giant conceded. 'But still nevertheless, I let him walk away. As you know, well I have never done that before have I? Quite a step forward towards becoming civilised don't you think?' Barak added this most cheerfully his mood suddenly changing like the wind.

Ragnor shook his head in dismay he gave a bemused shrug then he uttered out several Viking curses, to him this still seemed like a damned stupid thing to chance just to become civilised.

Once again the two men suddenly stopped in their tracks to talk thus letting the others walk on even further out of earshot.

'The tavern of the Half Moon, tell me, will you throw in with me my friend Barak? Why we could clean up me and you - we could make a fortune from that place Barak. '

Barak knew well what his answer was going to be, but cleverly the ogre still appeared to be thoughtful over his reply. Barak did not want to offend Ragnor by being too quickly dismissive over his business proposal. After all Ragnor had come to his aid at the drop of a hat. Also on top of that the slayer supposed he had not been totally honest as yet about the forthcoming perils they had yet to encounter. Still though, for now these little bits of information would keep for a little while longer.

'Alas, for now I think I must decline Ragnor, well at least for the present anyway. However, you are of course correct in your assessment of the financial security of your venture, but it is your venture and not mine. I aim to become a farmer, a dealer of horses and hunting hounds, a man of the woods and forests.'

Ragnor cursed under his breath, Barak would have drawn in customers to the tavern as does a flame to a moth. Why, drinkers would have come from miles around just to buy the ogre a drink, aye and buy him a drink from his own cellar; what could possibly be better.

'You mean it then Barak, what we spoke of the other night, when this adventure is finished then so are we both. There will be no more living by the sword, no more plunder, no more high adventure?' Ragnor asked this question somewhat sadly knowing that it would be the end of a violent but exciting era for both of them. Barak gave a grunt then nodded, aye and it was a most positive nod at that.

'What will a man like you do - what do you think you can do after your whole life's work has been that of killing and warfare? Selling horses and dogs? No surely not Barak? I do find that very hard to believe. No there can't be more money in that trade than owning a busy tavern,' Ragnor argued. 'Aye and in a tavern, which after all is your second home you would have at least some sort of chance. You could of course cook, you have a love of it, and I my friend have a love of eating it, as does everyone else. Why, there would be rogues, gamblers fighters and swordsman, men such as you are used to spending your time with. From far and wide these men would come to the tavern, this just to meet and drink with us, we would be rich men with big beer bellies and purple noses. Aye Barak we would be stinking rich surrounded by a sea of drink and pots of money.' Ragnor said all of this most enthusiastically. 'So tell me what on this earth could possibly be a better way of making a living - answer me that Barak? ' Ragnor was as ever a stubborn man and he was obviously not going to give up easily on his valid case for both he and Barak going into the tavern business.

Barak though once again shook his big bucket head.

'But I am already rich Ragnor, aye and I am as you put it stinking rich at that,' the giant argued.

'Ah, yes but you could be even richer still,' Ragnor countered quickly. 'There is no such thing as too much money, aye and these are your frequently spoken words and not mine Barak, you could be a lot richer.' Barak puffed upon his pipe then he sighed a little wearily, Ragnor was a man who did not like to take no for an answer.

'Aye my friend and I could also be a lot deader,' Barak said in a slightly dismissive tone. 'These inns, these taverns can be dangerous places, as everyone friend and enemy alike knows just where and when to find you Ragnor. And of course you can never know who will walk through your door next or how many of them there might be. No my friend, for me it will be over when we pull in back at the Salmon River by the great northern wall of Hadrian. '

Ragnor looked up at his giant friend straight in those black dangerous almond eyes. 'I know you well Barak, better than anyone. I think you do all of this for the boy Hassan then?' The giant was thoughtful for but a moment as he sucked merrily upon his pipe then painfully on his sore tooth, then he gave a positive nod.

'Aye I do this for the boy for the most part, but also for myself, Ragnor. You must understand I no longer want to hunt down men for bounty or fight foes that I do not even know or have a grievance against. On my return I will hunt only the wild beasts in the woods and meadows or the fish in the rivers. I would sit in my garden within the castle walls and smoke my pipe. This or lounge upon my porch in the woods with a jug in one hand and my good dogs lying at my big booted feet, this while the boy fishes in my pond for my supper. Which by the way Ragnor is now well stocked with many fine trout,' Barak said proudly.

'There I will listen with great pleasure to the sounds of the dark forest, the howl of the wolf, the roar of both the red stag and the big brown bear. Hassan will make a fine man one day and a fine trader too unless I am very much mistaken. Also the boy can grow anything at all, be it either fruit or vegetables or even the much cherished weed. The lad grows that now even as we speak, though perhaps in all truth he knows not what it is that he cares for. ' Barak said this with raised eyebrows and a crafty chuckle. 'When I am gone to my grave he will be wealthy beyond his dreams, aye and know this already, the boy can read and write fluently in three languages and studies many more,' Barak said proudly. 'But be sure of this Ragnor when you do buy your tavern, twice in the year in the springtime and with the fall of the leaves. Then I will come to your tavern and I will drink with you. Mayhap with some fortune who knows you might even chance to buy me a one back every now and then,' Barak joked. 'Who knows Ragnor? We might even talk Aulric into leaving his little island and his castle to come for a drink, perhaps he will bring with him the Prince Kye.' Barak said though in all truth he doubted this was an event that was at all likely as Aulric seldom wandered far from the wall of Hadrian.

'Well, I would not wager on that visitation Barak,' Ragnor said with a crooked smile. 'You know as well as I do that Aulric is tied to that castle of his just as a carrier pigeon is to its roost.' Barak was in total agreement but said nothing as he sucked on his bad tooth and then his pipe as they walked toward the ship.

'Oh by the way Barak how is your tooth?' Ragnor asked of a sudden.

'It still hurts,' Barak replied.

'Good,' Ragnor answered with a smirk.

With these final words said and no more spoken the men were off and away aboard the Falcon, and on with the next chapter of their journey.

Soon Barak would have to tell his good friend Ragnor what they must expect on the remainder of their trek. Soon and soon enough, but that time was still not yet, no it was not quite yet.

Barak while saving Ragnor a troubled journey, was not so lucky as he puffed upon his pipe and pondered. Barak knew well what lay ahead. Though his journey lay far away the slayer could remember almost every footfall.

This time though the trek was in reverse.

From the land of the Britons they would have to sail to the Germanic coastline. This of course was to be the easiest part of the venture.

Next came the Baltic with its Ports and Taverns.

Beyond this last point of civilisation came black stagnant oceans where swam all manner of scaley horror. Should the falcon have good fortune and not succumb, there was more.

Barak and his companions would reach a shingle shore. Here they would beach and rest, hopefully without any wounds to lick. From the beach all being well their adventures would travel inland.

Ahead lay forests, rivers and snow capped mountains. If the elements of the beasts did not lay them low, there was more.

Beyond the mountains lay the desert, the steppes and the open plains they would have to cross. In these places, along the way, bandits and savage tribes of Nomads abounded.

Once on reaching the open plains, then came the Mongol's small slant eyed horsemen with perhaps not the best of attitudes. Once and only once all of these obstacles were overcome will they have arrived.

A narrow gorge flanked by mountain walls that lead to towering gates, gates that hid behind them the somewhat secret kingdom of Krozakistan. Strangely perhaps after all they had been through here lay the real danger.

Barak puffed once again on his pipe. The giant smiled wryly as he thought how lucky his companions were, not knowing what lay ahead.

Chapter Twelve

The Falcon was not long out of the harbour before Barak turned his attention to the prisoner. There were many questions that must be asked and also they must be answered, and it was time now for these questions to be put. Barak turned the lock and opened the door to the small holding cabin that held the Krozaky warrior.

'Come out of there if you are still alive and you are able,' Barak commanded. 'For I would like to speak a little with you now,' the giant said gruffly.

'Why don't you come in and get me,' was the bold and immediate reply from the prisoner within.

Barak laughed aloud, it was a booming but never the less chilling laugh.

'Alas, sadly I cannot do that my boy, would that I only could. '

Barak had left his home so long ago and he was now familiar with so many accents and dialects that his own language now was almost lost to him. So for now they spoke together in the tongue of the Britons, doubtless the young warrior had learnt the language to help him with his mission.

Thus the warrior who had been knocked out without seeing his attacker was totally at a loss as to who it was, or indeed what it was he was speaking to.

'Why is it then that you cannot enter the cabin - are you afraid of the dark perhaps? Or mayhap is it that you are merely afraid of an unarmed man? Mind you, I am a Krozaky man and believe me that makes a great difference,' the warrior stated bravely and somewhat arrogantly.

Barak gave out a grumble then a growl upon hearing this.

'I cannot enter into the cabin you fool because I am simply too big to do so,' Barak replied somewhat coldly.

'Too fat more like it,' the warrior next said to himself out aloud in his mother tongue.

'Enough of this nonsense,' Barak said angrily, also in the language of his people. 'I have not spoken thus in thirty years. Well, apart from bits and pieces to my dogs, or to Hassan. But anyway besides that it all comes back to me now,' the giant muttered out loud.

With that Barak then reached into the holding cabin and plucked out his struggling black garbed countryman. Into the light of day the giant hauled him, into what had now turned into a cold but sunny autumn afternoon.

The Krozak warrior was a fine looking young man with a jet black goatee beard that was well trimmed and tidy. As for the rest of his facial hair growth, well, that was something which would not trouble him for some time yet. This warrior was also tanned and hawk nosed with black flashing dangerous eyes about him, indeed the young man was true to his breed.

At once the young warrior glanced quickly about him at the large hairy itchy strangers who stared at him with cold blue eyes.

'Barbarians,' he snarled with more than a little contempt for his captors. At this time the warrior was shielding the sun from his dark eyes, dark eyes which had become accustomed to his equally dark holding place.

'It was these barbarians who dressed your wounds, it was they who gave you food and water, know this, you live by their hand. Well at least you live for now anyway,' the giant hissed coldly.

Barak with this said then released his hold upon the young warrior who was perhaps no more than in his early twenties.

'You know my language, so perhaps you are not as totally uneducated as I had first expected,' the warrior said bravely.'

'I could speak your language long before you were even born,' Barak retorted angrily.

Still blinking in the bright sunlight and trying to focus on the man before him, the Krozaky warrior looked down upon the wooden deck where he now stood. And then he looked down at a pair of great booted feet standing just a yard in front of him. At first the warrior had thought the deck was some sort of split level affair. Of course it was not however and so this man towered above him, oh and he himself was by no means a short man. Now the young warrior blinked as his eyes became a little more accustomed to the sunlight. What moments before had been merely a gigantic silhouette appeared to him now to be much more, aye and very much more.

'Barak,' the warrior hissed out both in utter shock and horror. 'No, oh no, this is not at all possible. '

On hearing this, the giant grinned broadly revealing those fearful white fangs as he stood huge with the sunlight at his broad back. Barak next removed his link helmet and scratched at his big bucket head. His massive powerful tattooed body and his shaven skull made him look a most positively demonic thing.

As with everyone else who met the slayer for the first time the warrior found to his horror that Barak's description was not at all exaggerated, oh no indeed it was far from it.

'Tell me boy what treachery, what misbegotten misguided reason had you to travel to the land of the Britons? Aye and then once there cause such heartbreak and misery for my friends?' Barak demanded to know as he replaced his helmet.

'You can speak and understand their language, so I now I will speak to you in their language also. What you say to me now these men all here will also understand. Know this fool, these warriors are Norsemen not Britons. Still despite this each and every one of them will understand what we say in the tongue of the Britons. I can twist nothing but neither can you, believe me you will know their feelings well enough. Though I must say to you I do doubt very much you will care for what they think, or indeed what they might say. '

In somewhat of a daze the young warrior gazed about him at the mean and hairy hostile faces. Of course there was it must be said not a friendly one in sight, but then again that was little wonder.

After but a moment the young warrior had a question for Barak.

'Tell me, the young girl, is she well? Tell me, is she safe?' the warrior asked a little urgently.

Barak on hearing this was quite pleased in his own way as the warrior appeared sincere in his concern for the princess. After all, part of his duty had been to keep her from all harm and away from Wraif and his uncouth and immoral louts.

'Yes, yes she is well and she sails homeward now even as we speak,' Barak answered with a low and rasping hiss.

With just a trace of a smile the young warrior gave a slight nod of his head. 'Good,' he said almost in a whisper. 'And the others, my friends and cohorts of the Imperial Black Guard - what then of them?' he next asked raising his voice a little. 'Are they also prisoners aboard this long and snake like vessel of the northern barbarians?'

Barak shook his head slowly.

'No' the ogre replied very simply. 'They are not prisoners here on this vessel, nor are they prisoners anywhere else for that matter. '

The warriors of the imperial Black Guard were more of a brotherhood than just simply an elite fighting unit. Since the legion was formed years ago their loyalty to each other was unwavering and also unflinching, death to them was better than any sort of dishonour. Now the warrior was both thoughtful and silent for but a short time. Not one man about him spoke, and as it so happened, well it was not at all necessary for them to say a single word.

'So, so they are dead then, my brothers in arms, my kinsman, my friends, they are all dead men are they not? ' the warrior asked plainly.

This time Barak nodded his head to the affirmative. Once he had confirmed the Black Guards' sudden violent demise, the ogre knew exactly what to expect from the proud young warrior. Still though, it was an honest enough question and the warrior would have an honest enough answer.

'I killed them all, the men on the boat and also those in the tavern,' the giant answered sternly and coldly. 'You alone have survived of your number, I let you live only for the simple fact that I have a need of you,' the slayer said sounding ever more icy and uncaring.

With a sudden scream of both anger and bitter hatred the young and anguished warrior hurtled forward, his arms outstretched towards Barak's huge neck.

Far faster than a man of his years was entitled to move Barak seized the man with one hand on his throat and the other on his black waist belt. In but an instant the warrior was first held high aloft above Barak's head before he was next hurtled most effortlessly through the air to land with a heavy thud on a pile of ropes, chains and sailing canvasses.

Another foot to the left and the warrior would have been impaled either upon an anchor or a whaling harpoon, and that of course would certainly not of helped matters in any way for anyone.

'Good throw eh Bull Neck?' Ragnor said with a cheery smile as he nudged his big scowling companion.

Bull Neck growled then muttered something that was no doubt not in the least bit pleasant or in any way complimentary concerning Barak.

Barak the meanwhile paced across the deck with purposeful and gigantic strides Rudely he hauled his countryman back onto his black booted feet. Now, now was the time for some answers. It was the first time in the young man's life, a life that had been dedicated to warfare and battle training when he had felt totally and utterly helpless. All his years of hard rigorous training in combat he knew would avail him nothing here. Against the awesome power of this huge and most terrifying antagonist he was totally and utterly powerless.

'Who sent you to the land of the Britons? For why, and for what reason?' Barak demanded. 'Speak fast and truthfully boy, for alas I am a man who, it must be said, has arrived at a strange time in his life. And sometimes, well my patience I suppose that it just fails me. You do I hope understand what I say to you don't you boy?'

Once again the young warrior was dangling in the air, this time held fast by his throat in one of Barak's huge hands. At this present moment in time he felt like little more than a child who had misbehaved and been caught out.

'Aye and also fool, these days I am alas never quite sure what I am going to do next. It must be old age I do suppose.' Barak continued to say this as the warrior dangled at the end of his out stretched arm. After a short while dangling there the warrior after a deep and painful swallow spoke up.

'Kill me then Barak, it is better that I die here and now than betray the rules and the code of the Krozak brotherhood. After all the legion of the Black Guard is sworn to defend all that is true to our kingdom.' The young warrior answered this defiantly but with some difficulty, his windpipe being a little sore. 'You Barak, why you are no more to me than a deserter, aye you are a deserter to your people, your country, and your very crown. ' Bull Neck smiled, the treasonous fool liked very much what the young warrior was saying.

Barak for the second time in what had been but a matter of moments released his grip upon the young warrior. With a scowl the giant then looked about him at Ragnor and his ever bloodthirsty crew. All there had a sort of morbid interest as to what Barak would do next with his very disrespectful country man. Bull Neck for his own reasons was more interested in what the black clad warrior would do with the knife he had let him keep. Barak of course being Barak, well he knew only too well he was being observed as to what his next move would be. So with this thought in mind perhaps with this proud cocky young fellow a change of tactics might be a little more fruitful. Aye, it might also be a little more prudent Barak thought to himself.

Aye perhaps a little tenderness, a little compassion might be for the best on this occasion.

'Speak, speak to me in any tongue of your choosing, then I in turn will answer you in that same tongue. But first though boy you must tell me your name, when you have done this and once I know who you are.' Barak then halted with what he was about to say, he paused but briefly to take in the cold chill sea air into his lungs after this, the ogre said on. 'Then my lad once I have your name, then I will tell you all about my sad and bad life, also of course my reason for leaving my land, well our land. This, I swear I will do, you have my solemn word upon it. And my word boy, I will give to you before you even speak or answer one word to me, is this agreed?'

Now as the young warrior peered up at the face of death, he realised he had nothing to lose now, well nothing but his life. But then again only one second ago the young warrior thought he had lost that anyway. The young man was silent for a moment or two he was trying not to shake with fear while he gathered his ravaged wits about him.

However this of course was not an easy task, but then again he thought somewhat gloomily to himself nothing ever was or had been of late. After the warrior had managed to massage a little life into his bruised neck he spoke out bravely.

'I am Tark, I am the son of Atark,' the young warrior stated proudly. 'My father many years ago was sword master, also the master of arms to your father for some long time. I do also believe that as well as this my father was also his friend and his confidant. Do you remember Atark, do you remember him? Tell me, do you recall my father at all, Barak?' the warrior asked eagerly, hopefully.

Barak at once smiled on hearing this, it was a warm sincere smile as the notorious cold blooded killer remembered back into his happy childhood days long ago.

Ragnor dispersed his men at this point the excitement after all was over now, and as ever there was always much work to be done about the dragon ship.

'Yes I do in all honesty remember him,' Barak said with another slight smile. 'Your father was not only a good swordsman Atark was a good horseman too. In fact it was he who put me on my first pony - did you know that boy?'

Tark at this point looked a little bewildered by the ogre's statement because as it so happened he did not know that bit of information.

Perhaps, just perhaps his family's royal connections were stronger than he had ever imagined them to be.

'We will walk a little, Tark son of Atark'. Barak said this in a softer and an almost kindly tone. 'This good dragon ship is a long one, and I think a few circuits of the vessel should give you your sea legs. Also, I think it best at this point to speak in our mother tongue, though speak it to me slowly when you must ask me anything. I believe that I speak it mostly only in my sleep these days. And of course in slumber, well I have no one to correct me if my words are muddled. I speak also to my animals in the tongue of our fathers, but then again they are quite unable to correct any of my verbal blunders, if you know what I mean.' Barak had said this with yet another slight smile.

'Anyway let me speak to you now for a moment or two without any sort of interruption. It will be easier for me that way, you do understand?' Barak asked as the men began their first lap of the longboat. 'When I am finished with what I have to say Tark you can ask me anything that you wish to know. I will neither lie to you on this occasion, nor will I evade any of your questions. But in return, when this is done and your interrogation of me is over then I will ask you my questions. And then I will expect from you the same honesty and truthfulness, so, are we in accord Tark son of Atark?'

At once the young warrior nodded his still throbbing turbaned head in eager agreement, the warrior wanted to know a lot more about this huge tattooed man.

'I never lie, Barak,' the young man said proudly and adamantly, 'never.'

Barak gave a weary worldly sigh then the ogre ground his teeth together hoping that his painful back molar would dislodge itself. Sadly though for Barak it did not, obviously this offending tooth intended it would give him pain for some while longer.

'Well I do lie,' the giant continued on a little wearily. 'Well at least sometimes I do, but only when absolutely necessary, also this is of course always for the greater good you must understand boy? And so that is exactly why I said to you now I will not lie to you on this particular occasion, understand?'

Tark turned away from Barak and the warrior gave just the faintest of a reluctant smile Here indeed was a man who was very different to all others he had ever met. Mayhap this was a good thing or then again perhaps it was not, at day's end only time would tell. In but a short while the warrior thought silently to himself, well then he would no doubt find this out. Only then would he decide whether or not to chance his hand, this by plunging a concealed dagger hidden in his boot, into the giant's black heart. First though the young warrior had decided he would at least listen and discover what sort of man it was he walked with on the deck of a dragon ship in the middle of some cold grey forsaken ocean.

Slowly unhurriedly the ogre and the man from the Black Guard did another lap or two of the ship in more or less total silence, this before Barak at length began once again to speak. The giant rubbed out his pipe and replaced it inside his thick tan leather waistcoat then once again he spoke.

'I smoke too much Tark I must cut down, this even though most men who know me say I cannot, please believe me one day I will.' Once again the young man found it hard not to smile at the giant's strange open sort of words.

'My dear mother she died giving birth to my brother Zark, though doubtless you of course already knew that?' Barak said starting off the conversation as he turned his back upon the wind and put a large hand inside of his waistcoat. Now to the young warrior's amusement the giant once again pulled out his long pipe which was still warm, it of course being stubbed out only moments ago. Urgently the ogre stuffed its bowl full of black weed then relit it from one of the ever burning braziers. 'But perhaps young Tark, I will cut down on the smoking after this venture is over. For I do find Tark the odd drink and also a little smoke helps me to relax,' the giant explained this before getting on with what he was about to say. 'Anyway you knew of the death of my mother even though it was long before your time, this I know.'

Tark gave a most positive nod.

'Of course I knew this, after all it was not a secret. And I also know from talking with the old soldiers of my legion this was a dark day for our people. She was much loved, she was much respected, and my father I know he thought much of her. I remember he spoke much of your mother to me when I was a child.' Tark said this with more than a small trace of sympathy in his voice.

Barak looked thoughtful as he took a long deep draw of his pipe before once again continuing. This conversation he thought to himself might prove to be a harder one than he had first anticipated, nevertheless still the ogre went on with what he had to say.

'Well this sad tragic loss was the ruination of my father as he loved and doted upon my mother. Now there were to be many dark days ahead, oh and many dark months aye and even darker years.' Barak said this most sadly while he was sucking in a most furious fashion upon his long clay pipe.

175

Now the two men moved slowly towards the secured horses as the beasts munched uncaringly on their feed of good hay and the best of ground oats.

'For almost three long painful years my father grieved,' Barak continued whilst puffing upon his relit pipe. 'Still though, despite his grief, my father ran and ruled the kingdom as ever he had done, both wisely and justly. Barak then paused and looked skyward toward the heavens before he spoke again. 'No one ever saw him grieve as I did, no one could ever envisage the great lord's loss and his sad despair. Through the day he went about his daily duties sitting with the so called nobles, the law givers and the ancient scribes.' Barak paused for a moment, the slayer cursed then sucked once again upon his long pipe. 'And of course there were also the elders, the advisors, as well as the other official liars who had never done an honest day's work in their lives.' Barak puffed away yet again and with even more angry gusto, the great slayer did so hate the establishment. 'When once these fools were gone, my father would lock himself away, then he would drink strong vodka till he could drink no more. For him to be able to drink no more, well, you must please believe me, that was a lot of vodka.' Now the agitated looking giant took another long puff upon his pipe before saying on.

'His love for my mother, well I tell you boy that must have been a great and a most wonderful thing indeed,' the giant said as he almost whispered these words.

Barak at this point then turned about as he affixed Tark with a blank stare.

'Aulric, he whose son you struck down with your black arrows and whose daughter you chose to take away. He puts me very much in mind of my father. You, you by your actions, you turned my friend into a useless broken thing.' When Barak said this he spoke calmly, very calmly, there was not even a trace of the bitterness in his voice that he truly felt.

Tark made no reply to Barak's cutting reproachful remark, after all what he had done was by order of his peers. And also after all said and done he was only a soldier obeying orders. Well that at least was his somewhat sad feeble excuse for these recent events.

'But that is of no matter to you I suppose, as you of course had your somewhat inglorious mission to accomplish for the Black Guard.' Barak said this with a wave of a hand as he turned about and filled up the wooden water buckets for the thirsty horses.

Now the giant walked up the line of tethered and hobbled horses watering each one of them in turn as he went along. Tark could not help but gasp in awe as he beheld the great gelding for the first time. Of course this was doubtless the giant Barak's, mount, the young warrior had never seen such a huge hairy legged beast before. Why it was even bigger than Commander Gortak's big black stallion, aye and it was bigger by far. Unhurriedly the giant watered his big gelding as he spoke softly to the great beast in his own tongue. Barak at that time seemed to forget Tark could understand exactly what he said to the great snorting, hoof stamping beast.

Barak, his conversation with the horse over once again continued with his tale.

'On the eve of my brother Zark's third birthday my father seemed a little more cheery, more forthcoming than usual. We sat and we drank in the evening, we talked of hunting dogs, fast horses, brave eagles and such like.' Barak silently reflected upon the past as he puffed away upon his pipe. Tark looked skyward as Barak's black eagle called from the top of the billowing masthead. The great bird seemed to call for no other reason than it wanted to be seen and noted. Tark looked up at the huge eagle with a certain amount of pride, after all the great black bird was the symbol of his people. Barak spoke again and the warrior listened, aye and he listened most intently.

'We talked just like any father and son would talk, my father loved to hunt just as I do. I have always loved the chase of the stag and the boar, or the hare in the meadow with a pair of fleet hounds in fast pursuit. Barak once again fell into a moment or so of deep thought. 'Do you also enjoy these things boy, do you enjoy the hunt,' the giant asked honestly and plainly.

Tark gave a very enthusiastic nod. 'Of course I do Barak I am a Krozaky so I like nothing better,' the young man replied keenly.

Barak for a moment went once again silent and he seemed to drift off to another place a distant place. After a while in his deep musings the giant began to speak once again.

'Well anyway we planned that night on the very next morning we would rise from our beds early and ride out together to hunt the red stag. I still remember it even now as though it were yesterday. I could barely sleep that night just thinking of the excitement of it all. Next morning we took my father's two best dogs, a pair of black snake headed beasts bred from the hardiest, the fastest of all the steppes hunting dogs.

'My father's and his fathers before, it was their forebears who had brought these swift dogs with them when our people were still no more than nomadic warring tribesmen,' Barak declared this with a growl. This, as the giant was, a man who was ever proud of the Krozaky's fierce steppes heritage. 'Do you know the lake road, the winding road that leads up into the tall pine forest, Tark?'

Tark gave a positive nod.

'Aye I know it only too well, I fish that cold deep lake whenever I do have any free time on my hands. '

'Good, then that makes the story all the easier to tell,' Barak said puffing out ever more clouds of smoke from his clay pipe. 'Well, well on that morning we set out before the cock even crowed its noisy annoying wakening call. At that time it was midsummer and also it was a most glorious morning. Already the mountain mists that lay in the deep valley had begun to clear as the early morning sun burnt them away. Through the night there had been a brief but most violent summer storm, this had lasted no more than an hour, if even that. Anyway along the lake road we raced head on my father and myself at a furious gallop, both upon fast fiery spirited black stallions. These stallions were bought at some cost I must say from Arab horse dealers. But believe me boy, these animals were bought with my father's own coin.' Barak did not want Tark to think the tax payers' money had been spent on such a lavish uncalled for luxury. Such liberties put down as expenses, well these were reserved for magistrates and all of the other official vultures. 'My father's horse was young and only part broke, it was a bigger, faster thing than mine. As well as this it had also bolted to boot, the creature was off and away and had galloped a short distance ahead of me. ' Once again at this point the giant seemed agitated and most unsettled as he puffed away with gusto on his pipe. 'In a bend in the road by the old dead black tree, the tree that has stood in that place forever, well the wind from the storm had brought down a less robust tree. 'Barak paused painfully, seemingly recalling those last few moments of his father's existence. 'I remember my father looking back at me as he galloped on, his face was so joyous at that time. At least I suppose his last living moments in this world were not ones of grief and sorrow. ' Barak cleared his throat and he seemed to struggle somewhat with his words for just a moment or two.

At length and after a little while, the slayer once again continued with his sad tale.

'Well his horse it shied, aye the beast jinked suddenly away from the fallen tree and my father was thrown heavily to the ground. As you more than likely know he was a very big man. Anyway my father landed very hard and very badly.' Barak paused for a moment as he sucked upon his pipe, the great ogre now looked increasingly gloomy and sad. After another long puff upon his pipe then once again Barak spoke. 'After that heavy fall your father's king, and my own father well he alas smiled no more. Barak once again stalled for a moment in gloomy reflection. 'Neither did I, well at least not for a very long time.' Barak now turned his attention once again to the big gelding as he most gently stroked its muzzle. 'From his dead finger I took this very ring.' Barak said while showing the young man the eagle crest of their country. 'This gold ring he wore upon the middle finger of his right hand as do I,' the killer said showing the young warrior the ring. 'It is the two headed eagle, it is the symbol of our ancient clan, the very symbol of our people. Dare I say it; it is I suppose the symbol of my kingship.' Barak paused as he stroked the great head of his war horse as it nuzzled gently up to him. Slowly the giant then turned his face towards the great beast hiding his emotions from the young man. After all, the ogre well he supposed he did still have a bad reputation to keep. Moments later after a cough and a sneeze the

178

ogre put down hay for the big horse, then Barak spoke up once again. 'Anyway as you no doubt know, Tark son of Atark, my father he was burnt upon a high funeral pyre and turned into ash. Aye and also that mighty fire I so clearly remember, it seemed to scorch the very midnight sky itself. This though at day's end, well it was what my father wanted upon his death. So of course Tark, this being the case, this was what the King had to have, his last wish. '

Barak next coughed, spat and then took himself a drink of vodka from his gourd. Tark politely declined the offer of a drink from the ogre and so Barak said on.

'Straightway, the nobles, the magistrates and the high born social climbers bickered and argued amongst one and other. Each, all and every one of them, well they were all looking to secure ever more power and influence, for themselves aye and for themselves alone. Oh aye these worthless carrion argued and haggled thus even as my father still smouldered away upon his funeral pyre. I spat as I cursed each all and every single one of them,' Barak said hatefully and angrily. 'It was for themselves, and themselves alone these fools had aspirations for mind you. Oh aye these worthless dogs had not one single thought for the common people, no, none at all. ' Barak this said then spat onto the deck in hatred and contempt, next the slayer ground the spittle into the boards with a booted foot. 'My brother Zark was ever sickly pale and weak, he had fallen into a dreamlike sleep at this time. Looking back now as I do so often of recent, I wonder to myself if this slumber was perhaps not induced by the black lily. But no, then again this treachery and treason perhaps did not happen at that time. No Tark, of course I am being foolish and suspicious, as it was much later when things went wrong in his life I think. '

Barak paused in gloomy reflection, perhaps the giant was thinking what could have been, aye and also just what might have been had he stayed and not rode off into the wild.

'Anyway for better or for the worse I rode away from that place. My home, my brother, my country and kingdom, I left behind me. Life in the palace and the great halls with its courtroom full of deceit and lies was not for me, no not one bit of it. Know you this the palace. It was stifling and was becoming more corrupt with the passing of my father. Also such places, well they lacked the honesty and the honour of a battlefield. Not of course that I had ever been on one Tark, but only because I was too young mind you.' Barak then sighed and shrugged, the slayer next puffed again upon his long pipe.

'Alas boy, I am a man who can run only his own life in some sort of order, Tark,' the giant explained honestly. 'Being so the very idea of presiding and ruling over thousands of souls, this I found more than a little daunting. I never wanted to be a king, no I only wanted to hunt, to fish and throw myself giddily into any battle that was afoot. Aye it was adventure that I sought then in those far off days, not affairs of state. I wanted to spend my time with heroes not

179

cowards and most certainly not dangerous liars. Barak refilled the water buckets then he walked the line of horses yet again. 'In truth though Tark, there are times now that I do wonder very much to myself. Aye I wonder to myself did I do the right thing riding off as I did, was I indeed wrong in my actions? My father had often said to me he would trade his palace most gladly for a woodsman's lodge and the freedom to work and to roam wherever it was he chose to go. Indeed, it was with these thoughts in the back of my mind I rode off out into the vast unknown. It was with these thoughts I rode out into the vast wild wilderness, perhaps my boy I was wrong,' Barak said again with a shrug. 'After all at the end of it, I am but a man just as you are. Me, I am not a god I am not a demon nor am I a devil. Oh and also perhaps I am not now even a king, Tark son of Atark.'

Barak was a man who could ever and always win men over with his openness and his honesty when it was well applied. Now also as it so happened it was these very frank straight spoken words that now brought the hitherto proud young warrior down onto his knees.

'You wear the ring of kingship my high Lord Barak, aye and I say to you now that you are my Lord and also my king. With this being so my Lord, then I do now swear I will serve you, you and no other,' Tark said this most passionately as well as most humbly. 'My life it is forever yours, it is yours to command unto my very death. I do swear this now upon the ring of our people. I Tark, son of Atark will serve you as my father served your father king Bartok, right up until the very end of it all.'

Barak raised his dark eyebrows in surprise at this sudden turn of events, and then the ogre gave out a grunt and a low growl of satisfaction.

'Good, aye good enough boy, but get up now Tark, you must never kneel before me or anyone. Oh no, oh no never kneel, not to me and like I say not to anyone for that matter. For one thing you will surely get a bad back, for another too much bending will make your breeches baggy,' the giant said with a grim smile.

Tark at once arose, next the young warrior bowed slightly then pulled himself up to his full height whilst he blew out his ample chest.

'I will tell you all it is that you want to know my Lord,' he announced with another bow of his head. 'First of all I will tell you that the man who is called Bull Neck discovered a dagger hidden in my boot, he chose to say nothing and he let me keep it.'

Barak once again raised his black eyebrows, in mock surprise this time.

'Oh surely not, well I always knew he was a treacherous dog,' the giant hissed as he turned about and glanced over his shoulder. Even now Bull Neck was eagerly watching what transpired between Barak and the black clad assassin, also perhaps at this particular time the stammering fool was also praying. Would the

180

black clad warrior give him away or would he suddenly plunge the dagger into the giant's heart he wondered? Indeed, did the warrior even recall that it was he Bull Neck who had searched him? For at that moment in time Tark was only in a semi-conscious state, these were thoughts which would trouble the oafish traitor for some time yet to come.

'Never mind boy, at day's end that fool will get what he is long overdue soon enough,' Barak said as he turned his head about to face his new recruit.

'I would kill him for you now my Lord, aye this could be my first task for you,' the young man offered very eagerly. Barak though had other plans for the treasonous Bull Neck.

'Thank you but no, oh no my boy, that as you put it is a task I am saving for myself.'

So it was that afternoon on the dragon ship Tark pledged his undying allegiance to his new lord and master, his new found king. Later on throughout the long perilous trek Tark would further enlighten Barak as to the treachery and the intrigues of corrupt and current palace life.

On that night the Falcon did not dock, but instead the dragon ship sailed on ever eastward. Barak he had now taken Tark under his wing and the men talked much as Barak as ever prepared the evening meal. Tark however did find it very strange that his king was cooking for a ship full of big bearded barbarian pirates. But then again over these next weeks and months the young warrior would find so many other things that were so very strange and very different about the giant Barak.

But in the meanwhile, well, a would be back stabber was most uneasy as he went about his daily duties.

Bull Neck was a fool but he was still ever watchful, the oaf was perhaps aware of the new found friendship between the black clad assassin and Barak. But then again he thought to himself, was this merely a clever ruse by Tark to make his mission to slay the giant a little simpler. These troubled thoughts would cause the oafish Bull Neck to lose much sleep in the future weeks and months ahead.

Meanwhile as Bull Necks pea sized brain caused him much grief Barak had slowly roasted a dozen piglets over the braziers. Also the ogre had laid out wooden plates of fruit and boiled vegetables to keep away scurvy and thus provide a balanced nutritious diet for the mainly flesh eating Vikings.

As an added bonus there were water melons, dates coconuts apples and oranges, this as well as carrots turnips and garlic cloves to thin down the blood.

Thus in his own way Barak strove to keep the unhealthy, healthy, this if only by a better diet.

Hastily the Vikings, who were ever ravenous things devoured all in sight, even all of the fruit and vegetables. With this done the Northmen next washed their food down with a large quantity of good German ale. Lothar, he had very kindly sent them on their way with several barrels of beer, aye and at cost price at that. And also as well as that piece of generosity the fat German had further thrown in two large skins of his best vodka for Barak. This was a gift that had of course greatly pleased the toothsore giant, and as for Lothar well he was now rated of course a true friend.

'Where is big Borz by the way? I have not seen that fat drunken waster nor have I heard you talk of him Ragnor?' Barak asked as they sat about drinking and feasting. 'Does he perhaps captain another dragon boat for you Ragnor? And if not where then is the great oaf?' Barak enquired as he leaned back against his saddle while he blew smoke into the chill night air.

Borz was a good man, aye also he was a good friend of Ragnor's in fact they had grown up together and sailed the oceans for oh so many years. Barak quite rightly thought it was strange the big fat jovial Viking was not sailing with them on such a hazardous mission.

Ragnor swallowed down a mouthful of beer then he spat and cleared his throat before speaking in reply to Barak's question.

'Ice bear, it was an ice bear that took him off, we were high up in the Arctic Circle by Svalbard. No Barak we were even past that frozen place,' Ragnor said more than a little sadly. 'There we were trapped by the ice, we were held fast for a full month or more even. Aye we could not move the Falcon one way or another even though I had men working day and night breaking the ice from around the Falcon's hull. And this just so the vessel was not crushed by the ice you understand? Ragnor grumbled. Barak at this time was sat down smoking and drinking and of course already fearing the worst. 'Aye freezing it was, without doubt the coldest that I can ever remember it. No I tell you Barak I have never known such a bitter cold like it. ' There was now a rumble of agreement from those few of Ragnor's men who had survived that freezing ordeal.

'We lived upon fish that we caught through holes bored into the sea, sometimes we caught the odd seal which we ate raw, we had no wood to burn you understand. ' Ragnor gave off a shiver at the very thought of that freezing winter. 'Anyway one day Borz was fishing alone when an ice bear, a huge white thing with eyes blacker than even yours took him off, quite simply he was never seen again. Aye I do remember the day well, if only I could forget it,' Ragnor said gloomily. 'Borz was alone but from where I stood at the bow of the boat I could see him sitting upon an old metal bucket smoking his pipe as he fished away patiently. I shouted and I waved to him unaware of the danger, he waved back with that silly toothless smile of his across his big fat hairy face, then the next moment he was gone forever. I watched it, a snow white monster dragging him away into the icy mists of beyond. I could do nothing, nothing, the beast was too fast, too strong and Borz he was alas gone forever. ' Ragnor said this in a low mutter his big heart was once again breaking with the very sadness of his good friend's demise.

ON hearing this sad news the ogre puffed the faster upon his pipe and drank the deeper of his vodka. As it happened the slayer was particularly fond of the honest, brave, and ever jovial Borz.

'Aye Borz, he was not only a brave man he was also a good honest man. ' Barak said this most sincerely whilst raising his voice as well as his cup of vodka in salute to the unfortunate pirate. 'Aye, a good man, a good Viking and also he was a good friend to each and all aboard the Falcon,'' Ragnor roared out in total agreement. All there of the savage brotherhood next also raised their drinks to the memory of the well liked helmsman.

That night Tark listened intently to every word spoken, the young man was no fool, he had already acquired a good command of both the Norse and the language of the Britons. Tark listened carefully, saying very little but learning much, with the passing of each and every day the young man became more educated in the ways of these big hairy carefree barbarians.

Obviously these were well travelled men that by fate, as well as accident, he had thrown in with. Many of the longest served men had sailed to places that to him seemed quite impossible. Unbelievable places, places that were neither charted or recorded by either map or even word of mouth. The Norse spoke of a land inhabited by beardless red men that dressed in skins and feathers, these red skinned black haired men knew not of iron or steel or armour. Their far away land apparently teemed with all manner of game and their many rivers overflowed with fish. Here there were deserts, forests and mountain ranges, vast plains that made the never ending steppes just seem as nothing. When Tark was alone with Barak he had decided to learn more of this distant place, but not now, oh no, now was not at all the time.

Anyway the night wore on and sleep eventually overtook them all one by one. And as all slumbered the big hunchback Loki steered the Falcon as it soared speedily across the grey waves like some great phantom. On that following night Ragnor suggested they would put in somewhere to eat and drink. Also by mooring up this would give the horses a chance to stretch their legs and eat fresh grass before they sickened. Perhaps the Falcon would dock only once after this stop before arriving at length at the headland on the eastern coast. Or then again mayhap this would be the very last stop. Either way it would be there on a shingle beach where the Northmen must leave the Falcon and travel for many weeks and months overland.

Chapter Thirteen

It was dusk when the Falcon pulled into the small port that was set in a sheltered, most cosy welcoming cove. The men at once tied up alongside similar types of ships as their own, of course though these vessels were nowhere near as fast as the Falcon. There were some half a dozen raiders from Jutland and Friesland already moored along the harbour wall, the ships bobbed up and down in the rising tide. These boats were sleek well crafted vessels and were not unlike the Falcon at all in shape or styling. However, these were smaller vessels, vessels which were more designed for rivers than the open sea. The owners of these longboats were apparently in high spirits as their out of tune singing could be heard even as the Falcon was secured with its thick ropes to the iron mooring pegs of the ancient well used harbour.

'We are in for a good night Barak' Ragnor said, his hairy face beaming with anticipation and delight. 'I know these rogues, aye these men they too hunted Wraif,' Ragnor said waving the dead man's chain at Barak. 'But it was us who took him, it was we who took the prize, he and his sea dogs are dead by our hand, our hand alone. Aye and all of this without a single man of ours lost,' Ragnor said proudly.

Barak did not smile or did he gloat on hearing these words, the ogre merely gave a solemn nod. At day's end to his eternal regret he had after all slain six of his own countrymen. Six of his own citizens, six of his own warriors that night he had butchered and Barak had not cherished that sad fact at all. Perhaps, the giant had thought to himself later after the fray that he could have perhaps played that bloody onslaught another way. Aye and then mayhap he would have had those six dead warriors at his back now as well as young Tark. Still though what was done was done and of course it could not be changed or be undone. The dead of course were dead forever, the dead could not be brought back to life, or could they?

'I still have much to learn from young Tark,' Barak said to Ragnor as they headed off down the busy street that ran the full length of the harbour walls. And I think also my friend that you yourself have much to boast about in these crowded taverns. You know, with the unfortunate Wraif's sudden if not sad demise,' the giant added with a cynical grin.

Ragnor did not disagree he merely gave a very cheery smile then a nod of understanding at the giant's truthful statement.

'Aye you are as ever quite correct with your guesswork Barak my friend, but to me now you do seem a little lost. Tell me is all well with you Barak?' Ragnor had asked this question after Tark left them and wandered off to buy drink as well as some smoked eels and four roast chickens for supper.

'Yes Ragnor I am fine, all is well,' Barak answered perhaps a little unconvincingly. 'Please my friend, do not concern yourself about me. But tonight it is my intention to learn the full meaning of this plotting, scheming outrage then I will know how better we all stand in this sad business. I have made many mistakes in the past, now I feel it is time to atone in some way for my many sins. Believe me Ragnor I am only sorry that I had to involve you in this messy most complicated affair. For believe me there is still much danger ahead to come my hairy red bearded friend. Aye Perhaps even more danger than you might care to think of. ' After making this somewhat long winded statement the giant it must be said looked more than a little glum.

Ragnor though, knowing the giant's moods, well the big burly Viking merely laughed out long and loud at the slayer's words. Aye and this was a true Norse laugh, a blustery, carefree, could not care less laugh. And then before the laughter died the big Viking clapped the giant upon his broad shoulder.

'My good friend, life it must have its dangers, it must have its pitfalls, aye even its very end no matter how brutal Barak. Because else and otherwise, well I suppose it is not worth the living, is it?' The big Viking laughed loudly once again as he boomed these words out loudly and honestly. 'Why Barak if I die upon this day or this very night, then I care not one bit', the Viking laughed. 'The worthless man that I hunted, well he is a dead and gone thing now. So now my friend with my own task completed I am now a most happy man. And now, well now we will finish the rest of our dangerous quest, finish it together.' Ragnor as ever was brash and uncaring, and aye indeed he was typical of the very best of his kind. 'You are better than a brother to me Barak, also at day's end we both know that we should have been dead things many years ago.'

As it happened, Barak, well the ogre agreed with every word spoken by the big boisterous Norseman. 'Anyway besides all of that my large friend, will you return to the boat with your new fawning recruit Barak?' the Viking asked jokingly.

Barak gave a most positive nod of his big head then he even afforded the big Viking a thin smile.

'Aye together myself and Tark will stand the first watch, not that I suppose one is needed. We will talk, the young warrior from the Black Guard and I, then tomorrow my hairy friend you will know just as much as I do.'

Once again the big men grinned broadly then the warriors clenched their hands in honest friendship, they said no more.

So the friends parted company and after the customary grunt and a nod they then went their separate ways. Ragnor, well he headed off with all his crew to the nearest noisy tavern to meet up with the Jutes, the Geats, the Friesians and all of the other sea going rogues. And then once there with a drink in his hand no doubt the Norseman would indulge himself in a bit of bragging and boasting, for of course after all he had a story to tell. And with his flair for the dramatic the big Viking was more than keen to tell it. Tonight he supposed to himself neither he, nor any of his crew of rough ready rogues would be putting their hand in their pockets very much. In the meanwhile both Barak and Tark returned to the Falcon with their smoked eels and their roast chickens to feast upon. For some time the two men sat relaxed by one of the braziers aboard the Falcon. Here the men warmed themselves and here they talked with some ease about fleet horses fast brave dogs, aye and of course about the hunting of the boar and bear. All of this the men spoke of, this as well as the fishing for the giant salmon that abounded in the many rivers of their far off homeland.

At length after all this lighthearted talk Tark felt comfortable in the company of his new king and mentor. It was then the young man began to talk in some detail as to the constant plotting and underhanded scheming going on within the Krozaky palace.

Of course for years there had always been talk throughout all of Krozakistan of the now notorious legendary Barak. Talk of his great adventures, his conquests, wars, battles and his duels with both men and monsters alike were epic affairs. Barak had become notorious, a living legend who was without doubt the greatest slayer who walked the known earth. No creature could best him and no man could stand against him with lance or sword, or anything else come to think of it. But even so, it was still also true that no man could stand against the ravages of time forever. And now at fifty years of age surely he was a spent and a somewhat jaded force. Surely now after all these years the great slayer must be weakening, tiring, not now could he be the man of fable that he once was. Now surely the living legend must be growing old and sodden with the endless drink he swallowed and the black weed he constantly puffed upon day in and day out. Aye, surely now his keen mind along with his huge body must be sent weak by the powerful weed he was reported to smoke almost nonstop.

Well that was at least what the schemers and the would-be rulers of Krozakistan were relying on, aye it was this simple fact that these deceivers had all banked upon. However, these men were fools though, for Barak was just as big bold and as strong as ever he had been. Aye, the great ogre had neither mellowed with the coming of age nor had he become fat and jaded. No the slayer was indeed still the same man, still the myth aye and perhaps even the same monster of fireside stories he had ever been.

Anyway this detail aside, apparently, and according to Tark there were two brothers who were the main plotters and deceivers in this sinister underhanded affair of treachery, deceit and corruption. These brothers had hoped, if not expected for Barak to either die on his passage through on his perilous route to save the Prince. Or perhaps he would be provoked into a swordfight; this no doubt by a foolish Roman gladiator with an over active mouth. Oh yes the brothers' influence was far reaching and the giant's approach had apparently been well broadcasted. Thus many things many events were now slipping slowly but surely into place. Should and could Barak despite all and everything manage to return to his kingdom, to overcome the threat of fools who overestimated themselves. Also should he survive the lurking groups of assassins which no doubt would dog his long perilous journey. Well these slight drawbacks, as well as the wild man-eating beasts of the forests and the mountains the ogre must encounter on his trek. Once there in his homeland should he ever reach it, well there was always the age old method of the poison in the cup or the arrow in the back. One thing however these conspirators had not reckoned on was the still unwavering awesome power of the man who would at length confront them. Time it seemed had in no way been a great enemy of Barak. No the great ogre was still much as he had ever been, the slayer had neither weakened nor had he even mellowed.

In the meanwhile the young, much won over Tark was more than confident of the people, both the common folk as well as the vast formidable Krozak militia. All of these would embrace Barak as their King and their saviour. Well, this once the people as well as the rank and file had seen and met with him.

Tark went on and explained as to how the two brothers had tricked bribed and threatened their way into a position of power. Those who would gainsay or challenge the brothers in any way either met with some grizzly horrible death or else simply just went missing altogether.

As for the Prince Zark, well he was just as weak and sickly in body as he had always been, apparently Barak's brother was a tall pale withdrawn figure who was seldom even seen or heard of. Zark was of course no warrior; no the Prince was an artist a poet and also apparently an inventor of strange machines even. Still though the Prince to his credit had a love for his people, however he seemed unable to muster the strength to resist the dangerous brothers and their many lackeys. Indeed the Prince Zark was a man who was very much alone, alone with no one to either turn to or rely on. Oh aye these brothers through their devious conniving and their murderous ways had made quite sure of that. Tark swallowed down his smoked eel, the young man was now beginning to enjoy their strange burnt flavour. Quickly the young warrior washed the smoked eel down with some beer then he spoke up once again.

'I also fear our journey back to the land of your people, my Lord, will not go totally unhindered,' Tark said this more than a little gloomily. 'As alas the brothers they have gypsies, rogues, cut throats and thieves in their employ. Oh aye my Lord the brothers have deserters and backstabbers a plenty to aid in their deceit. On our overland journey to meet with the brigand Wraif by the shore of the Dead Sea we camped at each night fall with many a cut throat. These unworthy scum were all paid for and bought men by the brothers, it was these men who fed and guided us to the coast. '

Barak as ever was most attentive, missing nothing. The ogre let the young man say on without any sort of interruption.

'Aye another thing my lord Barak, when we left the garrison gates we were a hundred men strong, Black Guard warriors all. But yet only I and the other six of the brotherhood made it to the sea to meet with the pirate Wraif. And by the way our passage to the shore was well guarded we had only the wild beasts to settle with my Lord Barak, not the renegades who will doubtless be in wait for us.'

The giant smiled broadly, but still he said nothing, the ogre finished off his own smoked eel wiped his greasy hands on a rag, then he lit up his much used pipe.

After a few relaxing puffs upon his beloved pipe, followed by a big swig of vodka Barak then spoke up in a slow and deliberate fashion.

'You forget Tark that I have already made this long perilous journey once before, you also forget I was alone then. Aye and also I was nothing then but a gangly spotty boy at that time, younger than you are even now. '

Tark went silent, the young warrior did not want to even imagine how he himself could have possibly fared on such a long dangerous journey alone. Why this homeward trek was going to be bad enough in the company of the good brave warriors he was in league with now. Barak smiled most casually then the ogre sighed, in truth the slayer now looked a most relaxed man. With a sigh the ogre took a drink of vodka then he laid his big bucket head back upon his expensive Arab saddle relaxing himself. Barak, well the slayer now looked like a man without a single care in the whole world.

'Trust me boy we will prevail, aye you must trust me lad we will win through. For my hairy rogues, well these brave souls are quite simply much bigger and much more dangerous than the other rogues we might meet up with on our path home. Aye these Vikings despite all and everything else are damn good at killing people' the ogre said with a wry smile. Tark now swallowed down a piece of chicken then halved the carcase and shared it with Barak's big dogs and in a gulp all was gone. 'Aye and also we have as a further insurance my good faithful, somewhat slightly unhinged animals?' Barak suddenly went on. 'Well my boy, I would match each of my pets for courage against any savage forest beasts, for they are fearless things that have so far never let me down.'

Tark at this particular moment in time had no answer to Barak's positive most confident words. And so the young warrior merely shook his head in sheer wonderment at the giant's apparent indifference to their somewhat dire situation. Next each man swallowed down a mouthful of vodka as they both suddenly laughed out loudly together at the dangers that lay still somewhere ahead for them. Tark very wisely declined a puff upon his king's pipe He did this most politely of course. As now, well the young man was drinking more than ever he had done in his life and also he did not want to add the sins of smoking to his bad habits. Aye over these last few days while in his king's company Tark had barely been fully sober. So now the last thing the young warrior wanted was to start smoking as well as the heavy drinking. As to Barak's strong black weed, well that extra indulgence would surely kill him off before the rest of the adventure had even begun.

Anyway, after a rough raucous night with the Geats and the pirates from Jutland, Ragnor along with his men made their way more than a little unsteadily back to the Falcon to sleep off their night's free drink. Even before the Vikings awoke that following morning the horses which had been grazing all night inside a walled field by the side of the harbour had been secured back aboard the vessel. Sven and Stefan, well these lads were proving to be more than capable grooms, the horses were always well fed, well watered and well cared for. Yes the boys in many ways were indeed proving to be a great asset on this trek. Barak, as well as their uncle Ragnor were both well impressed with them.

Fortune favoured Barak as the wind on that morning's sail picked up, it blew well in their favour and it was barely daylight when the Falcon slipped silently out of the harbour.

For three days and three nights, the brisk wind carried them along speedily ever nearer the distant shore where the men would at length leave the Falcon beached. This once done then the warriors would make their way through forests over mountains and across deep treacherous rivers as well as the vast steppes and the barren deserts.

However, on the fourth day of their voyage a fierce storm brewed tossing the Falcon about so badly that neither man nor beast could scarce keep their footing. Still though as good luck would have it the Falcon was only hours away from what would be their last civilized stopping place on their sea voyage. As the storm raged the fierce wind coupled with the rain almost cut their weather beaten faces apart. Despite this hindrance Ragnor expertly steered his dragon headed longboat between the harbour's narrow sea walls into and alongside the huge stone walls of the harbour proper.

Then with this done the ship was at once quickly well secured to the stout moorings in that ancient sheltered Baltic dock. At once the horses were unloaded then the beasts were found comfortable shelter. Hastily the animals were fed with hay and grain in a large but rickety stable at the back of a roomy old coach house called the Whale Inn. From here in this prosperous harbour wagons took fish, crabs, lobsters and the like as well as the spoils of the sea raiders inland. Aye inland these hard earned spoils of the sea and the less hard worked for stolen booty went into the busy markets, villages and towns of the unruly hinterland. Then with this task once done only a little while later these wagons would make their return journey. However this time though carrying a different cargo, now they returned with grain, bread and red venison meat aboard. Aye this, as well as towing along behind them livestock, beasts such as cattle, sheep, pigs horses and goats.

Apparently according to Ragnor this bustling port was the last Roman stronghold along the wild Baltic. And also it was a garrison town that fair heaved with thriving activity, second only in size to the Hundsruck.

These next few days here, well the place would be even more crowded, somewhat busier than usual. It was that time of year for the slave fair, all would make money here, all would be happy and prosperous. Well that of course was unless you happened to be a slave. However, this of course was a somewhat unsavoury event which nevertheless was always good for the town's resident market traders and the other ever greedy businessmen who as ever lusted for money.

As always Barak was ever in charge of purchasing the meat the fruit as well as also all of the vegetables which would be required for the rest of their still long perilous journey. His own supplies of fruit and vegetables and the others which had been purchased along the way had all been consumed over these last few days. So, this final intake of food, drink and also of course weed would have to last them all until the warriors next hit land. Once there the intrepid party of Norsemen would begin to hunt down their own food.

Only in some cases when the Vikings eventually landed at the far off shore, then their prey food would in turn also be hunting them. Still though that was a problem that could be worried about on another day, as for now once the weather cleared the giant would familiarize himself with this packed thriving market place. The food, well that must be bought at the last minute and could be awhile away yet as there was no telling as to how long this storm would last.

Barak secured for both himself and Tark a room above the coach house which stabled the horses. It was not as expensive as Barak had thought it might be, in fact truth said it was free. As the innkeeper, well the fellow was no different to any other in the innkeeping trade. He was fat, shrewd and with very few teeth in his big bald head, but nevertheless the man had a bulging money belt. And also the innkeeper being a shrewd man knew only too well the notorious fearsome painted giant was good for business. However this was a simple fact that did not concern the great slayer in the least. As Barak at this particular time in the journey, well he sought only warmth and comfort. For the ogre knew only too well they still had much sailing ahead, aye and also much hardship after that sail. And so this place, well here was his last chance to lie in a soft bed then take a hot bath in the mornings before he sat down to eat his ample breakfeast. And quite honestly the ogre well he intended to make the most of his stay here in this storm battered place.

In every tavern along the harbour, even in the other drinking houses in the winding back alleys of the prosperous bustling town there was standing room only, not a seat or a table in sight. Every stick of furniture had been removed to allow more customers into the premises and of course what was not there could not be broken. Every stable housed both men as well as beasts seeking shelter from the fierce storm that had even grounded the ever screeching hungry sea gulls.

Ragnor posted his non-smoking men with the horses, this so that no fool there would fall asleep with a charged up pipe. Also in these wild parts, horse thieves just as well as pirates were in abundance. With this being the case the beasts must be well guarded lest desperate rogues try to make off with them in the middle of the night. After all the Norsemen had carried and tended these horses so far, soon it would be their turn to return the favour and earn their corn.

'It looks like this bad weather could last for some days Barak.' Tark said this after both he and Barak had left a public Roman sauna. Now both of the men at this time were feeling quite clean and pink, indeed they were much refreshed after their long hot sudsy soak.

Barak gave a grunt of agreement as he looked skyward at the black storm clouds as they raced ever rapidly by.

'Aye boy I do think you are right on that score. You know a man he can fight the beasts of the woods, the serpents in the sea, or even armed men with a sword in their hand and hatred in their eyes. But believe me no man can fight the forces of nature, no man can fight the elements,' the giant answered profoundly.

'Not even you my Lord Barak?' Tark asked with a cheeky smile.

'No, no lad no, not even me' Barak grinned, the ogre he supposed was beginning to like this young man. 'So forget the weather for now, come with me my boy. I will buy you your drink and we will roam the taverns here in this place whatever it is called. Then lad we will see what we will see and we will hear what we will hear. For believe me it is an uncertain thing if we will ever pass this way again. Barak said this while looking up at the ever darkening skies. 'Better still boy, here, you can buy the drinks.'

Barak next pushed a heavy purse of Roman silver coins into the young man's hand.

'Do not protest, do not say anything. I am your king remember, therefore I must be obeyed in all things?' Barak said this as he smiled down at the young man.

As already said Barak had begun to like the young man, anyway the ogre thought it would be nice for someone else to buy the drinks for a change. And this even if it was with his own money. Tark well he had also at the same time grew to like admire and even worship his giant monarch more with each passing day.

Barak using his keen instincts in turn now also trusted the assassin not to stab him in the back. And of course he had also learned much about his brother without even being bullish in any way. A little bit of information here, a little bit of information there, everything now was slowly but surely patching itself together into place. Either way it was apparent these devious brothers were behind everything bad and treacherous that had so far transpired in Barak's kingdom. Zark his brother, well he apparently was merely a puppet in their hands, no more that, he was only a pawn in a very dangerous game. In complete contrast to Barak the prince was unwell, he was by all accounts a weak feeble creature. Indeed Barak's younger sibling was quite unsure of what was happening all about him. Still though, even with all of his failings and falterings the Prince Zark had, according to Tark, entered himself into a much prized and esteemed tournament of the longbow. Aye and then to everyone's' surprise and amazement the prince had won it. This contest which was held every year was an open invite to any man in the land, any archer be he common or noble or otherwise. It was a contest to try their hand at a series of targets both tiny objects and fast moving things. Apparently the prince's marksmanship was uncanny and it had transpired he was a master archer and a bowman without compare. Zark had beaten the much despised brothers who had between them won the contest for the past five years or so.

Tark himself had entered the competition in the past along with other members of the Black Guards. And while always being in the last dozen of a thousand entrants Tark to his shame and disgust could never manage to beat the much despised brothers. So for Zark to succeed in such a win of marksmanship over the decadent, very dangerous siblings, well this was indeed a great achievement. As expected the brothers however had of course not been in any way noble in defeat, no far from it. Both of them had cursed Zark and cried out aloud in their private chambers. Then in their rage and fury the siblings had beaten their cringing servants whilst in an orgy of drink and opium.

Barak on hearing this was for his part beginning to dislike and despise these brothers more with every conversation he had with Tark. But little by little the ogre was also starting to understand the workings of his own brother. Well at least Barak liked to think he was beginning to understand.

For two more days then two more nights the wind and the rain raged, aye it was as bad a storm as Barak could ever remember. In fact so dark was it that indeed it was hard to tell the night time from the day. Roof tiles crashed down onto the cobbles killing more than one man, trees were uprooted and toppled to the ground. Why two huge Roman galleys slipped their moorings, smashed together then sank into the harbours waters with only the top of their masts visible. This of course was a Roman misfortune which it must be said brought a broad smile to Ragnor's red bearded face. So fierce was the storm the parade of slaves in the town square was put off until better weather arrived. After all no one there wanted to buy a snotty shivering thing that might die on them.

As ever and always the tavern keepers prospered, these shrewd men praying for more wind and rain, this of course to contain their many sheltering customers. Ragnor on seeing the prosperous smiling innkeepers once again relentlessly pestered Barak to buy in with him in the Half Moon Inn.

But Barak had merely smiled, the ogre had then advised him they had best conclude their present affair before setting out upon yet another one. Still the two friends talked and drank while they diced on a tavern's bar counter. After all there was nothing else that anyone could do but wait out the storm. So as the men had so often done in the past they would all just have to sit out the weather and just make the best of it. Oh and of course as ever still enjoy themselves while they tarried there.

Upon the morning of the fifth day at the harbour town which was by the by known as Varnak, the sun shone brightly as the wind and rain finally abated, all now was as calm as a mid-summers day. Now, now it was time to buy in the supplies that would be needed for the rest of the journey.

Barak arose at first light and at once the giant quickly washed, shaved then dressed himself. Now the ogre as ever was most keen to be about his business of bartering in the narrow winding streets of the busy market. Barak loved nothing more than to trade, to haggle with the storekeepers and street traders over fruit meat and livestock, aye and he was good at it too. Though Ragnor was always most quick to point out that Barak mostly received his goods cheaply because the market traders were merely afraid of him. Most bargains were obtained cheaply quite simply because the traders felt too intimidated to haggle quite as fiercely as was their norm with other less fearsome looking customers. However, this was an accusation of course that Barak both resented and most strongly denied.

Tark was by now Barak's most constant companion. The young warrior was given back his weapons as Barak had charged him with the honour of guarding the king. Which as it so happened in this particular case, well of course it was his good and noble self.

This day the very last that was to be spent at the bustling harbour town of Varnak was of course a most important one. As there must be provisions bought that would be fresh and not overripe, these meats and fruits must both last and not rot. The live animals to be slaughtered later for food, these creatures must be strong, healthy and free from any disease. Because of course these beasts must be strong enough to survive the remainder of the voyage to feed the ravenous Norsemen. So livestock, such as chickens, geese and other wildfowl would have to be both fat and in good condition. As also would any goats that were to be purchased. Barak as has already been said was particularly most partial to goat meat. Aye also any prepared meat purchased from the market traders would need to be fresh killed and salted. As the flesh, well it was good for only two or three days at the very most. Barak followed by Tark with his two great dogs in tow moved freely through the crowded streets and alleys of the bustling harbour town. As the masses of buyers, sellers as well as the townspeople that had gathered parted gingerly at the giant's approach. Varnak it was not a German town, though it was of course populated by more Germans than those of any other nationality. Indeed Varnak was a most bohemian, most cosmopolitan place. Arabs, Turks, Spaniards even Egyptians were everywhere, moving all about the busy streets and the narrow winding alleys. The sounds and scents of Asia and of the Orient as well as those from both eastern as well as western Europe were everywhere and all about them. Barak well for now he at least quite liked and supposed he was enjoying this lively very interesting place.

Behind the giant and Tark there followed a very large fat man with a big fat bulbous purple nose. This fat man drove a four wheeled mule cart, and this fat man was also a very drunk, very loud fellow. He was of course a German; the noisy fool was also not surprisingly called Horst. Loudly the driver of the mules shouted in a most blustery abusive fashion for the crowd to move aside and be out of his way. Perhaps the perspiring fat man would not have been so bold and blustery had his business not been with the giant? Anyway the fat man was sat behind two ancient worn out mules, these sad overworked underfed beasts drew behind them the large flat four wheeled cart. And it was this rickety badly maintained conveyance that carried the supplies Barak had so far bought on that cold but fresh sunny morning.

Makeshift wooden cages carried all manner of feathered creature. As well as these birds, several big billy goats along with a one eyed ram had been bought; this ram of course was purchased at a very bargain price. Fruit and vegetables were all there, bananas, dates, carrots, onions and turnips were all tied together in bunches, or sacked and stacked alongside the livestock. Now there was only the liquid refreshment and the feed for the animals to be located, then bought and paid for. Hay, grain, fresh water for the beasts was all purchased for a very reasonable price. All of this, as well as kegs of frothy beer for the Norse, also of course a good supply of both vodka and strong black weed from a smelly Baltic trader for Barak's own consumption. After all, if things did go sadly wrong as so often they did, then why die an unhappy man the giant had reasoned?

Barak growled angrily to himself as he picked at his broken back tooth, this tooth was once again becoming ever more troublesome and most painful with each passing day.

'Hear that Tark?' Barak asked of a sudden stopping in his tracks. 'Up ahead of us there is a commotion - sounds like a fight or perhaps it is a riot of some sort.'

With not another word spoken Barak was off with giant strides up the winding cobbled street towards the town square and the direction of the uproar. The closer Barak approached the square the greater the smell of cooked food pleasantly assailed his nostrils. Roast chicken, smoked fish and even grilled horse chestnuts his keen senses could detect. Oh yes, there were all of these aromatic appetising temptations as well as the obvious wonderful sizzling noise of a wild boar roasting over a nearby spit. Perhaps, with a little luck Barak thought to himself there was a hanging or some other merry social early morning event in progress. Either way something interesting was going on, aye and by the by it was far too soon for the slave market as that less entertaining event was not till noon. But either way it was plainly obvious to Barak something else must have packed the narrow streets out leading all the way to the town square.

Chapter Fourteen

Barak invested in a large long smoked eel as he strode along toward the noise somewhere ahead of him, the ogre swallowed the fish down almost in an instant. Why, it would be hard to suppose a big black cormorant could have done a quicker or better job of it. Still, with the hunger upon him and with a plentiful supply of food readily available almost everywhere about him. Well the giant next invested in three plump roast chickens one each for his huge dogs and of course the biggest one for himself. Tark after just breakfeasting a short while ago was not hungry and declined the offer of a roast bird. Barak looked about for his eagle which had been with him earlier she was however not at hand. Doubtless she was off somewhere now laying waste to the many seagulls flocking about the busy harbour. Without delay the big dogs devoured the chicken's carcasses, bones and all just as instantly as did their master. Indeed, if it had been an eating competition between man and beast it would have been very hard to pick a winner between them.

Tark however, well as said he did at this time not choose to dine at this particular moment, this not merely because he had no appetite. No, the sensible young man sensed danger here, any hunger he might have had, well it had suddenly left him. And anyway after all, it was always a lot easier to move with speed on an empty belly.

Barak pushed his way somewhat rudely through the mixed crowd of townsfolk as well as a dozen off duty soldiers. Of course the giant was most keen to see what all this early morning commotion was all about, as ever the ogre was not long in finding out. Now though what the great slayer suddenly saw before him contorted his face with a rage and anger. And also it brought a most fearsome snarl of displeasure to his thin scarred lips.

There before him bound upon a heavy twenty foot link chain, a chain that was secured to a stout pine pole inset deep into the cobbles a man or something that looked somewhat similar to a man struggled against three tormentors. And these three laughing fools were armed, one, with a long bull whip while the other two heroes wielded long red hot pokers. With such vicious weapons these cowardly men jabbed and lashed at the unfortunate creature with an element of safety, as they knew well both the chain's strength as well as its length. Before Barak's very eyes the trio of half drunken fools laughed out loudly and in a most annoying fashion. These tormentors mocked the creature as did the large crowd of unworthy onlookers who encouraged them on with their cruel cowardly torture. Here after all Barak quickly concluded was a most worthless audience. The crowd or rather mob was packed with lesser men who threw left over food as well as insults and anything else they had in hand at the huge chained creature.

'What is it Barak?' Tark asked looking on in both horror and wonderment at what he was witnessing. 'Is it some sort of huge deformed man? Or is it perhaps a beast my Lord, from a bygone time? For my Lord that thing is like nothing I have ever seen before; the creatures power, it is immense,' Tark declared, awe struck at the creature's appearance. Barak did not reply, the ogre merely grunted and growled then ground his teeth together in a most alarming manner. Now Tark sensed his master was about to do something, but what the young man wondered? Best now, Tark thought to himself to get Barak away from this disturbing affair, aye and just as quickly as possible.

'Still, come my Lord, we must away and leave this place for we have no business here. Also, this nonsense whatever it is, does of course not concern us in any way. ' But big Barak, well the ogre he thought differently, this nonsense it did concern him. And the ogre had already decided he was about to make it his business to do something about this most unfair situation.

The chained creature's power as Tark had noticed was indeed awesome, the thing it was perhaps a creature that stood a little over medium height. But the beast was broader in the shoulder and also at the neck than either Barak or Bull Neck put together. Also the thing moved in an ape like way, but yet strangely it was obviously more reptilian than simian. About the creature's waist a thick iron girdle held the beast firm to its chain which in turn was attached to a thick timber pole inset deep into the cobbled ground.

And as for the three antagonists who beset this unfortunate creature, well they were three parts drunk. All of these men were brown skinned, brown eyed hook nosed fellows with oiled tousled blue black hair. Also these antagonists were most gaudily and colourfully dressed in silks, satins and velvets. Aye these brightly dressed fools were all well put on with thick gold chains about their necks, their fingers the meanwhile bore thick gold horse head rings. Beyond these men, at the far side of the square there were several bow topped brightly painted caravans. Big heavy hairy legged coloured horses stood beside these living wagons in a most lazy docile fashion. Sitting outside upon the steps of these horse drawn caravans there sat dark skinned hook nosed women. These women had about their heads brightly coloured silken scarves, huge hooped gold ear rings hung from their pierced ears. Old wizened dried up crones that were selling lies to some of the town's many fools. Aye this the crones did while younger prettier girls danced and paraded themselves about on a made up stage. Other types of fools were beguiled by these lithesome creatures and those particular fools readily threw their hard earned money into a big floppy velvet hat. For some unspoken reason these easily led men were obviously expecting something that of course would not be delivered.

'Gypsies,, Barak hissed out under his breath. 'Horse thieves, deceivers that hail from the bowels of Asia aye and even beyond.'

Barak then once again suddenly turned his attention to the huge chained captive beast. This creature was a hairless thing and its skin was warty while the colour of its flesh was of a slight greenish hue. Also its eyes were large and yellow, indeed most frog like in appearance, this beast whatever it might be, was naked save for a dirty tattered leather loin cloth. Now the thing, it cowered as it lowered itself toward the ground, but yet Barak sensed the great beast was not afraid. No, instead the creature was cautious, the thing was patient, wary, also the beast was waiting for one mistake to be made by its antagonists.

Encouraged by the cheering crowd of onlookers the three men moved forward together, two of the men burnt the beast upon its huge back with their two long metal rods. And this, these cowards did while the third man, a man with a tall lop sided feathered hat used his bull whip. With a loud crack the thick hide whip cut a deep bloody gash across the beast's massive shoulders.

At once in a magnificent rage the creature ran forward with such a speedy powerful dash as to pull itself onto its backside as the beast hit the end of the chain at full pace. Now the creature's huge flat webbed feet pointed skyward, suddenly the crowd roared out in laughter, the man with the feathered hat postured while he took a smiling bow.

'What on earth, what is happening here Barak? Tark asked somewhat nervously. 'For the beast, whatever it is, makes no sound, is the creature, is it perhaps a mute thing? Else, why does the creature not cry out in its pain and suffering my Lord? '

Tark never received an answer straightway but instead the young man shuddered as he heard Barak let out a low growl like some sort of angry lion.

'It is a halfling, Tark, a swamp troll of some sorts that is if I am not very much mistaken. And quite simply, well, the creature makes no cry of pain or despair because the beast has its pride about it. Aye the unpretty thing has apparently a lot more pride than this miserable rabble here in the market square, or these three cowards that taunt it.' Barak said these words with a strong element of both sympathy and admiration for the great green creature. The giant though well he was obviously however less impressed with its tormentors. 'And look you there Tark', the ogre continued pointing a long gnarled finger. 'It bleeds Tark, look my boy the beast bleeds red just the same as you and I. Do you see that boy? The great green thing bleeds red,' the enraged giant growled out.

Tark felt of a sudden most uneasy as this was a most strange tricky situation to be in indeed. Now he wondered just what this new Lord and master of his was going to do about it all.

'It is a most crude and most primitive beast my Lord Barak. Indeed it is a most unattractive thing, a creature from the past. Also this after all is said and done is no business of ours my Lord,' Tark suggested a little timidly before going on a little more. 'Aye and also my Lord Barak have you forgotten your pledge? Forgotten that you, as well as the Norse, are on a quest for your good friend Aulric?' Tark said these words almost pleadingly.

Barak said nothing in reply, the ogre was silent for but a moment. However the slayer was not being ignorant nor was he ignoring Tark, no he was merely thinking. Thinking as he always did about any given situation he was about to involve himself in.

'For one thing Tark,' the giant said at length. 'Well, I don't like the odds here. Aye and for another, well this halfling he or it could come in quite useful for us on our present venture.' The giant then turned about slowly and he looked down at Tark full in the face. 'Remember this Tark, I never ever do anything, and I mean anything at all you must understand, without a good reason. '

Barak of a sudden casually bought another roast chicken off a skinny man who smelled strongly of garlic and he passed it over to Tark to hold for him. This of course the ogre did after he had first took a large bite out of it.

'Here my boy hold this for me, I won't be too long.' Barak said this whilst wiping his hands on the back of a town guardsman's red cloak. At once the guard turned about angrily and he was about to say or do something. Ah but then on seeing who or what it was who had used him as a kitchen towel, the guard merely gave a slight bow toward the giant and slunk back into the crowd. Barak after a polite nod to the cringing guardsman strode forward to the forefront of the ever increasing hostile and very noisy crowd.

Barak who up till now had been hooded under his black wolf skin cloak threw back his head covering to reveal his ferocious countenance.

Now the troll's attention was at once diverted as it noticed the huge towering ogre. Aye the thing peered past and beyond its puny antagonists. Now the beast stared towards this new strange looking and very huge man. Or indeed was it a man, for if it was, then this was like no other man that he or it, had ever before clapped its yellow eyes upon? Or perhaps and mayhap this huge very different looking newcomer was like itself in some sort of way or other. Was this newcomer to the crowd perhaps some sort of subhuman creature? Or was it perhaps merely another human that had grown much bigger than all of the others. Had this huge stranger with the brightly coloured skin come to further torture and humiliate him it wondered?

Fearfully the crowd hushed itself at once into a deathly silence as they beheld Barak's most fearsome appearance. Something most certainly was afoot here on this cold but sunny morning. Aye this show was perhaps going to turn out to be even more exciting than had even been promised. And, as it so happened, even these fools could not have been more correct in that hastily drawn assumption. Most of them there in the crowded square had by now heard of Barak's arrival

199

in their busy well run most prosperous harbour town. But the good people of Varnak had heard nothing about the slayer giving some sort of side show performance to entertain the masses.

The trio of drunken noisy laughing gypsies were enjoying their work so much that the fools seemed oblivious to the sudden death-like silence which had fell all about them. Being so the laughing fools simply continued on with their cowardly torment of the chained creature, aye and they did this with an ardent fervour.

It was more than obvious to Barak that these most worthless of men truly enjoyed their work.

And as already said one of them was armed with a vicious looking whip while the other two men were armed with red hot pokers.

Now the tallest of the three men, a dark skinned lanky hook nosed gypsy, the one with the plumed hat and a colourful waistcoat. Well this man drew back his whip for yet another lash at his chained captive. However his bloodied bullwhip on this occasion would cause the hapless creature no more pain, not on this day or any other come to that.

Barak put a huge booted foot on the tip of the bullwhip as it rested for just that moment too long on the cobbled town square.

Drunkenly the hook nosed gypsy tugged in vain at his snagged whip before angrily turning around to see just what the cause of the problem was. The gypsy was of course a past expert with this wicked weapon, so why he now wondered had it snagged upon something. Why was his well used lethal leather giver of pain now suddenly inactive?.

Well, he was about to find out.

'Good morning to you fool,' Barak snarled as the gypsy turned about then peered skyward up to face him.

Now the gypsy was not laughing, instead he was at once dumbstruck with fear on seeing the towering giant glowering down at him. For the first time in his whole life the fool struggled to speak, struggled to say something. Aye alas the fool just did not have the words on this occasion. In one gold ringed hand the gypsy held his long thick blood covered bull whip while in the other a goatskin gourd of steppes vodka.

Barak smiled a frightening sort of smile; it was of course the sort of smile that only Barak could indeed smile.

'Ah, I see that we have refreshments here as well as entertainment, good, very good.' This, the ogre said while he seized the man by his colourful silken waistcoat and then pulled him near to him. 'I have dined a little early today, so now I feel I must have a drink my fine feathered friend,' the giant hissed. With that said Barak then took a very big swallow of the vodka which he had seized.

200

After this swig the ogre licked his lips in blissful satisfaction. 'And now my little peacock, well now we must continue with the rest of the morning's menu, with just a few changes though.' Barak announced this out loudly so as the crowd could hear his every word. Oh and Barak now chuckled away in a most disturbing fashion as he shook the gypsy about like a child's rag doll.

'Now fool, now I will toast you with your own drink you stupid cowardly posturing peacock,' the giant growled out angrily. 'You have so far this morning entertained the crowd, so now my foolish friend in turn you must try to amuse me,' Barak sneered. 'For now my little feathered fool it is time for a complete change of roles.' At this point the brown skinned gypsy was now being held high aloft in one hand while Barak drank from the gourd with the other hand.

And then with that said Barak next hurled the gypsy showman straight towards the chained and bloodied troll. Well this the giant did after of course he had taken yet another big drink of the doomed showman's vodka.

'You are the master now creature, do with him what you feel you must, the fool is yours.' Barak said this to the troll, not even knowing if the strange creature could understand a word he had spoken to him, or it. But apparently the creature did understand Barak as it just so happened. So next, with what appeared to be no effort at all the troll promptly snapped both the back then the neck of its former antagonist. With this task easily done, the great green beast then threw the lifeless corpse amongst the stunned crowd as if the gypsy were no more than a rabbit.

'Well, well that was what I call a good throw by the creature my Lord Barak, aye the gypsy I think flew a lot further and a lot higher than I did,' said Tark with a wry smile.

Barak grinned at this as he turned to his newly recruited body guard, who had it seemed at least a sense of humour.

'But you are bigger than the skinny gypsy Tark, aye you are a lot heavier too,' Barak replied. 'And also besides that, I did not try too hard with you boy as I did not want you to go overboard and land in the sea. For in there you might have drowned, and this before we even got to know each other. Aye and that I think would have been more than a little sad, don't you boy?'

Tark nodded in agreement then he smiled broadly to himself at Barak's cold ever practical reasoning. Oh and the giant was still smiling as the two remaining gypsies rounded angrily then foolishly charged drunkenly forward. Wildly both men ran towards Barak with their red hot pokers held aloft. After all they had just lost their elder brother as well as their clan leader, so perhaps at that particular time neither of them was quite thinking altogether straight. For if the fools did have their wits about them then they would have been off in the opposite direction at the gallop.

'I must protect you my lord and king,' Tark said as he passed Barak's chicken back to him; the young man next drew his keen curved sword then stepped forward.

Barak stood motionless, well apart from resuming feasting on his well done roast bird, now he would see just what Tark was made of. Barak ordered his dogs back as they marked the armed men's advance and were as ever keen for blood. Now the giant watched with a certain amount of pride as his new guardian and protector laid the two gypsies low with ease. Both of the men fell at once stone dead onto the cobbled town square and there they lay without so much as even a murmur or a twitch.

Tark smiled proudly as he casually wiped his curved blade clean of blood on the cloak of one of the dead men before sheathing his sword. With this once done the young man most politely gave a slight bow towards the smiling Barak.

'You are saved, well at least for now I think my Lord.' The young warrior said this with a broad smile also with an element of sarcastic humour to his voice.

Barak gave a grin followed by a slight nod of thanks with his bucket sized head.

'Good man, you are my rock, my saviour young Tark. Indeed, I just do not know for the life of me how I have survived these past many long years without your presence,' said a jovial smiling Barak.

'Obviously by sheer luck my Lord Barak,' Tark answered back cheerfully also very sharply, 'by sheer luck'. It appeared to the slayer the once starchy young blackguard was at least beginning to acquire a sense of wit as well as a sense of humour.

Almost at once the two men laughed together, now Barak knew for certain Tark was for him, that the young warrior was truly on his side. He had gained, the giant thought whimsically to himself, not only an ally, but also a friend.

As also would this very able and somewhat shocking looking troll be if things went according to Barak's plans.

Barak took another chicken from the skinny garlic smelling street vendor's tray, the ogre next moved forward in a gentle slow fashion towards the swamp troll.

'Eat,' the giant said as he slowly reached out with the hand that held the plump warm chicken towards the most wary suspicious looking troll. This great green creature after all said and done had no reason at all to harbour any friendship or be trusting of the ways of men.

'Eat, eat, keep yourself big, keep yourself strong, for strength and power my friend it is all and everything. Do you understand me? Do you indeed understand what it is that I say to you? ' Barak then next stood back a pace or two to give the creature some breathing space, some thinking room. 'For if you do not understand my words then know this I can speak to you in many other tongues.'

Now the troll averted his gaze from the giant for just a moment as it looked about at the stunned silent onlookers. He, or it, was all the while wondering to itself if this was not just more trickery from the cruel world of savage and heartless men. Still the beast was a starved thing so it accepted the chicken gladly and gorged upon the flesh hungrily. In fact, the creature quite simply just flipped the chicken into the air then on its descent swallowed the bird down whole in one go, aye bones an all. The creature's mouth of a sudden had simply opened as big as a bear trap, and the roast bird was gone in a single gulp. Barak had raised his black eyebrows in shock, surprise not to mention sheer admiration. Strange how it was, but little things like this they for some reason always quite impressed the giant.

Barak while still impressed by the creature's eating habits next drew his ivory handled dragon sword from its scabbard. Brightly the keen blade shone as it glimmered frightfully in the cold clear morning sun. Still though the big green beast did not flicker nor did it draw back from Barak as the giant approached with his dragon sword in his huge right hand. Instead the creature for its own reasons trusted this huge strange looking man though in itself it did not truly know why. Barak with a grunt next strode forward and the slayer raised his dragon sword aloft. By the by there were still fools in the crowd who thought Barak might slay the troll as a part of the morning's entertainment. However though, this of course was not to be the case at all. With a swish the giant's keen slender blade of the fabled dragon sword sliced through the thick chain as though it were no more than a rotten piece of mooring rope. Now with this done the swamp troll, well he was at long last at liberty, aye he was at last a free thing. All the crowd gasped in sheer amazement at the way the slender sword had cut through the thick heavy metal links. Most, if not all there had expected the blade to shatter into a hundred shards leaving the giant to be left standing in the market square looking quite stupid.

'You are a free thing now, aye now you can go wherever it is that you want to go - wherever you will,' Barak said this as he sheathed his sword and affixed the beast eye to eye.

'I myself, I Barak will have the harbour black smith remove that iron girdle also that chain from around about you. You are free my friend, do you understand me? You are a free thing to go just where you will?'

For just a moment or two the troll's emotions seemed to get the better of him, freedom, well this of course had long been his dream. Next the creature lifted up the loose length of chain that was still attached to the thick iron girdle about his waist. He, or it, held this in his huge webbed hands as he stared at the chain for a moment or two. And then the creature blinked its big yellow eyes as it took a few steps forward toward Barak, the crowd withdrew fearful of the beast. This crowd were not so brave or noisy now Barak thought to himself. No, now these bunch of worthless jackals were cowed, and now the crowd of fools began to mutter nervously amongst themselves.

'My thanks to you, my Lord Barak,' said the troll after some little time had passed by. The creature said this with a strange croaky sort of voice. 'But tell me, aye please tell me if you can where in the world will I go to my Lord? Do you think that just perhaps there is a place out there for such as me anywhere?' Then the creature after saying this paused, it next blinked its big yellow eyes before once again speaking. 'And indeed my Lord what on earth can I think to do when or if I ever do get there? Aye for just as you see I am a halfling. I am neither a human nor am I a troll, yet because of this I am despised by both.' Now the creature next blinked its yellow eyes again as its long purple forked tongue whipped out in a most snake like fashion. Straightaway the halfling sensed the fear and hostility all about it. This though was of course something which was nothing at all new to the creature. 'Have you my Lord? have you perhaps anywhere a place for a beast such as me?'

Barak gave a thin smile as this indeed was the answer to the question the slayer had quite expected. Also the answer the giant would give, well this would be a one the halfling also so wanted to hear. Barak paused for just a second in time before replying to the powerful very dangerous looking creature.

'Well yes friend, we, my rogues and I, well we do always try to help out the oppressed and down trodden whenever possible.' The giant then once again paused for but a moment as he scratched at his trimmed white chin beard. Once again the slayer ran his keen black eyes over the powerful green halfling. Here was something or somebody that could come in very handy in a fight, here was a new recruit. 'Yes, oh yes, you could always come along with me and my friends,' the giant said this with a casual shrug of his huge shoulders. 'Why we can sail the stormy seas, we can roam the rugged land, climb over mountains high, travel the deserts and steppes. Then with this done we can hack our way through the very darkest of forests to slay the beasts that lurk there, we can live a life of adventure and daring.' Barak then paused for a moment to swig down a mouthful of the dead gypsies' vodka before continuing with the exciting outline of the halfling's life to come.

'For we can after all my green friend do only what we are born to do. Aye and all of this in the very short time we have left to do it in, if you know what I mean?' Barak paused once again but only briefly before he continued speaking to the strange green warty creature. 'Anyway besides all of that, I do honestly think I will have need of you. Aye, we my friends and I, we will also have need of your strength and your power on our current venture,' Barak added as he took another drink. The great green crude primeval creature reacted to Barak's flattering words with a polite bow and a flick of its forked tongue.

'My Lord, I am yours to command,' the troll thing said simply as he next gave another bow of gratitude to his huge colourful liberator.

'Good, oh that is very good, even better than I had expected,' Barak whispered this to himself under his breath.

Tark was at this moment numb with relief also dumb with disbelief, but either way the warrior was greatly impressed. This new king of his was shrewd and cunning beyond any belief. Why now, Barak had even won over a most primitive and fearsome looking beast. The young warrior watched open mouthed and mesmerized as the troll lurched forward then knelt down on the cobbles of the bloodied market place before Barak.

'Aye I can do this, and I will do this, for now I am at last a free thing. I am free just to do as I want and as I please. Free I am, free after years of being sold on from side show to circus then sold on again to fight in the arenas where I slew both men and the wildest of beasts. Barak once again smiled to himself this big green warty creature certainly had all the credentials he was looking for. Now the troll peered up at Barak from his kneeling position. 'But these link chains and this heavy belt of iron must stay with me forever my Lord. 'Until the day that I die I will keep them upon me to remind me of my past,' the troll said this with more than a hint of both hatred and bitterness.

Barak raised an eyebrow in surprise, strange, he would have thought the troll would want to be well rid of those heavy unhappy shackles. Barak's thoughts and musings though were suddenly very rudely interrupted.

As there was of a sudden the sound of many a trumpet aye indeed it was a noisy and most uncalled for fanfare. As it happened this was a fanfare that heralded the approach of the town prefect. After this noisy introduction just a few moments later some sixty or more Roman marines arrived tramping the cobbled streets with their winter fleece lined boots. Along with them to the fore of the company of marines four bearers carried aloft a most regal looking chair litter.

Aye a big black slave stood at each corner of the expensive ornate conveyance, four tall stout men of equal height all of them dressed in lion skin robes. All four of these men shivered in the cold morning sunlight, the slaves were not long to these climes and the weather was not at all to their liking. Now the elaborate velvet drapes of the regal chair were drawn back just a little as a strange decadent looking so called noble man peered out into the bright chill daylight. Here was the town prefect and the odd looking fellow was noble only by a dubious birthright, this fellow was neither a moral nor was he in any way a pretty man. In all fact, well the unpleasant looking thing had not one single redeeming feature about him to boast about. After a short while in passing for observing all and everything about him, then a little more time for some dim thinking. Well then it was that the inbred looking Roman noble spoke, aye and this it must be said was not in any way a cheery sound.

'There is a disturbance here on my town square, why and how so is this? For I do forbid it,' he rasped out with a very unhealthy sort of voice. 'Who dares to come here and upset the peace and the harmony of my holdings here?' This the prefect asked whilst peering all about him with his dark beady rat like eyes. For some reason either perhaps because of bad eyesight, or be it too much bright winter sunlight. Or even perhaps just because the fool had used too much opium that morning the prefect seemed not to detect the towering glowering giant.

Suddenly through the crowd a much overweight, much over dressed, over self-obsessed merchant pushed his way rudely forward to address the Roman Lord of Varnak.

'My Lord Prefect,' the man said bowing lowly while clasping a heavy gold link chain that hung about his fat sweaty neck. 'I, er, well, we here, the good folk and citizens of this town of Varnak we came here this day, well, this very morning for to observe some sport, some cheery entertainment. This fat man who was a prominent merchant in the vicinity looked quite out of breath as he stated his complaint. 'Aye the morning's venue however, well it was spoilt my Lord Prefect, yes it was completely ruined.' Now the fat perspiring merchant said this as he gave yet another bow then a very furtive sidewards glance toward the impassive indifferent looking giant.

Slowly the man inside the chair litter pulled back the curtains a little more as he looked down into the crowd searching for the man who had just spoken to him. The prefect was a slightly built most misshapen man with short lank dyed black hair, both his arms and legs were nothing more than skin and bone. Also his egg shaped head appeared far too large for the rest of his feeble wasted body. Aye this particular Roman nobleman was even more badly bred than any of the many others Barak had encountered. His dark beady eyes were alarmingly close together, also this so called prefect had huge batlike transparent ears. As well as having all of these physical afflictions the fellow also stank of rank decadence and decay. Aye, he was obviously an unwashed thing; the prefect was obviously not a great bather at all. No, far from it, here was rather a man who disguised himself with a strong heady perfume. And this the unwashed fool did instead of simply immersing his sad pathetic body in warm sudsy water. By the by, this Persian perfume or whatever else it was he doused himself with. Well, this gave off stale most unpleasant fumes, this rather than any sort of endearing enhancing scent.

'Entertainment!' the prefect exclaimed suddenly as he looked down upon the fat merchant. 'Why, yes, I came here myself on this very chill morn to witness a good piece of troll baiting, I like nothing better you know,' he replied with a low unpleasant hiss. The prefect next looked about him into the silent crowd then once again he spoke. 'So my good citizens of Varnak, why then, is that disgusting troll creature standing there unchained and at liberty in my own town square?' he asked most put out. On hearing this, the Troll flicked out its purple tongue as it moved a pace forward with violent intentions. Barak though he motioned the angry insulted beast to stay his ground, the creature without any complaint silently complied. Barak as it so happened was more than in the mood to handle this situation.

'Also and further more tell me this, why, oh why do I see before my very eyes three dead bodies?' This the prefect further enquired with a shrill most offensive and an almost inhuman voice as the corpse of the gypsy leader was dragged forward by members of the crowd. Now the prefect after asking this question and receiving no answer from anyone next focused upon Barak. Aye the foppish inbred fool affixed the ogre with a weak and watery eyed stare. 'Ah yes, yes I do believe that I see the reason for this carnage standing right before me now,' he cackled. 'You are the barbarian, yes you I do suppose are Barak, are you not?' The Prefect asked this most obvious question while pointing an accusing boney finger towards the grim faced giant. Barak for the first time in his whole bloodsoaked life felt that right now he should declare to this fool he was a king. And this just to outrank and shame this fool, however the ogre did not. Barak though instead spat upon the cobbled ground in sheer total contempt for the freakish looking prefect. And the grim faced ogre made no answer to the question put to him by the Roman official. Aye the giant chose at this very moment in time not to speak to the likes of this arrogant inbred so called aristocrat.

Now the big sweaty fat man with the overly large gold chain once again began with his protestations.

'I insist upon this man's arrest my Lord Prefect. After all, it was he who freed the Troll who then in turn slew Darius; Darius the gypsy king. Aye then his servant, well, this other man here, the one dressed in black, well it was he who slew the other two entertainers. He is of course a murderer my Lord Prefect.' And this the fat sweaty merchant said while pointing a fat sausage sized finger toward the stone faced Tark. By the way, Tark while not being bothered at being accused of being a murderer, well, he was not in the least bit impressed at being called a servant. Barak though in the meanwhile, found the menial title given to the proud Tark something that was quite amusing.

Well at leastways to him it was.

On hearing these words the prefect pulled a sour face whilst he listened intently to the fat merchant's bitter complaints. This he did as the sad looking fool sucked in opium from a large rounded vase. 'You then like gypsies, Artios, I take it? ' the prefect asked of the overweight but very wealthy merchant. Both of these two men, the fat merchant and the decadent prefect obviously knew each other quite well. No doubt this familiarity had been in the past an unsavoury corrupt union at that. A business arrangement that was made through bribery, corruption and a certain amount of deceitful back handed deeds no doubt.

Fat Artios the merchant, well, he suddenly felt the giant's cold black almond eyes upon him, now the fat man began to perspire even more. Nervously, nay fearfully the merchant took a whiff of snuff from a small ivory box before answering the prefect's question.

'No, no not particularly sire, but when the gypsy king was most brutally slain then thrown into the crowd, the corpse struck me a glancing but messy blow. As you can see my Lord my tunic and toga has the gypsy's blood upon it. And the garment, well, it is of course made from the finest silk, from Persia you know, very expensive, very distressing,' the fat merchant grumbled bitterly. 'Oh and also of course my Lord Prefect you must remember that the gypsy king Darius brought much trade to your holdings here. Yes the band of gypsies always brought with them good and useful slaves from afar. This as well as fine horses. The travellers brought gold and silver, as well as precious gems. All of this as well as the fastest of dogs and fine hunting hawks. True it is that the gypsy Darius made a lot of money here in this place of yours my Lord. But it is also very true you must remember the gypsy king also spent a lot of money here in this place of Varnak. Aye what is more, that money was spent here before ever leaving and moving on to the next town or village.' This the big fat merchant Artios finally added in his stirring defence of the gypsy king Darius and his gaudily clad kinsman.

As the prefect considered these words carefully he, after but a moment, nodded his odd looking head in total agreement with the fat merchant. After another thoughtful moment the prefect peered with beady rat like eyes down at the giant from his high regal chair.

'This is just so Artios, just so, please believe me I am in total agreement with your every word as it so happens.' And now the prefect said this as he scratched at a scab or something else that was equally unsavoury at the end of his weak pointed chin.

'Oh well what a surprise?' Barak muttered to himself as he took a drink of vodka from the dead gypsy's gourd.

'You, you Barak, I have heard you defeated the unbeaten gladiator Maximus, well, so at least my informants do tell me barbarian.' Now the prefect briefly paused, he looked dreamily about him then continued with what it was he had to say. 'Aye and then, then after defeating him, by all accounts you decided to let him live, let him walk away unharmed. Tell me, tell me barbarian why did you do this? For I was not aware, that you were a man who brimmed with compassion and mercy for those you had bested.' Oh and this question the prefect enquired of the giant almost accusingly.

After some deliberation and of course another quick drink, Barak decided he would answer the prefect's question.

'Well in all truth, I must say it was not hard work to defeat the Roman swordsman,' Barak answered evenly. 'And why I decided to let him live, well, quite simply because of this very reason. Your foolish champion was not then, nor ever could he be any sort of threat whatsoever to me.' Barak after saying this of course took another drink.

'No? oh no surely not,' the prefect said raising his thin greying eyebrows in surprise at this statement. 'But this fellow Maximus was a champion, and he was a champion in Rome itself,' the prefect countered. Smiling broadly the giant shook his mail clad head as he chuckled away to himself before replying. 'Champion or not the answer is still the same one. This fool of yours was no threat to me at all, and this as he quite simply was nowhere near good enough with a sword, do you understand? In fact any of the rogues who sailed here with me, any one of them could have done the same job just as easily as I did. Now do you see what I mean, Prefect? Do you now take my meaning?' Barak asked this with a thin smile. 'Know you this, what for swordplay that might impress you pampered Romans, well this has always I must say failed most sadly in any way to impress me. '

Barak took another drink then he smiled once again to himself this as the giant knew only too well how much his answer perturbed and irritated the arrogant town Prefect.

Now it was the Roman who sucked quite furiously upon his opium pipe as his beady eyes narrowed in both hate and anger toward the giant.

'I must say that I have of course heard of you Barak, but, then again who has not? You have after all earned great infamy, great notoriety over these past long years as a slayer. However, barbarian, that particular accolade is not always a good thing, if you take my meaning. '

Barak merely shrugged in a most indifferent fashion at these words, then the ogre walked nearer a yard or two toward the litter. Next the slayer halted as he lit up his pipe from a nearby eel smoker's brazier. Braziers thankfully were always ever plentiful in these noisy bustling harbour towns, aye and this even more so as the winter chill drew ever nearer. In fact every stone's throw something or other was getting roasted, smoked or grilled somewhere along the bustling crowded streets.

'I also have heard you slew the magistrate's scribe at the garrison in Vindolanda, aye and in a most gruesome way at that. Now this barbarian is a most disturbing, most unlawful act, it is also of course cold blooded murder. And at day's end no matter what the reason for this murder the scribe was in truth an official of Rome,' the prefect went on smugly.

Barak smiled next the ogre chuckled outwardly, he did so to simply annoy this fool from Rome. Aye it was no more a ruse though the giant chuckled outwardly he growled inwardly, he did not like this strange inbred looking little man. Oh no the slayer he did not like him one little bit.

Barak after a long draw upon his pipe decided he would now explain things to this wretched little man.

'I have already been told this, that what you have just said to me. I was told this very same thing by a young Roman centurion in Vindolanda. His words meant nothing to me then, and so neither do yours now,' Barak said with a sneer of contempt. 'Also it did not bother me, the slaying of a treacherous jackal who by the by hailed from my own land, and still his demise it does not bother me now. Because at day's end if a man needs killing, then I will of course gladly kill him,' Barak said calmly. 'Please believe me on this prefect I need no permit or permission from Rome, the Emperor or anyone else. In fact I always do just as I please, understand?' Barak said this with a sneer of utter contempt. 'But I suppose that is quite simply the way it is with me, as after all I am merely a cold blooded killer.' Barak had said these chilling words with a grim uncaring smile as he inhaled the strong weed deeply then blew smoke most casually skywards.

Meanwhile the Roman governor, prefect, magistrate, keeper of the peace and whatever other title he would have bestowed upon himself fumed. Why, why this was pure insolence the prefect had never heard anything quite like this before in his entire life. Here he was in his own market square being addressed as if he had no standing or high position at all. The sixty marines were now becoming most unsettled, as Barak after all was not renowned for backing down, this no matter what the odds. When the foolish prefect next spoke he said nothing that would cause the marines to rest more easily inside of their armour.

'By Roman law, murder, well that is sufferable by the death penalty, once convicted and this is death without trial. You as you are nothing more than but a foreigner and have also admitted to the slaying, well I do suppose I could have you executed even now as we speak. '

On hearing these most foolhardy words all whispering amongst the rank of soldiers ceased, all about went deathly silent. Now the marines looked about into the crowd searching for those who had accompanied the ogre, all the while the soldiers were cursing under their breath. It seemed to each and every one of them this drug deluded Prefect was obviously some sort of a madman. Why it seemed the fool was hell bent on bloody confrontation with the gigantic slayer. How many men were with Barak anyway? Every soldier there wondered this anxiously to themselves as their troubled heads pounded under their helmets.

Forty or perhaps even fifty men or thereabouts they knew had sailed into port, hopefully most were doubtless still in a deep drunken slumber. Barak was as far as all there could see alone, well save for the mysterious looking man in black robes and the two huge dangerous looking dogs. The troll with any luck would doubtless be off seeking a road to freedom, hopefully the beast would take no part in the fray, or would it? Still surely sixty trained marines, all veterans at that, had nothing to fear, common sense would surely prevail here? Perhaps, just perhaps the giant would turn his back on the prefect at any minute now, then just wander off brooding and cursing off into a nearby tavern. Perhaps if all of their gods were with them this was possible, then again this was Barak. Being so, such as he was, well the ogre might and was indeed most likely do almost anything. Also on the other hand while the giant might not value the position or the opinions of the prefect in any way. In the past the ogre was and always had been a good friend to the rank and file of the Roman army. Yes, hopefully with every known god willing perhaps all would pass by here today without any further incident.

Well perhaps.

Barak now most casual like stretched his huge arms skyward as he moved his neck this way and that until it creaked itself into place. After a grunt and a groan the ogre next blew more smoke hoops casually into the chill morning air. And this as the slayer had decided for now at least he would listen to this soon to die fool.

'The good Emperor Septimius Severus he is weak, he is poisoned so they say,' the prefect cackled spitefully. Apparently the prefect was not an admirer of the Emperor nor did he really like this cold place he had been sent to preside over. A posting in Spain or Egypt or even Greece would have suited him much better, as at least these places were warmer and more civilised. 'Septimius our noble Emperor, well he may not be able to offer you protection for much longer Barak.' This the Prefect said this while pointing a crooked finger toward the giant. Of course this indeed was a most foolish and a most unwise statement to address toward the grim glowering ogre.

Barak inhaled deeply then to calm himself he drank down more of the dead gypsy's vodka. These foolish misplaced and empty words as expected had both angered and offended the ogre to the very extreme.

Indeed it would be no lie to say that the giant almost choked upon his last mouth full of drink.

'Protection, what protection, tell me you foolish looking thing, what protection have I, Barak, ever needed from Rome or anywhere else for that matter?' Oh and the ogre snarled this out angrily once he was recovered from his choking fit. 'Not from the Emperor, nor from Rome and most certainly not from the likes of a skinny little bad bred fool like you. No, not I, I need no help from anywhere or anybody, Barak has never needed protection.'

Never in his whole life had the prefect been spoken to like this, so now it was the prefect's turn to almost choke. Next the prefect scowled angrily on hearing this insult, he sneered with total hatred and contempt for Barak. Now there was no doubt about it the fool was obviously fuelled with the opium. Possibly even something else that gave him a fool's courage, but being the fool he was then therefore the prefect did just not seem to understand what danger he was in. After all that childish worthless chain of office which hung about his scrawny neck, it meant nothing at all to Barak. This chain was accompanied with a short cane with a golden eagle on top of it, aye a gold painted eagle at that. Well these so called emblems of Roman power they of course were no more than worthless trinkets that held no threat to Barak, useless articles that meant nothing at all. Still though despite this, the foolish Roman prefect seemed quite oblivious as to the obvious danger he was now ever speedily getting himself into. Thus being so then the fool said on, digging his own grave with every foolish word.

'You have not asked my family name', the prefect said haughtily.

Barak puffed upon his pipe then shrugged indifferently the ogre next gave out a weary yawn.

'Something long winded, something regal, aye and matter less no doubt, anyway it would be a name that interests me not at all,' the slayer replied with total indifference. Now the giant paused for a moment as he drank then smoked once again before speaking. When next the slayer spoke he was smiling, however this was a cold cynical smile that carried no mirth with it. 'Tell me this prefect is it your sister who is your mother? Or failing that, is it your brother that is perhaps your father? Tell me fool which of these obvious mix ups is it?' the giant demanded to know. 'For I can see most plainly, that you are without any doubt a most sadly and badly bred thing.' Barak said this, both mockingly and boldly without any hesitation whatsoever. 'Why if you were the pup of a running dog or something else bred for some sort of a purpose. Something that is at all useful, then no doubt the owner of said beast would have drowned you at birth, aye and this even before your very first yelp.' Barak said all of this whilst he sneered hatefully. Now it was that the ogre's black blood was beginning to boil up with rage inside of him. Within the crowd of onlookers and even amongst the marines many bit upon their lip while struggling to contain their laughter at Barak's scathing words. However whilst the marines also enjoyed the prefect's baiting by Barak, they still feared how everything would end. This prefect was indeed a cruel arrogant man and he was a man who was disliked by all who knew him.

Dimly now in his opium induced stupor the prefect began to take even more offence, his bat-like ears detected the giggling around about him. Oh and also he was of course insulted shocked and exasperated by the giant's most insulting words. Being so now the sad looking fool stuttered and spluttered while he struggled in vain trying to get his own words out in reply. As of course this badly bred thing was not in the habit of being ridiculed and mocked. Yes and mocked so openly and brazenly, and this in his own town square at that. Anyway at long length the fool gathered together his battered bruised wits about him, or did he?

'I could order your arrest now you great barbarian oaf, aye and even your execution at my pleasure if I so wished it,' the prefect at last managed to reply shakily. Barak's total lack of disrespect to his high rank his office and also his family title was something that he found was quite unbelievable. All of his worthless pampered life the prefect had looked down with sheer disdain, even disgust at all that was not Roman. Anyway Barak did not appear so high and mighty from where he now sat upon his ornate high backed chair. Well the foolish prefect might have briefly thought this, but as for his four black bearers well those four men felt most intimidated. Aye and all four of them discovered there was much more to dislike about this place, than the mere cold weather.

Barak rubbed out his pipe replacing it inside his waistcoat. The ogre then took another drink of vodka, next he took a pace forward.

'Then why not order it, you freakish looking little fool?' Barak dared loudly. 'Order my execution or even my arrest then let us just see what happens next here in this place of yours.'

Sweaty Roman palms slid nervously toward their sword hilts at exactly the same time as Ragnor and a score of his large hairy rogues arrived at the square. Oh and this by the way was more by good luck than any good judgment. The big Norsemen at once rudely pushed the crowd aside as he and his warriors moved to the fore to show themselves. Ragnor wanted this so the warriors might be seen and so thus be accounted for. Ragnor was brash and rash at times but nevertheless he was not a fool. In the here and now the big Viking would sooner make the Romans stand down by a show of force than lie in concealment letting it come to certain swordplay. All of the sixty marines looked on with more than a little trepidation at the big burly well armed men of the north. Big shields, big swords and wicked looking double headed axes they all carried, each man of them suddenly produced from under their cloaks bronze helmets with eye slits and nose guard, these the Norsemen next donned in readiness for battle. These Norsemen as has already been said were all large ferocious evil looking men who loved to fight. Being so then this of course was not a good way to start the day every marine there thought to himself. Barak did not know the name of this fool prefect nor was he interested in learning his name, the fool of course was marked for death anyway. However by pure chance the ogre was to learn his victims name anyway.

'Cicero, my high noble Roman Lord,' Horst said as he stumbled forward half drunk and unwashed as usual. His one good leg was not working quite as well as it should be, this of course being due to the effects of the vodka. The German was apparently or so he had said still celebrating Barak's easily won victory over the Roman gladiator. Well that was at least his excuse for his present condition though it was not that the German ever needed one to get himself intoxicated.

Now the Prefect Cicero glared down hatefully and arrogantly at the fat drunken unsteady German. Cicero, well, he regarded all of these tribal northern earth worshiping fools with total contempt and utter disgust. What Rome wanted with them or their cold freezing wolf infested wastelands was a total loss to him.

'You, what do you want you shambling foolish German idiot?' the prefect asked somewhat sharply.

'I want to resign my position here at the Hundsruck my Lord,' Horst slurred with a drunken grin across his fat red face.

Cicero seemed somewhat taken aback at these words, surely this fool was not in the employ of Rome he thought to himself.

'Resign, resign from what you idiot, what position do you hold?' the prefect sneered. 'And by the way you shambling German fool this place is Varnak not the Hundsruck. Why you worthless drunken fool, you don't even know where you are,' the prefect snarled and sneered. 'But either way, you unwashed barbarian' whether in the Hundsruck or Varnak what employ could Rome possibly offer such as you?.' The prefect enquired this with a snidey aristocratic sneer. 'Who are you? Aye and indeed what on earth are you? ' the Roman asked with yet another snidey grin of contempt.

Horst who was as ever an attentive drunk had noted the Roman nobleman's disdain and his obvious contempt. But as the drunken German cared little or nothing for the Prefect's opinions he of course took no offence, so he said on. 'I no longer wish to be the town's lantern lighter, in this town or any other.' Horst said this with a hiccup a burp then a very loud fart. 'I am about to change my career you see prefect, aye I am now to become a pirate, I am to sail the seas.' Horst stated this fact both proudly and also very loudly. 'I have now had enough of this boring place, or for that matter the other boring place where I thought I was in the first place , if you know what I mean? Aye and also, besides all of that, well it was after all your fop son who ran me down in his chariot. Perhaps that accident took place here, but then again perhaps not,' Horst next explained. 'Aye and to his shame the fool did this when he had left his boyfriend's house in the middle of the night, this no doubt after a lovers' tiff. You know what boyfriend I mean my Lord, don't you? That black curly haired Marcus or Macro or whatever else they call him. '

At once there was a loud peel of laughter from the crowd as well as a subdued chuckle from each and every one of the marines. Of course the prefect was less than amused at this accusation, in fact he became beside himself with both embarrassment and rage. Aye the fool was so enraged that words for the moment quite failed him. Horst however was not similarly afflicted so the drunken German said on as he rocked unsteadily upon the cobbles of the town square.

'So my noble Lord I suggest that if you do want any heirs or other offspring to follow on in your smelly Roman sandaled footsteps. Well I do strongly advise that you get a young wife of your own sire, aye then you must just get on with the job yourself. '

Now there was yet more laughter from the crowd aye even the marines found it hard to hide their broadening smiles. And all of this in what was becoming a most precarious and dangerous situation there was still at least some humour to be found.

'Yes, you had best get rid of that dried up creature of a prune-faced wife of yours. Aye get yourself a new one with something to hold on to other than a wig,' Horst advised this most strongly to the fuming and much embarrassed prefect, relentlessly, above yet more peels of laughter the German went on. 'Because, alas my Lord Cicero I do think that your son the young Constantine. Well I think that fop will stop with the hairy backed garlic smelling Marcus, well anyway for at least the foreseeable future.' Once again there was more laughter and more whisperings amongst the mostly Germanic crowd. 'I also further think that everything will prove a very big disappointment as regards your future plans to further your family tree.' Once again at these words there was more spontaneous laughter, this time though it was a roar, it was not in any way a sedate or subdued chuckle.

Horst, who was ever the comedian, at once took an unsteady bow which in turn increased the tempo of the ever increasing crowd's raucous laughter. By now the enraged very agitated Cicero had totally lost his sense of direction. This, and also what little common sense the fool had ever possessed, not to mention his poor sense of humour. And when a man, any man, no matter how noble or how well bred he might think he is. Well when this fellow loses three such senses, then of course there is always the promise of trouble ahead.

Lord Cicero by now, well the fool had already went well past this point of no return, oh and then some.

'Marines, I order you to arrest these men, arrest them now the black garbed killer and also the giant, take them and put them both in heavy irons.' Cicero commanded this angrily and of course most unwisely. 'I will decide what their fate is to be later,' he shrieked out like some sort of demented old crone as he frothed at the mouth in rage.

On hearing this madness spoken by the foolish prefect Barak shook his big head, then the ogre spat upon the cobbles angrily.

'Bah, I suddenly sicken with looking up to the likes of an inbred fool such as you are.' Barak snarled this out as then with one hand he flipped over the prefect's chair sending it crashing heavily to the ground.

Well, well by now the big Negro bearers had seen quite enough, these big black slaves would endure no more as each and every one of them had seen quite enough of Varnak. Aye and so now each and every one of them took affright and were off down the nearest side street not knowing what to expect next in this cold place of lunacy and mayhem. Not only was this a freezing rainy windswept place, it was also fraught with all manner of horrors and dangers. With this being so all four of them had no intention of stopping their running until the inadequate sandals fell from their big frozen feet.

Now there was a hushed silence, a silence that seemed to go on forever, as all there stared at the shattered chair litter. Barak drew his dragon sword as he advanced in a slow steady fashion towards the marines. For some reason this bodyguard had no centurion with them. No officer no commander, no leader at all save for the worthless prefect. And as for that sad pathetic figure, well that fool now lay a cowering whimpering creature, soiling himself whilst huddled inside his broken shattered carriage.

Any man of that troop of marines who said he was not fearful as to what might happen next, he would have been a liar. Barak though in a most honest and diplomatic fashion would next put these fears to rest.

'I have no argument with any of you men, and if it pleases you then I would like to keep it that way.' Barak said this with his sword pointing downward toward the cobbles. Now the marines on hearing this most welcome news rested their sweaty hands from their sword hilts. Oh and this was as each and every one of them all sighed with a sudden and welcome relief. Barak at this reaction he also at once sheathed his own dragon sword. Ragnor, also as well as the Roman soldiers gave a grunt of contentment at this reprieve, the big Norseman had lost not a man against the pirates. However against trained marines though and with more of them about somewhere to back these ones up, well that would be a different sort of fight. Though not that a hard fight worried any of the Vikings, no far from it, in fact under normal conditions these men would have welcomed the fray. However these were not normal circumstances. Every man there knew that they had a hard task ahead of them without also having a pitched battle now, aye and this battle on Roman soil. Barak though was apparently undaunted, the ogre knew well these marines wanted no part of this folly brought about by a worthless useless thing. Aye and he was a thing that merely by his so called nobility had been given rank and station over decent and honest men.

'The arrogance of Rome, this has long been its downfall Cicero.' Barak said this with a scowl as the ogre turned his attention to the prefect. Now the slayer drew back a velvet drape to reveal the cowering, cringing so called nobleman. 'Should I kill you now fool I wonder, or should I not?' Barak asked himself out loud. 'Look you at your marines my high Roman Lord, their swords are sheathed, those men will not defend you. And this is not because your soldiers are cowardly men in any way, no, but because these men have neither love, nor any sort of respect for you. Truthfully you must ask yourself Cicero, who would?'

Cicero stared back both tearfully and fearfully now at the towering Barak. Whatever he had drank, or smoked that had made the prefect so brave earlier, well now it was fast losing its potency. Aye the drugs and the drink it was now indeed wearing off and very fast at that. Even though the prefect was obviously doomed to death, not one soldier of Rome reached towards his weapon, nor indeed were they going to.

'Cowards,' Cicero hissed out hatefully. 'I will see them all in hell, every single one of the marines will die for their cowardice. ' he declared. 'And I do swear it, I will see them all crucified down to the last man,' the prefect threatened hatefully. The soldiers at these words became once again unsettled, worried at the Prefect's sudden defiant venomous outburst. It seemed now they either faced the blood thirsty Barak with his ever growing number of barbaric friends, or a slow lingering death upon the dreaded cross.

Tark was a soldier, being so then he respected other soldiers, this even if one day he might have to kill them.

'You must slay him my Lord, kill the fool,' Tark whispered in a hushed low voice, the young man also said this with some conviction. 'Or as you know yourself Lord, these honest soldiers here will all suffer death, a most horrible death at that.' Barak merely grunted in reply, as Tark had just said the prefect must of course die. For if he was allowed to live then the pompous arrogant fool would surely crucify every marine present for not coming to his aid.

Not of course that in such an eventuality it would of availed anything, well apart from more deaths in the Empire.

Rank and file Roman soldiers revered and respected Barak, the gods, Roman or otherwise, only knew the men of the legions had good reason to. As after all, the giant had stood with the legionnaires leading them as a commander into battle for long enough these many past years. It was perhaps true that Barak did prefer the company of wild wanton uncouth barbarians. Perhaps these barbarians suited his wild unruly nature better, or perhaps it was because these men were bolder gamblers and better drinkers than the men of the legions. Still though despite all of this the ogre had nevertheless fought many a hard battle alongside Roman foot soldiers, in all truth he had found them never lacking in courage. True these men fought more like some sort of automatons than with the wild passion of the savage barbarians, but still despite this their courage was unyielding.

Barak now pulled back more of the crimson drapes embossed with the roman eagle to reveal where the still quivering prefect Cicero lay. And of a sudden the high born Roman prefect was not so brave or so bold now. Aye the Roman nobleman no longer appeared to be so full of his own self importance and arrogance as he peered up and ever up into Barak's black eyes. It was now that the giants keen senses twitched at the prefects rank stale smelling perfume. Oh and close up well the winging fool looked even more degenerate and inbred. Apart from his strange shaped head, his too close together eyes and his almost transparent bat like ears. Also the Prefect's teeth, were needle sharp, the teeth were more ferret like than that of any human, aye and that with Barak's included. So all in all, Cicero was not a thing that any parent would be proud to say he or she had brought into the world. Still though, the bad bred thing would not be gracing these cobbled streets or any other streets for much longer.

'You are to die this day Cicero,' Barak said plainly with a slightly crooked smile. 'But not by my hand you must understand.' At these words the prefect was struck speechless, both his mouth as well as his tongue failed him. 'No, oh no I would not soil my good sword, or even a bad one come to that on the likes of such as you,' Barak hissed out through clenched gritted dog sharp teeth.

217

Tark glanced at Ragnor who looked just as mystified as he was as to Barak's frank statement to the prefect. Was it the Viking who was going to be the executioner of the Roman Prefect Tark thought to himself, or was it perhaps going to be he himself acting as the slayer? As after all he was now Barak's official bodyguard. Or even mayhap it would be Barak's other new found enlistment. Was the strange looking Halfling to be the death dealer here in the still crowded town square of Varnak? It was however with some element of relief to Tark that it was to be neither one of these three possible candidates.

With a sudden command from Barak, spoken in his native tongue, the giant turned his back on the cringing whimpering Roman. Now with his orders given the ogres two great hounds dived into the broken timber and the velvet drapes as the great brutes seized their hapless victim. Cicero had time only for one brief girl like scream, after this he was done, he was gone and the fool was no more a living thing. Aye at least for Cicero it was all over very quickly, over in just a matter of a few seconds. Now with the crowd witnessing this horrific most grizzly scene they then at once quickly broke up, dispersing down the narrow side streets. Many of them were vomiting as they made their hurried departure from the market square; the fat merchant Artios was one of the first to flee. Aye and for a fat man Barak was quite impressed at just how quick the merchant moved. Now, just as Barak had planned it the locals were in fearful dread of what butchery would or could come next. This crowd after all had urged on the gypsies and so they were in some part accountable for the goings on of that morning's so called entertainment. Aye also the Troll was a free thing now, free to wreak any havoc or revenge that he or it thought was due for his gross mistreatment. Of course as well as this he was now with his new found friends, aye and they were a most dangerous looking collection of friends at that.

Barak at length calmed himself down once more and the ogre took a deep swig of vodka, then yet again the ogre sucked deeply upon his long clay pipe.

'You do drink and also smoke far too much my Lord Barak if you do not mind me saying, perhaps you should abstain from these unhealthy habits for a short while.' Tark advised the giant with an element of humour in his voice. 'For one day my Lord Barak, I really do fear it will be the vodka or the weed that will be the very death of you.'

Barak before replying intentionally took another long drink and then another big puff upon his pipe.

'Aye, so they keep saying,' Barak replied dryly with a casual and a dismissive wave of his huge hand.

'And also my Lord you must remember you do not get any younger with the passing of time,' the young Krozaky said as he smiled in a cocky most confident fashion.

Barak then took several long strides till he was standing right next to his newly promoted bodyguard, the ogre bent down as he whispered in Tark's ear.

'Aye and so it is my young friend, everyone keeps telling me that also,' the giant hissed in mock anger. With this said then the ogre coughed violently after inhaling too much of the strong weed. Barak next looked skyward, turning his attention toward a flock of screeching seagulls that soared overhead. These sea going vultures no doubt had every intention of finishing any scraps of the prefect's body left by his big dogs still chewing on the corpse. Now the giant coughed reluctantly again as he spat black phlegm onto the cobbles. After this untimely unpleasant occurrence the ogre once again turned his attention to his smiling young countryman.

'Aye, you may well be right in your dark morbid deliberations as regards my future health boy. But know you this and best you know it now. True it is that the drink or the weed might carry me off to the bowels of hell itself. Yes my socialising habits might well kill me in the end. Yes, I think all of that is very true, very true. But also there is something else, which is also for sure, something else that is for certain. And that my boy quite simply is this, unless the swordplay vastly improves in these younger generations of so called warriors, gladiators and would be duellists. Well then I do think young Tark I will doubtless live on forever, perhaps ending my life fighting these useless warriors with the aid of a walking stick while sitting in a chair that rocks.'

Tark on hearing this laughed out loud, the young man shook his black turbaned head as he wiped tears of mirth from his dark eyes Tark liked very much Barak's quick but grim humour. And also as it so happened, mayhap the great ogre was quite correct in what he had just said. For after all there was quite simply no one about who was near good enough to take the ogre out and slay the giant in fair combat. Yes, more than likely Barak was correct in what he had just somewhat jokingly said. It would more than likely be the weed or the drink that one day would lay him low, not an enemy's sword.

With this said the giant said now turned his attention to the marines, marines who were standing at a bit of a loss as at what next to do. This the soldiers did whilst their former prefect was still being feasted upon by Barak's dogs. By the way the breaking of bones, the tearing of scrawny sinewy flesh had made quite a few of them go not surprisingly most ashen. Barak of a sudden took a few measured strides forward toward the front line of marines as the killer had something to say. Being so then of course now the giant would just as ever say it.

'I know you soldier, for believe me I never forget a face, and that be it friend or foe,' Barak said this suddenly as now he was addressing one of the front line marines.

Now all of the marines stood still like some sort of switched off automatons in ranks of five wide. At this particular time on this very eventful morning these men were in all truth not quite knowing what to do now the much despised Cicero was a dead thing. Well the fool was not only dead, by now he was also mostly eaten by the huge dogs.

Of course the soldier who Barak had addressed, he indeed felt greatly flattered that the giant could remember him. Aye and remember him from a campaign he had taken part in some ten years earlier on the much warmer African coast.

The soldier motioned to speak but Barak with a wave of a hand motioned him to silence.

'Tell me nothing soldier let me remember, you, you are not a Roman are you?' Barak declared this knowingly, his brain inside of his big bucket head was working overtime now. Aye the giant was thinking hard, his ever quick brain was turning back the years putting all his memories into some sort of order. Now the marine Barak had addressed smiled with an element of pride, perhaps Barak did remember him, and this was not some sort of a wild random guess.

'You are a Spaniard, aye and you are a Spaniard from the snow capped mountains if my memory stands up, are you not?' the giant enquired as he smiled confidently at placing the man.

Of course on hearing this, the man was most impressed, the marine went to speak but Barak with yet another wave of his hand motioned him once again to silence.

'Say nothing my friend for I know much more, know you this, any man who has stood at my back in battle or warfare.' Barak paused at this time before continuing. 'Well please believe me, I do not ever forget who or what these men are about.' Even though Barak was being friendly and cordial, the Spaniard found this very disclosure made him feel a little weak at the knees. However, weak at the knees or not the marine was most impressed and flattered the great ogre Barak apparently forgot nothing from his black and blood soaked past.

Briefly the ogre paused for just a moment then the slayer smiled as he spoke up once again.

'Tell me my friend, tell me are you well, and are you fit Ferdinand?' Barak asked this question after only but a moment's thought. And the Spaniard, for Spaniard he truly was could for a moment say nothing so amazed was he with the killer's memory. Barak grinned, as he recalled all inside of that big bucket head of his, then the slayer said on once again. 'I see your leg wound has healed where the Moor's spear hit you.' There was at once on hearing this declaration excited mutterings amongst the other marines. Long had the Spaniard told that some time ago he had served with Barak, oh and also long had he been doubted, even ridiculed at his somewhat unlikely tale. Now though his truthful story he had told to younger men than himself, well it would be at last verified.

220

'Aye, aye I am well my Lord Barak,' the soldier hesitated for a second or two then he spoke. 'Though under this helmet my head is now grey, my hair is no longer black, aye and, also it is a lot thinner than it once was back then.' Ferdinand answered this with a slight bow of his head toward Barak.

With a grunt the giant shrugged, Barak smiled at these words then the ogre put a hand upon the man's shoulder as he gave out a little chuckle.

'Aye my friend, but remember this, you must be thankful you still have a head at all for your grey hair to grow out of, Ferdinand. As please believe me that was indeed some savage bloody battle that we fought long ago upon the shores of the silver sands.' Ferdinand silently made no argument on that account, as the battle after all had been no more than sheer butchery for both warring sides. Barak though as ever, well he saw warfare on a much more cheery note. 'Still though my friend, despite all and everything, it was at least a good glorious most honest well fought battle was it not? Big Barak asked this question of the Spaniard with a grim smile. 'Aye and more importantly we at long last slaughtered our enemies, it was we who prevailed, we won the day after all,' Barak added this with a sigh of fond reflection. Ferdinand nodded in agreement but then the soldier looked suddenly a little troubled.

'True that is, but for me it was a glory marred by great sadness my Lord Barak. For I lost my brother on that final day of battle, he fell on those blood soaked sands,' the Spaniard said sadly.

Barak sighed again and the slayer sighed a little sadly to himself this time.

'Ah yes your brother Domingo, I do remember him well also. Aye he was a good man, a good swordsman and a good soldier, but at least my friend his end was quick and clean. You can believe me on that Ferdinand, for he was at my side when the dealer of death found him, believe me he felt nothing. And as for his slayer, well, I took care of him with a swordstroke,' the giant said honestly.

Ferdinand's lip suddenly trembled with emotion, the Spaniard then gave a bow of gratitude for both Barak avenging his brother's death and at last knowing how his younger sibling met his end.

Barak's memory, well it must have been incredible the Spaniard thought to himself. After all Ferdinand's brother had only been in the tenth legion a week or so before his sudden violent and very premature demise. Why he was no more than a raw recruit, only twenty years old at that time. And yet here the giant could call him to mind in an instant, and this after barely meeting with him. Now though the great Barak spoke of him as if he were an old friend almost.

Ferdinand bowed once again, the Spaniard was over awed by the giant's sheer presence as well as his memory. Ferdinand was also amazed at how the giant had remained unchanged over the years since last the two men had met. Barak, well the ogre of course most politely returned the compliment with a nod of his own big mail clad head. Melancholy thoughts of the long past were suddenly pushed to one side as now the present time was of course of the utmost importance.

Barak wanted no ill, no misfortune to befall the marines for his bloody actions of that day, as always and as ever the giant had a most cunning plan. Suddenly a grim smile crossed his tattooed face as the ogre smiled broadly revealing those, wolf like teeth.

'Mad dogs from the street, it was mad dogs that killed your worthless prefect,' Barak boomed out of a sudden. 'You here, you soldiers of course cannot be held at all responsible for the ways and habits of mad dogs.' Barak smiled to himself, the ogre was quite proud of his plain simple little plan. 'Now do you all here know why this butchery was done, why it was done in this most unsavoury way?' the giant asked all those before him.

Perhaps it was that Barak had formulated this plan after and not before the big dogs had knawed upon Cicero, however no one there was to know that.

At once there came a nod followed by a satisfied murmur of relief from the hitherto very worried marines.

'So you will not face the cross and be most dreadfully crucified, no far from it; you will live long. Also I do think you will forever remember this most interesting day, well this until your gods, whoever they might be, carry you off,' Barak said with a thin smile. 'And so now my friends, well I do hope also that you all understand my somewhat bloody actions?' Barak asked this question almost imploringly. Tark once again was most impressed by his king's ability to win over men. 'And if you can do that alone, well that is good enough for me, to hell with the likes of rubbish such as Cicero. What battles had he ever fought in the name of Rome or the Emperor, aye or anyone else for that matter? No, no you here, you men are the power the pride and the glory of Rome, not him. Believe this, so it was such as the fool lived as nothing, then so he also died as nothing,' Barak sneered. 'My good dogs, believe me, these beasts would have eaten him all down if the fool was worth the eating. But look you all now, the prefect or whatever he called himself, well he was not even good enough to be dog food. Look you at my dogs, they leave his chewed upon remains even now. ' Barak declared this in genuine surprise at his normally ravenous hounds declining meat, even bad meat. 'I do just hope the dogs are not both ill' Barak added with a genuine concern in his voice that caused the marines to laugh amongst themselves. 'Now though, now we will let the seagulls, the gannets and the street vultures such as rooks and crows fly off with the rest of what is left of him.'

All went silent for a moment after Barak had finished with his damning condemnation of the demised and much despised prefect. But then after this grim thoughtful silence there was a short period of uproar. It was now, now for the first time did the marines draw their short swords. Albeit if it was only to clash their blades loudly upon their long rectangular eagle emblazoned shields, this, the soldiers did in a loud salute to Barak's ever wily cunning. And amongst them there was none who saluted louder or longer than the very emotional tearful Spaniard, Ferdinand. Barak as well as through his wits and his guile also in some degree to his honesty had made this day's law breaking and most gory event no more than some sort of misdemeanour. Mad dogs had slain the prefect, after this was done the beasts had merely ran off through the bustling crowd into the forest. These imagined dogs would of course obviously be depicted as rabid creatures, much like Cicero, Barak supposed. Anyway nobody, but nobody in the bustling harbour town of Varnak would gainsay that story no matter how far fetched it might seem. And this in fear that their very lives would be forfeit by the avenging giant, as this was after all the giant's own somewhat sinister plot. So, now no soldiers would suffer the agony and the misery of the cross, all would be peaceful and harmonious once again. Well hopefully at least it would remain so, this until the next time that perhaps big Barak paid a visit to Varnak.

Barak now took the last drink from the deceased gypsy's gourd then the ogre spoke up once more in a gusty and bullish fashion.

'I myself will write a lengthy passage to my good friend the Emperor Septimius Severus. Aye and also I myself will tell him that I bore witness to this tragedy as to the tragic sad demise of the brave and most noble Cicero.' Barak after this obvious lie then spat onto the cobbles in disgust once these words were spoken. Apparently even the slayer's clever dubious lying had at times its limitations.

But still besides all of this, there was yet another roar of wild raucous laughter from both the Norse and the marines alike, Barak had once again became the hero and entertainer.

Thus as ever enjoying the adulation, and of course his admiring audience Barak once again said on.

'For I must as it so happens write to him anyway,' Barak said as he smiled wryly. The giant had at this moment an adoring audience hanging onto every word he said, and anyway he was quite enjoying his own sense of humour.

'It is a letter concerning a matter of the utmost and greatest importance,' Barak added with a serious tone to his voice. 'Yes, it is indeed a most important delicate communication I must send off. ' Now all about him as the giant spoke the crowd listened with a great eagerness and interest as to what Barak's next witty comment would be.

Now the giant drank from a fresh gourd kindly offered him by the unsteady Horst, then the slayer smoked upon his pipe briefly whilst he deliberated his next words. On such merry get together occasions as this was turning out to be, well, timing was very important. With a final puff upon his pipe and a wry smile Barak spoke again.

'I hear there is to be built in my honour a statue, this statue is to be built in the senate of all places. Oh yes and also perhaps there will be even another one built, aye and this at the very gates of the great arena of Rome itself, in the Coliseum.'

All of the marines applauded madly seeing the importance and significance that was bestowed by this great honour. Like most of them Barak was a foreigner, these men were mostly auxiliaries, Germans, Spaniards, Gauls even Huns as well as a few Goths. So for the proud pompous Romans to honour the giant in such a way, well this filled each and every one of them with a certain amount of pride. For up till now it was unheard of for a foreigner to have a statue built in their honour, this either in the Senate or the arena or anywhere else for that matter. The Norse men though in all truth were not quite sure what it was, they applauded and simply clapped and cheered loudly because Ragnor did so.

Barak, after another swift drink went on with himself once again.

'Of course it would greatly displease me should the statue or perhaps statues be short or fat or skinny, or undersized in any way,' the ogre said most sincerely. Now there was another roar of laughter and Barak had to wait some while before he could continue to speak once again. 'These monuments dedicated to my apparent greatness, must in truth be both noble and handsome in bearing. Oh aye, indeed these lifelike images must depict all of my most finest and endearing features.' Barak said all of this with an element of passion and some amount of light hearted sincerity, this as he stroked his trimmed well kept white goatee beard. And of course the giant was not at this present moment in time in the mood to be humble or modest in any way.

Once again there was yet another round of long, loud laughter from what remained of the crowd and the marines. This merriment was next of all followed by even more wild and raucous doting applause. Barak smiled broadly on hearing this adulation as next he then bowed and saluted his doting audience. And then with this final act done the satisfied ogre waved his fond farewell before finally making his way alone from the market square.

Later on that day the big noisy seagulls of Varnak would no doubt later swoop down and finish off what was left of the hapless luckless prefect. However in the meanwhile Barak would head off towards the Falcon to organise the loading and storing of the supplies for the remainder of their voyage. Though not of course before stopping off at the tavern where he had previously been both sleeping and drinking while the storm had raged these past days.

With the storm abated all was just as ever in the taverns and being so then the tables and chairs were laid out once again in readiness for hungry, heavy pursed diners.

Barak, as he had scheduled, went to the tavern, hurriedly the thirsty ogre drank down a gallon of good ale then he dined upon a large well cooked rabbit and squirrel pie. At this time Barak could see no sign of a single Viking or of the creature which he had left in Ragnor's and Tark's company. Once his dining was over and done with the slayer next with huge strides was off toward the Falcon for a quick inspection of the supplies and livestock. Barak of course as ever wanted to see with his own black eyes that all was well, that all was safe and secure. Now Barak glanced skyward, the skies were darkening once again, the wind was blowing chill and strong, perhaps one more day in the tavern would not hurt. Aye and also another day's socialising would give him more time to become familiar with the big green halfling. And if the creature could drink as quickly as he or it could eat then the thing would certainly make a good drinking partner Barak thought cheerily to himself. Aye and anyway after all Varnak was the last civilization the travellers would see for some time. Indeed mayhap it was the last civilization any of them would ever see, this if the so called gods and bad luck was against them.

Well, this was if civilization you could call it. For what after all was civilized about the whipping and burning of either a man or beast in the name of a morning's entertainment. Aye and a beast that was chained in heavy links to a pole in the middle of a market square at that.

Barak after a short search of the harbour front swung the doors open to a tavern where here at long length he found the Viking. Ragnor of course had in the meantime been visiting several other drinking establishments. Now Ragnor, Tark, the creature and a collection of the Norsemen were all sitting drinking about a long table. In this tavern there was plenty of room for tables as now the slave fair was on. And of course a dead prefect after all was not about to spoil the day for the worthless buyers of human flesh. Barak smiled as he glanced all about him. Barak at this particular time was followed by his own small company of Norsemen who had been stacking and packing the supplies aboard the Falcon. Now in anticipation of a good day's drinking Barak's scarred, tattooed face broke out into a most warm smile. All about that crowded smoke filled place there was some sort of non-sensible activity going. Drunken pot bellied men diced and arm wrestled, and there was also a sad skinny fool of a juggler with one eye who kept dropping his eggs. On top of this nonsense there was a fat, middle-aged belly dancer in the corner of the room making quite a fool of herself in front of a bunch of drunken simpletons. Almost immediately, a fist fight broke out between two big fat red faced men. These fools fought over the price of a scabby worm ridden hunting dog that itched and scratched at itself a lot. However their pathetic fight was to be in vain as the sad looking dog skulked out of the back door, this on the arrival of Barak with his two great hounds at his side. Anyway the itchy creature in Barak's considered opinion was not worth a flagon of the Briton's wishy washy ale.

'Ah this is just my sort of place today, what say you Ragnor, is this not a fine drinking house?' asked the giant as he walked over to the long rectangular table where the big Viking sea lord was seated. Ragnor grinned broadly then grunted in reply as he shoved yet another fat pork sausage into his hairy mouth, he nodded keenly in agreement. Ragnor as ever these days was more interested in knowing how much money the place was taking. This with his ambitions still firmly fixed on being a fat purple nosed innkeeper with a purse full of money and a cellar full of drink.

Of a sudden this place had strangely and quickly calmed with the appearance of Barak accompanied by his half dozen or so evil-looking followers. Since the ending of the storm and the savage affair in the square earlier that morning the taverns of Varnak had all been full to capacity. Aye and this with those who were not there to witness the killings as well as those that were. Now each and everybody in the town of Varnak had their own story to tell of how the gypsies and also the disliked prefect had met their grizzly end. Though this of course however was something that did not concern Barak one little bit. Later on in the day, after the slave market perhaps sanity and order to some degree would return to Varnak. In the meanwhile though, the price of frothy ale and huge breakfeasts swelled the purses of every tavern in Varnak.

A long pinewood table which sat next to Ragnor's was suddenly politely vacated by some dozen or so dark skinned men. All of these fellows wore turbans and were dressed in flowing colourful robes, obviously slavers from Persia who had done their dealings early. Men from the desert, this was plainly obvious to Barak, and not only by their expensive attire. True to type these peddlers in misery drank not the good beer or cider; also they turned their arched noses up at the tasty fat pork sausages everyone else under the roof greedily consumed. Some people apparently just did not know what tasty meat they were missing Barak thought to himself. But this, the ogre pondered on but briefly as he shouted out loudly for a little service, and of course as usual well it was not long in coming either. At once there was a quick switching of seats as Barak sat himself down to drink with Tark, Ragnor and Loki; a little reluctantly the ogre sat also with Bull Neck. Oh and of course most importantly he sat himself down next to their new recruit, the big green and quite shocking looking troll.

This strange but very powerful creature sat there silently listening intently to every word spoken by all those around him. Next after a brief little run down of the days occurrences the Troll was given food and drink, these of course he both consumed very quickly. Then and after this brief gorging, well the thing next even puffed for some time upon Barak's beloved clay pipe. Very kindly the giant thought the creature needed something a little stronger than ale after the events of that very busy morning. As after all, it was not yet mid day and already four men had been done and accounted for. Aye and it was true though it was albeit that these were all bad and most worthless men. Oh yes this indeed was a market day that would be long remembered in the Roman harbour of Varnak. Anyway, the strong weed more than anything else seemed to put the creature at some sort of ease with himself and all that went on around him. Casually now the great green warty thing stretched out his broad flat webbed feet toward the fire then he or it lay back in his high backed chair with a most strange look about it.

Now at this very moment in time the atmosphere in the busy bustling tavern was very noisy but never the less cordial and in good spirit, aye and also the drinks as the norm came quickly and lasted not long at all.

'I would sail on the evening tide Ragnor, tell me can we do that sea master, is that possible? ' Barak asked as it drew nearer to the midday.

Ragnor nodded in a half hearted fashion, he too as it so happened would like another day of drinking in Varnak. Though in his professional capacity as the captain of the Falcon the Norseman felt obliged not to suggest such another days stall.

'Aye, oh aye we can do that, but why Barak? Why miss this tide we have now and this good steady wind? There is still time enough to sail now you know, well that is if we hurry on but a bit,' the Viking added cleverly.

Barak paused, the ogre was thoughtful for but a moment before replying to Ragnor's well-put question.

'Well, to tell you the truth my good friend, I just wanted to see how much money this tavern takes in the next few hours. Now the giant was leaning across the table and was speaking in a most crafty whisper, as ever the wily Barak knew only too well how to stall the Viking when need be. 'It is slave market day, this being so then it should get very busy in here, don't you think so Ragnor?'

Ragnor beamed as he drummed his gold ringed fingers upon the solid pine table in a most happy boisterous fashion.

'Ah then my friend, so you are interested in buying a share of a tavern after all?' he grinned. 'You know what, well I knew it Barak, oh aye my friend indeed I just knew it,' the Viking next said on merrily. 'As after all you are a man of money, a man of means and property, aye you are a man not at all unlike myself I must say,' Ragnor said all of this whilst puffing out his chest and hunching up his broad shoulder. 'Why, we together we could buy one tavern then another, aye and then even another one after that. Why Barak together we could take over the whole drinking trade along the Baltic coast you and I,' Ragnor went on most gleefully. 'My loyal sea rogues, why they would become our barmen, our tavern's guards and of course our best customers. We would thrive we would prosper, to hell with the cold salt sea I say. I would sooner drown myself in good drink rather than in a freezing salty sea any day. ' Then with this said next the Viking Sea Lord touched cups with the giant in a toast to their prosperous future behind a bar counter. Aye and anyway one more day in another tavern after so many spent in the past would not after all do them any harm.

Barak though of course had no interest in going into the innkeeping business, and that was here or anywhere else for that matter. However Barak did want to relax the Troll and talk with him, the ogre wanted to find out exactly what this strange creature was all about. Aye and this was far much more preferable instead of just putting him straight aboard the Falcon then sailing off toward the distant horizon.

Also that was of course assuming the huge green creature had not changed his mind, and perhaps now had other plans for his future. This though Barak had thought to himself was most doubtful, aye most unlikely. And also as for their current adventure, well there was still plenty of time enough to do what they must do. But as ever in such delicate matters thought it was best if the task was all done right, aye and done right the first time. As there alas would be no second chances here upon this most perilous dangerous, even foolhardy trek. And in all truth the first careless blunder the bold adventures made along the way, well it could well be their last. As for the big green Troll, well, with a bellyful of drink and a few more puffs of Barak's pipe the tale that the creature told was indeed a one of great sorrow and woe.

Barak as ever by his cunning and by his kindness had won the fearsome but very useful creature over. Once again, for a final time Barak had offered him or it, or whatever else the noble thing, was a purse of gold to go wherever it was he wished to go. True, earlier the Troll did say he wished to travel by either road or sea, just to go wherever his saviour Barak would wander, and to hell with the dangers. Barak though despite his plotting and all and everything else was now letting his conscience get the better of him. It was plainly obvious this creature had suffered much in his life without enduring yet more hardship. Unexpectantly, now honesty as well as his conscience was somewhat troubling the ever calculating giant. Barak to his credit, well, the ogre did point out to the Troll this quest was not at all an easy one, as it was fraught with all manner of peril and hidden danger. Now this was the Troll's last option, the big frog could leave with a purse full of coins or the creature could take his chance with his new found friends. Barak now with an almost clear conscience offered him a part in their non profit making venture, a venture that could quite possibly bring about his very end. In all truth Barak supposed he was a bit disappointed with his own honesty, as this of course was no way to gain and recruit good warriors, green or otherwise.

After all everything that could have been plundered had already been taken, so it was blood sweat and tears all the way now, this right till the very end of it. Anyone or anything with a brain and armed with this information would have taken the sensible course. Aye, they would have taken the money offered then ran off in the opposite direction just as rapidly as possible. However though, the troll of course being a troll, well the thing picked the most non-sensible course, this by deciding to sail on the evening tide with the rest of the brave but foolish chancers. Anyway the day wore on as eventually darkness fell, soon it would be time to leave the warmth and comfort of the still very busy most interesting tavern.

'Tell me my green warty friend, before I do order and pay for the rest of these last drinks in this tavern, have you by chance a name to be called by?' Barak enquired reclaiming his pipe from the yellow blinking eyed troll.

Now the troll shook his big green newt like head slowly and perhaps somewhat sadly.

'No, no I have not a name my lord, well at least not a one I ever liked, or none you could ever say,' the troll replied after a quick flick of his forked tongue.

'But your human mother did she not give you a name then?' Barak asked, this after puffing upon his pipe then very generously passing it back to the halfling.

The big troll puffed out a cloud of dense smoke then the creature paused as he spoke in that croaky reptilian voice of his. It was a voice which was becoming by the way ever croakier with the more weed he smoked.

'Aye but it was a troll name so believe me like I say my Lord you could never hope to pronounce it.'

Next the troll blinked again the lenses of his yellow eyes, these lenses flicking sideways instead of upwards and downwards as do humans.

'Anyway my lord, pray tell me how is it you knew that it was my mother who was the human part of my make up Barak?' the troll asked after another heavy puff upon the giant's pipe.

Barak smiled craftily before he replied, the ogre wondered with interest what reaction the answer to the troll's question would bring about.

'Because my large green friend, I can't see many men wanting to force themselves upon a female swamp troll, if you know what I mean,' the giant answered with just the hint of a cheeky smile. 'After all the female sex of that particular species, well these are not things of great beauty are they? ' the giant chuckled. 'Oh and also of course I do know the females swamp trolls are twice the size of the males, so believe me this would be a task that would take some doing in the first place. No, no your mother without any doubt was a human I would think, in fact I would gamble my good dragon sword upon it,' Barak added in a most confident fashion.

There was complete silence for a moment or two about the long table as no one knew quite how the creature was going to react to Barak's matter of fact explanation of things. After all this was not a human thing sitting there in front of them all, well at least it was not entirely human. With a flick of its tongue the troll blinked again, then the creature passed the clay pipe back to Barak, this only after very politely first wiping the mouth piece clean upon a table napkin.

Slowly then after but a moment he or it held out a huge long fingered webbed hand toward Barak in friendship.

Next the troll's slightly forked purple tongue flicked out as it did so every now and then as once again the great green warty creature blinked those big yellow eyes.

Barak took the huge broad webbed scaly hand and the ogre shook it warmly, there was much power in that handshake.

'I meant no offence to you by my words, you do I hope understand this?' Barak asked in a kindly tone of voice.

'None taken my lord Barak,' the troll replied, his eyelids rolling side wards once again. 'You know, I have never thought of that, that of what you have just spoken to me I mean Barak.' The creature said this with a strange grin, a grin that revealed a ridge of hard even looking blunt but powerful teeth. 'About my mother, I mean her being a female human. For strange as it might seem, I think she and my father were quite happy living together as husband and wife. '

On hearing these words all about the hitherto noisy table went suddenly silent at the halfling's strange statement. Why Ragnor almost choked upon his drink before dropping his goblet to the floor. And also Barak for once, perhaps for even in the first time of his life appeared most shocked by this statement, aye even the great ogre was struck totally speechless. Barak's pipe at once fell from his open mouth, why the ogre next even spilled his drink all over the place. Now it was the halfling who smiled, knowing full well the shock he had just caused by his words, at least all the men around about him supposed it to be a smile. After this smile the Troll spoke up once again.

'I have as you see many failings, also many short comings, of these I am well aware of the halfling said in a low reptilian hiss. 'But being a bastard however, well that I suppose is not one of them' the halfling said on proudly. 'I was you see born in wedlock, as strange as that may seem to you all,' the halfling added with another strange sort of smile. With this both said and, heard by every Norseman there, the silence became quite deadly for a moment or two.

It was silent though only until Horst got the gist of things and understood just what was being said here about the long table.

'Well then creature you are indeed different to us all here my none too pretty friend,' Horst slurred as he rose unsteadily to his foot. 'Well, apart from being a big green warty thing with yellow eyes and a forked tongue I mean.' And this, the drunken Horst chuckled while dribbling beer all over his unkempt beard. 'For you must know this my noble beast, very few of us here, well, with the exception of Barak who of course as everyone now knows is royalty. Well very few of us here knew both of our parents,' Horst said honestly with a drunken lopsided smile. 'In fact, I must say this here and now, aye and in all honesty,' Horst then burbled loudly before continuing whilst taking another drink of his vodka. 'Well I for one, well, I never met either one of mine, parents I mean.' Horst said this with a carefree could not care sort of shrug. 'So perhaps, just perhaps my large hairy friends that is the reason why I am a worthless drunkard. Aye and also the reason why mayhap I find myself in the company of an unhinged ogre a big green lizard and a host of blood thirsty murdering Vikings,' Horst added with a smile followed by a loud belch.

'And my friends if that is so, if that is the case for the way I am, then I will salute them both for deserting me as a babe,' Horst said these words with watery eyes. In truth the drunken German was becoming quite emotional, still he went on. 'Because my friends, well I do suppose I like the rough but nevertheless honest company I keep.' Horst said this while raising his drink aloft then consuming a good amount of it in a single gulp.

Now the table was briefly deathly silent for a moment before suddenly it erupted into a rough but most honest mirthful merriment. The troll, as well as everyone else there were now falling about in fits of uncontrollable laughter, this at Horst's honest, somewhat profound statement. Even the morose ever miserable Bull Neck, well not even that oaf could help himself from suppressing a crooked lopsided sort of smile. Now, now for the first time in his whole life the troll was at long last at some sort of peace with himself. The halfling now looked about him and he saw a huge drooling red-bearded hunchback in the shape of the none-too-pretty Loki.

Then there was Bull Neck who he had noticed stuttered and stammered at even the mention of Barak's name. Also Bull Neck had those odd coloured eyes as well as an even odder most unpleasant disposition. Of course perhaps most importantly there was the gigantic most fearsome looking much tattooed Barak. People in the streets as well as the taverns turned their attention to stare in horror towards him more than anyone else amongst the motley company of large hairy misfits. Men who by the by were mostly incomplete, as not many of these rough but amiable men had two eyes, two ears and a full nose about them. Aye at least half a dozen of Ragnor's men had patches over one eye or the other whilst pieces of their noses and ears were either sliced off by the sword or bitten off in a savage drunken brawl of some sort. Indeed it was only the black garbed warrior Tark and the two young boys who appeared to look anywhere remotely normal. Aye each and every one of the crewmen they were a wild wanton unkempt unwashed lot. Men who were covered in animal skins as well as bits and pieces of captured armour from a dozen or so nations these fierce warriors had clashed with in the past. And also these Norsemen wore cleverly designed bronze horned helmets with nose guards and eye slits upon their scraggy raggy itchy red heads. Indeed, these men were more animal in appearance at first glance than perhaps they were human. Why, in this busy bustling inn no one even gave him a second glance, now he was at last a freak amongst freaks. Yes the halfling was for the first time in his entire life a most happy contented large green creature.

Ragnor suddenly arose and he banged loudly upon the stout table as he ordered up more drink, this as well as a roast chicken for each and everybody. Oh and this of course the Viking put upon Barak's bill. On the arrival of the roast birds the troll as much expected impressed everyone as he swallowed his chicken down whole and in a single gulp. To Barak perhaps more so than even the other watchers this was most impressive, so impressed was the ogre he very kindly bought the creature several more chickens. Fat plump well roasted birds that all went down exactly the same way as the first and just as quickly. So all in all, well it turned out to be a most pleasant cordial afternoon, being so the warriors drank on and the bold band of warriors feasted as was their norm. Indeed this was the old Norse way, aye this more or less was the code of their violent often short lives. Drink much, eat much, laugh and make merry for the now, as tomorrow perhaps death awaited them. After feasting till the Vikings could neither eat nor drink no more, still three parts drunk the ragged party of men set sail upon the evening tide. Aye and this, the sea wolves did whilst singing out loudly their ancient defiant bloodthirsty songs of the sea. Now, yes now it was that the rest of the bloody reckless adventure would start a proper yet again.

For many days the adventurers sailed on with a good but cold wind at their broad backs, there were no more ports, no more harbours, no more towns or hamlets. And as bad luck had it well at long length the voyagers were becalmed. Nothing now though would deter Ragnor's reckless crew, so next the oars were struck out into a cold and grey lifeless sea. With no wind to assist the Falcon for many more days the seafaring warriors rowed on, then rowed on again. Wearily the Norsemen slept then woke yet again while others of their brotherhood had taken their place at the oars. Once rested the shift of huge determined men changed places only to row once more until even their iron hard hands blistered whilst their hearts pounded inside of their huge chests. Still though one way or another, their far off destination would be reached, aye this no matter what.

And all of this while strange fearful beasts raised their huge ugly heads above the black stagnant waters dripping with stinking dead seaweed, blinking as the things did so at the voyagers with huge rounded eyes. However, the ugly stinking beasts were unsure of these large bold trespassers, and so the monsters were much more cautious than usual and their hunger left them. Perhaps in time there would be easier prey coming soon to feast upon, easier victims, and easier meals. So with this being the case thankfully these slimy beasts sank their big ugly heads back again into the cold black depths of their stagnant watery abode.

Dense fog came as quickly as it went but still the stout long dragon ship moved on slowly ever steadily towards its eventual destination.

Ragnor, his instincts honed to the sea almost from his very birth forged on as if he had done this voyage a hundred times over, none there aboard ever doubted him. The big Viking, well, he was after all a master mariner and Ragnor had no equal in his knowledge of the seas and the oceans.

Through black clouded rain filled skies and foggy freezing days that turned into even colder nights. And then nights that turned into even darker days the

Norsemen rowed on without any murmur or even a single complaint. Indeed so dark was it that at length not one man there aboard the Falcon knew the difference between night and day. Neither the sun nor moon nor the stars up above were seen, aye and all of this for who knows how long? There was after a long length of time when all aboard the Falcon were weary and worn out from their efforts. It was only then when Barak and the huge swamp troll manned the oars that pushed the Falcon ever forward, ever onward. Relentlessly the giant with the great green beast pulled on the oars while the men slept and rested themselves. Stroke for stroke together the ogre and the troll rowed through the fog and the ever gathering gloom. Perhaps now inside of their own minds each great beast tested one another seeing who would first weary from these strenuous exertions, however none did. And so with this being the case, and with the great united power of these titans the Falcon had made good her time across the still dark monster filled waters. Those following days that passed by were hard to calculate due to the constant fog and darkness. But then and at long last the Falcon was beached upon the very shingle bay from where Barak had last left these shores many years ago.

Chapter Fifteen

Once the dragon boat was beached the horses were unloaded, without any delay the beasts were quickly put to work. Speedily the Falcon was next dragged up high and dry onto the shingle beach. This was after a bit of a struggle due to the steep incline, still nevertheless here was to be the Falcon's final berth place. Here the dragonship would rest until the vessel was required once again, well that was of course if anyone was alive to sail it. This cove, this haven was a secure place that was far beyond the reach of even the highest of winter tides. Next the horses after their labours were unharnessed and loosely hobbled, this done the beasts were set free to graze upon the sharp but nutritious dune grass. All about there was fortunately an abundance of driftwood, aye and this was sad broken wood. As this timber, well it was the wooden bones of ships from every country that had ever put a vessel out to sea. With this amount of ready fuel available several huge well stacked roaring fires gave these rogues all the heat and light the warriors had missed of late. Aye these dancing flames gave the Norsemen all a warm most cheery feeling. On that night Barak killed off the rest of the livestock, now in great merriment the warriors drank while feasting around the blazing crackling camp fires.

Chickens, turkeys and geese were all either roasted or went into one of Barak's huge cooking pots to make a thick most welcome warming broth. Meanwhile the Norsemen lounged about lazily, talking and laughing loudly before the blazing fires. Now after the ordeals of the past, the warriors sapped strength, as well as their spent energy was slowly but surely returning to them.

'Will we leave this place in the morning at first light Barak?' Ragnor asked this question as he tucked greedily into yet another roast chicken. It was at it so happened the third one the Viking had already hungrily consumed, well that as well as also two big bowls of thick broth.

'No,' Barak answered as he threw a dead but still feathered chicken into the air for his own big black eagle. At once the great black bird swooped silently down from its perch upon the mast head of the Falcon seizing its supper in mid air before returning to its post to eagerly devour the chicken. 'Your men have done well Ragnor so we will let them rest late; noon, aye noon is early enough to continue on our long journey. We have been a long time aboard the Falcon and your men have rowed many painful leagues.' Barak explained this as he crushed a fat roast chicken carcass between his sharp teeth then swallowed some of the flesh before saying on.

'The men will need all their strength returned to both their bodies and their souls, so I will not sicken them now,' the giant went on, wiping grease from his mouth. 'Do not worry my friend there is time a plenty to get to the palace for the antidote. You know me well enough in fact I suppose no one knows me better.' Barak said as he ran a huge hand over one of his dog's great broad heads. 'And I would sooner travel a little slower in a more careful fashion than charge off at a fast pace that sickened both man and beast. '

With these words said, Barak wiped his hands clean on a rag and then he relit his pipe. Barak at once blew out a cloud of smoke as he looked about him at those who had heard his words. To a man the Norsemen muttered amongst themselves in total agreement. After all, it was far better to fight rested and well fed than be tired starved and foot sore.

'We have two day's march on the sand dunes, Ragnor and this is hard going, most tiring.' Barak paused after saying this, and then next he gave to each of his dogs a roast chicken which had been left for some time to cool.

'We have food and fresh water enough for two, perhaps even three days Ragnor,' Barak explained. 'I have kept back cured sausages, smoked fish and a good quantity of boiled eggs. So we will of course not starve on our travel,' the giant assured everybody. 'I also have German beer a plenty, six barrels of it. And this beer you can pour into your gourds, the remainder we will strap to the horses in the kegs. Of course this refreshment is just to ease the weariness of our long trek. ' Barak took another blow of his pipe then smiled he was quite pleased with his careful forward planning of things so far. 'Also, I did of course not neglect myself. I have purchased a good quantity of vodka and a sack of black mountain weed; this will help me to think in times of the darkness that lie ahead?' Barak said this with a broad smile as he lounged most casual like before a raging fire.

At this the Vikings all laughed and joked amongst themselves whilst cheering the giant most heartily. Now the Norsemen had good food and drink a plenty, and in all reality these rugged warriors neither needed nor wanted for themselves any more than that.

'And now before we do go any further my friend, well I will tell you all of what lies ahead of us. And then you must on hearing what I have to say, decide if you and your men, are still with me or not, Ragnor,' Barak said as he leaned his back against a washed up tree stump.

Intrigued the Norsemen came in closer from their individual fires with their frothy beer and their well cooked meat. Silently then the Viking brotherhood gathered about in a tight circle just to hear what it was the giant had to say to them. So then it was while sitting there with the savage but loyal Vikings in attendance Barak drew out a rough map in the shingle. And all the while the giant went on and told the silent listeners of what terrors and dangers lay ahead of them. Human foes were one thing, but what natural obstacles and what maneating animals would be encountered on their way, well that indeed was another story.

After some time silently pondering the map etched in the shingle, and of course, thinking about the giant's almost honest breakdown of the journey. It was the red bearded Ragnor who rose from the circle of his hitherto feasting and drinking reavers. Who, it has to be said had become suddenly strangely quiet, in fact the Norsemen were totally silent and even a little subdued. Also, as implied the ravenous feasting and the boisterous drinking had also lost some of its former revelry and gusto.

'So, once across these mountainous dunes we are on the sand flats, yes? And here is where we can feast upon small reed deer is it not? Well this is of course very good Barak,' a smiling Ragnor said. 'I do as you well know like venison. Aye I think perhaps it is my favourite of all meats, though I do like boar and bear meat also. Oh and also I think after chewing upon cured sausages and smoked fish, well venison will be a most welcome feast.' Ragnor was smiling now and even chuckling in a half drunken fashion to himself as he deliberated on his next words. 'Aye and by the sounds of it the rest of our adventure is truly an adventure, just as you said it would be Barak. No, I must say that you do not disappoint us my large friend, in all truth it can be called nothing else but an adventure.' Ragnor said this out loud in a loud bold and blustery voice. 'You have just as ever not let us down Barak, has he my men, my brothers?' Ragnor declared with a booming voice.

'Well, you know me, so of course I do try not to fail, Ragnor,' Barak said with a wholesome laugh.

There was at this point a chuckle from Ragnor's crew of warriors, a cautious chuckle, but a chuckle nonetheless.

'So when we have walked for some days across these flat fenlands we will arrive at this black forest of yours you say?' Ragnor said with a smile as he took a mouthful of beer from his gourd.

Barak smiled, sucked upon his pipe and then he gave a slight nod. Ragnor, the giant suspected was now in the chair and in the mood for a light hearted jibe, aye and no doubt a jibe at his expense.

'Once here in this dark most dangerous forest you say we must then repel huge bears and packs of ravenous wolves that abound there. And these creatures you further say, are most partial to the flesh of man, am I right so far Barak?' Ragnor asked this after another mouthful of ale and a final bite of his roast chicken. With this done the big Viking belched loudly then tore what was left of his chicken apart and fed Barak's huge dogs with the remains of the carcase.

'Yes, oh yes you have got it all right so far, Ragnor.' Barak said this with a knowing smile as he began oiling his beloved dragon sword. Now the giant smiled again, he chuckled to himself as he wiped the blade lovingly clean with a rag then replaced it back into its leather scabbard.

'Then, when and after we have fought with the wild beasts of the forest and hopefully drove them off back into the wild, we will once again begin to forge on. And with Odin's help and with much good luck we will hopefully emerge many days, even weeks later, to walk from the dark forest. With these perils hopefully overcome we next have a river to cross then Barak, is this so?' Once again Barak gave a nod but once again the ogre said nothing in reply so Ragnor continued. 'Aye and you do say that this is a great wide river. Aye and also it is a river that is black and deep, slow moving in some places while being wild fast and rampant in others. But here Barak, so you say, the salmon are large and the fish are many for us to eat and gorge upon.' Ragnor said this while rubbing his ever growing belly in mock excitement before continuing with his entertaining break down of their coming journey. 'Ah but alas, there are also great slimy beasts lying under these waters, beasts that would in turn feast upon our flesh also, yes? There had been an ever growing sniggering amongst the pirates, now though that sniggering was turning into more of a loud chuckle as the Norsemen were all quite enjoying this light hearted baiting of the giant.

'Well Ragnor, after all I never said this venture was going to be easy all of the way did I?' Barak said with a good humoured smile.

'Aye true, true, this is all very true Barak, you made no such promise,' the Viking chieftain agreed with a broad and cheery smile. Ragnor then ran his ice blue eyes over his smiling men and then after but a moment he continued with his evaluation of the situation. It must be said the big Viking was in all truth quite enjoying himself on his make believe podium. 'With Odin willing it, we can hopefully escape from the bears and the wolves of this dark and grim forest, maybe even avoiding the serpents that lurk in the depths of the black river if our luck holds out. Ah but you then further say Barak, we must make our way up some steep treacherous mountain pass. Aye and a mountain pass which of course by that time of year will doubtless be both icy and snowbound. '

Once again Barak offered no argument and the ogre gave another nod of agreement. And this was followed by a broad grin as the giant waved his huge sausage sized fingered hands in a care free and dismissive fashion. At this little conversation the slayer thought to himself well, it was after all becoming quite amusing. Ragnor after taking time to pause for a moment once again continued with his giant baiting. 'Oh and then, well if I am not much mistaken Barak? You further say we must speak in whispers once in these lofty peaks. Aye and this because there are often, snowfalls brought about by a sudden sharp noise in these snowy heights? '

Once again Barak gave another positive but uncaring nod as he took a deep swallow of vodka which in turn was followed by a long puff upon his pipe.

'Well winter comes early in this place, but alas no one can help the weather, Ragnor, you of all men should know that. This being that you are a fearless and most intrepid Viking explorer,' the giant sniggered.

Ragnor though was unabashed by Barak's obvious sarcasm. So the big Viking briefly paused then he continued speaking once again after he took another swallow of his frothy beer. All of this talking, well it was turning out to be very dry work.

'In these snowy peaks you further say the great mountain lion lives. And of course these creatures you tell us are huge fanged things, with teeth in their heads longer than a Persian's dagger,' Ragnor smiled then smirked before continuing.

'Aye and also you do say this to us, do you not Barak?

Once again the giant smiled he gave an uncaring shrug before puffing lazily upon his pipe as he stretched leisurely in front of the raging fire.

'Yes, yes I do say this, but these Lions they are a rare beast now, and not nearly as common as they once were years ago.'

Ragnor raised his bushy red eyebrows in mock disappointment and then he spoke.

'Well how truly sad I am about that, as I was of course so looking forward to meeting up with one of them in the midst of a blizzard on a winding icy road. Why this exciting event would after all be a good and entertaining story to tell over the bar counter in our tavern Barak, would it not?' Ragnor said this with a cynical smirk.

Now of course this humorous comment brought not a chuckle but a roar of laughter from Ragnor's rough band of men, Barak it appeared was not the only one with a sense of humour.

However, the ogre as ever was quite unflustered and he was enjoying Ragnor's humour almost as much as the Viking and his followers were.

'Exactly, why these are my very thoughts also Ragnor,' Barak said blowing smoke hoops into the windless starless night.

Ragnor continued with his giant baiting once again having to raise his voice now over the rough mirthful laughter of his men. As all there noticed the big Viking was quite enjoying this little show he was putting on. The initial shock of Barak's explanation of what horrors lay ahead of them was passed. And this was now becoming to the brave and intrepid Norsemen no more than just another adventure to tell in a tavern or over a camp fire in the years to come. Ragnor wiped beer froth from his big beard then continued with Barak's humourous and entertaining interrogation.

'Then and once up and over this mountain, well that is of course if we are not all eaten alive by beasts which should have surely died out many years ago or crushed and swept away by a snowfall. Next we will descend down to the windblown harsh and frozen steppes that lie far below us, how inviting!' Ragnor paused at this point after his lengthy long winded speech making sure that all about him were still paying him their full attention, and they were. And so with this observation made then once again the very talkative Viking continued. 'Here somewhere on the these windswept steppes or upon the barren desert you further say these accursed nameless brothers could well have an ambush of some sorts planned for us, do you not? '

Barak chuckled and kicked another log onto the blazing fire as the ogre spat black unhealthy looking phlegm into the pepples. Next the giant ground his teeth together as he cursed with some gusto his bad broken back molar, as now it was paining him yet again. But then after cursing and failing to dislodge the tooth with his fierce grinding the great Ogre sighed heavily, next he yawned and stretched out his great arms. With this task done, the giant burped loudly while he took another draw upon his long clay pipe before speaking.

'Deserters and untrained rabble Ragnor, cowardly bandits, we can kill them all, kill them just as easy as we did Wraif and his bunch of sad fools,' Barak announced with much confidence. 'We will take their horses, we will eat their food, drink their beer and vodka and also whatever other refreshment these fools have about them.' Barak said this with an element of some glee as well and as ever with his boundless confidence. 'Aye, and who knows my friends, what other treasures and trinkets these rogues have gathered in their saddlebags. Oh yes and all this treasure accrued from over their many years of robbing and thieving from hapless desert travellers Ragnor?'

Now the Norseman on hearing these encouraging words raised his bushy red eyebrows as the big Viking smiled in gleeful expectation. Of a sudden Ragnor seemed to forget that this trek for him was supposed to be a non-profit making venture.

Barak seeing that Ragnor was speechless with the very thought of spoils elaborated a little more.

'Why, for all we know Ragnor these fools could be decked out high and low with gold and silver, aye and all manner of other priceless gems,' Barak went on raising his voice over Horst's ear bursting snoring.

Ragnor paused for just a moment before speaking while he took for himself another little drink.

'Gold, gold! Aye and gems too you say Barak?' Ragnor asked thinking here he might beget the funds for to buy a tavern, perhaps even two. True it was the big Viking had booty enough back home in the cold stark north to buy the biggest and the busiest of inns. But still why travel all that way, just to explain things to his fat wife, his foppish son and his useless daughter, all that way across rough winter seas just to say he was done with all of them? Aye, all that long way northward, when he could stop on his way back with enough coinage to become a fat unhealthy purple nosed but prosperous innkeeper?

Barak gave an unhesitating nod in answer to his friend's question, then he puffed once again upon his long clay and much loved pipe.

'Aye spoils a plenty these rogues will have Ragnor, and of that I am most certain. But to be honest, I just hope these fools have some good weed about them, for by then I will be running myself a little low you know,' Barak said with a troubled sigh.

Ragnor had to laugh out loud at the giant's words, just as did all of his rough men, Barak as ever was the optimist. Why, the giant not only hoped for riches, not that he wanted any for himself, this bonus would be for the men. No, it was only strong weed and drink that the ogre would be craving for when the time came.

'What about the swamp, Barak? Why have you not told him about the swamp?' Tark said in a hushed whisper as he moved close up to the giant.

'Ssshh be still boy, I will tell them later about the swamp, well if need be, too much information in a single go, can often spoil things you know. Besides, Ragnor as you must well know by now has no liking for swamps, bogs or even marshes.' Barak suddenly pulled himself up onto his huge feet then the ogre coughed, spat and sucked on that annoying back tooth of his. 'Enough of all this, what will be after all will be,' the giant stated boldly and in a most matter of fact fashion.

'Anyway besides all of that and what lies ahead of us, we still do not have a name for you as yet, my green scaly friend.' Barak said changing the subject and turning his attention to the very relaxed contented looking troll.

'Then you pick me one my Lord Barak,' the troll said, this with his great webbed feet outstretched toward the blazing fire.

Barak gently stroked the head of one of his great dogs whilst deliberating; the ogre was thoughtful for but a moment before he next spoke. Our Troll is our friend, he must have a good name, the name of a warrior, Barak reasoned to himself. For but a moment the giant was thoughtful as he poked at his irritable back tooth with a piece of broken twig. Of a sudden a name came to mind, aye and a good name at that.

'Ragnor, your friend, my friend and a friend of all sitting here about these raging campfires, I speak of the now deceased, much missed Borz. Borz he was a good man, no, a great man was he not?' Barak asked this question already knowing what response and what answer to expect from the savage hairy faces about him.

Ragnor gave a most positive nod, and then the Viking chieftain said on.

'Aye, he was a brave uncomplaining sort of man. And, also Borz was my friend as well as yours, why he would have followed you or me into the pits of hell itself if we were only to ask it of him Barak,' Ragnor said this both honestly and proudly.

Aye, and perhaps, well unless it was the smoke from the fire, then almost tearfully.

Barak nodded in solemn agreement, there was now a moment's silence as all who knew Borz gave a moment's thought to the dear departed most well liked Viking.

'I think that our new enlistment, I think he also has such brave and noble qualities as Borz, and in such matters I am not normally far wrong.' Barak said this with a measured amount of reverence and emotion. 'Perhaps you more than all men know this to be true Ragnor,' the slayer added looking his friend straight in the eye. 'Borz I think would be a good name to give to our large green friend here, what say you my brothers?' Barak asked passionately. At once the Viking chieftain gave a nod of agreement then Ragnor looked to his men who had warmed to the troll greatly. Aye the Norsemen had to their credit welcomed the creature into their violent savage brotherhood. To a man they seemed most pleased the troll or halfling or whatever the creature might be was taking on their dead brother's name.

'Are we all here then agreed? Ragnor asked rising to his feet and standing in the glare of the firelight. 'I ask you all here and now, on this rank smelling shoreline, are we in accord and as one in the giving of the name of Borz to this, this er, er. '

Barak grinned and next helped Ragnor out of his stammering.

'Halfling,' Barak said seeing that Ragnor was in some confusion as how to address their latest large and greenish recruit.

As one now the Norsemen all arose, with their drinks in their hands held high aloft the warriors toasted most loudly and proudly the newly named Borz.

'Is the name then to your liking?' Barak asked as the halfling rose to his huge webbed feet and took a bow. His purple forked tongue flicked out whilst his yellow reptilian eyes with their horizontal black pupils glanced about him into the ranks of barbarians. These barbarians by all accounts were now his brothers, brothers to the bone, and indeed brothers to the very end of it all.

For a moment the creature was it seemed quite lost and overcome by all and everything, dare it be said, even almost tearful with emotion.

'I like it,' the troll at length hissed out in his croaky rasp like voice. 'Aye it is a good and a strong name Lord Barak, I will try to do this name justice,' the creature said with another slight bow of his reptilian head toward the men now gathered about him.

Now there was at once a great roar as the fierce Norsemen saluted their new clan member and brother-in-arms, the halfling now had at last a family, now he belonged.

A young tall blonde headed Norseman with a patch over his right eye, a man who Barak did not know greatly sang an out of tune ballad of death, destruction and gore gained honour. Aye and as said, well he was far out of tune, oh and also of course the words did not rhyme. Still, and but only moments later the whole shaggy crew were screeching away to the same ballad.

'Well Borz, you are most certainly one of us now, so how do you like it? Barak asked with a satisfied grin.

At once the trolls yellow eyes blinked, the lenses moving rapidly from side to side and his tongue flicked outwards as he made a most curious cackling noise. Barak assumed this quite correctly was to be laughter of some sort. However the halfling was unable to give an instant answer, he seemed choked and far distant. After a while, and at length though the creature managed to speak.

'If I die on this very night or even tomorrow I will die a most happy thing,' he said his croaky voice quivering with emotion. 'At long last, I feel that I am of some sort of use, and also that I am amongst friends. For almost a hundred of your years, I have cursed almost every single day of my very being,' he said passionately.

With this said the Halfling spoke no more and then he without another word took himself off and away into the gloomy darkness of the night to be alone with his many thoughts. Now he was free at long last, and the creature swore silently to himself he would stay that way. But whatever horrors did lie ahead of him, well in all truth he cared little. For one thing was most certain the halfling knew well, whilst in the company of his friends, he would never ever be a slave again. Death to him, well that was something which was far more preferable to shackles, chains and the savage cut of the whip.

'A hundred years, he said a hundred years, how so Barak?' Ragnor asked a little mystified by the Halflings strange statement. Barak shrugged as he sucked upon his pipe, then he took a long drink. Now with this done the ogre smiled broadly then he laughed out loudly.

'He is a swamp troll Ragnor, well at least in half,' Barak explained. 'Left be, and without any further life threatening accident, he is only half way through his natural life. In fact now that I think about it, I do suppose he is still growing.' Barak said this with a chuckle that turned into more booming laughter.

'And this, this is something that amuses you Barak?' the big Viking asked, a little concerned about his friend's sanity . Now the giant shook his big bucket head, he was still laughing loudly. Barak placed a huge hand upon his friends shoulder.

'No, you hairy fool, but it certainly pleases me. Why, the creature, it is almost twice my age. Now, now, well now I feel like a boy again,' the giant laughed.

Ragnor gave a bemused shake of his head, and after another drink or two the Viking retired to his berth, this was becoming with every day's passing an ever stranger mission.

On that following day the party of slayers slept late then breakfeasted, and then with this done the Norsemen pushed on across the strength sapping dunes. Two hard days later of foot slogging the party arrived at the sand flats amongst the needle sharp reed grass. Here the men were relaxing whilst enjoying themselves hunting the small but very plentiful red deer. And all of the men feasted well that night, each deer was only about the size of a small goat, and in all honesty these deer were not the best of runners. So between the huge but fast dogs and the black eagle the deer were an easily caught prey. Perhaps while this was not a great sporting event it meant the ever hungry company of northern barbarians were all well supplied with fresh tasty meat.

Some days later as yet another cold dusk fell the adventurers arrived at the verge of the sinister, most eerie looking black forest. Still the mighty Norse however were undaunted, sinister and eerie it might well have been but that was a problem for another day. And so just as the warriors had done since the start of their adventure the men ate, drank then rested themselves well on that dark cold night. Whilst, all the while the warriors slumbered, from deep within the dense dark forest there came the most fearful roars of the great beasts therein.

'It grows colder now my Lord Barak, it looks like snow I think.' Tark said this as he joined Barak on the very edge of the perimeter of the circle of fires they were the only ones of their number awake at that time.

Barak made no reply, but instead the ogre stared out intently into the blackness of the vast dense forest that lay there stretching out before them.

'We will lose men in the forest, you do of course know that Barak?' Tark said a cold shiver running down his back as he said this. Barak turned slowly about and faced his young countryman and then the ogre rubbed out his pipe with a huge thumb.

'Get some sleep lad,' the giant said in almost a whisper. 'For, I do think you will have much need of it, aye and this all very soon.'' With that said Barak spoke no more and followed by his dogs he moved toward one of the fires. Once there the ogre laid himself down both atop and under his many thick bearskins to get some sleep.

All of the heavy drinking had ceased now even though there was still drink a plenty in both the goatskin gourds as well as in the barrels strapped to the horses and mules. From here on in it was a time for the utmost caution, it was a time for every man there to have his wits about him.

'He is, I think unsettled, the big man.' Ragnor said as he suddenly rose from where he had been slumbering, the Viking walked over to Tark. Together the men watched as Barak now lying down under his thick wolf and bear skins grumbled and cursed away to himself. Then as always a big dog had laid itself down on either side of the giant pressing up close to their master providing him with both extra warmth as well as security. Above them the winter skies had become alive, all of a sudden aye these last nights had been dark dreary evenings. Now though a thousand cluster of stars studded and decorated the ever colder night skies. A shooting star went plummeting by then another, and yet another one after that. A wolf, a big one by the sound of it, sang and howled at the moon in the distance, its cry was soon answered by a chorus of its fellows. Barak's big dogs lifted their big broad heads as they both growled out a low but intimidating challenge to the beasts of the wild. Briefly the great boarhounds rose and stood over their now slumbering master before settling down once again to lightly sleep. And also the great black she eagle called out in the night, she was beyond somewhere in the dark and out of vision. But the men she watched over however, well these men to her credit were always in her sharp sight.

'You have been friends a long time Ragnor I think, you and my King?' said Tark a little dreamily.

Ragnor's pale eyes stared into the dark almost black eyes of the young Krozaky warrior. Seemingly he was searching for some sign of treachery, but the Viking well he found none. And so with this being the case the Norseman spoke, he did this both honestly and frankly. 'Forever lad, me and your King we have been friends forever. I would die for him, as I know he in turn would die for me,' Ragnor replied openly and honestly. Tark nodded realising just how good friends his King and this red bearded barbarian were. It was Tark who next spoke up.

'Barak, he is like no man I have ever before met Ragnor, once I swear that I hated him with a passion. I had even sworn to slay him if I could.' Tark glanced over at the snoring giant, now the young man hesitated for a moment before once again speaking. 'Now though he is like a brother, a father, a friend and a leader. Barak is not only my King, he is all and everything to me. His power, his strength, his intellect and his reasoning, his very being itself, oh no, he is like nothing at all I have ever encountered before in my life. Aye and believe me Ragnor, I have moved among many scholars, among many learned men. Yes and also the so called great men of war, but these men are as nothing compared to Barak. Why, even the glowering Commander Gortak, who is by the way the most feared and respected of all the Black Guard's brotherhood, he also is as nothing compared to my Lord Barak, nothing.' Tark said this with an honest passion.

Ragnor gave a grunt followed by a nod of his hairy head in total agreement to these words then the big Viking spoke in a low hushed whisper.

'Over these cold dark nights ahead of us boy you will hear many whispered stories, dark tales concerning Barak, some of them are lies, some are true. No matter, we will sit down together soon you and I and then you will learn what sort of man your King truly is. Also I in turn will learn from you, learn all about your great and powerful kingdom that lies still far ahead of us. Tell me now, is this agreed young Tark?' asked the big Viking chieftain.

'Yes,' Tark said with a proud but boyish sort of smile. 'I think I would like that Ragnor, for in truth we have spoken little together you and I so far on our journey.'

Ragnor put a big hand that was adorned with his heavy gold rings upon Tark's shoulder.

'And so would I lad,' the Viking said warmly. 'But I will tell you a tale now my young friend, and this for you to sleep upon on this cold and starry night in the middle of nowhere. You can believe it if you want or discard it if you will, to me it is matter less if you think me a liar or you think me a fool,' the Viking said this in all earnest. Ragnor then looked about him a little cautiously as the two men stood there on the edge of the safety of the perimeter of glowing firelight. Once satisfied he would not be overheard Ragnor decided to continue with his most unsettling midnight tale.

'A score of years ago in the insect ridden jungles of some nameless African province ruled by Rome, we went there me and that great dozing ogre over there. Once again, like I have already said it was for the Eagles of Rome, the pride of the Emperor that we fought in those days. Though this was always for good pay mind you, my services well they are not cheap you must understand,' Ragnor added before continuing again. 'The Romans, well, their legions could not hold this dark septic place that was as rich in gold and gems as Solomon's mines. Know this boy, men I have no fear of, Tark, no it was the tiny things that bit and stung and drove me quite mad, you know lad I do so hate swamps', Ragnor hissed. Tark bit upon his lip at these words and somehow the young man managed not to laugh, no that was something he would save for later. Ragnor the meanwhile continued with his tale. 'Anyway the Emperor's best legions of Rome had been slaughtered and butchered down to the last man. Why in truth these unfortunate men had even been feasted upon in this foul accursed place by the tribesmen. A dozen long boats I had along with me at that time, aye and all of these were full of good Norse fighting men,' Ragnor said reflectively. 'Chosen men, hand picked and picked by myself from the very best and the boldest warriors I could find from all of the Northern sea raiders. These warriors were daring fearless men who were afraid of nothing and no one, do you understand me boy?' Ragnor pressed a little urgently. Tark at once nodded as he licked his lips in eager anticipation of a good meaty story; the young man as it happened would not at all be disappointed.

'We were promised a high bounty and a great reward if we could only put down the demonic power which the elite Roman legions had failed to overcome.' Ragnor now suddenly looked about him into the darkness almost fearfully. As this was not at all common knowledge, and nor was it a well told tale the big Viking was now about to tell. In fact it was an episode in the giant's long exciting life the ogre had seemed to try and totally put behind him. Barak had no fear at all of either mortal man nor even the wildest of savage beasts, but the dark and sinister unknown, well that to him was a terror he chose to avoid, well at least when at all possible. Aye for such dark magic and witchery, well this was still something which unnerved him, oh aye this unsettled the slayer no end. 'You know I hated that campaign, lad,' Ragnor said bitterly. 'I hated the jungle, the heat and the sweat, the snakes and the scorpions, for indeed it was a most terrible place. Oh aye give to me the frozen wastes anytime.' Ragnor now pulled over his head the fur hood of his long wolfskin cloak against the cold and he smiled, as this cold but clean germ free weather was much more to his liking. At least in the cold climes, well everything that could or would kill you was big. Being so you could at least stick a sword in the creature before you died and were sent on to heaven or hell. Ragnor after a moment or two of reflection went on with his dark tale. 'Anyway on top of all that and everything else, we ended up fighting our last days in a stinking accursed reptile filled swamp. I tell you Tark, I will never fight in a swamp again, disease, leeches, all manner of slimy, biting, stinging, creatures there were lying in that stagnant stinking place.'

Tark had to smile on hearing this, as now he knew why Barak had not mentioned the swamp to the big likeable Viking.

Ragnor drank deep from his goat skin gourd of beer before once again continuing with his most sinister story.

'It was in this dark most dangerous place, it was here where Barak had his teeth filed sharp. Aye and this most painful operation was performed by a black fuzz headed witch doctor with but one bright blue eye and a most demonic look about him. You see young Tark, to defeat these eaters of men, Barak so to speak, well Barak had to become one of them if you take my meaning.' Of course these chill words caused a cold shudder to run up Tark's broad back bone. Ragnor paused, seemingly reading the horror that crossed the young warrior's face then once again the Viking continued with his strange tale.

'As ever and always, Barak, he was a most cunning and clever man. And thus being so the great slayer divided the cannibal tribes, in time Barak became the leader of all and each and every one of them. Aye and also, as each and every tribal leader stood in his way, well Barak merely goaded and insulted them into a fight. Barak as you will learn lad, well he has always been so good at insulting people, in fact I know of no one better. And so then of course, well your Lord the great slayer fought these unfortunates, and also of course he promptly killed them all, then took their place.' Tark had to smile to himself on hearing this as it certainly seemed to fit in with Barak's way of planning things perfectly. 'But there are dark forces at work out in these places boy, things that are not normal to either you or me. Dead men can get up and walk, dead men can rise up from their shallow graves, and believe it or not these cadavers can come to life.' Tark next gave off another shudder at these whispered words. 'Well, if life is what it can be called,' Ragnor added. 'Either way lad I have seen this myself, aye and on this I give you my sworn oath, so you can believe me. ' Ragnor said this most sincerely as he swallowed down another mouthful of beer, this both for good measure and also for a little courage. Even now, after all these long years the telling of this tale still filled him with a certain amount of fear, this as well as an obscene dread.

Of a sudden Tark became even colder and it had to be said he was a little afraid of what the Viking would say next. Was then his King Barak a cannibal as was sometimes rumoured, this, the young man wondered more than a little gloomily to himself. After all, Ragnor was most sincere in his words, and this obviously was no mere child's tale to idle the time away.

Ragnor recorked his drinking gourd then he continued with his somewhat grim and sinister tale.

'Well, these defeated tribes, they summoned up their dead from the very pits of hell itself to fight against us.' the Viking said this in a hushed whisper. 'We had slain our living foes but now, now my lad we had to fight their Zombie dead also.'

Tark at once took Ragnor's gourd of drink from the Viking's hand, he uncorked it then took a deep swallow, aye and all of this was without even being invited.

'How did you do all of that Ragnor if the many legions of Rome with their trained soldiers were cast aside and devoured?' Tark asked nervously. Ragnor gave a wink and a wry smile before answering.

'With cold steel and fire, this backed up by also a great deal of courage my lad. Oh and of course Barak's wily cunning,' Ragnor answered plainly. 'First off, we silenced those accursed voodoo drums, and next we butchered each and every one of the tribal witch doctors. Then, and with this done, we next sought out their undead Zombie legion in the dense jungle. Once found, well we then hacked them to bits while the creatures still slept in their graves in the daylight hours.' Tark shuddered fearful at the very thought of that living nightmare. 'Still though boy, at length we won through, the man eating tribes and the Zombie warriors, they were no more. '

It was Ragnor's turn now to take another long and deep swig of good German ale.

'You know boy, I lost more good men in the filthy swamps to snakes and other slimy crawling creatures than I did in battle. Unseen things, things that pulled and sucked my men down under the fetid waters then made off with them. Aye young Tark, I lost more to the serpents and other creatures than I did to the human man eaters,' Ragnor said this with a scowl, then a thoughtful sigh before speaking once again. 'Then on top of all this, as well as the snakes, the crocodiles and all the other ravenous serpents. Well if those creatures weren't enough there were the big black leeches, these and other nasty, stinging, biting little things that had to be burned from our bodies with red hot blades.' Ragnor spat with disgust as he recalled those dreadful hateful days. Dark days, and days when he and his men all struggled chest deep through stinging swamp reeds toward the river where his longboats lay guarded and anchored. Of a sudden the Viking smiled and he glanced skyward into the cold starry skies above him. 'Still my boy, at least there will be no more swamps for me,' the Viking declared still not knowing just what it was that lay ahead of him. 'Aye, give me the cold the frost and the icy rain, and even the deepest of snow anytime, instead of those bug infested septic pits.' Ragnor, once this was said gave a grunt then he wiped beer froth from his great red beard. Now the big Viking seemed somehow relieved he had shared his nightmarish burden with the young warrior. Tark, in turn, felt a little dishonest at not mentioning to Ragnor he would after all have to face at least one more deadly swamp before he became a prosperous purple nosed innkeeper. 'Anyway lad I will now bid you a safe and a warm goodnight my young friend,' Ragnor said patting the young man on the shoulder. With not one more word said, the Viking chieftain turned his back walked off and laid himself down beside his men, and just like the resting wolf Ragnor was off to sleep in but an instant.

Tark after a moment or two well he also went and lay himself down to sleep by the comforting warmth of one of the many fires. However all of a sudden, Ragnor's words came disturbingly back to him. Barak, his great king, his mentor and his hero, was he then after all his greatness, was he still some sort of a cannibal? Tark thought to himself. Or had that filing of the teeth perhaps been only a clever cunning deception and no more than that, and the whole shocking affair was just some sort of a mere clever ruse. Aye, aye surely this dark episode in Barak's life had all been no more than a trick, and this merely to fool his enemies. Yes even the filing of the teeth, this no doubt was only to make the cannibals think the great slayer was one of them, and it was no more than that.

Anyway, the young man for his own sanity's sake chose not to ponder too long on this somewhat sinister thought. At length, and after a few more drinks of German beer from a discarded goatskin gourd Tark covered himself well up and fell off to a good night's sleep under his bearskin coverings.

When the Norsemen all arose that following chill morning, and when the warriors had shook themselves free of cold and sleepiness. It was then they looked upon the dense black forest stretched out in front of them. And the stalwart Vikings perhaps did this it must be said with just a hint of dread and grim foreboding. For as far as the eye could see, from the east to the west, the forest it stood there before them. Indeed the forest was in appearance just like some sort of great towering black wall that barred their way ahead. Still though, despite all and everything, it was never the less an obstacle that must after all be dealt with. So as always and ever the company of men first breakfeasted, after this then the Norsemen smoked and drank unhurriedly. As now the men of the north let warm life creep back into their bodies over the freshly backed up camp fires.

Then, once this dining was done, and the warriors were warm and fed, this until they could eat no more. Well, it was then the warriors saddled up the horses and advanced at a steady walk toward the dark woods that lay not far ahead of them.

A rota had been set up from leaving the ship on the shingle shore, a rota that gave every man some time at least on horseback, time to rest his weary legs. Vikings, it must be said, while being at home in the stormiest and wildest of seas, well they were neither the best of horsemen, or were they good marchers. Still though, the men from the far north were a rough and ready bunch and always did their best. And what is even more important the Vikings did all of this without any sort of complaint.

Horst, due to him having only the one leg and that being a gout ridden one at that had rode Barak's big gelding since leaving the Falcon. Luckily the Arab saddle held the ever drunken German secure with its high back and equally high fronted pommel. This had been the first time Horst had ever thanked the Roman fop for driving his horses too fast and over recklessly. Horst was a man, who it must be said, never had any love for walking and this even when he had two legs under him.

Meanwhile Barak had marched on tirelessly over every foot of ground saying that he was far too big and heavy to burden the other smaller horses.

And as it so happened, well this of course was more than likely quite true.

'We will have to carve our way through there Barak,' Ragnor said this as the company of men now stood but only yards from the edge of the dark silent forest. 'Those thin but spiny lower branches must all be cut back, or else they will flay both man and beast alike,' the Viking added with a curse.

Barak spat then merely grunted, as of course the ogre knew only too well what must be done in the here and now. Aye and also now the sky above them looked angry and dark with snow clouds, and also not a sound was there about them. Strange this was, as only last night in the darkness all manner of sinister threatening roars growls and eerie howling broke the silence of the night. However, here though, well here it was a nocturnal place, the creatures of the black forest for now, they at least slept.

It was now the riders dismounted as they stared impassively ahead of them into the somewhat dark and gloomy wild. So thick and close together were the trees of the dense pine forest the horses would have to be led in single file for the rest of the way. Aye and both man and beast must follow on while a pathway was cut out ahead of them. Only the one legged drunken Horst would remain saddled. Even then, he would have to crouch behind the gelding's big head and broad neck just to avoid being knocked to the ground by the higher outstretched branches. Barak and Tark, well they of course were the only ones among the travellers who had come this way before. Aye, only these two men knew how dark, impossible and dangerous the black forest was to travel.

Now all those there stared ahead into the blackness and the silent gloom of the forest. The straight tall pine trees towered skyward, almost it seemed till at their highest point they touched the ever greying snow filled skies.

'I don't suppose there is, perhaps, a hidden pathway through this place, dotted with taverns is there Barak?' Ragnor asked with a grim sort of smile. 'Please my friend, tell me there is.' The big Viking was smiling now, just as were all of his men, the warriors to a man sensed this was at last what they had been brought along for.

As to the slaying of the pirate Wraif and the rescue of the princess, well that had been truthfully the simplest part of this mission and ongoing adventure.

Ragnor continued light heartedly looking for better news, which by the by he knew well would not be forthcoming..

'Or is there even a place where it is perhaps less dark, a place where it is not so thick with branches Barak?' Ragnor continued to ask hopefully. 'Aye even a place mayhap, where we could walk upright instead of having the flesh ripped from our very bones by those spindly low branches?'

Barak made no reply, instead he merely shook his bucket sized head then he moved to the side of one of his big gaunt and patient grey mules. Now the ogre rummaged about for a moment or two in one of his big hessian sacks. Then, and after but a little while the ogre produced two short double headed steel axes. Aye and these axes, well they were both oiled and honed, and of course being Barak's property, well they were of course razor sharp. As was everything else of Barak's made of any kind of metal and that be no matter if the implements be either weapons of war or even simple garden tools like a spade or a garden hoe.

'Well, there might not be a pathway through the forest right now, or right this very minute Ragnor, but there soon will be and you can believe me on that. ' Barak said this with all of his blustery confidence after he had examined the cutting edges of his axe blades. 'Now stand you all well back, give me some room to swing these blades.' And this the giant commanded as he spat onto the ground which was thick with old pine cones and pine needles.

Of a sudden with a growl and a grunt the giant turned himself into a great swishing, swiping windmill of a thing. Now the ogre became a huge automaton that hacked and slashed up and down, left and right at the lower of the outstretched horizontal branches of the pine trees. Of course these were a hindrance, and were an obstacle, aye these branches were an enemy, being so then they of course had to be removed.

For seven nonstop hours and only later as the light faded did Barak finally cease his most tiring of exertions; the slayer at length drew to a dead halt. Barak with his work done groaned and growled then dropped the axes from his now sweating and blistering hands. Despite the cold of the day sweat from his shaven bald head trickled over his forehead. Some of this ran down his big arched nose and some into his black eyes, stinging them. Now the giant undid the leather cords that held his thick hide waistcoat fastened, once untied he threw the sweat soaked garment to the ground. As for the chain link helmet, well that he had discarded hours ago and Tark now held that tattered piece of headwear safe for him. Now for the first time since he had started out upon hacking his way through the forest the giant turned about to face the way that he had just come. Not once since the ogre had started with his exertions had he looked over his broad shoulder, no not once. Always the slayer had forged on, ever and onward not looking back at all, Barak had focused only at the obstruction what lay ahead of him. Now though in all truth he was weary, the ogre had moved ever forward hacking away as fast as he could walk, as ever Barak had been unwavering in his advance. Now the giants mighty arms and face his broad shoulders and thick neck bled from the flying pine needles and the splintered wood from the shattered branches. Both blood and sweat mingled together and this concoction made small streams that seemed to flow all over his gigantic tattooed body.

'Gods.' Ragnor muttered out in sheer astonishment as he observed the unharnessed Barak devoid of his waistcoat. 'I do believe the great ogre is fitter and stronger now than he was when first we met all those long years ago,' he declared.

Barak despite being no longer a youth, well he was in awesome condition. The slayer was still thin at the waist while massively broad at the chest and shoulders. Oh and also his arms were pumped up with blood, this because of his strenuous efforts. Aye and so now these already huge arms were bulging with power. Naked now apart from his hide knee breeches and his stout leather boots, the slayer stood there rubbing his itching and sweating back against a tree with such ferocity that it shook.

'We have done well today,' the giant said lowering himself down onto his backside and resting his broad bloodied back against a tree.

On hearing these words it was a most impressed Tark who spoke up.

'No, no we have done nothing, done nothing but follow on in your wake. It is you who have done well on this day my Lord Barak. ' Tark said taking a step closer to his king and offering him a drink of water from his canteen.

Barak now gave out a mock scowl of anger.

'Water, water!' the ogre exclaimed. 'You Tark, you, dare to offer me water for refreshment and this after such a hard and lengthy day's toil? Give me my vodka boy, or else just let me go dry,' Barak growled out. 'Aye and set up the camp fires for it grows dark. And your gods, well even those misguided fools only know you have plenty of branches to use for the burning,' the giant chuckled. So at once as Barak commanded a ring of brash for perimeter fires was quickly set up six paces apart for their safety. Later once this was done there was next a big central fire hastily made up for the Warriors warmth and comfort.

Barak had by now while this was being done swallowed down several mouthfuls of vodka. Now with the giant feeling a little refreshed he rose to his big booted feet. 'I will not drink that water you so miserably offered me as refreshment, but I suppose I do have some sort of a use for it,' he declared.

Tark held out the goatskin gourd of drinking water toward the giant. Barak took it and then poured the contents over his bald head and massive body, washing away the sweat and blood from the sharp pine needles as he did so.

'Now my friends, now we will eat, now we will drink and we will as always enjoy each others' company,' the giant announced loudly. 'It is of course venison once again,' the ogre announced as he stretched stiffly and also a little painfully skywards. 'Aye and I no doubt will have to prepare and cook that also I do suppose?' the ogre rumbled, pretending to be a little put out. 'I tell you now you bunch of rogues, not even your mothers looked after you as well as I do,' the giant said with a smirk. Tark passed his king another gourd, this one though was full of vodka. After this when Barak had taken a long swallow the young blackguard held out a brand of kindling for the giant to light his pipe. The ogre gave a nod then thanked him as he would of course enjoy both, more so as the smoke would be the very first of the day.

Barak had done much on that day, aye and well he knew it, the ogre was he supposed quite entitled to be proud of himself. Now though as the evening drew in it was time to eat drink and smoke strong weed, aye it was a time to enjoy a good well earned rest. Despite the aches and the pains bestowed upon him through the day's labours the giant felt good in both body and mind. Barak's great strength as well as his endurance had been tried and tested to the very limit Despite the physical effort the ogre had, he supposed, quite enjoyed the honest toil. But still gratifying or not, on the morrow the slayer had decided as much as he had enjoyed that day's labours others could help in the hedge pruning. Weary but content Barak after affording the men a decent wholesome supper then lay himself down and slept a deep and dreamless sleep.

However, still it was though despite all and everything, it was the giant who had awoke first among all the men that following morning. True it was the ogre did rise a little stiffly and he was more than a little bit sore, not of course that was something he would ever admit. But nevertheless the ogre shook the light covering of frost from his bear skin pelts which had kept him warm throughout the chill night. And then after but a moment to reflect on yesterday's hard toil Barak threw fuel on each and every fire. This the ogre did to warm up the men as they still slumbered around and about their dying flames. It was at that time every morning as in the evening when Barak walked with his dogs whilst he checked over the horses. All though thankfully was well. At length after a pleasant and an uninterrupted smoke on his long clay pipe by a camp fire, next the men were aroused from their slumbers. On that first morning awakening in the forest the men had dined but briefly upon dry slices of venison. With this dining over the men were ready and eager to be on their way once again, deeper now the company of warriors ventured into the black forest. Barak had spent the day before showing the men how the brashing and the thrashing must be done, now though it was the turn of others.

Bull Neck whatever his many faults was not at all a lazy man, so it was he who took up the challenge of hacking his way through the forest; this with a certain amount of relish. Aye indeed the great oaf set off at a furious pace with the keen axes, he was of course trying to match Barak's achievements of the previous day. And in truth to his credit for a while the crude brutish Bull Neck impressed. But then though, after three hours Bull Neck found to his own disgust he could not keep ahead of the men who followed on behind him. Still though despite this, well it was without doubt a brave enough effort after all was said and done. The rest of that day two large Norsemen worked together swinging the keen blades, this for short periods only before resting and then passing over the axes to fresh men.

Barak by now was already gone. The giant had gone on with his dogs scouting the road ahead. At this time the slayer was also accompanied by, Tark and the halfling swamp troll. Barak would now scout and hunt up some food while the Norsemen hacked away at a pathway through the forest. In the meanwhile Barak's huge black eagle soared somewhere high up above them in the snowy cloudy heights. She screeched and called, but however this thankfully was a joyous call not an alarm call, so far all apparently was well.

It was turning dusk when Barak eventually rejoined Ragnor and the rest of the Norsemen. The company of warriors had come a fair way through the forest and the giant was both pleased and impressed with their progress. Also the evening's camp was already set out neatly with plenty of stacked branches to burn. All of the fires were lit and the horses tethered on lines of rope lashed securely between the towering pine trees. Barak for his part had brought back with him a half grown black boar his huge dogs had hunted down and slain. Half grown or not this was still a big beast though and carried enough meat on its bones for everyone to go to their beds well full of meat. Barak's dogs had run the creature so hard it had little fight left in it when the huge beasts had eventually closed in for the kill. Still though Barak's huge dogs after their efforts looked both stiff and sore, aye the hounds were bruised and even bloodied in places from the boar's vicious curved tusks. No matter, as the hounds were of course bred for this sort of work, and anyway just like their master the huge dogs seemed to thrive upon pain. Indeed the more the beasts bled, then the more the dogs fought on with savage determination. Barak skilfully and quickly butchered the boar into great slabs of red meat, this the ogre placed into his cooking pots with carrots and onions, and also with spices from afar.

Meanwhile Tark sat around a camp fire as he told Stefan and Sven in some detail the tales of the day's exciting hunt. All the while the boys sat silently almost trance like as Tark told of the crashing headlong chase through the dark forest. And then of the cornering and slaying of the great black beast against a pile of wind fallen trees.

Barak in the meanwhile split open the boiled boar's head, this he gave in two halves for his big dogs to devour then after this next the ogre gave his eagle the creature's tongue. Oh and for the young boys the giant gave each of them a curved dangerous looking tusk as a gift a reward for their hard work caring for the horses.

Aye, the brothers after all had looked to the beasts carefully, feeding, watering and grooming them. And this the lads had done as well as checking all else was well, looking to the food animals before their slaughter making sure the beasts were secure and safe and wanting for nothing in the way of comfort.

Both boys smiled broadly, as of course both were proud and thrilled at their gifts from the giant. Now at once these tusks would be boiled up then scraped clean to remove blood and sinew. With this done next the tusks would be polished up, and this with oil as well as a lot of elbow grease. Finally once all of the cleaning and polishing was complete the tusks would be lashed with a leather thong to become a permanent decoration about their broadening young necks. Doubtless in years to come when the great slayer was no more, and the boys then being men would receive many a free fireside tavern drink. All of this merely for the telling of their tale as to how they had come to own the large curved tusks given them by Barak. Well, well that was of course providing the brothers survived this most dangerous exciting adventure, and lived long enough to tell the tale.

As the Norse warriors sat about the fires that night feasting and drinking whilst telling tall tales and singing ballads of heroes long past. Of a sudden the snows they had all so long expected came to them. The snow came a floating down light and gently at first, but soon and only a short while later the snow began to fall a lot heavier. Aye and in almost no time at all, all about the warriors was as light as day and of course a most snowy white.

'Your men did well today Ragnor, aye they have covered a lot of hard ground. How did you work this?' Barak asked showing a genuine diplomatic interest as he sat chomping contently upon a lump of well cooked boar meat. Ragnor looked pleased, it was nice to be complimented, this even by a long time friend. Now the Viking after a quick drink went on to explain just how the day's work had been delegated and so accomplished.

'Well Bull Neck took the lead and took up the axes first, aye Barak he set away by himself, like a demon Bull Neck was.' Ragnor said all of this whilst giving a nod of gratitude toward Bull Neck. 'Aye a good day's work he put in, a good man, a good worker too,' Ragnor added. 'And then later after a long length when the Bull was finished and done in with his work, I then tried a different tactic. Aye I worked one man upon one axe each, and this for short periods only. When it was time the men would change over and rest. This did work much better, but it was only Bull Neck who could work, and swing both axes together. '

Ragnor had said these words of praise out aloud. So loud, that Bull Neck who sat near one of the perimeter fires could hear his every word. Ragnor would if he could defuse this tricky unsettling situation between Barak and Bull Neck if at all possible. It was for the best, if these men could only resolve their differences and at least make some sort of a grudging peace. For then, he, Ragnor would at least sleep a little better at night. Of course the big Viking had already been told by Barak about the dagger, the blade being left unchallenged whilst hidden in the boot of the Krozaky warrior, Tark. This of course was not good, oh no, this of course was not very good at all. But still Ragnor was reluctant to accept this was a deliberate and devious act on Bull Neck's part. In truth Ragnor was beginning to push this incident foolishly aside, regarding it as more of an oversight than any act of treachery. Tark, well he might have been mistaken in this and perhaps only thought Bull Neck had indeed discovered the dagger. When after all perhaps the oafish fool had not made the discovery, aye surely the Bull had merely over looked its presence. As Bull Neck after all, well he was not the most astute and observant of men. So being the case, well perhaps this was all just a very sad very bad unfortunate mistake. Well perhaps it was, but then again perhaps it was not. Nevertheless, what at length would be, it would be.

'One more night into the dark woods Ragnor and then we must be even more alert. We must have less drink and have more guards posted by the outer fires throughout the night.' Barak said this as he now tore into a rib bone of the boar ripping it apart with his sharp teeth with ease.

'Wolves? ' Ragnor suggested as he held out his big bare feet toward the big inner fire for a little warmth and comfort. 'And so soon Barak, I had not expected the wolves to come visiting till we were much deeper into the forest.' Ragnor said this as he took a swig of beer from his gourd.

'Yes, wolves,' Barak answered with a slow uncaring nod, and this just as a wolf howled in the not too far off night. 'And by the sound of it as you can hear, well these wolves are not too far away from us now, two days, three at the very most.'

Even as Barak finished speaking, another wolf howled out a reply mournfully and eerily in the distance causing the great dogs to stir from their dozing with both their tails and hackles up.

'Tell me then have you any good news for us then Barak?' Ragnor asked with a crooked half smile.

Barak laid his broad shoulders against his high backed saddle, which at most times he rested his big head upon, for now though it merely propped him up. Now the giant just like Ragnor had his feet extended toward the fire as the ogre warmed the soles of his booted feet. Barak looked about him at the other half dozen raging perimeter fires and the men who cheerily sat about them. Good uncomplaining men, men with strong arms, strong backs and also most importantly stout hearts to go with all of this.

Barak grinned, or perhaps he growled or leered well anyway it was one of the three. Next the ogre took a deep drink of his vodka then he inhaled deeply of his well used long clay pipe. With all this done the slayer gave out a smile of utter satisfaction. To look at him you might have thought Barak was lounging about in safety in some luxurious palace, surrounded by dancing girls and foolish jugglers. Aye and that he was not in dangerous and dire straits in some wolf infested freezing snow-deep forest.

'Yes, I do have some good news for you as it so happens,' the giant said as he propped himself up and reached inside of his leather waistcoat. 'Here,' the ogre said as he threw a piece of old linen he had bound into a small parcel towards Ragnor. 'Tonight my hairy friend I want you to forget about the snow, the cold, even the wolves. Aye and this even though, these beasts of the forest may well dine upon us at a later date.' Barak said all of this in a most relaxed carefree manner. 'This gift I have is for you and your brave men,' the giant smiled knowing that this little present would be a most welcome one. 'I know you and your rogues relish this particular kind of fungi, just as much I do my smoke. Though I must say for why, well in truth I am not quite at all sure,' Barak said puffing most contentedly upon his pipe. 'I myself tried them once long ago and I had nightmares for a whole week after. '

Ragnor opened the linen parcel which was held by a thin fabric cord, on seeing what was within at once his bright blue eyes fair danced with glee in the firelight.

'Mushrooms!' the big Viking exclaimed aloud. 'Aye, and the right sort of mushrooms they are at that Barak, where did you find them, tell me?' the big Viking demanded urgently.

Barak shook his head from side to side as he chuckled away to himself.

'No, oh no for if I told you that Ragnor this quest would be over here and now,' the ogre said taking another deep draw upon his long pipe. 'So take these mushrooms with my blessing and get your madness over and done with Ragnor before the wolves come.' Barak after saying this gave a shrug then a broad grin which in turn followed by a long sigh. 'Who knows my friend, these might after all be the last bit of fungi you ever have, well at least in this life anyway.' Smiling broadly the big Viking chieftain looked about him at his gathering brotherhood of nosey warriors. Barak smiled as if reading his friends very thoughts. 'Don't worry Ragnor there is plenty more where those came from, well at least for tonight's madness.' Barak next laughed as he indicated with his pipe toward one of his hessian sacks. And so on that cold and starry night, well it was most certainly a different one to any other, aye and it was a very different one indeed.

This was the time of year now for the magic forest mushrooms to bloom and also to be at their most potent. Barak was most fortunate to find these treasured valued fungi in the forest when he hunted down the boar earlier. Well at least these mushrooms were valued by the Vikings anyway. All it would have taken was one more hard severe frost and the fungi would be all gone, killed off by the cold until the next autumn of the following year.

Ragnor and his ferocious but loyal clan put great store in these mushrooms, as had their forebears long before them. Now the fungi once unwrapped were straightaway laid out to dry before the fire. A little later when once dry and flakey the mushrooms were crumbled into the boar broth then stirred into the soupy substance. Eagerly the Norsemen drank this concoction down most readily and greedily, this while others of their number smoked the fungi in preference to drinking it. Later, and after but a short while had passed the potent forest fungi began to take its mind changing effect upon the Norsemen. And then it was that Ragnor and his brotherhood of sea wolves, well they began to behave most oddly indeed. In fact it would be most true to say the warriors all turned stone mad. True, indeed this was going to be a very strange and noisy night ahead. But also at the same time it would also be a peaceful night of cheery friendship and the very highest of fellowship.

Barak, well the ogre also felt most contented also, for the ogre had supposed he at least owed his friends and comrades this one small indulgence, this before the perils lying ahead of them.

Slowly, but ever so slowly, the Norse began to change once again with the taking of ever more of the forest fungi. Now in their drug induced state the Norsemen howled and danced about in a manic frenzy as they champed, smoked and drank down the potent mushrooms.

Tark, the halfling Borz and the giant Barak however took no part in their strange primal celebrations, nor did Horst who was by the looks of things apparently passed out with the drink. But still, the three remaining observers did look on with great interest. Oh yes and all three were most amused by their comrades' strange antics. At least Barak thought to himself while the Norse all feasted greedily upon this gift from the forest well, for now at least the valuable drink was left alone.

Later on that following morning as a bulging eyed and headsore Bull Neck took up an axe, as did big Loki who also by the looks of him was not quite himself. This, of course was to be the start of their shift to cut and hack a pathway through the black forest. However, before the headsore Vikings, who were still recovering from their night of devouring magic mushrooms, troubled a single twig a most curious thing happened.

Borz walked, nay strode passed both men and saying not one word the troll advanced toward the as yet untouched tree line. Now the halfling's great chain at this time was swirling and swishing all about and above him in a deadly arc.

Some fifteen feet of heavy link chain which was still attached to his iron girdle about his warty waist. Oh and of course, well this was not a light thing in any way at all to wield. Yet now, it appeared these cruel fetters had become almost a part of him. And just as the halfling had earlier said to Barak he kept this chain as a reminder of those dark days. Oh and also those heavy links as it so happened were a most formidable weapon. Aye, Borz's chain was just as effective as the axes, if not more so, as the heavy links tore down with ease the protruding lower branches that barred the way ahead.

Ragnor smiled over at both Bull Neck and Loki who both looked perhaps not in the best of fettle for hard work anyway.

'Looks like you can rest for a while,' he said still smiling broadly. 'For somehow I just don't think for one minute, that our big frog will be tiring very quickly, if at all.' And just as expected by all and everyone the big green creature did not and the Troll worked his chain all day right up until the light faded. Aye and then also for the next two days following, he, or it, did exactly the same, and this without any complaint. With this being so, the men merely had to march on behind the tireless reptilian saving their much needed strength for the perils ahead. Perhaps this was just as well, because now, now the Norsemen were in the dark domain of the big fierce forest wolf.

Chapter Sixteen

Just as upon every other night the company of adventurers camped that evening and banked up the campfires till the flames raged and crackled fiercely. Later under the safety of the firelight the Norsemen went out in numbers and brought much brashed wood back into the circle of flames. For now to leave that circle of the beacon of firelight alone in search of fuel, well, that would have indeed been a most dangerous folly.

Beyond, out of eyesight there were many long fearful howling cries from the nearing large wolf packs as the beasts gathered in the gloom yonder. Now the horses were tied tightly by their bridles to a picket line stretched between the tall trees. And also as an extra precaution the skittery beasts sensing danger were hobbled by their front legs, leaving their powerful back legs free to lash out at the wolves; wolves which were sure to come very soon in search of food. Why, even now the great loping things gathered in some numbers in the darkness beyond the firelight. Now to make matters worse the snow came down at the warriors in heavy flurries. This as the cold wind grew in its ferocity bending the tall trees till they creaked and groaned. Cauldrons of venison and boar meat simmered away over the fires but no one apart from Barak and the Troll seemed at all hungry. Why even the ravenous Ragnor seemed to have suddenly lost his appetite. All of the Vikings had now put on extra bearskins, this both to protect them from the cold as well as the teeth of the forest wolf. And also of course this made their appearance look a much larger and a more formidable target for the wolves to tackle.

Borz suddenly rose from his crouching position as he swallowed down a steaming lump of meat the size of a man's head. After this flesh was consumed the great green creature made a most threatening and snake like hissing noise, this while the halfling next slowly unfurled his heavy chain from about his huge shoulders. All of this as his forked tongue flicked in and out at a rapid pace as the creature looked all about him into the wild. Just as the Vikings were, the halfling also was now garbed in both wolf and bear skins to cover his hairless body. Of course the halflings cold blood did not relish this weather one bit and so now barely an inch of him was visible.

Above, perched high in the swaying trees the big eagle shrieked and screamed as the feathered killer flapped her great black wings in eager expectation of what was soon to come. While far below the big dogs stalked about stiff legged, their tails and hackles up. Barak's hounds too were growling in growing anticipation of the battle they also knew would not be long in coming to them.

259

Far below her, there in the clearing within the ring of fires the she eagle would make this place her killing area. Sven and Stefan the meanwhile, well these able lads would guard the horses. Both of the capable youths were each armed with long bows while their arrows were stuck in readiness in the snow at their feet before them.

'Stay by the horses heads, be sure to keep away from their back ends lads,' Barak advised. 'But most of all, you must keep well away from my big gelding. One kick from him, and please believe me you will end up in either Svalbard or Valhalla itself.' Barak's words raised a chuckle from Ragnor but before the chuckle had even died from his cracked hairy lips. Well it was then and in only a heartbeat or two the ravenous wolves of the forest were upon them, the creatures came unafraid and in a headlong rush.

Oh and by the by this was no small disorganized attack by a small pack of starving desperate wolves. Oh no, no this was more like a well planned and well thought out military assault. Why there must have been at least one hundred wolves involved in the first attack upon the encampment. Big raggy rangy beasts, huge things, creatures that were mostly black in colour. Well at leastways these forest wolves had more black about them than any other colour in their thick winter coats. It was plainly obvious straightaway these hungry canines sought to drive the horses off into the woods. Once this task was completed then the wolves could later hunt the horses down and feast upon them at their leisure. But thankfully though, the horses were all too well tied, too well secured. Aye and also the beasts lashed out in a panic sending several wolves yelping off in pain into the snowy shadowy gloom beyond the firelight. But then though there came of a sudden an agonized cry and a savagely mortally wounded Viking named Olaf. He who was the blonde one eyed singer by the pebble beach was dragged off into the wild never to be seen or heard of again. Next there was another fearful cry and Luft, a good swordsman and a good helmsman was done for. He also was twitching and thrashing about wildly while his throat was being ripped out. Now the deep snow all around about the Norsemen was fast becoming stained a deep red with gore and blood and this from both man and beast.

'Stay within the circle of fire,' Barak shouted out loudly as he lopped off the head of a large and savage she wolf.

Barak's huge dogs of course also did their part, as no single wolf was the equal of either one of these big red killers. And even though the big dogs were still a little stiff from the boar hunt the great hounds still both obviously relished the fray. Barak's great eagle swooped down from her perch, and easily almost with disdain the great bird scooped up one of the pack. With this done she next simply flew off with it, aye and just as an owl might as easily do with a rat. Over and upward the great bird flew, over the trees she soared then dropped the wolf from a great height, this before returning for another of the pack. Now the battle was on in earnest, it was every man for himself as the warriors rolled about through the flames and the blood soaked snow that reddened more by the second.

Five of Ragnor's men were down and dead, dragged off away as no more than things for food now. Perhaps thirty huge forest wolves had been slain while even more of them were wounded and cringing out in the shadows beyond. And all of this savage brutal carnage had all happened in only a matter of a few fast heartbeats. Now though as the battle heightened even more wolves joined in the fray, bounding and loping open mouthed into the firelight from the dark forest. These beasts had food enough for now to last them with the five big men their pack had taken and dragged off, but the wolves still wanted more meat, more blood.

Aye in all truth this seemed now that it was no longer a mere hunt for meat alone. Oh no, the big wolves of the dark forest wanted much more than that, as this duel in the forest was now more like all out war. Still, it was as expected a war the Norse would rise up to and relish; every single man there played his part. Well after all they had too, for these men were all each and every one of them fighting for their very lives.

Bull Neck who of course was just as foolish and as brash as ever had run off into the darkness after a wounded wolf. However, then the oaf had at once become set upon by others of the large pack. In all truth and to his credit, a lesser man than the great fool would have died there and then. Torn asunder and ripped apart in the now crimson snow by the large savage wolf pack. However, not so with Bull Neck and three or four wolves the oaf brained with his cudgel before being overwhelmed and brought to the ground by the pack. As much as Barak had no love for the man still the ogre with a curse went never the less bounding to his aid. Now the giant he was slicing all and everything apart in his wake. Together he and Bull Neck beat away the wolves and returned bloodied but unbowed to within the ring of fires. Of course Barak received no thanks for his concern from Bull Neck. Indeed the fool he looked more embarrassed for having to be rescued, even more so by Barak.

The troll's chain meanwhile it was deadly, and in Borz's steady advance the wolves parted then broke, the creatures of the forest were unsure of this new and most fearsome beast. At long length after much blood was shed the tide of battle changed and it changed for the better. But still it changed not soon enough and by now Ragnor had lost another two good men to the wolves.

Ragnor cursed angrily and he fell upon the back of a wolf that tore into one of his dead men as it feasted upon his still twitching flesh. With the rage of a true berserker the big Viking stabbed at the wolf and throttled the life out of it. And aye he even bit into the beast's ear in his wild vengeful fury. Aye and this Ragnor did until the beast was no more than a dying twitching thing itself. Of a sudden a big black wolf flew over Barak's head, kicked with such force by the big gelding it was long dead before thudding its body against a tree trunk.

Meanwhile big Loki slung a dying wolf into a raging fire where the creature howled away its last living moments. After this he moved with surprising speed for such a lumbering and misshapen man off into the gloom. Aye off into the gloom he went, and this reason was to help the bloodied Bull Neck back onto to his feet. And this as the big fool had once again left the circle of fire in pursuit of a wounded crippled wolf. Bull Neck as ever and always was a man who just simply did not seem to ever learn by his mistakes.

All there now within the ring of fire were bloodied and were most weary from their exertions. But still this was no matter as the warriors had by now won through, and victory at last it was theirs. At last the big wolves of the forest were all gone, now aye the man hungry killers had retreated back into the shadows with their bushy tails tucked firmly between their legs. Still though victory was at a cost, seven of Ragnor's brave men were now dead and dragged off for food. Why there was nothing of their broken bodies to mourn over or to even send off to the gods on a fiery pyre. As well as these dead there were also many more men who were wounded, and young Tark, well he sadly was one of them.

Aye and this was a most strange and curious thing though, for the young warrior had not one serious bite mark upon his body. In fact not one single bit of his black clothing had been even torn or was it bloodied. Tark had about him only a single huge and bloody lump, this upon the back of his turbaned head. Oh and this of course was not what could be called the usual wound a large wolf could inflict upon a man.

Barak scowled and growled angrily at this discovery and then the ogre spat blood from his bad tooth into the already reddened snow. Obviously the ogre had of course already noticed Bull Neck had used his much loved and lethal club against the wolf pack. And also this wound inflicted upon his countryman, well it smacked strongly of Bull Neck's work. Barak bent down onto one knee as he scooped up the black clad warrior as if he was no more than a babe. For now this mystery would have to wait, but only for now, for the slayer he would in due time have his answers, aye and all of them.

Tark with good care would survive his wounds and the young warrior would live to fight another day. After all he was young and he was strong, but most of all Tark was a proud Krozak warrior. Barak for now at least would have to put his dark suspicions to one side lest his black temper get the better of him. Still though on the happier side over fifty wolves lay dead and many others would die of their wounds beyond in the deep dark woods. Barak was now confident about the wolf pack, confident as well they would not come again, it was over. The Norsemen had all been challenged and tested now and the blood trade was in their favour, the next stop was the river. With this in mind the bloodied but victorious Vikings rested in that clearing for a day or two. Now the warriors bound their wounds and rested their bodies while regaining their strength, all but Tark however. As for now at least the young warrior hovered somewhere between life and death. And still even as the wolves feasted upon their fallen friends and comrades, so now did the Norse in turn feast greedily and venomously upon wolf flesh. It was days later much rested and with their wounds in repair that the Norsemen travelled on through the forest unmolested. Even so it was some weeks later while hampered by terrible weather until the company of men finally reached a broad river. A river just as Barak had said flowed ever slowly in its dark, deep depths. While at the same time its shallow waters were white and angry elements bouncing over the sharp protruding rocks, indeed it was almost as if this waterway was two separate rivers.

In these last long weeks since the wolf attack, Tark with much rest and good care had slowly begun to pull himself back together.

And on that night by the river the Norsemen, as undaunted as ever, sat and talked together around the central fire, just as they had talked over many nights since the fight with the forest wolves.

'Our people Barak, do you know of our true history? I mean from where and whence we came from before there was a Krozakistan? ' Tark asked this question whilst holding his hands out towards the heat of the fire.

Barak smiled, he was both pleased and relieved to hear the young man string a few words together without faltering. Why of late when Tark had spoken he sounded little better than the fool Bull Neck.

So indeed these words were pleasing, this as the young warrior had spoken very little in fluent fashion since the attack of the forest wolves. Indeed the young man had slept for days on end, moving in and out of consciousness. Barak, since Tark's dubious accident had constructed a makeshift sledge and Tark had been drawn along upon it by one of the horses. The bitter cold the lad had not felt as he had been kept warm by the many newly acquired wolf pelts. However had it not been for Barak's potions, his wolf meat soups, as well as the general doctoring and caring of the young man, Tark would have doubtless died. Indeed, sometimes over these last weeks the young man had merely existed in a kind of half dead limbo. Aye the young warrior appeared to be more dead than alive. Still, still and right up till now, Tark could remember nothing, nothing at all of how he came by his injuries in the battle with the wolf pack. Barak so far had kept his own council on his views of things, and the ogre had said nothing to anyone, not even Ragnor. And of course this was even though Barak strongly suspected it was Bull Neck who had dealt the cowardly blow to the back of Tark's head.

'Yes, yes, I do boy.' Barak said this after some while, as he was chewing most contentedly upon his cured wolf meat. 'I do know the full long history of our people. I do suppose you would you like to hear it?' the giant enquired. Tark gave a most enthusiastic nod sadly though this nod hurt his still very sore head. Anyway sore head or not the young man made himself comfortable before the fire. And now the warrior looked forward to hearing the story that Barak was about to tell him about his people, even if this tale he was about to be told was perhaps merely an invented one by Barak. Still, then at least the young man thought to himself it would nevertheless be no doubt entertaining. Oh and just as always and ever with his new found king, mentor and friend the young warrior would not be at all disappointed.

Barak, well, he also decided to make himself a little bit more comfortable. So now the giant threw more wood onto the already raging crackling fire. With this done the slayer next stretched out his long legs toward the fires comforting heat. As was ever the norm for the ogre Barak had his long clay pipe in one hand and a drink of vodka in the other. Borz by now had his own long pipe which had once been owned by one of Ragnor's men. Aye it had been owned by one of the unfortunates who had been slain and dragged off into the forest by the wolves. Now, well, the deceased Norseman had no longer any need of the pipe, being so Ragnor had made a present of it to the likeable halfling.

Looking a most contented thing the troll puffed away quite happily on dried out river reed mixed with just a little of Barak's own potent weed. Barak's weed had to last after all and it doubtless would be a while before he came across anyone who would be carrying this relaxing valuable substance.

Barak, once he was comfortable, with all around him listening intently he then began with his story.

Well this was of course after one more puff upon his pipe, that as ever was followed by one more swig of vodka.

'Our people are the last descendants of the Kurgans, a race of warriors who roamed the steppes long before Rome was ever even heard of,' the giant said proudly. 'The Kurgans were a huge and a fierce race of warriors. Oh and also the Kurgans were an unforgiving people with a passion for harsh warfare, indeed it is said they had about them a craving for blood. '

Ragnor on hearing this pulled a hairy face of mock horror.

'No, oh no, surely not Barak,' Ragnor said with a chuckle and a sarcastic smirk. 'And I in my ignorance, I had thought to myself your forebears were all poets and minstrels.' These sharp witted words of Ragnor's brought a peel of laughter from everyone about, of course none there laughed louder or longer than Bull Neck. Anything, anything at all even said in jest that belittled Barak the jealous wayward oaf found spitefully amusing.

Barak shook his big head then scowled then next he cursed his bad tooth before spitting venomously into the raging fire. But all of this mind you, it was only in mock dramatics, well apart from the bad tooth.

'My ancestry is recorded in the ancient library within the great hall of the Empire of the Krozak people.' Barak said this, both proudly and sternly while fixing Ragnor with an icy stare. Of course the icy stare though was also no more than a ruse. 'Meanwhile Ragnor, your unknown and very doubtful pedigree, this is merely scribbled in a most child like fashion upon cave walls that drip with ice. Why even now the only thing you can read is a childish sailing chart. Aye and this with arrows and dolphins and seagulls etched upon it instead of real writing.' Barak said this in a most matter of fact fashion also quite forcefully and with some element of dramatic conviction. Ragnor though on hearing this, well the big Viking at once bristled at these most unflattering and slanderous words, so of course his reply was instant.

'So Barak you think it was my childish ignorance that has taken you to places only a few men have ever seen or ever will,' Ragnor retorted angrily after swallowing down a mouthful of ale.

Barak though just as ever and always was not in any way at all lost for an answer for Ragnor's question.

'Bah, we were in all truth lost, aye you got us all lost in the sea mists and the fog Ragnor,' Barak argued back light heartedly. However the big Viking, well he was not in the least bit amused by the ogre's humour.

'I took you far far away into the land of the red men did I not?' Ragnor countered, his temper becoming a little heated. After all said and done, he, Ragnor, was a famed master mariner. A great seaman and navigator, and he was not some mere foolish chancer who had put out to sea hoping to find some mythical uncharted land by luck and by luck alone. Indeed, Ragnor had set out looking for the very place he had eventually after some hardship discovered. Aye Ragnor had achieved this task when hundreds of Viking raiders and explorers before him had failed, failed and died in the trying. Barak though for the moment, well, perhaps he was in a bullish and somewhat provoking mood.

'Bah it was the tides and the winds did that, aye it was the elements took us there, like I say, we were lost,' Barak continued to argue.

'Ask Bulgar and ask Tor; they were both there with us,' Barak pressed jokingly now. Ragnor though, well, the big Viking he once again missed the giants somewhat off hand sense of humour.

And now he was about to explain just why.

'I would ask them Barak, but alas the wolves have carried them off into the woods for meat, or do you not remember that part of this adventure?' Ragnor replied, this with mixed emotions of both sadness and anger in his voice.

Barak almost at once cursed his own ignorance. Indeed, the ogre had busied himself so much in the caring of the young Tark he had quite forgotten about his other fallen friends and long time comrades. Aye Barak had chosen to busy himself with the caring of the living and not the grieving of the dead. Still however now the giant sighed heavily then shrugged wearily regretting his careless words. Barak next took on about himself a most sad expression.

'Forgive me, please forgive me all that are here,' the giant almost begged. Ragnor was much taken aback on hearing this, in truth the Viking could not last remember when he had heard Barak apologise for anything. Once again the giant continued in humbling himself before his friends. 'For, yes Ragnor, I do of course remember only too well the slaughter in the forest. Aye and it grieves me a great deal the loss of such men, please believe me on that Ragnor,' the giant said this most sincerely. 'For now my friend if I am not much mistaken, well that leaves only you and I remaining who can remember that which we saw long ago in the land of the red men,' Barak said solemnly. Now the great ogre paused for but a moment amid the deadly silence. Barak next a little uneasily puffed upon his pipe, took a drink, then he spoke up once again.

'Please believe me I meant no offence by my foolish words Ragnor, I am most sorry if you were offended,' Barak said again with much regret. 'You are a great mariner, aye and also a great friend and that my brother is quite simply why you are here with me now.'

Ragnor gave a slow nod then a thin smile which was followed by a grunt of approval at the giant's honest and sincere words. Barak assumed most correctly he was forgiven for his moment's lack of sensitivity There was then a brief moment of sullen and thoughtful silence. This as Barak, Ragnor and all the brave bold men sitting about them remembered their fallen friends.

After a moment or two of silent contemplation it was the giant who first amongst them shook off his melancholy broodings.

'Anyway that is another story for another day, our tales of red men and distant places, Tark.' Barak continued after another long puff upon his pipe and another good swig of vodka. 'Now then, can I get on with my history lesson? ' asked the giant in bit more of a brighter spirit. 'After all the boy here needs education, and so education he shall have,' the ogre blustered.

Ragnor grunted in agreement and nodded his hairy head as he pulled his wolf skin cloak about him. Oh and by the by this was a cloak which had grown somewhat in size of late as it now having three more thick winter wolf pelts having been stitched on to it.

'Now then my friends where was I? Oh yes.' Barak took another swig of vodka then he puffed upon his pipe once more before continuing with his tale. 'Our people Tark, well in all truth I do suppose they stumbled across our kingdom by mere chance. Aye mere chance, and no more than that my lad, oh by the way Tark, are you warm enough boy?' Barak asked fussing over the young warrior like some sort of a mother hen.

'Yes, oh yes my Lord I am warm enough, go on please with your tale,' Tark insisted a little embarrassed by his king's attention. As after all the young man had over thirty big savage Vikings listening to all that was being said to him.

Bull Neck could not help himself and so the oaf sniggered like the big idiot that he was at Barak's concern for the young man. Barak of course being ever alert to all things heard the fool however, the slayer chose at this point to ignore him, well at least for now.

The giant after spitting into the fire with silent contempt for Bull Neck then continued once again with his story.

'We, our people that is, we had moved away from the cold wind blasted steppes to escape the worst winter there ever was. We also had at that time long ago, famine and plague, this as well as a long bloody civil war to get over. Aye, civil war Tark, with family fighting against family, so all indeed was not well, no not well at all my lad. For weeks and months, months that turned into years we, our people roamed the steppes, the plains the vast tundras and the great beyond. All the while we were looking for good grass for our many beasts and a place to eventually settle ourselves down. '

For a moment the giant paused, as expected the slayer took a drink then a deep comforting draw upon his long pipe. Barak with this done, looked about him. When the ogre was satisfied all there were giving him their full undivided attention he once more continued with his story.

'One night, in the middle of a cruel fierce storm our people cold, wet, weary and footsore found themselves high upon a vast plateau, a plateau that was unknown to our nomadic tribe. At this time our people were badly beaten by the wind and the rain, now they were exhausted and spent, aye and now they could go no further. So this being the case the tribes of our fathers camped there on this plateau for the night. You must remember all of this took place oh so many hundreds of years ago Tark.'

The young man gave a knowing nod, he was not totally ignorant of the history of his people, and this story he knew was well recorded and documented in the great library of the capital itself.

Barak though, well in all honesty he did not know the young man was so enlightened, the schooling in the military academy had obviously improved.

'I will show you the writings of this someday Tark, perhaps on our return,' Barak promised before once again continuing. 'Anyway, shortly before dawn great huge gates which were inset into the very rock face of the mountains themselves, creaked ever slowly open. These gates had gone unnoticed during the time of the fierce wind lashed rain storm the night before. Only cleverly constructed winches and strong pulleys, not to mention the aid of several elephants could have made this at all possible, so heavy were they. Huge heavy gates, gates made from iron and bronze and also a heavy black wood as thick and long as a guard man's pike. I say this Tark for the benefit of the others sitting about us here. As you of course have seen these same gates and so you can of course vouch for their size. '

Tark at once gave a most positive nod of agreement as to Barak's description of these massive city gates.

Barak paused again for another drink and another puff upon his pipe before once again continuing with his interesting tale. When Barak did tell a tale a man should have plenty of time put aside to listen to it, as the drinking and the smoking in between did take up a fair bit of the day or night.

'From behind these magnificent huge gates strangers appeared. These were small and slight figures with an eerie somewhat sinister look about them. Small frail things they were, with bodies a man with good eye sight could see straight through to the world beyond. These creatures had arms and legs as we have and indeed were similar in shape, though they were less than half our size. While their bodies were small these beings had about them large egg shaped heads with huge orb like eyes; these folk were obviously not of this place. Oh no my lad these beings were not of this earth of ours.'

Silently the Vikings sat about the raging fire spellbound and in total silence. Now the Norsemen were neither eating their meat nor even drinking their much loved ale. Big Barak after a brief pause for dramatic affect then once again spoke on.

'These creatures were by all accounts hairless and apparently sexless things,' the giant said quite blankly. The slayer took another long draw from his clay pipe and looked about him at the men who sat still in silent wonderment at his strange story.

'Then these things were devils or they were demons Barak, for I myself I have heard of such beings before,' Ragnor put in breaking that deathly silence.

Barak gave a grunt and shook his head in total disagreement.

'No, oh no far from it my friend, they were a most kindly compassionate race of beings. Beings with a knowledge and an intellect that far exceeded any of the other so called higher civilized nations. Why the Romans, the Greeks, the Persians and even the Egyptians were no more than cave dwellers by comparison to these strange little folk. Anyway our people were most kindly invited to stay and live among these strange but harmless beings. Know this, behind those great undefeated gates, there stood lofty silver towers and dome shaped temples of gold, great ornate halls and palaces. All of the streets were most neatly cobbled and there was a good working sewerage system which ran perfectly throughout the entire great city. Aye and this sewerage system was and still is far superior than anything in Rome. Then beyond that great city there lay lush forests and great rambling grass plains rich with all manner of game. Also the rivers there were many. Here these waterways ran both fast and lazily off into the great beyond. Aye and also, as you already know Tark, these rivers are still teeming with the very best and the very biggest of fish. Oh and also there was and still is as I have already said good and plentiful grazing for our horses, camels, cattle, our sheep and goats. There were no other tribes or clans beyond those great gates to war with, only our people Tark. So this being the case our people grew strong and wise under the guidance and influence of these strange but kindly beings.'

Tark smiled proudly, Barak's tale was much the same as what he had read over and over again since being a small boy.

'And what of them Barak, what happened to these strange beings?' Tark asked as he sat now in cross legged wonderment.

As after all reading something was one thing, but being told it by your king, well that again was yet another.

'Well they were long lived things Tark, or so it was at least written, living up to three or four times the life span any mortal man could ever have hoped for. But still, gradually over many years these strange little beings all perished with the passing of time. You know that it is said amongst our ancient people Tark, and it is an old saying. I think that it is a wise one also, well it is said that, "only the rocks live forever".' Barak with this said took for himself a long drink and a blow of his pipe before speaking once again. 'Everything else with the passing of time will perish, or dry up and simply blow away into dust,' the ogre added thoughtfully perhaps thinking of his own demise. 'Still and nevertheless, in that short time of bonding and education with the strangers, much indeed did change and transform our savage nomadic tribes.'

Barak paused, the ogre was thoughtful for another moment then he once again continued, after of course yet another drink and another puff of his strong weed.

'These folk did after all bring our fierce ferocious forebears together, not as a mere clan of warring thieving barbaric tribesman, but as a great nation, a great kingdom. Aye and also a kingdom that has never known the sorrow and shame of defeat in battle. Up till now our land has known only glory, respect and compassion for its people. We, the Krozaky, we do also have compassion for other people. Aye, we do have much compassion, well, just so long as the fools have sense enough in their heads to leave us well alone and keep out of our way,' Barak said this with a slightly dangerous smirk as he glanced over at Bull Neck as he sat hovering over in the firelight.

Tark smiled proudly, the young man liked this story, the tale though he had read it many times before made him feel good inside, it also helped him forget the relentless pounding in the back of his skull.

'Umph,' Bull Neck suddenly grunted as the fool sneered most unwisely. 'Ssstories ffor the weak mminded, if yyou ask mme.' This, the half drunken fool stammered out eventually and louder than what he had thought. Bull Neck had drank a great deal that night, aye far more than was at all usual for him, far more than was prudent given his moronic attitude. As it happened, well the big uncouth oaf of course he seemed to have something upon his small and simple mind which was troubling him no end.

Ragnor cursed under his breath at Bull Neck's foolish remarks and there was at once a hushed deathlike silence around the raging campfires.

As after all if Ragnor had heard the foolish Bull Neck's words then so had the ever sharp eared slayer.

Barak was angry, indeed he was very angry and the ogre was most quick to reply to the Norseman's somewhat snidey remark.

'Well if that is so you stammering stuttering fool, well then you should be most pleased by my fairy tale. And that because Bull Neck, you yourself are such a weak feeble minded thing.' Barak replied this instantly as he most coldly affixed Bull Neck with an icy glare.

Bull Neck, well the brainless fool was most unwisely becoming quite annoying once again. As well as this, also Barak had not forgotten for one moment about his silence over the concealed dagger in the boot. Nor neither of course had the giant forgotten about Tark's cracked skull. Bull Neck was the only man that night, who, was armed with a cudgel, aye and also he was also the only man who had something to fear by Tark's good health. Doubtless the fool wanted to silence Tark on the off chance he had not yet spoken to Barak. Not spoken of how he had found and yet carelessly overlooked the curved dagger hidden inside the warrior's long black boot. For surely, if Tark had of informed on him then even in Bull Neck's dimness of mind, by now he thought he would surely have been a dead thing. Barak though was a most complex man, and the ogre did what he wanted to do just when he wanted to do it, oh and also how he wanted to do it.

'It is no secret that our dislike for each other is a mutual thing Bull Neck,' Barak went on never shifting his glare from the oaf s piggy mismatched eyes. Bull Neck felt suddenly uneasy now as he scratched at his bald head then fingered his forked red goatee beard nervously. If he had been innocent in any way, then he would have returned the glare and made a fight of it and to hell with the consequences. But of course the oaf was not innocent and the simple fool had become that which he hated the most, himself. For, he was a traitor now aye and well he knew it. Aye and also even the fool that he was, well he knew now in his poisoned heart that the giant Barak also knew it.

'I could gut you now just like a fish, oh and just as quickly, aye and also just as easily you great clumsy oaf.' Barak snarled this out with his dark temper slowly rising. 'Why, I could slice you and dice you, and I could have you tasting just like a suckling pig. Aye, with some added peppers and a few spices from the east you would taste quite delicious, for once in your life you would be of some use Bull Neck,' Barak sneered. 'Aye, even if this was only as food to feed decent men upon.'

All there amongst the Norsemen were silent as it had long been whispered Barak had a somewhat dark cannibalistic nature. However, so far there was never any actual proof of this grizzly and macabre claim. And in truth there were not many, if any of the brave bold sea raiders who wanted to accuse the slayer of being partial to a bit of human flesh.

A worried looking Ragnor snarled, spat and then cursed as he rose suddenly to his feet looking about him into the wild as he did so. Next the big Viking felt the hilt of his boar's head broadsword as his ice blue eyes searched the woods about him for something that was not at all there.

'Bull Neck, get you up and on your feet, stir yourself man, look you now to the horses yonder. Get up man and do not linger, take big Loki with you for company. For I swear I have heard something moving about in the gloom and the shadows beyond, go now look to the horses do not delay.' Ragnor said this out loud. Also he said it abruptly with an element of urgency in his voice, but of course this was indeed a false urgency.

Grudgingly together with the lumbering Loki the rebuked and downcast Bull Neck moved somewhat reluctantly away from the warmth and glow of the central fire. Now, now the foolish man would have to stand watch over the horses and spend the rest of the night by the smaller perimeter fires. True it was the fool would be colder there, but still despite this misfortune with a little good luck he might at least see the light of day once more with those odd coloured eyes.

Oh and nevertheless fool though he was Bull Neck knew as well as all there sitting about the raging fires Ragnor had neither seen nor heard nothing in the dark gloomy beyond. Aye sadly those about him, his Norse brothers, also knew exactly the same as he did. Ragnor had merely created a ruse, aye a clever ruse and nothing more and this to banish Bull Neck off into the night before he was slaughtered. Still though the simple fool supposed reluctantly to himself Ragnor had however more than likely saved his life that night. For fool though he was, Bull Neck understood only too well now Barak would kill him just as soon as look at him. Barak though for now remained silent and this even though he knew well enough it was Bull Neck who had clubbed Tark back in the forest on the night of the battle with the wolves.

As a brooding Bull Neck threw some wood upon the perimeter fire he turned and stared ever upward at the towering scowling Loki. The big hunchback muttered some very uncomplimentary oaths then pulled his wolf skin hood over his lop sided head as he turned his head away. Loki at this particular time was both very angry and deeply ashamed of his friend's behaviour. Mumbling curses Bull Neck the meanwhile pulled his own black bearskin cloak tight about him as he squatted down over the fire uttering curses of his own, all of which were directed at Barak. It was on that cold night the oaf swore to himself upon Odin's very soul, Barak, no matter what, he would not live to see out this venture.

In the meanwhile Barak puffed rapidly upon his pipe, this of course was the ogre's own way of trying to simmer himself down before addressing the Viking chieftain.

'Congratulations my friend, your powers of observation are improving with your old age Ragnor. Why they have become now even keener and more acute than my two boarhounds lying here before me in a restful slumber,' Barak said this evenly to Ragnor as he calmed himself.

'Aye, aye perhaps this is so,' Ragnor replied with a wry smile sheathing his big broadsword, the Viking next yawned as he stretched himself sky ward. 'I suppose you are right at that Barak, I think my senses are improving.' Ragnor said this with a sigh of relief as the foolish Bull Neck still had his thick head upon his thick neck.

Also the big brawny men about the fires gave of a chuckle of relief and a somewhat nervous sigh as the very tricky situation eased itself. Whatever these big savage men were to each other, they all relied on a fierce code of self preservation. These warriors watched each other's broad backs, and to a man these men would die without hesitation to protect their clan brothers. Bull Neck, despite his many faults was, at day's, end one of them, aye and he was a vital member of their brotherhood at that. But still despite this, all there knew something underhanded must have gone on these past days for Barak to goad and insult him into a fight.

Just as the same all there knew Bull Neck would not back down from anyone, even against Barak if he felt there was a just cause. However on this night though Bull Neck was cowed and silent, on this night the Bull did not rise to the ogre's insults. And indeed it was obvious to all that Ragnor had stepped in and most cleverly saved his hide. Aye and also all there knew without that clever intervention Bull Neck could by now be no more than a dead thing. What was perhaps even worse the fool might just of ended up being sliced and diced up for supper as big Barak had so forcefully put it. For a while after their low nervous laughter the big Norsemen sat about the fires drinking silently, perhaps even a little gloomily. Now the big Viking chieftain watched carefully the thoughtful expressions upon his warrior's bearded faces, Ragnor for now had seen quite enough for one night.

'Well, now might be a good time for us all to get some sleep Barak don't you think?' Ragnor asked this question plainly as he next affected a long drawn out sort of yawn. Barak gave a grunt and nod of his mail clad head in agreement, next though the giant glanced briefly over to where Bull Neck and Loki sat about the fire. This was a fire they had now banked up somewhat for warmth and comfort against the cold night ahead. Sadly it was only a shame Barak thought to himself, that the big honest Loki should have to suffer Bull Neck's company for the rest of the cold night. Still, the giant thought once again merrily to himself, Bull Neck well he, after all would not be about for much longer. Well at least ways the treacherous dangerous fool would not be about if he had anything to do with things.

'Aye, aye my friend, why not have a bit of an early night?' Barak answered simply as he laid himself down upon his black bearskin by the fire. Without another word the other Norsemen seeing Ragnor lie himself down all followed suit. Now quickly the men finished their drinks off and turned in for the night huddling under their heavy winter skins for warmth against the bitter chill.

Ragnor though well he had to have one last word before his blue eyes finally closed.

'Anyway my large ill-tempered friend, what happened to all of that compassion and forgiveness those strange wise little men bestowed upon you and your people Barak?' Ragnor asked this question with a wry grin whilst lifting himself up from his bearskin bed.

Barak paused then he turned over in his bed to look at Ragnor before answering his well put question.

'Well like I say, all that was a very long, long time ago Ragnor my friend,' Barak replied blankly. 'Oh and as you well know, compassion, well this can dry up just as easy as a river bed. And so now my friend, I will bid you a goodnight.' With that said Barak snuffed out his pipe, finished his drink, then huddled himself under his skins to sleep.

On that following morning the men awoke to find themselves in a foot of deep crisp snow, this was all around about and also on top of them. Though in all honesty the climate had now warmed a little despite this snow, now it was not at all cold in any way. Well leastways the weather now was perhaps not as freezing as it had been.

Slowly the company of men arose and at once shook themselves free of snow, next with this done the men went into the forest and did what they had to do with themselves before day's start. Then and when once this task done the men returned and sat around the fires warming their bodies while they talked and breakfeasted.

'Strange place this, aye and strange weather too Barak,' Ragnor remarked looking skyward at the racing white snow clouds above him.

Before the giant could even make a reply to Ragnor's observation the Norsemen were without any warning whatsoever assailed by a most ferocious blizzard. Still, the party were most fortunate that the horses were well hobbled. For if not then the beasts would have without doubt gone off at the gallop into the wild. Now and unable to continue any further because of the blizzards ferocity the men left their clearing and at once retreated back into the shelter of the thick dark forest. Barak though just as ever was not disheartened by this event, as all along the ogre had expected such wild and fickle weather. Once in the comparative safety of the forest the giant lit up his pipe as he stared outward and upward as the tall trees were tossed this way and that. And as said the ever patient giant was in no way put out by the savage assault from the elements in any way.

So, for now at least as many times before the travellers would simply have to sit out the storm. Then later when the storm was finally spent and blown out the men would continue on once again with their journey.

For two days more that white blinding blizzard blustered and raged all about them keeping the Norsemen pinned to the spot. All the while the tall trees creaked and bent as they bashed together off each other at their highest point. Here during this storm their time though was not at all wasted. Now the freshly skinned wolf skins were scraped, cleaned and dried before being stretched and stitched together. All of this hard but necessary work was done to make shelters and windbreaks. These skins once prepared and cured were tied tightly between the close standing pines. Of course during this time as was the norm the fires were stacked high and the remainder of the ale was broken out from the two remaining oaken barrels.

Seemingly the tension of the incident between Barak and Bull Neck was forgotten and now was a time for high fellowship and feasting.

Barak had made tasty broths from the remaining wolf and boar meat and despite all and everything the savage hardy Norsemen were not in the least put out or troubled by this new setback. As Barak had always said in the past the men must always be kept happy and contented to get the best out of them. And as ever and always the big burly Vikings were of course a most uncomplaining cheerful hardy lot. Aye and if things did go bad, as they so often did, well the giant felt at least he could not wish to die in better company than these brave souls. Well that however was with the one exception of their number of course.

When the weather finally broke several days later the Norsemen once again marched on. The warriors crossed the freezing river at an angry shallow stretch. Here the fast flowing river almost took the legs out away from under them. However holding on to horse's tails and each other's girdles the warriors crossed without incident. And so now with their crossing complete it was time for them to catch their supper. Without any further ado the Norsemen gaffed salmon with much success and camped now on the other side of the river that very night. Once again though on that night the accursed weather changed yet again, going from being mild to bitter cold. Well in truth it was a lot more than cold, aye indeed what a freezing frosty night it turned out to be. Aye and all of this with also a wild savage howling wind. This wind carried with it hailstones the size of a big man's clenched fist behind its rage. Indeed this accursed weather was ever changing, aye and now it had changed for the worse once again. Still, as always and as ever in such situations big Barak was quite prepared for the every occasion and no matter what that might be.

This side of the river was a treeless barren place, and it was a place without shelter of any sort. Now, well now the intrepid travellers were open in every way possible to all of the most inhospitable of elements. Barak with a sort of satisfied smile turned about and from within his mule packs pulled out make shift tents made from sail cloth. Quickly, these tents were at once easily lashed together and erected. Up till now in the dense forest the ogre had felt these tents had not been so far needed. However, in the here and now the tents were a most welcome asset. Of course the tents were a flimsy somewhat precarious shelter that offered little in the way of warmth. But never the less the canvas would at least keep the men dry and free from the blow and the bite of the ice cold winter wind. Later once the hail had ceased its downpour the Norsemen sat themselves contentedly around their raging camp fires fuelled with dried out drift wood from the river.

There in the firelight as darkness fell these tough, rough and ready men ate, drank, talked and laughed out loudly as they went over their adventure so far. Oh, what a tale they all had to tell once back in their far off homeland. After eating and drinking their fill each of these warriors with their own thoughts retired to their tents. Once there the men slept a restful and a most well deserved sleep under their thick wolf skin and bearskin coverings. All slept well, all that was but for the giant Barak, the slayer kept himself alert, he did not choose to sleep that night. No, the great ogre he did not sleep at all, as here was a most dangerous place. Barak alone, with his great dogs of war and his huge black eagle for company stood watch over the small encampment. As the beasts of this river, well these large dangerous creatures apparently were not at all confined to its mysterious depths.

Far from it as these, man eating beasts had been known in the past to slither and slide ashore in the dead and darkness of night and make off with those who had foolishly thought they were safe from reach, safe from harm. But on this cold blasted night, well, that at least would not happen, not while Barak stood his watch. On the following morning sadly for Barak and his followers the weather grew even worse. As now there came upon them a freezing wind from the north east, this as well as more bruising hail and sky cracking thunder. Here was a thunder followed by forked lightning that seemed to split the very sky open. This thunder and lightning distressed the horses so much the beasts almost bolted and were off hobbles or no hobbles. Still though despite all of this, Barak had thought it wise to be at least some distance from the river. This being the case after packing the horses the Norsemen moved on just a little bit further for safety's sake. Oh aye and also it must be said the ogre did not relish in any way another night without his much loved sleep. Wearily after fighting their way through a flesh stinging gale the party after a hard march camped once again just as dusk fell. Once again this was amid a ferocious attack of giant hail, hail that killed another one of Ragnor's hard uncomplaining men.

Gunnar he was called, a large flame headed man with a good sense of humour as well as a good sword hand he would be sadly missed.

To look at the big broad red bearded man you would have sworn the Norseman had been brained by a club. For such was the injury to his hairy head under his thick dented bronze Viking helmet. Ragnor fumed and growled angrily, he was

275

eight men down now, seven to the wolves and now one to a big bit of frozen ice. Ragnor rumbled and grumbled as he growled away to himself. Now the big Viking prayed for enemy warriors to slay rather than fight with the wild beasts and elements of this stark unforgiven land. Anyway besides all and everything the men had a hasty supper then rested overnight. Barak on that cold windy night slept like a log under his bearskins and for once was not the first to rise.

'I thought it best to let you sleep my Lord,' Tark said as he offered his king a gourd of vodka to revive him. Barak clicked his huge neck into place and he spoke.

'Is someone else doing the cooking boy, as I smell meat?' said the ogre after a long swig from the gourd. Tark shook his head and spat upon the ground away from the wind before replying.

'No not really my Lord, that is the Viking Gunnar yonder upon a pyre, he makes his way now to Valhalla.' Barak took for himself another drink and cursed at the loss of another good man as he rose to his great booted feet. Later, once with this sad task completed and with heavy hearts at the loss of their friend as ever the band of warriors moved relentlessly ever onwards towards their destination.

Chapter Seventeen

Three hard days later the Norsemen stood at the foot of a long winding mountain pathway. And here was a pathway that disappeared from sight off into the grey snow filled clouds which rose high above them.

'We could still go onwards a little Barak, there is still a little light left for us to find our way.' Tark suggested as the men halted for a brief moment and peered skyward.

Barak did not hesitate in his answering straightaway. The slayer shook his mail clad head.

'No lad, it is light only because of the fresh snow that has fallen and not because of the time of day. Aye and these fierce beasts of the mountains, well I do suppose such creatures do come alive at night to hunt.' The giant said this while looking upward into the snow covered rocky heights whose lofty peak far above them was hidden by mist and cloud. 'Please believe me lad it is best for us to bide here for tonight. Aye here we will eat and rest, then start on the upward trail in the morning as fresh men. Ragnor, what say you to this, are you also in accord with my feelings? ' Barak asked of Ragnor who was now plucking icicles from his big red frozen beard.

'Aye, aye my friend I do agree with you Barak,' the Viking replied as he eased himself down more than a little stiffly from his horse.

'And I too agree with you Ragnor,' Horst grumbled in a drunken fashion. 'For I have sat upon this great snorting beast of yours Barak for far too long now.' Horst complained bitterly as he slurred out his words as usual.

'Then think yourself lucky you are riding the horse you drunken German fool,' Barak growled. 'Aye riding the beast, and that you are not leading it as I have done these last long miles Horst,' Barak replied a little angrily. 'For the good and noble beast that it surely is, has nevertheless these past hours stood heavily upon my feet several times.' Drunk or not Horst as ever was not stuck for an answer to the ogre's complaints.

'Well you must think yourself a most lucky man Barak, for at least you do have two big feet for the big horse to stand upon my Lord,' Horst said with a belch and a chuckle.

Ragnor sniggered at the drunken Horst's quick remark to Barak, as did everyone else within earshot.

Even the halfling now named Borz also chuckled in that peculiar way of his, and this as his purple forked tongue flicked out and tested the air.

Barak at once looked up to the stormy heavens above him as he muttered out curses. Why oh why the great slayer wondered to himself, why on earth had he brought with him a fat one legged German drunk. Still wondering the giant with a grunt shook his big bucket sized head as he savagely ground his teeth together. Still the ogre was wishing in vain to loosen his aching back tooth which by the by was still plaguing the very life out of him. After but a moment of his luckless tooth grinding the giant gathered his thoughts together, he next spoke up.

'Aye and anyway Horst,' Barak said after a moment or two of thinking and deliberating. 'I had thought I had seen you dragged off into the forest by a big black she wolf. Or was that perhaps merely wishful thinking on my behalf?' Barak remarked at length as he lifted the always unsteady German down from the big gelding.

'Oh aye, aye that you did my Lord, your black eyes they as ever did not deceive you,' Horst replied whilst steadying himself upon the treacherous ground underfoot. 'Yes my Lord that what you think you witnessed, well you most surely did, if you know what I mean? Alas though for the foolish slobbering beast, well it had seized me by my wooden leg you understand my noble Lord? Horst explained with a chuckle. 'Aye and the wolf, well it did I must say look a most stupid thing as it ran off into the forest with a length of willow wood in its jaws.' Horst chuckled, spat then took a drink of beer from his gourd before once again before speaking. 'I retrieved my wooden leg the following morning from the snows when we collected the dead bodies of the wolves for meat,' Horst added with a grin which revealed what little teeth he had left in his fat red faced head.

Barak merely shook his head and lit up his pipe, doubtless he thought to himself he could never cease with his smoking and drinking when in the company as such as the German. On that evening the company of Norsemen camped once again, this amid raucous laughter at the ever drunken German's most humorous story. Now Barak with a few drinks in him and heady with weed remembered why he had brought Horst along with him. As it happened, well the drunken fool to his credit did quite simply cheer everyone up. Aye and besides that, well the German was quite easily a better drinking partner than any of the Vikings. Horst could at least drink strong vodka without falling into the fire or setting his beard ablaze whilst trying to light his pipe. In fact the Rhinelander as it happened had more chance of stopping upright than any of the Vikings. Aye and this was even though the ever drunken fool had only the one leg to support him.

Anyway, the band of warriors spent another chill but otherwise safe night camped at the very foot of the mountain. And then after breakfeasting they then pressed on up the mountain pathway the following day. By the by this it must be said was a most slippery treacherous hard going passage from the very first footfall. Also that following day of their trek was exactly the same, aye and the one after was also a living walking nightmare. Only Horst was mounted now and he sat somewhat unsteadily aboard the gelding while the other horses were led riderless in single file up the treacherous winding pathway. A slip now for either man or beast would of course spell certain death as they crashed through the mists to the ground far below. However the fresh fallen fluffy snow that had drifted down through the sleeping hours. Well this snow at least offered the company some grip to walk upon, perhaps though this was only a dangerous deception. Aye, as under that white fluffy blanket of snow there was the thickest and most treacherous of ice. Also of course this rock hard ice was most dangerous, and so of course being so then it had to go. Now very carefully the ice was chipped steadily away with war axes and scattered over the side of the mountain pathway. All of this was achieved by the four or five men who had gone on ahead of the main party. Slowly, slowly but ever surely the diminishing group of warriors climbed onward and ever upward. Till at long last just as dusk fell and after many cold uncomfortable days on that mountain the warriors reached the broad craggy summit. Throughout the length of this summit, near the very roof of the mountain itself, there ran an ancient rock tunnel. Obviously this was a tunnel that had doubtless been there since the beginning of time itself. This ancient tunnel was entombed inside the frozen rock walls of the mountain. Aye and here it was a most stark affair with thick deadly looking lance like icicles hanging most precariously from its frozen roof. Aye and without any doubt, these dangerous looking ice spears could skewer both man or beast in an instant should they ever break off. Still though despite all of this frosty grandeur this stark cavern would have to put the company of weary men up for the night as outside now another fierce snow blizzard was born.

On the following morning all being well the party would be on their way once again ever eastward towards Barak's still far off Kingdom. Aye after hopefully a good night's sleep and a well deserved rest the warriors would embark on their downward descent to the steppes far below. So for at least on one night on their cold perilous travels the warriors would at least have above them a solid roof over their hairy heads. Aye, and a real roof at that, this other than the coverings of flimsy canvas and animal skins to stave off the wet and the cold. Meanwhile outside of the long rock tunnel the fierce blizzard whipped up the fresh falling snow, this wind hurled the snow into the air to meet and collide with the snow that was still steadily coming down from the heavens above. At once this merging created a thick snowy curtain, a curtain that was most difficult if not impossible to peer through into the bleak beyond.

'What was that?' Tark asked as a long tremendous roar echoed throughout the length and breadth of the tunnel. In but a moment the big dogs at once rose to their feet, their hackles and tails were held up high while their lips were drawn back in a threatening snarl. On this night due to the lack of timber lying about the warriors of the north had now only two large fires for comfort and warmth. As always the uncomplaining warriors sat about the fires warming themselves as best they could as icicles formed on their big red beards. Meanwhile Norsemen struggled not to freeze to death as their supper cooked and simmered away in Barak's big pots. However freezing or not as ever the big Norsemen made no complaint.

With a cheery look about him Barak stirred the meat lovingly while adding more herbs and spices as well as a handful of sea salt for flavour.

'Are the horses well? Tell me lads are the beasts all secure?' Ragnor asked of his nephews. At once the boys without any hesitation gave a positive nod in reply to their frozen bearded uncle. Still though nevertheless the youths without any complaint or even being asked all the same went and checked the horses over once again just to make sure.

As it happened the horses did seem a little more nervous than usual that night when they had left them chewing away at their fodder.

The lads had took along with them the big dogs and their weapons, the brothers looked about nervously as yet another long and fearful roar brought every warrior to his feet reaching for his sword or axe.

Borz arose to his feet his tongue flicking out while his yellow eyes rolled in his newt like head.

'Mountain lions, my Lord Barak?' Tark asked knowingly. The giant's eyes narrowed as he puffed upon his pipe then took a drink of vodka before nodding.

'Aye lions, there are two of them out there, and they are alas big ones at that,' Barak replied. 'When I hunted out our supper of mountain goat earlier I saw their tracks plainly in the deep snow, the cats have been tracking us now for over a day. '

Ragnor blew through his frozen lips and shrugged indifferently.

'Bah, only two cats Barak, why they would not dare chance an attack against so many armed men, no not two of them' Ragnor said this in a most dismissive fashion. Barak, well he did not at once reply and so Ragnor rambled on. 'No, surely these beasts would not be so reckless or foolish, would they?' Ragnor asked this question and then he answered it for himself, this the big Viking did while tying his long hair back behind his broad neck.

Barak took for himself another mouthful of vodka, then the ogre sucked upon his pipe before replying.

'Perhaps,' Barak shrugged with a casual indifference of his own. 'But either way my friend, they will not attack us tonight, no the lions will not attack here,' Barak replied quite confidently before continuing. 'But know you this, aye and know you all this now. Within two nights of our descent, before we hit the tree line below us the cats will come for us. Aye the lions will come looking for meat, and alas, we my brothers, well we are that meat. '

On hearing the giant's honest and profound statement a shudder was sent through each and every one of the big Vikings' very souls. Death, well this was something which did not frighten the warriors in the least, why these Norsemen had lived with death all of their lives. Ah, but on the other hand, being dined upon by huge man eating cats, well this fate was something totally different. Barak, with his words once said, smiled broadly revealing his wolf sharp teeth.

'However my bold and brave brothers, as it so happens well we too will have need of fresh meat by then. For after all my loyal brave hearts, we must also eat, agreed?' The giant had said this as he broke off from his broth stirring for a moment to sharpen his dragon sword with his fire stone. 'Also it has been a long time now since I last tasted the flesh of big cat. Aye, and know you all this, if cooked right which of course it will be, then I must say I like the taste of lion. Please believe me its taste and flavour are very good, very good.' Barak had added this enthralling piece of information with a lick of his lips. And so, with this slight off hand reassurance from Barak as to the gastronomic qualities of lion meat, most of the men of course ate a hearty supper. Even in these freezing conditions, with their bearskins laid on frozen ice that not even the fire could thaw. Still these heroic Norsemen at least managed to get some sort of a restless sleep on that freezing ice cold night.

And also, just as Barak had said, the warriors sleep went unhindered apart from the biting cold which repeatedly awakened them with their teeth chattering inside of their hairy heads.

On that following freezing misty morning just as the warriors left their cold rocky sanctuary Barak found fresh tracks in the snow blown into the mouth of the far end of the long tunnel. Alas it must be said these large tracks were not something that brought a great deal of cheer to the intrepid travellers.

'Ice bears; these pad marks look more like the tracks of ice bears than mere cats!' Ragnor exclaimed in both surprise and horror. Barak gave a grumbled nod of agreement and also a resolute sort of sigh.

'Aye my friend they are big, yes indeed I do suppose these tracks are very big.' Now the giant said this while crouching down and spanning a paw print with one of his own massive hands. Even with Barak's massive spread of fingers the slayer could still easily fit his outstretched hand inside the lion's paw print, aye and this with still plenty of room to spare.

'So my Lord Barak, last night, these beasts were in and under the very same shelter as we were?' Tark asked this in open mouthed horror as he looked about him from the mouth of the rock tunnel for signs of more tracks, or indeed the beasts that had made them.

'So, these creatures that hunt us down for food were in fact our room mates for a while? ' the young warrior mused out aloud.

Barak once again nodded.

'Aye it seems so, the creatures took shelter here, but it is a very long tunnel lad. And also the wind was in the lion's favour, so my dogs could not detect them. Neither myself or Borz caught the cats scent either, aye, it is just a shame my big eagle has flown herself off somewhere,' the giant muttered to himself, a little disgruntled at his birds untimely absence.

'Anyway, these big cats are a hunting pair, and the beasts are both cunning, and no doubt very clever. Aye and also there is no doubt the creatures will make their attack when we least expect them to, or then again perhaps the lions will attack, just when we most expect them to.' Barak had said this while puffing upon his long pipe. Ragnor at once grunted then the big red bearded Viking shook his hairy head in total disagreement.

'Bah, you speak in riddles Barak, true the lions might be big, but still they are after all only big cats,' Ragnor said with quite a dismissive tone in his voice.

Barak ground his teeth together, the slayer was not angry at Ragnor, no just angry at that back tooth, still as ever the thing just would not move.

Now after his tooth grinding, Barak turned about and looked into his friend's pale blue eyes, but the ogre had decided to say nothing in reply. After a moment or two of searching the heavens Barak shrugged and sighed as he looked searchingly up at the snow filled clouds above them. After that brief moment of thought it was then the slayer spoke.

'Still, regardless of what you Ragnor, or indeed what any one else thinks we can do nothing. Well nothing but wait for the lions coming, so for now we must go on down the mountain and not linger here.' Barak said this as his keen black eyes searched through the freezing mists that surrounded them. Carefully the giant studied every rock about him which was big enough to conceal these savage deadly ambush creatures. True it was the lion's tracks lead away from where the warriors now stood out into the misty beyond. However, that though was a mere detail, and so of course meant nothing at alas these most deadly of creatures were renowned for back tracking and springing sneaky well thought out ambush attacks upon their prey.

Wolves, well true they had cunning a plenty, and that was in no doubt, but also the wolves of the black forest had great numbers. So it was those killers were able to charge into the warrior's ranks while loping around their camp fires like some sort of an avenging army. However, here though on this freezing mountain there were only two large cats, but then again, these apparently were very large cats. Barak suspected quite rightly the lion's attack would be an entirely different one to that of the forest wolves. Aye and over the next day or two the ogre would as always and ever prove himself to be more than correct in his clever guesswork.

On that cold dusky evening when the warriors camped on the first day of their dangerous descent the snow was still falling heavily. And this whilst the cold cutting wind had not ceased or given up at all in its almost spiteful efforts to hinder the Norsemen. Scavenging fuel on their descent the wood and brash the warriors gathered could only afford one large fire for them to huddle about for warmth. This life giving fire the men had set away between a crop of huge fallen boulders from the white iced over frozen mountain. Unselfish as ever toward one another the men of the Viking brotherhood very fairly changed places in their sitting and lying positions around the flames. This of course was quite simply so all of the men could at least warm themselves at some time throughout the night. No wind breaks of either wolf skins or canvas material was erected to protect them from the chill freezing night. Barak explained this for a simple reason, as it was of course better the warriors could see just what it was hunted them down for food.

Aye it was best the big bold Northmen could all see what was coming directly at them before their very throats were ripped out and they were carried away for food. Once all this was explained it was Barak alone who sat away from the warming flames of the camp fire. And instead of this glowing comfort the ogre by his own choice huddled under a great black bearskin cloak with his broad back pressed against a huge rock near to the horses. Barak did this alone and with only his huge faithful boarhounds lying at his side. The giant had most kindly declined the company of Tark and the halfling, this for his own reasons. Barak had simply, but quite politely told them both he wanted no distraction and most of all no conversations on his watch.

Silence and patience now the ogre supposed was the key to slaying these huge mountain lions. Well that of course when coupled with a lot of cunning and even more good fortune.

Barak's great black eagle was much missed, she had of course taken herself off and away several days ago, this of course was a great disadvantage as she saw all about her. Still though she was near to her home in the ever snow capped mountains. Perhaps, the ogre thought to himself that now she must mate, mate for the first time in her life. It had been ten summers now since Barak had found her as a small sickly chick in an eagle market in the hinterland. In a rage the giant had taken the chick without paying for her, this after firing many insults at the vendor. As of course the fool was a vendor who had no right to have her in his possession in the first place. Still somehow the fool did have the chick, but either way that was another story altogether. Anyway the giant had taken the young bird, he had fed nurtured and lavished much time and affection upon her. Then and later on with the passing of time she had grown not only to be a creature of great speed and power but also a creature of great loyalty. True it was she was gone for now aye and at a time when she was most needed. Nevertheless despite this drawback Barak was both confident and hopeful the great black eagle would not be gone from him for too long. Soon enough, the she eagle would return to big Barak. She had not, nor would not desert the giant who had cared for her and raised her from being no more than but a fluffy chick. Still though Barak thought to himself as he ground his teeth together whilst cursing his sore one, she could have picked a better time to go a missing.

'I think I am the safest man here in this company of hairy rogues!' Horst exclaimed suddenly and loudly as he swallowed down his vodka while he feasted most uncaringly upon well cooked mountain goat.

Barak looked over from where he sat as Horst continued to ramble on in his usual smiling half drunken state.

'Yes, I will, I am most sure be the last man here among us all that these big cat beasts would want to eat I do think. '

Now there was a moment of two of silence, and then quite unusually it was Bull Neck who eventually spoke up.

'Wwhy ddyou ssay tthat, yyou are a llittle ffat man, ggood llion ffood?' Bull Neck said with a snidey sneer. Bull Neck, well, the foolish oaf did not like Horst one little bit, but then again the drunken German in all truth didn't like Bull Neck very much either.

Horst winked without any notice from the other Norsemen at Ragnor, and then the German smiled as he chewed greedily upon his goat flesh, washed down with yet more vodka. Horst of course as ever was a man who could well handle his drink, the gods only knew he had years of practice at it. Ah but even when well drunk, as already said, he was ever quick witted and had an answer for all and everything. So now the drunken German said on and explained himself.

'Because, you great lumbering fool, if these beasts are as wily as the Lord Barak says them to be then they will leave me till last.' Horst was still smiling most mischievously when he called Bull Neck a fool. And this as only the great slayer Barak had ever called and insulted the oaf in such an off-hand and uncaring fashion.

Bull Neck bristled inside at being insulted and called a fool by this fat one legged German drunkard but of a sudden the oaf felt Barak's dark glare upon him. And so quite wisely and also surprisingly for an idiot devoid of common sense the oaf sat there and he said nothing. There was for a long moment a drawn out silence, none there about the campfire spoke as they all awaited Horst's next words. Indeed Bull Neck and everyone else sitting about the fire looked a little bemused by Horst's strange yet most profound statement.

Smiling broadly the very unsteady German looked about him at the circle of big brawny savage looking red bearded men. These men were without any doubt big brave souls, aye the warriors from the north were without any doubt bold in the extreme. Also as well as all of this these large fellows were also good cheery company. Aye and this whether that be either in a busy bustling tavern back in some sort of semi-civilisation or around a campfire on a frozen mountain.

However, there were still times that Horst found the Norsemen not at all perhaps the quickest witted bunch of men he had ever put his time in with.

Aye and that was from one who was in a more or less permanent state of utter intoxication.

All blue Icelandic eyes were now upon Horst waiting for him to give some sort of explanation as to his most confident statement. Horst as ever was smiling his lop sided drunken smile, and this whilst he looked about him at the simple savage faces all about him, after a moment the German spoke up.

'Because of course, well I only have but one leg you great hairy Viking fools,' the German said suddenly slapping the top of his good leg and bursting into rough laughter. 'Why, even you scurvy slow witted pick pockets would have more sense than not to choose a roast chicken with but only one leg when there is another by its side with two legs.' this he declared whilst in fits of laughter.

As the German had well expected there was a moment of silence, this while the Vikings slowly grasped the significance of Horst's well chosen words. When at long last the company of rogues realised the German's reasoning of things, well, the Norsemen all laughed out loud, long, most heartily around the single camp fire. Well apart that was from the brooding ill-tempered Bull Neck. For that particular fool, just as was his norm, merely thought the German drunkard was as usual in some way mocking him and him alone. Bull Neck was a man after all with many issues, oh and of course most if not all of these were bad ones. Bull Neck grunted out an insult of some sorts directed at Horst then the unhappy soul rolled over in his bear skins and went instantly off to sleep. This though was not before briefly thinking to himself that once Barak was dead, then the little fat German would soon follow on in his path.

Anyway, as the light of a new dawn approached the shivering men stirred themselves slowly into life placing what logs were about upon the dying fire. As the men talked and joked as was their norm no matter what. Well, there of a sudden came from behind a rough patch of thorn bush a most terrible and pitiful scream. One of Ragnor's men had moved himself beyond the sparse bushes to relieve himself from his night of mild sensible drinking. For now there was not a man amongst them, who was making himself defenceless by taking in too much drink or weed or anything else for that matter. However, the unlucky Kartor, well alas he had merely taken himself too far away from the safety of the crowd of men. Most craftily now, well the luckless warrior had been simply carried off as a dead thing up a steep shale bank to become nothing more than food for lions.

And oh indeed this was a formidable bank with fresh fell snow lying atop of ice and ice which in turn lay over the top of shifting shale. So steep and treacherous underfoot was the incline that not even the dogs could follow in the huge cats' wake. These mountain cats had huge hair covered pads that were designed over thousands and thousands of years past for this rough rugged terrain. Now all that was left for the company of Norse men to see of Kartor was a red sash taken from one of Wraif's men as a trophy. Well, this along with a thick gold chain, as well as a pool of blood and gore in the deep snow. Just as Barak had expected it was most silently and most cleverly these big cats had stalked and hunted down their prey. Waiting, watching and lurking patiently never too far away from their intended victims. Cleverly the cats used the wind always in their favour, this so not even the hunting dogs' keen senses could catch their scent. Nor for that matter did Barak's animal keen senses or had the halfling become alerted to the big cat's presence. And so now Kartor, who was by no means a light man to carry off was done, gone and lost for now and forever after.

Up the steep shale bank the big Viking had been borne away, aye, then up even higher again over a high craggy rock wall, this all by one single powerful beast. Oh and ever and so easily had this well thought out task been accomplished. Why the big brave Viking warrior had simply been taken off limp and dead in the lurking mountain lion's huge fanged jaws. Barak who was more than an able tracker noted the paw prints of the mountain lions showed the bigger one, the one that walked in front of the pair of killers did the carrying off. It was more than likely this larger beast did the killing and most of the thinking also. The one in the rear was a slightly smaller beast judging by its still very sizeable prints in the deep snow. Now this left the giant in no doubt this beast, obviously the she cat, had cleverly dropped back to cover her mate and their victorious retreat. Oh yes there was no doubt about it in Barak's mind, these lions indeed were most cunning clever and dangerous predators.

And being so with this thought firmly in mind big Barak intended pressing on with all haste before even more men were lost to these clever, cunning and very large cats.

'We can do nothing more here my friend,' Barak said grimly as he turned about to face a most solemn downcast looking Ragnor. 'We can do nothing now except break camp then be once again on our way down the mountain,' the giant said whilst putting a reassuring hand upon Ragnor's shoulder.

Ragnor cursed then spat out angrily as he kicked the bloodied snow into the cold air. 'I swear Barak on Odin's beard, I will have this beast's hide for this killing of my man,' the Viking snarled venomously.

Now Barak who had moved to walk away turned about and the huge slayer affixed his friend with an even stare that belied his sorrow at the loss of another brave Northman.

'Both of them Ragnor, we will have both of them, aye and please believe me we will have them sooner rather than later,' Barak promised. 'Come Ragnor we must go now, we must away,' the giant said as the band of gloomy warriors turned and left that place of butchery. Once more the long faced Northmen set off down the steep and treacherous pathway that would eventually lead them to the steppes. These were Steppes though that by the way still lay far below the thick grey mountain mists.

Over the next two days of their slow slippery slide on the ice pathway which took the warriors ever downwards Ragnor lost another two of his good men to the big cats. These were Thal, and young Brule whose father had earlier been taken by the wolves of the forest. Both of these were from the brotherhood, good, strong and brave uncomplaining men Why, Thal had sailed with Ragnor for many years and Brule, well, Ragnor had known that young man all of his short life. After his nephews Brule was the next youngest of their dwindling company, younger even than Tark. All of these good dead warriors, and yet of his company of armed most capable men he had not as yet lost one of their numbers to a blade, an axe or a longbow. No, no it was wolves and lions, aye and even the hail that had accounted for the end of these brave souls.

Barak seeing how upset Ragnor was at the loss of his friends and kinsmen had at last seen enough of this cold blooded calculated slaughter. Being so now and with this being the case as always and ever Barak had a plan to end the carnage. Now the ogre would explain it to Ragnor and then he would simply set out to do it. Well at least the ogre indeed would try to do it, this or he would die in the trying.

'We have a horse that is badly lame, Ragnor,' Barak said on a mid-afternoon the same day the last man was taken off, and this as another cold night drew in upon them. Aye and all of this whilst the snow kept falling down steadily amid another flesh numbing howling freezing gale, a gale that cut into unprotected flesh.

'You must leave this unfortunate beast here with me Ragnor and then you must go on ahead with your men down the winding mountain trail. Tark and Borz will stay with me, but this of course only if they wish to do so.' All of this the big Barak said in a most calm and matter of fact fashion before yet again continuing. 'If this is so, and they will bide with me, then together with the aid of my good and faithful hounds we will kill these man-eaters once and for all. ' Barak had said this whilst grinding his teeth together, the ogre was still trying in vain to dislodge that accursed tooth. 'Aye Ragnor, I swear we will kill these beasts once and forever, for believe me I think these lions' time upon this earth, it is long past now. ' Barak growled this out in a most matter of fact fashion.

Ragnor though, and perhaps for the very first time since knowing Barak doubted the ogre just a little on this call. As after all's said and done, these were not just normal beasts they were dealing with, oh no far from it. And so now a very worried Ragnor next voiced his concern for his long time friend's safety.

'Barak these cats, well I think they are cats only in name alone my brother, why I do suppose they are bigger than ice bears.' Ragnor said all of this with a worried look about his frozen and much weatherbeaten face. Well, that was what face you could see under his great frozen beard, a beard which now had even more small icicles hanging upon it than ever before. Oh and also this big frozen beard, well it hid almost all but the Viking's pale eyes as they watered with the cold under his frozen bushy red eyebrows.

'I know I have already said this only moments ago Barak but by the size of their tracks I would say these cats as you call them are as big as an ice bear. Perhaps the beasts are even bigger; tell me, am I far wrong with my guessing? Or mayhap then perhaps I am correct my large and stubborn friend?' Ragnor asked with an element of concern in his gruff voice.

Barak made no answer not wishing to distress his friend with the truth, but Tark, well he did straightaway and honestly reply to Ragnor's question.

'Bigger,' the young warrior said looking all about him while trying to peer through the driving snow into the wild beyond.

Ragnor cast another worried glance toward Barak.

'Surely, surely my friend we had best all stop together, don't you think so Barak? Ragnor asked this question hoping he could perhaps dissuade the slayer from this newly formulated plan of his. This even though the Viking knew he was wasting his time. Ragnor's answer came back to him just as he thought that it would.

'No.' Barak said this firmly and with a slow shake of his great head, a great head that was as ever encased in his battered chain link helmet. This well worn helmet now though, well, it had a thick wolf skin lining under it links for warmth. 'This pair of killers, why together they would have us down to some half dozen men by the time we reached the foot of this long downward road. For alas Ragnor, sadly for us this is a long winding trail that is just made for ambush,' Barak explained. 'Please believe me my friend one by one these cats will take us off into the wild. Feasting upon our flesh, then returning for more men when their hunger once again returns to them.' Barak said this while affixing Ragnor with an honest and even stare before continuing. 'These beasts will think as you do, think that three men and a couple of dogs are but easy prey. With their cunning the lions will think us an easier target than you and your larger company of men,' Barak added as he struck his flints together and lit up his pipe. As now the giant at this particular time of the day was in sore need of a smoke.

Now Borz gave off one of those strange grins of his as the creature was both proud and pleased Barak wanted his company on this dangerous task. Oh and also the halfling he kind of chuckled to himself a little proudly as the giant passed him off as being a human member of their number. Though only the gods could know why Borz was so proud of that most dubious accolade. For in truth and at the end of the day the world of men had alas done him little enough favours in the past. Aye and also perhaps Barak was not doing him any such favours now by enlisting him on this most dangerous of lion hunts.

Ah but then again, Borz thought somewhat cynically to himself, in truth he had enjoyed himself over these last months. Besides all of that it was also Barak who had given him back his long yearned for freedom in the first place. And so therefore, and with this being the case then he would be proud to fight alongside his large and colourful liberator and the young Tark. With both Tark and the halfling Borz to assist him on his mission Barak now wanted everything under way.

'It darkens now,' Barak said stirring Ragnor from his dark musings 'Also the weather it worsens, so quickly now you must press on down the mountain for just a little while longer. Take yourself a good distance away from us and I swear to you all will yet be well,' the giant said trying to reassure his worried friend. 'But hear this, you must travel safely and camp cleverly. Make sure that you secure the horses well, light the fires and stay close to each other, be ever armed ever alert. Do you understand me Ragnor?' Barak asked affixing the Norseman with an eye to eye stare. 'Do you understand me my friend? Tell me do you truly hear me?' Barak asked once more.

Ragnor gave a grunt followed by an unconvincing nod of his hairy head then the big Viking removed his bronze helmet as he scratched at his raggy red frozen beard with one hand and his head with the other. Ragnor struggled to speak but alas he was not quite quick enough to get the first word in, but of course Barak was.

'We three will stop here in this place. We together will await the coming of the beasts.' Barak continued to say as he inhaled the strong weed. 'Trust me my friend, all will be well Ragnor, over there is an opening in the rocks for shelter.' Barak said as the ogre then nodded towards a small rocky overhang. This overhang it would at least offer them some sort of shelter from the freezing biting wind, oh and of course concealment.

'The lame horse will stay here with us as bait for the cats, who knows perhaps by now the creatures tire of man flesh,' Barak said with a cynical smile.

Ragnor still had not the words to reply to Barak's grim humour, nor did he have in him the inclination to debate the situation. After all so far on this venture he had lost almost a dozen good friends and fighting men, aye and still not one of these to another armed warrior. Oh aye and above all else, the most damning thing about it as far as Ragnor was concerned was that only one of these men had been giving a proper funeral. One out of all these good men, aye and that, that was only because he was brained by a giant hailstone and not carried off and eaten by a savage beast.

After a bit of thought and with a resolute grunt the big Viking clasped Barak's hand in friendship as he gave a respectful nod toward both Tark and Borz. Then with this done the Norseman quite simply and without another word spoken about the matter turned about and trudged off down the mountain pass leading his weary horse behind him.

Barak watched silently and thoughtfully as Ragnor with his men and horses disappeared into the mists and into the ever growing blizzard. All that Barak could do for the here and now was to sit and wait for the coming of the lions. Still though the trio of hunters or perhaps they were prey afforded themselves the luxury of an adequate fire. This whilst they sat down at the mouth of their small cave ever alert ever watchful. Meanwhile the lame horse was hobbled only a stone's throw away before them by its front legs. Oh and by the by this noble hardy creature to its credit and true to type was undeterred by the severe weather. So with great fortitude the beast now nuzzled away the deep snow and then it fed upon the tasty mountain moss that lay underneath. While it was true to say that the horses of the Briton's were neither the biggest nor the fastest of beasts, well to their credit they were at least strong and hardy animals. Aye and also these creatures were the most honest of things.

Barak had garbed and padded out the lame horse in wolf and bearskins, this the ogre had done to protect it both from the bitter cold and also from the fangs of the lions. Barak at times had more compassion for loyal faithful beasts than he ever had for wasteful useless men. And in all truth sadly there were of course always plenty of those worthless beings mooching about. So if at all possible the slayer would if he could, like to save the horse rather than have it eaten by the ravenous mountain lions. Barak now sat beside the camp fire with a gourd of vodka in one hand and his pipe in the other awaiting the coming of the lions.

Suddenly the giant afforded himself a grim smile as he mused over those unworthy souls he had encountered in his past and then sent on to hell. Oh aye, there were plenty of men he had met in his life time that he would sooner use as lion bait instead of the pony. Bull Neck of course was one of them in fact that worthless and useless stammering treacherous fool was at the very head of the list. Barak was suddenly stirred from his dark musings.

'Do you think the lions will come to visit us this night my Lord?' Tark asked this as he tested the tension of his longbow. Tark had already stuck arrows into the snow before him at the mouth of the overhang in readiness for quick flight.

Barak blew out smoke then the slayer gave a grunt and a most positive nod in reply to the question.

'Aye lad, the lions will come to us, and what is more the beasts will come for us very soon,' the giant said with great confidence. 'Look you now my boy,' Barak said pointing a finger towards where the horse stood hobbled. 'See how the horse is becoming unsettled, and my dogs also they are vexed; the creatures approach us.' The giant said this with a grim smile, also a low growl of eager anticipation. This as one way or the other, Barak wanted this affair settled, and he wanted it settled now. 'What say you Borz, do the Lions come to us? ' Barak asked rising to his feet while sniffing the air like some sort of wild thing. Now it was the halfling's turn to rise to his big webbed feet and look about him as all the while his purple tongue flicked in and out of his great mouth sensing out the freezing snowy wilderness.

'Aye my Lord Barak, the beasts of the mountain are near us now, they are beyond in the cover of the mist and the blizzard.' Now the halfling blinked and his tongue flicked out rapidly. Next, the great green creature hissed as he slowly unwound his lethal chain from about his broad warty shoulders. For the creature too, it, just like Barak, needed a reckoning with these mountain beasts, beasts that had slain and eaten several of his new found friends.

Barak once again sniffed the air in a most bear like fashion.

'Yes, I agree with you Borz, the lions do come to us.'

It was also obvious to Tark by the fearsome snarling of Barak's big dogs that they were also expecting some sort of immediate company.

Tark at this point felt a little put out and a little inferior to his huge comrades, for he at this present time could neither see hear, nor smell anything.

'It is my very intention to dine upon mountain cat and not horse this night, do you understand me?' Barak growled out addressing no one in particular. 'We end this duel here and we end it now, one way or the other, are we all agreed?'

Barak with these words spoken next put out his pipe with a thumb then the giant took a long swig of his much beloved vodka.

Both Tark and the halfling said nothing in answer, but then again they did not have too. Instead they merely nodded their heads in solemn silent and somewhat grim agreement as to the giant's murderous intentions and dark wishes.

Barak was not overly armed and he had brought along with him for this most dangerous death hunt only three throwing spears.

Two of these spears were his own weapons that the giant had brought along with him for the journey and also he had with him Horst's Roman throwing spear. This was a spear that he had of course in the recent past already had a certain amount of success with. Now, hopefully once more the spear would bring him good fortune and it would not let him down.

Still, though, while the cats were nearby it never the less could still be perhaps another long and unsettling hour or so before the deadly felines finally decided to make their cunning and attack.

But it was not an hour or so, it was longer than that when the mountain lions at long length came on the attack. And this the large felines did even more bravely but less cautiously than had been expected by the giant. Of a sudden as a gust of wind even more powerful than the others that cut flesh like a blade. Well this gale whipped up fresh fallen snow, the meanwhile the huge cats charged through the already soft deep snow in a sudden, violent blinding rush of speed and primeval power. Barak's idea of perhaps saving the lame horse was in hindsight no more than sheer lunacy. This as the poor unfortunate beast was down and out and a dead thing in a matter of no more than a few seconds with its throat ripped out. Why the unfortunate beast was even being torn apart and feasted upon as the men and dogs approached as swiftly as the deep snow allowed them toward the bloody carnage.

So fierce was the ever growing blizzard now the men had to close much nearer than they had intended with the mountain cats and this just to make it even possible to see the huge creatures plainly. Aye and when the lion hunters did finally see the blood covered carnivores even Barak was much impressed. As oh what huge fearsome beasts these lions were, even bigger by far than Barak had imagined them to be. In all truth Barak had to grudgingly acknowledge to himself these mountain lions were magnificent beasts and creatures well worthy of slaying. Amidst the mist and the snow blown up by gusts of wind the lions stood now defiant and unafraid over the dead horse with their huge mouths and fangs dripping with blood and gore. After all this was their prize, it was their trophy and their meal, obviously they were neither going to share it with these humans, or would they abandon it. However that bold stubbornness as it so happened well suited Barak just perfectly

As magnificent or not Barak had already of course decided he was about to slay them both, well either that, or the Lions would have to slay him.

Barak's big, eager and fearless dogs were as brave and as bold as ever were commanded to stay their charge until the big cats had been weakened up a little. Of a sudden just for an instant there was a brief lull in the wind. And in that heartbeat of time Barak hurled two of his throwing spears with blinding speed at the larger of the two cats which was obviously the male. One spear glanced off one of the lion's great foot long teeth as it travelled towards the animal's throat. And then after but a heartbeat the next spear thrown, caught by the wind, fell short and stuck harmlessly into the side of the already dead horse. Barak had better luck with his third spear as it drove deep into the big cat's left shoulder bringing about both a roar of extreme anger and pain from the fierce mountain beast. Now the smaller one, well if smaller one the female mountain cat could be called given its size and power. Well the she bounded forward bravely far faster than a beast of its great size was ever entitled to move towards the offending warriors.

Tark had said earlier he was a good and a capable archer, and the young man did not lie, as this indeed he most certainly was. Five arrows Tark fired off quickly into the body of the fierce female beast before it was amongst them. Five arrows and five hits, but still the creature would not and could not be halted or would she be denied her most determined attack.

Barak was brought roughly to the ground by the angry creature amid a veritable blur of snow cloud and warm spurting blood from the female lion's wounds.

Tark meanwhile had been brushed to one side by the big cat's charge as she passed by him, his longbow was now shattered useless and broken, sadly so was his left arm just below the elbow.

Onward she charged and crashed full force into the giant slayer knocking him to the ground.

Barak now lying upon his back had seized the great beast by its long fangs as it sought to lock them about the giant's big link clad head. However, the ogre at this particular time was apparently not put out, far from it in fact he was laughing like some sort of a madman. Oh and also now the dogs were into the fray atop of the great female beast ripping into the back of its neck and shoulders snapping the arrow shafts that protruded here and there all about its great tawny body. Barak's great dogs were now in a mad fighting fury, and they were lost in a desperate blood rage to protect their master.

It was now the big halfling troll also rushed bravely in to join the fray with his heavy chain twirling dangerously above his newt like head.

'Leave me, protect young Tark!' Barak shouted to Borz as the big male cat painfully rushed forward as best it could towards the young injured Krozak warrior. Straightway, without any hesitation or thought for himself the Halfling sprang forward placing his body between Tark and the great furious male lion.

Tark was struggling as best he could to get back onto his feet now in the deep snow. But with his left arm broken and the footing bad underneath him this of course was no easy task. Painfully he at last pushed himself upward with his good arm and was once again upon his black booted feet, albeit a little unsteadily. Now though the young warrior at this time felt dizzy, sick and also even a little faint. And all of this as he looked about him as if he were in some sort of a dream, or be it rather a nightmare. Behind him Barak lay prone still upon his back holding the smaller but still huge female cat by its tusk like fangs. Despite all and everything the giant was still laughing out loudly as though he was enjoying every second of this life or death struggle. This beast the ogre thought most confidently to himself was after all a much lesser beast than he was. Barak still held the lion firm and the big she cat could not move an inch such was the giant's great and awesome strength. Now, and possibly for the first time in her long ferocious life the lion knew now just exactly what fear was all about. And for this reason, as now she was no longer the great slayer and the invincible huntress, now she was the hunted, and now she was the prey. It appeared that she had finally met her match with an even greater slayer, this in the shape of Barak.

Suddenly the giant snapped out a command and the dogs reluctantly left their master to throw themselves into the other bloody fray against the big male cat. Tark had managed to pick up one of Barak's wasted spears and then throw it with his good arm at the larger of the two cats.

However this was not a death dealer and like Barak's earlier throw it also drove into the creature's left shoulder. Aye it struck a hand's width away from the now broken javelin the giant had earlier hurled. Still despite its wounds the cat had managed to seize Borz by one of his massive green legs then the creature slung him like a child's rag doll high into the air. Oh and the halfling landed with a terrific thud against a frozen craggy rock several yards away. Such a violent impact would have killed even the strongest of men instantly, but not the halfling however, Borz was straightway upon his big broad feet and attacking the cat with his flaying iron chain. Indeed Borz seemed more annoyed and even embarrassed than hurt in any way by what could have been a fatal throw.

Tark at this same time had lost his footing, now the warrior slipped then fell with a curse into the snow just as the two dogs charged by him. Now the great hounds next fell upon the cat with a blood lust the likes of which the young warrior had never seen before. Why these huge red dogs seemed almost as mad as their master who was still laughing loudly and who by now had snapped the neck of the smaller cat. With this task once done Barak then hurled the lion with an element of disdain to one side.

Now with the giant once again upon his great booted feet and looking madder than hell itself at all about him Tark wondered just what exactly next was about to happen. By now as expected the ogre was bloodied and blowing heavily, Barak also bore a deep hole in his left shoulder where one of the great Lions great teeth had skewered him.

Tark felt at this time totally and utterly useless, as now he could alas do nothing but watch and remember a fight, nay a battle he would never in his life forget. Before him Borz had his iron chain wrapped about the big male cat's hindquarters. And meanwhile the troll with his immense power was heaving the creature this way and that while the dogs attacked its face, its huge long black maned throat and powerful neck. This big male lion had in its long violent past and over many long years on the mountain been the victor of many bloody fights and so far the loser of none.

Nothing though as everyone knows however lasts always and forever. There was of a sudden a long painful howl and Barak's bitch was thrown roughly to one side to land many yards away in a bloodied broken heap. This as her mate the big dog still seized the large mountain cat under the throat and could not, nor would not be dislodged from its bite. Despite desperate roars and flaying claws and all and everything the big dog bravely held on firm, it would not loose its grip.

Barak glanced momentarily over at his broken bitch then with an insane fury about him the ogre came forward with a most fearful and furious headlong rush. This rage was also something that Tark would remember till the very day that he died. The giant had by now pulled out his ivory handled dragon sword to smite the great lion and end the epic battle on the mountain. But then for some reason and at the very last moment as he closed upon the lion the slayer cast his beloved weapon down into the blood soaked snow. Barak next ordered off his big red dog from the cat Most reluctantly the dog obeyed and now it moved sadly toward the broken whimpering bitch. With the big dog dismissed Barak next turned his attention toward the Halfling.

'Borz my friend, no offence but be gone from this fray, the lion it is now mine to war with, understand?' Without any argument and only a nod of his newt like head the halfling drew back, releasing his chain from the big cat's hindquarters. And then, with this done with a ferocious growl the giant threw himself about the head of the beast. Aye and all of this with no regard for its great dagger-like teeth or its gaping ravenous jaws. Very soon, the lion's fearful defiant roars turned into cries of pain as the hate filled giant choked the very life right out of its huge body. Not satisfied with this revenge for the loss of his beloved bitch the ogre then snapped the lion's huge neck just for good measure.

The great cat, the master of the mountains had won many heroic victories in its long past, but after this day, well the lion it would of course win no more. Now, the giant rose from the side of the dead lion with blood covered outstretched arms, blood that was both his as well as the lion's. Still in a most fearful rage the ogre next roared out both his sadness and also his triumph towards the stormy heavens. Stiffly aye even painfully the ogre moved toward the side of his brave faithful red bitch as she fought and gasped for the last moments of her life. The big red dog at this point had left its long time mate and now set itself in a raging fury upon the carcass of the male lion ripping and tearing away at its face and throat out of sheer hate and fury. After all, the big red dog had lost his only mate so now whether dead or not the great hound would exact some sort of revenge. Barak the meanwhile had went down onto his knees as he spoke softly and stroked the bloodied face of his bitch in a most caring loving fashion. She whimpered painfully as she pushed out a paw towards her distraught master, now Barak's bitch lay upon her side with blood flowing freely from her mouth and nostrils.

Borz was uninjured despite the heavy throw and so now the halfling helped Tark back onto his feet once again.

Barak looked sadly up from where he knelt over his dying dog and then he spoke.

'Are you well my boy?' the ogre asked of Tark. 'Tell me lad, are you an unkilled thing? ' In a dreamlike state, the young man could not at first give an answer as he was much concerned as to his lord's own well being. But at length after a moment or two he found his tongue.

'Aye, aye I am well my Lord Barak, my arm it is broken but that I suppose is nothing on such a day as this. For in all truth my Lord I had expected to die here in the snow upon this very day.' Tark said this whilst speaking very shakily but also very honestly.

Barak was relieved upon hearing this though he merely grunted then he addressed the halfling.

'And you, Borz, are you also a living thing? Aye and if so, tell me are you still complete? Aye are you still whole and intact? ' the giant enquired with yet another glance toward his upright companions.

Large yellow eyes rolled the purple tongue flicked out as slowly the newt like head nodded.

'Aye, I too am well Lord Barak, but tell me master what of yourself? This the halfling asked while not being quite sure as to what blood belonged to Barak and what blood belonged to the huge mountain Lion. Barak's face, throat and neck at this time were covered in gore and his left shoulder pumped blood from the puncture wound made by the female Lion

'I live Borz my friend, that I suppose for now is at least enough,' the giant answered somewhat sadly and dismally. 'Oh, and please do not call me master, you have no master now, remember? Borz made no reply, he merely gave another slight bow of his head. Tark was about to speak again voicing his concern for Barak when the sound of cantering hoof beats made him turn his pounding head about.

'Ragnor, why, how are you here?' Tark asked of the open mouthed Viking.

For once in his life the Norseman was silent for some moments to come as he took in all and everything about him, then, after but a little while he spoke.

'Snow, snow blocked the way ahead, our path, it was barred and our road down was impassable. So I rode back here to see how you fared.' Ragnor was riding alone, save for his nephews Sven and Stefan, behind them the riders had saddled horses in tow, Barak's gelding being one of them. Now the Viking cursed under his great red frozen beard at the sight of his blood soaked friend kneeling over the whimpering body of his dying bitch.

'Barak, Barak my friend, please do not die on me, not now, not here of all places.' This the big Viking said in a sarcastic fashion hoping in vain to bring at least a little cheer to his long time friend. However this ruse did not work and it appeared for the first time since the Norseman had known the giant, Barak's grim humour had for once left him.

'Leave my gelding here with me Ragnor, then go, aye and go now.' The great slayer commanded this while not lifting his black eyes from the dying bitch. Barak's voice, well at this particular time it was wavering more than just a little.

'But Barak,' the Viking protested, 'you are hurt and by the looks of things you are hurt bad,' Barak said nothing in reply to this, instead the slayer spat then swallowed but he still did not raise his eyes nor turn his head in the direction of the Viking.

Gently the giant stroked the ears of the dying bitch before replying to Ragnor.

'Hurt, well hurt or not you must leave me Ragnor, and leave me now,' the giant insisted as he forced snow into his shoulder wound. Even with the fight over the giant's blood was still up and his heart was fast beating, mayhap the cold snow would help slow the blood loss. 'Go now, go. I will join you soon enough my friend. Waste no time and in the meanwhile make good the fires. Prepare for a feast, for tonight we will dine upon those beasts that would have dined upon us,' the giant growled out sadly yet triumphantly.

Now the two young boys at this point were tearful, aye and they would have dismounted and gone to the side of the dying bitch had Ragnor not ordered the lads to remain saddled. Obediently the boys complied though they sobbed their hearts out and were broken at the sight of the dying hound before them. Still though the young boy's grief was as nothing compared to the great slayers. Even now the giant still did not rise to his feet, nor did he cast a glance towards a concerned but very bewildered looking Ragnor.

'Go,' the ogre repeated trying to hide the emotion in his quaking, shaking voice. Barak paused for a brief moment, collecting himself together before speaking once again.

'I will drag the cats down behind me to dine upon for our supper, but first I must attend to my hound.' Barak next stalled for another moment or two and then he spoke gently but firmly. 'She, my hound has but a short time left to live, so go now be off, leave me here, leave me now,' the ogre said most sadly. 'If you were ever my friends, and I know that you are, then do as I bid of you all, leave me.'

Ragnor who was by now totally speechless waited until Tark and Borz were mounted then turned his horse about and made off back down the mountain. And so it was that silently, reluctantly and much saddened by the giant's own sorrow the small group left that place. Barak the meanwhile knelt there in the snow as the life slipped away from his brave and faithful bitch. The small group of riders had not ridden far when the big red dog of a sudden howled out its sorrow and its misery at its life long mate's final demise. And this the great hound did while Barak roared like a wounded beast at the oncoming of darkness and another cold starry night, a night his good and brave red bitch would never see. Grim faced the riders rode from that place down the winding pathway atop the heavy snow that made it safe at least for the horses to carry their weight. And this as the treacherous ice was now far below the snow's ever-increasing depths. Being so both man and beast travelled now down the winding mountain road in comparative safety.

After a short while of riding Ragnor turned around in his saddle and spoke to both Tark and Borz.

'I do not understand it,' Ragnor said out loud. 'Why, in all these years of knowing that man, I have never seen him so grief stricken and so saddened. Good friends we have lost to war and the very years themselves, but never have I seen him so utterly ruined, so forlorn. ' Ragnor said this in total disbelief at his friend's sorrow over the death of his big red bitch. Next the Viking then reined his horse to a standstill on the mountain pathway and whilst still turned around in his saddle he addressed the young Krozak warrior.

'Oh and by the by Tark, know you this now boy. Barak does not, nor never has he had names for those cold blooded red killers of his.' On hearing this slander the young brothers scowled angrily at their uncle's harsh words. But still the lads sensibly held their tongues and said nothing, this out of respect for their protector. However though only for the moment would they be silent.

Tark was reined up close beside Ragnor's horse now as the snow slowed then finally stopped its falling from the heavens. The young man gave a most proud and knowing smile before giving an answer to Ragnor's words. Words that seemed to suggest in some way, that his master was not at all close to his huge hounds. Tark next drew in a deep breath of cold mountain air and then he spoke out. Now he supposed was as good a time as any to enlighten the big Viking.

'She was called 'Rose,' the young warrior said with a slight lopsided grin. Though, in fact despite the grin, the warrior was almost tearful with pride and emotion for his master's sorrow and grief. 'Aye, in our tongue, in the tongue of the Krozaky people, her name it was Rose, in fact it was Red Rose.'

'Rose!' Ragnor exclaimed totally taken aback by Tark's most unexpected statement.

'Aye, Rose, the bitch she was called Rose. Aye and also the bigger dog her mate, he has a name also, and that name it is Thorn,' Tark said proudly.

Ragnor sat atop his mount open mouthed, totally speechless on hearing this, as so were his young nephews.

'You of course were not to know this Ragnor,' Tark said feeling for the big Viking. Ragnor now looked most downcast at not being privy to this information 'My Lord Barak he spoke to the dogs by name in his own tongue' Tark explained. Ragnor glared skyward then downward as he cursed his own clumsiness. Next the big Viking bit upon his lip until it bled as of course he did not wish to unman himself in front of his companions.

Oh aye and even more so his own nephews, oh no that would of course would never do.

'Perhaps my Lord Barak, well, just perhaps he has more heart and humanity about him than we all will ever know,' Tark said this proudly as now he was almost tearful himself.

However of the five riders there on that cold, downward mountain pathway that lead through the mists, the snow and the ice. Perhaps, the only one who suspected the giant's heart was as big as his great head was the halfling. For after all, had it not been Barak who had saved him from a life of misery and hell, had the great ogre not given him a totally new future. True as it so happened, the future looked like being a very short and a very bloody one. But then again at day's end it was he who after all had chosen it. Aye, he did not take the offered coin and be gone and off to who knows where. Truthfully, Borz, well he or it or whatever you would call the being did not regret one single moment of this adventure, and to his credit nor would he.

Without another word spoken the party rode off in grim silence down toward Ragnor's encampment, once arriving there they made ready the evening fires. Now the company of Norsemen were just below the tree line so there was brash and timber aplenty for fuel. Aye and also now on that cold starry night the men of the North would all look forward to eating the beasts which as Barak had said had intended to dine upon them. Barak at length eventually arrived at the camp, both cats the slayer dragged behind his great horse tethered to long leather plaited ropes. His remaining big dog Thorn was lame and bloodied as it walked stiffly and painfully behind the bodies of the dead lions. As for the bitch Rose, well she had of course died soon after the small party of riders had left the grieving giant. And now the noble hound lay deep in the earth with a mountain of huge stones on top of her broken body. This at least apparently pleased the Lord Barak that no unworthy scavengers would ever taste her flesh.

Barak dismounted painfully from his big gelding as he entered the glowing encampment of ringed fires. The ogre just like his remaining dog Thorn was also a little stiff and sore from his exertions. Thoughtfully though, the ogre was straightaway offered vodka by a most concerned Ragnor. And of course at once Barak drank this down eagerly before pouring a little upon the hole in his punctured left shoulder wound. Barak winced and cursed at the pain, then drank down another mouthful of the wonderful clear liquid. Later and after more drink and weed to fortify him then a hot iron would have to be slapped against his wound to seal it and stop infection. But first as just said the slayer would of course take in a few drinks, this of course just to ease the pain. Ragnor had spoken to his men, he had advised them not to be cheering and back slapping Barak on the victory over the lions. As true this was a time for great celebration after all the great fanged lions were now dead things, but alas so also was Barak's big red dog.

In the firelight the Vikings were stood about in admiring astonishment at the size and power of the great tawny cats. But still being always and ever hungry things well the warriors from the frozen North now had rumbling bellies. As despite their admiration for the great cats awesome power they were now of course looking forward to tasting their flesh with great enthusiasm. Yes the warriors so far on this venture had supposed eaten most things, so feasting upon mountain lion, well that seemed quite an ordinary run of the day event to them now.

Barak moved a little lamely toward the fire for warmth as the Norsemen poked and prodded at the dead cats examining in awe their foot long sabre like fangs. Now in need of a smoke the giant put a bloodied hand inside his waistcoat and felt for his pipe. The slayer was in desperate need of an intake of weed as well as a good drink he thought to himself.

However though and sadly on top of all and everything else Barak was to be bitterly disappointed.

'Oh this is not a good day,' the giant muttered as his beloved pipe fell to bits in his huge bloodied hands. 'Oh no, oh no this is not a good day at all,' the ogre mused out loud.

'You know Tark I have had that long pipe for over twenty years,' the giant grumbled as he somewhat sadly threw the pipe's remains onto the fire. With a blink of his yellow eyes and a flick of his long purple tongue the Halfling stepped forward to save the day.

'Have mine, my Lord,' Borz said as he offered whilst lurching forward and holding out his own recently acquired pipe.

'I think that perhaps my halfling throat is not quite cut out for the smoking as yours is, in fact I do think the smoking is killing me.' Barak gave a thin smile then a nod of gratitude as he accepted the pipe.

'Very wise my green warty friend, I only wish I had your strength and determination of mind, then perhaps I too would cease with the smoking. As you say, it is I suppose not a healthy habit after all.' Barak next sighed wearily, this, the ogre thought to himself one way or the other would be a day never to be forgotten. The giant once again thanked the Halfling most kindly before he lit up the pipe after cleaning and filling it with his own strong weed. This pipe was just as long as his last pipe but it was made of wood rather than baked clay. True it was the giant much preferred a clay pipe, but then again, a smoke after all was a smoke. Aye and after all that had happened on this long hard day he was now in bad need of one. Barak took another drink of vodka and of course as ever it was a long one. All eyes were upon him now in gloomy wonderment, the Viking brotherhood, well all but for one felt for the ogre. Barak took yet another drink then growled inwardly to himself as he drew deeply from the new pipe. It was as it so happened, a quite pleasing smoke and much better than he thought it might have been. Ragnor looked on with a most worried look about him. This, the big Viking did as he was still concerned about his large friend. But nevertheless Ragnor had no intention of fussing about the giant in front of his men. Another drink of vodka followed by another puff upon his pipe, then Barak creaked his massive neck into place. Thorn by now had lain itself down by the young boys who stroked and spoke softly to the sore and weary and by the looks of it heart broken animal. Ragnor of a sudden looked less gloomy he smiled as he stared across the fire toward his huge friend. Now, now it was that big Barak had that savage grin of his back upon his scarred and tattooed face.

'Well, my men, my raggy brothers of the frozen north, tell me, just how do you like your lion served? ' Barak roared this out, the slayer was now shaking himself free from his dark sad broodings at the loss of his beloved bitch. Still though the great ogre thought to himself, she, Red Rose had after all had a good and a full life. Oh aye she had lived well, died well and then gone on honestly.

At these words spoken by the giant a great loud and sincere cheer rang out from the host of Vikings. As ever it was only the ever brooding Bull Neck who did not celebrate Barak's victory over the huge fearsome lions who had feasted upon members of his brotherhood. No, that great fool would of course sooner have it that it was the lions who were feasting upon Barak's body. For Bull Neck's moods were becoming ever darker and longer as inside of him his hatred for the giant grew ever stronger and even more malevolent. However, Bull Neck's shortcomings at this particular moment in time were of no matter. Being so for two whole days the men feasted there in that place upon the lion's flesh. Also as it so happened the flesh was a most tasty meat and provided a most welcome meal. The travellers were still at this time trapped by a wall of snow from the avalanche and their way forward, well for now at least anyway. In this time of idling away the hours the giant stretched and cleaned the lion pelts, the ogre then also cleaned and polished up their tusk like teeth. These great killers, the beasts of the mountains were now only to become no more than ornaments, trophies and trinkets that would adorn a burly neck. But, this as ever and always, well it was always the savage price of defeat. On the third day in their encampment the fickle weather, well it changed yet again. Now there was a tremendous rainstorm and a heavy non-stop downpour in the late evening, this washed away the snowy mountain that had been so far barring their way downward. So being thus released on that following grey drizzly morning the warriors began to wind their way downward through thick slush and mud. Once again ever downwards they went, downwards towards the base of the mountain that still lay far below them. Somewhere down there under those swirling rainy mists lay the lowlands, the lowlands and the vast rolling steppes.

Chapter Eighteen

Some days later in the mouth of a wide shallow cave the party stopped at dusk. This the men did amidst a torrent of driving hail and forked lightning that opened up the belly of the night sky. Barak's jaw had by now doubled in its size with poison from his bad tooth making his face look lopsided and freakish.

Barak at this time was both in agony and misery but despite all his efforts, still his tooth would not be dislodged. Great mountain lions the giant had fought and slain as well as the forest wolves, yet it was a bad tooth that was still his daily nonstop tormentor. Similar to everything else concerning the giant, this offending tooth appeared to be both a strong and a stubborn thing that would just not go away. But anyway brooding and fretting over the damned tooth would not help anything. So the giant simply got on with things and he busied himself with his cooking of the three mountain goats he had hunted down and caught earlier in the day. There was of course still some lion meat left over to eat, the cold temperature had at least kept that flesh edible. Aye so there was meat a plenty, but Barak well the ogre could eat nothing, and this much to Ragnor's distress.

'You must eat Barak, aye you must eat to keep up your strength and your power. After all, who knows, the chewing of the flesh might cause your bad tooth to come away from that great square jaw of yours,' Ragnor said offering his friend a slab of cooked goat meat.

Goat, well it was, as already said, Barak's favourite meat, and as ever the slayer had cooked it to perfection, but alas the ogre could barely open his mouth to speak let alone tear into meat.

Both men stood there together at the opening of the cave looking out into the black of night. Barak and Ragnor were silently pondering over where they had both just come from, oh and of course where they were bound for. Before them somewhere out there beyond the ghostly mists lay the vast expanse of dry deserts and rolling plains, as well as the wild windswept steppes. Further on behind these blustery steppes, lay their final destination, the land of the Krozaks.

Only the Mongols, the bandits, the camel and the jackal and other creatures of the night could survive in its most cold and hostile vastness.

Ragnor nudged Barak then the big Viking turned to look back into the cave with an element of pride at his brutish men, men who as ever drank whilst they laughed and feasted. As long as these rough band of men had a supply of food and drink then it seemed that little at all on this earth could in any way dishearten or undaunt them in any way.

Aye Barak he too turned his throbbing head towards his chosen killers, the ogre knew well he could not have a better bunch of rogues to watch his broad back.

'Eat, eat my friend else you will waste away into nothing,' Ragnor said as he once again offered Barak the goat meat.

'Oh and by the way, tell me how is your shoulder that I so lovingly and slowly sealed for you with a red hot iron?' Ragnor asked this question with a most wolfish grin. The pain of the red hot iron against torn flesh would have made most men pass out, or at least scream and shout while they wrestled with those who held them. Barak however, well the slayer he needed no holding or restraining. Nor did the stubborn bucket headed giant need a stick between his fanged teeth. True the ogre had growled grunted and snarled as he was prone too. As this of course was the norm for Barak, also of course he had ground his teeth together viciously still hoping in vain to lose his bad one, sadly though he did not. Later when the task was finally done and the wound sealed with fire the great blustering slayer had cursed Ragnor for being so slow and clumsy in his doctoring. Apart from that though there was nothing, Barak he had merely spat out a mouthful of bile from his mouth into the slushy snow.

'My shoulder it is fine, it is my back tooth that still hurts me,' Barak rumbled. 'Aye and anyway Ragnor did I ever tell you that you do cluck on like an old mother hen?' The ogre continued as he rubbed the side of his face before continuing. 'As for the meat, well perhaps I will eat it later, before I lay myself down to get some sleep,' the giant mumbled on painfully. 'For I do suppose you are true in your words Ragnor, I must eat, even if it is only to keep up my strength for the long journey ahead. '

As the two men stood at the mouth of the cave talking in honest friendship they were spied upon by unfriendly eyes, unfriendly odd coloured eyes. Bull Neck had become ever more a skulker in the dark, ever more the snake in the night. Bull Neck had become now no more than a lowly jealous deceiver. Also, on top of all this the oaf had a poison contained in a small gourd, this as well as the poison in his black twisted heart. Bull Neck had purchased this deadly potion from an alchemist on their last port of call at Varnak. Secretly, furtively the treacherous deceiver had stolen himself away down narrow alleys to find this dabbler in the black arts. After a while in searching the fool had eventually found the witch that he sought, aye he found the evil crone in a secluded dark and dingy den.

Patiently, the Bull had waited there in a small ante-room while the ancient old crone went about her dark unholy business. All the while as she conjured the witch had cackled with joy as she ground and mixed the deadly potion. Apparently the old crone was happy in the fact that her creation would bring about the demise of some unfortunate victim. Hemlock, mandrake and wolf-bane she had ground together. This done next the witch added something else just as equally if not more nasty. Something, that was even more deadly, more gut wrenching than any of the other ingredients in the small phial.

Venom from the marsh viper, no man, whoever he might be, giant or otherwise could survive this most deadly of cocktails; now the poison was complete. Barak, being a creature of habit took himself for a short walk with his one remaining dog every night before retiring to his berth. And this night being apparently no different to any other so Barak took himself away. On his walk the ogre stopped and stared upward toward the cold starry night skies as he spared a thought for the lost Vikings and of course his brave bitch. So then it was in this short time Barak was gone when Bull Neck made his move.

Barak had laid down his steak of goat meat on a wooden plate on top of his high backed saddle. And this meat the ogre had promised Ragnor he would eat on his return from his nightly walk with his dog.

Bull Neck feigning sleep had heard all of this and so was of course overcome with an evil joy, as tonight would be the night.

Aye and so it was in this short time that Bull Neck had managed to pour a little of the poison onto the meat. Only a little of this foul potion was all that would be needed the witch had assured him to complete the desired result. So many , peppers and cloves of garlic did Barak apply to his own meat the almost tasteless potion would not even be detected, well until of course it was too late. All that Bull Neck had to do now was to wait, to wait then to watch the giant die an agonised death.

Barak however on that particular evening, was not returning quite as quickly as was his norm from his nightly walk. Now the slime in his mouth from the rotten tooth spoilt and polluted the taste of his vodka. Being so then Barak had drunk little of his beloved clear liquid that night, not enjoying the taste of it. Neither would sleep come at all easily to him because of the throbbing pain from the bad back tooth. So of course with no alcohol to help him doze off into his slumbers, well Barak surmised this was going to be a very long night. Still, the giant supposed to himself, he at least could still suck upon his pipe with a certain degree of satisfaction.

Bull Neck was not the greatest of thinkers, nor was he the best of drinkers for that matter. Besides, the fool had drunk down overly much ale and even some vodka on that particular night. Of course the deceiver had consumed this amount just so he might have the courage to perform his act of black treason and utmost cowardice.

Aye, the big idiot had swallowed down far too much strong drink, thus the oaf had fallen into a deep and drunken slumber. It was a sleep Bull Neck slipped into soon after the fool had applied the poison to the meat. But had the treacherous man been awake and alert then he would have seen Barak on the return from his walk give his supper to the halfling Borz. Borz had awakened on the giant's return and looked longingly at the big steak of goat meat. And as it was, well only Borz could both enjoy and stomach the hot mouth burning sauces and peppers that Barak took with his meat.

Borz being Borz, well of course the thing did not chew upon his meat. No as was the norm for him, he merely swallowed it all down in a single go. Any human, would have died there and then on the very spot, aye died writhing and convulsing in agony. Aye, any man, even a giant would be done and dead in moments after only their first bite of the meat. Borz however was not human, well, as it has already been said he was at least not all human. Now for possibly the first time in his long tortured life this was perhaps going to be the only occasion that Borz was grateful for his mixed breeding. With a most painful hiss, Borz dropped down onto the ground clutching at his gut in total agony, now his reptilian roars of pain awoke each and every one of the sleeping men.

Startled, at once, the warriors with bleary sleep filled eyes grabbed drowsily at their weapons in a panic thinking all the while they were under attack from either beast or man.

Bull Neck, already grinning with triumph at these roars of agony sprang very unsteadily to his big flat feet. The fool, he tottered there beside the fire with an idiots smile about his fat red face. However, this foolish smile across his fat porky face was not a long lived one. What on earth had happened here Bull Neck thought dimly to himself? Why was it not Barak writhing his last painful moments of life upon the floor of the cave?

'What is it Borz? What is it that has happened to you? ' Barak asked urgently as he dropped down to one knee at the halfling's side.

While Borz had dined upon the goat meat Barak still unable to sleep had been standing by the cave entrance sucking upon his pipe.

'Poison, there was poison in the meat you gave me my Lord,' the halfling rasped out painfully as his yellow eyes rolled about this way and that in his newt-like head. All there, including even the quick thinking Barak were at some loss at what to do to help their green reptilian friend. Borz however had in his pounding head and churning stomach his own remedy in mind for a quick recovery.

'Give me vodka, give me vodka quickly my Lord Barak,' the halfling demanded as the men gathered about him while he struggled to stand himself slumped up against the cave wall.

Barak did as he was asked and at once the big green halfling most urgently swallowed down a good deal of Barak's gourd of drink.

Oh aye, and this drink was not however going to be down for very long. Borz with great fortitude and a little help from Barak fully rose himself up, bravely the halfling staggered to his big broad webbed feet. With this done still reeling and retching he moved outside of the cave's entrance, once outside the halfling was most violently and horribly sick.

Barak seeing that Borz would survive the poison at once turned about and straightway the ogre affixed Bull Neck with a cold steely accusing stare.

Only he amongst all of the men there had harboured him any bad feelings, only he would wish him any harm. That poison had not been intended for Borz, no it had been set to kill another, set to kill Barak.

'You, you are a traitor, aye and you are a coward,' Barak snarled moving forward rapidly toward the guilty looking Viking.

'You, it was you who did this to him; you Bull Neck are nothing but a cowardly ditch dog that needs putting down, aye and putting down right now.'

Bull Neck said nothing in reply, after all there was nothing left to say, he was discovered and well he knew it. So now with all lost Bull Neck merely spat and cursed his bad luck as he reached for the heavy cudgel at his side to defend himself. What the poison could not and did not do then perhaps his heavy oak club could.

'Hold Barak, we have no proof that this was the work of Bull Neck,' Ragnor shouted this out urgently and most unwisely. All there among his own men thought of Barak with only admiration and reverence. The Norsemen valued Barak's judgement in all things, even if that judgement was against one of their own closely knit brotherhood.

Barak, on hearing Ragnor most carelessly glanced over his broad shoulder towards the Viking chieftain. Foolishly this the ogre chanced whilst the heavy club of Bull Neck smashed with a dull thud into the side of his big square jaw.

At once Ragnor instantly cursed himself and his stupidity for distracting the giant, had he now got his friend killed he thought grimly to himself. Now in a fury Ragnor then went to draw his own great boar's head broadsword. Now, now he would if needs be slay the traitor himself. However, the big Viking, would as it happened not be troubled with this task. As it happened Bull Neck's blow, a powerful blow that would have killed any other man, had done nothing more than simply thrown the giant into a fuming rage. In fact Barak stood there before his assailant still on his great booted feet, aye and also the ogre was also looking most put out. Only a heartbeat passed then in a sudden blinding fury Barak was upon Bull Neck like a cat upon a mouse. Seizing him by his great neck, a neck that had given the disgraced Viking his name, the angry giant next slung Bull Neck upwards high above him. Indeed, so high was Bull Neck hoisted that the failed poisoner's bald head smashed heavily off the roof of the cave.

Bull Neck though was still a Viking warrior, thus being so the brotherhood just momentarily had mixed feelings as open mouthed they witnessed what was going on before their very bleary eyes. Indeed several of the younger men were

306

most confused as just what to do next. Now the Norsemen looked nervously and anxiously toward Ragnor for some sort of guidance. Was he, their chieftain, going to stand by and watch one of their own being battered to a pulp before their very eyes? For in all truth most of the men were still half drunk as well as much confused and did not know exactly just what was going on about them.

Ragnor cursed, not wanting to believe just what it was he was seeing, or for that matter, what Bull Neck was being accused of. It was then with his head in a total spin as what to do next that Ragnor noticed there upon the cave floor a small dark glass and leather bound phial. Also what was so damning was that the suspicious looking phial was still attached to Bull Neck's thick broken leather waist band.

In the meanwhile Barak by now had bounced his would be assassin off every wall of the cave; this the irate ogre accomplished with apparently little or no effort.

'Poison,' Ragnor shouted out loudly as he uncorked the phial then sniffed just that faintest hint of its contents. 'Bull Neck is guilty as accused, he is now no longer one of our brother-hood!' the big Viking bellowed out angrily. Big Ragnor felt now both let down in the very extreme, and also deeply ashamed. Aye the clan chieftain was ashamed that he should have harboured and trusted such a worthless wayward man. Not only had Ragnor trusted Bull Neck, but the big Viking had also held his second man in high esteem. Oh and also after all and everything else, well Bull Neck had been his friend over these last violent but exciting years. Aye and in work as well as in battle Bull Neck had not once ever let him down, and so this now though was a very sad shameful day.

With Bull Necks shame and cowardice plain for all to see the others of the Viking brotherhood scowled and growled angrily. And this as the Norsemen slowly with sweaty palms sheathed their weapons, weapons that had just been edged an inch or two from their scabbards. Weapons that to their eternal shame might just of been used to protect the worthless Bull Neck from the vengeful Barak. Now realising their terrible mistake the Viking brotherhood spat in disgust, all there were deeply ashamed that one of their numbers could stoop so low as to use poison to settle a grievance. After all is said and done, poison was a women's weapon, a traitor's weapon, a coward's weapon.

Barak by now was atop Bull Neck, the ogre held him down by his throat with Bull Necks broad back pressed down hard upon the cave floor, the traitor could not move a hairs width.

Now, but too late, ashamed of himself, the big Norseman had little or no resistance left to offer up in any sort of fight against his massive antagonist. And at this moment in time his black shame, this disgrace it had made Bull Necks great strength desert him. So now, well he was laid there a most bloodied, beaten, and disgraced warrior. Fool though Bull Neck was even he now knew that he was nothing in the eyes of his brothers, no he was nothing at all.

In all of the many follies he had ever made in his violent brutal but hitherto honourable life, this shame now sullied all and everything. Oh aye, every brave deed every act of courage in warfare would be cast aside and forgotten now.

'Tell me, tell me, will you live Borz?' Barak asked this question plainly whilst looking over his shoulder. The slayer was now turning his attention to the halfling who still stood propped up at the mouth of the cave.

With an immediate and positive nod the big green halfling coughed and spat as he grasped at his throat with a huge webbed hand. Oh and all of this while his big yellow eyes rolled skyward.

'Aye, aye, I will live, please believe me I will have no more than a bad stomach in but a little while my Lord Barak. As after all the venom of the marsh viper, well it is thankfully in my blood anyway,' the halfling cackled trying to make light of this very bad affair.

Borz as it so happened was also a creature of great heart and compassion. While he was more than pleased to have swallowed down the poison meant for Barak, well the Halfling also knew that Bull Neck was an assassin. Aye and indeed he was in all truth a most cowardly assassin at that. Still despite all of this, Borz, well the halfling nevertheless did not relish at all the thought of witnessing Barak slaying this foolish wayward man. Mayhap with this being so, then perhaps the great green halfling also had a great amount of humanity in his huge warty body.

With a savage grunt big Barak pushed himself up and away from Bull Neck in sheer disgust, now the ogre stood towering over his would be assassin. Now the great slayer appeared lost for words as all about there was a deathly silence whilst the Norsemen waited for Barak to slay Bull Neck. However the ogre to his own surprise, as well as those of the brotherhood had no such plans.

'I must have grown soft of a sudden you great fool, for I will not kill you Bull Neck. No. This is because you are I think not worth the killing.' Barak stated this calmly as his black rage was now suddenly abated. 'I also think now, that you are perhaps a man who is already a dead thing. Oh aye, aye now you are dead, both to yourself and you are dead to what few friends you ever had. ' Barak said this more in pity now than in any anger. For the giant knew only too well no warrior could live with this self inflicted shame; sadly for Bull Neck it was all over. Aye and fool though he was the big bloodied Viking in his swirling dimness of mind also realised this to be a sad and stark fact of life.

Bull Neck wiped blood from his face as he looked blearily about him into the ice cold blue eyes of the Viking brotherhood. Now though, well this, it was his brotherhood no longer. So now to a man the warriors turned away from him, now these hard but honest men of the north showed him only their broad backs. Bull Neck was shunned and rejected, he was now no longer a friend, he was no longer a Viking. In fact to these men of his former brotherhood he no longer even existed.

Slowly painfully the shamed and disgraced Viking rose unsteadily to his feet. And this the fool did as his bald head spun with the battering dished out to him from Barak. It was now that the lost and foolish Bull Neck felt sick and disgusted with himself. Why oh why had he become the man that he had become he dimly wondered. Bull Neck slowly turned about on himself towards his one time friend and his chieftain Ragnor, for what reason he did not even quite know.

Ragnor though, well the clan chieftain could not even face him, so instead he hung his hairy red head in black shame for a man he once trusted with his very life. Ragnor was gutted and was deeply ashamed of this man, a man who had long been well respected in their violent but sacred community. Now the Viking chieftain, well, he decided that he would never look into those odd coloured eyes ever again. So now Ragnor, well he had also decided to turn his back upon the worthless poisoner.

Bull Neck, knowing all was lost sighed deeply as he then turned and looked about him both sadly and even tearfully. For one more time, for one last time he stared at the backs of his former friends and comrades. Now the fool more than ever was deeply ashamed and disgusted with himself. Indeed big Bull Neck, once a great and feared warrior, was now a most sorrowful and pitiful sight to behold. His bitterness and black hatred as well as his ever growing jealousy of Barak had twisted and festered inside him. This hatred had turned him into something that no warrior should ever have become. Big Loki was the last of the savage brotherhood to look into Bull Necks odd tear-filled eyes. Now out of compassion the hunchback Loki motioned to speak to his one time friend. However his lips failed and the words would not come to him. So now with nothing spoken, the hunchback just like the others of the brotherhood also turned himself about to face the cave wall. Bull Neck knew only too well now that he was neither a good man, nor, what was even more important to him, a good Viking. Being so there was but only one thing he could do now to atone for his sins to his warlike gods, oh and of course his warlike friends. So Bull Neck deciding his own fate with a sudden scream of shame and despair picked up a nearby sword then made a headlong dash for the cave entrance.

'Odin my Lord, will you receive me? Bull Neck screamed this out as he jumped out into the darkness. From there the traitor disappeared over the edge and into the mists of the abyss far below. For Bull Neck both his bitter life and this quest was now over, in fact everything was over, over forever. For a moment there was a deathly silence with no one quite knowing what to say, except of course Barak.

'Oh well, I do suppose this is goodbye then Bull Neck,' Barak said indifferently as he moved toward the cave entrance to help Borz stand himself up straight.

'Well my warty friend, I do suppose you saved my life by eating my steak,' Barak said as he smiled warmly toward the halfling.

Borz gave a slow nod of agreement. 'Aye, aye perhaps, but you had saved mine first my Lord Barak, and so we are even now I think,' the troll croaked painfully. Barak smiled once again then chuckled light heartedly. 'As you say my friend, we are even Borz,' Barak replied with a slight bow of his head.

'Ah, well that at least is a good thing,' the giant chuckled to himself while spitting out blood, gore and also a very large molar. 'Well, at least that fool Bull Neck managed to do something right for once. Aye, the idiot knocked out my bad tooth with his cudgel before he took leave and left us.' Barak at this particular moment in time had a quite cheery expression about him now. 'Aye and also at least before the fool died, he did manage to string a few words together without making a mess of it. ' The giant had said this with just the trace of a faint smile. Barak next spat out another mouthful of blood and slime into the slush, and this as he peered over the edge of the mountain pathway. 'There is still a long way down ahead of us Ragnor,' Barak remarked as he spat once again into the abyss and the mists far below.

Ragnor with his hairy face a mask of unhappiness at the very thought of Bull Neck's treason scowled, then sneered before replying.

'Yes, yes I suppose there is still a long way down to go my friend, Barak.' Ragnor said this more than a little grimly. 'But as for that fool Bull Neck, well I do suppose he had already let himself go a long way down.' Now with his emotions in ruins the big Viking added this statement somewhat sadly and ashamedly. Still though as always and ever what was done was done, so of course then it could not be undone. Ragnor suddenly growled to himself, then he snarled like some sort of forest beast before turning toward Barak. Still distressed and much ashamed by Bull Neck's behaviour Ragnor gave a slight bow toward Barak, this of course was politely returned.

Big Barak knew exactly what his longtime friend's thoughts were, simply because the ogre would have felt exactly the same if the boot was on the other foot. Imagine that if on some mission one of Barak's men for whatever reason had attempted a kill upon Ragnor. Well of course his death would be swift, after all Barak and Ragnor were brothers to the very bone. With sharp knives the two men, when drunk one night many years ago in some nameless tavern or other had cut their flesh. With this accomplished the men then had pressed together the wounds so that the blood mingled. So as said the ogre and Viking were brothers by the very blood to the bone.

'You, you Loki, you are promoted.' Oh and this Ragnor suddenly exclaimed with a loud shout whilst clapping the huge hunchback upon his drooped shoulders. 'Aye and raise yourself up in spirit man as you unlike your shameful friend are a great and noble Viking,' Ragnor added earnestly. 'What say you my lads?' Ragnor shouted out to his men, hoping to raise their spirits up from the very pit of shame and despair for their former clan brother.

Sadly though there was however, only a half-hearted murmur in reply and but little more than that. Ragnor at once scowled in bitter disappointment, this was not quite going as he had planned. Viking loyalty to one another and each and every member of their brotherhood was a strong, most a fierce bond. All there now knew of Bull Neck's treachery, but still nevertheless in the past he had been their friend as well as a brave fighting companion. All of these things and all of these deeds were hard to forget in but an instant of sheer lunacy and disgrace. Now at this moment, the Viking Sea Lord, clan leader and ferocious chieftain thought it most necessary to speak out. Aye it was time now for him to voice his opinion over this sad and most messy affair.

'Bull Neck, as you all know was once my right hand man, he was also my close friend and my brother just as he was yours.' To a man the Viking brotherhood stood silent as they listened to every word their chieftain had to say to them. 'This is not in any way easy for me to say. ' Ragnor said this with his voice filled with a strong emotion that he could not conceal. 'But in simple truth, the Bull had turned into nothing more than a poisoner, aye in truth he had become a most jealous and wayward man.'

Ragnor said these words boldly but was obviously visibly perturbed and upset by that evening's sad turn of events. Still, the big Viking thought to himself, these were words which had to be spoken so he said on.

'All of the great strength and courage that he once had, so much of this had gone, it had deserted him. Sadly this was replaced by jealousy and bitterness and above all hatred, aye and hatred for one of our own brothers.' Ragnor now steeled and hardened himself for what he was next to say.

'For if Barak is not entitled to be called a brother to our clan, then I say neither am I, and I will stand down if this is your opinion. Choose another to lead you, if you think me wrong or Barak is guilty in some way or other. But I will remind you now that it was not Barak who killed Bull Neck, though he was well entitled to do so. No, no the big oaf, perhaps to his credit killed himself not being able to live with his guilt and his black shame.' Ragnor then paused as his pale eyes scanned his warriors, their savage heads now lifted instead of staring at the rock floor of the cave. 'Anyway my brothers I think that is enough said on this sad and bad matter. Aye and we will speak no more of the traitor on this night or on any other night for that matter. '

Ragnor then paused and took in a deep breath of cold sharp chill night air before he spoke once again.

'Well my brothers I do have a thirst upon me now. Aye and also no sleep will come to me on this sad and shameful night. ' Ragnor said this as he picked up a gourd of German ale. 'Now, I ask you who will join me now to toast in our brother Loki as second and next in command? For in all truth Loki might not be a thing of great beauty, but nevertheless I would trust him with both my life and yours,' Ragnor declared this while raising Loki's long and heavily muscled arm aloft.

Loki now looked at both bemused and much baffled thing as this sudden promotion he was not at all expecting.

Now though at this time there was no murmur, but instead there was a roar of savage approval from the remaining Vikings in favour of Bull Neck's none too pretty replacement. And also, while all there knew that Loki might not be the handsomest of their brotherhood, it could not be denied that the big hunchback's courage, integrity and honour had never been in any doubt. And also as Ragnor had said Bull Neck's name after this night, well it would be spoken of no more.

Chapter Nineteen

Several hard and long days later, amid hail and rain and a fierce biting wind the warriors reached the foot of the mountain, a mountain that had claimed even more of the brotherhood. From here after a good night's rest and a bellyful of goat meat they then set off across the rolling barren frozen plains. For a week or more the warriors relentlessly rode and walked steadily if not hurriedly ever onward. All the while and just as ever a cold biting wind was forever in their hairy faces. This as the plains sand stabbed at their uncovered flesh like so many ant bites. Later the band of warriors camped one cold starry night weary and much battered about by the savage unyielding elements. Now, though there was little food or water left, the ale, vodka, and even Barak's weed was running alarmingly low. Still, no one said this was going to be an easy venture and not one man among the Vikings complained, grumbled, or even looked downhearted for that matter.

And so, just as ever and always big Barak had found the Norsemen to be the very best of travelling companions.

'When this sand storm eventually, if ever eventually, abates, tell me is there any game around to hunt, Barak?' Ragnor asked this of Barak who had just returned from a scouting mission. Apart from Barak all the other men were warming themselves around a camp fire at the end of another days march.

'Damn the hunting, aye and damn the food too, is there not about this windswept place an inn or a small cosy wayside tavern? ' the drunken German asked hopefully. 'Surely Barak is there not a snug little hamlet hidden somewhere about this freezing vastness?' added Horst with a hiccup. 'For know you this Barak, if things do get any worse, then I will be in the greatest of dangers of sobering up.' This the German added with a weary sigh before saying on. 'You know my big friend the very idea of being sober, well I think that frightens me more than an executioner's axe.' When the laughter died down at the German's ready wit, Barak, grinned broadly and then he spoke up.

'We have no need to hunt for our breakfeast or our drink,' the giant said shifting his weight about in his high backed saddle before dismounting. 'Food, strong drink and also a good supply of mountain weed will be soon brought to us, aye and at the gallop and at first light. Well this is of course providing I am not very much mistaken in my judgement. Which as you all well know, would be most uncommon,' the giant added a little smugly. Barak had said this with a broad smile, indeed the ogre looked most gleeful as he unsaddled his big horse. With this done the ogre then sat himself down cross-legged in front of the

313

campfire. Barak, he was now at this time smoking the last pipe full of his beloved weed.

Now all of the Vikings looked about them, then at each other wondering just what on earth Barak was talking about. Barak though, well, the mirthful ogre would now educate his bold companions.

'Dawn raiders. They will come to us at first light screaming and cursing from the east, and just in time for breakfeast,' Barak added after a puff upon his pipe. 'Before sunset I glimpsed them with my Persian spyglass, the fools were riding on the horizon. These pirates of the plains know that we are here and they have known this for these past days. Please believe me their food and drink will all be ours very soon my friends.' Oh and the giant explained all of this in a happy most matter of fact sort of fashion. 'As well as food and drink these robbers have horses a plenty. Being so this of course means that every man here will have his own beast to ride, a horse, or even camel,' the ogre added this even more cheerfully.

Ragnor at once glanced over at Tark, to see if the young man had been privy to this newly announced information.

However Tark shrugged and indeed the warrior looked just as taken aback and as baffled as Ragnor was, as in truth, well he was as much in the dark as was everyone else sitting about the campfire to this news.

'So, just how many men are they then Barak? How many dawn raiders are we expecting arriving for breakfeast?' Ragnor asked this question with somewhat of a sarcastic tone to his voice. Now the other Vikings around about chuckled, this while all there eagerly awaited the giant's reply.

The answer it was not long in coming.

'Oh just about fifty or so I do suppose,' Barak said in reply to Ragnor's question. 'Aye, but no more than fifty, no, they are just a small band of knaves and desert cut-throats.'

Ragnor next coughed and gagged on his last mouthful of beer upon hearing this so called good news. Once the Norseman was once again calm and composed then he spoke.

'Aye, aye my friend but that is a small band that still outnumbers us Barak, we are not as many as we once were you know?' Ragnor said doing a quick head count. As the big Viking was now a good few men down from his original thirty eight fighting men. Though in all truth the two boys had now earned the right to be called true warriors, aye and then some.

Barak yawned and was instantly dismissive of Ragnor's negative opinions.

'Bah you worry too much my hairy friend. These riff raff are after all not our match Ragnor; we will slay them all, then take what is theirs and make it ours.' Still smiling the giant had said this most casually and also very confidently, he went on. 'Believe me Ragnor this is no more than a gift, a gift of food, drink and fresh supplies of everything that is needed. Think of this my hairy friend, there will be no more foot slogging and no more walking. Everyone will be mounted on either a horse a mule or even a camel if they are bold enough. Oh and come to think of it, well I do like eating camel nearly as much as I do goat,' the giant said with a lick of his lips. 'No, no you must trust me the morning light will bring us an easy victory. And anyway, you have long been complaining about fighting the beasts and the weather instead of armed men Ragnor.'

With these profound words said and no answer coming back in argument Barak yawned stretched then he rose suddenly to his great booted feet. Once again the giant yawned as he clicked his huge neck into place.

'But first my friends, there is much work to do before we sleep; we must be well prepared for their coming.' Barak then at once and without any further ado had the Vikings dig a long deep channel all about their encampment, a sort of waterless moat so to speak. As luck would have it their rounded shields proved to be the perfect digging implement for this strenuous work. Later with this important task accomplished and when the sandy ditch was deep enough to come up to a tall man's chest and was just as wide, Barak stopped their labours.

Next, the linen and sail cloth tents were stretched tightly across the entire void. These were held down in place on each side with sand and the odd wooden stake here and there. With all their tasks once completed the Vikings stood back in the early half light as they looked at one another smiling in a most confident self-assured manner. Soon with the rising of the sun and in the full light of day there would be foemen to fight. Oh aye, armed foemen and not wolves and lions and the dreaded elements they had struggled against these past long months. Men with swords that they could kill and slaughter, oh what a good and glorious start to the day the warriors all cheerily thought.

'Now let them come, Ragnor,' Barak snarled happily as he was both pleased and confident with the night's work. 'We will backfill the trench with their dead bodies, then once more be on our way. Ah but this we will do only after breakfeasting first of course,' the giant said with a chuckle. 'You know Ragnor, I think I am quite looking forward to this early morning distraction, also the exercise it will be most beneficial.' Barak said this as he took the last puff upon his pipe and his weed finally ran out on him. 'Well, as long as I get a breakfeast then I don't really care how I get it.' Ragnor said this as he removed his bronze helmet and scratched at his hairy head.

'Tark, how is your arm now boy?' Barak asked of the young warrior.

'Much better Lord, either way I can use both hands for sword play, you must remember that I am . . .' Barak somewhat rudely interrupted Tark before he could finish that what he was about to say.

'Black Guard, yes boy, I almost forgot, so of course you can use both hands with a sword,' Barak said with a grin. 'Anyway,' the giant said breaking off from his banter with his countryman. 'It is time now for a little sleep men, these fools will wake us up in plenty of time for the fight. No doubt they will come over from that hill with the morning sun at their backs whooping and screaming like mad things. I know them well or rather at least I know their kind. These foolish chancers hope to catch us half drunk and half asleep. However, alas for these desert rogues, well it is us who will be catching them. ' The giant said this with a most fearful smile.

As ever the warriors had total faith in Barak's planning so without a care the men of the north lay down their hairy heads to catch up on some well-earned sleep. Screaming, charging raiders would awaken them and this with plenty of time to arm and prepare themselves for the early morning fray. And as it so happened thankfully all was very much as Barak had said it would be on that cold but sunny morning on the desert plains.

Riding upon horses and camels hook-nosed brown skinned bandits came galloping full tilt downhill toward the encampment thinking to catch their victims dozing and unaware. But oh, oh what a shock the raiders received and what a tremendous foolish blunder did these raiders realize they had made. However this enlightenment came all too late as horses, camels and their luckless riders were pitched forward headlong into the surrounding trench. Only a dozen of these men, those who were sat upon slower decrepit animals avoided the slaughter and the carnage of their fleeter companions. And these men, being the brave souls they all were, spun their sad beasts about and headed back off in the direction from which they had just come. So alarmed were these luckier raiders by the slaughter of their comrades that any pack animals in tow were loosed and at once discarded. Indeed it was only their own miserable sad lives that the raiders wanted to save at this particular moment in time, not their ill-gotten possessions. Possessions that were won from the past, and were won from more successful missions against lesser men.

After the effortless and total rout of the nomadic bandits the men of the North were most elated, now the Vikings were once again in the most highest of spirits. So far the band of Norsemen had still up to this very moment lost not one man in sword play since leaving the Salmon River. Only the savage elements or the wild beasts of the forests and the mountains had cost them any men on their venture. No prisoners of the raiding party were either taken or interrogated, all were slain. This onslaught had been brief and had been bloody, aye, that early morning fray was all over very quickly.

Tark did say after the failed raid he had recognized several of the dead men as rogues under the pay of the treacherous brothers. These men had been the Black Guards' guides and escort to the mountain. But whether or not this particular raid was under the brothers' instruction or merely an ambush to secure horses and loot, well they would perhaps never know. Nor would Barak or Ragnor in all honesty care, for it was now they who had the horses, camels and pack mules laden with all manner of creature comforts. These raiders, just as Barak had expected, hailed from many tribes and religious persuasions, thankfully not all in their number were followers of Allah.

So as well as a bonus of having food, drinking water and also a good quantity of good black mountain weed there were also plenty of barrels of weak but drinkable ale. Aye, and also to Barak's delight there was thankfully a good supply of strong steppes vodka.

To the giant Barak the ale was wishy-washy stuff, even worse than the brew of the Britons, good only for rinsing your mouth out after a heavy night's real drinking. However, the black mountain weed and also the steppes vodka, this of course was most definitely a welcome bonus. And also there was another most welcome early morning gift that would help the weather-ravaged men along the way ahead. Some half dozen yurts were strapped to the sides of several of the tall gaunt looking mules and camels deserted by the fleeing nomadic raiders.

Yurts were a rounded living accommodation made from bent saplings that were when erected covered in camel and goat skins, then lashed together with strips of hide. Even a man as big as Barak could stand upright in one of these cleverly well put together constructions. Also these most welcome accommodations of course offered the travellers warmth as well as shelter from the biting wind. Fires could also be lit from within their robust confines, the smoke escaping out through the highest point where a gap in the overwrap was most cleverly left open.

Also as well as all these new found practical aids there were sacks of plunder to be shared out amongst the Norsemen. Gold and gems, silks, satins, furs and exotic spices, all of these in the past were no doubt robbed from hapless camel trains. Over these years the bandits apparently had their fair share of good luck as they roamed and raided these inhospitable wastelands. Luck though however, as everyone with a brain knows only too well, cannot of course last forever.

There were also in the many sacks and chests some most valuable and interesting medicines and potions. Amongst these were Persian healing lotions, as well as exotic spices for cooking, which Barak would of course claim for himself. After all no one else there had any interest in these lotions and potions, or even knew what they were for that matter.

Ragnor just like Barak also wanted nothing in the way of gold or booty, oh and certainly he had no use for any silks or satins. At day's end the chieftain could always borrow from his now wealthy kinsman if needs be. Aye these men were after all his friends and his brothers in all and everything. These rough rogues would not deny him any gold needed to invest in a tavern on their way back homeward. For now though the big Viking was just pleased to have killed a few men and have better sleeping accommodation. All of this comfort as well as plenty of food to eat and an ample amount of ale to drink, no matter how weak it was. Vodka the Viking could drink only in small quantities. He had found over

317

the years drinking vodka with Barak was not at all healthy. The last time Ragnor had went drink for drink, well, tried to go drink for drink with the giant he had been ill for a week. Aye and even after that terrible gut wrenching week was up, well even still, he had not been very good for much.

Anyway and also as an added bonus there was a bandit's camel that had broken one of its front legs while tumbling into the trench. Straightaway the unfortunate beast was of course instantly dispatched by Barak, then butchered just as quickly. And all of this on the very spot where the creature had fell. Oh, and this butchering was swiftly and expertly completed amid yet another storm of flesh bruising giant hail.

This hail however Barak simply ignored, the ogre after all was looking forward to camel steaks for his breakfeast.

So once again it was the weather that was proving to be their main antagonist, not the feeble forces of poor pirates and inept plains bandits. Now that cold and sunny morning had turned suddenly as black as night as the hail fell driven by a savage north easterly wind.

Barak had talked with Ragnor for but a brief moment giving him advice as to how and construct the yurts, this while the ogre put the unfortunate camel quickly out of its misery. Then with this once done and in the next short while as Barak had pressed on with his butchery the Northmen set about erecting the captured yurts just as quickly as they possibly could. Unfamiliar with this practice it took the Norsemen some little time to achieve perfection. Still despite this, quite soon all of the men were under their most welcome recently acquired shelters, all now were sitting about warming themselves around their camp fires.

As Barak had always said from the very off, this party of men would get to their destination when they eventually got there and not before. To Barak it was more important for both flesh and spirits to be kept high, the men were not to be sickened on their long perilous and most arduous of journeys.

Years ago when he was a young and fresh commander to the Eagles of Rome Barak was in a sort of constant competition with his Roman equals and counterparts. Not of course that the high ranking men of the Roman militia thought Barak was in any way their equal. Oh no, to them Barak was nothing more than a bloodletting savage, a barbarian, an inhuman ogre, a freak even. But soon enough these high born aristocratic Roman commanders would all learn very differently as to the folly of that most foolish assumption. These fools in their crimson finery would sit atop their fine prancing Spanish horses all day long, posing and posturing while looking ever so regal and noble like. And then in their pride and their arrogance these same fools expected their weary men to jog along obediently and faithfully behind them, this on blistered sandaled feet. All of this was expected while the weary footsore men were sweating and roasting inside their plate armour. Carrying with them also as they went along their weapons of war, their drinking water and also their own food, field rations and bed roll. At the end of all this long hard day's footslog, the tired soldiers would be expected to wage war on behalf of glorious Rome. Ah though not for Rome alone, no there were of course the considerations and demands of their proud illustrious commanders to take into account. A victory, no matter how costly to his men, would give the high born officers the glory and the adulation of battle they craved for. Alas the rose petals, the fanfare of trumpets and the adulation of the crowd, these were not rewards for the men of the legion. Aye this even though it was their sweat, blood and tears that stained the ground on which they had warred.

This though however was a brutal tactic of war that of course did not and could not ever work. It was and still is a stark fact men with sore blistered feet simply do not move very quickly in time of battle. Also men who have little or no love of their leader, however illustrious his supposed breeding might be, these men are of course simply just not willing to throw their lives away, and this merely to bolster a spoilt uncaring aristocrat's military career.

Barak, however, well he was a very much different sort of man to the proud Roman generals. In the past the giant had marched alongside with his men on his big booted feet. But only the march, mind you, never ever the famous body draining Roman jog trot. On such occasion the ogre quite wisely much preferred to be saddled. Still though, all in all Barak's simple fair policies of war had thus far always stood him in good stead with the rank and file, the men of the line. Keep the men happy, fresh and well fed and they will fight all the better for it, that at least was the ogre's policy. Grind the men down, make them weary and mutinous, then this action will without doubt bring disaster to all and everything.

For two days more, unable to move with the savagery of the elements, the men of the north feasted and rejoiced as the giant hail bounced harmlessly off the yurt's tough outer skin. By now the victorious Vikings the meanwhile had shared out the bounty of gold and gems amongst themselves. It would be true to say they were all most happy with the reward for their easy victory. And so at least if they were all going to die on this adventure then they would all die very rich men. Bards minstrels, poets and fools alike would sing loud and long of their heroic deeds. Aye and this, long after they were gone on and turned to ash or dust. After all this was an epic adventure indeed that they had undertaken, death to these rough rogues and reavers it meant nothing at all now. Somehow and in some way these warriors would all be long remembered as heroes by their far distant kinships. And so this savage immortality it comforted their fierce souls, aye these Norsemen would be legends each, and every one of them would be spoken of as heroes.

With this in mind then our band of huge hairy warriors pressed on once more. Now and with the unusually cold desert left behind them the warriors would next encounter the swamp. So once again as the hail abated on the third day then, as always and ever the intrepid party moved onward in an ever eastward direction.

However so cold was it now that the warriors crossed the frozen swamp without any incident at all. Indeed there was also no sight or even a sound of anything reptilian or swamp-like at all. Well that was of course, save for the company of their own friendly Troll. All of the bull rushes, swamp reeds, swamp willows and the like these had all perished and died, then just disappeared under the frost covered snow. In fact once the riders were out of the other side of the former dreaded stinking bog no one there except Barak, Tark, and of course the troll would even have known a swamp had existed at all. As for Barak, well he thought it more prudent not to mention there had ever been a swamp at all to cross in the first place. After all said and done what Ragnor did not know would never hurt him. From here and perhaps with luck in three or four weeks hence of uninterrupted travel the band of warriors would be standing at long last before the great gates of Krozak itself. Once there and from then on all would indeed be revealed, this be, it for the better or for worse.

Barak of course had every intention of meeting with his younger brother as soon as it was possible, and the ogre would achieve this by whatever means was necessary. Oh and of course the slayer also certainly had very dark murderous intentions of a meeting with the two conniving brothers. Two brothers whose very names the ogre still did not even want to know, well not yet, not until he was within the walls of the kingdom itself. One way or another everyone was going to get exactly what was coming to them, and that was something the giant had promised to himself a long way back in the journey.

After continuing on with their travel there was another freezing windy night spent within the comfortable confines of the yurts. Aye and also it was another noisy blustery night of high spirits and good fellowship while dark camel meat roasted slowly over a blazing fire. Well cold outside that it was, but inside, the men some seven or eight to each yurt lounged about without their great wolf and bearskin cloaks and their winter clothing.

Indeed big Barak sat cross legged at the fireside, sweat glistening from his broad brow so warm was it within the cosy accommodation. Meanwhile the giant as ever puffed away quite contentedly upon his wooden pipe, a pipe that by the way he had now become most accustomed. After a moment or two of thought the giant next glanced casually about him at his strange companions. To his immediate right sat the huge green and warty troll. A troll which he now greatly liked and much respected, Borz after all had great courage as well as great strength. Next and then to the giant's left side, there sat the one-legged and ever drunken German, Horst. Also Horst, despite his many failings, was nevertheless a man Barak had a lot of time for, and if nothing else he was always entertaining. Ragnor and Loki sat opposite, sitting side by side with their huge red beards sticking outward dripping with beer and grease from the remains of the camel meat. And as ever the pair of them looked both uncouth and primeval things. As has already been said the savage Vikings lacked all manner of social graces. Also by now on this evening the Norsemen were more than half-drunken things. And, apparently they were celebrating something or other by the singing of an out of tune song. Indeed looking about him Barak supposed Ragnor's young nephews and Tark were possibly the only ones there of the company who looked at all remotely civilized or even human. Oh and as for Barak, well, the ogre knew only too well his appearance did not quite conform to the norm, that though, well it was something which bothered him not one little bit. As for the rest of the Norsemen who also sang feasted and drank in the adjoining yurts, well, these mostly incomplete fellows in all honesty were only a little better in appearance than either Ragnor or Loki.

Well then again, no, perhaps these warriors were quite a bit better with their looks than the most unpretty looking Loki.

'Well, this must be just like being at home with the family Ragnor? ' Barak said with a sly grin as he very unusually kicked off his big boots when in company and warmed his huge feet by the fire. In mid swallow the big Viking drained down another goblet of beer, he then belched, farted and hiccupped almost at the same time.

'Family, what on earth would you know about family, Barak?' Ragnor asked with a crooked mischievous smile.

'We here, we Norsemen are your family, aye and we are the only family that you have ever really known since you rode away from your kingdom all of those many years ago.'

Barak took no offence at these words, no far from it the ogre merely grinned knowingly as he glanced at the staring pop-eyed Viking.

True the ale was weak, wishy washy stuff, but one look into those wide pale eyes told Barak it was the smoke from the black mountain weed that was affecting Ragnor more than the ale. The warmth, also the confined conditions about them within the yurts of course meant everyone about the ogre was getting a free smoke of Barak's strong weed.

'Oh, I am in no doubt that you have countless illegitimate offspring to the harlots of Rome, Barak,' Ragnor continued. 'Aye and perhaps you have even more bastards in all of Rome's other fine but decadent cities you have visited whilst in its employ. But still my friend that is not exactly family is it?' Ragnor asked this while beginning to slur his words a little.

Barak at this accusation did not burst into laughter as might have been expected. No, rather the giant frowned and looked quite offended, then the ogre took upon himself a most serious sort of expression.

'Ragnor hear you this, aye hear what I have to say' the ogre said pointing the sharp end of his pipe at Ragnor. 'The painted courtesans of Rome, or indeed any of the other floosies who hail, from anywhere else for that matter. Well these sad poor creatures hold no attraction for me, not now, not ever for that matter.' Barak said this evenly without either a trace of mirth or anger.

'No! oh no surely not,' Ragnor exclaimed out loudly and insinuating by his tone he never believed a word of it.

'No!' Barak replied back instantly and also a little sternly.

'Why so then big Barak, tell me are these women not at all comely enough creatures for you to have wiled away your time? ' Barak took a deep draw upon his pipe before answering the Viking's question.

'Aye, comely enough I do suppose they are, and also these females are mostly disease ridden things.' Barak replied puffing away heavily upon his pipe now in apparent agitation. 'Aye and believe me Ragnor, I for one have had no wish to be spending the rest of my life scratching and riving away at myself for one night's lustful pleasure with one of those sad things. Aye and then to wait on in agony for years just so that eventual madness and blindness would doubtless carry me off to my lime filled grave. No, oh no, oh no Ragnor, that is most certainly a fate not meant for me, my hairy misguided Viking friend.'

Barak with this said then took for himself a good long drink of vodka.

'This is all very true my Lord Barak, yes it is most very true,' Horst said joining in with the conversation with a lopsided sort of drunken smile. Horst, like Barak, was on the vodka not the ale, and the German as ever was certainly not being slow about the drinking of it.

'Floosies, floosies, well they of course are creatures of the night, sad things that are best left well alone,' Horst further added after another long swallow of drink. Ragnor though was less convinced as to Barak's past good behaviour, and he was about to say as much.

'So now you try to tell me Barak, that all of these long hard years you have done without the company of women?' Ragnor asked this question while pointing a gold ringed finger toward the giant, aye and somewhat accusingly at that.

Now the giant rumbled and grumbled away to himself as he drank then smoked before giving his answer.

'No, oh no not at all Ragnor,' Barak answered a little sharply. 'But unlike you and your hairy Vikings,' Barak paused then took another drink, 'good men and brothers to me though you are, well I am a little more picky. Aye, I suppose that I am a little more selective in my choice of a bed warmer than perhaps you are. Why everyone here knows that any old she goat would do well enough and suffice for you Ragnor,' Barak next stated blankly.

Barak after making this statement instantly apologized to the nephews of Ragnor saying he was sorry if he had offended or embarrassed them with this remark about their esteemed uncle in any way. As for the youths, well the lads were sitting so silently sniggering at the insults being hurled about the ogre had quite simply forgot their very presence.

However, the other men lounging about were not so restricted so they laughed out loud long and openly, this while the blonde youths chuckled shyly behind their shirt sleeves.

Ragnor sneered scowled then cursed next the offended Norseman spat a little angrily into the blazing fire before speaking.

'You have long been famed for your expertise in your choice of horses dogs and huge things that fly and hunt Barak.' Ragnor hissed this out while pointing a finger at the giant. 'But strangely, I have never as yet heard anyone sing out your praises over your choice of a woman.' The big Viking said whilst blowing his chest out and yet again pointing a challenging finger at the giant.

Barak took a deep drink of vodka as he retracted his big over warm feet from the fire. These feet as it so happened weren't the only thing that was getting a little hot around here. Yet again the great slayer took another long slow puff upon his pipe. Barak did this whilst the big Viking awaited some sort of guidance and advice from the giant as to how to choose a good woman. For Barak, the Viking knew only too well, would always have the last word on all and anything. Of course Ragnor was correct in his assumption. So now with Barak being Barak, well now the giant was about to educate all and everybody within earshot.

'From the small nameless villages, from the hamlets and the farms, these are always the best places to find the right sort of women. Not noisy taverns, pleasure houses and most certainly not the narrow streets and dingy alleyways that crawl with filth and decay,' the giant said with a sneer. 'No, no oh no, you want a good honest farm girl, and you want one that is not too thin and bony mind you. Oh no these women must, must have plenty of flesh about their bones, but on the other hand, nor should she be overly fat either. Well furnished, yes she should be a well furnished thing, with big thighs, I particularly like big thighs' Barak explained in all honesty. 'Aye this Ragnor, yes this is my choice of women. Clean and strong hard working country girls, girls who know the land and are neither full of their own self-importance nor are they ashamed of what they are. ' Barak paused as he took another drink then pointed the tip of his long pipe toward an open mouthed Ragnor.

'Aye and also know this my friend, you can always make a good deal with a farmer for his wife, or his sister, or even his daughter for that matter if she is of age. Aye, a farmer, he will not see a traveller go lonely; anyway it is only for a night or two you know?' Barak said this in such a straightforward matter of fact fashion that it brought tears of laughter to everyone's eyes. Now the Vikings all fell about quite out of control with themselves. In fact, so loud did they laugh that the men from the next yurts came to find out the cause of all the wild revelry and merriment.

Barak though for the very life of him just could not understand either their mirth or for that matter their bewilderment.

'What is it, what did I say that you all find so amusing?' Barak asked earnestly and out loud so he could be heard over the booming laughter.

It took some time before Ragnor could pull himself together and he was even able to reply to the giant's question.

'You mean to tell me, you great big oaf, that you simply walk up to some farmer and then ask him if you can borrow his wife or his other closest female relation for the night?' Ragnor asked, his face, well that which was at all visible behind his bushy beard, was bright red with his laughter.

Barak took another deep draw upon his pipe followed by a swallow of vodka. It was plain to see these fools sitting about him were not good dealing men at all the ogre thought to himself.

'Well why not Ragnor? As after all, fair exchange is no robbery so they say,' Barak argued.

'Aye, and know you all this, I do not rob the rustics in any way you must understand? Oh no, no far from it. Indeed, I do always try to help them out by giving these folk some coin, farm life after all is a hard way to make a living you know? Aye and also, I always make them a fair honest offer for their women folk. Why I do suppose that it is just like the hiring of a horse really,' the giant said on most sincerely.

Barak to say this now had to raise his voice so that his words could be heard over the raucous laughter of the Vikings. Unabashed and in innocent bewilderment Barak said on, after all these fools obviously needed educating.

'Why, there is nothing I think better than to wake up in the countryside with a fine strong woman of the land lying next to you after a long night of affection. Aye and then a little later on to rise up and get dressed, to sit and enjoy a big farm breakfeast with the rest of the family. Oh yes, this I do think is a most wonderful thing. Later on, and with this done then relax with a drink and a smoke or two. Oh and then the next step after this friendly socialising is to have a relaxing bathe in a hot tub, true bliss.' Quite unintentionally Barak had caused yet another loud outburst of uncontrollable laughter. And still for the life of him the bemused ogre could not quite understand the reason for the Norsemens' riotous mirth. Ragnor now was quite unable to speak and the big Viking could not manage even a single word, as now his uncontrollable laughter had rendered him useless.

'You have no morals about you at all my lord Barak, no you have none at all,' Tark at length managed to say clutching at his sides in such fits of laughter as to give him a stitch.

Barak looked greatly offended at his young countryman's harsh uncalled for words. And this as the ogre thought he at least would have understood the straight forward honest business transaction.

'Tell me how many fishing boats have you back in your mountain fjord Ragnor?' Barak asked suddenly and bluntly of the hysterical Norseman.

Ragnor, after some time, managed to calm down his laughter and was once again in at least some sort of control of himself.

'Six or seven perhaps, why do you ask me that Barak?' replied the still smiling and chuckling Ragnor.

'You can sail only one boat at a time, so why then do you have you six or seven?' the giant asked seeking to entrap his hairy friend.

Ragnor took himself a mouthful of weak ale, but in truth he had trouble swallowing it such was his mirth. And this, the big Viking thought to himself was one of the most amusing nights he could long remember.

At length after a little while Ragnor found his tongue and was able to answer the giant's question.

'People from inland, these folk would come to my village to fish, these farmers have no boats of their own so they borrow mine,' Ragnor replied this

while still chuckling away to himself and not quite seeing what was coming next.

'Ah, I see, so do you give these boats of yours freely to these people then Ragnor?' Barak asked this already knowing what Ragnor's answer would be to his cleverly put question.

'No, no of course not Barak, I take money for the use and for the wear and tear of the vessels. Not for free, no never, not charge, well that would indeed be a most foolish thing to do,' the Viking replied while putting a drink to his hairy mouth.

Barak on hearing this smiled and leant forward across the glowing fire.

'Well, I too give money for wear and tear; I give it to the farmer for the loan of his wife, it is the same difference is it not?' Barak once again had to shout this out loud so that he might be heard over the almost insane laughter of the Vikings.

Barak once again looked most agitated as he puffed upon his pipe wildly, then swallowed down more drink to calm himself.

'Aye and know you all this, you bunch of cackling fools, not once in all these long years have I ever been denied a woman by these rustics,' the ogre declared proudly. 'I am not a thief or a robber you know, well at least not all of the time, and I do pay a fair price for my female company. Oh aye the farmers have always took my coin without complaint. Aye and what's more they were right glad of it, oh aye they were'' the ogre further explained. 'And what is more, well these rustics waved me off on my way the morning of my departure. Yes and let me tell you they were amongst the most happy and cheerful souls you ever did see. Though, I must add without sounding too boastful, the men folk never looked half as happy as did their chubby red cheeked women!' Barak said this with a most satisfied smile.

For several hours later the company of big Norsemen were still laughing hysterically, to the point of each and every one of them acquiring an acute stitch in the stomach. It had apparently never even crossed Barak's mind the poor farmers were quite simply terrified of him. Being so any deals that were transacted, well, these deals were only concluded as the farmers feared greatly for their very lives. But then again, perhaps in this particular case ignorance was bliss.

At length, the wind and the hail abated and the Norsemen travelled on for several weeks more without event, this of course was a most refreshing change.

Chapter Twenty

On the very eve of the band of adventurers reaching the gates of Krozakistan, Barak and Tark rode out together from the small encampment. It was not yet quite dark when they left and both men knew exactly where it was they wanted to be. After an hour or two of steady trotting over very unsteady ground the riders eventually reached their destination. This was at the mouth of a long straight canyon that was flanked either side by high cliffs. Here the riders slowed down to a walk then reined in their sweating horses to a standstill. There, in the distance before them the men could both make out the dim flicker and glare of torch light. And this inviting brightness came from the city's torches, it came from the streetlights and the braziers of the well guarded battlements. Aye and also the warming inviting glow came from the very houses of the good citizens of Krozak.

Of a sudden the giant swallowed, it had been over thirty years now since he had last set his black eyes on that comforting glow.

By now it was full dark and freezing, oh and also it was the most windless of nights. Above the riders there was no moon, the skies though were studded with a million glowing stars. As well as these static beacons of light there were also great numbers of shooting stars that hurtled across the skies. These were more bountiful and larger than the likes of Barak in all of his wanderings had never seen before. Why it appeared the very heavens themselves were putting on some sort of show for the two homeward bound travellers. Was this then to be taken as an omen? Aye was this to be taken as some sort of a sign of welcome? Or then again was this perhaps a damning rebuff? Now Barak the great ogre thought this darkly to himself as his big dog let out a long low growl of suspicion at its surroundings. Barak now spoke softly to his remaining big dog and at once the hound calmed itself.

Anyway, after but a short while the riders moved off from that place and next the men reined their horses in under the shelter and safety of a craggy overhang in the rocky canyon. This, the riders did amidst yet another sudden storm of large and painful hail. Hail that once might have unsettled the horses now bothered them not in the slightest, the beasts were by now well used to it. The towering mountains either side of the narrow canyon seemed to reach up to the very star studded skies above. Five hundred good men could hold this narrow passageway against ten times, no twenty times that number, aye and hold it forever if need be.

Barak was silent and watchful. He seemed to be studying whatever it was that lay somewhere in the darkness ahead of him. It had been so long since the slayer had ridden this rocky path and the last time he did so, well it was of course in the opposite direction. How would he be received by the men of the Black Guard the ogre wondered to himself? After all he had slain six members of the close knit brotherhood. Would he be welcomed here? Would he be treated as a friend and their leader, or would he be their foe? Was he to be a saviour to his people? Or was he simply going to be thought of merely as some sort of a traitor, a deserter even? What lies and poisonous words had these treacherous brothers with their fellow conspirators spread amongst the rank and file of the armies of Krozakistan? Aye and what had the common people, his people, what had they been told about him, the giant wondered silently and somewhat grimly to himself.

'Barak, my high Lord, tell me, is all well with you?' Tark asked becoming a little perturbed at his master's long time of silence.

Now the giant appeared agitated as he ground his wolf sharp teeth fiercely together and he moved about a little uneasily in his high backed saddle. 'Yes, yes all is well my boy, do not concern yourself or worry about me,' the giant answered most unconvincingly.

Tark though was in no way whatsoever going to be stalled or put off by his master's somewhat lame reply. Something he sensed was most sadly amiss here and the young warrior, he would to his credit not be denied an honest answer. No the young warrior would know just what it was that troubled his king. With this in mind, he then spoke bravely.

'I would not normally call a man such as you, who I consider to be both my king and my friend, a liar. However though, well you do sore tempt me my Lord Barak.' The young man to his credit said all of this, frankly bravely and honestly.

Barak grunted and growled then he reached for his goatskin gourd that was slung over the front pommel of the Arab saddle. Uncorking the gourd the giant next drank long and deep of the vodka. With his thirst quenched, well if thirst it was, Barak turned and fixed the young man with a strange stare. This though, well it was a stare that was not in the least bit threatening or terrifying.

'Those words King and Lord, well these words mean nothing to me Tark, yes such titles mean nothing to me at all, but the word friend, that does. Aye, it means to me a lot, and know you this, I now consider you as a good friend to me boy. Know this also, I am most sorry that I slew your friends and comrades, for these were also my own countrymen. Alas though, things do happen in life, in everyone's life, that are neither just nor are at all fair.' Barak said sadly. 'Like I say my boy I am most sorry for their deaths, aye truly I am. '

Tark could not straightway reply as he was choked up at his Lord's frankness and honest sincerity, so now he took himself a drink of ale from his own gourd. Tark had tried the vodka and found that it was altogether far too intoxicating a beverage for him to keep his wits intact. Well at least when he was drinking the strong clear liquid with Barak that was. What vodka he used to drink back in the garrison had made him roaring drunk. Now though after these past months, well that amount would barely make him slur his words or cause him to make an unsteady step. Perhaps after all the drunken German, Horst, was right, practise did make perfect.

'You know the other night as we all sat around the fire and there was talk of our families, do you recall that conversation Tark?' Barak asked totally out of the blue.

Tark, who had regained his composure somewhat by now, gave a nod of his black turbaned head.

'Aye my Lord, what of it? ' he replied keeping his conversation brief lest he once again faltered and perhaps unmanned himself in some way.

Now it was Barak's turn to stall and hesitate and to become a little cautious with his next few words. Indeed should the ogre continue with what he was about to say to the young man, or should he not, the great slayer wondered? Perhaps it would be wiser and more prudent to merely say nothing and just turn his horse about him and trot back towards the encampment. For some reason though, a reason which was even unknown to himself Barak after some hesitation and deliberation decided to speak on and confide in the young warrior.

Though this information, it could wait a moment or two until he took another swallow from his gourd.

'Many years ago Tark, when I first left this place that now stands spread out before us, I did not, as is the common belief of seemingly the whole world, go headlong straight away into an orgy of full blown warfare and bloodletting with all and sundry. No this I do most strongly deny, as my boy well it is quite simply just not true.' Barak then paused whilst he took another swig of vodka, next the giant cursed as he had no flints or fire about him to light up his pipe. Totally out of character his lighting flints the slayer had most carelessly left behind in the yurt. Perhaps, now on top of everything else his wits had also begun to leave him.

Tark at this point had made no reply choosing to let the great warlord get on with his tale in his own time. And oh what a tale by all and any accounts this would prove to be. Aye indeed it would be a revelation, and a most sad and heartbreaking revelation at that.

'I wandered away from this place and as you now know I covered exactly the same perilous ground that we have ourselves just travelled. Of course I was only a boy back then, not much older than Ragnor's nephews. Oh, and I was, as you already know, all alone at that particular time. Many strange beasts and many men I did slay before I at long length arrived at the shingle shore were now lies the Falcon. ' Barak then paused for just a moment for another drink. 'By then I had walked many long and weary miles, this as my horse had run off and was doubtless killed by the wolves of the forest. Anyway, at that dead and stagnant sea, I found on the beach a broken rotten hulk of a ship, it was a galleon, a roman vessel. No doubt it had been a slaver that had in its murky past dealt in hardship, cruelty and misery. Now though it was a washed up broken thing, so I suppose the vessel had in some ways at least repaid some of its former sins.

Now its tattered fading sails bore the black cross upon a white sail, the Roman cross of death,' Barak said solemnly.

'Ah then it was a plague ship that you had stumbled upon my Lord?' Tark put in knowingly.

Barak gave a slow nod of his huge head then the giant took yet another drink of vodka from his goatskin gourd.

'Aye, a plague ship it most certainly was boy, the disease though had long since died out before I boarded the broken hulk. Aye and also the huge gulls of that place, big noisy things that you have seen for yourself, well these sea going vultures had eaten every black disease carrying rat on board. Oh and also the birds had pecked clean every bit of flesh off the dead mariners' bodies. This being so Tark it was only white skeletons I did find aboard, skeletons and nothing more.'

Tark now leant forward in his saddle keen for more information.

'Were there chests of gold my Lord? Aye, surely there was treasure and loot aboard, Lord Barak?' Tark had asked this question both hopefully and expectantly.

Barak though merely grumbled and then shook his head in reply.

'No, no my boy, no there was not a single coin, these men had been banished off to the mercy of the sea, these men had simply sailed away to die wherever they would. So this being their fate they had no need of gold or silver or anything else for that matter.

Both men then briefly acknowledged a moment's silence for the long deceased mariners. Ah but only one moment's silence mind you, then Barak once again continued with the telling of his tale.

'And so lad, it was the wind and the tides that brought those unfortunates to be beached upon the same shingle shore where now lies the Falcon. Perhaps these men were all dead before they floundered, or mayhap the mariners died later where I found them, who knows?, Barak at this point turned his great gelding about and the horsemen left the cover of the overhang.

Thankfully the hail had almost stopped by now and the ogre could just as easily talk as they rode on their way back to camp. Suddenly as they did so, in the far off distance, there was just the slightest hint of a faint but certain rumbling.

'Thunder, my Lord Barak?' Tark suggested this while pulling his horse to a halt so he could listen to the distant rumbling a little better.

Now the slayer sniffed the air with his keen nose before replying to his young countryman.

'Perhaps,' Barak replied simply, though in all truth the ogre did suspect something else far more sinister and dangerous than the mere sound of thunder.

Slowly and carefully the riders picked their way back along the rocky trail back toward their encampment.

Barak talked constantly as they went along revealing a tale that even Tark, who had grown to know the man well over these last months found very hard to believe.

Aboard the Roman slaver Barak had secured for himself a large rowboat. This was one of many aboard the vessel and after close inspection it turned out that it was the best one. Luckily for Barak this rowboat had been painted and cared for, its underside had been tarred and weather proofed. And as a bonus also the small craft had stout oars and a row of seats, aye and it was of least a decent size to be put to sea.

True it was not perhaps a dragon ship by any stretch of the imagination, but never the less at this particular time it would have to do. Barak said he had managed with the salvage available to construct some sort of a mast and gather up lengths of sheeting for a make shift sail. Then later after his construction was completed he would take his chance with whatever fate it was that lay ahead of him in the great salt sea. Sooner he would face that unknown danger than retrace his steps to his homeland with his tail tucked between his long legs.

Barak had left the shingle shore armed with a Persian sword which had been a present from his father. Even now he still had the weapon, the sword was back in camp wrapped up in rags all oiled and sharp just as it was when his father had given it to him all those long years ago. Barak had also taken with him a Krozakian longbow and a quiver full of long shafted arrows with black eagle feather flights. These weapons Barak had as well as a strong curved dagger and a good skinning knife, oh and also a small spiked fighting shield. Barak at that time had wrapped about him a thick black bearskin cloak and breeches and tunic of stout leather, in fact very similar attire to what he now wore. Upon his very large and still growing feet the absent prince had worn stout knee high boots very like those he was now heeled in.

All in all, the giant supposed that his fashion sense had changed very little over the years but only back then the young Barak had a mane of thick black hair. This was long thick hair that had about it a most curious reddish tint. For countless days Barak had rowed and rowed then drifted in and out of sleep and then woke and rowed on again. Until at long last, he finally left the dark stagnant waters of that dead stinking septic sea far behind him. Barak had not starved however on his voyage as he had taken with him a fresh killed deer. As well as this nutritious meat, Barak had shot from the skies many screeching mocking seagulls. These, well these to be honest, Barak found were tasteless things, still, nevertheless it was meat of sorts. Most carefully this seagoing carrion Barak had roasted over a small brazier, a brazier that was perched upon a rectangular Roman shield. Barak had salvaged this brazier from the captain of the slavers no doubt once luxurious cabin. Even back then, aye even as a boy, Barak was most able and adept at forward planning for almost any eventuality.

Anyway, Barak explained that the wind and the tides bore him ever northward now and the blood in his veins was beginning to freeze a little more with each passing day. As a further setback the supply of wood he had taken with him was spent. Being so, well now he had no means to keep himself warm in the dark days ahead. All in all, Barak had thought at the time, his adventure was going to be a short lived one. Surely he supposed that he would die there frozen to the very oars of the small craft. But the fates or the gods or the devil himself however had other plans for him. And so, almost as Barak seemed to drift off to heaven or hell or wherever else he was bound for, suddenly there came out of the freezing mists a ship. It was a dragon ship, a long low lean well put together vessel, not dissimilar to Ragnor's Falcon. After that though, Barak could remember no more, at least not until he woke up in a warm low stout lodge with a glowing fire. Barak though was awake but briefly, as feeling warm and safe he had drifted back off to sleep. Later on, Barak found out that the lodge had a thick turf roof atop it. Oh and this weighty roof acted both to keep in the heat as well as prevent the building from being blown out into the wild arctic sea. For many days he slept then woke then slept on again, in truth, Barak was perhaps deader at times than he was a living thing.

Many days later on one chill morning as the wind howled outside and the thunder of the cold far north fair shook the stout lodge he arose a little unsteadily to his feet. Barak had then looked about him; he was naked at this time save for a loin cloth. In the corner of the room, over a chair that was carved expertly with boar's heads and sinewy dragons, lay his clothes. All of these garments were laid there neatly, all washed and mended, his weapons lay next to them oiled and cared for. Barak did not stink of sweat and filth, so whoever owned the tidy lodge had obviously cared for him well, aye very well. Oh and also as well as this he had been bathed and shaved and his big feet were bound with linen. And this of course was for no doubt and no other reason but to keep them warm and stave off the frost bite. Happily each and every one of his toes was still there upon his huge feet, so he had to be at least thankful for that. This, as well of course being grateful for everything else these benevolent, so far unseen people had done for him.

Barak had next arose and dressed himself as quickly as he could, he was about to strap on his girdle and weaponry when he was distracted. Then all of a sudden Barak heard the alarmed cry of a young woman. And this above the howl of the raging wind, the crash of the ocean and the peel of the thunder. Without further thought Barak had rushed outside of the lodge to grab a small but strong Icelandic pony by its bridle. Obviously the pony had taken affright with the thunder and it would have been off, and off with the most fairest of women. Aye and she was a woman that Barak as a young man or even Barak as an old man had ever found her equal.

Tark listened intently to his Lord's tale of these years long gone by and of years that Barak evidently had never before even spoken of. Well, well that was at least not until now, not until this very moment in time.

'And so you settled there, in this place that was far to the north, for at least a little while then Barak?' Tark asked with an innocent smile.

Barak gave a nod and pulled his gelding's head up as it stumbled in the darkness.

'Aye, for a while I dwelt there boy, they were all good people. Also I was, I must say most happy in that cold wind blasted place which, by the by' was no more than but a small island. '

For some reason the young man felt a sudden warmth about his very being at the thought of his Lord and master living in some sort of harmony with apparent peaceful and decent people. True Ragnor and his rogues were decent enough in their own way, but peaceful, never.

'And the young woman, the one that you saved, did you become friends, lovers even?' Tark suggested this a little boldly. Barak drew in a deep breath of air, he hesitated for but a moment then answered.

'More than that boy, I married her; she was called Freya,' Barak replied proudly.

'Married! ' Tark exclaimed, embarrassed now by the clumsy question he had put to Barak, aye and he was shocked in the extreme at this revelation. 'But Ragnor, he said you had never once wed, aye and that you had never taken a woman as your own. '

Barak reined in his big horse, the ogre drank long and deep from his now only half full gourd of vodka.

'Ragnor is my friend but he is not my keeper, and anyway, a man must have some secrets,' the giant said almost in a whisper.

Tark was much taken aback, even shocked by this reply. 'Then why? Why, do you tell me this my Lord Barak?' Tark asked plainly. 'Why?'

Barak growled to himself, it was a long low growl before replying to the young man's well put and honest question.

'Because you are here, and because it is now,' the giant replied with a weary sort of sigh. 'And perhaps also because, because when I am dead and I am gone, there will be someone at least to tell why I am the way that I am. Why, why I am the killer that I am,' he further explained.

Tark moved to speak, but Barak silenced him with a gesture of a hand.

'We had a daughter,' Barak went on after another drink. 'She had tousled hair that was as white as the snow, she had the very bluest of eyes, far brighter than any summer sky. '

Barak said these words almost in a whisper.

'She was like her mother in every way, aye she was a beautiful little girl.'

Tark, well he said nothing at all now. For some reason, somehow deep down inside of him, the young man knew this well kept story was not going to have a happy ending. And sadly the young man, well alas, he was indeed most well and truly correct in his well thought out assumption.

'For almost five years I lived with those good kindly people, these folk were traders and fishermen, farmers and hunters. Not pillagers and killers like the cowards who came to our small village when I was away with the rest of the men. Away hunting the great whale in the cold grey sea.'

Tark held out an outstretched hand towards Barak.

'Vodka, my King, do you mind if I take a drink from your gourd?' Somehow Tark did not think that weak ale would give him the backbone required to listen to the rest of this story.

Barak shrugged and sighed heavily, then he passed over the goatskin gourd to the by now somewhat stressed out young man riding at his side.

'The child too, our child she was also called Freya, after her mother. And know you this lad they were all and everything to me. I needed nothing more and I wanted for nothing else in the world,' the giant said slowly and sadly. 'Not palaces, nor kingdoms or glory or fame did I crave back then on my frozen island home.'

Tark was humbled now and humbled in the very extreme. In fact, he was not quite at all sure that he wanted to hear the rest of this story. This man, months ago, he had set out to hate and even slay if that was to be the way of things. Now though this very same man had spoken to him not once but three times now. And when he had spoken, well he had opened up his great heart. Oh and this was heart that by all accounts to most people was a black and an unforgiving thing. However, how very wrong these foolish misguided folk all were. Firstly the great slayer had spoken of the loss of his father, a man who he had obviously loved most dearly. Then later on into their venture, why the great giant of a man had crumbled and almost broke down in tears and this at the death of what some might say was no more than a big savage dog. Now, and now there was this most woeful tale, a tale that was sure to become even more heart breaking and more soul destroying to the ear than all else he had so far been privy to so far.

Barak, after a brief pause to collect himself then continued on with his woeful story.

'When we arrived back at home and sailed up the fjiord, the three ships that had sailed away to hunt the whale were not greeted by joyous excited cries as was hoped for and expected. No, oh no all was deathly silent, well except for the cries of the mocking screaming gulls above our now troubled heads. Every man aboard our ships knew that all was not well here, aye and sadly every man aboard the longships was quite correct in their thinking. You see Tark, raiders had been to our village—sea wolves, pirates, worse even, slavers. Those of the village who had not been dragged off for slaves, were either killed or had thrown themselves upon the sea rocks far below the cluster of lodges. Barak paused now and he took a big intake of breath before being able to continue. 'My small daughter, along with her mother lay dead and broken there upon the ice cold rocks. My woman, my wife would not be taken, not be taken as slaves to be sold off and parted from each other, a quick death they chose rather than this.'

Tark could not help himself now and he sobbed out both loud and openly at his master's cruel heart break.

'Who, who did this black deed my Lord?' Tark at length muttered with some difficulty. 'Who was it my Lord, who did this to you and your family.'

Barak rumbled out a growl and a curse, the slayer then cleared his throat as he spat into the darkness, oh how now more than ever he wished he had brought his flints.

'His name was Azira, he was an Arab slaver. And an Arab slaver who had put together a large dragon boat full of every kind of rubbish that ever did walk, sail or even crawl upon the earth.'

Now Barak's almost black eyes narrowed hatefully.

'He was a man who was very much alike to the brigand Wraif then?' Tark suggested pulling himself together just a little.

'Aye, aye very much so, but only ten time's worse' Barak agreed. 'For Wraif was but an oaf, and a fool. Azira though, well he was both a cunning and cruel man.' Barak replied as he scanned the heavens above, almost as if the ogre was looking for some explanation to the very reason for his violent life. After a brief pause Barak went on. 'The dead of the village, were sent to their gods and laid upon huge fires, much lamenting was had for several days after. At length, my sorrow and my grief it turned into pure hatred, the blackest hatred I have ever felt or ever wish to feel again. Armed with this hatred it was then I left the island which had been my home. Aye and it was then that I hunted these bringers of sorrow in all earnest. It was a blood hunt, a death hunt, aye and a hunt I suppose that I have been set upon ever since.'

Barak once again suddenly found himself cursing for not bringing his flints, aye as he was in sore need of a smoke now.

'I was a little known young man back then, famed for nothing other than my great size and my raw strength. The good people who took me in, and gave me a family did not even know I could handle a sword. However those of them that still lived, well, they would soon learn otherwise. I had vowed to myself and the memory of my dead father, that before the time this death hunt was over Azira and his dogs would hear and fear my very name. Even in their deepest darkest sleep, I would be there with them turning their dreams into nightmares. I wanted them to know I searched for them, and also I wanted them to know in what manner they would die. One morning when I woke, I shaved off all of my long hair. I now suppose this was a symbol of both my hatred and my grief, I became at this time in my life both a bounty hunter and a mercenary. As this you must understand was a task that was simply necessary to finance my search for the Arab Azira and his henchmen. I also trained hard; I made myself stronger and faster with both the sword and the lance. Of course on my extensive travels I went to the best sword masters in every city that I stayed in as I scoured the earth for revenge. And this you must remember Tark, I had already been trained to the sword, lance and the bow from the moment I could walk.' Tark's mouth was dry now while his head spun in a total turmoil.

'I too have undergone the same rigorous training as you, perhaps even more so,' Barak went on. 'For by my father's own words, I was born to be a warrior king, and I was to have no equal in battle.' Now the young Krozak warrior shuddered and swallowed at the very thought of what tortures Barak had put himself through. As he knew only too well the harsh, cruel, and exhausting training that Barak must have went through to make him expert with all manner of weaponry. After all, it had been Tark's own father who had helped train the young Barak in the art of combat all those long years ago.

'One by one, here and there along the winding way myself and the dozen or so good men from the northern island who had sailed with me, and were still left alive sought out and slew all of Azira's henchmen and accomplices. Till at long last, after many more years, there was only Azira himself left alive. Aye, now there was only him alone left to kill. By this time I was also very much alone as the others from the northern island had returned to their homeland and to what was left of their families. All these men thought I was mad to continue further in my search for Azira.' Barak next shrugged then gave out a heavy sigh as the riders ambled their way back toward the encampment.

'But how could I have been mad, boy? For after all said and done, at long last I had found him. Aye, I had found the dog who had caused the death of my small family. I had set out from the cold north, heading ever southward across Europe and into Asia in my hunt for revenge. '

Barak spat onto the ground at this point, his blood still boiled, his heart was still black. It was black with hatred for the man who had slain his woman and child, if not by his sword then by his very actions.

336

'Anyway I found Azira in the middle of the vast desert; he had been betrayed by his own brother. There was, apparently no love lost between them, for what reason I neither asked nor cared as it was enough that he took me to him. Azira's younger brother, Kamiz, waited beyond in the dunes with a score of his own well armed men. He had, in all truth offered me help against his brother and his henchmen, but what I needed to do, I needed to do alone. This was, after all, a most private matter. '

Barak paused once again for a drink, Tark took one also, and a big one at that. He had seen at first hand the giant's sheer power and his total blinding ability with his sword. And so now the young warrior could only surmise and imagine in horror what happened next. He was not at all wrong in his assumption.

Barak wiped his lips and then went on with his tale.

'The tent where I found him was a large regal affair, a tent that belonged to a powerful and wealthy sheik. And a sheik with whom Azira was doing business, aye and he had for some time.. Apparently, at least so I heard, he was a Bedouin by all accounts. Anyway this man was not only a buyer of slaves, as well as this he was a dealer in fine horses, fast hunting dogs, hawks and falcons. Oh and this tent was as I have already said, a most lavish. most luxurious affair. It had within it, standing at guard some twenty armed men, these men were mostly moors. Aye and all around about, in the lesser tents perhaps some one hundred of the sheik's tribesman slept or rested themselves. Anyway it was almost midnight when I dropped in; midnight and dawn, these have always been my favourite time for the killing of my enemies.' Barak added this in a most matter of fact fashion.

'Well which of these times do you prefer my Lord, giving the choice I mean?' Tark asked this a little sheepishly, and almost wishing he had not put the question in the first place.

'Dawn, yes, I do suppose I much prefer dawn for the killing time.' Barak answered this plainly without any hesitation as a jackal howled in the distance.

'Why so my Lord Barak?' asked the young warrior keen to be further educated.

'Because at dusk boy, I suppose I do like my pipe in one hand and my drink in the other hand,' Barak replied in answer to the young warrior's question. 'While at dawn,' the giant further continued somewhat whimsically. 'Aye at dawn, this a red skied one if at all possible, yes that is my favourite killing time. And then, well then I do like my blood covered dragon sword in one hand, while holding my enemy's grinning severed head in the other. Do you understand boy?' Barak then asked with a grim leery sort of smile.

Now Barak's sadness of a few moments ago, it seemed to be replaced by a slight tinge of madness as his black eyes once again narrowed in his big head..

'Oh,' was the only word Tark could muster up in reply before Barak continued with his explanation of things.

'Unless of course it is an arranged duel, then it must always take place at noon, at midday,' Barak said trying to sound formal and civilized.

'As this of course gives the combatants time to prepare themselves for the fray, understand? Time to bathe and shave and of course breakfeast, also to make sure their property is passed on to those who matter. If you know what I mean? ' Barak then asked.

'Oh yes of course my Lord it must of course be midday, yes oh yes I do understand,' Tark agreed whole heartedly.

'Anyway where was I? Oh yes now I remember, well, I announced myself as I entered into the sheik's tent.'

Once again Tark could not help but shudder at what new horrors would no doubt be revealed to him in the next few minutes or so.

'At this time, I had already begun to have my body tattooed, my arms chest and neck were well decorated with my many tasteful images.' Barak paused for a moment taking in the night sky then continued with his tale. 'Azira, on seeing me, well the fool knew exactly who I was and what I was about. At once the dog cowered and screamed out in alarm for his men to come to his rescue; these men had sat themselves by the small oasis nearby. And these retainers of his were at this time smoking and feasting upon goat and camel meat. You must of course remember Tark the men of the desert touch not the alcohol or the pork. Fools, why they just don't know what delights they are missing,' Barak said this with a sneer of contempt. As the giant, well he never trusted or did he put any faith in a man who did not touch strong drink or eat pork.

'Fifteen men there were in total, fifteen heads I had lopped off and thrown into the life saving water of the oasis. Perhaps there might have been some half dozen more who escaped into the night, bah but that is of little matter. Anyway Azira now shouted out to no one, as they were of course by now all dead things.' Barak spat and gave out a somewhat weary sigh. 'I had not only gone there to kill my enemies Tark, I had gone there to die myself, my life, well it meant nothing to me at that particular time.'

Once again Tark shuddered, but this time more in grief and pity for the giant's sad mental state at that tragic time in his life. For if what the giant had earlier said was at all true, which Tark did not in any way doubt, then what Barak had become, a killer, then this, he had not set out to become by ways of planned intention. Indeed, it was very true that Barak was perhaps some sort of a monster. But in his defence the infamous slayer was a monster created from more than a little bad circumstances. Tark's considerations and thoughtful deliberations were interrupted as the giant continued with his grim tale.

'Death, well it was not over quickly, Tark, for Azira, no, my hatred was such that I could not merely slay the man with a single sword thrust. The moors within

338

the tent, who after all is said and done were merely no more than slaves themselves threw down their weapons and fled off into the night.

Aye and the wealthy sheik the meanwhile washed his hands of what was happening there before him. Oh Aye and instead the fool chose to suck upon his opium and turn his head about the other way. Doubtless he was praying, praying to whatever gods would ever listen to him as he did so. However though, just as I suspected, none did. '

Now Tark's spine went ice cold as the hairs upon the back of his neck stood all on end.

'What next did you do then, my king?' Tark asked a little hesitantly whilst almost dreading the reply.

'I sliced off every single limb of the screaming, begging dog Azira, leaving his head till last,' Barak growled angrily.

Tark at this point felt very sick and faint, indeed the young man had great difficulty keeping the contents of his stomach were it belonged.

Barak snarled and spat then once again continued with the grizzly conclusion of his tale.

'Then before my final stroke of my sword, I cursed each and all and every one of the gods at once. I did this, quite simply for making it possible that you can kill a man only the once for his sins.'

Tark's throat, by now, was once again too dry to talk, so he took but another little swig of what was left of the vodka. For by now, well there was sadly very little left of the uplifting liquid to drink down. Also, if things continued the way that they were, and Barak burdened any more of his past tragedies upon him. Then, Tark thought to himself he would perhaps end up with a drinking habit that was just every bit as bad as the giant's!

'The other Bedouin tribesmen that slept and the sheik, what became of them?' Tark enquired, this, with yet another element of regret for asking another stupid question in the first place.

Barak shrugged uncaringly, then he sighed as he pointed to yet another shooting star that plummeted earthwards.

'I killed the sheik and I also killed what men of his I could catch, or what men had the courage to stand and fight. As for the rest of them, well they, just like Aziras men, fled off screaming and cursing into the night.'

Little wonder, Tark thought to himself as he imagined the carnage and panic of that horror filled night so many years ago.

'Why then did you kill the sheik Barak, was he not an innocent party in this crime?'

Barak gave a slow shake of his big head.

'No boy, no, the sheik was not innocent in any way, in fact far from it. And so I killed the sheik to leave a message, a message in blood,' Barak explained. 'For after all, without the likes of the sheik and his greedy kind, well these uncaring men, the men who buy the slaves off fools like Azira simply to make profit would not be many. Being so then of course then Azira would not have had a trade, so could not peddle his cruelty and misery. '

Barak paused as the horses picked their way along the rocky road to the campsite.

'Oh and I of course, well, I would still have a family about me would I not boy? True, I would most likely have been a bad farmer and an even worse fisherman. But, I would have been a man of the land and the sea, rather than of the sword and blood. And also like I say, I would have had at least my family about me, my wife and my white haired curly headed child. ' With this said there was a silence for a moment or two before Barak spoke once again. 'Believe me Tark I would have been a most happy contented man to grow old with my wife, this as I watched my pretty little child grow. ' Barak said this with his voice full of both deep regret and also a most bitter sadness.

Tark at this point was rendered totally speechless. The young man had not the words to say a single thing in reply to his heartbroken king. Barak though to his credit, well, the astute giant knew this to be a sad simple fact only too well.

'Come Tark, we can still catch up on some sleep before morning if we hurry on but a little.' Barak suggested as the jackal howled once again and the distant far off rumble grew in volume.

And so with nothing more said on the sad subject the riders did hurry on a bit faster and indeed the warriors did catch up on at least a little sleep before breakfeast. Some hours later when Tark had awakened the much troubled young man wondered to himself if what he had heard last night was, perhaps, words spoken only in a dream. Aye perhaps that was all it was, perhaps the rigours, the hardship and the very adventure of it all had addled his brain. Aye and mayhap he had merely dreamt that Barak had been married and fathered a small white haired curly girl child on an island far to the north. But on the other hand if he had not, well then little wonder his new king, his new lord and master, his new god and his mentor was a stone mad killer.

Chapter Twenty-One

As the dark and the black of the cold night disappeared, it was replaced by an equally cold but bright clear morning. On that morning the warriors breakfeasted quickly upon oat scones and camel's milk then dismantled and packed away the yurts. With this done and the mules and camels all packed up and ready the Norsemen in high spirits saddled themselves and were off on the last leg of their long journey. By midday with their travel unhindered and give or take an hour, the riders would be at the northern gates of the capital. This huge gateway was one of only the four main entrances to the great city itself.

'Well at least the rain has kept away my Lord, I thought after last night's thunder we were in for yet another drowning, aye or even more hail,' Tark said this brightly as he rode alongside Barak. Of course the young warrior was looking forward to being home again, looking forward to seeing his friends and his comrades. Oh what heroic tales he had to tell them all. And oh, oh how his friends would all envy his adventure and his wild exploits with the Vikings and of course the legendry Barak.

Barak made no reply to Tark's remark about the thunder, instead the thoughtful slayer merely grinned knowingly as he sucked merrily upon his newly acquired long clay pipe. And this was by the by a pipe the ogre had taken from the body of one of the would-be and over ambitious raiders.

Ragnor urging his horse forward also had something to say as regarding the fickle weather.

'Aye, I heard it too, though it was the likes of thunder I have never heard before, why it even echoed. ' Ragnor put in, between swallowing mouthfuls of sand that was being whipped up by a sudden gust of wind.

Barak pulled a veil which was attached to his mail link helmet across his face so that now only his dark almond eyes were visible.

The wind was by now so severe that any naked part of a man's body that was exposed to the elements was stung most painfully by the sharp plains sand. In but a moment once again all of a sudden the fierce whipper wind died out just as suddenly as it had sprung itself into life.

'It is very easy to tell you have spent more time at sea than you have upon dry land Ragnor.' Barak said this to the big Viking as he pulled out his Persian spyglass from under his black wolfskin cloak. However though the giant's words went unheeded by the hooded Viking.

'There Barak, listen, I can hear the thunder again.' Ragnor said while sitting a little unsteadily upon his newly acquired and somewhat spirited desert mount. 'And yet look you Barak, the clouds above are cold looking things, but they are clear and move but little despite the wind.' The big Viking said this while pulling his hood up tighter over his hairy head and rubbing his hands together against the bitter cold.

Barak pulled his big gelding to a sudden and immediate standstill and next the giant scanned the distant horizon with his Persian spyglass.

'Oh yes, just as I thought,' the giant muttered to himself as he passed the looking device over to Ragnor.

After but a glance the big Viking cursed as he also looked through the spyglass toward the horizon. Now it was and only then, that perhaps for the first time since they had set out on this dangerous quest the Norseman looked like a man in total dismay. Total dismay as to the way things seemed to be turning out.

'Oh, oh what next I do wonder?' Ragnor growled out a little angrily. Now the Viking after a few Nordic curses then passed the spyglass over to Tark. Who on spying out the horizon the young warrior, well he also took it upon himself to let out a mouthful of enraged oaths at what he spied through the looking device.

'Mongols, there must be at least a thousand of the horse stealing, blood thirsty, nomadic murderers.' Tark said this out loud, as at this moment in time even his stout heart was by now sinking into his high black boots. 'All this way, and all these leagues across land and sea we have covered, for it all to end like this,' the young warrior went on a little angrily. 'Over oceans, wolf filled forests, black serpent filled rivers and mountain peaks were the ancient lion dwells. Over the endless deserts, then through the swamps and the freezing steppes for it all to end here so close to home, no surely not,' he exclaimed. 'Just for our mission to all finish here like this, no, no this cannot be,' the young warrior complained bitterly.

'Swamps, swamps, what swamps are you talking about lad?' Ragnor asked a little puzzled at the young warrior's choice of words.

Barak ever attentive was quick to cut in.

'Just a slip of the tongue,' Barak put in very quickly. 'I think the boy is tired, he misses his home and his family, if you know what I mean Ragnor?' Barak after saying this took another big puff upon his pipe before snuffing it out. Now with this done the giant took a large swig of his vodka from the refilled goatskin gourd that was always and ever close to him.

'What now my Lord Barak, what do we do now? ' Tark asked this question almost regrettably, as he always did. Aye and indeed the young man dreaded the answer he was almost sure he would receive from his giant monarch, this just as he always did.

Behind them now the big burly Vikings were gently drumming upon their big round shields with their broadswords, the Northmen were singing a low death chant. But in all truth, well, the Vikings looked not the least bit bothered about this latest turn of events at all. True they would more than likely all die here in this wasteland, but then again, well here was as good a place as anywhere. Oh and of course the warriors would at least be fighting with men and not with the savage beasts of the forests or the mountains. Aye and also the warriors would all at least die with a bloodied sword in hand, oh and they would all die rich prosperous men at that. All of this after such an epic adventure, an epic adventure that any Northman could only ever dream of taking part in. Besides, also on the good side of things, at least by the looks of these new foemen the Norsemen would be fighting warriors just as fierce and as unwashed as they themselves were.

As for the Mongols, while being sparse bearded and small in stature compared to the big burly full bearded men of the north, they were nevertheless most worthy foemen. Oh and also of course, well there were also plenty of these slant eyed little horsemen to go around.

Now the troll of a sudden smiled a broad honest smile as he reined up his camel alongside Barak. Borz was better off and more comfortable riding a camel, horses well they just did not seem to like him for some reason or other.

'I knew it was not thunder that rumbled away in the night my Lord Barak,' Borz explained with a strange sort of smile. 'And I knew only too well it was the distant sound of many horses that we heard.' Barak looked impressed as he doubted not one word Borz had just spoken.

'Oh aye, and tell me, why so Borz?' Barak asked plainly as to how the halfling had reached this very correct conclusion.

'Well, well everyone else, apart from myself that is, all thought it was no more than the roar of distant thunder,' the Halfling chuckled. 'But then again, everyone else here is not a troll my Lord,' he chuckled yet again. 'You see my Lord Barak, my skin it dampens at the hint or even the slightest scent of rain,' the halfling further explained.

Barak nodded in appreciation at this cleverly arrived reasoning as the ogre smiled toward the halfling most warmly. 'You know Borz, I had quite forgotten about that, I mean about you being a halfling.'

On hearing these words the troll clutched at the lion fang that now hung around his broad green warty neck, the lion fang Barak had given him to wear with pride for his part in the slaying of the great lions. Next the troll bowed his green sloped newt like head in gratitude at the giant's words, this as his forked tongue flicked out and he cackled in laughter. Here, in this company of barbarians Borz supposed he was neither thought of as a troll or halfling here he was only Borz a friend and warrior. Among these brave rough rude men breeding and appearance, it counted for nothing, nothing at all. Now, now and at this very moment in time he was sat beside a king, aye and he was also a king who was his friend.

Now the yellow eyes rolled from side to side and the long purple tongue flicked out several times before the halfling spoke.

'If I am to die here on this day my Lord Barak, then I must say to you I am a most thankful thing.' The big green halfling said this most sincerely and he also said it without any trace of fear in his croaky reptilian voice.

'Thankful,' Ragnor put in hastily quite bemused by that strange yet profound statement. 'Why? Tell me why be thankful Borz? Are you perhaps now gone stone mad or what?' Ragnor asked as the approaching cloud of dust kicked up by the Mongol horses drew ever nearer.

'No, no I am not mad Ragnor, no I am far from it,' Borz replied evenly. 'But I am most grateful, grateful and thankful to die here upon these stark windswept plains today amongst good friends,' he continued. 'Good friends aye and dare I say it, even brothers to the very bone,' Borz said boldly. 'Aye, for this is a death I do far much prefer, instead of dying at the end of a chain set onto a pole in a market square merely to entertain a crowd. To die here amongst my friends is one thing, but to die amongst those who hate, fear and loathe you, well that Ragnor is yet another. '

Now every man there in earshot felt humbled, aye humbled yet fortified by the troll's loyal and brave words. So with this thought in mind the banging of shields with their broad swords and the chanting of the Viking death song increased. It increased both in volume and tempo, not to mention a berserker's passion for war and glory. This place now to those of the savage Viking brotherhood was the field of Vigrior, it was the field of death. Here was the eternal battle field where every true Viking at his end fought with both his beloved gods as well as his dreaded demons.

Once again Tark repeated his question to his king and he asked it a little more loudly and a little more urgently this time.

'My Lord, my Lord Barak, what do we do now? Indeed what on earth can we do against such impossible odds?'

Barak merely smiled as he shrugged his huge shoulders in reply. Barak next glanced around and looked behind him, the giant smiled again. The big men of the north were in good voice, they were in fine spirits to die right here and right now. So, that Barak thought grimly to himself was at least one good thing in their favour. After a long silence and a weary but care free sigh, Barak spoke up.

'Well lad, if the Mongols charge us, then I suppose we will then have to charge them boy, if you know what I mean? Barak had said this in a slow matter of fact sort of fashion. 'Or, perhaps we might just have a little talk about this and that, who knows? Best we just wait and see lad,' Barak said with an uncaring sigh.

'As this after all could be no more than a mere coincidence that we have all arrived here at the same time on this barren place. You know these things can and do happen boy?' Tark at this ludicrous reply was rendered totally speechless, had the giant perhaps taken leave of his senses the young man wondered silently to himself.

Barak was still smiling as he explained this, in fact the ogre seemed actually amused by the somewhat dangerous precarious situation.

Tark though, well, the young man was of course not a Viking. No, and he was not chanting a death song, nor was he banging upon his shield while hoping for a glorious end. However the young man was a realist and this current situation was not looking good. Oh no this new dilemma was not looking very good at all. Tark of course was no coward though, and his thoughts at this time were of his country, his friends and his family. Aye and also of course of the girl that he had intended one day to make his wife, she had with great difficulty been put aside in his thoughts over these past months. Why he had not even mentioned her name to Barak, but now, now as Tark neared home she was ever on his mind. Once all this intrigue, the revenge and the wrongs were for once and all righted and settled, he would then go to her. Yes, but then and only then, and not until then.

What would happen to them he wondered gloomily, his friends and family should the evil brothers prevail? Indeed, if these dangerous ruthless siblings became the cruel rulers of his beloved Krozakistan, what then would become of them all? Tark pondered very darkly upon this possible tragedy until Barak roused him from his troubled musings.

'Anyway my young bodyguard,' Barak continued with a wry smile. 'These horse thieves, perhaps they might have just come here to this place, to surrender for their past sins. In which case my lad, then we will of course be merciful. I am not, you must all understand a man without compassion for the down trodden.' Barak, with these s misplaced words of comfort said rode off slightly ahead of his company toward the advancing Mongol horde. Oh and all the while the great ogre still had with him a grim and resolute smile upon his fierce tattooed face.

Now as ever and not wishing to miss out on anything Ragnor urged on his horse, he was of course followed by the now small group of brave warriors who still drummed away upon their shields. Slowly both factions trotted on towards each other till at length the fearsome warriors from both sides of the argument stood only yards apart on the cold north eastern steppes.

Barak had behind him less than thirty good men, a halfling a drunken German and of course the now very worried looking Tark. But to look at Barak, well you would have thought the ogre had every legion of Rome standing at his broad tattooed back.

A thousand fierce faces with sparse beards and almond shaped eyes all focused upon the giant and of course his strange mix of very large very hairy companions.

And as for the Mongols well these vicious looking little horsemen were all armed up to their mostly black and uneven teeth. Each man there carried with him several curved swords apiece, a selection of daggers and longbows as well as small rounded shields of hardened hide and studded with small sharp metal spikes. Also these riders all wore about them heavy padded fleece jerkins and long coats atop thick studded leather tunics. Each and every man of this large company of riders wore a thick fur hat with long ear flaps. While, their long braided hair reached down to their chest and was intertwined with strips of leather. Obviously these small hardy men were well adapted for the hostile weather of the deserts the plains and the tundras of their birth. The Mongols each sat atop small tough steppes ponies, these were hardy animals which could trot on tirelessly all day and all night if needs be, aye then fight a battle at the end of it. To the fore and to the centre of the group of horsemen there sat an unsmiling weather beaten man with a long forked moustache.

Tark as it happened had not been far off at all with his guesswork as to the numbers of these fierce little horsemen. As there stood now before them were perhaps some thousand or so riders, but not a man less than that. The man with the forked moustache had skin like dry yellowed parchment and he was flanked either side by what were his two scowling arrogant looking sons. It was he who was the Ruler of these men. He was the Khan, a godlike figure to these tough nomadic Mongol warriors.

Barak obviously undaunted by this show of force sat silently upon his huge gelding; the ogre was saying nothing at all at this point in time. No Instead the wily giant, well he chose to wait for the Mongols to open up the morning's topic of conversation.

Ragnor at this point raised a hand and signalled for his men to cease their drumming so spoken words could be heard.

'You are the slayer, you are Barak,' one of the Khan's sons said almost accusingly and in the language of the Krozaky.

Barak stared down uncaringly unblinkingly at the small sparse bearded young man. Then and after a pause of a moment or two the giant decided to answer the question put to him.

'Yes, yes, I am he, I am Barak,' the ogre replied simply and saying not another word after declaring that.

The young man's dark eyes narrowed upon hearing this.

'Then I am Taras, here is my brother Taachi and here is my father, the great Lord of the plains and the steppes.' Now it was the young man who paused just a moment for affect before once again continuing to speak. 'Here is my father, who is the high Lord Temudgin, ruler of all you see about you.' The young man said this proudly whilst bowing his head politely in respect to his father as he did so.

346

Barak also afforded the Khan a slight if not obvious nod of respect this was at once most cordially returned.

'Why, why are you here in this place Barak?' Taras asked after some thought for the correct wording.

Taras spoke the language of the Krozaky people, but this only after some slow deliberation and even then he spoke it with some difficulty.

Barak shrugged as he looked skyward toward the heavens then directly at the young somewhat arrogant Mongol.

'I need explain nothing, other than this,' the ogre replied. 'I go where I will boy and I take what I want, when I want it. Aye and this, well this I do even more so if it is mine to take in the first place,' the giant said icily.

Barak though, well the ogre now answered this statement back to the young man in perfect Mongol and not in his native tongue. 'The great Khan Temudgin! oh well oh well, I must say that I am most impressed,' Barak said with a slight smirk.

Taras while being mightily impressed with Barak's fluency in the Mongol tongue was less impressed with the giant's disrespectful attitude.

'You speak our tongue, how so?' Taras demanded. Apparently now the young man was a little put out as he would no longer be needed to handle any further negotiations. His sense of importance had so it would seem, now simply just vanished.

'What does he say to them Tark?' Ragnor asked with a worried look about his hairy face.

Death of course did not bother Ragnor, and here was as good a place to die as any he supposed. Still though, well he would of liked to have owned a tavern for at least a little while before he was a dead thing and off to sit in the great halls of Valhalla.

'For whatever it was Barak said, well that one there does not look too happy about it,' Ragnor continued nodding his head towards a scowling sour faced Taras.

'I know not Ragnor, Barak he speaks to them now in the way of the horse stealing Mongols, it is a savage and most primitive tongue,' Tark replied with more than a little amount of disdain.

'Are they happy do you think Ragnor? For we are well outnumbered here,' Loki said as he urged his horse alongside that of his chief.

Ragnor looked upward to the cold grey skies above as he blew through his cracked and dry lips.

'Well, well I was certainly right to promote you Loki, for you can at least count,' the chieftain said with a hint of sarcasm.

Horst freshly awoken by the drumming of the Vikings' shields had also made an astute observation.

'I wonder what these little horsemen drink? It must be strong stuff for them to have such a twisted agonized look about them.' Horst slurred out these words as he wakened from his drunken slumber and trotted his mule forward a pace or two. Horst's humour as ever broke the tension and brought at least a chuckle to the band of grim faced warriors. 'Anyway, if I am to die on this very day in the middle of nowhere, then I wish they would get it over with. I tell you Ragnor I am freezing here sitting aboard this stubborn bad tempered mule,' the German complained bitterly. Once again the drunken Horst's words brought another chuckle to all within earshot.

'You speak in the tongue of the Mongol people Barak and you speak it well, how is this so?' the other brother, Taachi, asked of the giant.

Barak made no answer, but instead the ogre glanced down at the still silent and inscrutable looking Khan as he sat there upon his small but sturdy pony.

'Know you this Barak we have been paid to kill you, kill you then cut off your head as a trophy,' Taras said in a most matter of fact and at least an honest fashion.

Of the two arrogant looking brothers Barak had already decided that he much preferred Taachi.

Now the giant gave a low and barely audible curse at Taras's bold statement. This boy of Temudgin's had little or no respect, and he obviously needed some education as to the way of things.

And this being so, well then education was of course just what he would have.

'Paid, paid by whom you snot nosed little whelp?' Barak demanded while shifting his weight about in his high backed saddle.

Taras of a sudden took a slight shock at the giant's hostile attitude and lost the use of his tongue. Thus becoming mute and being unable to answer Barak's blunt question it was his brother who spoke up.

'It was the usurpers, the despots that would take over your city and your kingdom from you, it was they who put up the gold,' put in Taachi a little smugly.

Perhaps, just perhaps, Taachi was just as obnoxious as his brother thought Barak to himself. Now the glowering giant affixed the young Mongol prince Taachi with a cold and an icy glare. Indeed, the slayer was not at all sure he liked this little man's arrogant cocky attitude. In fact the giant had now decided he did not like any of the small slanty eyed brothers one little bit. Still, the ogre had also decided he would do his best to hold his rising temper, well, at least for now anyway.

'Tell me this boys,' Barak purposefully emphasised the word "boys". 'Since when did the proud nomads of the windswept steppes take pay from those, who they themselves call usurpers and despots then?' the giant asked leaning forward in his saddle. 'Surely if you do indeed know these pick pockets for what they are, then why do you take pay from them?'

Barak had edged forward now a little upon his great snorting gelding, his big dog Thorn was at his side baring its great teeth at both of the brothers.

And as for these brothers, well, they were both silent now and not quite knowing how to answer the giant's straightforward defiant and of course well put question.

Barak turned about now to face the Mongol warlord, as he glared down at him from his huge warhorse.

'Perhaps, I was wrong to have thought so highly of you in the past Temudgin.' Barak had said this while urging his huge angry looking horse on a few more steps.

Both Taras and Taachi were bemused on hearing this as they failed to see the significance of Barak's words, words that were addressed so boldly and so uncaringly to their illustrious father.

Still the great Khan of the steppes remained silent as he looked on apparently unconcerned at what was being said about him.

'We were promised by the envoy of the brothers much money and much land. All of this we would receive if we could halt you here before you ever reached the city gates.' Taras said this regaining his powers of speech. Oh and also after a little while of thinking and pondering over the present very unusual situation.

Much of the young man's cocky confidence though had left him now, in fact it would be truthful to say that he felt most uncomfortable with the giant's ever increasing closeness. When if ever he wondered to himself was his father going to speak up and say something to this fearsome looking ogre.

'Tell me more boy, say on,' Barak said with a grim and unnerving smile. After a short while Taras managed to enlighten the giant further.

'Your head, er, er, it is to be placed upon a tall pole in the town square,' Taras replied more than a little uneasily. His nerve it would seem was now leaving him, still to his credit he said on. 'This loss of your head would be intended as a message to your followers and to your people that your day is now done.' Taras said at long length, but indeed this was a most hard and difficult thing to say to the glowering giant who edged his big horse ever nearer. For now the young man's mouth had gone dry and to his shame the fear inside him was ever growing. Also the young Mongol suddenly realised for perhaps the first time on that chill morning. Not one of the big red bearded men sitting atop their horses opposite him appeared to respect the superior numbers of the Mongol horde. Indeed these warriors looked most uncaring and undaunted by the possibility of almost certain bloodshed.

Aye and all of these red bearded men were big, oh yes, yes these ferocious looking warriors were all very big. The pale blue eyes of these riders had about them the look of men used to dealing with death, and they were obviously unafraid. Oh and what on earth was the huge green thing sitting atop a camel, the young Mongol next suddenly wondered to himself with an element of dread.

Barak once again moved the gelding forward another few more steps. This the slayer did, till he towered over Taras the elder of the two brothers. Of a sudden the ogre leant down from his high backed saddle so his vodka breath almost intoxicated the arrogant youth. Now, it was time for Barak to have his say and of course as always and ever the ogre would have it.

'For one thing boy, it is not the brothers' land to give away to the likes of you, or anyone else for that matter,' Barak rumbled. 'It is my land, mine and the land of the people of Krozakistan, do you understand me, boy? the giant snarled. 'Oh and furthermore boy, if you think you can take my big bald head from my thick neck, when thousands of better men before you could not,' Barak sneered. 'Well then boy, I think you must be setting about trying to do this task, aye and try now for I weary of the sound of your squeaky girly voice,' Barak challenged angrily. 'Perhaps then boy, let us see whose head it is topples first into the sand and is placed upon a pole for fools to stare up at.'

Now at such close quarters to the great giant, Taras, who was truly a proud and brave warrior was struck totally speechless once again. Well indeed did the hitherto arrogant youth feel even his fiery blood run just as cold as ice water. Now the young Mongol prince was unable to speak, he was unable to give any sort of answer to the angry giant.

It was now at long last, seeing his son might be in danger of losing his own head to the angry ogre, the long silent Khan suddenly at last spoke up.

'You look well big Barak, aye you look strong and just as fierce as you ever were. Aye and also I see that you have not changed in your attitude to life, or indeed death my large friend,' the Khan cackled. 'No, oh no, you have not changed at all over these many long years since last we met, big Barak. In all of these long and violent years of war and slaughter, you are still exactly as you have always and ever been, cold, unforgiving and uncaring.'

Barak grunted then gave a nod of thanks on hearing these most flattering and kindly words. Indeed the slayer thought briefly to himself those were perhaps some of the nicest things anyone had ever spoken to him.

With this said, the wily and wiry inscrutable Khan of the steppes pressed his pony forward toward Barak he was at this time still cackling away to himself. Next, the Lord of the steppes held up his outstretched hand toward the giant in friendship. It was now the big Barak smiled down at the Khan as he shook the small but strong hand warmly.

Once again it was a smiling Khan that addressed the giant slayer.

'Try not to change big Barak, for there are so few of us left now, so few stubborn uncompromising men in this already ever changing and most treacherous world. ' The great Khan said this softly with a crooked but friendly smile. Next the lord of the Mongols turned to his sons and the thousand or so baffled horsemen waiting behind him for a command. The Khan stood up in his stirrups as he spoke out loud so those that could hear his words past on what he said to those horsemen behind them.

'It was I who taught big Barak to speak our language, the language of the steppes. And this, well this was many long years ago when my father traded with his father, the great and mighty King Bartok.' Of a sudden the Mongol clan leader the Khan of the steppes clutched at his horses mane as a sudden fierce gust of wind almost blew him away. 'This was long, long ago indeed before most of you were even born. Long before I even knew your mother,' the Khan next explained to his open mouthed sons. 'Barak as we all know went his way and lived his life for his own reasons as he lived it. Much later, some twenty or so years ago, we met once again we met upon a distant battlefield fighting for good coin. Happily though, we were fighting on the same side that day, and so of course we won. ' The great Khan of the steppes said this as he was released from the genuine handshake. 'My father and his father were good friends, as we are, and as we always will be.' Unusually the Khan, the great Lord of the steppes then gave one of his very rare almost toothless smiles. Perhaps strangely to his followers, he was, well so it now at least seemed to all about him, apparently a very happy man.

Both Taras and Taachi were much relieved, their stern expression disappeared and the brothers actually managed to force a smile of sorts. 'That is a very big horse father, indeed I think it is without any doubt the biggest horse I have ever seen.' Taras said this after a drink of water from his gourd, the youth's voice was more friendly, and less arrogant now.

With a chuckle the high Lord of the Mongols nodded in total agreement at this observation, next the Khan smiled then spoke to his son.

'That is because my boy, the great beast quite simply carries the biggest man upon its back that you ever will see.' Once again the Mongol Khan smiled warmly as he chuckled away in a most childlike fashion.

All of the riders sat behind Barak, though ready to fight and die sighed with an element of relief that the Mongol lord and the giant were apparently on some sort of friendly terms.

Had a battle been afoot, the Vikings to a man were ready and game for it, this even though the outcome would of course not be in their favour. Still, after all

351

these many leagues it would be nice to finish the quest and at least ride into Krozak. Smiling, the Khan nodded towards Barak's companions as he gave another slight grin.

'I must say this to you big Barak, you do ride out these days in the must ugliest of company,' the Khan said with another chuckle. Barak conceded, as the ogre supposed to himself that was a point even he could not argue with.

'True, aye this is all very true, but no doubt that is also what I think my ugly company are saying about you and your men, Temudgin,' Barak replied with a thin smile.

'Surely not big Barak, surely not.' The Khan said this while revealing what few broken and blackened teeth he had in his boney skull like head. 'Any way, you know what they say big Barak, handsome is as handsome does.' At that Barak put his head back as he roared out with laughter at the Lord Temudgin's words. And now on seeing this laughter all there knew no blood would be spilt here upon the cold windy steppes, well at least not on this day.

So the King and the Khan talked most cordially there upon the windswept steppes for some little while. Now it was the men talked about their past and their present as it now stood for both of them, oh and of course they talked also about their immediate future.

Temudgin was no fool, and not now and not ever had he been one. As the Mongol, well after all he was both a clever and a mighty warlord. Oh and by the by, he was a warlord who had with him today for company only a fraction of those who he could call upon if need be. And also the Khan, it must be said that he was indeed a very enlightened man. His well placed spies and his secret informants from within the city of Krozak, they played their part well and knew most if not all that went on in the capital. For months these spies had informed him there had been a guest within the palace for some time now.

This guest was a mandarin, oh and also apparently he was a dark sorcerer of some notoriety by all accounts. And as well as all this, the wizard was both a powerful one as well as an evil one at that. Apparently this dark sorcerer had been cast out, banished by his sacred brotherhood for his dark and demonic practices. So powerful was he that it had taken the combined powers of thirteen others of his kind from the circle of magic to drive him out from the golden city. So, and by ways and means unknown to anyone the wizard now lavished and lounged in the comfort of the palace by day. Whilst in the darkness and the still of night the sorcerer conjured and practiced his dark witchery in the tall west tower.

'Oh no, oh no, not wizards now,' the giant muttered, a little put out at this new information. 'You know I have always hated sneaky creepy wizards,' Barak growled out to no one in particular.

Next Barak gave out a long thoughtful sigh as this whole affair was becoming by the minute ever the more intriguing and ever the harder to follow.

Of a sudden and apparently for no reason the Lord Temudgin changed the subject from the goings on in the palace.

'Tell me this big Barak, aye tell me, do you still take pay from the Emperor of Rome?' The Khan asked this question as he groomed his sparse beard with his short grubby fingers.

'No, no I do not,' Barak answered straightaway and simply. 'No, no not any more, I am retired from warfare now you know Temudgin, well at least almost.'

Temudgin on hearing this somewhat ridiculous statement could not help but chuckle away to himself.

'Well that is good, oh yes, yes that is very good my overly large friend,' Temudgin replied with just the faintest trace of a crafty smile. 'So then you must enjoy your retirement big Barak, for you above all others I do think deserve it.' Barak now affixed the small Mongol chieftain with a blank stare.

'Then tell me, tell me my overly small friend, why do you ask this question Temudgin?'

Temudgin shrugged, the warlord next smiled then chuckled once again.

'I myself, well I am not yet retired Barak,' the Khan answered with a slight shrug of his shoulders. Barak shook his head now, this as if he could read the diminutive Khan's very thoughts.

'Oh, oh I see, well I do hope that you enjoy your war with Rome.' Barak said this knowingly as he glanced about him at the many different standards of the Mongol clans held high aloft behind Temudgin. There, held proudly skyward were the totems of all of the mighty clans. Oh yes, here were the clans of the boar, the bear and the wolf as many others from across the steppes and tundra. Aye and all of these as well as those of the snake and the eagle, these tribal totems were all there before him held proud and high for all to see.

Now the Khan bowed his head and gave a thin smile, as it so happened, he never could fool or deceive the giant. Rome was a fading power now, and Temudgin after all felt that he should be remembered for ever in history for something or other. So why not be remembered for bringing about the downfall of the Roman Empire, then with this once done, starting his own great dynasty.

Later, when at length Barak parted company with Temudgin it was as allies and their boyhood friendship was renewed. Barak though, he had declined any offer of Temudgin's company as the slayer made off toward the city gates. After all, the ogre had no wish to look like some sort of invading force riding upon what was after all his own city and his own people.

353

Temudgin though, well the Khan did however say one very strange thing to Barak as they parted company on that cold day upon the windswept plains. Of course the shrewd and cunning Khan knew only too well that Barak had forsaken all gods. And this as they, well at least so the giant had long felt, had long ago since forsaken him.

Only Tengri, the Mongol god of the skies and the wind had for some unknown reason ever been a friend to the giant in the past, and that of course was even without the giant's asking.

Temudgin before the final parting of two old friends had something that he felt must be said.

'On the day of your reckoning big Barak, that by the by my friend comes to you very soon, ask of Tengri, for he will not let you down, as for some unknown reason the god likes you.' Temudgin had said all of this as he turned his pony about then trotted off into the wind blown dust. Strangely though, these were words Barak would not take lightly, nor would the ogre forget them. Nor would he forget the parting words of the wizened and ancient Mongol shaman, a man who was as old as the very mountains themselves.

This ancient white haired witch doctor had broken from the ranks of unsmiling horseman and he had approached the giant as he was about to ride off.

'Fear not the shadow of the devil big, Barak,' the toothless old ancient had said to him. 'For you will see this shadow, aye and you will see it very soon, but fear not ogre for this shadow, he is a friend. '

With these words spoken the witch doctor then turned about and rejoined his fellows, thus leaving Barak to ponder quite bemused and baffled at this vague riddle left to him. But Barak though, well the slayer pondered upon this only briefly mind you, for there was still after all very much to do.

It was decided as they rode along that Tark would gallop on ahead and announce Barak's soon arrival at the garrison to the legion of the Black Guards. The gate by which they would enter was at the garrison itself, this of course was the headquarters of their elite legion. Now it was still the same old question rolling about in the giant's big bucket sized head. Would these slightly unhinged Black Guards receive him with open arms? Or would he be rejected as a deserter from their ranks and a traitor to his people? Would his subjects be singing and throwing garlands? Or would these same subjects be shouting insults and throwing stones? Well whatever it was to be, either way the slayer supposed he would not have to wait long now to find out the answer to this long awaited question.

Meanwhile, within the walls of the west tower, the brothers, whilst in the company of the mandarin sorcerer, stared fixedly into a rounded mirror that stood on tall ornate legs.

Whilst the three men stared and glared into this mirror there was also many curses flying here and there, as none of them were impressed.

'The dogs of the steppes and the desert have failed me, aye failed me, and this after taking payment for the task I set them. Aye the accursed Mongols have not slain Barak,' the elder brother said spitefully to his younger sibling. 'I swear these accursed unwashed nomads will all pay most dearly for this treachery,' he next declared in a total fury. However the wizard, well it must be said he looked not the least bit surprised by this turn of events.

'It is of no matter my young lords,' the sorcerer said with an uncaring gesture of his thin bony hands, skinny blue veined hands with long painted fingernails. This tiny and somewhat frail looking sorcerer was dressed in the very finest of eastern silks.

A long black expensive gown the wizard wore and this gown was encrusted with shiny sequins and even precious gems depicting the earth, the moon and the stars of the heavens. Also the wizard had upon his skull-like head a black silken cap with a long thin hood, this hood tapered down to his scrawny waist. Upon his tiny blue veined feet the wizard wore expensive slippers. These were also in black and were expertly stitched together and made of both silk and velvet. By his withered appearance the wizard was obviously an ancient decaying thing, a thing that had lived far longer than nature had ever intended him too. However, ancient or not this undead thing was not lost for words.

'Follow my instructions my young lords, obey me without question and all yet will be well,' the wizard promised while giving a little bow of his skull like head. 'As please believe, me we can make this great painted oaf bend and buckle and do our will, trust me.' Now with this said the dark wizard chuckled and cackled as he toyed with his long wispy snow white beard that reached down to his red waist sash.

Now it was that the elder brother motioned to speak but his words were waved casually and dismissively aside by the still sniggering sorcerer.

'My kind lords I am weary now, I am in need of some much deserved sleep, for I have conjured and I have plotted all night long, this all for your benefit. ' The sorcerer said these words with a yawn that revealed ancient blunted and blackened teeth. 'But I must say this to you both now though, I for one had no faith in the savage Mongol horde in the first place,' the wizard cackled somewhat triumphantly. 'Now, tell me my Lords can you remember me saying this to you both? It would be true to say the wizard asked this question somewhat smugly. 'For they these Mongols are a most fickle and a most untrustworthy breed, they are only savage and primitive barbarians after all. So I for one my young Lords, well, I expected no more from the likes of them. ' Oh and the wizard said this with a most spiteful hateful sneer.'

'No, no, you must trust now in the dark arts for your final success and salvation. Yes you must trust in dark evil magic for the power that is due very soon to you. Oh yes indeed you must trust in me, you must trust in the black magic of Master Fong. For know this my noble lords I most certainly will not fail or disappoint you. ' This the ancient sorcerer promised whilst holding his hands together before him. Then the wizard gave just the slightest of polite bows before taking his leave. Saying no more the wizard shuffled off with tiny steps as he vanished off into an ante chamber for some rest, this after no doubt another unsavoury night's work.

These unloved brothers were both tall lean things with little flesh upon their long bones, aye they were pale and decadent looking in the very extreme. After a short time spent in cursing the Mongols, the brothers also silently disappeared down a secret passageway. And this no doubt was to do some sinister plotting and scheming all of their own. Once all was accomplished here, and when Barak was at last a dead thing, then they would have no need of the dangerous wizard. Ah, but how to kill him was the thing that for now puzzled and perplexed them.

Meanwhile, Tark had arrived within the city walls and he sat now with the garrison commander of the Black Guard. Well he and some of his highest ranking and most trusted men of the elite legion. There were perhaps some dozen grim faced full bearded men sat about the long rectangular table.

The young warrior wore proudly about his neck a foot long fang, a trophy from the female mountain lion. Barak had given this to him to wear just before Tark had set off for the garrison as after all up on that freezing mountain the young man had earned it. As said the halfling Borz wore the other one, aye and the great green creature wore the fang just as proudly.

'You say to me that we should welcome the long absent Barak back into our much troubled land Tark?' And this was the question the big burly garrison commander asked, or rather demanded gruffly. The elite company of high ranking officers were sitting now in a small tavern, it was a tavern that was owned and run by the Black Guards themselves.

This tavern was a private comfortable place where of course none but the soldiers of the Black Guard could drink and socialize therein. And here and now that was more or less what these men were doing, drinking and talking in an off the record sort of manner. Here at this particular moment there were no scribes or recorders, only the elite and the most high ranking soldiers of the Black Guard were present.

Tark gave a quick positive nod in answer to the big burly but somewhat over-weight garrison commander's blunt question.

'Aye, Barak is my Lord, he is my King, thus being so then he is of course also your Lord and King, Commander Gortak. '

On hearing this, the big garrison commander gave a grunt of disapproval at the young man's somewhat carefree and brash words.

Tark was it seemed to the commander, becoming just a little bit too big for his big black and very dusty boots.

Commander Gortak paused for a moment before speaking, and this as he detected a big change in the young man's attitude and bearing.

'I seem to remember Tark that when you left this place you were perhaps not so keen on Barak. In fact if my memory stands up correctly, well, you wanted to cut out his cruel black heart. Oh yes, these were your very words I seem to recall you saying young Tark.' The big and blustery commander said this as he leaned across the long oblong table towards Tark who sat opposite him. Now the big commander with an obvious intent to intimidate, he affixed the young warrior with a cold and steely stare with his dark pure blood Krozaky eyes. However though, most surprisingly to the big bullish commander, this was a cold stare which was unflinchingly and perhaps just as icily returned.

Oh aye this show of nerve was much to the shock as well as the surprise of the big gruff Commander Gortak. Most men of the Black Guard lowered their turbaned heads in a most subservient fashion when the commander affixed them with one his icy glares. Tark though however, well he was by now used to staring into much more dangerous, much more frightening eyes. So of course the young man was not impressed, nor was he feared in any way whatsoever by the commander's glare. And also as being an officially appointed body guard well Tark felt it now his duty to protect his king in words if not by action.

'Barak's heart is neither black, nor is it cruel Commander Gortak. I will pledge my life upon that,' the young man answered back both defensively and defiantly.

For now at least the collection of high ranking veteran Black Guards sat silent and impassive, they were all unwilling to pass any comment at this point in the conversation. Aye it was yet a little early in the day for any immediate judgment, as this after all was only little more than an informative debate. Commander Gortak, their big grizzled but much trusted, commander wanted to know the whys and the wherefores of everything concerning Barak. Oh yes, and the commander also wanted to know just who and how many warriors rode along with him.

After all, the way things were at the moment and with the poisonous words that had been spread about in the city, the kingdom, aye and even amongst the legions. Why this whole very tricky affair could actually provoke an all out civil war if it was not handled correctly. While the Black Guards were pledged to be loyal to the king as long as he in turn was loyal to the state and its people it had to be said the other many armed fractions were not so tied by honour, or perhaps foolishness. Cavalry regiments, foot soldiers, palace and city guards as well as the thousands of border outriders. All of these men could all turn against the elite ruling Black Guard. This should their decision be considered false or wrong or

357

badly judged in any way. And while the legion of the Black Guard were indeed the elite fighting force of the empire, of course not even they could handle such vast numbers of their counter parts, well not all at the same time anyway. It had long been reckoned that one Black Guard warrior was worth five lesser trained soldiers, but even so these men still could not prevail against such great odds if all went wrong. For now though this was all matterless, and several strong drinks of vodka later the debate over Barak still went on.

Tark ordered more refreshments as he pressed his case for support of his Lord Barak, the young warrior did this with the utmost vigour as it slipped into the mid-afternoon.

'By all the gods at once boy, I must say that you can certainly drink your share of the vodka now.' Gortak declared this loudly as Tark swallowed down yet another cup of vodka in a single gulp. 'You must have a lot of steppes sand in your throat to wash down or something,' the commander added with just a slight chuckle.

Tark smiled back broadly at the big commander before he spoke up and replied.

'You spend time with the Lord Barak as I have done these past months and you also would drink more than you ever thought possible. I swear to you all now about this table the man can smoke his strong weed and drink his vodka, then still fight and slay anyone or anything that lives and breathes on this very earth of ours.'

With a grunt the big burly commander leant back casually into his chair as he stroked his thick black beard, a beard that was tinged with grey.

As the commander stroked his ample beard he of course could not help but notice the huge fang that hung about the young man's broad neck. But as yet the commander said nothing. Still he pondered a little enviously, as one of those would look most impressive about his own ample neck the commander silently thought to himself. Meanwhile the innkeeper's assistant threw more logs onto a nearby fire then went into the kitchen to bring more drink for this collection of esteemed Black Guards.

'You do think a lot of Barak, don't you boy?' the commander asked, red wine running down his grey black beard. Truth said the big commander often turned a little nasty when drinking vodka so now quite wisely he had switched to the wine these last few rounds of drinks. Once, only months ago the Commander could have drank the young man very quickly under the table, but not now, no not now.

It was plainly obvious to all the young warrior had changed a great deal in these past hard months, aye and he had changed for the better and not for the worse.

Tark gave a nod of agreement to Gortak's question then he looked about him at the other high ranking Krozaky officers. Half of them now looked bleary eyed and three parts drunk Tark thought smugly to himself. For it was he, the young man who had set the pace to which the drinks had arrived at the long table. Aye and it was he also who had bought and ordered the drinks with coin given him by the giant. Barak to his credit had not sent him off to this meeting as some sort of a pauper, bereft of coinage. Of a sudden after a while of silence and contemplation Commander Gortak leant across the table and spoke in a hushed voice to Tark.

'Barak, then you think my boy, he should be accepted as our ruler? You think Barak should be our Lord and Master?' Gortak asked plainly. Tark took another deep drink then nodded in reply before speaking out aloud.

'Aye, aye I do, after all, the great slayer wears the double-headed eagle ring of kingship upon his right forefinger. This ring was given him by his own father, the great king Bartok, so aye, I do say Barak is our King at day's end.'

Tark was gaining in confidence now so he swallowed down another mouthful of strong undiluted vodka then refilled his cup yet again.

'Barak is my King, thus being so then as I have said before he is also your King,' Tark stated once again, both plainly and proudly.

At once there were mutterings from the Black Guard hierarchy, mutterings that were both for and against the words the young Tark had just so boldly and bravely spoken.

Commander Gortak smiled to himself smugly and proudly; now once again the big man leaned back in his chair. This big commander, well he also smoked the weed, but mind you not in the huge quantities that Barak smoked the mind numbing substance. Now the commander lit up his pipe. This was a long clay pipe most similar to Barak's favourite pipe which had been broken earlier in their mission.

As the big commander puffed out his first most relaxing smoke clouds Tark once again spoke up.

'We are all here bound to Barak by honour, at least let him speak to you then you will see for yourselves what sort of man the great slayer is.' Tark said, this while looking each man about him straight into their dark, somewhat suspicious eyes. Before Tark had left this place almost a year ago now he would not have presumed himself worthy to chance such a solid stare. The young man had though in such a relative short time, a time that seemed like an age, changed very much.

Now, thanks to the confidence given to him by his Lord Barak, well Tark supposed that he dared say and do almost anything.

Commander Gortak gave a nod of somewhat grudging agreement, then he took another drink of his wine followed by a puff upon his pipe before speaking.

'Thank you Tark for your assessment of the current situation. However though as it happens, well, we here in this room, we are quite learned, and so we need no such history lesson. Do you understand me my boy?' the commander next asked firmly.

Tark did not reply in voice, but the young man instead gave a grudging nod of acknowledgment. With this done the big commander said on.

'Now, now tell me lad, how many men ride alongside Barak? ' Commander Gortak asked plainly as he fingered an ancient dark scar that ran across his forehead to disappear under his black turbaned head.

Tark did not delay or dally with his reply.

'Less than thirty souls, these are Norsemen from the frozen far north. Believe me these are good men, big bold brave men. I like them all, aye each and every one of them I would trust with my life. And so would you, and so will you when you soon meet with them, you have my word upon it. Oh and also as well as these most able warriors, there rides with our king a most amusing German drunkard who has but one leg.' Now the big commander as well as everyone else sat about the table at this particular time were becoming ever more enthralled by Tark's tale. So knowing their interests were aroused the young man went on with his entertaining but factual story.

'But perhaps our strangest member in our group is a huge green troll creature. Borz, for so he or it, is called now, is perhaps to most an unsavoury looking creature. Still though putting his none too pretty looks aside he is nevertheless a most noble thing. Our Lord Barak saved him from a cruel beating in a market square. '

Commander Gortak somewhat astounded on hearing this sucked upon his pipe and drank his wine. With a shake of his much bemused head the commander next raised his bushy eyebrows in surprise at this somewhat strange revelation.

'A troll, a troll, tell me boy why would anyone on this earth want to save a troll? ' The commander asked this question looking once again more than a little bemused. 'These things are not human after all are they?' he declared between puffs of smoke. 'Why, these creatures are surely nothing more but wild slimy vicious beasts, well, at least so I have heard. Though Tark, I must both admit and confess I myself have never before seen one of these vicious and unholy beasts.'

Tark gave a nod followed by a shrug in only part agreement at the commander's sharp and in his opinion unkind words. For in all truth the young man both liked and respected the halfling. As after all said and done the big green creature had saved his life back there upon the frozen mountain in the fray with the lions.

Young Tark had learnt much from Barak, the young man was now both wily and cunning, aye and he would not be lost for words here in this company, not today or any other day come to that.

'On the day this troll was rescued, well I to my eternal shame tried to persuade my Lord Barak not to interfere in the affair, but our king, well he would have none of it,' Tark went on. 'Three men were set upon the troll, who is in all truth only a halfling and not a pure blood monster. ' Gortak listened now most intently as did the rest of the Black Guard elders to Tark's tale. 'This beast was chained heavily whilst tethered to a stout pole, this pole was in turn set firmly into the cobbles of a market square. This was a market square by the way that lay near the cold northern sea where it merges with the Baltic. '

Now all about there was complete and utter silence, while all there waited with great interest for the rest of this tale.

'My Lord Barak, well I suppose he simply just did not like what he saw there. So our King simply stepped boldly forward and threw the ringleader of the band of gypsies who taunted the creature toward the halfling. However, this our Lord did only after relieving the fool of his drink of course.' Several of these high ranking generals chuckled upon hearing this, none more than commander Gortak. Tark knowing full well he had the floor spoke on.

'At once the fellow, who was a gypsy by the way, was dispatched by the creature. Aye and then thrown with ease into the hitherto hostile crowd just for good measure.'

'Thrown?' Commander Gortak queried, a little bemused by these events.

'Aye, thrown, commander, just as easily as a child's doll, you must understand this creature has great strength' All about the elite of the guard looked most impressed. 'I, for my part, well I took it upon myself to slay the other two cowardly rogues. You must understand Commander Gortak I am now King Barak's official bodyguard.' Tark had said this very proudly. Still though the young man said this without bragging, boasting or lying, he was quite simply telling the truth. Why though a man such as Barak needed a bodyguard was something of a mystery, still commander Gortak said nothing about that particular subject.

Instead the commander merely gave a grunt of satisfaction followed by a nod of approval on hearing these somewhat strange events. Moments later there was also even a faint smile of pride as to Tark's actions while Commander Gortak congratulated Tark at becoming Barak's bodyguard.

'Then you did well my boy, and I am most proud of you, but now you must tell me this. What of the others of our brotherhood, the men of the Black Guard, what of those who went with you on this long dangerous trek. Tell me Tark, what of those who ventured with you to the land of the Britons?' the Commander asked bluntly. 'For you say now yourself that you have only for company the Norsemen, a one legged German and a halfling creature at your side. So tell me lad, tell me what then of your brothers-in-arms?' the Commander pressed a little urgently.

'For unless my memory fails me, there were a hundred of our warriors dispatched on this somewhat dubious mission.' Commander Gortak said this as he puffed upon his pipe whilst once again he leant across the long rectangular table.

Tark looked about him at the stern unforgiving unsmiling faces of his so called betters and superiors, then, the young man replied and he replied cleverly.

'I can say only this and say this alone, my comrades, my brothers-in-arms all died quick, they all died well commander,' Tark answered solemnly but honestly. 'But please commander, please for now press me no further at this moment in time as to their demise. Recalling it will bring me only sorrow and distract me from what must be said.' Tark it now seemed had spent too much time with Barak as now the young man could actually deceive without lying.

Without any hesitation the stern faced Commander gave a grunt of understanding, as of course he too had lost friends and comrades as a young man. And also just like Tark, it was some time before he could talk in any sort of detail about their fate.

Of a sudden the commander rose to his black booted feet, Gortak was a big man, much taller than Tark. Also the commander was also heavy set with a scarred tanned face and a big broken bent nose. Still while the commander's face might not have been at all pretty, well it did have that certain brutish honest look about it.

'Good enough.' the commander growled out as all about him, Tark included, also rose to their feet. 'Now my boy you must go, go and bring your King here to this place of the Black Guard, young Tark. And then once on meeting with this notorious living legend of yours we can perhaps decide a course of action to follow.' With this said the commander sighed wearily as he uttered out a low curse to himself before continuing. 'The Black Guards since time remembered have never betrayed their Lord; let us all hope this is a practice that is not broken. '

At the far end of the long table there were mumbled mutterings from several of the Black Guard hierarchy and veterans. Tark in all truth did not quite catch what these men were saying in secret to each other, but either way the young man was not impressed. Whispering, mutterings and behind the hand comments, these were actions that always smacked of treason and deceit. Aye and this also was something Barak had taught him to be wary of in the short time they had spent together.

'Just what do you mean by that hidden and whispered statement?' the young man bristled angrily. Tark put this straightforward question to the grizzled old wall commander, Commander Xarl. For it was he, it was this unsmiling commander who seemed the most set against the return of Barak. Commander

Xarl was a huge grey bearded man, in fact he was almost as big as Gortak. However, huge or not, he was much taken aback by Tark's aggressive stance and no nonsense attitude. So after stamping his feet in a most threatening manner Xarl calmed of a sudden and stood now speechless, unable to reply.

Tark however was not similarly afflicted no indeed he was far from it. 'Know you this I will not lead my Lord Barak into some sort of a coward's trap, if that's what you think. And this plotted by you commander Xarl, or anyone else here in this room,' the young man said defiantly.

Now the big grey bearded commander stood back in total shock at the young man's harsh words spoken so sharply, aye and this to his betters and to his peers. Indeed, the grey bearded Xarl glanced toward the garrison commander to help him out from this verbal attack. Somewhat reluctantly commander Gortak felt obliged to, but still despite the disrespect given to the commander he could see Tark's point. But then on the other hand Gortak could also see commander Xarl's reason for being somewhat anxious and a little suspicious of these recent happenings. On top of all that, these men gathered here were time served officers, generals, commanders and such, all with good reputations. No, Tark he supposed must be rebuked aye, he must be put firmly in his place. It was quite obvious to Commander Gortak the young man had recently spent far too much time in bad company.

'Cowards? Cowards? You would dare say that word here boy, in this place?' Commander Gortak asked much offended and taken aback at the young warrior's ferocious loyalty to Barak.

Gortak you must understand was not only the garrison commander and the most feared man in the legion of the Black Guards he was also Tark's blood uncle. Gortak's older sister had been Tark's mother. Since her death some years ago and the demise of Tark's father it was he who had brought Tark up and this as more or less his own son. But now, now all of a sudden it appeared he played second fiddle to a man who after all was a complete stranger, aye and him a king or not. And this of course was something that did not sit well with the big blustery commander, and as it happened, well things were about to get even worse.

'Aye, I would say that, and I would say that to you all right here and right now standing about this table,' a most agitated Tark continued in quite a rage. 'For if you do mean any kind of treachery to your King and mine, then stand you all well back from the slayer, use your longbows or your crossbows. For in fair combat, why the man would kill each all and everyone here in this room in a single go, aye and that with you all fighting together. Aye and the Lord Barak, he would do this without so much as raising a sweat on such as you. Anyway, at day's end what fights, what battles and epic wars have any of you here ever fought?' Tark at once demanded this while swallowing down another mouthful of vodka. 'Border skirmishes with worthless horse thieves and no more than that,' he said with a sneer followed by a defiant snarl.

'Not a war not a battle have you ever been in, why none of you here have seen what I have seen, nor do you know what I know.'

Now though the proud blustering Gortak found his nephew's words most hurtful and very disturbing, as did the other grumbling mumbling veterans, nevertheless they stood there in an angry subdued silence while Tark continued with his most passionate defence of his king and mentor.

'And when you use your longbows as you must to gain victory, then slay me as well for I will die hacking and slicing at the side of my Lord and King,' the young man said most passionately. 'Know you all this, aye and know it now, we of the Viking brotherhood, for I am now one of their number, we slew a boatful of pirates. These were pirates who were paid for from this very place, aye and we lost not but one man in the doing of it. And then much later on in our journey, we were again attacked, this but only days ago, attacked by men I met on my way to the island of the Britons. Oh and these men, these men were also paid by your masters, who, to my eternal shame were once mine. But yet again we prevailed we killed them all, and once again we lost not one man, this although these bandits were almost double our number.

'The barbarians, as you choose to call them fell one by one to the jaws of the wolf and the great lions of the mountains. Aye these creatures killed the Vikings, these beasts or the very hostile elements themselves. My Lord and your Lord, he now wears two great fangs about his neck from these dead beasts. One Barak killed with his bare hands, he snapped its neck as a lesser man might kill a rabbit, the other, well, the slayer strangled the creature. Barak gave me this tooth from the female beast as a gift, a trophy for helping him, the halfling Borz wears the other.'

Tark went on and he did neither stop nor did he falter with his honest tale. And all this while the generals the commanders and the respected veterans of the Black Guard stood open mouthed as they listened on in silent awe.

'Know you all this, also the Mongols of the steppes greeted us here on our approach this very morning.' On hearing this each and every one of the high ranking Black Guard stood about that long table looked most shocked and surprised at this new revelation.

'Aye and these were a thousand strong, the horsemen were led by the cruel, most ruthless Khan Temudgin. I tell you all now, I thought we were all to die there and then,' Tark hissed out. 'But no, no the horde offered the Lord Barak their swords should he be in need of them. Also know you all this, the Khan has a mighty army now, a hundred times bigger than that which we met before on this day.' On hearing this even the elitist hierarchy of the Black Guard had a worried look about them that they could not disguise. While they were silent though, Tark was not, he went on with his tale.

'Why, the Khan has united every tribe from the steppes and the deserts to ride behind him, this as he means to march upon Rome. Apparently, so Barak tells me, Temudgin means to make his place in history before he dies.' Tark next paused for a moment or two before continuing. 'But I tell you all here now, Temudgin would have just as soon rode here to this place to make war and glory. Barak thanked the Mongols but declined their offer as our king would not have their swords turned against his own people. Also know you this, these Mongols also once again were paid and bribed from this very place by the agents of the corrupt brothers.'

Now there were very worried mutterings at this point from the Black Guard veterans. Oh and also this most unexpected information caused commander Gortak to flush red with embarrassment and shame, for truthfully he knew nothing at all of this dark deceit.

Tark though was not yet finished with his so called superiors and betters, aye and he had more harsh truths to say.

'If any of you here think to kill him, or the men that ride along with him then you should think again,' the young warrior advised. 'Once, I had thought the warriors of the Black Guard legion were the proudest and the best of all, now though I am not so sure.' Tark paused as he ran his dark angry eyes over each and every one in the room of the tavern, then the young man spoke up again. 'But when I look at you all now before me, I must say that I am most disappointed. '

On hearing this, the big burly commander did not fume as was the norm for him, nor did he bluster, or did he even threaten to punish and discipline the young soldier. No, far from it, in fact commander Gortak was almost brought to tears of emotion by the young man's fierce loyalty. Aye and this was a loyalty not only to Barak but also a loyalty to a company of men Tark had known only a short time. But then again in that short time, well these men truly did have many an adventure by the sounds of it. Indeed it must be said Commander Gortak was greatly impressed.

'Say no more Tark, your loyalty to Barak and the Norsemen is most commendable.' Commander Gortak said this knowing full well he might upset the other members at this informal meeting. But in all honesty after these revelations of bribery, treachery and corruption Gortak cared very little at this point who he might offend. 'Let us not fall out with each other over this matter Tark,' the commander said taking a sip of his red wine. 'Bring your King here to this place we will meet and talk honestly amongst ourselves. Treachery, well this after all, it is not our way. Also I do believe that we made a grave mistake by dishonouring ourselves and agreeing to send our men to the land of the Britons. For, at day's end I do think we had no right to do this most doubtful and dubious deed.' Gortak said this more sadly than grudgingly.

Tark on hearing these most honest and even humble words from his uncle almost at once calmed himself. And so next and after but a moment to contemplate, the young man next gave a courteous nod to all at the table then with a twirl of his black cloak was off and away.

'Farewell my uncle, I will return within the hour with our King,' Tark shouted back over his shoulder.

At once the Commander politely returned the nod even if it was to Tark's back then he gave just the slightest hint of a proud smile.

'He is just like his mother, my sister was ever fiery, aye she was also the most obstinate woman in all things.' The commander said this as he shouted out for another round of drinks. Now though the next drink he would have though would not be red wine. Oh no it would be a very big vodka, this as the commander felt at this particular time he more than needed it.

Chapter Twenty-Two

And so, within the hour, just as Tark had promised the small band of warriors he had endured so much with at last stood at the great gates of Krozakistan. Huge elephants, three to each door heaved and struggled pulling on massive chains that were bolted on to the equally massive gates. Great winches at the same time strained and turned as well oiled cogs slowly but most surely caused the iron and bronze six foot thick ancient gates to creak open. Of a sudden there was dying daylight between the huge ancient gates, gates which had never been broken or breached in warfare.

Barak, who was of course never a shy sort of retiring man galloped forward. At this time the great slayer was alone and a little ahead of the rest of his party. Barak once inside the great gates twirled about on his great steed sending sand flying all about him. As ever and always the great giant, well he knew only too well how to make the most spectacular and most dramatic of entrances. In many ways the great flamboyant ogre was, he supposed to himself, just like some sort of entertainer. There were perhaps at that time some two hundred hand picked stern faced men of the legion standing at attention in two neat rows to receive their guests. Also these men were the biggest members of the Black Guards in the legion, each and every one of them were hand picked exactly for that very reason. Oh aye and it goes without saying that these men were of course all armed to the very back teeth. Just as also it goes without saying that the warriors were clad totally in their military black uniforms with black girdles and polished black boots. Each and every one of them wore a black turban with his black face veil pulled and tied firmly just under their dark piercing eyes. It must be said that these men looked both very impressive and also very deadly. Barak smiled proudly to himself as he cast his black eyes over these tall proud warriors who were after all his own personal guard. Well that was of course unless these men all wanted to kill him, then put his big bald head upon a high pole like so many others apparently felt they should. Now a few moments later the others of the giant's company trotted inside the huge ancient gates as they divided themselves and moved in even numbers to Barak's left and right flank. Somewhat unsettled the big dog Thorn looked about at the black clad men as it bared its teeth in a most threatening manner whilst moving nearer to the front side of its master's huge horse.

Commander Gortak stood to the fore of his Black Guard. He was accompanied by those who had earlier listened to Tark's blustering's in the garrison tavern. From behind this illustrious but somewhat unsteady group of esteemed blackguard veterans there came a low gasp from the rank and file as Barak dismounted his huge horse and approached the commander who was only a few yards away.

Gortak was a big man, no, he was a very big man, one of the biggest men if not the biggest in the whole legion. But in the here and now standing there against Barak, well, the commander looked like little more than a podgy little boy.

Commander Gortak was so taken aback by the fearsome impressive giant that he could not even find the words to speak. At once the commander lowered his gaze as the giant slayer approached him with great strides. Next the commander bowed his turbaned head in total servitude. All of these long years the commander had silently wondered to himself about Barak, he had wondered if they would ever meet. Aye and then if by chance he ever did meet Barak, how would he react to his truant but legendary king. Well, now the myth, the legend stood not a yard away from him, and so he had his long awaited answer. Commander Gortak was much awe struck, and also he was much impressed by the legendary slayer. Barak was in all truth it must be said even far bigger and bolder and much more fearsome in his appearance than the commander could have ever imagined him to be. True it was that his young nephew had painted a shocking, most frightening picture of Barak. However, that description had fallen short in every aspect, aye and it had fallen short by a very long way at that. Those of the rank and file since being children had all heard blood curdling tales of Barak's fame and description; they likewise were most impressed

Barak looked about him with great interest and also great pride at every detail of the ancient garrison. This place was just as he remembered it to be, oh aye, the ogre thought proudly to himself, the garrison was still very impressive to say the least.

Rows of well kept well stocked stables were to his right, whilst to his left were the billets, barracks and villas for the rank and file of the Black Guard. Married men with families, these all had their own well kept tidy villas. Meanwhile the single men lodged themselves in the clean very spacious soldier's quarters. After all these were the elite soldiers of the Krozak army, being so they quite deservedly lived accordingly.

There was a long silence, and then Barak finally announced himself as he spoke out both clearly and loudly to what was after all his own legion.

'By our law, the law of the Krozak people, my people and of course your people, even a King can be challenged if he is thought in any way at all to be unfit and unworthy to rule the Kingdom.' Barak with this said then paused for a moment as he looked about him into the ranks of the tall black clad warriors; then the slayer spoke on again.

'The King he can be challenged in open combat man to man, this by beggar, thief, knight or even a so called nobleman. Whatever, these noblemen are yet unknown to me,' Barak said this with a sarcastic sneer. In Barak's long held opinion all of the many titled lords and ladies he ever met weren't really up to very much. In fact it was well known among his close friends that Barak himself would sooner while away his hours with a dim witted farm hand, an uneducated labourer or even a friendly bar wench. Well in truth perhaps the slayer, given the choice, would have more time for the bar wench.

Anyway after a pause of perhaps a moment or two the great ogre and slayer of man and beast said on.

'This I do think is a good and just law,' the giant went on to say. 'As it is of course, a straightforward fight, it is no more than a duel to the death. And thus being so, well it involves no one else in this dispute. No others, no armies are involved and so therefore there is no civil war. Aye, there is no brother fighting brother or a father fighting with his own sons and kin. No innocents are hurt or killed in this dispute, so therefore it is just a private matter, aye this I do think is a good thing.'

The garrison, with its high gates and towering walls, as well as its surrounding cliffs, well it was like some sort of a huge amphitheatre, every single word spoken by the giant could be heard clearly and plainly. At this very moment the elite legion of the Black Guard stood silent and impassive while the giant spoke.

'I am Barak, I am Barak the bloody, I am Barak the butcher, I am Barak the deserter of his people if you like those words better! ' This the giant roared this out strongly and passionately. 'My father Bartok was your King, aye and he was a great King, and also he was a great father to me.' Barak's voice, it now wavered for just a slight moment then the great slayer once again continued to speak out. 'I wear this ring upon my finger it was my father's, this was his final gift to me. In fact this was his dying gift to me.' Barak said this whilst holding his huge hand high aloft for all to see the double eagle headed ring. With this done then the slayer spoke up once again.

'But this ring, this ring alone does not make me lord and master here in the land of the Krozak, this proud place of my birth. For whatever gods you all pray to, and know you all now that there are many, aye and most of these are worthless deaf things.' Barak's words of uncaring blasphemy brought a low rumble of mirth from the black clad legion, why even Commander Gortak chanced a thin smile. 'I will not trick or deceive you in any way by swearing my life upon a god, any god,' Barak went on. 'Know you all now, that I believe in none, I neither pray nor bow, nor do I beg to any of them.' Again the giant paused as he glanced about him at his attentive audience before once again continuing with what he had to say. 'For the why of it, well I do suppose that is my business alone, this is something anyway of no matter to anyone but myself. ' Barak then stalled for a second, this for affect before saying on.

'Nevertheless, I do know this, aye and you can believe me or not. I know only too well that I have been an absent and unworthy monarch. And being so, then perhaps I do deserve to be challenged.' Once again Barak paused as he ran his eyes over the proud warriors in front of him. 'Only you here, only you can do or undo that which I have done in the past. Aye, aye it is only you, only you alone here now in this very place that can stand and judge me for my past crimes and my many uncountable sins. '

Barak then ceased with his appraisal of his many short comings.

'Oh, oh he is good, is he not boy?' Ragnor whispered this to Tark who had moved his horse to the side of Ragnor's beast. 'This big killer is wasted, you know he should have gone in for politics years ago, don't you think so boy?'

Tark could not reply to the Viking's question at this particular time as his eyes were full of tears of honest passion and emotion for his King's moving speech. Alas the young man failed to see that while Barak was being truthful, this was also a clever, well thought out sermon to win over the legion. Barak after awaiting a clever amount of time said on with even better timing than the greatest of thespians.

'So, if any man here would challenge me for the right of kingship, he should do it now, right now, aye and in this very place. Send out word throughout the rest of the ranks of the fearless Black Guard warriors, let it be done here and now. This is an honest and an open challenge, aye also it is the very least you warriors of the Black Guard all deserve.' Now the great slayer paused for but a moment longer before continuing with his speech. 'I am Barak, and I have returned hopefully to put that what is wrong here in Krozakistan to rights.

'So let there be no more treachery here, let there be no more deceit and no more lies. Let there be no more dark plotting, no more underhanded scheming in this place of my birth. Now, now I do hope to atone for what wrong I might have caused and done to you my legion of Black Guard. Oh and of course also to my people and my brother Zark by riding away from here all those long years ago. If that is not to be, then so be it, but if I fail then at least I will die here in the place of my birth. Now the giant paused again, letting his clever words sink into the soldiers of the line before speaking up once again. 'For one thing is most certain, and that is simply this, There is not one here among the Black Guard who is good enough to lay me low in fair combat. ' Barak stalled again as he looked ahead and around about him into the ranks of black garbed warriors, then once again the ogre spoke. 'Which, after all is said and done is my own guard. Aye, you men are my own guard,' Barak roared this out proudly. 'So you tell me, who is it then, who is it who can possibly slay me?' The giant gave time for another short pause before speaking up once again.

'And I say this to all of you standing here now before me. If there is not one here to take up the challenge then there is no one at all, for you of the Black Guard are the very best of the best. You warriors are the bravest the proudest and the most courageous of all our great Krozak legions. You are after all the empire's imperial knights of honour, our elite, you are my elite.' Barak declared this with a long roar before affording these black clad paragons of bravery and honour a slight nod of respect. 'I swear he is getting better by the second is he not boy?' Ragnor said this with a wry chuckle.

'And I also swear that was the longest speech I have ever heard anyone make,' Ragnor added still smiling broadly.

'Be still and be silent you foolish man, whilst we await now the reply of the Black Guard you big barbarian oaf,' Tark hissed out a little angrily. 'After all, what do you know of kingship and knighthood and of high chivalry?'

Ragnor, well luckily for Tark the big Viking took no offence at the young man's emotional outburst. For after all said and done, Tark was little more than a boy. No, the Viking merely concealed another broad and knowing grin with his baggy woollen shirt sleeve. As has already been said the big Viking had of course known Barak for a very long time.

Oh and also Tark at once regretted his own words, Ragnor as well as all of his men knew well of honour, kinship and most of all loyalty. Anyway, the reply Barak was hoping for was not long in coming from the black clad warriors, or from the stern garrison chief himself. Commander Gortak at once dropped to his knees as did the rank and file of neatly turned out Black Guard. Next, the quite overcome Commander took Barak's huge hand and then kissed the ring of kingship.

At once there was an immediate roar of approval from the ranks of the Black Guard as they as one sprang to their big black booted feet. Indeed, this noise, well it was so rapturous it even managed to get the Viking's worn out horses to dance about upon their tired weary legs.

'Well, at least it looks like we do have some sort of an army now boy for our battle?' Ragnor said with a sly grin.

Tark made no reply to these words instead he trotted off to join Barak and his uncle as they were mobbed by the throng of overly excited Black Guards. Whatever lay ahead in the very near future, be it death or glory or both, Tark would embrace it. Now his destiny, be it for the better or for the worse, now lay with Barak, aye and this to the bitter end.

'Why don't you stand up commander?' Barak asked with a thin smile. 'Come stand, let us talk, for I have much to catch up on matters of state, oh and of course perhaps most of all dark treachery. '

At once the commander did as he was bade, with a bit of an effort Gortak pulled himself up onto his black booted feet, this as he stared upward in total awe at the towering giant. All that Tark said about him was true, big Barak was without any doubt the most fearsome man he had ever seen in his life. Barak next smiled revealing those sharp, wolf-like teeth. This by the by, well this was a sight that filled the commander with even more mortal dread. Commander Gortak glanced down at the giant's girdle where hung the much famed ivory handled dragon sword. Aye and this was a most famous, most legendary sword that had slain so many of the giant's enemies. Oh and apparently these many enemies were not always human foes. Atop the high backed high fronted Arab saddle of the giant's huge horse there lay the skin of the mountain lion in testimony to the brutal fact of young Tark's tale. The lion's great tawny mane covered the front pommel whilst the tail of the lion lay draped atop of the flaxen tail of the overly massive war horse. This, while two of its foot long sabre like teeth hung about the giant's huge neck. Anyway and besides all else, Barak's quick but well planned entrance into the city and the speech that followed, well it had apparently won the day. And so it appeared now that perhaps not surprisingly the great ogre for better or worse was once more adored by all and everyone.

'For almost thirty years, since being a boy, I have hoped and dreamt of this day, of your return to your kingdom my Lord Barak,' Gortak said sincerely.

Barak gave a grunt followed by a nod of thanks as he placed a huge hand upon Gortak's brawny shoulder.

'Well, I am very much happy your dreams have at last come true Commander. However, let us all just hope that these dreams do not turn into nightmares. Barak after saying this paused smiled and then he spoke again. 'Now, now my commander, can you answer me this,' asked a smiling Barak. 'I have two questions for you, aye and believe me these are most important ones.' Barak said this with an element of seriousness in his voice that worried the burly commander slightly. Were these questions something perhaps that he could straightaway answer. Aye and also could he answer them honestly the commander wondered silently to himself?

'First question Commander Gortak, have you plenty of food and drink here, here in this hallowed haven for heroes?'

Somewhat bemused the commander gave a slow but most positive nod.

'Yes, yes my Lord Barak, of course we have plenty of both.' Commander Gortak could not help but smile, as that question despite his reservations it provided a very simple answer. ' We have both a full cellar of ale, and a good supply of vodka. Oh and we have also of course a well stocked kitchen my Lord.' Barak stroked his snow white beard chuckled, and then he glanced skyward, perhaps Tengri did favour him in some way or other. 'Good, in fact very good Commander Gortak, I see at least some things have not changed.' The giant said this while remembering his childhood days mooching about the well stocked cellars and the kitchen of the Garrison.

'Now for the next question commander Gortak, can we have it?' Barak asked this question whilst his face was breaking into a wide and most mischievous grin.

It must be said Commander Gortak was much shocked and even taken aback by Barak's lack of protocol and decorum. In truth and as well as this, the commander also found the giant's sense of humour strange and new to him. Aye, this huge new found king seemed to be quite mad, but in a likeable sort of way. This apparent madness was, however, of no matter. As Barak after all was the newly returned king, thus being so he would be obeyed in all things. Well, at least by the Black Guard anyway.

At once the Commander barked out orders telling his ever attentive orderlies to prepare the best of food and drink. If the Lord Barak required feasting and drinking, then feasting and drinking he shall have. Aye and this banquet, it would be held in the great hall at that.

This hall was a huge regal place which had seldom been used over these past unsettled years of disruption and discontent. Many years ago when Barak's father lived, his birthdays as well as other happy functions would all be celebrated here. Aye and indeed here the King would come to drink and to talk and laugh with his favourite fighting legion whenever he had the chance to do so. For King Bartok, just like his wild wayward son had little or no time at all to socialise with titled and landed so called aristocrats. In fact, it was well known the king often disguised himself and disappeared into the second city to drink with the so called lower classes. True, these souls might have been poor people, but still a man had more chance of getting a drink out of one of them as a greedy penny pinching magistrate. Bartok, just like his son was a man who also hated and despised magistrates, indeed he hated any sort of pompous overbearing officialdom.

While the cleaning of the hall, the cooking of the food and the breaking out of great barrels of strong ale and vodka was being prepared, Barak, feeling dusty and travel weary took his brave intrepid fellows off for a well earned and long overdue bath. It was hot underground springs that supplied the constant warm water to the well constructed roman type baths. These lavish baths were all tiled in fine marble and perhaps there were some thirty or more of them in number.

Oh and also these baths ranged widely in both size and depth. Barak with Ragnor and his men had of course opted for the largest and the deepest of them all. This long wide bath started off shallow, hip depth, and then the bath ran slightly downward so that it was so deep at the other end even the giant had to swim to keep his big head above the warm water.

While soaking and lounging about in the warm water the men's clothing was taken away for washing and cleaning, oh and of course repair. Their chain link armour and weapons would be oiled and polished, oh and of course sharpened at the forge. With these most necessary tasks once accomplished the Norsemen would find both weapons and rejuvenated clothing laid beside their beds. Meanwhile, manservants brought soaps, scents and relaxing lotions which were poured into the warm sudsy water. Now possibly for the first time in their entire lives the Vikings were actually warm, wet, and clean all over, and this all at the same moment in time.

'Ah, I do love the feel of warm water upon my worn and weary body, don't you Ragnor?' Barak asked this of his friend with a satisfied stretch. Ragnor muttered something, he was apparently not quite as convinced or impressed as to what a little hot water could achieve. 'Oh, I do forget Ragnor, I suppose this is the first time for you, aye perhaps this is a whole new experience, to be clean I mean. ' Barak said this with a snigger as with his huge hands he splashed the big Viking in his bearded face.

Ragnor scowled a little angrily, as in his long held and considered opinion, well water was for sailing upon.

'I smell like a woman Barak,' Ragnor complained sniffing under his own hairy armpits.

'Well, you are safe with me Ragnor, because I must tell you now, you most certainly don't look like one,' Barak said in a fit of laughter.

Ragnor grumbled then cursed as he looked about the hot bath at the others in their company.

'Is Borz alright Barak? Look you there is he a drowned thing or what?'

Ragnor asked this question as he pointed toward the troll, who was now lying upon his back floating face up. Face up, but some foot under the water's surface and this with his yellow eyes firmly shut. The weight of the great chain he still wore about him would have taken any human to the bottom of the bath and drowned them without a doubt. However with the troll, well this huge heavy chain appeared to be as no more than a silken sash about his massive green body.

Barak nodded his head confirming all was well, and then the ogre momentarily disappeared under the surface of the warm now bubble filled water.

'Yes, Ragnor he is alright, in fact I think Borz is most well,' Barak answered when he resurfaced. 'He is after all half swamp troll, Borz is not all human remember, so he will not drown. '

Ragnor grinned at Barak's explanation as after all it was plain even to a blind man that Borz was not human. Ragnor had sailed to many places and encountered many strange tribes and peoples. Borz however was the first he had ever met with a green scaly skin' a purple forked tongue and yellow eyes. Aye and this was not to mention, his newt like head, or his huge webbed hands and feet.

Now though with a satisfied look about his face the troll had in fact drifted off into a blissful dream filled sleep. And also this was the first time in an age the great green creature had been both wet and warm at the same time, so now he intended to make the best of it. So to the halfling swamp troll, well, these warm baths were no less than sheer heaven.

Under the comfort of the warm water the halfling now took upon a most deep greenish and frog like colouring. Barak merely supposed this was the healing goodness of the warm water, somehow this was revitalizing his whole body. And just as ever, well it so happened, Barak's carefully calculated assumption was quite correct. All of the dried out skin and the old scars and wounds seemed to seal and heal, then mend themselves and simply disappear. Also it must be said the longer the submerged halfling was under water the happier and more contented he seemingly appeared.

'Borz is more at home in these warm waters that he now lolls in and lies under Ragnor, please believe me on this, see how relaxed and well he looks? Cold water our friendly Halfling can of course endure but he would find it not at all inviting. However these hot baths will both restore any lost power the freezing elements have sapped from both his body and soul over these last months. Trust me, Borz will surface when he is good and ready, aye and only when he finally needs to breath in air once again. Aye and I think when he does finally surface the noble, if not handsome creature, he will have about him even more strength and more sheer power. '

So with this explained, and the attentive Norsemen apparently both happy as well as impressed by Barak's reasoning Ragnor and his warriors from the north soaked there in the warm scented water for over an or so hour longer. Here the warriors soaked and rested themselves in the warmth of the hot scenty water. Why the men supposed that they even enjoyed it, though of course the Norsemen would never admit to this openly. Being so comfortably immersed the warriors bathed, allowing the warm sudsy water to heat the blood in their very veins. A while later much refreshed, the savage but very pink skinned and fragrant Viking party of men eventually emerged from the hot baths.

For most, if not all of them, it was more than likely the first time they had been truly clean since the day of their birth. Oh by the by the one legged Horst had also been scrubbed clean, even though it did take half a dozen large hairy Norsemen to accomplish this most tricky task. Bathing over the men then dried and dressed themselves in silken gowns and pressed their big feet into black velvet slippers. It was time now to relax with a drink and a smoke, and then with this done, time to catch up on a little sleep. Aye and a warm trouble free sleep at that, oh and this in a soft scented bed. Here the warriors could sleep unmolested in spirit knowing they were free from the attacks of wolves or huge mountain lions. Later after resting and donning their fresh cleaned attire, the warriors would join the commander and his elite Black Guard for a most monumental feast. So it was that after a while, after their bathing and their sleeping on soft beds the Vikings finally arose both relaxed and refreshed It was then, then that these Norsemen did in all truth make some effort in their appearance.

Their flaxen hair the warriors brushed and groomed then braided, just as also the men did with their great foot long beards. Clean and polished chain link armour was set into place over wolf and bearskin vests and tunics. Also their shirts and woollen leggings were clean and fresh as well as repaired. Now this material felt soft and comfortable against their skin. Not harsh and scratchy as it had been over these past months on their trek. Trophies of gold chains and gold rings were all of course worn with an element of both pride and prosperity. At length when the Vikings were eventually happy with their magnificent barbaric appearance they were led off to the great banquet hall of the Black Guard.

At once there was a great cheer and an earbursting clamouring of black steel breast plates as Barak and Ragnor with their party entered into the hall of the Black Guard. Oh and also this was the first time outsiders had been permitted here in this place of sanctuary. This was a great hall reserved for elite warriors, men of war, combat and of course the all important honour. But, as Barak had pointed out to the Commander Gortak, every one of these men who had sailed from the distant shores of Britain well, each and every one of them more than qualified for all of those accolades. Oh and of course neither Commander Gortak, nor anyone else for that matter argued the point with Barak. And so now without any further ado the informal feasting and the drinking began in all earnest. That following morning after the feast, and with just a handful of men about him Barak would talk with commander Gortak. Then it was, the ogre surmised, then, he would learn a lot more about the treachery within the palace. Oh, and of course the ogre wanted to know a lot more about his own brother, and what part if any he played in all of this dangerous nonsense. But all of that for now would have to wait, as now the intrepid party of most worthy men would feast. Ten long rectangular tables filled the huge most impressive hall and around about each table there sat a hundred men.

Ragnor looked about the great hall in total awe. Nothing he had ever seen, even in the service of Rome was as large and as ancient as this regal place. Why he doubted if even the fabled halls of Valhalla could compete with such splendid grandeur. All about him on the solid stone walls hung the most ornate and wonderful tapestries depicting past battles and other long ago heroic glories. Also there were cunningly wrought statues in marble, bronze and stone, these of kings and heroes of the bloody violent past. Oh and of course all of these impressive monuments were expertly cut and carved out by the very finest of craftsmen. About the huge hall bronze guttering that was six feet from the ground ran from corner to corner of the great room. This guttering affixed firmly to the walls was filled with oil, oh how it glowed and danced as the flames burned brightly. Here was a most simple but clever system that both warmed and lighted up the large room. Aye and here also was a heating and lighting system that was far more advanced than anything of its day. Oh and as for the feast that was laid out before them, well nothing in all the so called great civilized capitals of the world could compete with this most varied and ample fare.

Each one of the long and wide tables was laden with such red meats as camel, goat, lamb and beef, also venison and wild boar meat was in plentiful supply. There was also roast fowl such as goose, turkey, duck and chicken. Aye and there was all of this as well as wildfowl such as pheasant, partridge, bush grouse and even wild swan. Of course there was a large variety of fresh fish from the teeming rivers and well stocked lakes. As well as all this, there were large platters of over a score of different cheeses. Baskets of strange and exotic fruit were also plentiful, but these colourful fruits were perhaps laid out more for decoration than consumption. As an extra bonus there were tall glazed clay pots of strong weed and large glass and china jugs of all manner of drink placed here there and everywhere across the ancient tables. Ales, wines, ciders, mead and of course potent steppes vodka were laid everywhere about the food crowded tables.

Oh and of course all of this as well as scores of huge wooden barrels of beer sat upon strong wooden racks against the walls ready to tap into whenever needed.

Barak smiled proudly, this was a feast worthy of his Blackguard and also worthy of the men who had followed him on the dangerous journey to this huge and ancient hall.

Oh yes, the cooks, the kitchen staff as well as the hall all stewards had all well and truly done the revellers proud. Aye and this most certainly was going to be a night the big Barak and all there would long remember. Well, that was providing of course that the slayer was not soon assassinated. Perhaps, the giant thought briefly, he should appoint Borz, who still lounged underwater, as his food tester.

Now the Vikings, who were all pink and scrubbed up, were to be treated as most honoured and esteemed guests of the elite blackguard. As has already been said, outsiders were not allowed or invited into the great hall of the blackguards, and until this day, well it was totally unheard of. Why, not even any of the other Krozak legions had ever been invited to the hall. Indeed, nor had those of the other legions known or even heard of such a privilege being granted.

The Vikings were divided into small groups, so that one or two of their number sat at each end of every long table. By their side, there sat a most ancient and learned scribe. Oh, and also an equally ancient recorder. These ancients were indeed most learned fellows, scholars who were also fluent in any tongue known to man. Aye and of course, this including Norse. And being so, as the Vikings told the somewhat fabulous but true tale of their adventure and their epic journey. Well then, these scholars not only translated it to the warriors of the blackguard, but they also wrote it down for record. Aye and all of this in great ancient leather bound books, and books that were perhaps older than many civilisations. Oh yes indeed, now it was a most spectacular and vivid tale that the Vikings told to their speechless spellbound hosts.

Oh and what was more, much more. Well of course and as already said, all of it was true; well most of it. Here was a colourful, but semi truthful tale of cruel and wicked child snatching pirates. Aye and also tale of no good reavers and knaves, fools that were hunted down and slain for their cowardly sins. Next the Norsemen told of how the troll had been saved from the market square, and also of how the gypsies and the prefect had met their well deserved fates. Later, the Norsemen next spoke in some detail of the huge man-hungry wolves that ran amok in great packs of a hundred or more. Oh and this these ravenous wolves did in the deepest and the darkest of forests, forests that lay in the wild and untamed far beyond.

Later again, and after this the Vikings told of black rivers that abounded with shoals of teeming fish, these as well as with slimy man-eating serpents that dwelt therein. All the while the warriors of the Black Guard sat silently listening, seemingly spellbound by the enthralling tale. Still though there was even more to come. Now the Black Guard's most honoured guests next told them of great giant rock-hard hailstones. Hailstones that could crack a man's skull open just as easy as an egg. Why this rock-hard hail could manage this even through the warrior's thick bronze helmets. With this once explained, the Norsemen also told of the epic battle with the huge primeval mountain cats. These huge lions were obviously creatures from a bygone age, and things that should have long since died away into the pit of time itself.

Barak, he now wore two huge foot long fangs taken from the male lion about his massive neck, a trophy of that sad day when one of his dogs had perished so bravely in that glorious fray.

In some detail the men from the north went on, and next further told of how they were beset by desert nomads and how they had bested them all. Aye and this, the Norsemen had achieved without the loss of a single man. Then finally after all of these ordeals, when the warriors were almost at the city gates of Krozak, how they were confronted by the Mongol Khan Temudgin. Here the Khan had sat upon his small hardy pony with a thousand of his small sparse bearded warriors at his back. To a man each and every Viking thought that their perilous journey was over there and then. And so with this fate firmly in mind the warriors had chanted their death song as they drummed upon their shields. As now against such great odds they each of them readied themselves to fight to the very end of it. Many of the Vikings there had thought this was indeed the field of Vigrior, and here was the field of death. But of course this was not to be, and the Khan had embraced Barak as both a friend and as a brother.

Aye and also the Khan had apparently informed Barak it was the corrupt brothers who had paid him from their own purse to put a final halt to his progress. Temudgin was paid, so he had most honestly said, to cut off the king's head. Oh and this for no other reason so that the big bald thing might become a decoration, or even a trophy of some sorts.

Now here were dark words, and dark words that stirred the Black Guards up more than just a little. So now more than ever, aye and at the drop of a hat these men of the Black Guard were more than ready and eager for a little good old fashioned honest bloodshed. Aye, aye indeed these well trained warriors were ready for a bloody all out war. All of this for the honour of their returned king, oh and of course their elite brotherhood. And it was after all a noble brotherhood that had lately been wrongly used. Aye and the Black Guard had been treated to their despair and disgust, like little more than mindless fools. So now the story was over and indeed this had been a most stirring tale, no doubt of that. Also it

378

was a tale told honestly by the Norsemen. Now though the men of the Black Guard, well they were all keen to redden their swords and become a part of it.

By the by in the telling of the tale, well the Vikings were all under the strictest instructions to leave out the episode in the tavern, as sadly that was the unfortunate part in their adventure, when Barak had slain four of their blackguard brethren. Oh and of course the Norsemen also had to forget about the two unfortunate warriors on guard aboard Wraif's black dragon ship. Oh aye, their grim but quick demise was of course never to be mentioned in the telling of the evening's entertaining tale. Also to save any sort of embarrassment Bull Neck's treachery was also not to be mentioned. And this was as Ragnor as well as the other Norsemen were all of course most grateful to forget that shameful little episode. When the story was once over the Krozak warriors banged upon the great tables with their drinking horns, now the brotherhood all hailed the Lord Barak and his brave party of warriors over and over again. Every single man in the elite legion would have given ten years of their life just to have been part of such an epic adventure. An adventure that was of course now written down into legendry, aye and this would be a tale which would be told and passed on until the very end of time.

When at long last the feasting the drinking the backslapping and the handshaking came to an end it was a cold chilly morning. And so all now both Black Guard and Viking staggered off to their beds, oh and this as best they could. Now though, well this was the time for Borz to dine, aye now it was the huge green troll who feasted alone in the great hall. For many hours now the creature had soaked himself lying submerged in the warm hot spring water that filled the baths. When he had at long length emerged Borz had taken upon himself a most froglike and very bright greenish appearance. And in all fact, and if at all possible, well he now looked even more reptilian than ever he did.

His huge body seemed even more massive now, more vital as if it was puffed up with even more raw explosive power. Also the halfling's body did fair ripple with repaired and renewed muscle, the old scars and wounds had simply vanished. Also any strength that he or it might have lost in the past, lost by living a more human life style than was at all good for him, well this had seemingly been restored. So now after soaking and sleeping for all these long hours under the warm, strength restoring water the great green thing had awakened. And upon his awakening, well Borz was now indeed a most ravenous and starving huge green thing. So now the halfling was sitting dining alone, and well, well he quite simply gorged himself upon whatever remained upon the long tables. Aye and so this the great green creature did until he could eat not one more bite. However, it must be said though, well, that was some considerable amount of food consumed before the creature was finally well and truly stuffed.

Earlier while the weary servants were already clearing the tables away, and this when Borz had all of a sudden appeared dressed only in a loin cloth and glistening with power. Only one glance at this strange looking most powerful creature was enough to send them all scampering hastily off back toward the kitchen in total fright and horror. Aye and it was only once, once when this great green beast had finished with his eating and his drinking, would they show their ashen faces. Fish, well that was perhaps the least consumed meat of the night's drinking and feasting. This as the Krozak as well as the Norse had always favoured the red meat above all else. To the Troll though this detail was something that mattered nothing or little at all, flesh after all was flesh. Being so, Borz, well, the halfling started off with the fish, then, whatever was left he would just eat that up later. But either way, there would be that morning very little meat going to either the hunt kennels or to the pig pens.

Oh and as for the servants, well at least those weary tired souls would have an easy enough job. This, as now there would be only empty plates to carry away off to the kitchen once the halfling had finished with his dining.

When at long last Borz could eat not one more bite it was turning light, now the creature was a most rounded contented thing, oh indeed his big green belly was well full. The halfling burped loudly then he took for himself a deep drink of vodka, then another and another. Oh and this the creature did, well so he told himself to wash down the vast amount of food he had already consumed.

Well at least that was his somewhat feeble excuse, or was this perhaps because he had spent over these last months far too much time in the company of the ogre Barak. Well, Borz wondered this but briefly to himself as he next both belched and then farted loudly. Still though, at least he had managed to give up the mind numbing weed he thought quite proudly to himself.

Anyway once this eating and drinking was done the halfling rose up on his big webbed feet as he yawned and stretched himself skyward. With this done, then the creature gave off a most satisfied smile. After this the most contented halfling next retraced his frog-like steps back towards the hot baths to soak himself once again. Once there the creature yet again intended to submerge himself under the warm comforting waters, and have for himself yet another good long and well deserved sleep.

Whatever it was that lay ahead for him and his new found friends Borz had already decided his stay here, however short or however long it might be, was going to be at least a most pleasant one.

It was almost midday when Barak, well fed, well rested and well bathed, arose from his deep uninterrupted slumbers. The ogre then at once shaved himself, both head and face in front of both a long and large mirror in his chamber with his keen Persian blade. Once satisfied he was a large thing of great beauty, next the ogre once again bathed himself in the warm bath waters. Barak swam slowly past the still dozing Borz several times before vacating the water then drying and dressing himself. With this done after his leisurely soak and his unhurried swim Barak walked with his dog Thorn around the vast barracks of the Black Guard.

Borz by now had awoken and he accompanied Barak upon this casual and informal inspection. Next the giant inspected the large stables, making sure his big gelding and of course the mules, as well as the other animals had been well cared for. He found Stefan and Sven there and already the young lads were hard at work grooming, feeding, and caring for their charges. Happily the young lads were chattering away still most excited about the previous night's great feast as they did so. Barak well the ogre smiled to see the boys so happy and contented and in such high spirits, all was apparently well here. Why, even the bad tempered camels looked quite content as they chewed away on their hay and filled themselves with vast amounts of fresh water.

'Your great black eagle Lord Barak, has she gone now forever? Gone never to return to you?' Young Sven asked this, and it must be said the lad asked the question with a certain amount of sadness and concern in his voice.

Barak stroked the broad and powerful neck of the big gelding as the ogre fed the beast a carrot or two from a hessian sack. With a grunt the giant next slowly but positively shook his big bucket sized head.

'No, no Sven she is I suppose my friend, being so then she will return to me. Though I must confess, I do not know when exactly,' the ogre said this with a shrug of his huge shoulders. 'But still and nevertheless, I know that she will return when the time is right for both me and herself. Blackie, well, she was ever a good bird to me, aye she was ever loyal and always a most faithful thing.'

Both of the young lads sniggered just a little upon hearing this as Barak bent over to pick out a handful of carrots.

'Blackie! ' Stefan said, a faint smile crossing his handsome young face as he glanced at Sven in wonderment at the slayer's words. Barak, sensing a tinge of ridicule and even mockery, came at once to his own defence.

'Bah, that was but a name the young princess gave the bird, not one of my own you must understand my lads,' Barak said this with his face reddening a little under his tattooed countenance. On hearing these words the young boys chuckled and the giant, well, he felt suddenly a little uncomfortable. And so with this being the case, well the ogre at once excused himself for his embarrassing slip of tongue. Barak gave the big gelding another friendly pat on its huge neck and another carrot before making ready to leave. But just then, there above them there was a squeal as a pair of rats scampered across one of the beams. To the surprise of the boys Barak at once fell backward in shock seemingly and this over a bale of hay. The great slayer at this time was looking none too pleased, aye and more than a little put out. Borz on the other hand however was a much more cheery large green thing. This as the halfling's tongue shot out twice in quick succession and the creature with the greatest of accuracy accounted for both long tailed rodents.

'You know Barak, well I do think that I like a good fat rat nearly as much I do a plump chicken. ' Borz said this as the tail of the last rat disappeared down his throat. Grumbling and cursing Barak now pushed himself up from the floor as he next dusted himself down. Now though the ogre was more than a little embarrassed at stumbling over the bale of hay. But strange as it might seem despite Barak's heroics fighting all manner of huge man eating creature and slaying countless warriors. Well despite all of this, the ogre simply did not like rats. Come to think of it, the great slayer was not too fond much of mice either. Still, no one he supposed would ever really have to know that. As after all, a slip in a barn, well that could happen to anybody. Nevertheless though it was now time to go, this as mayhap more rats might suddenly put in an uninvited appearance.

'Look to the horses and mules boys, give them all double corn, keep them warm and covered with any blankets that are lying round about. As after all these honest beasts have carried us far and carried us safely, so they deserve to be pampered a little don't you think? Barak shouted these words back over his broad shoulder as he disappeared from the stables. Borz chose to stay with the young lads as there was still a fat rat running about he had aspied behind one of the hessian sacks.

With those parting instructions said to the boys and leaving Borz to his rat hunt, Barak next made his way off toward the council chambers. This to consult with Commander Gortak and his most trusted of captains. Of course at this meeting there would also be scholars, elders and scribes all about to record in writing that which was spoken word for word. For indeed there was much to discuss and much to learn before Barak would be making his next move against the traitors who would take his kingdom for their own selfish ends and means.

So now it was that Barak strode off in hot haste toward the council chambers of the Black Guard elders. Here and now the great ogre would talk with the past commanders and the so called learned men. Oh aye and mayhap, and just mayhap mind you, those who were still loyal to the memory of his illustrious father. But of course right now, at this very moment in time these men had sworn new loyalties. And those loyalties were to the present king, the returned king, King Barak

Down a long stone slabbed narrow corridor the giant slayer marched with an air of great urgency about him. These past hard testing months the slayer had spared the men a hurried and forced journey. However, now though the ogre would be about his own immediate business with a lot more gusto. Protocol and politeness to him were over with, now it was time to get down to the very crux of the matter at hand.

Perhaps a dozen or so men sat in that ancient council chamber. These men were just as had been expected retired commanders and aged scholars of long renown.

Barak was politely invited to sit at the end of a long table, this upon a great and aged throne like chair carved from some sort of heavy black wood. Once the giant was seated he nodded politely to each and all about him, then with this done the slayer began to speak.

'Temudgin, the Khan of the lowlands tells me that these accursed brothers. brothers whose names I did not wish to know until I had entered the gates of the kingdom. Well the great Khan of the steppes informed me, these fools now have a wizard to aid them in their black treachery. '

For a while there was silence, aye and this was a most puzzled and ominous silence at that.

'Temudgin!' one of the old former barrack commanders said a little accusingly. 'You have then spoken to the renegade and horse thief Temudgin?'

Obviously this fellow had not earlier met with Tark, nor had he been enlightened by those who had.

Barak gave a positive nod in reply, he well remembered this crusty old one eyed commander from when he was but a boy.

'Yes Commander Xantol, why I spoke to him upon the wind blown steppes only yesterday morning. '

Commander Xantol seemed both impressed and also more than a little flattered that Barak had remembered his name.

'Anyway, now that I am at long last here, and I have survived the long journey, tell me Commander Gortak, how are they called, these troublesome brothers? '

The Commander at once rose a little stiffly from his chair as it was the custom for anyone addressing the King to be upon their feet before speaking.

Commander Gortak put a large hand to his mouth as he cleared his throat and then spoke.

'The brothers are named Karl and Tarl my Lord, and perhaps it is only a year or two that separates them in their age. Karl, he is the older one, he is without any doubt the more devious and more evil in his plotting and his treachery. And as for the other fool, well he merely obeys and follows in almost slave like fashion as to the whims and fancies of his elder brother's endless plotting and scheming.'

Barak grunted and scowled then gave of a most unsettling sort of a snarl before asking his next question.

'What then of the wizard?' Barak asked this as he struck his flints then puffed upon his pipe thoughtfully. 'I have heard he is a dabbler in the dark arts, and that also he is a banished and a most corrupt creature. Temudgin also informed me that this wizard is a Mandarin no less.'

Commander Gortak now looked down toward an ancient white haired old man who sat at his right side.

'Zoltan, Zoltan can you hear me old man?' the commander bellowed out loudly as he bent over to address the white long haired and long bearded scholar.

The old man seemed to stall for a moment but then he replied.

'Yes, but you will have to speak up a little more Commander Gortak,' the ancient replied in a most irritable manner. 'There is no good whispering and muttering away like a spy or a deceiver,' he grumbled. 'I am now a little bit deaf you know my Lord Barak,' the old man next explained to his king.

Even under these most serious of circumstances Barak had to afford himself a slight smile.

'Oh no, surely not,' Barak muttered to himself.

Zoltan was an ancient old man, why in truth he was as deaf as a post when Barak was no more than but a lanky skinny long-haired boy. Zoltan would have rose up onto his feet out of respect for the King there and then was he able, however at present he was not. Also out of respect Barak motioned the old man to remain seated upon his boney backside.

'You are most correct in what you say my Lord Barak, aye there is indeed a wizard who aids the brothers. Why, he is even now hidden away in the west tower,' Zoltan answered a little shakily. 'And yes I do believe that by what has been reported to me, he is both an evil and a dangerous thing. This I think is an obvious assumption to anyone with a brain, or why else would he be in league with the brothers? As after all these brothers are also evil and dangerous things themselves of course.' Zoltan might have been as old as the gods themselves, however he was obviously still a wise and an astute old man. Barak thought this to himself as he listened intently to what the old man had to further say.

'This sorcerer, so I have learned by my various means controls a mirror. It is a mirror that sees all and everything beyond our towering walls.' Commander

Gortak at once gave Zoltan a look of disapproval; surely being in high command of the elite guard then he should have been privy to this so far unrevealed information. Zoltan ignored the commander's icy stare and continued with what he had to say. 'However, the wizard can see nothing that goes on within these city walls.' Zoltan added and he was at this time still ignoring Gortak's glare.

'How is this so?' Barak asked as the ogre poured himself a drink, this as he leant back in his great carved chair. Now the giant took a deep swallow of the colourless liquid thinking of course that it was vodka. However, sadly though he was most put out to find out that it was only water.

Barak now upon tasting the difference between his much loved vodka and the tasteless water let out an instant curse. As in Barak's long held opinion, well water was only any good when it was hot, bubble filled and sudsy. Zoltan shrugged in reply to the slayer's question, then the ancient chuckled at the giant's obvious drinking error. He was by the by the only man there brave enough to do so. Then, with his chuckling finally finished Zoltan once again began to pass on information to his king.

'The guardians of this place who welcomed our forebears here many years ago, they were powerful beings, this in mind if not in body. ' Zoltan said this and said it still with a toothless smile about him before continuing. 'Much of this wizard's black and hateful magic, it may well be practiced within our kingdom. But luckily for us, the gift of his dark vision does not at all work within the empire's mighty walls. With this being so we can all speak freely and frankly here within this great hall.' Zoltan then gave a slight even painful if not polite bow at the end of his informative deliberations. Barak gave a wry grin. The giant liked this old ancient, aye and apparently a lot more than the old man liked him he thought quite rightly to himself. Barak after his grim somewhat crafty thoughts then also gave the ancient wise man a bow of gratitude, this for his vital and important information.

'And my brother Zark, what then of him Commander Gortak, tell me what kind of man is he? ' asked the giant blankly.

Commander Gortak had no hesitation in his reply.

'He is a good man my King, but a man lost I think, aye he is I suppose perhaps lost to himself.' Barak on hearing these words cast the commander a somewhat puzzled glance. It was a glance that made the hitherto fearless commander feel somewhat uneasy. Still however, at length though the commander after a quick drink of water managed to say on.

'So, being your brother, well just like you, Zark is also my Lord, as you are.' Commander Gortak replied while still feeling quite uncomfortable under Barak's glare. Still though to his credit he never the less pressed on. 'But know you this my Lord Barak I do feel for him, for Zark, he has not your strength of body. '

The slayer gave a dismissive and indifferent grunt at hearing the commander's protective and sympathetic words. Barak at the end of the day was a man who respected only power, courage and honour. Aye and in truth the ogre could not truly understand weakness of any sorts. Perhaps this even more so with a man who was bred from the same parents as he was.

'Is my brother then, oh, and tell me without any lie or deception, tell me is he perhaps some sort of simple soul? Is he then merely some sort of a fool? Aye and also is he no more than some sort of a puppet to these deceivers, or what?' Now the giant asked this question with a trace of both anger and intolerance in his voice. Commander Gortak however was not going to be the one who would answer this question. Zoltan scowled, the old man cleared his throat as he sipped at a glass of spring water before managing to arise. Aye and also arise fully to his feet this time. Once upright and upon his shaky legs the long respected elder began speaking out in defence of Barak's younger brother.

'No, no your brother is neither a puppet nor is he a fool of any sort my Lord Barak,' the ancient croaked in a most perturbed and irritable fashion. 'He is as it so happens, a man of letters, he is a poet, a writer and an inventor of the strangest and the cleverest of machines. Machines, the likes of a butcher such as you, or even a so called wise man like myself for that matter, will ever clap eyes upon,' the old man said proudly.

At these stark and unkindly truths there was a deathlike silence about the place. Perhaps under these present circumstances Zoltan could have chosen his words a little more carefully. Still though, the ancient was undeterred by the fears of others, and so he went on with what he had to say.

'Please believe me Barak, like I have already said the Lord Zark is neither a simple soul as you put it, nor is he a fool of any kind. Oh no far from it, your brother is a good and gentle man, he is neither treacherous in his thoughts or is he a deceiver in his ways.' Zoltan seemed most vexed and put out at any slur Barak might have intended against his younger brother. For the ancient Zoltan in all truth had the greatest respect and thought most highly of Zark. Apparently the slayer's brother was in all fact the greatest intellect and the greatest thinker Zoltan had ever come across in all his long years. And to be thought so highly of by such a learned respected man as Zoltan, well, that in itself was indeed a great accolade.

Still though, once again Barak gave out a disgruntled growl and a grunt of total indifference. Though this perhaps the giant did not out of any sort of disrespect for his younger brother, no this was done much more cleverly. This was meant more as an act to provoke some sort of reaction, aye an opinion of some sort from those around about him. However though, and perhaps through sheer fear, well there was not a murmur. All was silent in the great hall, then after but a little while, once again it was the aged Zoltan who spoke up.

'Know you this, not everyone can be a fierce bloodthirsty warrior, a savage leader of mindless brutal men such as you are Barak.' Zoltan made this accusation with his voice shaky and breaking up a little with angry emotion. Commander Gortak on hearing these words at once reached for his pipe, perhaps a little of his own weed might calm himself down. As now at this particular time commander Gortak did not fully know who was due a heart attack first, his own goodself, or the ancient Zoltan. Meanwhile the old white haired man supported himself by leaning upon the long table in front of him, as he had apparently not finished yet.

'Oh and remember this Lord Barak, Zark is your full brother, aye he too is your father's son just as you are.' Now the old man said this as his voice was becoming a little more agitated.

Still, there was a hushed and deathlike silence as the ancient well respected Zoltan went on undaunted with what he had to say.

'Zark your brother, he is a man not at all like you, in fact to his credit he is most unlike you, aye and I thank the stars above he is a different sort of man. ' Zoltan said this while giving Barak a cold and icy stare with his watery brown eyes.

'As you already well know Barak, Zark is not a man of war. Oh no, he is not a man of blood and glory and savage uncalled for butchery. Oh no, oh no he is not at all like you, nor is he like your father King Bartok. As to your father I will say without a word of a lie, well, let us say he was never a man who shied away from the use of the sword. Indeed good man though he was, well your father would have always made a better battle Commander than a king.' Zoltan said speaking honestly. 'Aye in all truth, I think as many did and indeed still do, big Bartok would have been a happier man performing that bloody brutal task.'

Barak of course took no offence at these scathing words, simply for this reason, it was all the truth.

'Aye and you Barak, well you, you great big painted thing, you are of course very similar to your father in many respects. Aye, you are after all, well you are no more than a barbarian King.' After chastising the giant and his long dead father King Zoltan next turned his attention elsewhere. Commander Gortak had now puffed sufficiently enough upon his pipe to ease his stress. Now comforted by the weed all was well, being so he grinned accordingly. However this grinning did not go unobserved.

'Do not hide your childish sniggering behind your black baggy sleeve Commander Gortak. I am deaf, but I am not blind, nor am I stupid in any way,' Zoltan hissed out angrily.

Gortak thus rebuked and chastised by the ancient but wise Zoltan once again resumed his stone-like stern appearance as best he could. Also, the commander quite wisely said nothing at all in reply.

Gortak was a big bold commander but to his credit he knew his limitations, he did not want a verbal duel with the very vexed Zoltan, no, oh no, as that would not do at all. Zoltan, well he then once again began to speak up, and this just to enlighten Barak as to the merits of his younger brother.

'Zark, he is a gentle and a caring soul, aye your brother has much compassion and much love for his people. I do think he is very much like your dear mother, and that believe me is not a bad thing. Zark, well he is a great thinker and a great intellect. Also he is a kind prince with the greatest of ingenuity, aye and not to mention ability and imagination. ' Zoltan by the by had said all of this almost lovingly before going on once again. 'What imagination I wonder, if any, do you possess my Lord Barak? ' This the white haired old man asked as he pointed a boney finger out toward the grim faced slayer.

Zoltan with these last somewhat cutting words spoken then lowered himself slowly once again down on to his velvet cushioned padded chair. Now, and if indeed it came to pass the old man never spoke another word in his long life, well then Zoltan was most glad he had spoken these last ones to the glowering ogre who he had known since the time of Barak's birth.

'He is old, aye he is very old my Lord, perhaps, just perhaps the ancient Zoltan is gone senile even.' Commander Gortak said to Barak in a whisper seeking to defend the advisor's somewhat harsh and cutting words.

'No, no Commander, Zoltan is not senile, the old man is right, he is quite correct in what he says,' Barak countered without hesitation. Now the giant at this particular time, well he was a little humbled. Aye the great slayer was more than a little subdued by the old man's straight and forthright talking.

This as it has forever and long been said amongst the nations, aye and these civilized or otherwise. Well that was simply this, and that was the stark truth often hurts more than any lying slander. Still though, Barak had now supposed he had felt a little badly done by. Being so, well, the giant felt that under these present circumstances he should defend himself against Zoltan's hurtful remarks as regards his imagination, or rather the lack of it. Anyway Zoltan had spoken for quite long enough, and so now it was Barak's turn to speak up. And as ever and always Barak was determined both to entertain as well as educate his captive audience. Aye, he would also give all there before him something to think about, this including the crusty old Zoltan. With this intention set firmly in mind Barak cleared his throat and grudgingly swallowed down a little of the much despised water, no imagination indeed.

Still though, water did have its place, and that place was in a hot bath full of sudsy foaming bubbles. So now with his throat lubricated with the water the big Barak said on.

'Many long years ago, on one of my first great campaigns for the standard of Imperial Rome, I was ordered to take and destroy a great garrison. Oh and this, well this was a garrison that lay by the sea on a far off and distant land. Also, this towering garrison in the land of the Moors had stood for over a thousand years, and never before had it been taken in conquest. ' The giant then paused and took another drink, quite forgetting the refreshment was still only water laid before him and not something stronger. At once the ogre scowled and growled as the tasteless liquid went down his huge neck. 'I had under my command on this particular campaign some twenty thousand of Rome's finest fighting men. Well this, this as well as also another five thousand German mercenaries of my own. '

Barak paused now as he glanced all around and about him. Each and every one of the stern faced men of the militia sat there now in all eagerness, hanging onto every word so to speak. Aye this to hear the ogres tale, as doubtless they all thought it would be a most bloodthirsty one. Meanwhile the scholars the elders and the scribes merely sat in what was some sort of knowing dread of what was to come.

'For weeks and months we waged a glorious, most bloody and brutal war. Oh yes, yes it was quite a wonderful time.' Barak said this with a wistful smile as he glanced at the scowling Zoltan. 'We pulled sea rocks from the shoreline and bombarded the garrison walls non-stop day and night with our huge ballistas. Oh and they in turn, the Moors who held the garrison, well these horsemen would attack us at any time. Aye and this be it by either day or night with their cavalry of brave ferocious desert warriors. At long length, I began to run short of both rocks and food. Oh and aye, what was even worse, we were beset by nasty biting insects that thrived upon the bodies of the many dead. My men at this time were weary from fighting nonstop. Being so, then well of course they had no time for grave digging. This being the case, well the bodies of the fallen had stayed where they were laid.' Barak had earlier stubbed out his pipe, but now with the absence of anything soothing liquid wise he now relit it. After a few longs puffs the slayer grinned broadly revealing his wolf sharp teeth in full. Of course this was a fearsome sight, a sight which caused many a man in that great hall to give a cold and fearful shudder. Big Barak after inhaling and then exhaling a little more black weed, once again continued to speak and say on with his tale.

'But know you all this, sometimes even the broken bodies of the dead can become most useful things. Aye and I, well I am I must say a man who hates and despises any sort of waste.'

Now, well, now all there sitting about the giant looked pale and ashen. This as obviously all there had heard all manner of dark and sinister rumours as to their kings supposed cooking and eating habits. Once again the elite gathering gave a cold shudder, the scholars all dreaded what their savage wayward monarch was next going to say. Oh yes, how they all now silently prayed the great ogre was not about to disgrace the royal house. Disgrace and shame it with dark cannibalistic tales. As for Barak, well the ogre seemingly could read their very thoughts. In all truth the giant was finding his captive audience's apparent discomfort quite amusing.

'What did you think I did then for my weary struggling starving men Commander Gortak? Indeed my man, well, you must tell me what would you have done in my situation?'

Now the big burly Commander felt of a sudden a little faint, a little uncomfortable. Aye indeed all of these emotions he felt, this as he reached under his black robe for a small gourd of hitherto concealed vodka. Barak smiled broadly as Gortak passed the drink to his king. This of course the commander did only after he first took for himself a mouthful of the soothing liquid for himself.

'Medicine my Lords, my king and I, well we have the same affliction, aye, we have the same ailment.' Commander Gortak explained to the elders and scholars as he then very cleverly gave a cough then a slight bow toward Barak.

'Well, in all truth my Lord, such a situation would take some time in pondering over so I await for you to educate me. ' This the Commander added and thus evaded the giant's somewhat ominous question.

'Well, I did exactly what you or any other good commander would do with the bodies of the fallen, like I say I did not waste these dead men, no, far from it.' Barak had said all of this in a most cheery fashion.

Cheery or not all there, both the men of the military and academics alike expected the worst was yet to come. In a way though, these captive listeners later supposed they were quite pleasantly surprised with what Barak said next.

'Well with no more missiles available as the shoreline was emptied of rocks, then we simply used the dead corpses in their stead. Aye, we quite simply fired all of the dead men, dead men from both sides of the war, over the high walls into our enemies.' Barak said this with yet another cheery sort of smile. 'Clever eh Zoltan? good thinking, imaginative even don't you think?.' Barak further asked with a cheeky grin as he took a swallow of Commander Gortak's vodka before once again continuing with his tale. 'After our long bombardment with the corpses the very next day the garrison was deserted, there was not a man to be found, not a Moor in sight. Quite simply this was all because the defenders of the fortress feared the bodies of the dead carried disease, and the plague. So thus I secured yet another great and glorious victory,' the giant said proudly. Barak, well the cheery ogre then held out his huge arms as he smiled, why he even winked towards the ancient Zoltan.

'Now, now tell me Zoltan, tell me now that I lack imagination,' the giant grinned broadly.

Zoltan scowled as he shook his troubled head in total dismay, Barak, well king or no king he was most certainly a barbarian. Next saying nothing in reply the elder merely rose unsteadily to his feet and excused himself. Now, mumbling oaths and curses to himself he was helped away by a court assistant who was almost as frail as he was. True it was the great giant had not admitted to cannibalism as the ancient feared he might. But still and nevertheless, Barak, his own king was without any doubt a throwback to the old ways, the days of the Kurgans. Oh yes Barak was truly his father's son, alas he was a barbarian king. Zoltan knew well Barak would not alter, no he would always and ever be the same brutal thing that he was now.

No matter, it was established later that afternoon and agreed by all there Barak must go to the palace and ride to the city proper. Once there he would confront the brothers and their creeping crawling lackeys. They, these brothers, their henchmen and deceivers then of course must be slain and put to the sword. Of course this task could only be achieved once a just and rightful cause was proven to the respectable citizens of the kingdom. Not of course that the common folk would ask for such a reason. However, still, law and order as well as some sort of protocol must appear to be observed, well at least for now anyway.

Doubtless the city guard would, well it was suspected be at some sort of odds whether as to side with the brothers or their king. For even now these soldiers apparently had been fooled into believing Barak had betrayed his own people. Oh and then on top of this betrayal, Barak would no doubt beguile and trick the Black Guard into throwing in with him. While all the time the wayward giant King had planned to sack and destroy the city with both the Norsemen and the Mongols as his ferocious allies. Aye and all of this mayhem and butchery was deemed to be out of some blood-crazed hatred. Oh and a hatred that the great slayer had long harboured for his younger brother. Doubtless the other legions of cavalry and footsoldiers, oh and also the vast numbers of outriders had all been fed the same bellyful of lies.

However either way, whatever did lie ahead of Barak and his band of followers, well this was best met head on. With this being so, then on the morrow while the morning was still steeped in darkness. Barak with a party of Black Guards accompanied by the Norsemen, would ride from the garrison to the inner city then onto the royal palace itself. Once there at this place there would be many questions asked, aye and they must also of course be answered. Barak, well the ogre was not now in the mood for clever trickery or sly deceit of any sort.

Chapter Twenty-Three

On that following morning Commander Gortak saddled up the biggest and the best hundred men of his legion of Black Guard. Later, together with those who had so far accompanied Barak on his journey these warriors stood at the palace gates just as it broke light.

Already in that dim half light of dawn the riders had made their way through the narrow winding cobbled streets of the suburbs waking the slumbering townspeople as they went along with the sound of nigh on one hundred and forty men on shod horses. Oh, and of course a large green troll sitting atop a bad tempered camel called Moses. Thankfully the drunken German had not saddled his mule on that particular morning, as doubtless Horst as ever was still in a drink fuelled slumber. As said, after a while of riding, the company of determined looking horsemen drew up at the palace gates. These were tall strong iron gates which were locked with heavy chains and guarded by some twenty or so very uneasy looking palace guardsmen.

'Open these gates, open the gates in the name of the King!' Commander Gortak bellowed this order out loudly and it must be said with some relish. The Commander had no love for the palace guard whatsoever. Aye and indeed the Commander had been long looking forward to screaming out this long waited for command.

All the other legions of the Krozak militia took their turn in border patrol and putting down bandits and renegades but, to commander Gortak's disgust the palace guards however were excused from such duties. No, these so called soldiers did nothing at all according to the ever critical Commander Gortak. Well, nothing apart from parade up and down then polish their black boots and their shiny undented breastplates. Oh and this, well this as well as brush their plumed horse hair helmets then jump when these unworthy brothers said jump.

Aye these men were in his considered opinion only toy soldiers, and Krozak were nevertheless, no more than that. Aye, these fools were only lap dogs to the brothers and their fellow conspirators. So this being the case these men were therefore also in his opinion, traitors, and not to be trusted one way or the other. It was plainly obvious to Barak that commander Gortak, good man though he was, well he had something of a dark side.

'Anyway tell me this, why is this gate chained, you dog?' Gortak asked this question somewhat roughly of the captain of the gate.

'Why is our path here to the palace barred? Aye and why is it you stand there staring vacantly with a shiny but blunt sword in your hand, as if you were under some sort of attack?'

Commander Gortak's manner was not polite, he was as ever gruff and stern, indeed he was a most accusing man. Oh yes, it must be said the big burly commander was a man who lacked any kind of social skills whatsoever. In fact, it would be very fair and not unkind to say he was at times a very rude and abrupt man in the extreme.

At first the captain of the guard seemed unable to find his tongue, the officer dropped his sword as he stammered and stuttered out a sad reply. Aye and this he did much to the disgust and annoyance of the impatient Black Guard commander. At length though the Captain found his tongue and he spoke up. Though perhaps this very nervous young captain of the gate would very soon regret just what he had spoken.

'The Lords Karl and Tarl, it was they who decreed it so Commander Gortak,' the gate captain answered more than a little sheepishly.

'Oh aye, and why is that?' Commander Gortak demanded to know quite simply, and this whilst leaning forward in his black saddle that sat firmly upon his big black horse.

Once again the captain of the gate was hesitant, even fearful of the overbearing and bullying commander. As were the captain's soldiers who stood nervously looking about them into the ranks of fearsome looking black garbed riders. It was strange though these guardsmen all thought, how some of these riders seemed to have long red beards.

'The brothers, they fear most strongly there may be enemy agents afoot. Aye and perhaps these agents are already present in the capital at this very moment,' the captain answered somewhat nervously.

Barak and his band of men had ridden along the winding streets in the middle of the Black Guard riders. Being flanked this way the red bearded Norsemen were concealed, well at least to a certain degree. Barak after all did not want to cause any sort of panic in the streets with rumours of huge red bearded barbarians and a green troll thing riding along with him for company. But these bold brave warriors had come this far on the adventure and truly they deserved and had earned the right to be with Barak every step of the way. Ragnor and his men as already said also wore black hooded cloaks atop their armour and animal skins to hide them from the peering, prying eyes of the townsfolk.

Barak, not liking the way the conversation was going with commander Gortak and the gate captain' urged on his mount and moved to the fore. Once there the ogre reined in his horse alongside that of the Black Guard commander's black stallion. Both the commander and his mount were immediately dwarfed by the giant and his huge snorting, hoof stamping war horse.

Now the nervy young captain stared ever upward at the huge man atop the huge horse towering over the Black Guard commander. Moments earlier the young man was in truth much afeared, now though he was terrified. This particular morning he grimly thought as he swallowed with fear, well, it was not going as planned at all. One more hour and his turn of duty would have been over, one more hour and he would have been safe. What next he wondered briefly and bleakly to himself before this new and massive stranger spoke.

'Enemy agents, whatever do you think they mean by that my captain, not me I do hope?' Barak enquired this as he threw back his black hood to reveal his tattooed face. Oh and the giant, well he was of course quite unmistakable.

'Barak,' the young captain exclaimed fearfully dropping his reclaimed sword yet again from his already sweating hand. With this done the young officer almost just as quickly dropped himself down onto one knee, as did all the other guardsmen of the palace gates.

'We can tear these gates down or you can open them captain, what shall it be?' Gortak demanded this with a growl. Now, now the commander was growing a little impatient with this stammering unsure fool of a captain. Here was a captain who by his beardless pink face and his general appearance could not long have been out of the military school.

Perhaps, well just perhaps not even long out of school

'I have a key here at my side Commander Gortak, I can open it for you, aye and I will open it.' The young captain said this whilst fumbling nervously at his waist girdle for the suitable key to unlock the iron gates.

'Good, good that is very good captain, as that is exactly what I had in mind for you to do,' Gortak said with a cruel cynical smirk. Commander Gortak's loyalty was much appreciated and valued by the giant. However, his bullish attitude, well, that at this particular moment in time was not so welcome, no it did not at all impress Barak.

'Perhaps, it would help just a little, if you stood up and opened your eyes my captain.' Barak suggested this with a trace of sympathy in his voice. 'I am only your King if you so will it, I am not the Medusa or some other sort of demi-god. Please believe me lad, you will not turn into a stone pillar if you look upon me, you have my promise on that. '

On hearing this there was a low chuckle from Commander Gortak's men as the gates were now rapidly unchained and held open for them to pass. Now the company of men trotted briskly forward past the palace guards who stood with their heads lowered and their hearts pounding with relief. Doubtless these men thought to themselves they would all face some sort of punishment from the brothers. This for opening the palace gates without putting up a fight of some sort. However, had they been brave enough or foolish enough to do so, well this resistance would of doubtless been very brief, very bloody and a very one sided affair. Oh and of course no matter what, the gates would of still been opened either one way or the other. Oh aye and this no doubt with their bodies lying here there and all around them.

Why Barak alone by the looks of him could of slain each and all of the palace guards together, this without any assistance whatsoever from Commander Gortak and his elite killers. Anyway once inside the iron gates the riders began to trot across the vast parade ground that would lead them all the way up to the palace steps. This parade ground was a deep red tiled ornate affair with the most unusual elaborate cosmic designs of the planets and the far beyond cunningly etched into it. Indeed the expansive parade ground appeared almost like some sort of map of the heavens. This place of course was ancient, why these well laid slates were set long before Barak's forebears had arrived here in this place. Whoever it was who had laid and measured these deep red tiles were obviously master craftsmanship of the very highest quality. It was strange how as a youth Barak thought to himself he had taken the vast most impressive parade ground for granted. Now though after so many years away from home and travelling about as he had done. Now the well travelled slayer realised just how high the standard of workmanship was performed and situated, all this in his own home town. The Romans, well they of course and as ever prided themselves higher than all other current civilizations upon such intricate workmanship. Aye the Greeks' the Persians and even the Egyptians, well these civilisations the Romans thought were no more than some sort of a sub culture.

However this though, well this workmanship was far superior to anything Barak had ever seen in his travels in the Roman provinces or even in their larger cities. In all truth the giant had quite forgotten much about his own kingdom's capital city. Here, here was indeed a most regal and a most magnificent place with its high towers, its turrets and onion shaped minuets. Ahead of them now, only a good bowshot away there stood a delegation of city elders and of course the accursed ever hated magistrates. Oh and also of course, there were as ever the scores of other useless over paid fat lazy officials. These worthless fools had all been hastily roused from their dreaming scheming slumbers by their observant aides, aides that worked hard both night and day and slept but little. Still half asleep these pompous officials had at once hurriedly been dressed by others then gathered together at the palace steps.

So now it was these same fools, well they all apparently waited to greet these horsemen. Perhaps this was with open arms, though then again perhaps it was not. Behind these scores or so of long robed and most unhealthy looking officials there stood perhaps some two hundred of the palace guard. These men were all lined up in four rows of men, and it must be said they were looking quite splendid in their crimson cloaks and their shiny burnished plate armour. And also these men wore upon their hot and sweaty troubled heads plumed horsehair helmets, not unlike those of the officers of the legions of the Roman cavalry. Their brightly burnished oval shields they wore upon their left arm while their keen curved

395

swords were of course sheathed. Each and every man there stood to rigid attention with his long shafted spear held firmly in his sweating right hand.

Every man there of the palace guard, well they all not being unintelligent expected this was not some sort of early morning social call. To a man they knew only too well the rank and file of the Black Guard despised the rest of the Krosaky army legions. Aye and this perhaps almost just as much as Commander Gortak did. Barak had by now replaced his black hood over his big shaven head and fallen discretely back into the ranks to ride among his own savage Viking reivers. For now at least, the giant decided he would let the brash bullish Commander Gortak do all the talking.

Aye, but however, this was only for now.

Tark, who was reined in beside Barak had already informed his Lord that the brothers were not amongst the delegation who had ventured from the palace. It was much more than probable though these sibling conspirers had been roused from their dark slumbers. Aye this indeed was of course a much more likely fact than not. Barak was in no doubt whatsoever in thinking that these unsavoury characters would be lurking about somewhere. Apparently these brothers were nocturnal things at times, but still despite this they most eerily somehow missed nothing. Now no doubt the brothers were watching in secret each and every move made by Barak from some hidden vantage point or other.

'You come here to this place, to this palace uninvited Commander Gortak. This, well this is of course a most unwelcome trespass, it is a violation of your post.' It was a tall man who said this, a tall man with short cropped snow white hair and a most snidey look about him. Aye and he was a tall man who was dressed in a fine black mink gown that almost touched the ground. No doubt also this mink gown was bought and paid for by the sweat of honest workers who were of course less expensively dressed.

Commander Gortak spat in contempt at the speaker's words, then, the big commander added a grunt as he growled out an insult just for good measure. For he just like Barak had little or no time for pompous self-centered officials full of their own over-blown importance.

'Tell me this, since when was it in the capital of Krozakistan called a trespass for the king's guard to ride across the king's parade ground, Tilus? Aye and also since when was it the gates were ordered to be chained and locked and guarded by your armed palace fools?' Tilus, who was by the by, the senior magistrate and chief council advisor, would have spoken and countered sharply in reply had not the Commander quickly continued with his stern questioning.

'Oh and also, well this day if I am not much mistaken, is, if I remember correctly, market day. And yet here I see no bustling stallholders setting out their goods, and also I see none of our citizens here looking for early morning bargains.

In fact Tilus I see nothing but shiny polished soldiers. Well this and pallid weary looking Palace officials, fools, who to be honest know little or nothing at all.'

Barak now gave a thin smile, the slayer supposed he could not have put what the commander had just said any better himself.

'Aye and on market day Tilus, well this parade ground is open to each all and every one of our people. Oh aye, and also it always has been so,' Gortak added sternly and gruffly.

Tilus took a step forward as he descended the bottom step of the many that lead up to the most illustrious palace.

'Yes perhaps, but not any more Commander Gortak,' Tilus replied somewhat simply and more than a little smugly.

It was plainly obvious to Barak that both Commander Gortak and this unhealthy looking Tilus fellow had no love for one another.

'Why is that then Tilus? Tell me is everybody here and around ill or something? Or is there perhaps the threat of the plague about?' Commander Gortak growled this question out while peering down from his big nasty looking mount as he did so.

Tilus merely smirked and gave a carefree wave of his soft manicured hands. Of course these were hands that had never done a day's honest work in his whole miserable self-centred life.

'It is the High Lord Karl's orders, and that is quite simply all you need to know soldier.' Tilus said this with a sneer of supremacy as he put a hand upon the black rein of Commander Gortak's stallion. Almost at once the big black beast, which just like its master certainly had somewhat of an attitude problem bit Tilus quite viciously. Oh and this bite, much to the commander's obvious delight drew blood from the magistrate's right arm. Also quite surprisingly the blood was actually red, apparently magistrates were, so it seemed, human. Straightaway and at once the high ranking city official screamed out in a shrill girly like fashion. Why, Tilus sounded just like a young child as the fool at once drew back fast and almost fearfully away from the offending big black beast. This fool would be of little use in an arena or on a battlefield Barak thought to himself as he smiled behind his black face veil.

When and after a moment or two Tilus found his tongue, he then verbally vented his anger toward the rider of the beast.

'That thing, that thing you sit upon is indeed a most savage creature Commander Gortak, aye it should be muzzled like a camel, or better still killed and butchered for meat.' Tilus complained bitterly drawing himself further away from the unfriendly creature.

Of course the commander was most offended and less than impressed by these harsh offending words concerning his noble mount.

'Nonsense Tilus, my horse Thunder is a stallion and all stallions, well they do these sort of things.' The big commander said this most defensively as he patted his horse lovingly upon its powerful black neck. Gortak had already decided he would reward the stallion later for its good taste to bite the back stabbing and ever plotting Tilus. For now though he would rapidly change the subject somewhat.

'Aye and anyway, tell me this Tilus, since when were these merchant's sons given the title of Lords here in the capital? After all Barak's sibling Zark is the presumed king and master here, well that until the day his brother returns once again to us. '

Tilus sucked upon his injured arm, then he spat out blood before replying quite angrily to the commander's question.

'Zark as we all know is weak, also he is unwell, he has I believe taken to his bed some weeks ago with blinding headaches and the dizziness' Tilus had said this with a sly crooked sort of smile about his already snidey face. 'Why, it was Zark himself who requested that the brothers look to his kingdom and take care of all his official duties,' Tilus next replied coldly.

Once again Commander Gortak gave a grunt and a growl directed at the brothers worthless lackey Tilus.

'Your young weak-kneed captain at the gate spoke of enemy agents amongst us Tilus,' Gortak said this whilst leaning forward in his black saddle. A saddle that was designed much in the way as Barak's was, for comfort. 'What enemy agents would they be then? Better still you foppish fool, tell me what enemy do we face? ' Commander Gortak next sternly demanded to know.

'As after all, being the Black Guard Commander, then surely I should of been informed if we are upon the brink of some sort of war or deception of any kind,'

Tilus muttered curses as he scowled angrily and rubbed at his bitten arm.

'The foolish captain of the gate said this to you Commander Gortak did he? Well I do swear I will have him, along with all of his men, lashed until death for cowardice,' he next hissed out spitefully.

Barak by now had heard quite enough of this foolish nonsense, oh and also the ogre was fair fuming with rage. Now the angry giant urged his big horse forward with a kick to the ribs and at once the great beast bounded forward with such a leap it knocked Tilus down onto the red tiled floor.

'There will be no lashings here today you simpering fool, and nor for that matter on any other day, at least not to any soldier of mine.' Barak growled this out as he sat atop his horse glaring down at the now cringing Tilus. Today, well it seemed was a day the unfortunate Tilus was going to have no luck with big horses, or big men. 'Well, not so proud and haughty now are you, you worm? This the angry giant snarled out whilst pulling away both his face veil and then drawing back his black hood. Bending over in his saddle Barak next scooped up the palace magistrate and court official by his long scrawny throat, aye and this as if he was no more than a rabbit.

'Barak,' Tilus stammered, his voice wisely filled with fear and mortal dread of the great slayer. 'It is then true and not just rumour, you do still live and you are here now, here amongst us? ' he gasped out a little painfully.

Barak grinned as he glared down broadly and fiercely clenching Tilus tightly in his right hand.

'Yes, oh yes it is true, and by the by, you simpering pathetic fool, I am King Barak to you, you skulking dog.' Barak said this with a hateful sneer that made the other untrustworthy officials draw back up the palace steps in total fear. 'Oh aye, and yes you fool I do live, yes I am also here at last amongst you, you, and your fellowship of carrion.'

Tilus could not move one way or another, why he was so afraid that he could not even speak. Barak's black eyes were upon him and the high court official quaked with fear as he dangled in mid-air still held firmly by the giant's massive hand. As for Barak, well the ogre continued with his verbal assessment of the situation as he saw it.

'And I think Tilus, I think I have returned here not a moment too soon by the looks and the sounds of things.'

By now the other haughty court advisors and officials were backing even further away toward the regal palace two stairs at a time. It was quite obvious to them all Barak was twice as big and twice as dangerous as they thought he, or indeed anyone possibly could be. Gortak's dark eyes narrowed angrily as the Commander of the Palace Guard left his rank of soldiers and marched forward to stand directly before Barak. Next, the Commander of the Palace Guard first politely saluted the Black Guard commander then he bowed and saluted Barak. Oh and all of this he did before dropping down, as to what now appeared to be the custom, onto one knee.

Next this fellow quite boldly introduced himself.

'I am Kovan, I am Commander of the Palace Guard, and my legion of men will stand with you my Lord Barak. We will each and every one of us fight if needed at your side, this we will do until death or victory. ' Commander Kovan said this with some conviction while banging his right fist against his left breast in salute. Barak gave a grunt of obvious satisfaction whilst he smiled a little smugly to himself. The giant next glanced at the stern faced Commander Gortak who was obviously not impressed at Commander Kovan's actions. Commander Gortak obviously held all the legions other than his own Black Guard in total disdain and scorn.

But Barak on the other hand, well he as ever cleverly wanted all the friends and all the support he could get.

'Good, yes that is very good, but now, now stand up Commander Kovan,' Barak said with a gesture of his right hand. The giant did this after releasing his grip upon Tilus and dropping him roughly to the ground. With a dull thud the so called high official landed whimpering pitifully upon the hard cold red slabbed ground.

At once Commander Kovan rose to his feet and removed his plumed helmet. Commander Kovan was a tall, broad cropped haired cropped bearded man who was perhaps in his early thirties. Once again the palace Commander Kovan bowed politely then without another word he turned about and rejoined his much relieved men at arms. As the palace commander did this he gave Tilus who was now rising stiffly to his feet a glance of pure hatred. Now, now the men of the palace guard were much at ease with these sudden turn of events and had a most relaxed expression upon their tanned faces. Commander Gortak though merely grunted, as he still of course had little or no time for any legion other than his own elite Black Guard.

Barak thought it now time to make his intentions quite clear.

'I would speak with these brothers, you know, the brothers who you lackey for Tilus, aye and I would speak with them tonight. So Tilus and without fail mind you, at midnight bring these fools to the council chamber. ' Barak urged on his gelding, the ogre reached down then once again he held Tilus firmly by his scrawny neck and heaved him effortlessly onto his sandaled feet.

'Make it so,' the giant said, first shaking then dropping him once again roughly to the ground. Oh and by the by, well this little showing up of Tilus was something the men of the legions, both the Black Guard and the Palace Guard found all very amusing. So amusing the soldiers did not even try to hide their mirth in any way, far from it they all to a man laughed out loudly at Tilus's obvious fear and embarrassment.

'I think you will find these brothers of yours up there, high in the west tower,' said the ever observant Barak. 'As I do believe, I seemed to catch a glimpse of a glass lens blinking in the sunlight just a moment ago,' Barak said plainly.

Tilus now quaked as he knew only too well where the brothers would be concealed, the fact Barak also knew this by his simple powers of observation unnerved him no end.

'Oh, and I would also speak with my younger brother Zark, just as soon as possible, do you understand me?' Barak then ran his black almond shaped eyes over the other treasonous fearful palace delegates. Now these worthless souls at once cringed and cowered whilst drawing themselves away back up the steps, pushing their way through the neat ranks of palace guards as they went. Barak after saying what he had to say turned his huge horse about. Next of a sudden the slayer gave a most casual wave up toward the west tower, the tower where the brothers both watched and lurked.

Within that west tower the giant's casual well timed wave had the desired effect Barak had planned, this was panic, sheer panic.

'He sees us Karl, the great slayer he sees us, the ogre knows only too well that we are here in this tower and we are watching him.' Tarl stammered this out and he did so most fearfully and almost tearfully as he pressed himself back towards the wall of the lofty tower.

Karl cursed and scowled angrily, he was as ever most annoyed at his younger brother's lack of courage and backbone. 'Fool, fool go now at once and awaken the wizard, bring Fong, bring him here to me now,' Karl commanded of his younger sibling.

'But, but the wizard, he sleeps, my brother,' Tarl argued back a little sheepishly.

Karl mumbled curses under his breath and spat before speaking again.

'Then you must awaken him you fool, there is the door to his chamber, bring him here, bring him to me now,' Karl repeated impatiently. 'And then, then after you have done this, take the men who are under our pay, men who are still loyal to our cause and find Zark. Aye you must find him then hide the fool away from his brutish brother. So busy have we been of late with our plotting, well I have not seen the prince for what seems like an age. Who knows, perhaps with a bit of luck he is already a dead thing lying amongst the flowers in his garden,' Karl said this with a bitter uncaring sneer. 'But if you do perchance find him, tell him this. Tell him Barak is here in the city and we have heard through our spies the ogre means to kill him. Tell him also he must flee into the secret chambers and conceal himself if he is to live. With any luck that great savage ogre might have forgotten the very whereabouts of the secret chambers and passageways. For if he drinks the vodka and he smokes the black weed even half as much as they say he does, well then surely his pea size brain inside his pumpkin size head must be totally and completely addled by now,' Karl chuckled spitefully to himself.

Next the would-be king and despot Karl sneered in utter contempt and jealous hatred for the giant. No matter what, Karl had no intention of allowing this over grown tattooed fool to interfere with any of his plans for total and absolute power. Barak after all, so Karl mused, was no more than a primitive overgrown butcher. Still though he was a butcher who could trace his blood line back to the Kings and heroes of the savage Kurgans, oh and these men it must be said were all very accomplished killers.

Master Fong was straightaway awoken from his slumbers as Karl had ordered. He was it must be said not pleased by the sudden rude intrusion. Still though despite this the wizard did manage to assure Karl the stronger and the more determined of the two brothers he need not have cause for worry. And also the wizard assured him with a cackling laughter that all would be well. Before the week was out both he and his weaker sibling brother would be crowned joint kings of the coveted empire of Krozakistan. Fong had always known all the while that no mortal flesh and blood man could stand any chance against such an awesome and terrible slayer as Barak. Also even with all the poisoned talk that had been spread about the slayer these past months the Krozaky people and most of the armed men all still loved and adored their huge savage and most wayward monarch. Barak after all was their heroic saviour, he was their king, their god even to some of the more honest but feeble minded.

However, Fong knew only too well Barak was not a god. No, the great ogre, he bled and ached and he slept and he dreamt just as all other mortal men. Aye and the great slayer did all of this just the same as anyone else, and being so, then just the same as anyone else he could and would be killed. Without giving too much away to the brothers, Master Fong returned to his slumbers. The wizard did this while leaving the dangerous and treacherous would be King Karl a much calmer contented and happier man. Fong had no doubt in his mind that once Barak was dead and out of the way, both his brother Zark and even Karl's own sibling would be the next to die. Karl would have no need for either of them and after all why share a throne with a useless faint hearted weakling? This even if that weakling was your own brother?

Anyway, the paid agents of the brothers searched in vain on that cold sunny afternoon to find the Prince Zark and fill his head with yet more lies. However, also so did the newly won over palace guard who discreetly searched for the prince. Mind you the soldiers did this for better and more noble reasons. However, at long last the guards were ordered by Barak to search no more. Barak still well remembered the many secret chambers and tunnels that went here and there all about the palace and its vast grounds. This being so if his brother Zark did not want to be discovered for whatever reason, well then he would of course, not be found.

'Tell me what kind of man is he, my brother?' Barak asked this of the palace commander Kovan.

'After all you guard him, you talk to him and you know him, so, how do you find my brother as a man?' Commander Kovan was about to speak, when the giant suddenly silenced him with a raised gesture of his right hand. 'Oh and Commander, I would the sooner you tell me your honest thoughts and opinions about the man. Aye and not just say what you think I would want to hear, understand?' At the time of this conversation the men were stood on a large ornate balcony overlooking a vast well kept garden. It was a garden which was well cultivated and obviously well cared for.

This garden was of course now fruitless given the time of year but still despite this it was nevertheless a most wonderful place.

Commander Kovan gave a slight cough then cleared his throat before speaking up.

'Zark is a good man, a most caring man, and he is a man who loves both his people and his country in equal measure my Lord Barak. Your brother, the Prince is a man who writes and paints and makes things beyond the understanding of all and everyone. Why, even the brightest of our scholars both young and old have not his intellect. You know, even now he works on a craft he says will soon leave the ground and fly into the air like a bird. '

Barak on hearing this scratched at his white beard as he raised his dark eyebrows in sheer disbelief at what he had just heard. A flying machine, no that of course was something that surely was not quite possible the ogre thought to himself.

However though, Commander Kovan went on most enthusiastically as to the finer qualities of Barak's younger brother. Indeed the commander seemed just as impressed by Zark as was the ancient Zoltan.

'The good Prince likes nowhere better than the great library or this garden, everything here he grows and cares for himself, he has no servants or gardeners to assist him. Aye and also this is the very reason why I brought you here to this place Lord Barak.' Now of a sudden there was an element of concern in Commander Kovan's voice. 'I only just hope the prince is safe, aye, and that he is merely in hiding somewhere.'

Barak gave a grunt then lit up his long pipe, this as it was now time for a smoke.

'In hiding from me do you mean Commander Kovan?' Barak asked this question with a trace of guilt in his voice.

Now the Commander was suddenly rendered speechless, this as he was not quite knowing what to say to the giant at this moment. Zark, as it happened, well he could perhaps well be afraid of his own brother, knowing what lies he was doubtless told by the treacherous brothers.

Barak shifted his gaze from the palace commander as the ogre could see that he was making him more than a little bit nervous. Puffing out clouds of smoke the giant then next turned about and looked admiringly around the large neat well kept garden. True there were more pretty flowers, hanging trees and fragrant flowering shrubs than Barak would have grown back in Britain. But then again the giant being ever practical only liked to grow things he could later eat, sell, trade or even give away to the poor and needy. Still though despite this small detail, perhaps he and his brother would have a lot more in common with each other than he had at first thought possible. Barak turned about once again and faced the palace commander.

Then the slayer spoke.

'Know you this Commander, if these ill-bred brothers, if they dare harm my own brother, my father's and my mother's son. Then, well then, I would think these ditch dogs are either a lot braver, or a lot more stupid than I ever thought at all possible. ' Barak said this while putting a comforting hand upon Commander Kovan's slightly trembling shoulder.

'However, we will put this to one side for the moment, come now with me and we will take a drink of Vodka and rest our weary legs for a while. This searching, it is after all thirsty work my friend. Oh aye, also you must remember tonight at midnight we will hold court. Barak smiled after saying this, then the great slayer in a happier state of mind clicked his huge neck into place. 'Oh and by the by that little midnight meeting should at least be a most interesting affair, even if it is, I suppose not at all truthful,' said the somewhat cynical giant.

Later on and at day's end, just as it was so ordered by Barak, the midnight court was convened. Now Barak entered into the ancient council chamber and he sat himself down upon a huge throne-like chair at the end of a long rectangular and age old black wooden table. This equally ancient chair was also made of black wood and was most cunningly carved with symbols and perhaps writings of those who educated his people in those far off days many years ago. Oh and of course this was a true throne of court, a seat reserved only for a King. Barak had felt a little strange as the dusty covers were pulled away and he had been seated into the throne. As after all the last man to sit in this great chair was doubtless his father, and that of course was many, many years ago. To both his left and his right sat a variety of so called wise and learned men, oh and perhaps of course some that were not so learned. Most of these however were no more than high born social climbers who were only out for what land, monies and prestige they could secure for themselves.

Magistrates, nobles, scribes and elders as well as the various commanders from each and every legion of the Krozak army were also there in the great council hall. Aye they were all present and dressed up most regal like in their finery for this historic event. All of these high ranking men had been summoned and gathered together for this midnight meeting. This was not only as a matter of protocol, as also they might perhaps be witnesses to a possible double murder. Oh and this would be a possible double murder committed by their very large and very unhinged king. Anyway each and every one of them had been appointed and guided to their various chairs about the long table by the stewards and ushers of court. All in all Barak supposed well here was quite an impressive array of men of so called prominence. But also as ever at such gatherings most of the men here could of course not be trusted. Why most of these hopeless fools were not even worthy of note. In some ways Barak thought to himself this gathering of pompous idiots was little more than some sort of three-ringed circus. Who of them here were loyal? Who here were the deceivers and back stabbers? This, the giant wondered somewhat grimly to himself.

Barak looked about him at the regal splendour of the great hall. He was but a boy the last time he had accompanied his father to this hallowed place. Barak had brought along with him Tark for company but not only for company. Tark would come in useful to point out the names and faces of the court officials and military commanders. Nobody less in rank than a captain would be allowed into the council chamber if you were a military man. And so this being the case Barak had promptly promoted his young bodyguard up a rank or two. As it happened in the distant past, captains would often accompany their commanders or those who they were assigned as bodyguards to protect. Once they were within the hall these bodyguards would then act as no more than poison testers, tasting both the drink and any food that might be laid before their illustrious charges. However though, that would not be the case here. Anyway, if Barak wanted a poison tester he would have appointed Borz. Still though, there was laid out before them from one end of the table to the other, cold meats, fruit and a variety of cheeses. No strong drink though, sadly, it was still only water that was available to quench a thirst. Now the Norse though, well they were much more fortunate men on this particular night. When Barak had left them a little earlier the Viking brotherhood were all feasting upon wild boar and drowning themselves in good strong drink. Oh how the giant envied them. But still and nevertheless this business at hand had to be sorted out one way or the other, so it was best now just to get on with it.

After all there would be plenty of time to drink with the Norsemen after his business here was concluded. At the far end of the long rectangular table there sat two empty chairs, doubtless these seats were reserved for the still absent brothers.

'All are here about you now my lord, save for the brothers Karl and Tarl.' And this the newly promoted Captain Tark whispered as he stood behind the seated giant. Being a captain gave him right of entry into the council chamber by invite, but amazingly Tark was still not high enough in rank to qualify for a seat.

This was an act of protocol Barak found quite intolerable, but nevertheless it was yet another ancient law that must be observed and obeyed. It was also the law that all weapons must be discarded and left placed neatly in racks outside the council chamber doors.

Aye and this also the giant found quite unsettling. Barak had not been parted from his beloved sword since it was forged all those many long years ago. So with this being the case then he would be most keen to finish off his business here and be gone. Aye the slayer would hastily say what he had to say then have his death dealer strapped back upon his hip just as quickly as possible. However the fabled weapon was in safe hands. Because as well as the trusted Black Guard that flanked the corridor from one end to the other, well Thorn also lay guard over the legendary blade.

Barak sat back in his great chair as he looked about him at the pale and ashen features of the unhealthy looking council members. Barak, whose memory as ever was quite unfailing could remember many of them from when he was just a boy. Even then these men were ancient and dying things. Aye and even now

405

after all those long years ago the giant could still pick out the ones his father had said were wise and could be trusted. These honest men put against the deceivers, the backstabbers, aye and the others the long dead King had branded as no more than over privileged fools and liars. Barak was greatly surprised that so many of these men, both good and bad had still lived on to reach such old age. Ah but then again an honest day's work, this was never going to kill any of them, nor neither the clamour of battle come to that. Aye if these corridor creepers were ever going to die of anything then it was more likely from boredom the slayer supposed to himself.

This great hall or chamber itself was a huge lavish affair with oriental velvet curtains and lush thick carpets from Persia and beyond. Within the long airy room it had ornate cunningly wrought tapestries hanging from its high walls depicting heroic battles from Krozak history, battles that were fought out long, long ago.

Blazing torches stood out from their bronze fastenings set deep into the solid stone walls. Every six foot or so one of these torches blazed brightly, making the great ancient hall a shadowy and somewhat eerie place. Of course as well as these torches there was the lighting and heating from the oil filled guttering that ran from corner to corner of the great hall.

A tall bent-over man with a long white beard reaching down to his waist stood in attendance upon a raised and rounded dais. This unhealthy looking fellow was garbed as were all the council members and officials in a single long black robe, a robe that reached down to his boney sandaled feet. Also this robe was a hooded affair and the long hood sitting atop his head hung over his brow hiding most of his face. Perhaps though this was for the best Barak mused to himself as in all truth most of these ancients looked near to being soon mummified things and were not at all pretty. Aye and also if this meeting went on too long doubtless there would be a fatality of some sorts Barak thought whimsically to himself. Also this man, this usher, he carried in his right hand a six foot rod of solid gold, the rod had a most ornate and most decorative double headed eagle atop it. Unlike the painted eagles of Rome, this also was made of solid gold and it had bright red gems for its eyes. Why this ceremonial trinket itself could of bought all of Aulric's primitive kingdom.

'Is there no strong drink to be had in this place?' Barak asked in a low rumble already knowing the answer to his question. Tark and Commander Gortak had already informed him of the formalities of such a hearing, but the giant had hoped in vain the rules could have been perhaps made a little lax on this occasion.

However of course that was not to be.

'Only water my Lord Barak, it is the ancient law,' the tall hooded man replied in a monotonous droning sort of voice.

Commander Gortak who now stood to Barak's right, he would when the time came be seated on the first and nearest chair to the giant. However this would only transpire once all were seated and the council meeting had begun a proper. Gortak struggled not to laugh as the giant cursed under his breath at the ancient and outdated no drinking laws. It was no wonder his father had hated these council meetings with a passion Barak thought to himself.

'Aye this is an ancient law my Lord Barak,' the tall hooded usher repeated in the same loud drab voice. Obviously the usher or master of ceremonies or whatever else he was. Well just perhaps he was used to speaking to the ancient and the deaf, aye and he thought that Barak was in some way similarly afflicted. Barak raised his eyebrows in mock surprise at the hooded man's words.

'Oh no, surely not,' the giant muttered out a little louder than he had quite intended. A servant at once came forward with a jug of water and a drinking vessel in his hand. Barak most politely declined the offer of drinks but retained the drinking vessel. Next the ogre produced from under his wolf skin cloak his own midnight refreshment.

'I have here my own drink, it is spring water from the mountains, much better, much healthier, oh aye and I do swear by it.' Oh and the giant said this with a slight smile as he poured the vodka into the cup. 'Once bitten twice shy my lad.' Barak whispered this to Tark who had by this time great difficulty in controlling his laughter. Barak took a deep swallow of drink as he next congratulated himself on his own wile, then the great ogre spoke up once again.

'You, you Tilus, it is now the midnight hour, so, your master's tell me, where then are these fools?' Barak demanded this somewhat gruffly as the ogre was now becoming a little bit put out at being kept waiting. Aye and also, well, apart from the military men Barak supposed he did not really enjoy the company he was spending his time with. Tilus now looked a little fearful. However he had no time to answer Barak's question, as of a sudden the great doors to the council chamber were pulled open by the guards to permit entry. It was then that big Barak got his first glimpse of the brothers. Oh and the ogre was it must be said, less than impressed by their somewhat dainty and girly appearance.

'Here we have the diplomats, the brothers Karl and Tarl who hail from the noble family of the merchant traders Xenox.' This, the hooded usher announced in that same droning monotonous voice as the brothers moved forward in a most feminine fashion to stand by their appointed chairs. Noble, well there was that much overly used word again the giant thought to himself.

These two men, well if men they could be called wore identical clothing. Why these insipid creatures were even painted and powdered up in exactly the same decadent feminine fashion. Each one of them wore a long expensive silken lilac toga type dress, this flimsy garment reached down to their lilac silk slippers. Their fingernails were painted a bright red and these nails were long manicured things, not the hands of either a warrior or a worker. Also their lips, well these too were bright red. Their pale liquid eyes, blue eyes which were not that of a full blood Krozaky. These eyes had been powdered, aye and powdered a strange yellowish colour at that. This in all truth gave the brothers a most sickly and jaundiced look. Both of the brother's heads were shaven bald, and these shining craniums were fragile looking in the very extreme. Aye, oh aye these skulls would take no crushing at all when the time came to it Barak thought merrily to himself. Why the ogre would need no more effort than it would take to crush a goose's eggshell. Now and with their painted hands held together the brothers bowed, though this with a most sinister look to all those about them. Next the brothers paid their homage to Barak, this last and quite politely the longest of all.

Well at least these pair of fops had at least some sort of manners Barak silently mused to himself. Next one of these creatures spoke.

'I am Karl Xenox my Lord Barak and this is my younger brother Tarl,' the slightly taller of the two tall and very lean men said in a shrill girl-like voice.

Barak grunted in honest uncaring disgust then he took another swift drink of his vodka.

'Here Commander, take a drink,' Barak said as he passed the refilled cup to a smiling Commander Gortak. The commander swallowed down the vodka eagerly then passed the drained cup back to his King. Meanwhile big Barak stood silently staring at the brothers in shameful astonishment. Next the slayer refilled the cup and took another drink then offered this to a grinning Tark. Somehow the young warrior quite rightly assumed this formal court meeting was going to be like no other that had taken place in the great council hall. Oh and as for the giant, well he of course had no intention here in this courtroom of observing any niceties or formalities. What the slayer had to say would be said, and those who were offended by his words could quite simply leave. Or otherwise, well these fools could stay and be offended even further for all he cared. As after all he was the King, well at least for now he was anyway. Now the aged court usher, who looked like a man who had been dead for several days politely pulled back the two chairs set aside for the brothers. At once the sickly looking siblings seated themselves, aye and most daintily did they sit. Posturing and posing like a pair of painted courtesans. With the brothers so seated, then all of the others in attendance at once also sat their backsides down on the velvet padded chairs.

Oh and all of this while the brothers smiled in a sickly sort of fashion as they looked about them selecting out certain members of the court officials with their searching glances. However though, well not one legion commander gave any indication of any mirth at this blatant flirtatious encouragement. That in itself was good enough for Barak, now the slayer knew at least he had all of the legions on his side. Anyway, the giant wanted answers and he wanted these answers quick and without delay. Aye and indeed, the impatient ogre wanted these answers now, right now. Oh and it was to hell itself with the ancient protocol was the giant's ever growing sentiments. Answers, Barak wanted answers.

'I looked for my brother today, but alas I could not find him here in the palace, and nor for that matter was he in its grounds. Tell me, why was that then do you suppose?' Barak demanded this of the brothers, and getting straight to the point of things.

Tarl fidgeted with his robe like some sort of a rebuked child as he glanced nervously and fearfully all about him. This ogre seated at the other end of the long table was much bigger and even more fiercesome than he thought at all was possible for a man to look, well if indeed a man he was.

'I do not know my Lord Barak.' Karl answered the question evenly, and to his credit the elder of the two brothers held his nerve under the giant's cold glare. 'After all your brother is a most furtive and secretive man. Aye, the prince often hide's himself away for days on end, in secret places that only he himself knows. It is after all a very big palace, or have you forgotten that my Lord Barak?' Karl asked this question with a brave and daring smirk.

As for now the usurper felt he was safe here amongst these bookworms and court officials; however he was wrong to feel so, oh yes he was very wrong. For Barak as we know hated any kind of officialdom with a savage and an unyielding passion. Oh and also the giant after all, well he did not like this creature. Oh no the slayer did not like him one little bit. Barak now muttered curses to himself then took a deep drink from his cup draining it in a gulp. Now with his temper rising, the ogre instantly refilled the cup, he then at once drained the contents also in a single swallow. Now and thus fortified by the wonderful liquid Barak put a hand to his ear as if struggling to hear the words Karl had just spoken to him.

As ever and always the great and avenging slayer had a plan.

'Tonight, tonight alas my young creature, my deafness it is upon me, and so I do not hear you too well. This is due I think to too many knocks about my big bald head I do suppose.' The giant had said this with a sort of smile that next turned into a very nasty looking sneer. 'So, so now I will come closer to you, this just so I might hear what it is you have to say.' Barak rumbled this out as he rose and pushed back his chair with such a force it almost knocked Tark to the floor.

'You must be seated my Lord Barak, protocol must be observed at all times.' This, the ancient usher with the eagle-headed rod said with his droning voice beginning to break up a little with the excitement of it all.

'Deafness, aye deafness this is a most terrible thing my Lords.' This a smiling Zoltan said seeking to justify Barak's rude actions. Old Zoltan, well he was now most keen to see just what this brutal tattooed giant was all about.

'This is outrageous, scandalous!' Tilus protested and this the brother's lackey said just before he was slapped across the back of the head as the fast striding giant passed him by.

'Sorry, did perhaps my hand catch you by accident in my passing?' Barak said this whilst trying to sound concerned for the brother's worthless lackey.

Tilus, well he made no reply to the giant, as even that slight slap was enough to render him totally unconscious.

Tarl was now thrown into an instant panic and tugged frantically at his brother's lilac dress.

'Look Karl, look my brother, the great painted ogre, he approaches us.'

Karl cursed as he pushed his brother's hand away from him.

'You must be seated my Lord Barak, it is the law,' the ancient hooded man declared, his heart racing like that of a galloping horse.

Barak paid not the least bit of attention to the usher and this while several scribes with their grey heads lowered wrote down with some excitement the events of that very moment. Only a few long giant strides later and Barak was there standing towering over the brothers Xenox.

'I do strongly advise you both not mess with me in any way, you pair of powdered fops.' Barak snarled this out as he stood glowering down over the still seated brothers. 'For you must both believe this, I am indeed the ogre and I am the monster men speak of. Do you understand that? Do you, do you understand me you pair of fools? Barak demanded in almost a whisper so his threat could not be heard by others. Now at this time the ogre's fanged teeth were only a hand's width away from the brother's pale powdered faces.

At this point the usher had opened the doors to the council chamber to summon the guards of court, but of course despite his somewhat pathetic cries for help none came. Instead the guards of court stood there motionless, as did the vigilant but statue like Black Guards in the corridor. It was almost as if Barak's sudden and imagined deafness had also claimed their hearing as well. Deaf or otherwise Barak had something to say, so of course he would say it.

'Tell me now you badly bred things, who was it that gave the order for the Black Guard to leave this place, leave here and go to the land of the Britons? Speak up you pair of fools and speak up now while you still have a tongue in your empty heads to do so,' Barak demanded this in a low hiss. Tarl at this time was now a jibbering wreck of a thing. Karl meanwhile swallowed down a mouthful of water to lubricate his dry mouth before managing to speak up.

'It was your own brother Zark, aye it was he who gave out the order Barak. And I, well I as a servant merely carried out his request by calling upon the blackguard to do his bidding.' Karl answered this question trying with some difficulty both to look and remain calm.

About the ogre and the brothers now there was much whisperings and mutterings at the long table. However not one soul made a movement other than to strain their ears to hear what was being said between the giant and the elder brother.

410

'Liar, you do lie to me creature, and so tell me, why would my brother the prince want to do that?' Barak demanded to know.

Karl even under such immense pressure was as ever and always a quick thinker.

'He believed my Lord for his own reasons, unknown to me as to their origins, that you plotted to raid and sack this kingdom. Oh and what is furthermore he also believed you blamed him in some way or other for the death of your mother. Aye and because of this, that you were intent on slaying him.' Karl said this out loud so all there could hear him as he put forward his sad and flimsy defence. None there believed one word the elder brother had said. However though despite this the book keepers and the court scribes nevertheless recorded it down in Karl's defence.

And as for Barak, well the ogre he at once fumed at these words. In but a heartbeat the slayer would have perhaps crushed the skulls of the brothers there and then. Well this had he not been suddenly surrounded and mobbed by a dozen or more of the ancient council members. These as old as they were, had at last had seen quite enough of the sacrilegious break in ancient protocol. Besides the protocol, if they sat back another moment or two doubtless they would all see a double murder committed right before their very watery eyes.

Tarl at this point could take no more, so next and with tear filled eyes he was up and he was off passing the smirking Black Guard down the corridor as he hurried off to his chamber. Why the younger brother ran off whimpering down the long corridor so fast that Barak's great dog could not even have caught him had it given chase.

'My Lord Barak, my King you must be calm, please my Lord, please control yourself.' This the tall hooded court official gasped out between his heavy breathing and his death rattle-like coughing.

'Calm, calm myself you say? Barak declared angrily. 'Know you this, I should, aye and also I could so easily snap this lady man's treacherous scrawny neck like a dried out twig,' snarled the angry giant.

Karl who was ever cold, collected and in control of most situations, at this point, well, even he began to panic. Oh aye and in all truth the plotter thought to himself that his life was to be over there and then. So of a sudden he rose and begged the court officials to be excused, with this done and in an obvious fright he sped off looking most sickly to a small ante chamber. This as it happened was an ante chamber which provided a most civilized toilet facility. A toilet facility that made anything else of that day and age look positively primitive in comparison.

'Fong,' Karl gasped out in shock as he closed the stout door behind him. 'You here, aye and here now, how is this so?' he gasped clutching at his fast beating chest. The tiny sorcerer merely chuckled as he next tugged playfully at his long forked and wispy white beard. Karl for the very life of him failed to grasp what the ancient Mandarin sorcerer found so amusing.

411

'Why do you laugh Fong? We are after all undone here, it is over now and we must flee this place. Aye we must flee before we are all butchered by the great ogre Barak.' Karl stammered this declaration out most fearfully. 'This man, if man he is, no, no he is not a man. No Barak is a demon, Fong, aye he is a demon from the very pit of hell itself I tell you. ' Karl Xenox muttered this out with his normal cold composure completely gone now. 'Yes, Barak is nothing less than an ogre, an unstoppable demon from the very pit of hell itself,' he went on. The elder Xenox brother said this while his bitter tears stained the coloured face powder about his pale eyes.

Once again Master Fong merely chuckled, then the wizard offered out a goblet of a steamy frothy drink from out of nowhere to his patron and hitherto host.

'Drink this, my gentle Lord. I promise it will make you feel much better, trust me my friend it will make you strong, it will make you able. '

Karl, out of sheer panic and without question eagerly took the goblet and drained it down in a single shaky swallow. Its effect was indeed strange, aye and it was also instant. As of a sudden his world, well it went around and around in a swirl of smoky colours and vivid images. Every tattoo he had noticed etched upon the giant's huge body seemed to come alive, come alive then run and fly and slither before his very eyes. Karl Xenox next suddenly fell in a faint onto the marble tiled floor beneath him. But then when he arose only moments later helped to his feet by the grinning sorcerer, the despot felt strangely different.

In fact the most devious usurper felt very different. Now the wizard had something of great importance to say to Karl Xenox.

'You must go back into the hall now my young prince, you must challenge Barak for the right of Kingship,' Master Fong said firmly. 'Challenge the great oaf to a swordfight, aye challenge him to a duel to the death. Oh, and this duel is to take place in two days hence. In two days mind you Lord Karl, no sooner and no later,' Fong further explained.

Karl did not argue nor did he protest at this ridiculous request, instead he then simply nodded positively.

'Yes, yes I do understand Master Fong' he answered in dreamlike agreement.

And so next, the wizard said on.

'You must challenge the ogre to a duel, a duel for the insults, and for what he has accused you of this very night,' the sorcerer said with a thin smile. 'Oh and of course by doing this, then you also challenge him for the Kingship. Do you understand me Karl? The oafish ogre is still as yet, you must remember, still the King. Yes it is Barak who is the monarch here, and not that foolish dreamer of a brother of his. And with this being so the ogre therefore must accept the challenge you offer him. Besides that, because he is Barak, he will of course accept your offer. Oh aye and this even though he might not understand it. However my prince, this is matterless as then he will of course also die.

'And all of this even though by his very animal instincts and by what common sense he does possess in his big bucket sized head, the ogre will know only too well dark magic is at work here. However Barak's foolish pride and his even more foolish honour will my prince prevent him from objecting or raising an argument to your seemingly ridiculous challenge,' the wizard said this with a thin smile. 'So now then Karl Xenox, do you trust me? Oh and furthermore do you know exactly what you have to do, and also what you have to say when you go back into the great hall?' This the tiny frail looking ancient wizard asked whilst affixing his mesmerized host with his cold black slant eyes.

Karl, the now hypnotised looking plotter next answered the Mandarin sorcerer without any hesitation.

'Yes, yes I do trust you, and yes I do understand exactly what it is that I must do,' Karl replied still in a dreamlike state.

'Two days, only two days from now my friend and the great oaf Barak will be dead and gone. Oh and believe me, once dead then he will be soon forgotten and become a thing of the past. With the giant dead, it will be you who will be the rightful King of the great undefeated kingdom of Krozakistan. It is the law of your land, and being so no one in the kingdom can gainsay it. ' Fong said this while stabbing a bony finger towards Karl who had by now a strange and eerie smile about him.

'And for my part in the giant's downfall,' the wizard stalled, as if savouring this very moment. 'I Fong, I will summon up from the very grave, from the very pit of darkest hell the greatest and the most evil swordsman of all time. It is he who will fight in your place for Kingship and not you,' Fong whispered. 'This long dead master swordsman will take on your very appearance, and all who watch in amazement at this duel, well, these fools will think you are the hero, that it is you who are the victor of the one sided conflict. Why Barak, he will look like no more than a painted oversized fraud against the skills of the greatest sword master who ever lived, the legendary Ming.' The tiny ancient sorcerer was most convincing as he said all of this most confidently, and in a most matter of fact manner.

'Now my Lord Karl you must refresh yourself here for but a moment.' Fong pointed towards a font where warm water ran constantly, supplied from the same underground source as were the baths.

Karl, well he did most obediently and mechanically straightaway wash himself down in the marble font basin. Next the dangerous schemer admired his person in a long slim glass mirror affixed to the marble wall as he completely composed himself for his reappearance in the great hall. Fong was most correct in his straightforward statement. Barak had to die for the usurpers to make any sort of headway. After but a moment's dreamlike thoughts, Karl Xenox looked about him. Now the wizard Fong had simply vanished, aye he had simply disappeared off into thin air. It was then the scheming plotter and usurper to the throne quite

413

calmly left that place of his recent brief sanctuary. Above all the disruption, the clamour and the obvious confusion in the great council hall the elder brother returned and seated himself. Karl Xenox waited a moment or two giving everyone in the hall time to realise his return. It was then, when his presence was noted by all and sundry, he quite calmly rose to his slippered feet. Oh yes and it was also then he announced his brave intentions to cross swords with Barak. Aye and this was to take place in two days time and in the great arena just as Fong had directed. To say this challenge caused a great amount of confusion and bewilderment would have been a massive understatement.

'A duel, a duel my Lord, have you gone completely and utterly mad? ' This a still very dazed Tilus asked, pouring water over his throbbing head.

'No, no not mad, I am merely proud Tilus,' the usurper answered back plainly and impassively with that strange look about his powdered face.

'In two days hence and in the ancient arena of the capital, I do challenge you to a duel to the death, Barak,' Karl said, his expression at this time was doll like and his pale eyes were glazed.

Barak moved toward the elder of the brothers, the sweet over powering scent he wore assailed the ogres nostrils making him almost urge. Barak glared down at the elder brother knowing full well that in these few minutes Karl had left the council hall he had met somehow with the Mandarin wizard.

'Are you well Karl Xenox? For surely you must know you have no chance against Barak?' Asked the tall hooded official who croaked this out almost painfully as he steadied himself from falling by grabbing against a high backed chair.

The excitement of this whole very strange affair may well be this ancient servant of the courts very undoing before the next rising of the sun.

Karl Xenox completely ignored the tall hooded usher as he pressed on with what he had to say.

'For the honour of my noble family and for insults afforded me by Barak this night, as well as for the kingship I do offer challenge. Do you accept my challenge Barak? Karl Xenox repeated with a most confident tone to his shrill voice.

Barak did not for one moment hesitate in his reply and this even though he knew fine well the darkest of treachery and deception was at work here.

'Aye, aye you fool we will duel, and we will begin our duel at midday. Let this take place in the great arena in front of my people. And yes fool, it goes without saying this fight is to the death.' Barak said this while slamming his great fist down upon the table so hard that a crack formed down its whole length.

'So be it then,' the ancient hooded court official said weakly; by the looks of him he was still quite obviously in quite a state of shock. Aye and indeed the old man wondered to himself would he live long enough to witness this most oddly made duel.

With these final words spoken Karl Xenox still with a foolish sort of grin about him bowed first to Barak then to the council members. Then with this final act of protocol once accomplished he next padded off silently away to his quarters.

In the meanwhile book keepers scribbled away into their great leather bound books these strange and dramatic events of this very unusual midnight gathering.

'Well, that was quite a turn up was it not it Tark?' Barak said a little wistfully to the newly appointed captain Tark who had by now left his place and strode quickly to be at Barak's side. 'One minute the man, girl boy thing or whatever else it was is quaking with fear in his girly slippers. Oh and by the looks of things on the verge of soiling himself or herself or whatever the creature just might be. And then next, only moments later the vile lady thing challenges me to a duel, aye and a duel to the death. Very strange, very odd don't you think so my boy?' Barak added as he toyed with his thick gold hooped earring and took another drink.

Tark had about him at this particular time a most concerned and worried look. Since meeting with Barak he had been well educated. Aye indeed, he had for himself a most exciting time and the most highest of adventures. But the young man had noticed however while grooming himself that very morning his jet black hair was greying a little about his ears. Oh yes, life with Barak could certainly age a man Tark silently mused to himself.

'Karl Xenox, he is no swordsman my Lord Barak, no he never was, and he never will be.' Tark said this in a confused mumble also he looked most agitated as he said it. 'I do not understand this, my Lord, and nor do I like it. Why the fool has no chance against you, you or anyone else for that matter, no he has no chance at all. '

Commander Gortak too, well he looked most perplexed as he swallowed down a mouthful of vodka offered him by the giant.

'Magic, dark magic is afoot here, aye and dark cunning magic at that my lord.' Tark said this in a whisper as Barak thanked the various delegates and officials that filed past them making their somewhat rapid departure. Oh and all the while these dumfounded delegates were muttering and mumbling as they went on their way.

'I don't know about you Commander, or you my boy, but I for one need a good drink. And aye, aye I also some good company to go with that drink, do you understand? Barak said this as he strode off down the corridor after first picking up both his big dog and his beloved sword.

It was all that Tark and the commander could do to keep up with the fast striding giant as the men made their way back to Barak's private chamber.

Once there, Barak lit up his pipe and inhaled deeply before blowing the smoke out into perfect rounded hoops. Barak next poured out three drinks of vodka, the ogre had about him at this particular time a most disturbed and agitated look.

'Witchery, sorcery and black magic, Oh I do hate these things,' Barak declared this of a sudden as he drained his goblet dry then gave it an instant refill.

Tark was most sullen now, aye he was thoughtful and silent for a moment, indeed the young man he did not know quite what to say at this particular point in time.

Barak now moved to the small window in his chamber and looked out at a cold clear and star studded sky.

'Be sure on the morrow to bring me black lily petals to grind into a potion we might send off to Aulric.' This the giant said between puffing upon his pipe and swallowing down another mouthful of vodka.

'My Lord Barak that is a task that can wait for now surely,' Tark protested sounding a very worried young man.

Barak shook his big bucket head as he toyed with his earring, the ogre had a habit of doing this lately since losing his bad tooth.

'No, no it cannot wait Tark, the eagle, my black eagle she will soon return to find me here in this place. I know her well, and she will come back to me hopefully before my duel with whomever or whatever I fight in the arena two days hence. Then the antidote you must send with her to Aulric. If I am to perish in the arena by foul means, this is your final task for me, so please lad do not fail me in this request Tark son of Atark. For this, as you well know is a most important undertaking that has been assigned to me.'

Commander Gortak swallowed down another drink then he spoke up with his voice full of concern.

'Why fight magic my Lord? Why do you not simply call out the Black Guard and put down any who oppose us? Starting with the Xenox brothers and the wizard first,' the Commander suggested. Barak after but a moment's silence then shook his head.

'No,' the giant answered back quite simply. Barak's whole demeanour had suddenly changed since leaving the council hall and the slayer was not quite himself at all.

It was Tark now who was swallowing down great gulps of vodka as he knew only too well all was not right with his Lord.

'Flesh and blood, this whether it be that of man or of a savage beast I hold in no dread. I have no fear of anything that bleeds,' Barak explained after another drink.' But in the arena two days hence? I know well, it will not be the powdered fop Karl Xenox I draw swords against. That my friends is a most certain fact. '

Tark and commander Gortak also both knew this to be true and were both much afeard for their master's well being.

'Call it off my Lord, go to the council with your suspicions of deceit and treachery. Surely not even you can after all defeat black magic with but a yard of steel.' Tark said this imploringly. Commander Gortak was silent, but he was much impressed with the obvious friendship his nephew had with the king.

'And why not boy? ' a voice asked from behind them at the entrance of the doorway to the small but comfortable chamber. 'Aye, why not Tark? Tell me why not lad? After all, Barak has beaten black magic before. Or have you forgotten so soon that what I have told you on our many nightly talks Tark? Barak, well, he has before this day defeated zombies and the undead, aye and indeed anything else that has foolishly stood in his big booted path.' This was a half drunken Ragnor who stated this proudly. 'The slayer is after all my closest friend, aye the big man is Barak, and he is without any doubt the greatest warrior I have ever known. Oh and by the way, I will stand all wagers in favour of my large friend here. Aye and that be whether the great slayer fight god or demon, or even both of these sort of fools together and at the same time. Thor and Odin included,' Ragnor added this defiantly and with a growl of confidence.

Inwardly Barak growled and grumbled then the slayer cursed himself for these last few moments of weakness and self doubt. Ragnor's words of confidence had stirred him, after all was said and done, he was Barak. Aye and he was so far undefeated in all and everything that was at all nasty and violent. Aye after all he was undefeated by man or beast, or even the zombie creatures he had put to their final rest all those long years ago. Anyway and besides all of that, there were things to settle in the here and now, important things at that. It was now, now at long last time to atone, time to put right that which was wrong and corrupt in the empire of Krozakistan.

His father he would have expected it of him, no, his father King Bartok would have demanded it of him. And also at day's end it was only he, he Barak who could now put right that which had been made wrong in his place of birth. The slayer had no choice but to win in the arena, as to lose to whatever it was he fought was not in any way an option. Should the brothers and the sorcerer prevail, well then all decency morality and honour would most certainly disappear and be lost forever in his Kingdom. Tark suddenly smiled then the young man laughed as he spat venomously upon the tiled marble floor.

'You are of course right Ragnor, the man Karl, with or without a sorcerer to assist him is not worth that.' Tark said, pointing to the spittle upon the floor before stamping it in with his shiny black boot.

Barak drew his ivory handled sword, this blade was indeed to him a thing of grace and great beauty. On one side of the slightly curved blade there was etched into its keen flat surface a crouching dragon cunningly wrought by master craftsman. On the other side of the blade there was an inscription scribed in the same strange stroke like letters of its makers. Barak lovingly ran a gnarled finger over the perfectly carved very strange and mysterious lettering.

'Can you read it Barak? Do you know what this lettering says?' Tark asked as he poured out a drink for the Norseman just in case he was in danger of sobering up.

Barak at once gave a most positive nod.

'Yes, yes I can read it, I am not a fool you know,' he answered with a slight smirk. 'The inscription reads thus, simply, this sword forged from the star metal will never know defeat as long as its claim in war or battle is just and true. '

Ragnor sighed and then the big Viking shrugged as he took for himself a drink before speaking.

'Well then, there you are my large and colourful friend, you have nothing to worry about do you - so can we perhaps all be a little bit happier now. ' Ragnor asked this while drunkenly flopping his big backside down onto Barak's large bed.

'Oh and you must always remember this Barak, it is better to die sword in hand fighting your enemy, don't you agree?' Ragnor slurred these words out with a foolish grin about his hairy face.

Barak had to smile for it had been a long time since the ogre had seen the Viking chieftain so hopelessly drunk. Tark muttered his agreement as to the Vikings brave words as also did commander Gortak. But Barak, well the slayer surprisingly to all there shook his head in disagreement.

'No,' the giant replied quite simply.

'No!' Ragnor exclaimed with a shocked voice. 'Then tell me my friend how is it that you would wish to die Barak? Tell me, just how would you choose your final demise to be if not sword in hand and enemies at your great big booted feet?'

Barak grunted and growled in a contented fashion as he puffed upon his long pipe then swallowed down more vodka. The ogre next gave off a most wolf like grin before making his reply.

'Many years from now, sitting in my lodge in the forest or outside on my porch, after a good day's hunting and fishing. It is there aye, it is there by choice I would choose to meet with my end. With one drink too many and a last puff of good black weed, I do wish to simply fall asleep in a chair that rocks to and fro then never again to wake up. Aye and the last thing I wish to see in my long bad life is a big full moon, aye and also I would like to hear the sound of the wolf howling in the forest,' the ogre said most sincerely. 'And then at last when I am done, when I am no more than but a dead thing that cannot laugh or cannot rage as I am prone too. Well then my friends I would be taken to a high place and there be put upon a tall pyre. Aye and a tall pyre mind you, not some sad little thing, and then I would be burnt unto ash. For believe me my brothers despite

418

what you all might think, I intend for the drink or the weed to kill me and not the sword or the lance.' Barak said this with just the slightest hint of a smile. 'You know this liver of mine has been good to me. For the gods if there are any, well those fools only know I have not been good to it.' With this once said the giant smiled a grim and unforgiven looking sort of smile as he shook himself free of any melancholy thoughts.

'I will drink to that also you great monster, for I have been looking for more refreshment all of this night. ' Of course it was the drunken German Horst who said these words as he suddenly appeared and stumbled headlong into the room. 'Anyway, tell me how was your meeting, your meeting with the council my Lord Barak?' As ever the German asked this drunkenly as he helped himself to a drink. There were in Barak's chamber many flagons of ale and vodka strewn all about the place. And, also as always and ever Horst being a heavy socialiser never refused a party. Tark scowled and growled away to himself before being the first to answer the drunken German's question.

'The Lord Barak, he fights in the arena in two days from now, this of course is to the death.' Tark said these words most bluntly and in all truth the young man was perhaps a little irritated at the German's uncouth manners. However this grumpy irritation though was perhaps born more out of worry and concern for his master more than anything else. Tark, well, the warrior liked the German, and in truth the young man liked him quite a lot. But this whole adventure, well it now seemed to be unsettling him more with each passing hour.

Horst however, well here was a man who of course was apparently not similarly afflicted.

'Oh good, yes that is very good my Lord, then perhaps we can have a big party after you kill this unfortunate fellow.' Horst said this cheerfully with vodka running down his raggy unkempt beard and dripping onto the marble floor.

Barak shook his big head as he laughed out aloud at Horst's undying faith in him, the giant was still laughing loudly when he sheathed his much loved dragon sword and removed his chain link helmet.

'Why wait until then to party my little fat one legged German friend?' Now the giant said this with all of his confidence and his wellbeing restored to him, well for at least the meanwhile. After all when all was said and done, whatever had to be, well quite simply it had to be. Being so then brooding and fretting about it, well that after all, that would also help or achieve nothing. And so with this firmly in mind the small company of men then drank, aye they drank, they talked and most of all the small bunch of men laughed. The men talked of their friends, those who were dead and lost and gone forever. Each and every one of the men recounted old adventures till the darkness of night left them to be replaced by a bright cold and frosty dawn.

Chapter Twenty-Four

Barak slept on a little late that bright frosty morning. But then, when it was time the slayer rose unhurriedly and he breakfeasted alone upon a half dozen eggs, several slices of tasty cured ham and a string of thick pork sausages. All of this was washed down with a gallon of fresh goat's milk. Later with his breakfeast over the giant swam in the hot baths till almost noon with only Borz for company. Borz was already submerged looking most content under the warm water when Barak had arrived for his morning swim. Apparently and not surprisingly no Vikings according to Borz had bathed that fresh crisp morning. No matter, as being clean once in a lifetime was perhaps more than enough for the savage brotherhood. With his bathing once over and done with the giant left the sleeping submerged halfling still happily soaking himself a foot under the surface of the water.

Meanwhile Barak had already decided he would ride out into the country, this to think and contemplate. After all there was still much to do, oh and of course he could not fail in his quest. Be it monster, demon, false God or whatever entered the arena to face him, he must prevail, no, he would prevail. Now though the slayer would ride the winding road by the lake, the road that led out into the forest. This was the same long and winding road where his father the king died in his arms all those years ago. It was the giant supposed somewhat glumly on that day and on that very road which had changed his whole life forever. And this for the better or the worse of it, well he had not long to wait and see. Would he free his people in the arena by a victory, or by defeat would he enslave them? Borz had offered Barak his company for the rest of the day but Barak however had politely declined the offer. Today he would ride out alone and today he wanted no company, this no matter how good it might have been. Today would be a time for his thoughts and his distant memories as well as his future plans. Behind the garrison of the Black Guard there was a secret pathway which led through into the mountains and the woods. This little known pathway in turn led out to the old lake road. Aye and this was a good road for a strong gallop, oh and of course it also kept you clear of the hustle and bustle of the city itself.

By this time tomorrow the giant thought to himself as he hit the road at the gallop with his big dog lolling behind the gelding, he would be in the arena. In fact at this very time tomorrow it could all well be over, over one way or another.

Oh aye by this time tomorrow he could be a dead thing.

It took a little over half an hour for Barak to reach the turning on the lake road and reach the very spot where his father had died. Now on arriving there Barak

420

gave a thin smile. Many years ago, only days before he had left his place of birth Barak had placed a tall white stone pillar on the very spot where his father breathed his last. This task was something the slayer had done alone and by himself. Also this stone pillar was still a brilliant white and was obviously well cared for; this of course greatly pleased Barak.

Also to the ogre's bemusement there was a garland of fresh flowers neatly placed at the base of the tall pillar. Barak by now had now reined his blowing horse to a standstill. Then and just as the slayer was about to dismount, of a sudden he heard the hoof beats of a single galloping horse fast approaching. At once the giant kicked on the gelding and hastily concealed himself in a nearby thicket behind a dense bush of red berried holly. Only seconds later the lone rider rode into view, aye and at some speed at that. This most able rider was mounted upon a dapple grey mare. Oh yes and this was a fine legged beast which was obviously both very fast as well as very expensive.

With a tug of the reins the capable rider pulled in the speedy mare at the stone pillar, then he at once dismounted with a light leap from the high backed saddle. Landing nimbly the man next moved toward the tall pillar, he knelt down in a most humble fashion before it.

Even from the glade Barak could see this man was very tall, also he was a rangey lean thing rather than a broad fellow. The owner of the mare wore a light green velvet hooded cloak and silken leggings; the fellow also wore sandals rather than boots. All in all his whole attire was more in fitting with some sort of a palace party goer rather than that of a man riding out at speed on this bright but chill day. Barak's keen eyes could see the tall man was unarmed, well this unless his weapons were cunningly concealed somewhere about him. However, a curved ornate and expensive bow was secured to the rear and the side of his high backed saddle. Of a sudden the short hairs on the back of Barak's huge neck suddenly prickled and rose up a little uneasily.

'Zark,' the slayer whispered to himself as he nudged on the gelding from the concealment of the thicket to gain a better view. From within the tall man's silken vest he next produced then placed at the foot of the pillar carved in his father's image, a single black orchid. For but a moment or more this tall man seemed to pray. But then though at the sound of Barak's unhurried approach the tall man turned suddenly about to face he who intruded upon his daily visit. Oh and when the man noticed a rider approaching it must be said this well garbed fellow had a most alarmed look about his handsome fine featured face.

For now the cold but bright winter sun was in the man's dark eyes, this glare of course was blinding him more than just a little. At first glance the prince, for prince he was, had honestly thought Barak was perhaps a warrior who hailed from one of the giant black races. Aye and also as well as this, perhaps this man, the prince thought to himself, was the assassin he had for so long expected. As the rider drew nearer though the prince saw this huge man's skin was only dark by the colouring of the many tattoos that adorned his muscular body.

Of a sudden Zark recognised this gigantic horseman.

'Barak,' the prince mumbled in a low utter with just a slight hint of fear and apprehension in his voice.

Now only a couple of yards away the giant halted his horse as he looked down upon what of course was his own flesh and blood brother.

For a long moment neither man there could even speak, instead the brothers stared with an element of wonder at one and other. Barak for some reason had always thought he would be disappointed with his brother's appearance, however to his surprise he was not. Zark was very tall, as tall as Commander Gortak or even better in height. And although his younger brother was fine featured he was not a weak looking foppish sort of man in any way. When after what seemed like an age the brothers did eventually speak it was Zark who spoke up first.

'Tell me Barak, tell me have you come here to slay me then my brother? For believe me I do see the hint of death in those cold black eyes of yours.' Barak's sibling asked this most honestly as he rose again from laying the black orchid at the foot of the pillar and stood once again back up onto his sandaled feet.

Barak though shook his big bucket sized head, and next he at once smiled back in a most friendly fashion. Straightway any coldness Zark might have thought was in his brother's dark eyes, well such ideas simply disappeared.

'No, oh no Zark my brother I have come here to this place of ours to save you, not to slay you.' Barak said this almost tearfully as he stretched out his huge right knarled hand toward his younger sibling.

Zark at once threw back his hood as he smiled up at the ogre and the very living legend that was his own brother. He, just like his legendry brother had his head so close cropped that it was almost shaved. At once the men shook hands most warmly, this done Barak dismounted and he clasped his brother about his shoulders. Thorn, Barak's big dog at this time took itself away atop a hilltop on its master's command, the huge hound remained there ever watchful, ever alert to all about.

'You have the look of our mother about you Zark.' Barak said this as a huge friendly smile once again crossed his scarred tattooed face.

On hearing this, the younger brother smiled broadly revealing a mouthful of perfect teeth. These were of course very even teeth, and not filed in any way like those of his wayward brother.

'Aye and you, well you my very big brother, you have the look of our father,' Zark replied with an equally friendly and happy smile.

Zark could not of course remember his father but still there were enough portraits and statues about the palace to see the likeness between his father and his notorious older brother.

For a moment the brothers just held each other by the arms not quite knowing what to say at this particular point in time. But then, and after a short while, the men sat themselves down upon the bankside beside their father's pillar. And this was of course to talk and exchange news relating to the treacherous brothers. Of course the siblings after all, well they had so much to catch up on after all of these long estranged years. Yes, there was indeed much to talk about, also there was much to tell of the sinister goings on within the capital and the palace itself.

No one in the whole world knew the palace, its many chambers and the vast grounds as well as Zark did. Every secret corridor, every concealed passageway and every hidden doorway the prince knew only too well. Indeed the prince could move about freely undetected whether this be by day or by night, just like some sort of unseen phantom. Of late Zark told his brother he had not taken the medication given him by the brother's own private physician. No, no he had discarded the foul smelling liquid and he had simply poured the offending potion away. They, the brothers Xenox had after all these past weeks been too involved and too concerned with both Barak's approach to pay him much heed. Now the brothers, well they and their co-conspirators were in even more of a panic with the giant's arrival. Over these last few days Zark had felt a totally new and far better man without his so called medication. Aye and also now of course while he had hidden himself away in his secret corridors the prince had spied upon both of the brothers. Well also he had spied not only upon them but also their devious and wicked mandarin, the wizard Fong.

Zark next went on with his tale and his educated assessment of the present situation as he saw it. Also the Prince further explained all of what he had learned from his spying to a very attentive and also a very impressed Barak. Zark talked on explaining all and everything and just exactly what he had learnt and heard from his secret places. Oh yes indeed without doubt, this was an eerie and a most sinister plot.

'Know you this, the wizard can, and please believe me Barak, he will summon up a long dead warrior to take the place of Karl Xenox in the arena. ' Zark told this to his elder brother while placing a cultured hand upon Barak's calloused, gnarled and tattooed one. 'This duel in the great arena is all the planning of Master Fong. I tell you Barak my brother, Fong is a most evil and corrupt wizard who revels in the dark arts. Also this swordsman who he intends to summon up, he is some long dead cadaver by all accounts.' Barak listened on intently and silently letting his younger brother further educate him.

'Aye this corpse is a warrior from the orient, a duellist and a slayer who lived and died many centuries ago.' Barak now felt the need for a smoke so he struck up his flints and lit up his pipe as Zark continued with his tale. 'This warrior was, well at least so I understand from my spying, poisoned by one of the ladies at court. Apparently while being a great warrior this cadaver was not a pleasant person, oh no Barak, he was not a man who endeared if you take my meaning.' With this said Zark took about him a most serious and also a very worried look.

'You fight magic Barak my brother, this is not a flesh and blood enemy. Being so you must flee, for even such a warrior as you cannot defeat such an evil demon,' Zark said with his voice full of concern. 'After all, how is it that any man can do battle with the undead? Tell me Barak, how can you kill that which is already a dead thing?' the prince asked imploringly. 'No Barak, even a great slayer such as you cannot kill flesh which is already dead.' Once again these words were spoken by a very troubled and upset Zark. Indeed, these words the prince said whilst sobbing bitterly.

Barak now drew heavily upon his long pipe, in fact quite frantically. Aye and this the ogre did before uncorking a gourd of vodka and taking a long swallow. Now the giant growled angrily at seeing his brother so distressed. Barak after his smoke and his drink next spat venomously while he put a huge hand upon his brother's quivering shoulder. Zark in the meanwhile had declined both a puff upon the pipe and a swallow of vodka. Very wise, Barak had commented in a somewhat tongue in cheek fashion, this given the seriousness of the current situation.

It was true the ogre could have told Zark that he had dealings with the dead before, and also that he had made them dead once again. However for his own reasons the ogre chose not too at this particular time. After a moment's thought big Barak gave out a defiant growl, it was a growl that quite started his younger much more sensitive brother.

'Aye, aye I can win if I am fast enough and if I am good enough. Oh aye and also if I can lop of this cadaver's long dead head then believe me my brother he will be a dead thing once more. '

Zark, though while still shaking with fear, seemed to take heart from his brother's words, why he even managed to afford a faint smile.

'Tell me Zark, when you were secreted away in your hidden places did you maybe happen to hear of this zombie warrior's name?'

Zark did not have to think at all, at once the prince answered his brother's question straightaway.

'Oh yes, yes I did my brother, his name it is, well it was the Lord Ming. Does that perhaps mean anything to you at all Barak?' Zark asked hoping any shred of information no matter how unlikely might help his brother in some way or other fight this conjured up demon.

Barak upon hearing this dreaded name sighed deeply and the ogre gulped in a little air before swallowing down a little vodka. As ever Barak was well educated. And indeed the slayer had heard and also read much over the years of this fabled, long dead notorious and most hated swordsman. After but a moment Barak gave a nod then replied to his brothers question.

'Yes Zark, the swordsman Ming was a great warrior, but not in any way a noble man. In truth Ming was from the land of the Mandarin. True while this killer was trained and schooled by the warriors of the Samurai he was not one of their brotherhood. Ming was a warrior who fought without a shield, he fought in many countless duels, he was so the writings say quite an unbeatable foemen. Also so the stories go, Ming killed in combat the very best of his Samurai masters. Ming was a two handed swordsman, he was an expert with each hand. So obviously I must of course fight him in the same way to stand any chance of victory,' Barak added thoughtfully. Zark now looked most dejected, as this was obviously not good news.

'Is this then a great problem for you Barak?' Zark asked with a most worried and concerned look about his fine featured face.

Barak removed his chainlink helmet and scratched at his freshly shaven head, a head that was beginning to sweat just a little. Dead things, Barak did not like dead things and even more so when these dead things could stand upright and walk. Aye then even more so again when these corpses could bear arms and deal out death to mortal men. Still though the giant grimly supposed, he had in the past coped with the undead before. Being so then if he had to, then hell, yes the ogre supposed he could do it all over again. Barak of a sudden shook his big head as he freed himself from his dark musings.

'Well my brother, it would of course been a lot better if the warrior I was to fight was a live foeman I do suppose,' the giant muttered light heartedly.

Zark now looked most perplexed as surely his brother was not now going to continue with this duel? However though, well of course Barak surely was.

'What, then you do mean to fight in the arena, Barak?' Zark asked not quite picking up on the words his brother had just mumbled.

Barak nodded his big bucket head then after his scratching he replaced his link helmet atop it.

'Aye, aye of course I mean to fight, after all Zark fighting is all that I know. Oh and now to your other question. No it is not a problem brother for me to fight with a two handed swordsmen, for I too am expert with both sword hands. My father, well our father and the fight trainers of the Black Guard had seen to that detail when I was just a boy. I suppose my biggest problem is I do not have two swords, I only have the one. True my good and faithful dragon sword will be as good if not better than both of Ming's swords. '

Barak said this whilst blowing out a cloud of smoke into the air.

'After all, my blade was forged by better craftsman and also it was forged centuries later, and this from unbreakable sky metal. ' Barak was thoughtful for but a moment, and then the giant smiled broadly before once again turning toward his younger, most attentive brother. Barak after a moment of thought spoke out both proudly and confidently. 'Though I do have our father's sword Zark, I do have that blade. So of course if this sword was good enough for our father then it is more than good enough for me,' Barak said passionately.

For just a long thoughtful moment in time Zark said nothing as the prince quite simply just did not have the words at hand. But then after a short while of silence and thought the prince spoke out boldly.

'I will observe the fight from a secret place Barak my brother. I cannot, as you know only too well help you in the arena, as once there as you know yourself you are on your own. But know you this, while I have never taken a life before I think it is never too late to start.' Zark said this indicating toward his crescent shaped bow at the back of his high backed saddle. 'So you deal with the conjured up cadaver and I will do for the brothers Xenox and the wizard, my life on it,.' Barak's brother said as they embraced each other warmly once again. 'I do know your task is a lot harder than is mine my brother Barak,' Zark said almost tearfully. 'But know you this also I have every faith in your skill with a sword as well as your strength and courage. For after all, the masses say that you are the best, you are the greatest of all slayers, so surely not everyone cannot be wrong can they?' Zark asked with a grim smile. Barak the meanwhile puffed upon his pipe as he gave out a grunt and a nod before replying.

'Well Zark, let us for all our sakes just hope that is so,' the giant replied with a cynical smile.

At length after much talking and debating the brothers bade their goodbyes to one another, then after a final hand shake they galloped off in different directions.

And so now all Barak had to do was to win the duel with the dead man conjured up by the Mandarin wizard, this however perhaps would be a task that was easier said than done.

That night the eve before entering the arena, well this was a most quiet and subdued evening.

Barak on that particular night drank not a drop of the beloved vodka. Instead, the giant consumed only a little red wine and also he smoked very little of his beloved weed. After all Barak wanted a clear head for his midday meeting with this long dead master swordsman Ming. Also the giant said little to his friends about his meeting with his brother, and Barak said nothing at all about being further enlightened as to the history of the long dead Zombie warrior. If he had Tark would worry himself into an early grave and Ragnor would doubtless throw himself into the fray out of sheer anger and concern for his friend. Horst, well the German would doubtless fall over in a drunken state of shock and the devil only knew how the halfling would react. No the bits and pieces of heresay Barak calculated was quite enough for them all to know. Anyway, one by one Barak's friends bade him a goodnight as they left the slayer alone in his chamber to his thoughts and deliberations. All in all Barak supposed he did have some strange friends and perhaps an even a stranger family. Barak thought on this only briefly as he honed, oiled and sharpened his weapons for the forthcoming fray before putting himself to sleep.

On the morning of the duel Barak rose up early after an almost sleepless night. But this sleeplessness however, was caused more through the lack of drink and weed rather than anything at all to do with his nerves. Once up and awake the giant once again swam in the hot baths with the halfling Borz. In truth the halfling had more or less made that warm watery place his home over these last comfortable days. Later after a good swim the giant left the baths and began to prepare himself for the arena. Barak shaved his head and face and then cleaned his teeth with soot and a bark skinned stick till his wolf fangs were pure white. Next with this done the slayer groomed and dressed himself in front of a long mirror.

Today the ancient arena would be full to bursting point and the people of Krozakistan would see their huge infamous truant King for the first time in many years. Oh and of course just as many for the very first time. Barak, well the great slayer at least wanted to appear as the masses would expect him to be, impressive and most of all - frightening.

Today's fight would be more about speed and expert sword play rather than the brutal cut and thrust of things. Ming, well he would doubtless be armed with two swords made in the same mould as Barak's ivory handled weapon. These swords would slice through the heaviest scale armour just as easy as flesh. So with this being the case it made it quite pointless wearing any useless cumbersome armour in the first place.

Barak had already decided he would fight his ghoulish foeman barefoot, for now his big boots could stop by his bed. His thick breeches he replaced with a leather loincloth, even his thick leather vest and his chain link helmet he would discard for this fray. Also Barak's second sword would be the one his father had given to him all those many long years ago.

It was the slayer supposed a good honest blade and after all it had served him well in the years before he had acquired his dragon sword from the fierce samurai.

Ragnor complained most long and bitterly at Barak's lack of armour or shield to defend himself in the coming duel. But perhaps that was merely because the Viking was not familiar with the style of fighting he was about to witness.

It was time now the hour was near to noon, the giant picked up his weapons and donned his lion skin which he wore as a cloak. Barak now made his way to the stables and mounted his gelding. Next and slowly and somewhat regally

427

Barak made his way to the arena passing through the winding cobbled streets amid throngs of applauding soldiers and citizens that lined every step of the way the way.

Every street, every road every alley and roof top was jam packed with cheering men women and children. The men of the Black Guard who were on foot pushed their way through the screaming crowd with Barak following behind them atop his huge horse. At his side, also on foot walked Tark, Ragnor and of course the troll, who was hooded and wrapped in similar garb to the Black Guard, this of course so as not to cause alarm and panic to the general public. Already the remainder of the group of Norsemen sat within the arena watching and waiting for any kind of treachery. Only Commander Gortak was also saddled as he rode directly in front of Barak booming out orders for the good citizens to stand aside.

Once at the arena within its lofty walls Barak handed the reins of the gelding to a captain of the Black Guard. Barak bade his big dog Thorn stay with his horse as the gelding was led to a small arched alcove and secured there. Both growling and whimpering at the same time the great hound looked most uneasy as Barak stroked its broad much scarred head. But still nevertheless the big dog reluctantly obeyed its master and the huge hound padded off, then laid itself down patiently by Barak's gelding. There a disgruntled Thorn would not at all contentedly hopefully await for its master's return. Meanwhile Barak, after walking a few paces away had once again returned to Thorn, now the giant bent down and patted the forlorn looking dog gently upon its scarred head. All the while the ogre spoke to the dog in a most kindly and caring fashion. But then, the supposed uncaring ogre feeling thousands of eyes upon him broke off from this gentle petting. At once the giant rose, next he turned about and without any further ado with a determined growl Barak strode outward to the very centre of the huge arena. Now this ogre, this slayer, this king or whatever else he might or might not be was at once greeted by a most deafening roar from the packed out stands of the massive arena.

Not for over a thousand years had there been a duel to the death here within the walls of this most ancient but magnificent structure. The great coliseum of Rome no matter how impressive was little more than a farmyard corral compared to this awe inspiring extravaganza. Barak stood there in the centre of the arena and raised his huge arms skyward, this the slayer did to a roar of approval and adulation from the masses. Amidst this deafening adoration there opposite from out of one of the gladiatorial chambers another figure emerged. To all intents and at least outward purposes this appeared to be the figure of Karl Xenox.

This figure carried a helmet made of leather and bronze at its side; the thing waved to the crowd as it strode in marching fashion toward the giant. It, this human looking creature made no noise at all, perhaps the thing could not speak.

428

Now there were many more loud cheers of wild encouragement and hero worship, none of these however were for the hated despised and the supposed Karl Xenox.

'Barak, Barak, Barak,' echoed the cry from everywhere about the vast arena as every man, woman and child leapt about upon their feet in sheer jubilation..

As the figure neared Barak the thing placed upon its head, which was the likeness of Karl Xenox, the bronze and leather helmet. This was a plumed somewhat ornate affair with dyed red horse hair streaming down to the things waist. Also, here was a helmet with a full face shield, this with a grotesque mocking smile carved into the face visor. Unlike Barak the dead thing wore full armour, a breastplate, metal plate shin guards and metal forearm coverings. All of these small rectangular metal plates were woven into a leather tunic and thick quilted knee breeches. Aye and all of this attire was the ancient Samurai armour of years gone by. As of course this design or the fashion of this sort of armour had not changed any over the many centuries. And also this armour, well it was the very same armour Ming had been buried in all those centuries ago. Oh and this of course after he had been poisoned for his many sins.

Karl Xenox, well his double would no doubt have been a lot taller than Ming. But then again a sorcerer who had the power to make a dead man come to life and walk, such as he was capable of, well such as he would doubtless have little trouble in making the dead man's armour fit the fake Karl Xenox. Barak as ever had guessed correctly, as to the style of foeman he would be pitted against. This undead thing was also armed with two Samurai swords, just as Barak had suspected. Of course these blades were also ancient, though thanks again to Fong's magic now the swords were both well honed weapons. Oh and these once lethal weapons, just like the armour had also belonged to their long dead master in his violent corrupt living years. Once again just as Barak had expected these swords were almost identical to the giant's own undefeated blade. Oh, and now this creature was close up, indeed the thing had about it the very look of Karl Xenox. Well all that was, apart from the undead thing's eyes as these were mere black pits, black bottomless holes, just like the pathway to hell or even beyond. Besides this, well the undead thing stunk to high heaven of mummified death and foul corruption. Still though, the crowd from where they sat or stood could neither smell the thing nor could these cheering onlookers see into its black socketless eyes. And so, to these vast amount of onlookers as just was planned by the wizard, the crowd were of course completely and utterly fooled by the foul devious deception. To all there in attendance this would be a one sided fight made by a power mad opium-filled fool. Aye and he was a fool who had obviously lost his mind at the time of making his absurd challenge. Oh yes, Karl Xenox was all of that, he was no more than a dangerous fool, a usurper who had pitted himself against their true King and their true champion. And now, now this fool would die, and all of the common citizens as well as the militia were expecting this whole silly affair to be over in just a matter of moments. Barak

429

their long absent King would at last rid them of this despised and hated despot once and for all.

However though, this huge crowd of chanting cheering patriots were in for a most rude awakening. Barak the meanwhile discarded his lionskin throwing it down into the sand of the arena. Now and all at once the crowd roared once again in adulation at their King's huge and colourful magnificence. About the giants massive neck now hung the two huge great lion fangs these were to be his only armour against his dead foeman. Of course this armoury, worthless though it was, had the desired effect. And so now the great slayer just as he had planned looked savagely magnificent.

However and now with the thing stood only a matter of yards from Barak, well most unnervingly the undead creature managed a cackle of sorts. Next the thing affected a disgusting and a quite disturbing sort of leer as it peered ever upward with it socketless eyes at the giant. But of course the wizard had planned all and everything to perfection. Barak's own pride and ego would make him fight on without complaint, this even though now before him the ogre could plainly see dark forces were at work. Barak of a sudden fumed, the ogre snarled then cursed as he was often prone. This cursing was now directed at the thing now standing before him. Oh and then with this all done, just for good measure, the giant spat directly into the things face. Oh and of course this was just to make the ogres intentions quite clear to whatever it was that now faced him. So now, and with all and everything clarified then at once this fight to the death began between the Zombie warrior and the great ogre. However the only difference in this death duel as opposed to others was that one of the combatants was already deceased. No matter, as dead or not instantly there was a whirl of flashing sword blades, sparks flew and the crowd was hushed into an awed silence. Barak's fame with a sword was of course well known, but when and where had Karl Xenox managed to obtain such fighting skills the surprised onlookers all wondered to themselves.

From high atop the west tower the brothers and the sorcerer observed with great interest the ongoing battle taking place far below them. Again and again the combatants closed and engaged with each other sending sparks flying from their deadly blades. Aye and again and again the warriors parted without either fighter standing out as a superior swordsman to the other. Oh yes indeed these were most well matched combatants. On and on the warriors fought slashing and stabbing at each other, one hour, two hours, three hours went by. Aye and all the meanwhile the good citizens and the soldiers of the city stood open mouthed in bafflement and stark wonderment at what they were witnessing. As this was of course, it was a duel that by no means anyone there was quite expecting. By now all the spectators were thinking they would be sitting in a tavern somewhere celebrating the demise of the elder of the Xenox brothers.

'Should your corpse down there perhaps fail us in this duel with the ogre Barak, then you do know the crowd, as well as the Blackguard will tear us into bits Master Fong?' Karl Xenox said this in a most matter of fact and quite cold uncaring sort of fashion given his present predicament.

Master Fong gave a slight bow of his head, and then the tiny wizard smiled most confidently.

'Fear not, aye and look you now my young lords. Now the giant oaf bleeds, and soon he will, in but a short time also begin to tire. Ming though, well he is happily for us an undead thing. So therefore of course our dead warrior will do neither of these things, tire or bleed I mean,' Fong next chuckled. 'Trust me, your future kingdom is secure, indeed it is I suppose almost won. Ming, he is the master swordsman and the victor of a thousand duels.' Fong after saying this added a sinister cruel and cackled whisper. 'Soon, soon he will begin Barak's final punishment, Ming will quite simply cut Barak to bits,' Fong sneered. However the elder and shrewder brother was perhaps not filled with the same overwhelming confidence as was the wizard Fong.

'Perhaps wizard, but then again perhaps not,' Karl Xenox said this with just a slight lack of faith.

After all Karl Xenox had gazed into those black eyes, aye and also he had almost felt those fanged teeth about his scrawny throat. However, the wizard had never been so close to Barak, aye and he had not felt the fear of such an encounter. With this being so then he was not as terrified as his ward.

'There is no perhaps about it my boy, the outcome of the fight is assured,' the wizard countered, a little put out at the elder brother's lack of faith in his black magic. 'No fighter could ever prevail against Ming, as he was the master of the masters, and quite simply the best swordsman there has ever been. '

Still though however, there was that element of doubt in Karl Xenox's mind. After all the wizard had not stared into those cold black killer's eyes as he had. Aye and so now the despot intended on saying as much.

'Aye but did your warrior, did he ever fight a man, nay a beast like that down there?' Karl Xenox asked pointing towards the giant.

At that very moment though the top of Barak's left ear was sliced clean through leaving it a most pointed and bleeding thing. Now and at once the vast crowd let out a gasp of shock despair and disappointment, but most of all concern for their champion. To their horror this fight was not quite going at all the way these observers had been expecting.

With a sudden snarl the giant cursed angrily, nothing he knew only too well bleeds quite as much as an ear wound.

Barak in angry retaliation made almost instantly a downward swipe with his dragon sword. Fortune favoured the giant as now there was a deep cut that opened up the breastplate of the cadaver Ming. Though perhaps fortune was the wrong word, aye and also, the totally wrong expression altogether. As had there been living flesh underneath the armour instead of only mummified remains, well then the duel it would have been over. Blood would have gushed everywhere and Barak would have had an instant and glorious victory. However this of course, well it quite simply was not to be. So once again the crowd gasped, but they did not cheer as all was obviously still not well. Even so the masses arose as one from their seats intending to hail their hero. But alas they were instantly hushed into a grim silence. As strangely and once again, there was no blood, not even a cry of pain from Barak's foeman. No, to their shock, horror and dismay there was only a little dark ash that seemed to flake down onto the sand of the arena floor. What was happening down there in the arena before their very eyes, this, the good people of Krozakistan could only wonder to themselves in stunned horror.

'What madness is this?' Ragnor rumbled. 'What witchery goes on before our very eyes? Why Barak has just gutted that man standing before him, and not a drop of blood do I see!' the Viking exclaimed angrily.

Now it was quite obvious Ragnor had been so drunk the night before he had forgotten any hint Barak might be fighting a cadaver brought back from the dead. Tark muttered curses under his breath, as it was just as plainly obvious now Barak was not fighting a mortal foe. Commander Gortak stood open mouthed, he of course knew well the possibility of treachery and witchcraft. Though with a soldier's outlook he had chosen to ignore such an eventuality. Magic, well this dark mischief after all was surely a thing of the past, wizards and seers might have held some sway once, aye but that was long ago. Also the commander was under strict instructions from Barak to say nothing to elaborate on the situation. By Barak's orders the fight must run its course and must reach a final conclusion, aye and this no matter what. These were Barak's orders, perhaps they were his last ones, but still they must nevertheless be obeyed. Now though time pressed on and it was moving into late afternoon on that chill but sunny day. Barak though as it happened well he was right glad it had been cold, in fact the colder the better, aye and for this reason. As now both sweat as well as blood glistened from several deep wounds about his huge body. Another expert flick of one of Ming's ancient but lethal swords and Barak's right ear was clipped. Aye and so accurate was this cut it appeared just as trimmed and just as pointed and as bloody as his left ear, in fact the ears were a perfect match.

Now this thing, well it next seemed to give off a hideous and mocking laugh as it stood back a yard or two. With its socketless eyes the thing seemingly admired its handy work. Then after another hideous cackle, the creature with its next barrage of blows shattered Barak's Persian sword. Aye and this was of course the sword given to him by his father. Sadly, tragically even, the blade snapped off about a foot above the hilt. And the sword under these dire circumstances was quite useless now. So as things in the great arena seemed to go from bad to worse. Well the vast crowd was hushed into a stunned silence, as were also Ragnor and all of his big burly Norsemen. These were now all worried looking men seated in the front seats of the arena. Worried looking men who were looking and waiting for a signal from Ragnor to put a halt to this farce. Barak with another downward swipe of his dragon sword next sliced open the shoulder of the creature all the way to its waist. But then once again no cry of pain or despair was heard, and this as a little more black ash fell onto the sand of the arena. Of course by now the crowd as well as the onlooking warriors of both Black Guard and Vikings strongly suspected something was most sadly amiss.

'Our Lord Barak has struck that thing a dozen times, yet whatever it is he fights neither cries out or bleeds,' Gortak growled angrily.

'This is not a duel Tark, no it is sheer butchery,' the commander next snarled out. It now appeared that Commander Gortak must have been just as drunk as Ragnor on the previous evening his nephew thought to himself.

Tark wanted to speak out as Barak had confided in him more than anyone else as to what he would face in the arena. However, the big Barak had also further ordered him to say nothing more. Tark had in turn given his King an oath of silence and he would say not a word to anyone until after the duel. Though of course, what possible good that would do anyone was a matter that greatly confused the rapidly greying young man.

Angrily the Commander cursed his nephew's stubbornness as he turned his attention once more to the arena. 'Know this Tark your pledge is your pledge, but the next time our King strikes his foe and the thing does not fall down in a heap. Well, the whole legion of the Black Guard will be upon it and to hell with the whys and the wherefores of it all. '

Ragnor at first grimaced and then agreed with Commander Gortak. Oh and this as he looked toward the troll who already had begun to unwind his chain in readiness to assist Barak. As not surprisingly, well the troll too sickened of this butchery. Oh and of course the halfling had not forgotten that day in the market square when Barak had come to his aide.

Somewhat grimly Borz thought to himself, just as he had entertained the crowd in Varnak without any chance of victory, without outside intervention. Well, in the here and now Barak he felt was in exactly the same sort of troubled situation.

Now however, Barak of a sudden between the non-stop sword play stood back a yard or two from the cadaver. The giant was soaking in sweat, this as well as blood from both his body, his arms and of course the ear wounds. Barak was also blowing hard now, and the slayer, although he was loathed to admit this to himself, felt weary and sluggish. Aye in truth he felt quite spent and even a little dizzy, aye and all this through lack of blood. Well this and also of course with the sheer effort of the several hours of swordplay whilst fighting with a dead thing. Perhaps now the great slayer thought briefly to himself, it was his time to die. Aye and perhaps he had always been destined to die here in the great arena of Krozak, his place of birth.

Now and high in the west tower Fong with the jubilant brothers were just about to celebrate Ming's victory over the tiring giant, perhaps though these fools did their rejoicing a little bit too early.

As it was then, when the great giant glimpsed his immense shadow upon the bloody sands of the arena's sandy floor in the last fading light of the day. Huge and bloodied the slayer now appeared. Aye and with his pointed ears, well he looked like some sort of fiendish giant elf. Why indeed, Barak did suppose, he looked like the very devil himself. It was then the bloodied ogre remembered the words of the Mongol shaman. For it was he who said to Barak, the slayer would see very soon the devil. But on seeing him he was not to fear, and was to take heart, for this devil he was a friend. The Khan had also spoken and he had said to call upon the Mongol god Tengri when in a time of need. Barak though, well the slayer decided he needed only one miracle at a time, and any favours Tengri owed him could for now wait. Of a sudden the giant grinned and then the great slayer laughed out long and loudly. Next Barak stood back another pace or two away from the cackling creature, this as he looked once again upon his own huge shadow with a savage pride.

Barak's ferocity and tenacity, this as well as his stubborn nature had made him refuse to yield, refuse to despair and buckle against the undead warrior's macabre immortality.

So now Barak looked above him as he roared long and loud into the heavens above. The skies were ice blue, they were cold and clear and all in all, the slayer supposed to himself this was a nice day. Oh aye, and also now it was about to get a lot nicer. Oh and also with this uplift in his spirits, well, there was, the giant thought in the far off distance a most familiar black speck soaring in the crystal clear heights. Barak roared out once again like some great injured beast, and then next the slayer folded his weapons across his huge bloody chest as he gave a slight bow to his undead adversary. However though, and just as expected this creature most rudely did not return the compliment. Oh no, instead the revolting thing merely cackled out yet another hideous laugh.

'What is the Lord Barak doing now Ragnor?' Commander Gortak asked anxiously sweat pouring out from under his turbaned brow.

Now, now the big Viking of a sudden lost his perplexed and worried look as he smiled broadly. Aye and this as Ragnor sheathed his broadsword, a sword which he had already drawn in readiness to join the fray.

'He is ending it now, aye that is what the great slayer is doing commander, he is ending it.' Ragnor said these words with great pride and also with the utmost confidence and conviction. 'Barak, has I think at long last finally had enough of all this nonsense.'

No sooner had Ragnor spoken these words when Barak spun about with all the speed, ferocity and strength that was left in his worn out bloodied and punished body. Ming with all confidence anticipated the move, and the thing had already swiftly put up his two swords to block Barak's strike. However, this ferocious blow struck from the maddened giant was more than any metal forged upon this earth, or any other could ever withstand. Oh aye, and that was whether these blades were held by a living man, or held by a dead one. Now Ming's ancient swords at once gave way to Barak's sheer power and of course his famed dragon sword. In but an instant the blades snapped and then shattered into a thousand shards with the impact. Now and at once the crowd first gasped and then cheered wildly as Ming's head bounced from his decayed body with a dull thud onto the sand stained red with Barak's blood.

Instantly, the vast crowd were upon their feet standing upon their benches chanting Barak's name over and over again in a frenzy of relief. These ecstatic, much relieved observers were now dancing, cheering and celebrating most wildly their King's great victory. Still though, the crowd were apparently not aware or even concerned there was no blood to stain the sand from the headless warrior. It was now also that the giant roared out long and loud, this without doubt of all his victories he regarded as the greatest of all. Not only had he defeated the so called greatest swordsman of all time, he had defeated Ming when he was a dead thing.

Barak after his loud and long roaring then stabbed at the eyeless head with his broken sword impaling it upon the broken blade. Next the victor held the obscene thing high aloft above him, this though Barak did after first removing the undead thing's helmet.

No doubt this was the fate Barak would have suffered should he have lost the fight to the creature. Now though it was time to enlighten the hitherto patient and very anxious observers as to what they had all been witness to.

'This is not the head of Karl Xenox, no, no this is foul witchery,' the giant proclaimed. 'I have fought an evil and an undead demon in this arena this day,'

Barak roared out into the crowd. Several times over Barak had to shout this out till at length the jubilant crowd was silent and listened to their King's words.

Of a sudden the crowds' cheers of worship and adulation, well, these cheers now turned into cries of hate filled anger and vengeance. Now, the brothers were at last so it appeared going to get just that which was long overdue to them.

'There, there high in that west tower balcony stand the traitors responsible for this deception.' Barak roared this out while flicking the long dead head into the sand in disgust before next the giant pointed his father's broken sword toward the traitors.

Cursing and scowling with bitterness Karl Xenox fumed whilst the wizard fumbled with his long wispy beard, and the younger brother trembled with fear.

'Enough of this, we are alas undone,' Karl Xenox hissed out hatefully. Now his deadly game was up and the plotter knew only too well he had nothing to lose, well nothing but his life. So with this in mind the elder brother next grabbed a bow from his lesser cringing sibling as he made ready to bring down Barak. After all this was an easy enough shot he mused to himself, Barak if nothing else was a large enough target to hit. Aye and well the despot might have done for the slayer had not a black shafted arrow passed through his own skinny turkey neck. Oh yes, and this black shafted arrow in turn pinning Karl Xenox to the equally skinny neck of his cringing brother, instantly and locking both together by the same well-aimed arrow. The scheming brothers toppled as they seemingly danced together for a moment or two before plunging far below to the cobbles and their deaths. Barak turned about and gave his brother Zark a wave of gratitude. True to his word Zark had just as promised secreted himself away in the opposite east tower. Also, just as promised Zark had done once and for all for the scheming worthless Xenox brothers, once and for all.

Master Fong spat while he cursed venomously at the turn of what he had thought were quite impossible events. Still, perhaps all was not lost, well at least not for him, as now he would magic himself away and be gone from here. Aye there and then the sorcerer would have been off and scampered away. No doubt, and then next he would have at once made himself invisible and thus impossible to find. Well this, the ancient wizard would have done, but for that distant black dot in the cold blue skies high above him. Oh and the black dot, well it was getting ever bigger. Also now, the big dot descended upon the wizard from a great height, aye and also at a great speed.

'Blackie, you are at last returned to me,' Barak uttered these words whilst smiling most broadly to himself. 'You have come back to me, just as I knew you would. ' The giant at this point looked most cheery at the return of his big black eagle. Oh and of course also the timing of the great bird's return, well it could not have been any better. 'I had thought I aspied you through my blood and my sweat, I knew well you would come back to me.' Barak had muttered this away quite proudly to himself whilst wiping stinging sweat away from his black eyes.

Now though the great black eagle folded back her wings as she swooped downward toward the wizard with a blinding speed. As ever and always the great eagle struck her target with a deadly accuracy, and also a very dull thud. Only seconds later the great eagle was carrying Master Fong kicking and screaming in terror from the balcony of the west tower off into the far beyond.

This the great black she eagle did just as easily as a hawk would carry off a rat or a rabbit. Master Fong continued to scream, kick and curse as he was borne off ever higher away towards the distant snow capped mountains. Now after centuries of wrong doing the Mandarin's days of evil plotting and dark conjuring were obviously over. What was also just as obvious was the great eagle would eat first before returning and being reunited with her jubilant master. Mind you, not that the noble beast would get a great deal of flesh from the scrawny wasted and ancient sorcerer's rotting carcase.

Barak was now stood in the centre of the arena looking quite magnificent. The giant was dripping with his own blood and sweat and he was standing over the long dead corpse of the swordmaster Ming. Beneath the clothing and the armour the thing was no more than ash and dust that even now fell away as it crumbled into the sands of the arena.

Commander Gortak had by now mounted his black stallion and rode into the arena with Barak's huge gelding in tow, Thorn was of course bounding on behind. Reining his horse in by the victorious giant the commander at once sliced away a piece of his black cloak and handed this to Barak to dab upon his now most bloody and very pointed ears.

Tark and Ragnor had both ran behind the horses, Ragnor was most keen to greet his bloodied but victorious friend. Oh and the ever greying Tark the meanwhile was eager to greet his victorious King. The young man arriving by his master's side at once kicked the corpse angrily and the thing crumbled once and for all into the bloody arena sands.

'Barak, you were ever the most fearsome man I have ever met, but I do swear now you look even more like the very devil himself.' Ragnor gasped this out, as the big Viking was a little out of breath after his brief but unexpected run.

Barak, well he merely gave a grunt as the slayer fingered his bloody and pointed ears, tenderly. True they did hurt quite a bit, but in all honesty the ogre thought once the ears had healed perhaps they would look most becoming. Well at least the ears looked quite fetching upon the shadow cast across the arena floor. After all the giant in his own odd way was as ever and always a strange and perhaps somewhat vain man. Barak now thought it necessary to inform those about him they had no reason for concern at his new deformity.

'Aye, aye well you know, I do think once my ears are healed over. Well they could perhaps make me appear even more handsome, well if not handsome then perhaps more interesting,' the giant chuckled away to himself.

'My brother you are victorious you have survived the duel with the walking corpse.' Zark panted this out in somewhat painful gasps as he too had run full tilt from the east tower all the way down to join his brother in the centre of the arena.

'Of course I did win the duel Zark, was there ever any doubt about it?' the giant asked light heartedly. And this even though there were times in the duel when Barak thought his day was up, this but only briefly mind you.

Oh how wonderful he would look, and how magnificent, Barak thought suddenly to himself as he examined the fresh scars about his body.

Now it was all the combined forces of both the palace guard and the Black Guard could do to keep the ecstatic and jubilant citizens from over- running the arena and mobbing their beloved champion. By now and kindly assisted by the troll the drunken Horst had also arrived at the centre of the arena.

As ever, and Horst felt it only right being one of Barak's oldest friends that he should have his say on the matter in hand.

'Aye, aye you have done a good day's work Barak, you should be most proud of yourself, as it appears you have killed a dead man.' Horst slurred these words out with a lopsided drunken smile. 'Though I must say this to you my large noble Lord, this victory did take a little longer than I had expected. In fact and in all truth, well, I do think I fell asleep at one time,' said the ever drunken and ever unsteady German.

'Ming was a master swordsman you drunken German fool,' Tark protested immediately.

'Aye, he was a slayer brought back from the dead Why this undead warrior was undefeated in over a thousand duels.' Barak next replied in defence of his most recent performance. Horst apparently unimpressed' shrugged and sighed as he dribbled a little vodka over his beard before answering.

'True, true this is all quite correct my Lord Barak,' Horst answered with that idiotic drunken smile of his. 'But he was also you must remember, a lot older than you are my noble Lord. ' Horst said this with a friendly smile followed by a hiccup while passing Barak a gourd of vodka to celebrate his hard fought victory. 'So old was this fool, in fact my Lord Barak, well the poor soul simply fell to bits, shame on you' Horst added with a loud belch.

'Idiot,' Barak snapped as he thought to himself just what the drunken onelegged German had said to him. Still Horst's words did as ever make everyone else in earshot burst into rough mirthful laughter.

After the giant caught the ever drunken Germans humour, well he also gave a broad smile. A broad smile that turned into thunderous laughter, next the ogre shook the German's hand as he slapped him playfully on the back so hard the fool almost fell into the sand. Only then was it Barak took a well earned and a very long drink of vodka. With his thirst quenched the giant soaked the black tatters of Gortak's cloak with vodka before applying it to his now pointed very elf like ears. True this medication stung and it hurt like merry hell itself, but still at least this application would kill off any chance of infection.

Vodka, aye indeed this was a fine godly concoction that could heal both body as well as soul Barak thought briefly to himself before addressing his brother.

'Well, that was indeed a fine shot you made earlier my brother. You killed two birds with one stone so to speak, my thanks to you. ' Barak said this to Zark with a slight bow of his big and now blood spattered head.

Zark shrugged then smiled almost nervously, next the prince returned the bow to his elder sibling. Now any traces of the mind-numbing drug, the prince had been taking over these past years. Aye and a drug mind you, for a condition he did not even have in the first place, had completely worn off. Prince Zark was now vibrant and he was very much alive, oh yes very much so.

'You, you Barak have given new life to me my big brother, aye and a new meaning to my very being.' Zark said these words while clasping the blood soaked slayer warmly by his huge shoulders.

Barak of course made no complaint, but nevertheless in his present delicate condition this embrace did hurt quite a bit.

'Aye and you have saved my life Zark, as had you not toppled those painted fools in the west tower well then, I suppose I might be lying there in the sand next to what is left of that thing.' Barak said these words thoughtfully as he stared down at a pile of ash and little more else. 'And so now it is me who give you thanks Zark. Your marksmanship with a bow is everything I needed it to be on this day. And also you are not only my brother you are my friend, oh and in this you have no choice' Barak chuckled. Once again the brothers embraced in friendship as they shook hands warmly. 'You have already thanked me Barak,' Zark said having to raise his voice above the clamour of the joyous citizens so his brother could hear what he was saying to him. Barak was thoughtful as he kissed the eagle ring upon his finger.

'Yes, but before I thanked you as my brother, this time I thank you as my King.' And this the giant said whilst putting a huge bloodied hand upon Zark's shoulder.

For just a short while, Zark intelligent as he was, he nevertheless became a little unsure as to what Barak was exactly saying to him. But then after a moment or two in deliberation the prince collected himself together and he spoke.

'What is it then? You do not want the Kingship, Barak?' the giant's younger brother asked a little astonished at his sibling's revelation.

Straightaway without any hesitation the giant shook his big bucket head which still dripped with sweat and blood.

'No, no, it's not for me, kingship, or the protocol and everything else that goes with it. Oh no, oh no this is not for me at all. And as I have always said, since the time of our father's death, well it never has been. In all truth, I would never have returned back to this land, but for to collect, then deliver the antidote. The antidote which will release my friend's son, who was shot with the sleeping poison, from his limbo.' Barak said these words to his brother both honestly and sincerely.

Zark shrugged as he shook his head in total bewilderment, why he even laughed somewhat nervously a little. Next the prince who was now to become a king appeared much more confident and happier with himself. Zark, well he truly loved this place of his birth, also he loved all these people in the land of the Krozak. After all, this said and done was all the prince had ever known, aye and doubtless all he ever would know. Barak was now and just as he ever had been an untamed savage. Aye and King or not, he was a wild thing who would not or could not be changed. Even at this very glorious most heroic moment, and after all of these lost years in the abyss. Zark knew well his legendary brother would not and could not possibly fit in with the trappings of modern day civilization.

Zark supposed quite rightly his elder sibling was a throwback to the savage and fearsome Kurgans, those fierce nomadic warriors from whom his people were long ago descended. However, still in many ways his huge wayward brother had a compassion and a kindness about him. Oh aye Barak had a softer more caring emotion about him, even though this was an emotion the slayer foolishly seemed reluctant to show. Anyway and all that besides, Zark knew only too well Barak had made for himself his own life. A life that lay far away from the land of the Krozak, and to this distant place for better or for worse he must return. Barak now felt as ever it was time to for him to organise things.

'Commander Gortak, you once told me you were willing to serve me, aye and die at my side if needs be, correct?' Barak asked this as he turned to face the big burly Black Guard commander. Commander Gortak without any hesitation whatsoever at once gave a most positive nod in reply to the question.

'Aye, to the death, and even beyond that if needs be my Lord Barak,' the commander stated bravely and proudly.

'Good, nay that is very good Commander' Barak replied simply before putting his next question. 'Tell me then, will you serve my brother Zark in the same brave and loyal manner?' Barak asked evenly. Once again without any hesitation at all, the big Commander answered straightaway.

'Aye, if you are indeed once again intent on leaving us my Lord Barak, then yes of course I would serve your brother. Zark would then in your stead become my one and my only Lord. ' Commander Gortak answered this well put question as he bowed low to Barak's younger brother then next banged his black gloved fist on his broad chest in salute. Barak was thoughtful for but a moment then he spoke, an explanation for his actions he felt were needed.

'At day's end, well I am what I am Commander Gortak. I am no more and I am no less than that, my mould is set and it is cast. Aye and alas this cast cannot now be broken,' Barak explained. 'Understand this, I cannot be shackled to kingship and courtrooms, protocol and all of the other foolish rules of establishment, they are not my life. For such an existence, I do think would kill me. Aye and this just as sure as the cadaver's blade would have done, had I let it. But only I think the establishment would kill me a lot slower,' the giant added honestly.

Gortak shrugged a little sadly, this the commander did at the very thought of both he and his country losing Barak for a second time. However, after a moment or two fighting with his emotions, the stern faced commander gave a nod of agreement as to the giant's wishes. Barak now not only said on, he also listened. Commander Gortak once satisfied with his future duties and obligations then pledged his undying loyalty to Zark. Why the commander even swore an oath to be me more hospitable to the other Krozak legions. Aye and that even included Commander Kovan and his palace legion with their plumed helmets and shiny breastplates. Although this did take some persuading by Barak, and also a lot of will power on own his behalf. Still though, this was a small price to pay, as the big commander liked very much this huge giant who had briefly been his King. Oh yes and he would miss him greatly once the slayer was gone and away for a second time. Still Gortak supposed, well if nothing else he had at least met with the great legend. Aye and it was more than true that he had not been disappointed at all with what he seen. Barak had proved to be an even greater slayer than the commander could have ever imagined. And as said, well at least after all these long years he did get to meet the great slayer. More than that even, for he had ate with him, drank with him and laughed with him. And then while Barak was in the great arena fighting for his very life, and this against a dead thing. Well the normally bullish and brutish commander felt like he had even bled with him. Now Commander Gortak of a sudden shook with emotion, it was an emotion though which he conquered before once again speaking.

'Sadly, well, I agree, I do believe every word you have said to me to be true. This life of politics and diplomacy would do just as you say to a man like you my Lord Barak. Rules, protocol and the very establishment of things, these would I think bring about your downfall and perhaps even your demise. You are a great slayer my Lord Barak, greater even than I ever imagined or expected. Oh aye and this you have proven here today in the ancient arena and in front of a crowd of your own people, people who love you.

Gortak stumbled with his words for a second or two as once again he was choked up with emotion.

'Though I must admit my Lord, there were at times in the fight when I thought you were undone,' the Commander said in all honestly. 'Still my Lord, not a swordsman in the world, or even in the hereafter, none of these could have achieved what you have succeeded in doing on this most glorious of days,' the big commander said proudly.

Barak, well the great slayer for once said nothing, the ogre made no reply to these honest words. However, Barak's very strained and weary look indicated that he himself also thought this could well have been his final hour. Of a sudden though, the giant grinned to himself as he touched a sore and much clipped ear. Apparently the Mongol wise man was right and he had seen the shadow of the devil which was of course his own. However, despite all and everything, the ogre was still quite sure in his own mind he had not called upon any god to help him in his duel to the death. Aye and this was including even the god of the wind Tengri, a fact which had greatly pleased Barak. However, all of this was for now of no matter as Barak stood there in the arena after a great and a glorious victory. Oh yes, and this was a victory that would be wrote about and sung about till time's end. There now amid the cheering and the high spirits Zark was proclaimed the new King of Krozakistan. And as for Barak, well the slayer somewhat sadly surrendered his father's treasured ring of kingship to his younger brother. Perhaps for Barak this was one of the hardest and saddest things he ever had done in his long bad and wayward life. Still though and after all, what had to be had to be, and anyway this was done now and the ring of kingship was parted with. Barak was no longer a king, Barak nevertheless though was still Barak.

Being so then all of a sudden amid the heady clamour of things, Barak now felt the urge to drink, feast and to walk the streets of the capital. Oh and this of course whilst he mingled and spend time with his countrymen. So, Barak being Barak, well the giant did exactly just that very thing. Aye and indeed what a night was made of it. Why each and every man woman and even child of the city drank and danced as they sang and rejoiced. And all in all the remainder of that most unforgettable day turned into a most glorious and happy affair. Street entertainers such as fire eaters, jugglers, bards, minstrels as well as every sort of vendor possible were selling every kind of food and drink on the crowded streets. All of these folk prospered well, but also as well as this they enjoyed the night and the revelry that went with it. Oh aye and this until the good people of Krozak could eat drink sing and dance no more.

Much later and at long length the good and happy citizens of the capital eventually retired to their beds. No more were these people under threat from the brothers or their foul followers as those unworthy brothers had now for the most been stamped underfoot into little more than soup by the good citizens of the capital. Their day it was done, and now a new kindly era had at last arrived in both the capital and the empire. Tilus and all the other surviving lackeys of the plotters were promptly given a well deserved beating for their past liberties. Then with this done, they were next sent packing without a coin to their name into the wild outlands. Once there, and out in this cold harsh wilderness doubtless these worthless fools and lackeys were destined to become no more than dinner for the wolf or the bear. And in all honesty, well that is all these fools were good for.

On the following day's dawn it was bright and cold, but still nevertheless it was a cheery enough morn. Aye it was also of course a fine morning for a fast brisk ride sat astride a good horse. This the giant thought as he opened his black eyes and prized his blood dried ears from his red stained pillow. Now with this painful task accomplished the slayer next at once lit up his long pipe and puffed away quite merrily whilst sitting upon his bed. True it was the ogre felt more than just a little stiff, aye and more than just a little sore. Still despite all of this Barak nevertheless felt good about himself, why a few more puffs of weed, followed by a swig of vodka and he would feel just fine. Now though the victorious slayer would rise, he would go now and bathe himself in the warm baths. Later after this Barak would eat and drink as he prepared himself for the coming day. So after bathing in the warm waters and eating down a hearty breakfeast of a string of sausages and a half dozen eggs, Barak then began to doctor and repair his still hurting ears. Later once this task was completed then he would think about his future and look forward to the rest of his life. Those devils and demons that had in the past haunted his sleep for so long, well now these nightmares had all been laid finally to rest.

Chapter Twenty-Five

With his wounds and his pointy ears doctored with potions the ogre had applied himself Barak examined his reflection, this in the full length mirror inside of his chamber. True the ogre had to stoop quite a bit to do so, but this was of little matter. After the duel in the arena a collection of palace physicians had mobbed Barak with their own remedies for his injuries. Barak though had dismissed them all choosing to repair himself just as he had always done in the past. Now Barak as he stared into the mirror grew reflective, so much had happened to him in his violent but quite glorious yet very tragic life. Also now the giant for no apparent reason thought of his wife Freya and of his little curly white haired daughter. Barak wondered sadly what might have been, aye and what could have been on that cold little island, had not the raiders came and wrecked his life. Brooding though as ever achieved nothing, so with a resolute growl the giant as ever put these sad thoughts once again aside for now. Soon enough, well, that if there were any sort of heaven he would meet with them. Sooner than that though Barak would see and be reunited with his adopted son, Hassan, yes the small boy was at least some comfort to him. A little later on that day, once more and for the last time Barak saddled up his gelding and revisited the turning in the lake road. Aye the lake road, the slayer rode there at a steady trot to the place where his father had died so many long years ago. As it happened a trot was perhaps all Barak's aching, throbbing body could endure. On arriving by the white pillar which was his father's marker the giant dismounted and sat for a good while. Oh and this with his mind in a whirl as he thought of so many things. Once again as he had done so many times in the past, the melancholy ogre wished he was home in his lodge in the forest with young Hassan. So much had happened to him over these past long months the slayer felt truthfully and also a little sadly he would never quite be the same man again.

Barak now sat stroking the scarred head of his big dog Thorn, then next the slayer stroked the breast of his great black eagle as he spoke to it softly. Suddenly the giant chuckled as he thought back to the screaming wizard who was borne off to become no more than food for his great bird. Next a still smiling Barak secured in a small phial, the antidote that would revive the prince to one of the eagle's powerful legs.

'Ah, if only I could be home just as quickly and as safely as you are to be Blackie. ' This the giant said with a weary sigh as he hoisted the huge black bird aloft then watched as it soared off high into the cold clear blue skies above. Barak observed for a good while until the great eagle almost disappeared from sight. And then at last after a little while she was eventually lost in the far distance.

Suddenly as the great bird disappeared from view the great slayer felt a little downhearted, a little more alone.

After all the long hard trek ahead of him back to Brit was something Barak was not at all looking forward to. Wolves would be there for sure, big cats quite possibly, but the cold, the ice, the snow and the bitter biting winds were without any doubt a certainty. Of course also there would still be the possibility of attacks and raids from bandits. Later on, and after enduring all of these hardships there was the long voyage home. Aye and this was a voyage over rough, cold and unfriendly seas. Now of course the weather would have even worsened and the full bite of winter would be upon them. All in all, Barak thought to himself, he was perhaps getting a little too old for all this young man's adventuring danger and heart pounding excitement. Barak sat brooding darkly upon this return passage until his thoughts were most pleasantly interrupted.

'You can be home from here in but a matter of days from now my brother,' a voice from behind him said cheerfully. It was of course Zark, and he had ridden out a little earlier hoping to find his elder sibling. By simple deduction the newly made up king knew of course exactly where he would find him. Also apparently by all accounts, well Zark also knew just exactly what it was his giant brother was thinking.

'My flying boat is completed. I tested it myself this very morning, though in truth I have flown the ship many times before. Now though once again the vessel is ready to soar off into the cold blue skies. Why even a child could steer this craft and master its workings.'

Zark went on with both an element of pride and excitement in his voice about the vessel he had constructed.

'And I of course will give this vessel to you most gladly Barak. After all, my brother, a ship, whether it flies or not, in exchange for this ring and a kingdom, that seems to me a good trade.' Zark said this with an easy most relaxed smile, these last days had seen a great change in his well being.

Barak on hearing this blew through his lips, but the slayer was a little uneasy and did not straightaway reply.

'A boat that flies in the sky, forgive me my brother, but I find this very hard to believe.' Barak said this while hoping not to offend, but in all truth perhaps he was a little unsure if his brother was at all serious. Zark gave a shrug, the new king let out a long sigh, and then he put a long fingered hand upon his brother's shoulder.

'Do you think a boat that flies in the air instead of one that floats upon the water harder to believe than your good self fighting with a dead man? Aye and this was a man who was long dead, a cadaver, who by means of black magic was conjured up by a wizard?' Zark asked somewhat jokingly.

445

Barak lit up his pipe as he raised his dark eyebrows. The slayer was a little taken aback by the comparison being made. Still though the giant supposed Zark did have some sort of point to his well put argument. And also Barak had heard of course from no less a person than the old but wise Zoltan his younger brother was somewhat of a genius, and was quite an inventor. For a while the brothers sat there talking as they watched off into the distance searching for a trace of the great eagle. But she was gone now, yes now she was winging her way back toward Aulric upon her huge black wings. After some little time spent talking of this and that the brothers rode off to a secret place of Zark's, aye a secret place high upon the towering cliffs above the lake. And then once at this secret place the giant was struck totally speechless at what his black eyes saw there.

Barak was sat astride his great warhorse, this whilst he stared ahead of him in open mouthed amazement. As now there before him the ogre gawped at some strange machine, a machine the likes of which he had never seen or had even heard of before. Even the great battle machines of the Romans, Persians Greeks and Egyptians were not as well constructed as this thing before him.

This craft was to all intents and purposes built as some sort of dragon ship by its elegant and clever design. Aye for it was indeed a long lean thing with tied down sails that protruded out from the sides of its hull. These sails once spread out would act like some sort of huge horizontal wings that could cut the air and the thermals in a most natural manner. Also a most sophisticated system of cogs ran here and there about the stern of this strangest of vessels, these were perhaps less natural. Nevertheless they all looked very functional. Oh and all of these mechanics were linked to each other by thick leather belts, and fixed at the stern of the strange machine there was a massive propeller this was no doubt for drive and also a little giddy up.

This vessel also had a single huge great crimson balloon at its centre, this was made from silk or satin or some other fine light yet very strong material. Some sort of strange brazier and a large set of blacksmith's bellows sat directly under this big balloon, obviously to increase its inflation if needed.

Barak after all was not devoid of the fundamentals of things concerning science and engineering, as after all he had been a most well educated child. Still apparently though, the slayer had not been as well tutored as his genius brother.

'Barak, Barak.' Zark said his brother's name twice to stir him from his trance-like state. 'This ship is big enough to take you and all of your men, aye and at a push even that big horse of yours as well. ' Zark said this more than a little proudly and confidently about his apparent genius, oh and of course his own inventive handy work. 'I have tried the vessel many times Barak in the past, mostly in the dead of night while all sleep. She flies and also she steers very well, I call her the swan boat. For I believe that was the name our Father lovingly bestowed upon our mother, the "Swan". '

Barak was silent for a moment, as the slayer seemed deep and almost lost in his thoughts. Aye the "Swan", that was indeed the name King Bartok would call his Queen when in privacy and away from court. For their mother she was indeed like a swan, the queen was tall and graceful, lean and long. Zark for a moment or two said no more, choosing to let his elder brother come around so to speak. Barak of a sudden gave a grunt and reached inside his vest for his pipe. Zark quite correctly, he took this as a sign that all was well with his large brother. Now the brothers dismounted after another moment or two of deliberation. Once on foot, well then Zark proudly showed Barak about the most ingenuous and impressive vessel.

Up till now Barak thought he had seen most things, after all he had travelled far in his brutal lifetime. And in truth because of his hunger to learn this as well as kill, Barak had put in much time with great philosophers and great engineers. None though, no, none at all, had ever shown him anything quite like this.

'And you say you built this craft all by yourself Zark? ' Barak asked totally amazed at the craftsman ship and the imagination that had gone into the construction of this magnificent ship.

'Yes, oh yes I started it long ago, long before the Xenox brothers ever came into my life to cause their complications and ruinations. You must remember Barak, our library it is both vast and very extensive. I took both the detail and the workings from a book handed down from the ancients. Those strange little beings who took us in and educated us all from savagery and barbarism all those long centuries ago. Well, at least most of us anyway,' Zark said with a snigger. Barak smiled at his brother's jibe, but he said nothing. Zark next paused, and this as he ran a proud eye over his vessel before continuing to speak. 'You know, these folk were indeed a most incredible people my brother, and they were of course quite obviously not of this world. '

Barak shook his head in sheer bewilderment as he gazed upon the vessel, and also while he struggled for something to say.

'Well whoever they were, and wherever they came from our hosts were no more incredible than you are my little brother,' Barak muttered to himself totally amazed at Zark's engineering achievement. Both men were stood aboard the flying ship now as Zark showed his awestruck brother about the well put together vessel.

'This airship steers like a ship upon the sea, only you ride the air waves in the sky as does your great eagle.' Barak was once again totally speechless for yet another moment, Zark though was not. 'The body work I constructed from the feather light metal the ancients brought here. This metal I had gathered together over the years, I melted this down in my forge then moulded it section by section into what you see now. As you know this metal is as strong as steel, ah but also is as light as writing parchment. ' Zark went on his voice was shaking with rising excitement, ah but then a worried thought crossed the scholar's mind.

'But your men who came here with you, will these Norsemen trust in it Barak? Will, will these Norsemen who have followed you here, will they sail in the swan boat? Aye my brother, will these rogues of yours even dare to board the vessel? And then, would your rogues shoot out from this cliff top on those steel runners? The steelrunners that will give you both lift and speed then take you into the heavens Barak?'

Barak merely gave a dreamlike shrug, this was he supposed to himself all a little too much for him to take in. At length though and after some little while passed the giant managed to make a reply.

'Why not Zark?' the slayer said after a few moments studying the strange vessel. 'After all, these men from the cold northlands have dared everything else asked of them to arrive here in this place.'

With a thin smile the newly promoted king gave a humble nod upon hearing these most honest of words. Zark next checked the fast moving clouds above them and the feel of the wind with a silken handkerchief he held high aloft.

'Perfect,' Zark said with a beaming smile and a small child's giddy excitement about him. 'You must now gather up all of your men Barak, do this and you can be off from this cliff top at dusk. By the time you reach the black forest to the west, the stars will be out to guide you back to your far away island.'

Barak could not help but be impressed, the black forest, that place lay long and arduous weeks or months away travelling by horseback yet apparently it was only hours away in the flying machine. Of course this was obviously news that pleased the giant greatly judging by his broad smile.

'It will be done, come Zark we must away now and prepare for our voyage through the air.' Barak said this as the brothers without any further delay left the flying ship and returned to their horses. Barak had mounted his horse a little stiffly, as yesterday's exertions troubled him more than he care to mention. Still sore or not at least he was alive. Barak, after one more final glance at Zark's amazing construction clicked on the big gelding and the brothers galloped off back into the city.

Though it would be true to say that Barak perhaps galloped a little more painfully than he would have liked to. Some while later Barak along with Ragnor and his crew of rough and ever ready reavers stood in awe before the strange most wonderful vessel. Horst as drunk as ever was draped almost unconscious with the drink over a horse. The German had of course been celebrating most vigorously since Barak's great victory in the arena.

Borz looked about him at the other warriors as his tongue flicked in and out and his great yellow eyes rolled in his newt like head. In truth although he would never admit it the halfling was perhaps more than a little nervous and fearful. The halflings great fear as it so happened, well it was of heights. Oh aye, and this even more so when there was nothing under him but air. Borz, perhaps for comfort now glanced at his broad smiling Viking crewmates. These men obviously by their smiling faces were greatly impressed by the strange and wondrous craft. And so, seeing the Norsemen seemed not a bit concerned at leaping from a cliff top in a strange craft. Well this gave Borz at least a little more courage.

In all truth the big burly grinning Vikings, well they to a man found this longboat a most godlike conveyance. Oh aye, and perhaps it was a vessel that might sail them all off to the very halls of Valhalla itself.

Aye and this before being skewered by a broadsword or hacked down by a great war hammer.

Both Commander Gortak and Tark, well both men stood statue like and aloof whilst silently observing the goings on all about them. At once and with all confidence the Norsemen giddily made themselves familiar with the sails the riggings and the workings of the strange but wonderful vessel.

'Can you fly it, do you think Ragnor?' Barak asked as he looked over the mountains edge down at the rugged ground far below them. Barak, well he just like Borz had some misgivings at the very idea of throwing himself along with his friends from the top of a cliff. Not so Ragnor however, the big Viking boomed with rough laughter as he slapped the giant across his back.

'Of course I can fly it Barak!' Ragnor exclaimed out loudly. 'After all, it is only a ship is it not my friend?' Ragnor answered with a carefree quite excited shrug of his shoulders.

Barak made no reply to Ragnor, for as just said the slayer, just like Borz was not too keen on heights. Still though, if this craft would get him back home in two or three days as Zark had said, then he was all for it. Barak lowered a ramp by the stern of the ship and walked his great horse aboard the flying vessel. Without a hesitant step the huge gelding boarded the flying ship followed by Thorn. Both animals much to Barak's delight appeared unconcerned in the least at their new surroundings. Now the giant gave a satisfied grunt This he thought to himself as he swallowed down a large mouthful of vodka was at least a good sign. Tark was stood by Barak's shoulder at this time, open mouthed the young man looked about the strange wonderful craft in sheer amazement. Everything the ancient Zoltan had ever said about Zark was true, Zark was indeed a genius, he was an amazing inventor. Of late the young captain had grown from being a brash and over confident boy into becoming a good capable unbiased young man. Now he was indeed a man who in any company of even the bravest of warriors could hold his own. Oh and all of this, well, he owed to the towering giant. Oh and as well to Ragnor, the halfling and the others who had accompanied him since he was taken prisoner of course. Still though now his journey was at last over. Aye and he had played his part, and also he liked to think he had played it well. Now the young man would speak, and he would address his king for what would be the last time.

'I would come along with you my Lord Barak, but in all truth I feel my place is here.' Tark said these words with some difficulty as his voice was trembling with emotion. The young man's brief attempt at being indifferent and stern, well this was harder than he had anticipated. Now as Tark watched his companions make ready to leave, well in all truth the young warrior was broken. Yes and perhaps all he would say or even do in these last moments was after all only pretence. Aye and it was no more than only a proud front that he put on to impress his stern uncle, or even himself. After all he had been on such an adventure over these past months, and such friends he had made, well he would never forget any of them.

Commander Gortak as ever stood stern and proud as he next gave a bow toward Barak and slapped his huge fist against his heart. Then the commander gave a nod of respect to each and every one of Barak's company of men as they filed by and boarded the flying ship. Now Commander Gortak stood by the edge of the cliff next to Zark, both men were rocked with passion and emotion, but neither of course would show it.

Barak clasped Tark's hand and gave a polite bow, this was returned and without a single word spoken the young man with tear filled eyes and a trembling lip left the flying ship. Barak meanwhile just as ever grunted and growled as he mastered his own emotions. At length the ogre felt he could speak without making a fool of himself.

'Look to my brother Gortak, advise him and guide him as I know you will. And oh, of course also offer him the friendship and the protection of the Legion of the Black Guard. ' Barak said this as he was hanging from the rigging at the stern of the flying boat. There was so much he would like to say to his brother and these bold guardians, but now there was so little time. 'And as for young Tark, well I hope you are as proud of him as I am Commander, for he is a credit to both you and your family.'

Now on hearing this it was the stern face of the commander that cracked as he unashamedly wiped tears from his dark eyes.

'The wind is right you must go now my brother, the wind will not wait, not even for such as you. ' Zark said this urgently as he next cut through the anchor rope tethers. Thus freed from its moorings at once the flying ship slid down its metal runners and was away over the edge of the cliff and onto the thermals.

Now there was much excited shouting and waving of hands, but of course little could be heard above the rush and the roar of the wind as the flying ship slipped into the great abyss.

'Tengri preserve us all!' Barak roared out for the first time in a long time calling upon a god for some assistance. Oh and it was an assistance that by the way the ogre felt he was long overdue. 'Take me home' the giant bellowed as he steadied his tethered horse and talked kindly to his great hound. And aye, now the great god of the sky and the wind just as the Mongol Shaman had said listened, Tengri indeed favoured Barak. Next the cold but welcome wind came in an all powerful rush as it scooped up the flying boat and set the vessel speedily upon its way westward toward the setting sun.

'Goodbye my brother!' Zark shouted as the ship first dipped then rose high above the small group standing upon the cliff edge. 'Oh and look after my mules.' Now the flying ships huge wings were outstretched and the big red balloon was inflated with hot air from the bellows and the brazier.

Barak shouted his goodbyes as he waved his arms about until his brother the commander and Tark disappeared into the far distance and into the gathering dusk. For a heartbeat there was for the ogre just a brief moment in time some sad melancholy and reflective thoughts.

However Ragnor though was not similarly afflicted and the big Viking was quite obviously enjoying being the master of this new, and very different craft.

'Oh I wish I had something to race, I wish I had something to hunt Barak.' Ragnor roared as the wind blew his mane of red hair back over his broad shoulder and he laughed out long and loudly.

Barak swallowed down more vodka and as ever shook himself free of his dark and somewhat sombre broodings.

'You do have something to hunt you old sea dog, catch up with my black eagle, well if you can. She has some start on us that is true, but still, she lies somewhere ahead of us. Take me back to my island Ragnor, take me back to Hassan, take me Home.'

THE END

IMPORTANT FOR 2017

We are delighted and very excited to announce the coming release of our new game that will be available on iphone and android devices.

It is my hope that you have enjoyed the book, if you have then I am sure you will love the game, also to note… Now you have read this book you should have a head start in playing the game.

New Game available soon on mobile devices from late 2017.

Please check out our website for the latest details

At http://sagaofbarak.com/

Printed in Great Britain
by Amazon

25593698R00251